HOW COULD A MAN BE SO STRONG— YET SO TENDER?

She was able to resist Rafe Valero when he behaved like other men—ruthless and ravenous. But now as he held her in his arms, she sensed a different Rafe Valero, a man who cared about her more than he cared about himself.

As he looked down at her, his dark eyes burning into her flesh, she began to respond. Her arms twisted around him, her heart cried out for the sweetness of his touch.

"What"—she barely dared whisper the words—"what are you going to do now?"

For a second his eyes seemed to laugh, but there was no laughter in his voice. "I am going to love you Kristy— the way you were meant to be loved. . . ."

Estelle Houle
Read
V 9.

Sensational Reading from SIGNET

CHEYENNE STAR

SUSANNAH LEIGH

A SIGNET BOOK

NEW AMERICAN LIBRARY

PUBLISHER'S NOTE

This novel is a work of fiction. Names, characters, places, and incidents either are the product of the author's imagination or are used fictitiously, and any resemblance to actual persons, living or dead, events, or locales is entirely coincidental.

NAL BOOKS ARE AVAILABLE AT QUANTITY DISCOUNTS WHEN USED TO PROMOTE PRODUCTS OR SERVICES. FOR INFORMATION PLEASE WRITE TO PREMIUM MARKETING DIVISION, NEW AMERICAN LIBRARY, 1633 BROADWAY, NEW YORK, NEW YORK 10019.

SIGNET TRADEMARK REG. U.S. PAT. OFF. AND FOREIGN COUNTRIES
REGISTERED TRADEMARK—MARCA REGISTRADA
HECHO EN CHICAGO, U.S.A.

SIGNET, SIGNET CLASSIC, MENTOR, PLUME, MERIDIAN AND NAL BOOKS are published by New American Library, 1633 Broadway, New York, New York 10019

First Printing, June 1984

1 2 3 4 5 6 7 8 9

PRINTED IN THE UNITED STATES OF AMERICA

Prologue

Only her eyes betrayed her.

Morning Star stared in fascination at her reflection in the dark still water of the shallow stream. The youthful, pretty face in that murky mirror might have belonged to any young maiden of the tribe. Shining hair, rubbed with grease, fell in two dark plaits onto her shoulders, and her skin, tanned even after a long, bitter winter, blended into the darker brown of a well-worn buckskin robe. There was in those features, soft and feminine, yet carved with a strong chisel, the same quiet dignity that had sustained the Cheyennes through centuries of toil and changing fortunes.

If only it weren't for her eyes . . .

Picking up a bucket from beside her on the bank, she dipped it into the water, diffusing the image into little ripples of light. The rusty metal pail disappeared, then came into view again, an ugly, ungainly thing, like all the white man's tools, no match for the comfortable waterskins she had used in the past. Another reminder, she thought bitterly, another visible proof that the buffalo were gone and they would live on the white man's charity forever.

Almost unconsciously, her eyes slipped back to the circle of tepees, outlined against blue-green pines on the slope behind her. Scattered patches of snow, startlingly white in the early spring mud, caught the sunlight and tossed it back in her eyes. Squinting, she tried to catch a sign of motion in the camp, but she could make out nothing. All seemed quiet and deceptively sleepy, as if everything were as it should be—as if today were a day like all the others that had gone before.

But *he* was there. Morning Star rocked back on her heels, her eyes still scanning the silent camp as she searched for the

5

man who had been there since dawn. Yes, he was there, whether she could see him or not—and he would still be there when she made her way back again.

As she rose, her lips pursed automatically, whistling for the mangy yellow mongrel who never failed to race out of the woods at her call. The gesture surprised her, and she stood for a moment with a startled look on her face. It was funny, she thought, the way old habits crept up on you. Wolf-Dog. What an absurd name for such an unprepossessing beast. How old had she been when she chose it for him? Six? Fourteen years ago, then. Fourteen long years of fighting to keep him out of the cooking pot.

Well, no point dwelling on it now, she reminded herself with a sudden firmness. The past was the past, and yesterday was over. All she could do was deal with today.

The camp as she approached seemed even quieter than it had from a distance. Tall conical structures of buffalo hide, gray-black with smoke and age, looked almost unreal against the biting crispness of a cloudless blue sky. Here and there, a woman scurried across the clearing in the center, her back bent with the weight of firewood or water. A handful of old men could be seen squatting beside glowing embers in front of one or another of the lodges, silently puffing on their pipes or enthralling wide-eyed grandchildren with tales of brave deeds in days long past. Otherwise, no one was in sight.

If only the braves were there! Morning Star paused at the edge of the clearing and looked around with a helpless surge of anger. If only the strong young men were in the camp, then *he* would never dare prowl so freely among them. And she would not be afraid.

But the braves were not there. A sudden, unexpected vision came to her eyes—dark hair cropped so short it barely framed slender features; full lips; a wide, thoughtful brow; gentle laughing eyes. Bitterly, she brushed the thought aside. The braves were not there, and for all she knew, they might never come again. She dared not waste her tears on them now.

Pulling herself together, she began to assess the camp again, seeing this time things she had missed before. The eerie sense of semidesertion that had seemed to hover over the place was only an illusion. From the darkened doorways of silent tepees, eyes were peering out, curious, frightened eyes of old women and children huddled together in the shadows. Behind one of the lodges, that of Blue Thunder, half a dozen of the younger women had gathered in a small group. The old man's granddaughters, Morning Star suspected, although she could make out none of their downcast features. The sight of a familiar head bobbing up suddenly in the center of the group brought with it an unpleasant jolt of memory. It had been Wades-in-the-Water, the youngest and prettiest of Blue Thunder's granddaughters, whom he had sent to her at dawn with a warning.

"There is a white man in the camp," the girl had told her. "A stranger. I have seen him myself. He is very tall and his eyes are black, like the eyes of an Indian—or one of the Spanish white men who terrorize the Comanches in the south."

Morning Star had held her body absolutely rigid. "A man?" she asked cautiously. "What man? Who is he?"

Wades-in-the-Water had looked fairly surprised. "He has a name. A white man's name. Rafe Valero. But does his name really matter?"

No, Morning Star had to admit, it did not. It did not matter at all who the man was, only *what* he was—and neither she nor Blue Thunder had any doubts about that.

"Grandfather says you are not to be afraid," the girl had added quickly. "The man does not know our camp—he has in his head no knowledge of the ways of Indians. All you have to do is keep moving. Mingle with the others when you dare, slip away from them if he approaches. As long as he does not get too close, you will be all right. If he does . . ."

She did not finish the thought. She did not have to. They both knew only too well what would happen. If the man did get close to her—if he caught more than a glimpse from the distance—he would see her eyes. And her eyes were not black, like the eyes of an Indian. They were a piercing blue.

Morning Star began to circle the tepees, still searching the clearing in the center with anxious eyes, when suddenly she saw him. He must have been there all the time, sitting on the ground in front of Blue Thunder's tepee, talking with the old man, but his hair was so black, his erect body so motionless in its fringed rawhide jacket, he almost seemed to fit in. Only the youthful set of broad shoulders and trim, lithe legs crossed carelessly in front of him gave him away.

But why there, of all places? she wondered, puzzled. Why

would the stranger come to Blue Thunder, a man too old even to sit with the old-man chiefs of the tribe? Surely it would have made more sense to seek out one of the four civil chiefs, like Brave Eagle, her own father. Could it be that he did not speak even a few words of Cheyenne?

A wave of relief flooded over her as she realized she had stumbled on the truth. Blue Thunder, with no more than a rudimentary knowledge of the white men and their language, had been right about this Rafe Valero, after all. He did not know the ways of an Indian camp. Setting her bucket down behind one of the tepees, Morning Star hurried across the narrow space that separated her from the old man's grand-daughters and slipped boldly into their midst.

Wades-in-the-Water looked up at her approach, giggling a little, then clapped her hand across her mouth to stifle the sound. The others, too, seemed surprised to see her, but as they recovered their composure, they threw her looks that ranged from support to admiration. Her daring had appealed to their own high spirits. Only Singing Cloud, the oldest of the granddaughters, greeted her with a frown.

"What are you doing here? Haven't you caused enough trouble already?"

Morning Star answered her with a sharp look of her own. Singing Cloud, indeed! With a name like that, the girl should have been a pretty creature, all smiles and gentle passions. Instead, her lips seemed perpetually pinched together, recalling the way she looked whenever she saw a group of young braves flocking around Morning Star's tepee and none coming toward her own.

"I haven't caused anything, and you know it!" Morning Star retorted hotly. "I would be the last person in the world to have invited that man here."

"Invited, perhaps. But provoked? That is another thing. Did he come here just by chance, do you think—or did he come because he heard there was a woman with blue eyes in the camp?"

"That's not fair. No Cheyenne would have told the white man about me. Besides, men like that have been making trouble in Indian camps since long before I arrived. This did not start with me."

Singing Cloud hesitated, uncertain for a moment. Then the malice returned to her eyes.

"And I suppose it is not your fault that the braves are gone? You are not the one who always stirred them up, pleading with them to remember the pride of their Indian heritage? Well, my friend, they are remembering it now—and some of them will not come back. Does it bother you that your own husband is among them? Or have you already forgotten that you are a bride?"

Morning Star felt as if all the color had drained from her cheeks. The gibe struck home, more than she cared to admit. She *had* made those very pleas, and she was paying for them now. But to say she had forgotten she was a bride! How could even Singing Cloud be so mean?

"Perhaps if you had a husband of your own, you would not be so vindictive."

The embarrassed silence that greeted her words made her instantly ashamed of herself. Now it was she who was being mean and spiteful, trying to punish someone else for her own secret fears.

"I'm sorry, Singing Cloud. Truly I am. I have no right taking things out on you, any more than you do to take them out on me. Our young warriors rode off in retaliation for a savage raid in which the Blue Coats killed old women and children. There is nothing I could have said that would have made them do that. And nothing that might have held them back."

Turning her back on the girl's petty malice, she made her way to the other side of the group and, taking care to keep her back to the stranger, she sat down on the ground. She dared not look around to catch a glimpse of his face, but she was near enough to hear his voice. It was unexpectedly husky, yet somehow soft, tinged with traces of an accent she did not recognize.

"Do you think, old man," he was saying quietly, "that because a man and woman are white, they do not grieve for the loss of their child? Or that their grief will last no more than a month—or a year? These people I am telling you about loved their daughter deeply, and she was stolen from them. All they ask is that she be returned. Is that so unjust?"

The words were no more than Morning Star had expected, but there was a quiet conviction in his voice that was somehow unnerving. Again she was tempted to turn, but again she resisted. There was a brief pause, then the man went on.

"All right, let me go over it again." He spoke slowly so Blue Thunder would understand. "Maybe something will jog your memory. The girl I am looking for is named Kristyn Ashley. Her father, Benjamin Ashley, owned a small shop in St. Anthony, north and east of here. He also owned a farm on the outskirts of town where he lived with his young immigrant wife, Astrid, and their children. It was fourteen years ago—that would have been the autumn of 1862—when Kristyn was taken from them by Indians. Perhaps Dakotas . . . possibly Cheyenne. The child was six years old then. She would be twenty now."

Morning Star held her breath as she waited for the old man's voice to reach her ears. It came at last, thin and muffled, difficult to understand for he made no effort to pronounce the words correctly.

"I do not know these names, Kristyn . . . Ashley? St. Anthony? No, I do not know these things."

And he didn't either, Morning Star thought, half smiling in spite of herself. White names meant nothing to the Indians, even the ones who had taken time to cultivate their alien ways. A man, a town—even a time of year. Autumn would not be autumn to Blue Thunder, but the Moon of Changing Seasons, or the Moon When the Plums Turn Ripe.

"Don't you?" The stranger sounded cool, almost amused, as if he understood more than he was letting on. "Let me describe the girl for you, then. She was a slender child, but even at six she showed signs of being tall. She would stand out among the Cheyennes. Her hair had coppery highlights, though they would have darkened to auburn by now. And her eyes were blue."

Morning Star turned at last, unable to resist the temptation any longer. She was careful to keep her eyes averted, but the man was not looking at her. He was half turned away, staring at the wrinkled, expressionless face in front of him.

If Blue Thunder caught the significance of the man's words, he did not show it.

"There are many with blue eyes among our people. I know that, white man, and you know it. Your people come here, your men. They see our women, and they want them. But they do not take them away when the time comes to leave. The women stay here, and their children, and many with blue eyes play in front of our tepees."

"Not many," the man replied calmly. "Some, perhaps—but not many. Besides, this girl has an identifying mark. I will know her when I see her. And when I do, I will know I have found Kristyn Ashley."

He rose and brushed the dirt from his pants with the wide-brimmed hat in his hand. To Morning Star, it looked as if he was going to leave, but he lingered a moment longer.

"I do not ask you to tell me about the girl now, old man. I ask only that you turn your mind to it when I am gone. You are wise, and I know you will do what is right. These people, these white parents, have been deeply hurt by the loss of their child. They want her back because they love her very much. They would not have searched for her all these years if they did not. Or spent so much money on it. The woman especially grieves for her daughter."

For the first time, Blue Thunder's eyes seemed troubled. "I know a mother's heart, white man, yes . . . I know this thing you speak of. Think you I would cause a mother pain?"

Morning Star sensed a deeper meaning in his words, and she knew the stranger heard it, too. Leaning forward, he pitched his voice so low she had to strain to hear it.

"It will be better for the girl, too. I have seen your camp. Your children walk around with gaunt, hungry faces. The feet of your young people bleed in the snow because their moccasins are so thin. If you love this girl—if anyone here loves her—tell them to let her go. Even a mother's heart can understand that. Kristyn Ashley belongs with her own people."

Kristyn Ashley. The words lingered even after the man they called Rafe Valero was gone and the sound of his voice no longer carried to Morning Star's ears. Kristyn Ashley. The name sounded vaguely familiar to her, although she was not sure why. Did she really recognize it? she wondered. Or was she only afraid that she did?

And who were these people? This Benjamin Ashley and his immigrant wife, still grieving for the child they had lost fourteen years ago? Didn't they know she would not be their little girl anymore? That she would be a woman now, with a life of her own, and that she would not want to come back to them?

Morning Star remained where she was, crouching in the mud beside the tepee, until she was certain the man was out of sight. Then, casting a hasty glance over her shoulder to make sure he was not lurking nearby, she retrieved her water bucket and made her way to her own lodge. Once inside, she would be safe, for the time being at least. Even with the braves gone, the white man would not dare to violate her privacy by lifting up flaps she had pulled tightly over the doorway. He would have to cool his heels somewhere on the edge of the camp, mulling over his talk with the old man and hoping his words had had their effect.

Not until deepening shadows pitched the interior of the tepee into darkness, telling her that dusk had eased into night, did she dare to come out again. The air was cool and smelled of burning pine, and she felt safer than she had for hours. Bold as he was, it hardly seemed likely that the man would venture into an Indian camp at night. And even if he did, the moon was still low, and the circle of tepees cast long, sheltering shadows on the earth.

In the pale moonlight, the camp looked almost normal again. Wisps of gray-white smoke curled out of the tops of several of the tepees, and the smell of grease and wild herbs told her the women were busy with their evening meals. Bright patches of light marked the places where open fires had been laid, and shimmering sparks leaped like fireflies into the night.

Hungry tongues of flame lapped around a pile of pine boughs in front of Blue Thunder's tepee, and Morning Star began to move toward them. Now that she felt secure again, she was curious to find out what other things the stranger might have said. Curious, too—though she doubted those impassive features would give anything away—to find out how Blue Thunder had reacted to the stranger's impassioned plea. She was so sure of herself in the darkness that she moved quickly, barely paying attention to where she was going. Only as she neared the spot did she raise her eyes to take in the circle of light cast by the glowing bonfire. When she did, she stopped cold in her tracks.

There, seated beside the fire, as calm and careless as if he were among his own people, sat the white stranger.

Morning Star's heart jumped into her throat and she felt a moment of panic, as if she had already stumbled into the firelight and been seen by the man. She could not help admiring him—how many white men would dare to sit among their enemies in the dark? How many Indians, for that matter?

But she feared him, too. Feared him more than she cared to admit. This was not the man she thought she had seen that afternoon. This was a man with a force and daring she had not anticipated.

Backing into the shadows of the tepee, Morning Star crouched alone in the darkness, unable to take her eyes off the man. There was something compelling about him, something so intense and magnetic she could not have leaped up and run away even had she wanted to.

He was like no one she had ever seen before. The effect of his height, far from being diminished by the darkness, actually seemed to be accented by the casual way he sat on the ground, one knee pulled up, the other leg stretched out full length in front of him. He was garbed in denim and rawhide, the frontiersman's habitual costume, but his jacket, cut to emphasize broad shoulders, tapered into a slender waist, and the muscles in long, lean thighs showed through the fabric of his trousers. His hair, worn long for a white man, caught the flames until it seemed to dance with black fire; his features were rugged beneath a deep tan.

There was, Morning Star thought helplessly, an almost hypnotic quality about him. A kind of force that drew her toward him, even against her will.

Perhaps it was his eyes. Dark, brooding eyes reflected the flames, holding her captive even as they blazed out challenges she could not understand. They were so different, those eyes. No Indian would let his soul show in his eyes like that. Strength and sensitivity, pride, passion, arrogance—all these combined to create in him a sense of virility as exciting as it was threatening. Morning Star felt a subtle warmth seep into her veins, a strange, familiar warmth she could not place. Only slowly did she realize what it was.

She was looking at this man the way she had looked at her young husband the night he first came through the doorway of their lodge!

Blood rushed to her face as the full impact of what she was doing swept over her. Now she was doubly grateful for the shadows that hid her shame. Feminine worth, in the rigid code of her upbringing, was measured by modesty and virtue. No Cheyenne woman would ever let herself look that way at a man who did not share her tepee. Especially a woman who was married to someone else.

Just at that moment, the man turned, fixing his eyes on the shadows as if he had the power to penetrate the darkness and see where she was crouching. He *knew*, she thought, intrigued and horrified at the same time. He knew she was there, and he knew how she had been looking at him.

Anger mixed with the sudden fear that surged through her veins, and she directed all her contempt outward. The smugness of the man. The arrogance! He was used to women looking at him like that. He was actually used to it—and he thought only one thing when they did! Shifting her weight forward on the balls of her feet, she prepared to rise and flee into the darkness. Let him think what he wanted, it would do him no good with her! A white woman might be ready to feed that masculine vanity of his. A Cheyenne never would!

Only when she saw him move, rising before she could pull herself to her feet, did she realize what she had done. Fool, she cursed herself bitterly. Fool!—but it was too late. She might as well have gone up and whispered in his ear that a woman with blue eyes was in the camp! It did not matter what had attracted his attention to her. The attraction was there now, and nothing could stop him from coming closer.

Nothing—save one thing. Jumping impulsively to her feet, she tensed every muscle in her body. The Cheyennes were a proud people—the men protected their woman with a passion as fierce as any on earth. If the stranger kept on looking at her like that, if the watchers in the fire-touched shadows thought he had only lust on his mind, even an old man would fight to the death to save her.

But the gesture came too late. Morning Star saw the man take a step forward, then pause, a slow smile beginning to touch the corners of his lips, and she knew without words what had happened. Away from the shelter of the tepee, away from its low, protecting shadows, the rays of the moon were as bright as firelight. The man had seen her eyes.

She tried to run, but she was no match for him. He caught her before she had gone more than a few steps. Jerking her roughly backward, he whirled her around to see her face. Even before Morning Star felt his hands grab her sleeve, ripping it in his haste, she knew what he was looking for. There was a scar on her arm. A long discoloration of the skin, not as noticeable as it had been when she was a child, but still clear to the eyes.

They realized the truth at the same moment. This woman he was looking for—this Kristyn Ashley—was her.

I

The Moon When
The Ponies Shed

One

It was not a good day.

Kristyn sat in a corner of the kitchen and pushed her lower lip out as far as a six-year-old lip would go. But if Mama even noticed, the girl could see no sign of it. Sucking her lip back, she propped her elbows up on the table and stared with wide blue eyes at a kettle bubbling on the wood stove.

No, it was not a good day at all. And it was so unfair! Just the thought of it was enough to make Kristyn begin pouting all over again. She had only been trying to help. When the water started to boil and Mama was nowhere in sight, she had pulled a chair over to the stove and climbed up on top of it. If Mama had come in a minute later—just one little minute! —she would have had the tea brewing and everyone would have been proud of her instead of furious.

And Mama *was* furious, there were no two ways about that. Of course, Mama was easily frightened—she kept on remembering that time when Kristyn was a little girl and had dropped a pot of steaming water all over herself, burning her arm—but it was silly to keep on fussing like that. She was much bigger now; she could handle the kettle perfectly. Mama had to stop thinking of her as a baby and treat her more like a grown-up, the way she did with the boys.

Papa appeared in the doorway, and Kristyn threw him a tentative glance, making her eyes as wide as she could, just in case. When he did not look at her, she let out a little sigh and admitted defeat. Sometimes Papa could be the most understanding man in the world, and a little girl could coax anything she wanted out of him—but not when Mama said no. Once Mama made up her mind, that was all there was to it, and even Papa did not try to change it.

19

"Astrid, are you ready? We're going to be late."

It seemed to Kristyn that Papa looked positively gallant in the dark coat he always wore to town. He was years older than Mama, of course, and his dark auburn hair was generously flecked with gray, but there was something distinctly dashing about him.

She decided to give him another try.

"Papa, couldn't I . . . ?"

"That will do, Kristyn," Mama's voice cut in sharply. Kristyn turned to see a red-headed eight-year-old at her mother's side. "You are to stay here while Joshua comes into town with us. Thomas and John will look after you. I want you to be a good girl and do what they tell you."

"Oh, Mama, I want to come, too. Please." To her humiliation, tears began to spill out of her eyes, making little spots on the crisply pressed yoke of her dress. "I want to come to the store with you and Papa. I'll behave myself. I promise I will!"

"No, Kristyn. You have to learn not to do dangerous things. I've told you that over and over, but I can't seem to make you understand. If the only thing that impresses you is punishment, then that is what you shall have."

Astrid glanced quickly away, determined not to let her daughter see a flicker of doubt in her eyes. She could not bear to hurt the child, but for the life of her, she could think of no other way to handle the situation. She could still remember how terrified she had been that last time, when all she could smell was burned flesh as she dressed her daughter's arm and prayed that the injury would have no serious effects. Even now, it pained her to see the angry red scar that always reminded her of the incident. Kristyn was a good child, willing and helpful, but she was high-spirited, too, and mischievous, making her hard to handle in a way the boys had never been.

"See that you mind your brothers," she said gruffly. "And maybe we'll bring you a treat from the store."

Kristyn puckered up her face to keep from crying again as she watched her mother cross the yard toward the wagon Papa had pulled up from the barn. Astrid had always been something of an enigma to the child, and she was a little afraid of her, as she had never been with her more approachable father. Even now, even angry as she was, Kristyn thought

she had never seen anyone quite so beautiful as Mama. She
was a tall woman, with hair so fair it almost seemed white,
and she looked astonishingly young, though Kristyn knew she
must really be quite old, at least twenty-eight or -nine. But
there was any icy quality to her beauty, a kind of aloofness
that set her apart from other women, and to her young
daughter, she seemed more a fairy-tale princess than a flesh-
and-blood woman.

Josh lingered in the doorway after his mother had gone.
His freckled face twisted into a decidedly smug grin as he
turned to face his sister.

"You aren't going to get any candy," he gloated, pitching
his voice just low enough so Mama couldn't hear. "I'm
going to eat it all up, and there won't be one piece left for
you!"

Kristyn glared at him resentfully. Sometimes her brother
could be fun and she liked to be with him, but other times he
was a loathsome toad!

"I don't care. I don't like candy anyway!"

"You do, too! You're just jealous 'cause I get to go and
you don't. You're a dumb stupid girl, that's all."

"I am not!" Kristyn punctuated her words with a sharp jab
that brought a yowl from Josh.

"Ow! Kristy hit me! Mama, she hit me!"

"No, I didn't!" Kristyn was furious. The little beast! No
matter what she did, he always went running to Mama! "He
called me a stupid girl. Anyway, he deserved——"

"Kristy!" Papa's voice stopped her in mid-sentence. "Not
another word, do you hear? And you, Josh—come here. Any
more of this squabbling and we'll leave you behind, too."

Josh was too shrewd to say anything else, but he threw a
gloating grin over his shoulder as he trotted obediently across
the yard. Kristyn longed to stick her tongue out at him,
making the most vulgar sounds she could manage, but her
mother's cool blue eyes were on her face and she could not
find the nerve. Waiting by the side of the house, she scratched
little patterns in the dirt with her toe and pretended she did
not see the wagon roll out of the yard. Only after they were
gone did she wander over to the fence, climbing onto the top
rail to watch as they disappeared into the distance.

Really, it *was* unfair! Today was supply day, and supply
day was Kristyn's favorite thing in all the world. For the last

year and a half, Papa, eager to make a better life for his young wife and his children, had virtually given up running the farm and opened a small store in town. Every four or five months, a wagonload of new supplies would come in from the East, and on the day they were due to arrive, Papa would take the younger children into town with him. Now Josh was going to have everything to himself, especially the brightly colored candies that Mama only let them sample a few times a year.

She hoped he would get sick on them. He probably would, too, considering how green he had looked last time. She hoped he would get so sick he would throw up on the drive home! It was the only bright spot in an otherwise dismal morning.

After a while, Kristyn got tired of sitting on the fence and, sliding back to the ground, she turned reluctantly toward the house. She knew only too well what Mama had meant when she ordered her to "be a good girl." She had meant that Kristyn was supposed to stay inside and not get in her brothers' way as they did a man's work in the fields.

Once it would not have seemed so oppressive, being cooped up in the house, for Kristyn was one of a large family. Her father had been married long ago to a woman who had died, and she and Joshua and John had enough older half-brothers and -sisters to keep the house rollicking and filled with laughter. But now they were all gone: Richard and young Benjamin with farms of their own, Caroline carried off suddenly in that terrible epidemic of scarlet fever last spring, Charlotte following a brand-new husband to her own home in Nebraska. The only one left was Thomas, and he and Kristyn's older brother, John, now eleven and too old to be taken on outings, had stayed behind to tend to the chores.

A tuneless whistle blew in from the fields. Looking up, Kristyn saw Thomas cutting through the tall grasses, a sickle slung over his shoulders. Her eyes narrowed as she watched him, and the tantalizing beginnings of an idea formed in her mind. Autumn was harvest season, and harvest was far too busy a time for a teenaged boy to keep track of the comings and goings of one little sister. Besides, in another minute Thomas would be too far away to see her.

Her eyes turned briefly toward the silent house. She did not know if her brother John was behind one of those darkened windows, idly looking out, but she did not worry about that. John had never been mean and devious, not like that nasty little Josh! Even if he caught her, he would never go running to Mama with the tale.

Her feet felt light, as if they had grown wings, and she skipped across the yard, darting through a narrow break in the shrubbery that led down to the creek. Papa had ordered her never to go there by herself, and usually she obeyed Papa, but today she did not care. If she was going to be punished anyway, she might as well be punished for something she had done.

The creek was fuller than usual, for it had been a rainy summer, and ripples of water cascaded over the rocks like miniature waterfalls. The trees had begun to turn, and the banks were a burst of scarlet and amber and gold. Kristyn studied the leaves carefully, picking out the ones that were bright yellow with green veins showing on their surface and tossing them into the rushing current. She loved watching the water carry them away, like canoes maneuvering the charging rapids of a mighty river.

She had just started to follow her leaf-boats down the current when she heard a noise behind her. A soft, rustling sound, like a snake slithering through the grass. Catching her breath, she turned very slowly to see where it was coming from. Could Thomas or John have figured out what she was up to and followed her so quickly? At first she could see nothing through the red and gold foliage that formed a screen along the bank. Then a face began to emerge out of the multicolored background.

For a minute she was not frightened—only curious. The eyes in that face, dark eyes in a dark-skinned face, seemed almost as startled as hers. Bright streaks of red and white ran across prominent cheekbones and a high forehead, and long braids hung down on either side.

An Indian! Kristyn had never seen Indians before, but she knew all about them, and suddenly she was afraid. The leaves slid under her feet as she backed away, down the bank again and into the icy water. The creek was deeper than she had thought, and the current tugged at her skirts, threatening to drag her down. Cornered and helpless, she began to scream.

Oh, please, she thought desperately, calling out to the brothers who now seemed terrifyingly distant. Please don't be so far away you can't hear my cries. Please, *please*, come and help me.

The agony that followed would be forever blurred in Kristyn's memory. Only isolated sensations remained. The feel of the water swirling around her waist. The look on the man's face, impassive beneath its mask, relentless as he plunged into the stream to follow her. The shrieking assault of other Indians. The sight of her brothers, racing toward her with nothing but a sickle and a long branch, hastily snatched up, in their hands.

And the sounds. She threw her hands over her eyes, but nothing could block out the harsh, terrible sounds of that one-sided battle. And then—a silence even more terrible. She eased her fingers apart, peeking cautiously between them, but all she could see was her brother's sickle, broken and useless on the ground.

She knew then that it was over. Turning her head away, she lowered her hands and waited quietly at the edge of the stream for the man to come to her. When he did, she saw him lift his arm, and she recoiled instinctively. But to her surprise, he only took one of her long red curls and twisted it between his fingers as he called out to his friends. It was a moment before she realized what he was up to.

Her hair. That dreadful, brutal savage wanted her hair!

With a burst of horror, she pulled away, wincing as the curl tore out of his grasp. He was going to scalp her! He had killed her brothers, and now he was going to kill her—and scalp her in the process! Crying out in fear and fury, she flung herself at him, pounding clenched fists against his chest, kicking his shins savagely with the points of her shoes. So he thought he could get the best of her, did he! Just because she was a little girl and could not fight back. Well, she would show him! She would kick and claw until she had forced him away, then she would run and he would never catch her again.

The startled Indian, caught off guard, could only mute the fury of her attack by catching her shoulders and lifting her, feet still flailing, off the ground. To Kristyn's disgust, he did not seem harassed at all, but laughed, as if her spirited outburst amused him. Enraged, she redoubled her efforts, but try as she would, she could not make him relax his hold, and soon her strength ebbed away. She waited, terrified, for the man to pull out his knife, but he only tossed her over his shoulder and carried her to one of the waiting horses, like Papa might carry a sack of flour to a farmer's wagon. Setting her down in front of a crude wooden saddle, he drew his lean body up behind her, holding her in a grip so tight she could not move.

The horse started forward, and Kristyn turned, catching a sickening glimpse of crimson on the gold autumn leaves behind her. The Indian put a firm hand on the side of her head, forcing her eyes into the folds of his tunic. This time she did not resist. There was no will left in her to fight. She was tired, much too tired to feel anything but the jogging of the horse's stride as she allowed herself to be carried across windswept meadows with a smell of winter in the air.

She was too frightened during the day that followed to be more than dimly aware of the changing landscape. Cottonwood groves along the familiar stream gave way to scattered box elders on the hillsides, their leaves spreading a mantle of color across the slopes. Here and there, a shallow pond broke the monotony of blowing grasses, and wild ducks, startled by their approach, rose out of the rushes with an alarmed flapping of wings.

The men spoke only occasionally, calling out to each other in harsh, guttural words Kristyn could not understand. She did not look at her captor, but she had a strong sense of him in the unyielding arms that surrounded her and the rough feel of his shirt against her cheek. The smell of him was strange. Not comfortable and masculine like Papa, with the smells of the farm and Virginia tobacco, of homemade soap and fresh earth just turned by the hoe. About this man there was only the scent of grease and rawhide, wild horses and smoke from wood fires, and a hundred other things so unfamiliar she could not put a name to them.

Darkness had already settled over the countryside by the time they reached the Indian camp. Kristyn, too terrified to be sleepy, stared with wide, unblinking eyes at the great circle of tepees. They were imposing structures, perhaps ten or twelve feet tall, constructed of crude wood-pole frameworks covered with animal skins. Some displayed strikingly primitive patterns on their sloping sides, others had been stained a solid red, but for the most part their conical shapes showed only the drab grayish tan of aged hides, blackened by the smoke that seeped through vents in the top. The crimson reflection of a dozen open fires gave an unworldly air to the scene.

The normal activities of the evening were already in progress as they rode into the center of the clearing. Old men squatted around the fires, recounting *coups* of battles long past and handing long-stemmed pipes with carved stone bowls from one to the other. Children shrieked excitedly, darting back and forth between the tepees, disappearing into the darkness one minute only to reappear the next. Near one of the fires, just close enough to catch the warmth of its rays, a group of women sat on blankets and tossed long, rounded sticks into the air. Loud bursts of laughter echoed through the night as the sticks landed in jumbled patterns on the earth. A pair of lean dogs, their matted fur the same gray-tan of the tepees, snarled at each other over some scrap or bone that had been cast away. Yapping at their heels, a fat, playful puppy, too little yet to make a tempting morsel for the cooking pot, tried unsuccessfully to get their attention.

The smell of the place was as strange as the smell of the man who had brought Kristyn there. An odor of smoke hung in the air, pungent pitch-pine, mingling with cottonwood and chokecherry, dogwood and the tangy sharpness of witch hazel, and the scent of fresh-cooked meat, singed by flames, seemed to linger on the night wind. The bitterness of coffee beans, roasting on heated stones, only half masked the odor of sweat and rancid oil, smoky rawhide and urine and buffalo dung that pervaded the camp.

Their arrival created a flurry of interest. Men and women alike left their fires to crowd around the party of braves with their captive. Kristyn sat absolutely straight in front of the saddle, barely daring to breathe as she stared down at them. The men were clad in loose tunics of buckskin or some other animal hide, with leggings to match, all decorated in fringes and surprisingly elaborate beadwork. Even the soft moccasins on their feet had colorful patterns on them. Strings of assorted shells and bear claws dangled around their necks, and their long braids were wrapped in fur or otter skin. The women were dressed in much the same style, in long tubular sacks fashioned out of cured skins, or occasionally thin blanket cloth that must have been procured at some store or trading post.

One of the women detached herself from the others and, stepping forward, stared at Kristyn's captor with dark, haunting eyes. The man must have answered with a mute gaze of his own, for the woman's face softened, breaking into what seemed a smile. She raised her arms, and Kristyn realized, to her horror, that she was expected to slide down into that unwelcome embrace. She tried to resist, but the man pushed her forward.

She was conscious only of the smell of the woman, all grease and wood smoke, like the man before her. The smell, and the fact that her arms were thin, her hands hard and calloused, not soft like Mama's. Not soothing. The woman did not try to force her when the child shied away, but laid her hands instead on the girl's shoulders and guided her into one of the tepees.

Sputtering embers from an ill-tended fire in the center cast a faint red glow over the interior of the circular structure. The air was hotter than Kristyn had expected, so stifling she could barely breathe, and the tall, sloping walls seemed to close in on her. She stood very quietly where the woman had left her, just inside the entrance, and tried as hard as she could not to be afraid.

The room was utterly alien, with nothing to make her feel comfortable or safe. The walls had been lined with hide, much like the skins that covered the outside, but cleaner and creamier, and someone had made a crude attempt to decorate them with cornhusks and tufts of red cloth. More skins had been laid on the tamped-earth floor, providing a ground cover and at least partially shutting out the cold. Buffalo robes, piled directly on the floor, formed sleeping pallets, which had been made into makeshift couches by the addition of willow backrests at the ends. Buckskin pillows, embroidered with porcupine quills, had been scattered throughout, and baskets and bags of various shapes were piled against the liner. Much of the smoke escaped through a hole at the top of the tepee, but the air was still hazy, stinging Kristyn's eyes and making her throat feel raw.

The woman did not speak. Taking a pair of thick robes from one of the pallets, she spread them out at the rear of the tepee, fluffing them up in an attempt to make them look inviting. When she had finished, she raised her hand, beckoning to Kristyn, and the child stepped reluctantly forward. She did not know which was worse, her fear of the dark eyes that never seemed to leave her face or the dread she felt at sinking down into that awful, matted fur. In the end, fear won out, and she pulled the foul thing over her head, shutting out all the sights and sounds of that terrible place.

They left her alone for a long time. The noises outside were already beginning to die away when Kristyn felt hands tug the robe back from her face. Peering out, she saw the woman squatting in front of her. A strange object was clutched in her outstretched hand. Kristyn stared at it for a minute before she realized it was a crude doll. Its body, crafted from deerskin, was dark with age and so shiny it looked as if it had almost worn through. If it had ever had painted features, they were half rubbed away now, and its dress, beaded like the dresses of the women outside, was shabby and torn.

Kristyn could not bring herself to touch the thing. It was old and dirty, and it smelled. Just like everything else in that place, it smelled! She had an old doll, too. A rag doll Mama had made for her when she was just a baby. It was every bit as faded as this one, and ragged, but at least it did not smell.

Just at that moment, the flap that served as a door opened, and a young boy about the same age as Joshua appeared in the tent. He was dressed like a little warrior, with a fringed buckskin tunic and a pair of feathers attached to a band on his head. The effect was more comical than coy, for a pudgy potbelly peeked out from underneath his short tunic. His face was round, his eyes black and curious. In his arms, he held the puppy Kristyn had seen playing outside the tepee.

He spoke not a word, but went over to the girl, slipping the dog from his arms into hers. The puppy whimpered a little, as if in protest, then wriggled around to lick her face with a wet pink tongue. At that, the tears Kristyn had been holding back burst out in a sudden torrent, and she buried her head in warm fur, sobbing out all the grief and terror in her heart. She was still clutching the dog hours later when she finally fell asleep.

When she woke up, she found herself alone in the tepee. The dog was still with her, curled up like a little yellow pillow at the foot of her pallet, but no one else was in sight. Thin rays of hazy light trickled through the edges of the closed doorway, telling her that dawn had broken and the day's activities had already begun. The sound of fat sizzling on the fire drifted in from somewhere outside, and surprisingly inviting aromas reminded her that she had not eaten for twenty-four hours.

The flap of the tent opened suddenly, and a round face burst into the room. Startled, Kristyn pulled the furry robe up to her chin, hiding everything but her eyes. It was the boy she had seen the night before. He looked at her for a moment, then dropped the flap and vanished as abruptly as he had appeared.

The whole thing happened so quickly, the girl might almost have thought she imagined it had not the flap opened again and people come swarming in. There were too many of them for her to take in all at once, and she sat quietly on her pallet, more confused than frightened. Only a few faces stood out that first morning. The woman who had made the bed for her, laughing now, younger, prettier than she had looked before. The tall, strong man who had taken her captive. Another man, someone's grandfather perhaps, with brown, wrinkled skin and spaces showing between his teeth when he grinned. And the little boy, bright and lively as ever. They seemed animated now, excited, as voluble as they had been restrained the night before. Kristyn could not understand a word they were saying, but she knew they must be talking about her, for they kept pointing to her, then toward the open door, then back at her again.

She had thought then that they were looking at her hair. It was a long time before she learned their language well enough to discover what it was that had really intrigued them. It was a story she never tired of hearing.

"Tell me," she would beg the woman she now called *nágo*, mother. "Tell me about that morning."

And Buffalo Calf Woman would set down her tools—the bone awl and sinew thread she used for sewing, or the stone maul that pounded jerky into pemmican.

"Are you sure you want to hear that old story again?" she would tease.

"Oh, yes," the little girl would plead, climbing up onto her lap. "Please, *please*, tell me again."

The woman would bend down, kissing the up-turned brow, and run her hands down red curls, darkened with buffalo fat and tamed into two long braids.

"We were very happy that morning, little gift from the

spirits. We had just lost our own daughter, Yellow Fringe, who was exactly the same age as you. That was her doll we gave you that morning, though I think you did not like it then. We were very happy because Heamma-Wihio, the Wise One Above, had sent us another little girl to take her place. But we were sad, too, because she was crying. It is always sad when a child cries.''

The little girl would squirm impatiently.

"But her eyes," she would coax. "Tell me about her eyes."

"Oh, her eyes." The woman would laugh, as if she had not known all along what the child was looking for. "Her eyes were very blue. A paler blue than I have ever seen. 'Look,' I said to Brave Eagle, your father. 'See the morning sky through the doorway of the tepee. See how clear and pure it is, with one white star still twinkling on the horizon. The child's eyes are like that. Pale and blue, shining with tears like the last morning star.' "

"So that's what you called me!"

The child could contain her excitement no longer. The impersonal "she" of the story became "me" again, and she liked it that way. The woman never failed to laugh as she gave the girl one last hug and picked up her work again.

"That's what we called you, your father and I. We picked your name for the color of the sky at dawn. Morning Star."

The girl would wriggle off the woman's lap and sigh with satisfaction. It was a nice story, she thought contentedly. All the nicer, of course, because it centered around her.

And a nice name, too. Morning Star. Soft and pretty and melodic. It was the name she was to be known by for the next fourteen years of her life.

Two

"You're doing it all wrong!"

Morning Star tried not to laugh, but she couldn't help herself. Little Bear looked so funny, scowling down at the clumsy pattern he had traced in the dirt with a willow stick.

"No, I'm not. That's just the way you showed me."

"It is if you want to stand on your head to look at it." The boy had written the first letter of the alphabet, all right, but he had it exactly upside down! "That isn't an *A* at all. It's a *V* with a funny line through its middle."

Little Bear scratched his head thoughtfully, then broke into a quick grin. That was one of the things that delighted Morning Star most about her young playmate. Nothing could keep him solemn for long.

"Of course it's an *A*. Look!" Leaping over the markings, he gazed down at them from the other side. "Now it's right side up. You see!"

The logic was enticing. Morning Star tried to keep her lips from turning up, but she did not succeed. It was hard to stay serious with someone like Little Bear.

"That's all right for one letter. But what are you going to do when you write a whole sentence? Jump back and forth every time you read it? Or turn the paper upside down and every which way? If you want to write the white man's language, you have to do it properly."

She picked up several strips of jerky from a pile beside her and, laying them on a large, hollowed-out stone, began the tedious task of grinding them into pemmican. She had been more than a little surprised the evening before when Little Bear came to her and asked if she would teach him to read and write. In the two years she had been with the Indians, she and the boy had learned to speak each other's language, switching from one to the other as they chatted and played together. But to read and write? That seemed unnecessary. Especially since she had nearly forgotten herself.

She had not been alone in her skepticism. Broken Arm, Little Bear's father, had been equally doubtful. But in the end, he had deferred to the judgment of his elder brother.

"Let the boy learn," Brave Eagle had said in his quiet, authoritative way. "It can do no harm. The white men are many. We are few, and growing fewer all the time. Perhaps the day will come when it is wise for an Indian to understand the ways of his enemy."

So Little Bear had come for his first lesson, though not without certain difficulties. The Cheyennes had no written language of their own, relying on the spoken word in their communication with each other, and the boy found himself bewildered by the rigidity of a system he could not understand. To him, the symbols he scratched in the earth were just that—symbols to be used by the men who created them—and he could not resist turning them around to please his eye, the way a medicine man might rearrange the symbols he painted on a tepee.

Morning Star turned her attention back to her work. The heavy stone maul beat out a slow, monotonous rhythm as she ground it again and again against the jerky. It was amusing to watch Little Bear, even if she didn't know why he was putting himself to all that trouble, but she couldn't waste any more of her time on him. Not when her own task was much more important.

Nothing was more vital to Indian life than a good supply of pemmican, and this was the first time Morning Star had been entrusted with its preparation. She had even made the jerky herself. Some time before, after the last buffalo hunt of the season, she had been given a portion of fresh meat to cut into strips, just thick enough to hold together, but so thin the flies could not blow them. Skewering them on long sticks, she had let them dry in the sun, bringing them inside at night to protect them from the moisture. Now she would pulverize them with her stone hammer, and when she had finished, she would mix the resulting paste with dried chokecherries and store it in a rawhide parfleche where it would keep for several months. In a hard winter, when game was scarce and the frozen earth would not yield its roots to the digging stick, pemmican might be the only nourishment the family would have for days, even weeks, on end.

The autumn sun was warm on her back, the smell of the meat so familiar to her nostrils she found it hard to remember a time when the Indian camp had seemed alien and threatening to her. Only sometimes, when she thought back on that first night, did she catch a glimpse of a frightened little girl, burrowing deep into buffalo fur, her arms clutched around a little yellow dog—that same spoiled scoundrel who now followed at her heels wherever she went.

The thought always made her laugh. The very people who had seemed so strange and terrifying then were her family now, and she loved them dearly. She was intensely proud of her father, or *nihu*, as she called him. Brave Eagle was one of the four civil chiefs of their band, and when the entire tribe gathered together for celebrations in the summer, he would sit with the leaders of the other bands and the four old-man chiefs on the Council of Forty-four. Buffalo Calf Woman, or *na'go*, was not of equal importance, of course, for women were not important in the Cheyenne way of things, but she had soft, gentle eyes and a ready laugh, and she was never too busy to pick up a little girl in her arms or brush away tears. There was even a grandfather, *na'go*'s own father, who, according to custom, lived in the tepee next to theirs where he could be cared for by his daughter and her family.

Then there was her brother . . .

Morning Star looked up, trying to catch Little Bear's eyes, but the boy was too engrossed in the task he had set for himself. Not that Little Bear couldn't be exasperating—sometimes he seemed every bit as impossible as the redheaded, freckle-faced brother she could barely remember—but she liked having him around all the same. Of course, he was not really her "brother," being not the son of Brave Eagle, but what the white men would have called his nephew. Among the Indians, however, family ties were strong, and a man never thought of his brother's children as anything but *ná*, son, and *náts*, daughter. And when the children of brothers played together, they did not say to each other "cousin," as they might have in English, but rather "brother" and "sister."

Besides, she thought, laughing a little to herself, Little

Bear might as well be her brother, he spent so much time in their tepee. Since that very first night, when he had slipped the puppy into her arms, she could hardly remember seeing him take a meal in his own lodge.

The lazy afternoon stillness was broken by the wailing cries of a baby. Owl Woman's newborn, Morning Star thought, laying down the maul to rest her arm for a moment. Why was it that Owl Woman always seemed to have so much trouble with her children?

From the woods behind the camp, a bony yellow dog streaked into the clearing. It took him only a second to spot the meat in the hollowed-out stone, and he loped over to give it a hopeful sniff. Little Bear looked up just in time to see Morning Star swat him with her hand.

"You spoil that beast too much," he said, laughing as he took off one of his moccasins and aimed it at the cur. Wolf-Dog, undeterred, slunk away a foot or two and lay down in the dirt, whining expectantly. "Wolf-Dog! Only a girl would pick out a name like that. Why, that dog looks about as ferocious as you do!"

"I was only six then," Morning Star reminded him indignantly. "Besides, he was just a puppy. How was I supposed to know he would grow up to be so—so scrawny."

The sound of their laughter drew Buffalo Calf Woman out of the tepee. Morning Star flushed guiltily as she turned and saw her in the doorway. She was sure her mother had been trying to rest; she looked so tired and drawn lately, much older than she had that night two years ago when the girl first saw her. Besides, the baby's cries were much clearer out here. Morning Star could not help remembering the terrible pained look on her mother's face, only three months ago, when she had given birth to a child of her own, a little girl who did not live to cry even once.

But if the sound brought back unhappy memories, Buffalo Calf Woman did not show it. "Owl Woman is going to have to do something with that child," she said, her eyes sparkling with silent laughter. "She is much too soft-hearted to hang the babe on a tree."

Morning Star laughed, too. Poor Owl Woman. She had had four children in as many years, and each one seemed more trouble than the last. Indians delighted in indulging their children, coddling them constantly and giving them nearly everything they wanted, but there was one thing they would not tolerate—crying. In a society where warfare was a way of life, and stealth frequently marked the difference between life and death, one crying baby could give away an entire band. It was a lesson children learned early. When affection and pampering failed, a mother was expected to take her howling offspring out in the woods and tie his cradleboard to the branches of a tree, leaving him alone until the offending sounds had stopped. Two or three doses of this was usually enough to teach the most willful child that tears and tantrums were not the way to get what he wanted.

"Do you want me to help with the sewing, *na'go*?" Morning Star spoke a little too quickly, but the crying had finally stopped and she did not want her mother to think about it again. "Or shall I gather firewood for you? You look very tired."

"No, I am fine," Buffalo Calf Woman replied, shaking her head. She *was* tired—she had not felt like herself for a long time—but it worried her that her daughter could see it. "Finish the pemmican. That is more important. Besides, you are still a very little girl. Even the biggest load of firewood you could carry in your arms would be nothing at all. I will go myself."

Morning Star sighed as she watched her mother walk slowly toward the river. Really, it was frustrating, always being treated like a baby. When was *na'go* going to realize that she was growing up and could do her share of the hard work, too? Turning back to her pemmican, she caught a glimpse of Little Bear out of the corner of her eye.

"Why don't you help her?" she burst out impulsively. After all, Little Bear was two years older than she. "Your arms are long enough to gather a big load of wood. Besides, for all you're accomplishing with that alphabet, you might as well do something useful."

"Me?" Little Bear was so surprised, his voice came out in a squeak. "Help with the chores? That's women's work. Men don't gather firewood."

His expression was so indignant, Morning Star could not keep from giggling. "You're not a man—you're a little boy. And men do too gather firewood. At least, I . . . I think they do."

She was on uncertain ground now. She had an image of

tall, strong men, gathering up great loads of wood and piling it behind the house, but she was not as sure of it as she once would have been. Her life with her white family seemed so far away now, she no longer knew if things were real or if she was only imagining them.

"Well, I will be a man soon." The boy drew himself up as tall as he could and took a deep breath to push out his chest. "I don't have time to gather wood—or draw pictures in the dirt." With a disgusted look, he threw the stick aside, as if he had only taken it up in the first place to humor her.

"Oh, Potbelly . . ." Morning Star bit her lip to hold back the laughter. He looked so silly, all puffed up like that. "You are such a funny boy."

He gave her exactly the look she had expected. All scowls and flashing eyes. And not because she had said he was funny, either, but because she dared to call him Potbelly. At ten, the boy had outgrown his baby fat, but not the nickname it had inspired. Whenever she wanted to get a rise out of him, Morning Star knew just how to do it.

The ploy did not fail her now.

"I told you never to call me that again," he retorted furiously. "Nicknames are for babies—and I'm not a baby anymore!"

"Of course not." Morning Star was almost sorry she had teased him so mercilessly. It was too nice a day to quarrel, and anyhow, she had the feeling he was right. Didn't she hate it herself when people treated her like a baby?

"*Nágo* told me that every Indian is given a name shortly after he is born," she said, eager to change the subject. "It is usually chosen by a male relative of his father. He might have a pet name when he is younger—Curly or Fragrant, or something like that—but he always takes his own name back when he grows up. From now on, I promise I will always call you Little Bear—except when I'm mad at you, of course."

The jest was lost on him. "I'm not going to be known as Little Bear, either," he told her, his face as solemn as she had ever seen it. "Someday I'm going to be a great chief. Not a civil chief, like Brave Eagle, but one of the warrior chiefs. Little Bear is not a name for a warrior. *Nágo* was right—most men and nearly all the women *do* take back their birth names when they grow up. But sometimes a man feels he needs a new name. You know, something that tells people what he really is. Like . . . Kills-by-the-Camp. Or Wooden Leg, because his thighs are so strong he can run for miles without stopping.''

Morning Star stared at him curiously. She had never heard of this custom, but it made sense now that she thought of it.

"What name are you going to take?"

"I am going to be called . . ." The boy paused, glowering at her as if daring her to laugh. "I am going to be called Man-Who-Lives-with-the-Wolves."

"Man-Who-Lives-with-the-Wolves?" The look and the words had exactly the effect he had hoped to avoid. "What a silly name!" Just imagine, funny, good-natured Potbelly, trying to live with wolves in a dank cave in the forest! Who would pound his pemmican for him then—or gather his firewood?

"Silly, indeed!" a voice behind her agreed.

Turning, Morning Star saw Little Bear's best friend, Running Deer, emerge from behind the tepee. Being a year older than the other youth gave him a certain status he never seemed to forget.

"Man-Who-Lives-with-the-Wolves? Don't tell me, little friend, that you fancy yourself as a mighty chief. A warrior leading your braves into battle. You'd better get that idea out of your head—you don't have it in you. Stick to being a scholar."

Still laughing, he pointed at the letters scratched in the dirt. Little Bear looked embarrassed as he rubbed them out with his foot.

"I suppose you think you'd make a better leader?"

"Of course." Running Deer grinned easily. "But don't worry, my friend. When I am a great chief, I will always find a place on my Council for you."

Morning Star felt her temper begin to rise. Like all of the younger children, she was a bit in awe of Running Deer, so much cleverer and more confident than the other boys. But when he was smug and sarcastic like that, it was easy to forget how much she liked him.

"Little Bear could too be a warrior," she retorted hotly. "He is just as strong as you—and just as brave! You had better be nice to him, Running Deer. Someday he may have to find a place on his Council for you."

Running Deer turned to her with a mildly surprised look,

as if he had just noticed she was there. Then, with a nonchalant shrug, he looked back to his friend.

"Did you hear, I have a pony of my own? My father's
brother took it last month in a raid. He was going to give it to
his own son, but I'm a better rider so the family decided it
should belong to me. Do you want to see it?"

Little Bear's face showed only a flicker of emotion, but
Morning Star knew what he was thinking. He was excited
about the horse, but he couldn't help wishing he had one,
too. It was hard having a friend who was older and always
got everything sooner.

"What is he like?" he asked, curiosity getting the best of
darker feelings. "Is he a good mount?"

"A black-and-white pinto. And, yes, he is the best horse
you can imagine. But come and see for yourself. I'll let you
ride him if you like."

Morning Star grated the maul roughly across the hollowed-
out stone, taking her frustration out on the pemmican, as the
sound of their excited voices faded in the distance. She might
as well not have existed, for all the attention they paid to her!
They had not even bothered to say good-bye. She would have
loved to go with them—she could ride as well as Little Bear,
even if she was two years younger—and she longed to join in
the fun. But, no, just because she had been born a girl instead
of a boy, she had to stay behind and tend to the chores.

Not that she minded doing her share. She was glad to take
some of the burden from Buffalo Calf Woman's shoulders,
even if her arms did ache so much she could hardly stand it.
And she would do more, too, if they would let her. But it did
seem sometimes that the boys had all the fun!

The passing seasons did little to tame Morning Star's rebellious spirit. It was not that she did not enjoy her life with the
Indians; quite the contrary, she seemed to thrive on the
challenges of nature and even the hard work. Each spring,
when the Moon of Green Grass had come and it was time to
break camp, Brave Eagle would stand her up against one of
the posts that had held back the door flap and measure how
much taller she had grown since last year. And each fall, with
the approach of the Deer-Rutting Moon, she took on more
and more of the tasks involved in setting up the tepee for the
winter, until slowly, she found herself slipping into that

vague half-world between childhood and maturity. But try as she would, she could never quite get over the feeling that it was indeed the boys who had all the fun. And the girls who got stuck with the work.

"I don't see why I can't do everything Little Bear does," she blurted out one warm summer evening as they sat before a crackling fire in front of the tepee. "I can ride as well as any boy my age—and I can hunt, too! And I'll bet I could beat them at their silly games if I tried!"

Buffalo Calf Woman set down her awl and looked up with troubled eyes. "It would not be seemly, Morning Star," she reminded her quietly. "A woman should know her place."

But to the girl's surprise, Brave Eagle seemed more amused than disapproving.

"Why not let the child play with the boys if she chooses? She is as tall as they are, and as strong—I cannot think she will be hurt. And she is right. She *can* ride as well as any of them."

"Oh, *nihu!*" Morning Star could hardly believe her ears. "Do you really mean it? You won't be sorry, I promise you. I'll make you proud of me. Did you know *na'go*," she said, turning to her mother, "that there was once a woman warrior among the Kiowas. She was very famous—and she even had women to skin her buffalo and build her tepees, just like a man does!"

The alarm deepened on Buffalo Calf Woman's features, but Brave Eagle only laughed. The girl's childish enthusiasm did not worry him. With her blue eyes and lightly tanned skin, she already showed signs of becoming a great beauty. When the time came, there would be more than enough suitors for her, and she would slip naturally into a woman's role.

"Enjoy yourself, daughter," he said indulgently. "Be a child while you can."

Morning Star took to her freedom with an exhilaration that caught even Brave Eagle off guard. She did not, of course, neglect her chores, knowing that that would be the surest way to make her father change his mind. Nor did she disassociate herself entirely from the other girls, for one of her favorite hours came late in the evening when they all clustered together in the shadows just beyond the flickering firelight and watched the women play at their games.

She was especially fond of the Awl Game, the very game

the women had been playing the night Brave Eagle rode into camp with her. Choosing up sides, they would draw four lines along the edges of a blanket, two for the dry rivers—terrible places because you had to start over if you landed on them—and two for the flowing rivers, which were safe. There was much laughter as the women threw down their gaming sticks, flat on one side but rounded on the other, and marked their positions with an awl on the blanket. Recklessly, they gambled on the outcome of each toss, challenging each other with everything from a handful of glass beads to embroidered pillows and willow backrests, and even on occasion a recently cured hide or warm buffalo robe.

But as exciting as those evenings were, it was the boys' games that appealed most to Morning Star. They may have been designed for a practical purpose—the preparation of youths to serve as future warriors—but they were rollicking good fun, too. Morning Star could only stand on the sidelines and watch Throw 'Em Off Their Horses, for she had no mount of her own, but she was only too ready to add her lusty cheers to those of the other spectators. Dust rose from a hundred hooves, forming clouds around whooping figures and rearing horses, as the boys charged at each other with all the fury of a real battle, until only one—the "warrior chief" of the afternoon—was left seated on his horse.

But all the other games belonged as much to Morning Star as to the boys, and she quickly proved she was more than a match for anyone her size and age. She was best at the game they called Kick the Ball, for she was quicker than the others, and her childish foot would lash out to capture the hair-stuffed leather ball from under her opponent's toes before he even had a chance to see it. But she also liked Hit the Ball, a kind of primitive field hockey played with a wooden stick, and she never shied away from the Swing-Kicking Game, the roughest of them all. She was determined to swing and kick with the best of them, showing no mercy to the hapless boys she wrestled to the ground—and taking care not to whine or cry when the action went against her and she got more than her share of bruises.

Only on rare occasions did she still find herself left out of the boys' activities, but when she did, it stung even more bitterly than before.

One morning, Dull Moon, one of her mother's brothers,

came to tell them he was ready to dispose of several horses he had captured the week before in an especially daring raid. The youngest, a spirited colt, would go to one of the boys in the family, and in an unexpected burst of generosity, he declared the contest open not only to the sons of his brothers, but to the sons of his sisters and their husbands as well. Morning Star, listening quietly just outside the tepee, felt her heart sink. Dull Moon, of all her parents' relatives, was the one who least approved of the way she had been indulged. There was not a chance in the world she would be included among the boys this time.

The more she thought about it, the more frustrating it seemed. The competition would be a bold challenge to the skill of every boy who took part. The colt, unencumbered by either saddle or bridle, would be led into a clearing in the woods just outside of camp, where everyone in the village would have gathered to watch. There, in that strange setting, with the sound of the crowd in his ears, the animal would be as frenzied as a wild stallion. The boys would try to mount him, in order of age, until one of them managed to stay on his back. He would be the one to lead the colt back to pasture and tether him beside the horses in his father's herd.

At the appointed hour, Morning Star stood with the others at the edge of a grassy ring and watched a half-dozen youths strut out into the center and circle arrogantly around the horse. Their raucous jests and harsh cries rang in her ears, and she struggled to choke back her envy. If she could not win the horse for herself, then at least she wanted her brother to get him. But the contest was to be in order of age, and Little Bear was the youngest. How likely was it that he would even have a chance?

Yet, turning her gaze toward the horse, she was not so sure. He was a magnificent animal, a fiery sorrel, lean and long legged, and his mane whipped like flames in the wind. Whinnying defiantly, he threw back his head, giving Morning Star a glimpse of his eyes. Dark eyes, wild—flashing with challenge. For all her disappointment, the girl had to laugh. Not one of those cocky, overconfident boys would have an easy time of it that day. She would not be the least bit surprised if Dull Moon led the colt back riderless to his own herd when it was over.

How she wished she could try her luck with him! She had

never broken a horse, but she knew how it was done. It was said that the Comanches took the head of a wild horse between their hands and exhaled into its nostrils, forcing their breath into its lungs, making it a part of them—subjugating it to their will. That is what she would do with this horse. She would go up to that fiery, unfettered spirit, just as a Comanche would have done, and show him with her own breath that she was his master!

Not that she would have the chance. Sighing, she forced herself back to reality. Brave Eagle might indulge her all he wanted, but in the eyes of the rest of the tribe, she was only a girl, and there were things she could never do. Whole worlds would be closed to her forever, no matter how desperately she longed to taste them.

An expectant hush fell over the crowd. The boys moved slowly out of the ring, leaving Red Hawk, the eldest, alone in the center. He hesitated awkwardly, then strode up to the horse, looking him right in the eye. I am not afraid of you, he seemed to be saying. Do not think I dread the ordeal that lies ahead.

His bravado was sadly misplaced, as Morning Star had known it would be. Red Hawk was not a good rider, and it showed in the clumsy way he tangled his hands in the colt's mane and braced his feet one last time on the ground before leaping upward. The horse was more than ready for him. The instant the boy left the earth, the spirited animal gave a sideways shimmy, twisting his torso sinuously beneath that assaulting form. Red Hawk landed unceremoniously on his belly on the colt's back and, toppling head over heels, slid onto the dirt on the other side. The roar of laughter that greeted his failure went a little way toward soothing Morning Star's disappointment.

"What a fine rider!" someone said in her ear. "Why, Red Hawk stayed on that colt at least half a second!"

Morning Star recognized the jeering tones of her brother's best friend. As usual, Running Deer brought out mixed reactions in her. She could not help feeling flattered that the youth had chosen to stand beside her—she was at an age where she was just beginning to notice boys as something other than playmates—but he had an uncanny knack of always making her lose her temper.

"Wait until Little Bear's turn," she snapped. "Then you'll see some riding!"

She regretted the words instantly. Running Deer's soft, answering laugh told her that he was indeed waiting for his friend's turn—and he would be no gentler with Little Bear than he had with the others. Morning Star knew she should not care so much. Her brother himself did not seem to mind, but somehow she could not bear to have him exposed to Running Deer's sharp tongue.

One after another, the boys tested their mettle against the horse, and one after another, they failed. Finally there was only one left—Little Bear. Watching him, Morning Star was aware of her own conflicting emotions. She was excited for him, but she was afraid, too, and she found herself hoping not so much that he would win the horse, but that he would at least acquit himself well.

He began promisingly enough. He did not bluster like the others, but circled slowly around the colt, giving them both a chance to size each other up. Only when he was sure of himself did he edge cautiously forward, placing one hand lightly on that long, sleek neck. When the gesture brought no reaction, he braced both hands firmly and swung up, hooking his leg over the horse's back. Still the animal did not move, and Morning Star dared to hope that her brother's cautious manner had broken his resistance. That hope was shattered an instant later when the colt reared suddenly upward.

It was a dazzling display of energy. Little Bear tried desperately to hold on, but he was no match for that surging fury. The horse reared again, then one more time, arching his body backward, and the boy slid down into the dust of his hooves.

"Right on his rump!" Running Deer's laughter was infuriatingly smug. "So much for Great Chief Man-Who-Lives-with-the-Wolves!"

Morning Star spun around. Wasn't that just like Running Deer? It was three years since he had overheard that secret, and he had stored it in his memory all this time!

"I think you are the meanest boy who ever lived! I—I . . . I'll show you!"

Anger carried her out into the center of the ring. Only when she caught sight of Dull Moon's dark, scowling features did she realize what she had done, but it was too late to turn back.

"I want to try, too!" she cried out boldly. "None of the boys could do it. Why not let me? Or are you afraid a girl will show them all up?"

Dull Moon was too surprised to do anything but throw a questioning glance toward the sidelines. Astonishment mingled with the irritation he had felt when the last of the boys failed and, for once, he offered no objection. Brave Eagle did not reply to the query in the other man's eyes, but it seemed to the watching girl that the corners of his mouth turned up and he inclined his head in the faintest hint of a nod.

Morning Star needed no more encouragement. Trembling with excitement, she turned back to the colt, blocking everything else out of her mind. Remembering how successful Little Bear had been at the start, she forced herself to move with the same quiet caution. She was well aware that this moment was more important for her than it had been for any of the boys. The men of the tribe had bent their rules for her today. They would not give her another chance if she failed.

The horse seemed to sense a difference in her manner. He pawed restlessly at the earth, but he did not try to back away. Moving her hand slowly, Morning Star laid it on the side of his neck, as she had seen Little Bear do, and waited until she was sure she could control the trembling in her fingers. Then, remembering the Comanches, she drew herself up on her toes and cupped her hands lightly around his nostrils. The feel of her breath was soft and warm, as startling to her as it was to the colt.

She moved away tentatively, half exhilarated, half frightened by what she had done. To her amazement, the horse seemed confused, unsure of himself for the first time, and she realized suddenly that she had stumbled on the one way to deal with him. Do the unexpected. Make a move he had not anticipated, and he would not know how to thwart her.

She did not hesitate to press her advantage. She might have a second before the colt moved again, she might have two—there would be no more than that. Catching her breath one last time, she hurled herself onto his back, trying to show the same grace she had seen in her brother's movements. Only, unlike Little Bear, she did not try to find a fingerhold in the horse's mane, but threw her arms around his neck.

It was all that saved her. The horse reacted instantly, rearing back with a savage, twisting motion. Too late, Morning Star realized she had underestimated him. On the ground, she might be able to confuse him—mounted on his back, she was utterly at his mercy. Digging her knees into his sides, she clung frantically to his neck, praying that she would at least manage to stay on as long as the boys had. Then suddenly, just when the strength in her arms was about to give out, the horse drew his front hooves back to the earth and stood still beneath her, as if nothing had gone on between them. The only motion was the impatient toss of his head, a light, careless flick of his mane into her face, as if to say: All right, the game is over. We've had our fun. Now let's go for a ride.

Morning Star held herself straight and rigid on his back. Had she really won—or was he only playing one last crafty trick on her? Slowly, she drew one hand back from his neck, careful to keep her fingers twisted in his mane, and then as slowly followed with the other. When he did not try to bolt or rear again, she knew that victory was truly hers. He had accepted her. She could ride him back to pasture if she chose, and he would not give her a minute's trouble.

She did not have any illusions about what she had done. This was not a wild stallion she had tamed, but a colt that had obviously been ridden before, perhaps by a young child, for he seemed to tolerate her weight better than that of the older boys. Still, the laughter and shouts of approval that came from the watching crowd were sweet to her ears. She was a girl who had tried what only boys had the right to dare—and she had succeeded!

Flushed with triumph, she sat absolutely still on the horse and let her gaze sweep around the ring. Only when her eyes stopped on a slender figure standing by himself a little in front of the others did she feel her first qualm, and the warmth began to drain out of her body. Little Bear. All she had wanted was to keep people from laughing at him, and now she had wounded his pride even more! She, a girl, had succeeded where he had failed.

But to her surprise, the dark eyes that gazed back at her flashed only with excitement. Little Bear was a better sport than she had given him credit for. Leaping into the center of the clearing, he whirled around to face the spectators.

"My sister is more a warrior than any of us here today," he called out in clear, ringing tones. "No one will ever make fun of her in my hearing again!"

There was jesting in his voice, but he was serious, too, and Morning Star realized with a little thrill of pleasure that he was proud of her. Not jealous, as she might have been had he won the horse, but generous and proud.

He was laughing as he turned to her.

"Allow me to lead your horse to the pasture, my sister."

Morning Star leaned forward, laying her hand on his for a second. It occurred to her how much support this boy had always given her, right from the beginning.

"Not *my* horse, Little Bear," she said softly. "*Our* horse. You are my brother, and I will gladly share him with you."

Three

Morning Star crouched in the cold in front of last night's embers and listened uncomfortably to the reedy wail that came through the doorway of the tepee. She was two months short of her thirteenth birthday, but even then she knew that the cries of a newborn ought to be loud and lusty, not thin and frail like this.

The wind that swept through the camp still held traces of a bitter winter just ending. Across the clearing, Morning Star saw Brave Eagle coming toward her with a load of wood in his arms. She watched silently as he kicked the coals to set sparks flying again. It made her feel funny to see her father doing woman's work, although he did not seem to mind. The days immediately before and after the birth of a child were the only times masculine pride allowed a Cheyenne warrior to gather firewood in his wife's place or fetch water for her from a nearby stream.

At least this child had lived. Morning Star glanced at the closed tepee doorway. Three times before, in the days since she had come to her Indian family, Buffalo Calf Woman had given birth, each time to a stillborn child. This child might be small and feeble, but it was alive. And it was the boy she was sure her father had hungered for in his heart.

Perhaps it was a sign.

She turned toward Brave Eagle, but his face was rigid and closed, and she sensed he did not want to talk. Yes, it had to be a sign. The past year had been a difficult one, growing harsher and harsher with each passing moon. Perhaps at last things were going to change.

It had begun the summer before. For the first time in Morning Star's memory, the buffalo had not come. No great herds thundering across the plains, no cows with their calves, not even a stray who had gotten cut off from the others. Time after time, she had watched the men ride out of camp, and time after time, they had come back again with only their bows in their hands and nothing but an occasional antelope or mountain sheep across the backs of their horses.

The first to feel the hardship was the old grandfather. He did not complain, but every time Morning Star looked at his pinched features she knew he longed for the days when a man could feel like a man, and sons-in-law provided more for their wives' fathers than a watery soup made of wild roots or a tough slice of dried prairie turnip. His skin was so thin it almost seemed transparent, and sometimes she thought she could see a bluish tone in the veins that stood out on his neck and forehead. Soon it became apparent that the rigors of travel were too much for him as the band was forced farther and farther from familiar hunting grounds, and one of Buffalo Calf Woman's sisters was appointed to stay behind and tend to his needs. When she rejoined the others seven days later, she was alone.

Morning Star had not been there to hear her grandfather sing his death song, but she knew his voice had been steady, its timbre clear and penetrating to the end. When she had first come to the Indians, it had seemed strange to her, the way the old ones always seemed to know when they were going to die. Now the words sounded natural to her ears:

It is a good day to die!
All the things of our life are here,
All that is left of our people are here.
It is a good day to die.

There had been little time to grieve for him, for the Moon When the Deer Lose Their Horns had barely ended before tragedy struck again. The white men had made a harsh new treaty with the Cheyennes, but no sooner had they smoked the sacred pipe with the old-man chiefs than they broke their word again, taking back even the little land they had promised. The Indians, hungry and desperate, had sent Broken Arm, Brave Eagle's brother, with several of the other braves to try to reason with the Blue Coats at the fort. He had never arrived. On the way, he had run into a hostile war party, all fired up on the white man's liquor and spoiling for a fight. The wound he had suffered in the ensuing skirmish was slight, and when he returned to the camp, he was sitting straight and proud on his horse. But in the days that followed, the sore began to fester, and a body that had once seemed robust grew weak and wracked with fever. The medicine men had been summoned and the sound of their sacred chants could be heard everywhere in the hushed camp, but even their strong magic was not enough to keep Broken Arm from slipping into the sleep from which he would never awake.

Morning Star had been sitting silently in her father's tepee when Brave Eagle summoned Little Bear to tell him he would not see his father again. The look on the boy's face had been as painful to her as the news that brought him there. His jaw was set in a hard line, his eyes were fixed straight ahead, and she knew he was trying very hard to remember that a boy of fourteen was nearly a man in the eyes of the tribe.

"I am your father now," Brave Eagle told him gently. "You must look toward me as you once looked toward him who guided you safely through the first years of your life."

"Yes, *nihu.*"

Little Bear's voice was obedient, but Morning Star sensed the rebellion in his heart. How he must have longed to say, No, *nihu,* I will accept no father but the one who has left me. No one will ever take his place in my heart! But it would not be manly for a young warrior to display such tender emotions.

Brave Eagle, too, seemed to sense the boy's feelings. There was a heaviness in his face Morning Star had never seen there before. He studied the youth gravely for a moment, then spoke again.

"I have given much thought to your future, my son, and I have decided that you must make a sacrifice for your people. You are no longer a child; you cannot live in a child's world anymore. Tomorrow you will take a man's responsibilities on your shoulders. There is a mission school many days' ride from this place. The missionaries feed and clothe Indian boys, and teach them the customs and language of the white man. When the sun rises tomorrow, I want you to be ready to go to them."

Little Bear's face mirrored shock and disbelief. Morning Star, watching from the sidelines, knew exactly what he was thinking. Never before had he defied his elders, but how could a young man accept this thing without speaking?

"I cannot do that, *nihu*! I do not want to disobey, but I must stay here. Who would take care of my mother if I went? She has no one else now."

"Your mother will live with her brother, as is fitting. And you will go to the mission school."

Brave Eagle's eyes softened a little as he watched the boy. This was not a time to encourage spirit, it was a time to reinforce obedience, but discipline could be meted out with understanding.

"The white man is moving into our world, my son. You see that with your own eyes. Every year he takes away more and more of our land. Soon he will push us into barren deserts where no corn grows and no buffalo can live. The Indian ways will vanish one day, and the Indian will have to live in the white man's world. How can we do that if no man has the courage to go before us and learn the things that we must know?"

Morning Star was keenly conscious of the silence as Little Bear bowed his head obediently and turned to leave the tepee. He would not fight again, she knew, and her heart ached for him. She longed to throw her arms around her father's neck and beg him to change his mind, but there was a new hardness in his features and she was afraid. She held her hand in front of her face so he could not see her tears as she slipped quietly out of the lodge.

Little Bear was standing beside a fallen pine at the edge of the camp, his back turned toward her as he gazed out into the darkness. The moonlight was so pale she could barely make him out, but she sensed that he, too, was crying. She wanted more than anything in the world to go to him, but she knew she could not. His was a double pain that night, not merely the loss of a deeply loved father, but the loss of his place in the tribe as well. She could not add to his burden by shaming his pride in front of her.

She had not realized until that moment how much a part of her life he had always been. Little Bear. The funny, potbellied boy who never failed to make her laugh. The lively youth whose high spirits complemented her own. Somehow she had assumed he would always be there when she needed him. That they would grow up and grow old and always be

friends together. Now he was going away, and by the time
she saw him again he would be a stranger.

The baby began to cry again, breaking into her thoughts.
The sound seemed weaker now, so rasping and frail she could
hardly bear to hear it. If only he would stop for a minute. If
only he could get enough nourishment to sleep for a while.

Even a year ago, she would not have felt so useless and
frustrated. Then, there was still fresh meat and plenty of jerky
for a good, strong winter stew. Brave Eagle would have
whittled three branches into poles for her, and she would
have lashed them together, forming a stout tripod. Hanging a
buffalo paunch from the center, she would have filled it with
water and whatever food she could find: large chunks of
meat, and peas and prairie turnips, or perhaps the bulbs of
spring lilies or peeled stalks of sweet thistle. On a nearby
fire, she would have heated rocks—strong, tough rocks that
did not splinter from the flames—and thrown them into the
water until it bubbled and threatened to boil over. When the
stew was finished, she would take down the paunch and cut it
into little pieces so her mother could eat it and regain her
strength.

But now there was no meat, she reminded herself bitterly,
and precious little in the way of anything else. They had not
tasted fresh buffalo for more than a year, and even the jerky
had been gone for a long time. The antelope seemed to have
vanished from the forests, and it had been many moons since
anyone had speared a fish in the frozen streams. All they had
now were the rations the Blue Coats had promised them.
Bacon and sugar, hardtack, coffee and flour. Only the white
man's rations were like the white man's promises—thin and
rotting from the inside. The bacon was rancid and covered
with mold; the flour crawled with worms. How could a
woman who lived on rations like that have enough milk for
her baby?

The crying stopped, then began again with feeble little
gasps, like coughs or hiccups. Morning Star did not want to
look at the doorway again, but she could not keep her eyes
away.

"He is not going to die, is he?" she whispered.

A soft, scraping sound told her that Brave Eagle had risen
and taken a step toward her. She did not turn to look, but she

sensed him standing over her, and she knew that the fear in her voice had hurt him.

"That is not for us to know, daughter. Only Heamma-Wihio, the Wise One Above, knows if a child is ready to begin his journey up the Hanging Road to the heavens. It will be revealed to us when the time is ready."

"But he is so little. And we have had him such a very few days. It's not fair to take him from us now."

Brave Eagle dropped to one knee beside her and laid a hand on her shoulder.

"Nothing is ours to keep, my child. You know that as well as I. Not even our bodies belong to us. We walk the paths of this world only a brief time, and none of the things we have made will outlast us long. Nothing endures forever, only the earth and the mountains."

Morning Star drew herself to her feet and walked a few steps away, gazing up at the faraway mountains. How was it that a man like her father could take comfort in their cold, elusive presence? They did not comfort her at all. What did it matter that they would still be there, silent and unapproachable, after she and her parents were gone? Or the little brother she had prayed for every day since they had told her he was coming?

Everything had been done to assure his safe arrival. Buffalo Calf Woman had taken great pains to protect that new little life from the moment she felt it stir within her. Each day, she had risen before sunrise and taken long walks around the camp, for everyone knew that a baby's growth occurred in those early morning hours and the exercise would help him build his strength. She had been careful, too, never to stare too long at any unusual object or person so the child would not be marked when he came into the world. And when her time came, she had even asked Brave Eagle to bring presents to the medicine men, and they had come to sit in a circle outside her tepee. All through the long process of birth, the reassuring sound of their chanting could be heard, and their rasping rattles scared away the envious spirits that tried to steal the breath from a newborn child.

Even ignorant as she was, Morning Star realized it was a relatively easy birth. For the first time, she had not been shooed away, but was allowed to remain in the tepee, taking her place among the women of the family, even though she was not quite a woman yet herself. She was careful to stay quiet, not wanting them to change their minds and send her away. Pressing back as far as she could into the tepee liner, she watched with wide, fascinated eyes.

The tepee was swelled almost to overflowing, for all her mother's female relatives had gathered to offer support and to aid the two midwives. A thick robe, covered with straw, had been laid on the ground. On this, Buffalo Calf Woman knelt and, leaning forward, grasped the center pole of a heavy wood frame. Her face was strained, sweat soaked her hair and poured into her eyes, but she did not cry out, and Morning Star sensed more concentration than pain in her expression. When at last the child began to come, one of the midwives slipped between her and the frame and, using it as a brace, caught her up in a strong embrace. The other moved behind her and reached out to receive the child from the rear. When the delivery had been completed, the first midwife took a feather and tickled her throat, gagging her to force out the afterbirth.

The women all crowded around, talking at once and craning their necks to see. The midwife with the child gave it a hasty examination, then held it high in the air.

"It's a boy!" she cried, giving him a sharp swat on the rump to welcome him into the world. A howl of protest burst out of his tiny lungs.

Morning Star almost cried with relief at the sound. This baby had been born alive, not blue and still like the others. His cries were thin—not the hearty bellows she had heard every time Owl Woman gave birth—but at least he was crying, and that was all that counted.

The midwives fussed over the child, greasing his limbs and torso until they shone. Then they powdered him with dried cottonwood pulp and patted ripe spores of star puffball on the umbilical cord. Later, when the cord dropped off, Buffalo Calf Woman would sew it into a beaded buckskin bag, shaped like a lizard or turtle, and he would wear it around his neck to ensure long life. The placenta was placed in another bag. After the women had tied it securely with a rawhide thong, they took it outside the camp and hung it in the high branches of a tree. To allow it to be buried in the ground would cause the death of the child.

The placenta?

Morning Star turned back toward the doorway with a guilty start. The thin, tremulous cries, so nerve-wracking before, had stopped now, and the silence was even more frightening. How could she have forgotten the placenta? Every day for the first three days, she had gone to make sure it was still safe where the women had hung it. Today, for the first time, she had forgotten.

Without even pausing for a word of explanation, she left her father and began to race down the path that twisted into the woods. She did not know if her feet were guided by genuine faith, or only childish superstition, but that did not matter now. She had to get to that tree—she had to see that the bag with the placenta was still there. If it was, surely she could make herself believe that her little brother would live for one more day at least.

But when she got there, the bag was gone.

She stood at the foot of the tree, gasping as she tried to catch her breath. Could she have come to the wrong place? In her haste, had she taken a wrong turn and ended up in another part of the forest?

But no, it was the same tree. Slowly, her mind began to clear and she recognized details she had noticed before. The same gray-black trunk, the same thick leafless branches— only the bag was gone. She remembered again that eerie stillness those last few minutes in front of the tepee, and she knew now with a terrible, cold certainty what it had meant.

Even before she returned to the camp, she knew what she would find. The tepee was silent, as it had been when she left. Buffalo Calf Woman, too weak to walk, would be lying alone on her pallet inside, but it was not to her that the girl's thoughts turned. Almost unconsciously, her eyes sought her father where he sat motionless beside the fire. In his arms, he was holding a tiny bundle wrapped in a soft fur robe.

Morning Star knelt in front of him and reached out to clasp the fragile body that had felt so warm the last time she touched it. Together, father and daughter laid the child out on the earth and dressed him in a soft doeskin shirt, still much too big, since it had been made for the days when he would sit up and crawl around the tepee. Morning Star felt tears burn her eyelids, but she held them back, sensing they would add to the grief her father already felt. They worked hastily for they knew that the *tasoom*, the spirit of the boy, could not begin its long journey to the heavens while his body was still bound to the earth. When they had finished, they lashed his arms to his sides and tied him into the cradleboard that his mother would have used to carry him around the camp.

With the instinct of people who have lived in close proximity for many years, friends and family members began to arrive without summons. By the time they were ready to begin their slow procession toward the pine groves on the side of the hill, nearly everyone was there. Morning Star was free to weep now; indeed, it was expected of her, for the physical burden of grieving fell on the women of the tribe, and she let out her anguish in high-pitched wails that mingled with the cries of her mother's sisters and cousins. Had the boy lived longer—had he shown promise of being a great warrior, the mainstay of the family—she would have cut her flesh until it bled and made deep gashes in her arms and legs. But because he was only a small child, she had to content herself with tears alone as she watched her father hang the cradleboard in the branches of a tall pine, where the boy's spirit would be free to rise into the sky.

One by one the mourners departed. Morning Star remained behind, listening to the last echoes of their keening fade away until nothing was left but silence. She sat for a long time on the cold ground, her legs crossed like a boy's, and looked up at the cradleboard. She had not forgotten that the mother of a troublesome child would bring him out into the woods and hang him in a tree until he stopped crying. She did not know how much awareness the *tasoom* retained of earthly things, but she could not bear to think that her little brother might believe he was being punished. Or be afraid.

She knew, of course, that she was being foolish. Wherever the boy's spirit was now, it was not hanging on that branch with the poor shell of bones and flesh and skin that had once borne his name. The minute the cradleboard had been secured to the pine, his *tasoom* had ascended into the misty blue of the sky. When that blue darkened to black and stars appeared in the darkness, he would begin his journey up the Hanging Road to the home of Heamma-Wihio. There he would grow, as a boy should, on plains thick with buffalo and sweet with the smell of freedom. He would have his father's brother, Broken Arm, to call *nihu*, just as Broken Arm's son called Brave Eagle *nihu* on earth. And he would play the same games she herself had played, and learn to hunt like other boys, and ride into battle when the time was ready.

Still, the heavy weight did not lift from her heart, and still she could not seem to leave her brother alone. Never, as long as she lived, would she forget the terrible sense of pain she felt now. Twilight fell, and with it came the first evening star—the first stepping stone on that road that would take him away from her—and the earth seemed cold and lonely. Tears felt like ice on her cheeks when Brave Eagle came to find her at last and carried her back in his arms to the camp.

Four

With the passing of the next moon came the passing of Morning Star's childhood, and she realized with mixed feelings that it was time to leave her tomboy days behind.

The laws that governed the relationships between men and women were the laws of the Spirits, not the frail laws of humans, and they were more rigid than any strictures the tribe could impose. For all her longing, the girl could no more live as a boy than she could fly like the Thunder God into the sky and soar with him through the clouds. When the time came that she felt the bleeding that marked the end of her girlhood, like it or not, she passed into the world of the women.

Brave Eagle was proud, as Cheyenne males always were, when his wife came to him with the news. Indians doted on their children, but they took their joy not from keeping them little and dependent, but from seeing them grow and change. Once he had delighted in watching her childish ways; now he would take the same delight in watching her flirt with the young men who had been her playmates, and fall in love and marry . . . and bear children of her own.

And he would enjoy the antics of his grandchildren as he had once enjoyed hers.

Brave Eagle celebrated his daughter's coming of age as Indian fathers had celebrated since the beginning of time. Running through the camp, he had shouted to all within earshot: "Today my daughter has become a woman. I have shelterd and nurtured her all these many years. Today I claim my reward. She has grown to be a fine young woman."

In the old days, when times were better and a great hunter was a man of wealth, the festivities would have been more elaborate. Then there would have been many presents for friends and family—deerskins and soft buffalo robes, beaded moccasins and tufts of red cloth to decorate tepee liners—and perhaps Brave Eagle would even have given away a horse. But at least there had been sufficient game that last month, and as he ran through the camp, he could console himself with the thought that soon the men of the tribe would join him in a feast in front of his lodge. Meat would be roasted on skewers over an open flame, and with it there would be rice and dried apples from the trading post, fat brown sausages and bone marrow, plums gathered from the prairie, and wild honey to be sucked off of peeled willow sticks.

When the feast was over, he would pass the pipe, with its carved stone bowl shaped like the head of a horse. Not the white man's cigarettes, rolled in thin strips of newspaper, the way so many of the young braves did now, but a real pipe. He would light it solemnly, taking long, deep puffs before he passed it to the left, following the direction of the sun. And in those brief hours, before it was time to clean the pipe again, signaling that the party had come to an end, it would almost seem as if the old days had come back again.

Morning Star could hear the sound of her father's cries echoing through the camp, but in the tepee where she crouched alone in front of the fire, they seemed muted and far away. Loosening her hair, she undid first one long braid, then another, and ran a coarse buffalo-tongue brush through it until it glowed dark auburn in the last rays of twilight that spilled through the open doorway. When she had finished, the women came into the tepee and, circling round her, closed the door behind them. Laughing and joking, they removed the girl's clothes and, taking out brushes and pigments, they began to paint her body a vivid crimson. Then they wrapped her in a soft buffalo robe and drew her into a kneeling position in front of the fire.

No light still seeped through the doorway by the time they had finished. The coals cast only faint red shadows through the interior of the tepee. A burst of gold suddenly flared up, hissing and spitting into the darkness, and a pungent odor told Morning Star that sweet grass had been thrown on the fire, with juniper needles and a pinch of white sage. Leaning forward, she opened her robe and held it over the coals so the purifying smoke could pass through her body. The sensation was an eerie one. Her skin was warm, strangely tingling, and she wondered if it was the effect of the herbs she was feeling, or if it was only the sudden, bewildering knowledge that she was not a little girl any more, but a young woman.

When Morning Star's body had finally been cleansed to the women's satisfaction, they rose and filed one by one out of the tepee. After a moment, she, too, drew herself to her feet and, stepping outside, began to follow them to the Moon Lodge, a special tepee which had been set aside for the women to spend that part of each month when they could not come in contact with the men. Even rebellious as she was, Morning Star did not consider defying the custom. The blood of a woman was threatening to the masculine virility that ensured the safety of the tribe. Anything she touched during these days would lose its supernatural power. Her father's shield, blessed by the priests, the arrows that had been strengthened by their powerful magic—all these and more would be weakened by her presence.

The Moon Lodge was hazy with smoke, and at first, Morning Star could barely make out the figures of the women who were already inside. No deerskins covered the bare earth floor, and the sloping tepee liner was stark and unadorned. If anyone had ever made an effort to decorate the place with magical pictures and gay bursts of color, the smoke of countless fires had long since dulled them to a drab, uniform gray.

One of the women cast a handful of grease on the fire, and in the sputtering yellow light, Morning Star was startled to see gaunt, wrinkled features hovering over her. Drawing in her breath, she recognized Fire Crow Woman, her father's oldest female relative. Brave Eagle had told her often enough that the sister of his own father was a good and generous woman, but Morning Star had always been a little afraid of that sharp, hawklike nose and those penetrating eyes. She had completely forgotten that it would be Fire Crow Woman who was to meet her here tonight.

The old woman crouched down in front of her, bending her knees slowly, as if it hurt her to move. But her voice when she spoke was clear and surprisingly strong.

"On this day, my daughter, you have become a woman. It is my duty to instruct you, as the female relatives of my father's family instructed me many years ago. Listen carefully to what I say, for I shall not return to the Moon Lodge

again, and the words I tell you are words you would be well
to heed."

Morning Star nodded obediently. There was something
almost comical about the old woman, with her jaw so firmly
set and thin gray braids decorated with girlish beads, but she
was not even tempted to giggle. Fire Crow Woman had never
been one to prompt laughter in young people.

Reaching into the folds of her robe the old woman took a
long strip of rawhide and held it in front of her. Morning Star
stared at it, fascinated not so much by the thong itself, but by
the twisted fingers that were clutched around it. No wonder
they called the woman Fire Crow, she thought, trying not to
shiver. Her hands did not look like hands at all. They looked
like the talons of a bird.

"You know what this is?"

It was less a question than a declaration, and Morning Star
nodded again. It would be hard not to recognize the hide—the
chastity belt that was presented to every young girl on the day
she reached her maturity. When she left the Moon Lodge,
Morning Star would tie that long leather strip around her
waist and, after knotting it in front, she would wind it securely between her thighs.

"Take care to tie the hide wherever you go. Failure to do
so will bring great shame not just on yourself, but on your
entire family. Do not think that carelessness will serve you as
an excuse for forgetting. Carelessness will make even a pretty
girl look foolish in the eyes of men—and a foolish girl loses
her reputation forever. Even when you are married, always
tie the hide when you leave the tepee to gather wood or
water, or when your husband is away."

"Yes, of course. I understand." Morning Star was beginning to feel more at ease now, less afraid than she had before.
The woman did not seem so much severe as concerned. All
she really cared about was the welfare of her family.

Besides, Morning Star had to admit, Fire Crow Woman
had cause to be stern with her. Hadn't she flouted rules and
conventions often enough in the past?

"Do not exchange too many smiles or glances with a
young man," the woman continued, passing on to Morning
Star the same admonitions that had been passed to her when
she herself came of age. "Especially if others are near enough
to see. For then people will think you are foolish, and it will

be said throughout the camp that pretty Morning Star is easy and immoral. A woman who is immoral will never find a man to take her from her father."

She paused, giving Morning Star a sharp look, as if to see if she was listening. The expression on the girl's face seemed to mollify her, for she went on as before.

"If a young man comes to visit you in front of your mother's tepee at night, do not run from him or you will look foolish in his eyes. And do not send him away too soon, for then he will think you are impolite and have not been taught to value the attentions of a suitor.

"But do not let him stay too long—no matter how good-looking he is—for then he will tell himself that you love him, and what man can respect a girl then? Never say yes the first time he asks you to marry him. Always tell him you need time to know him better. Tell him he will have to wait a year or two before you make your choice.

"And never—never—let a man touch your breasts. For when a man touches your breasts, he believes you belong to him. Then he will tell all the other men in the camp, and what will happen to you if he decides he does not want you after all? No one else will have you, even as pretty as you are. No man wants a woman who is easy and immoral."

Morning Star tried not to smile, but she could not resist. She looked down quickly so the old woman would not see. How silly it all was. Do not send a young man away too soon, do not let him stay too long—do not be too forward with him, do not be too shy.

And above all—oh, yes, above everything else!—do not let a young man think you are foolish.

Foolish. How funny the word sounded, repeated over and over like that. Foolish, foolish . . . foolish! And yet, in spite of it all, Morning Star could not deny that the woman's advice was sound. Turning her head, she stared almost hypnotically into the embers of the fire. The Cheyenne world was a man's world; a woman had no place in it except through her father or her brother—or her husband. If no man claimed her, where could she go except into the fields, like those foolish girls who had untied the hide before their wedding night, or the women who had been divorced four times? No man would take her to live in his tepee then, but every man would come to her in the darkness, looking for the things no decent woman could give.

It was all so bewildering, Morning Star thought. Confusing, and yet in a strange way exciting, too. Rising from her place beside the fire, she stepped over to the doorway and stared out at the silent camp. In three days' time, or four or five, she would step once again through that same doorway, but the world she entered would not be the world she had left. She did not feel any different inside, she was sure she did not look any different on the outside either, but the difference was there all the same. People would look at her with exactly the same eyes, and they would see exactly the same thing—and yet it would not be the same at all. For they would not be looking at a girl anymore. They would be looking at a pretty young woman.

Pretty?

Morning Star set her waterskin down and peered anxiously into the marshy depths of the pond. The stagnant waters were dull with mud and a thin green film drifted across the surface. How she wished she had a piece of polished glass, the way the white women did, so she could hold it up in front of her and catch her image.

Was she really pretty?

Fire Crow Woman had said so often enough that night in the Moon Lodge, but was it really something she meant? Or was it only a part of the litany she recited to every young maiden at a time like that? Tentatively, Morning Star raised her hands to her face, trying with her fingers to trace the contours that suddenly seemed strange and unfamiliar. It had never mattered before whether she was pretty or not, only whether she could outrun the boys, or ride as fast as they could. Now she wanted desperately to know.

She ran her hands lightly along her cheekbones. High and strong, her fingers told her, hinting at a pride that was more masculine than womanly. Her brow was wide, too wide for true beauty. Her nose was finely chiseled, but her jaw seemed a bit too square, with just a hint of cleft in the center. Hers would be a striking face, she sensed. The kind of face a man would notice if she turned wide blue eyes his way, or brushed out her hair with coppery highlights that caught the sun. But was it a pretty face?

And would any man want her if it wasn't?

She lowered her fingers self-consciously, following the lines of a long, slim neck. They lingered briefly on the warm pulse at the base of her throat, then slipped downward, coming to rest on the front of her dress.

Never—never—let a man touch your breasts. The words sounded strange in her memory, filling her with sensations she could not understand. Curving her hands, she cupped them lightly over soft mounds of flesh. How embarrassed she had been when her figure first began to fill out; it had seemed so much at odds with her image of herself. Now she dared to wonder what it would be like to have a man touch her that way.

Flushing guiltily, she dropped her hands, banishing the thought from her mind as she picked up the waterskin and plunged it into the pond. What if someone had come by and seen what she was doing? Fire Crow Woman had just finished telling her not to be foolish—and here she was making a terrible fool of herself!

The waterskin was heavy, and she let it rest briefly on the bank as she glanced one last time at the murky pond. If only the water was just a little clearer. How she would have loved to know what a young man saw when he looked at her!

A sudden burst of laughter shattered the stillness. Spinning around, Morning Star was horrified to see a young brave standing in the rushes behind her. The amusement in his voice was echoed in bold, dancing eyes.

"Running Deer!" What if he had come a minute sooner—just one minute! "What—what are you doing here?"

"Perhaps I was hoping a pretty girl would take pity on me and lighten my heart with a smile. Or perhaps I was just cutting through on my way to go hunting in the woods."

The laughter in his eyes was hard to resist. There was no one in the world quite so good at manipulating people as Running Deer when he wanted to. If Morning Star had not known better, she would have sworn he was flirting with her. Or trying to get her to flirt with him.

"You were not hunting, Running Deer. You don't have your bow with you. Or your quiver filled with arrows."

"And what about you? What are you doing, staring into the pond with your waterskin beside you? Don't tell me you were trying to get a glimpse of yourself in the water."

"Certainly not!" Morning Star's cheeks turned pink, but she could not quite manage to feel as embarrassed as she knew she should. She had never experienced this kind of flirtatious banter before, and it surprised her to realize how much fun it could be. "I would never do anything like that. Besides, the water is too muddy. But surely you know that. You must have tried to see your own reflection already."

Running Deer laughed easily. "Well, then, if you weren't staring at your reflection, what were you doing? Waiting for a handsome young brave to come along and drink in your beauty with his eyes?"

The subtle emphasis on *handsome* was not to be mistaken, and Morning Star knew that Running Deer was as aware as she that the word applied well to him. He had never looked more dynamic—or more attractive—than he did that morning. His hair, dark and thick, was arranged in warrior's braids, and his eyes simmered like jet. He had stripped to the waist, although it was a cool day, and his naked chest was lean and bronzed and muscular. For the first time, Morning Star looked on him not as a handsome boy, but as a young man, virile and utterly sure of his compelling earthiness.

She dropped her eyes hastily. It would not do to let him guess what she had been thinking. Fire Crow Woman had warned her not to pay too much attention to any young man—and not to smile too often!

"And you, I suppose, think you are that handsome young brave?"

"If I am, you will tell me with a smile!"

"What?" Morning Star caught her breath uneasily. It was almost as if he had read her thoughts. "You are too sure of yourself, Running Deer. A smile is not so lightly given."

"Yes, I know. 'Do not smile too many times at a young man, my daughter.' " Running Deer pursed his lips into a tight circle, mimicking the sound of the old woman's voice. 'Or he will think you too easily won, and then he will not respect you. And do not glance his way too often.' "

Morning Star looked away, confused at the turn the conversation was taking. Running Deer was amusing, but he was disconcerting, too.

"I—I don't know what you are talking about. You aren't making sense at all."

"Aren't I?"

"No. Besides, you aren't supposed to know about things like that."

He laughed again, softly this time, as if her confusion had touched him. Dropping to one knee beside her, he teased her with his eyes.

"What a funny little girl you are, Morning Star."

"Little girl?"

"All right, all right. What a funny young woman, then. Have you forgotten that I have a sister only a year older than you? Do you think we didn't sit up half the night after she came home from the Moon Lodge, giggling and talking about all the things that went on? You would have done the same with your own brother, Little Bear, if he had not gone away to the white man's school."

Morning Star sensed a new warmth in his voice, and she wondered if she was responding to his kindness—or to the fact that she had just realized how devastatingly attractive he could be.

"Yes, I suppose I would. But that does not mean I am going to smile at you, Running Deer, just because you have asked for it. You can laugh all you want at the things Fire Crow Woman told me, but they are the truth. If you want a smile from me, you are going to have to earn it."

"Then I shall—and gladly. A smile too easily won is not a smile worth having."

He jumped lightly to his feet, reaching out to help her up. His hand was unexpectedly warm, and Morning Star felt her cheeks begin to redden again. They had touched each other often in the past, this young man and she, but then they had been children.

"Running Deer—don't."

"Why not?" His voice sounded deep and throaty in her ear.

"Because—because someone might come by and see."

"Would it matter if they did?"

"Of course it would!" How could he even ask such a thing? Didn't he know the shame that would be hers if anyone saw what she had done? "You know as well as I that it matters very much."

"Ah, but I don't. It is all right to take my hand for a second—is that what you are telling me?—but it is not all right for anyone to see. Why?"

"Because . . ." Oh, why was he twisting everything around like that? And why did he have such a silly grin on his face? "Well, because it isn't done, that's all. It's—it's . . . tradition!"

"Tradition?" The grin was maddening now. "And you, of course, have always been very traditional. You do everything just the way you are supposed to."

"Well, no . . ."

Morning Star's anger dissolved in a sudden rush of humor. It *was* ludicrous, after all. The little girl who played the Swing-Kicking Game and rode as well as a man—who was she to demand tradition?

"I'm not traditional about everything," she admitted. "I suppose sometimes it must look as if I'm not traditional about *anything*. But I do care about this. I will not bring shame on myself, or on my family. If you want to court me, you're going to have to do it properly."

Whirling away, she slung the waterskin over her shoulder and began to saunter slowly up the path that led to the camp. The sense of his eyes behind her, following every move, gave her an awareness of herself she had never known before. Her hips seemed to sway as she walked, and the edges of her skirt brushed against her ankles.

"Morning Star!"

His voice drew her to a stop, but she was determined to give him nothing more. Still, it was all right to smile—since he could not see her lips.

"Yes, Running Deer?"

"What makes you think I would court a silly girl like you?"

She turned then, letting her eyes play with him. This was the way it should be, she thought, intrigued with her own emotions. The girl in control, the young man begging for her favors.

"Foolish."

"What?"

"A *foolish* girl, not a silly one. That's the way Fire Crow Woman put it. A foolish girl like me."

She did not turn again as she followed the path into the trees and disappeared from his sight. She did not have to. His eyes had already told her what she needed to know. She *was* pretty—and he was going to court her.

The plaintive echoes of a flute drifted in on the first night winds that swirled around the tepee. Inside, Morning Star kept her eyes averted. But even without looking up, she knew that Buffalo Calf Woman was smiling to herself as she went about her evening chores, and Brave Eagle was pretending not to notice.

The magical powers of music had long held an important place in Cheyenne courtships. The sound of a young man's serenade was a plea of love, more eloquent than words could ever be, and the special medicine in the songs he played was guaranteed to touch the listening heart. The right magic, it was said, would weave a spell of love that even the most reluctant maiden could not resist.

The notes that filled the darkness were pure and haunting, and Morning Star knew that her young suitor had spent many long hours practicing in the woods before he dared to try his skill on the lady of his choice. The instrument he was playing had been crafted by medicine men, perhaps even Dakotas, for they were known to make the most powerful flutes. If so, Running Deer would have paid dearly for it, trading away a strong bow he had made himself or a robe from the first buffalo he had killed, but the price would seem small enough if it helped him win the wife of his choice.

Divorce was easy among the Cheyennes, but it was painful, too, especially for a man, who knew he must lose his children to their mother's family, and the idea of courtship was never approached frivolously. The medicine men worked long and hard on the courting flutes to ensure just the right sound. Sticks from willows or box elders were split in half and carefully hollowed out, then joined together again with glue and bound with rawhide strips until they were tight and secure. Five fingerholds at the top controlled the notes, and an air vent could be opened and closed with a piece of wood carved in the shape of a bird or a horse's head.

The sweet strains of music drew Morning Star to the doorway of the tepee. Firelight made a circle of gold on the earth; beyond it, the night was a deep, velvety black. Morning Star could not catch a glimpse of her suitor in the darkness, but she knew he must be able to see her, for the music stopped only seconds after she appeared. The wind felt cool against her skin in the silence that followed.

The reflected color of the flames gave a dreamlike aura to the young man who stepped slowly into the light, hesitating just at the edge, as if he had suddenly turned shy and nervous. Morning Star let her eyes run up and down his figure. The shadows made him seem taller than he was. His shoulders were thrown back, his legs apart and braced against the earth in a cocky kind of bravado. Over his arm, he carried a thick buffalo robe.

Morning Star's lips turned up in the briefest hint of a smile. How many times had she clustered with the other children in front of a young girl's tepee and watched as her favorite beau came courting? And how many times had she giggled and pointed her fingers in a mischievous attempt to embarrass them? Now the children would be flocking around her tepee.

She waited quietly in the doorway for Running Deer to come to her. The rules of courtship were strict, and she dared not disobey them. From now on, the young men would gather outside her family lodge in the evenings. Perhaps only one, as tonight, perhaps a dozen if she turned out to be popular, all waiting in line for a chance to be with her. They would come to the doorway one by one and, throwing a thick, furry robe over her shoulders and their own, they would snuggle deep into the privacy of its folds to whisper soft endearments or steal a secret embrace. But always, her feet would remain firmly on the ground, just inside the sloping doorway of the tepee, where her watching mother could see just what was going on.

She felt a moment of shyness as the buffalo robe brushed her shoulders, closing her in with the young man she had known almost all her life. So many new sensations to be experienced, so many things yet to learn. Who would have thought she could stand away from him like that, just a fraction of an inch—just so they weren't quite touching—and still feel the warmth of his body flooding into hers.

Perhaps it wasn't going to be so bad after all, this traditional code of behavior her elders were forcing on her. Perhaps there would be more than a few compensations for all the boisterous tomboy games she was giving up.

Running Deer seemed to sense her mood.

"You're sure you don't want to kick me in the shins?" he teased. "Or try to race me on your horse?"

Morning Star laughed lightly. This afternoon it had made

her nervous to think that this young man could read her thoughts so easily. Tonight she rather enjoyed it.

"You know me too well, Running Deer. No, I do not want to play the Swing-Kicking Game with you. Or even go hunting for buffalo. I know I will never do those things again."

"And you do not mind?"

His voice was casual, but she sensed a deeper meaning to the question, and she knew it was important. Not just for him, but for herself as well.

"No," she said softly. "I do not mind."

Five

"You have to make up your mind sooner or later." Running Deer's voice was uncharacteristically petulant as he glowered down at Morning Star. He was seated on the low-hanging branch of a tree with his feet dangling a few inches from the ground. "You can't expect an ardent young brave to play his lonely pipe outside your tepee night after night forever."

Morning Star threw back her head and laughed. How strange it seemed, all these years later, to remember that she had once been afraid even to smile at a man. Now flirtation seemed the most natural thing in the world.

"What a grouch you are this morning, Running Deer. I don't like you at all when you're this way. I think I'm going to ignore you."

With a toss of her head, she turned toward the woods and gave a long, shrill whistle. Only seconds later, Wolf-Dog came loping toward her. Kneeling down, she threw her arms affectionately around his neck. A howling wind caught her skirt and blew dried autumn leaves into her face.

"Sometimes, I swear you like that dog better than any of your suitors," Running Deer grumbled. Leaping down from his perch, he stood on the path in front of her, his arms crossed over his chest. "I should have been born with four paws and an insatiable craving for bones. Then you would have treated me better."

It was all Morning Star could do to keep from laughing again. "Why, what a thing to say, Running Deer. Some of my other suitors might have cause for complaint, but not you. Surely it hasn't escaped your notice that not another young brave has been allowed to bring a buffalo robe to the door of my tepee for many moons."

"But still you do not say the words I long to hear."

A discomforting intensity vibrated in his voice. Turning away, Morning Star ran her hand absently through the tangled fur on the dog's back. The first years of courtship had been fun for her, tantalizing, yet wonderfully safe, wrapped as she was in a soft buffalo robe under her mother's scrutinizing gaze. But lately a new element seemed to have been introduced into the process, an urgency she did not know how to handle.

"You are too impatient," she murmured awkwardly. "I told you, I don't like you when you're this way. I only like you when you're nice to me."

"Then tell me I may send my female relatives to your family bearing gifts, as a young brave does when he wants to marry a maiden. Tell me I may tie my horse in front of your tepee, and you will accept him. Or at least exchange rings with me, made of horn or metal from the white man's trading post, so the other braves will know a promise has been made and stop waiting by the stream for a glimpse of you."

Morning Star looked up uneasily. Only a ring—hardly an unreasonable request. The commitment would not be a final one. But still . . .

"I cannot make this decision so quickly. I need more time."

"More time?" The words fairly burst out of his lips. "I have waited six years already. That is time enough!"

"But we were children those first years. They don't count. And besides, six years is not a long time. My mother, Buffalo Calf Woman, waited from the time she was twelve until she had seen twenty winters before she agreed to share her tepee with my father. And everyone says she was the most beautiful maiden in the tribe."

"Well, that may have not seemed like a long time to Brave Eagle, but it does to me! I remember what your mother looked like when she was younger. She *was* beautiful—but not half so beautiful as you. Don't you know it's a torture for me to look at you and know I cannot have you?"

Morning Star shivered at the unconcealed longing in his tone. She had not invited it—she did not want it!—yet it called out to something unexplored and frightening deep inside herself. Confused, she lowered her eyes.

"You ask too much, Running Deer."

"I ask nothing!" he cried out in a burst of passion.
"Nothing—and everything! Take care, Morning Star. One
day you will wake up and find you have waited too long. No
one will be there to court you then. None of the other youths
who sit on the hillside, playing songs you don't even listen
to. And certainly not me!"

Morning Star watched helplessly as he strode away. How
cold he sounded when he was angry—and how terribly justified!
She tightened her hold on Wolf-Dog, but the mongrel, bored
with inactive games, wriggled his way out of her grasp and
raced back into the woods.

What was wrong with her anyway? she wondered miserably.
Surely any young maiden would be delighted to trade places
with her now—and *she* would not risk losing such a man by
dangling him on too long a string. Running Deer was not
only the handsomest young brave in the tribe, he was the
strongest hunter, too. The woman who married him would
always have meat for her stewing pot and buffalo robes to
warm her bed. What, then, was her excuse for holding back?
Why couldn't she just say yes and be done with it once and
for all?

It was not that she was afraid of the physical side of
marriage. At nineteen, her body was more than ready to taste
the mysteries of love, and the first stirrings of passion deep
within her had been roused to a pitch she knew must soon be
satisfied. Sometimes when Running Deer enfolded her in the
warm fur of his robe and pressed his body close to hers, she
wanted nothing so much as to give herself to him, utterly and
totally, his to do with as he would. Yet there were other
times . . .

Sighing, she looked up into the trees, still clinging to the
last of their dying leaves. There were other times, like today,
when the wind seemed to cry out to her. Hold out while you
can, don't give your heart too quickly—float away with me,
free and wild, into the heavens.

The wind continued throughout the day, and a heavy gray
cloud brooded in the sky. Morning Star had little time to
think of her confrontation with Running Deer again, for she
was busy helping Buffalo Calf Woman secure their tepee
against the coming storm. The smoke flaps at the top had to
be closed tightly before the wind could blow them away, and
while the older woman was driving pegs deep into the earth

to anchor the tepee cover, the younger one scurried around, searching for rocks to weigh it down. Only when they had finished did mother and daughter dare to sit inside at last, listening to the sound of the wind whining through the cracks and waiting for the rain to start.

But the storm did not materialize, and twilight fell on a world that was hushed and still. Morning Star stood in the doorway of the tepee and watched as the women carried burning coals from their lodges to rekindle bonfires in front. Slowly, the camp began to stir with activity. Men sat cross-legged in front of the fires while women tossed green twigs on the flames to drive away the gnats and mosquitoes. A little girl with a solemn face was setting up a miniature tepee on top of a waterproof skin so her family of dolls would have a dry place to sit. At the edge of the camp, some of the boys, bored after a day's confinement, had already organized a game of Swing-Kicking, and were shrieking and howling at the top of their lungs. The smell of moisture in the air was a welcome accent to the familiar odor of wood smoke and burning buffalo dung.

A tentative tattoo of drumbeats floated in from a clearing next to the camp. The dancing yellow flames of a huge open fire caught Morning Star's eye and she turned eagerly toward it. Cheyennes loved a celebration, and they took advantage of every excuse they could find to gather together with music and laughter. The success of the hunt or the birth of a baby, a victorious war party, a girl-child who had come of age, the beginning of a new season—even the end of a storm.

Morning Star joined the other young people who had already begun to gather in the meadow where the festivities were to be held. A harvest moon, full and orange, shimmered in the sky, and its rays blended with the fire to bathe the earth in a rich, warm light. Torches made of folded birch bark wedged into the forks of split green sticks had been set in a large circle around the blazing flames.

Inside the ring, dancers had already begun to form into a square. Morning Star took her place with the other young women who were lining up on the south side of the fire. Tall, flickering flames half obscured the lithe, bronzed bodies of laughing braves, positioning themselves in a line just opposite. The older men and women, as they arrived, filled in the east side of the square. To the west were the drummers and singers, by tradition all married men and all of middle age.

An expectant hush fell over the crowd as a pair of tall, angular figures, garbed in the deerskin robes and beaded headdresses of a woman, slipped gracefully into the center of the square. These were the *hemaneh*, the Halfmen-Halfwomen of the Cheyennes. The *hemaneh* held an important place in Indian society, often serving as second wives in the household of a married man, and their restrained masculinity added greatly to the collective virility of the tribe. A party of warriors would not willingly ride into battle without the *hemaneh*, not only because of their supernatural powers, but because they were skilled doctors as well and had strong medicine. Lovers, too, prized their services, for they concocted the most powerful love potions known to man.

The drumbeats slowly intensified, picking up the tempo of Morning Star's heart. Boldly, she looked up, searching through the flames for the one face that had the power to make her pulse race as wildly as the beating of the drums. She had always loved to dance, enjoying the subdued excitement of the beginning almost as much as the burst of activity that followed, but tonight everything seemed even more compelling than usual.

The men began to move first. They took their time, stepping to each measured beat as they snaked in a long line behind the women. Morning Star, like the other maidens, did not turn, but she was keenly aware of the soft padding of moccasined feet on the earth behind her. Then that, too, stopped, and for a moment, the only motion came from the *hemaneh*. Their movements were sensuous and peculiarly graceful, the strong force of a man, coupled with the subtle delicacy of a woman. When at last they paused, giving the signal that freed the maidens, Morning Star turned with the others.

The man who stood behind her was handsome and lively, but he was not the man she had hoped to see. Slowly, they began to move together, both with a kind of languid sensuality that matched the rhythm of each other's bodies. Ordinarily, Morning Star would have been delighted with her partner, for she was a skillful dancer and he could match her step for step, but tonight she barely even noticed him. Her body twisted from side to side, responding to the wailing sounds of the singers, but her eyes never stopped searching for Running Deer in that crowd of dancers. And her heart never stopped hoping he was searching for her.

It was almost a relief when the singers stopped their chanting and Morning Star could finally follow the drumbeats back to her place in the line of women on the south side of the square. The next dance, the one the elders called the Courtship Dance, had always been her favorite part of any Cheyenne festivity. The *hemaneh* were especially amusing that night as they pranced up and down the waiting rows of braves and maidens, pausing sometimes to wink at an especially bold young man, or to ask a pretty, blushing girl what partner she would choose for herself. The drums were silent when they had finished, the air filled with youthful giggles as they huddled together in the center of the square and whispered elaborately to each other.

It would be an omen, Morning Star thought suddenly as she stood on the sidelines and watched their exaggerated antics. If the *hemaneh* paired her off with Running Deer tonight, she would accept him. If they did not . . .

But there was no such word as *not* that evening. A special magic seemed to linger in the air in the wake of the storm, and the *hemaneh*, sensing tender dreams of love, did not play their usual pranks, but coupled young lovers with the mates of their choice. As Morning Star felt her hand being slipped into Running Deer's, she was aware of new sensations she had never known before. A kind of power beyond her control—a dizzying force that seemed to pick her up and sweep her away.

Even the music seemed different now, sometimes softer than she had heard it, sometimes pulsating with a strange, dynamic passion. She had performed these same steps a hundred times before—a thousand—but never had they seemed so intimate. So earthy. The beating of the drums vibrated through her body, and every slow swing of her hips was a promise that could no longer be denied.

How natural it all seemed when she was with him, and the sweet longings of her body could lull the foolish fretting of her brain. Perhaps that was the key to it all. As simple as that. All she had to do was stay close to him, laugh with him, let him embrace her tightly under the robe—and she would never doubt again.

The music continued throughout the night, but once the formal dances ended, the pairing became more casual, and young women were allowed to select the braves of their choice. For once, Morning Star did not flit from partner to partner, but lingered all night in the company of one man. And that man was Running Deer.

It was intended as a surrender, and he did not fail to recognize it. When he came to her lodge the following evening, there was a new confidence in his bearing, a kind of self-satisfaction that almost bordered on arrogance. Morning Star had never seen him that way before, and she was not sure she liked it, but she could not deny that there was a new excitement in their relationship. She could see it in the way he looked at her—and feel it in her own body when she looked back at him.

The muscles in his arms were firm and hard as he drew the robe around her shoulders and pulled her toward him. There was none of the urgency she had expected in his embrace, as if he could afford to be gentle now that he was sure of her, and his new tenderness brought out all the latent yearnings in her heart. For the first time since they had begun their courtship, she did not even notice Wolf-Dog's cold nose as he nuzzled at her ankles, hoping she would leave her suitor for a moment and come and play with him.

It was Running Deer instead who saw him.

"What?" he said with a laugh. "Aren't you going to dally with the little beast to make me jealous?"

Morning Star smiled up at him. "Do I do that?"

"Of course you do, heartless maiden. You play with me when you want him to come running. And you scratch him behind the ears when you want to torment me. Are you so sure of me now that you don't have to do that anymore?"

"Sure of you?" Morning Star dropped her eyes, letting dark lashes rest on her cheeks. "I should have thought it was the other way around. But, no—I am not going to play with the dog tonight."

"Then it is all over? You are not going to toy with me anymore?"

The words were not quite a question. Morning Star sensed a disconcerting sureness in the hands that caressed her now, so lightly and yet so bold, as if he knew she was his at last. Drawing her closer, he pressed her full length against his body. For the first time, she did not draw back, but let herself flow with the emotions, responding to the nearness of this man and the physical sense of his need for her. His hands began to move, slowly, subtly, searching for her breast.

She knew it would all be over in a matter of seconds. With that gesture, the touch of his hand on her breast, he would have made his claim on her and she would never dare turn back again. Fire Crow Woman had been right all those years ago—he *would* tell every man in the camp—and then she could never find another mate. One touch, one challenge, and she would never be able to say no.

Taking hold of his hand, she held it lightly for a moment, then drew it slowly back from her breast. She could not give herself away quite so easily—she could not make that final commitment from which there would be no release. Soon, yes . . . she knew she had to do it soon. But not yet. Not today.

Thoughts of Running Deer still filled her mind the next afternoon as she sat on a sunlit hillside east of the camp and gazed down at the circle of tepees beneath her. It seemed so silly when she looked at it objectively. She had all but said yes to him the night of the dance. Why couldn't she take this last little step and get it over with? Why couldn't she give herself to him completely and forever?

A sudden commotion in the camp below provided a welcome distraction, and Morning Star leaned forward to see what was going on. A rider seemed to have come into the camp—no, two riders—and everyone was spilling out of tepees and racing in from nearby fields to gather around them. Raising her hand to her eyes, she squinted into the bright sunlight, trying to make them out. To her surprise, she saw her own father, Brave Eagle, in the lead on his strong black gelding. The features of the man behind him were not clear, but the horse he was riding was her Fire-Wind.

Scowling a little, she drew her head back and stared at them. She had known her father was planning to go east that day, toward the spot where the white man's great iron horse belched clouds of foul-smelling smoke into the sky, but it had not occurred to her that he would bring someone back with him. Or that he would give the stranger Fire-Wind to ride! No one else had ever mounted her horse—except Brave Eagle, of course, and Little Bear in the days before . . .

Little Bear?

Morning Star caught her breath as she squinted into the
light again. She still could not see the man's features, but she
knew who he had to be! A surge of excitement raced through
her at the thought. Little Bear! Of course! Who else would
have come on the iron horse from places far to the east? And
who else would be riding Fire-Wind?

Forgetting that she was a woman now, and thus required to
behave with dignity, Morning Star hiked her skirt up to her
knees and began to race down the hill like the tomboy she
used to be. Little Bear was home! She had not realized until
that moment how desperately she had missed him. Little
Bear! Now she would have someone to laugh with, the way
they used to in the old days—and someone to talk to all night
long. She would tell him everything she felt, all her doubts,
all her confusions—and he would help her make up her mind.

She was gasping for breath by the time she reached the
crowd that surrounded the two riders. Without thinking, she
began to elbow her way into the center, not even caring who
thought her rude and ill-mannered. It was not every day a
girl's brother came home. No one could expect her to be a
proper young lady at a time like that!

Brave Eagle was laughing at her excitement, but she barely
noticed as she brushed past him and planted herself firmly in
front of Fire-Wind. Grabbing hold of the horse's reins, she
began to pull him around. The cry of welcome died on her lips
as she got a look at the rider's face.

The man on the horse was not Little Bear at all!

Dropping the reins, she let her hands flutter to her sides
and stared up at him in surprise. The man had Little Bear's
features, she could not deny that—the same wide-set eyes,
the same straight nose, the same full, rounded lips—but she
could see nothing else in him of the fun-loving youth she
remembered from long ago. Even his mannerisms were
different. He was of medium height, his build slender and
boyish, but he moved strangely, and the hands that held his
reins were smooth and uncalloused. The white man's clothing
fit him well: slim pants and a dark jacket, a white cotton shirt
open at the neck, high boots with heels on them and a pattern
tooled into the shiny leather.

It was a moment before she realized what had happened.
Five years ago, when Little Bear had gone away, she had

warned herself he would come back a stranger. Now she knew she had been right.

"Little . . . Bear?"

Her voice had a funny catch to it. The man seemed almost as puzzled as she as he leaned down and looked into her face.

"Morning Star?"

The incredulity in his tone stirred something inside her, and confusion gave way to indignation. Who was he to look at her like that? She was still the same Morning Star she had always been. She was not the one who rode away a Cheyenne— and came back a stranger!

"Why, what a dandy you have become, Little Bear. Even the white men must laugh at you, dressed like that!"

She did not get the response she expected. He did not quite laugh, but crinkly lines formed at the corners of his eyes, and his face was no longer solemn.

"Yes, of course it is Morning Star! I would have known that tart tongue anywhere. But surely, *na:sima*, I would have recognized nothing else about you."

Morning Star tried not to laugh, but she could not help herself. He looked so funny, with his eyes teasing her and his mouth almost ready to break out in a grin. This was Little Bear again, the same Little Bear she thought she had lost.

"No fair!" she protested lightly. "When I was a little girl, you could always make me laugh when I didn't want to. But now I am a young lady, and you must treat me with respect. How can you say I have a tart tongue when I am only speaking the truth? Besides, I haven't changed at all."

He did not answer for a moment, but gazed down at her in silence. The laughter was gone from his eyes, and there was a new look on his face.

"You have changed very much, *na:sima*. You were a girl when I went away. Now you are a woman. And a very beautiful one."

A flood of warmth seemed to accompany his words, calling back feelings Morning Star had long since forgotten. For the first time, she realized what had been missing in her relationship with every man who had ever courted her. Love was more than passion, more than just excitement. It was a sense of closeness, of being completely at one with another human being . . . a sense of sharing every secret of one's heart and soul.

The kind of sharing she had once known with the brother who was not truly her brother at all.

At last she understood why she had not been able to give herself to Running Deer. Because the man her body had chosen for her was not the man she longed for in her heart.

Six

Swirls of winter mist floated up from the muddy earth, softening the stark outline of deep green pines and giving the forest an air of enchantment. Ordinarily, Morning Star would have been captivated by the softness of the world around her, all mystical and white. But today, nature only seemed to be mocking her mood.

Frowning, she glanced over at Little Bear, seated cross-legged on a bare patch of damp earth, but he was so engrossed in the gooseberry shoot he was whittling down, he did not notice her. It seemed to her that nothing had gone right in the weeks since he had come home. She had been so positive that first day, when they had teased and joked with each other, that everything was going to be just the way it was before. Only here he was, trying to fashion an Indian arrow with fingers that were as clumsy as a white man's—and here she was, feeling more estranged from him than ever.

He did not even look right. He had put on a brand-new deerskin tunic, proudly embroidered by his mother with multi-colored trace beads, but he wore it self-consciously, as if he would have been more comfortable in a cotton shirt. His hair was cropped short, like a cowboy's, and his pants were the white man's serviceable denim, his boots the same tooled leather she had noticed before.

"Where did you get your new finery, Little Bear? You look more like a white man than some of the white men I've seen."

He paused in his work to look up at her. "Finery? Denim? But that's the kind of thing a workman wears. Or a farmer."

"And those?" Morning Star pointed with a brusque gesture at his feet. "I doubt if a farmer has boots as finely crafted as those. Or a coat like the one you were wearing when you came back. How charitable the white man must be! Dressing poor little Indian boys better than most of his own people!''

Little Bear laid the arrow shaft on the ground beside him and studied her with troubled eyes. She was dazzlingly pretty, even now, even when she was angry, but sometimes he wondered if he would ever understand her. Since he had come home, it seemed to him there was a new hardness about her, a new sharpness, especially in her dealing with him.

"No, the white man's charity does not go that far. No one knows that better than an Indian who has had to live on it. Not even the charity of those who dedicate themselves to the Christian god, the ones they call missionaries.''

He paused, hearing the bitterness in his own voice. She was bringing too many things out in him—things he had wanted to forget. Rising, he went over to where she was standing at the edge of the hillside, looking down into a mist-veiled valley beneath.

"You speak of the white man as if he were a single entity. *The* white man. But that is not so. There are whites who are generous, just as there are whites capable of great cruelty. All the clothes I have were given to me by a woman in the town near the school. She must have taken pity on me when she saw how ragged I was. Or perhaps she couldn't stand to look at me anymore—or smell me! White men are funny about smells.''

Morning Star wrinkled her nose as she glowered at him. If he thought he was going to make her laugh again, he was very much mistaken.

"If anyone smells funny, it is the whites. And you will never get me to believe a white woman helped you out of the kindness of her heart!''

Little Bear laid his hand on her arm, then pulled it back when he felt her draw away. "But there are white women who are kind, Morning Star. Why do you find that so hard to believe?''

"Because it is not true! Since when has any white man—or woman—ever been kind to an Indian? I know what you think, Little Bear. You think I am naive, but I am not. I know just what was going on in the minds of those white women when they pretended to be kind to you. You were just sixteen when you went to live among them. Your body was lean and hard, not soft like one of their own men. White women are easy and immoral, everyone knows that!"

He greeted her outburst with a look of astonishment, then began to laugh softly. So that was why she was so angry! Well, at least that was something he could deal with.

"She was a very old woman, Morning Star. Older than my mother. Or Buffalo Calf Woman."

Morning Star threw him a disdainful look. She had thought before that he did not know anything about white women. Now she was beginning to wonder if he understood women at all!

"What difference does age make, Little Bear? Why only last summer, the mother of Spotted Dog in the Havatanui band ran off with a man half her son's age. Spotted Dog sent many horses to the man's wife so she would not make trouble, but she wanted her husband back anyway. And do you know what the old grandmother said then? She said, 'Tell the woman I will send back her husband when I am tired of him.' That is exactly what she said."

Little Bear laughed again as he watched her toss her head, flipping long braids over her shoulders. How appealing she was when she showed her spirit like that. And how utterly transparent.

"So you think she was like that, too? The white woman in town? But she was not, I promise you. She was only a woman who had lost her own son and still had his things in the house. These are his boots I am wearing, and these were his denim pants. If the child of an Indian woman had died, you would not be surprised that she wanted to replace him. Why do you think white women are so different?"

"You were not a child," she reminded him. "You were sixteen. And in truth, Little Bear, I don't really care what that woman wanted from you—or any of the others, for that matter. I only know that you have been among the white strangers a long time, and now you are a stranger, too."

Little Bear turned away, glancing at the arrow shaft where it lay neglected on the ground. A stranger? Perhaps in a way she was right. Once he would have known how to cut zigzag lines in the surface of the wood to keep it from warping. Now his workmanship was crude and childlike.

There *had* been women like the ones she spoke of. One in

particular, delicate and blond, with laughter that cascaded like cool water through mountain streams, and long, flowing hair that seemed to catch the sunlight on the current. Easy and immoral, yes—and yet . . .

"No," he said softly, as much to himself as to her. "No, you do not need to be afraid of the white women. I did not give my heart to anyone all the time I was gone. No strangers will fill my dreams tonight. You have no reason to be jealous."

"Jealous?"

Morning Star's eyes flashed as she turned away. He had hit too close for comfort. Jealous, indeed! Maybe she *had* felt that way about him when he first came home, but she was not going to do it again. There were too many things about him she could never learn to like!

"I am *not* jealous over you, Little Bear. Why should I be? You are my brother. The affairs of your heart are no concern of mine."

He did not try to follow as she moved away from him, but waited quietly until he saw her pause beside an old oak tree. Resting her hand on the rough bark, she stared once again into the valley below. The fog seemed to be lifting, and soft gray-green hills were half visible in the distance.

You are my brother, she had said, uttering the words they had both avoided since the day he returned. Brother—sister . . . could these terms really have any meaning for them?

He could still remember the brief interview he had had with Brave Eagle the evening of his arrival. The older man had been alone in his tepee, sitting straight-backed in his place behind the fire as if he had been expecting a visitor. His face was impassive, but it seemed to Little Bear that his eyes were wary.

"I think you know why I am here, *nihu*. I have seen Morning Star again today, and I must tell you that I can no longer call her *na:sima*. Never again will I think of her as my sister. I want to court her, and if she says yes, I am going to make her my wife."

Brave Eagle had risen slowly to face him.

"This is not a thing a good Cheyenne says to his father, my son. It does not matter how you think of Morning Star. She *is* your sister."

"No!"

The word had an explosive fervor that startled them both.

Little Bear felt strangely like a child again, about to be scolded for defying his elders, but he could not let himself back down.

"No, she is not my sister. Her blood is not the blood that flows through my veins. There is no bar to our marriage if she will have me."

Brave Eagle studied him for a long time in silence. Then slowly, heavily, he bowed his head.

"In other times I would have forbidden this match. The girl is obedient, even if you are not. But these are not other times. The world is changing. I do not like it, but I can do nothing about it. Court her if you will."

Little Bear turned back to Morning Star, breaking off the painful memory. That was one of the hardest things he had ever had to do—hurt a man who had never been anything but good to him—and what had he accomplished by it? He had been so sure that day that he would be able to win this beautiful woman's heart. Now he was sure of nothing.

"You are not my sister, Morning Star. Even Brave Eagle cannot deny that. We were born into different families. There are no blood ties between us."

Her eyes seemed deep and brooding as she looked up at him, not so much angry now as sad.

"It is not the ties between us that frighten me, Little Bear. It is the ties that are not there. I know you do not share your blood with me. You do not seem to share it with anyone in the tribe. Sometimes I think I am more of a Cheyenne than you!"

The remark stung bitterly. Little Bear recoiled as if she had reached out and struck him in the face.

"I *am* a Cheyenne—and I am proud of it. But being a Cheyenne doesn't mean I have to live in the past. Cheyennes can look to the future, too."

Morning Star shook her head slowly. "I don't believe you, Little Bear. You say you are a Cheyenne, but you don't act like one."

"Why not? Because I wear these?" He stuck out his leg, tapping his heel on the ground. "Boots are more practical than moccasins. Or do you object to my denim pants? How is my mother supposed to make leggings for me? There have been no buffalo for many seasons. Should I ask her to take apart her tepee liner so I can dress the way you want? Is that how you would have me prove my loyalty?"

"Oh, Little Bear, why can't you see what I'm trying to say? No one cares how you dress. Or whether your hair is cropped short like a boy's or worn in the long braids of a warrior. It is how you act—and think—that counts."

She glanced around, catching sight of the arrow shaft on the ground.

"Look! What Cheyenne would make a careless shaft like that? Once you made finer arrows than any other boy in the camp, and you were proud of them. Now look! You haven't aged the wood properly, and it's so warped it'll never fly straight and true. And you don't even care! You just laugh at your mistakes. It doesn't matter to you anymore!"

"Of course it matters. It . . ." He paused, smiling a little at the words he knew she would not believe. "This is a part of my heritage. It will always be important to me. But don't you remember why Brave Eagle sent me to the white man's school in the first place? I want to teach my people, Morning Star. I want them to learn what I learned in that place. It's time that we hunted with rifles instead of bows and arrows, and tilled the soil the way the white man does. And began to read and write so that——"

"Read and write? That's what's important, isn't it? Not your heritage at all! You would rather spend all day with your face hidden in those books you brought back in your saddlebag. Or take up your pen and scratch out the stupid letters I've almost forgotten!"

Something in her voice caught his ear. A subtle sharpness he had almost missed.

"Is that what's wrong, Morning Star? That I can read and write better than you?"

"Of course not! It's just that I . . . well, I . . ." She broke off, feeling suddenly awkward and childish. "I do try to put the letters together sometimes," she admitted. "And most of the time I get them right. But there are days when I can't seem to remember whether a W is two V's right side up and an M is two V's upside down, or whether it's the other way around, and then I get all confused."

He laid his hand on the side of her face, trying not to smile at the pink flush in her cheeks. There were moments she was so touching, it hurt him to look at her.

"Shall I teach you then? The way you once taught me? It will not be hard for you because you already know the words."

"No!" She pulled back abruptly. How could she have let him touch her like that, when they both knew she did not want him? "Haven't you heard a thing I've said? The white man has never done anything but lie to us. He cheats us and steals our land. He leaves the carcasses of buffalo rotting across the plains, and for no better reason than that it amuses him to shoot them down! No, I do not want to learn white ways again. I do not want to move into that evil, deceitful world."

Little Bear took a step back, studying her intently as she trembled with anger in front of him. She looked so young at that moment—and so innocent.

"You do not understand," he said gently. "It is not for you to choose whether you will move into the white man's world or not. It is the white man's world that is coming to you."

"Then I will fight it! And so should you. How can you call yourself a Cheyenne and talk like that? What happened to the little boy you used to be? The one who was going to grow up to be the great warrior chief Man-Who-Lives-with-the-Wolves?"

He shook his head with a soft laugh. "That was a long time ago. People change, Morning Star. Little boys grow up. I did take a new name, but not the one I had planned then. I took the name the missionaries gave me at school—Stephen."

"Stephen Little Bear?" Morning Star looked at him with contempt. Wasn't that just like the white men? Forcing Christian names on their little heathen charges! "What a ridiculous name. It's not Indian—and it's not white. Now you won't fit in anyplace."

The words hit home, more than he cared to admit. Stepping away, he stared moodily down the slopes, but the mists had thickened and he could see nothing but an eerie veil of white. Would he ever fit in anyplace again? he wondered. He almost felt like an outsider among his own people now, and certainly he had always been an outsider among the whites. He could kneel on the hard wooden floors of their chapels hour after endless hour, until his knees ached and his legs felt as if they were going to drop off, but nothing would ever make his skin lighter or his alien ways more acceptable, even to the missionaries.

"Perhaps you are right," he said quietly. "I do not pretend

that the whites ever made me feel like I belonged, and I
suppose they never will.''

''Then why——''

''Because I have to! Don't you see, Morning Star? If we
cannot make a place for ourselves in a world dominated by
whites, there is no hope for us. We will not survive.''

''And is that so important? Mere survival? Oh, Little Bear,
what good is survival without honor?''

There was a sadness in her eyes he had never seen there
before. His heart ached at the sight of her. She was so
bewitching in all her moods. Laughter, anger . . . even pain.
He could not bear to think that he might lose her.

Reaching out his hands, he laid them lightly on her arms
and drew her toward him. This time she did not resist.

''There is honor in the white world, too,'' he said gently.
''Just as there is sometimes dishonor among the Cheyennes.
Honor is not something you find in the places you go,
Morning Star. It is something you carry inside yourself. If
your heart is pure, there will be honor in your life no matter
what paths you walk.''

He let his cheek rest lightly against her hair for a second.
The smell of grease drifted up to his nostrils, calling back
unwanted memories of roses and sweet perfume.

''Why do you rub your braids with buffalo fat like that?
Let me get you some scented soap from the white man's store
in town.''

Morning Star pulled away angrily, breaking the mood of
his caresses. Twice now, she had let herself be lured into
forgetting her resolve. It would not happen again.

''I am not a white girl, Little Bear. I am an Indian! This is
the way an Indian dresses her hair.''

''No, it isn't,'' he replied calmly. ''At least not all the
time. Some of the young maidens brush their hair until it
shines, and leave it soft and——''

''Some of the young maidens don't have hair that burns red
in the sunlight! I put grease on my braids so they will be dark
and everyone will know I am a Cheyenne!''

His face softened as he studied her, but his eyes were
steady. ''But you are not a Cheyenne. Why do you keep on
pretending? Just as leather boots and denim pants will never
make me white, all the hair grease in the world can't turn you

into an Indian. You are white, whether you like it or not. As white as the women you are so jealous of in the towns.''

Morning Star stepped back, stunned by the sudden chill she sensed in his tone. A new thought began tugging at the back of her mind, an ugly thought she did not want to acknowledge.

"Is that what it is?" she said slowly. "This strangeness that has been between us since the day you came back? You never really wanted me for what I am. You didn't even know what that was—or care to! You only wanted me for one reason. Because I reminded you of the white women you knew before!"

Without waiting for a reply, she whirled around and raced out of the clearing, following familiar paths deep into the silent forest. Scattered patches of snow were cold beneath her moccasins, and the mist swirled up around her face, half blinding her as she ran. How could he have pretended to want her when all the time his heart really belonged to the soft perfumed women he would never have? And how could she have let him do it? She had never realized before that love could be so painful—or so terribly humiliating.

She stopped at last, sinking down on a fallen log at the edge of a shallow ravine, too exhausted to go any farther. What a fool she had been to fill her head with silly daydreams. What a fool to think that old affections could be rekindled after all these years. Tomorrow she would seek out Running Deer, if he would still have her after the shabby way she had treated him—or one of her other suitors, if he would not—and tell him she would be proud to share his tepee. She was not going to waste any more of her life longing for things she could not have.

Dropping her head in her hands, she wept softly to herself.

Little Bear stood on a low ridge overlooking the ravine and looked down at the silent form of the woman he loved, all curled up like a little kitten on the fallen log. A soft white mist drifted around her, carrying her away from him at times, then bringing her back again. He had wanted so many things in his life. All those hours, kneeling on hard floors, praying to a god he did not know—all those long hours with the taste of the white man's salt pork in his mouth—what had sustained him then but the knowledge that one day he would come back and help his people? He would be the man to show them how to plow the soil and plant seed in even rows so they would not be dependent on the buffalo any longer. He would teach them to read and write, so no one would ever look down on them again.

Now all that was over—and all because a woman had cried.

Idle dreams? He smiled a little as he began to move down the slope. Perhaps. How could he persuade his people to farm when the farming implements the white man promised were never delivered? And how could he expect them to hold their heads high in a world where the color of their skin would forever set them apart?

He had thought of Morning Star as innocent and childlike only a moment before. Perhaps, after all, it was he who was naive.

Her hair was damp with mist when he reached her, her cheeks warm with the moisture of her tears. The eyes that looked up at him seemed to reflect the haunting mystery of deep mountain pools.

"Do you remember when you came to us?" he said softly. "That first night, when Brave Eagle brought you into the camp on the front of his horse? Your hair was loose, and it seemed to fly around your face. I thought then that the spirits had touched it with fire. That's why I came into the tepee—to see if it was going to burst into flames."

She smiled faintly, but her lips were quivering and she did not speak. Little Bear took her hand and touched it to his lips.

"Don't you see, Morning Star? That first image of you—that magical image—spoiled me for anyone else. I did not look at you with longing when I returned because you reminded me of white women. I looked at them, when I did, because they reminded me of you."

That evening he sat alone in the darkness outside her tepee and played the first notes of the song that told her his surrender was complete. If she wanted to be courted like an Indian, then he would court her that way. The flute in his hands was ordinary at best. There had been no time to seek out the Dakota medicine men, and no sturdy bows or fine new arrows to pay them with. Nor did he play it well, for he had had no practice, but he knew that did not matter. He had been away from the Indian camp too long. He would never be able to impress her with his athletic prowess—or his musical skill. If he was going to win her, it would have to be with warmth and laughter.

She did not keep him waiting, but came to the doorway almost immediately. The excitement that showed in his eyes as he stepped into the firelight was echoed in the slow, sweet yearning that filled her own body. She held out her hands to greet him, helping him unfold the buffalo robe and shake it out. The soft fur was warm against her shoulders, his body even warmer as he drew her toward him.

Morning Star could feel his fingers playing with the neck of her dress, not boldly, as another man might have done, but lightly, almost questioningly, and she knew he was asking permission to touch her breasts.

"I should not let you do this," she murmured breathily.

"Why not? Because a good Cheyenne brave does not do such things?"

She laughed softly, lowering her eyes. "No, Cheyenne braves always do things like that. At least, they try to. I meant, I should not let you do it because I will be ruined if you change your mind and do not marry me after all."

"And you think I will do that? Change my mind?"

"No. I do not think you will."

"And you?" He tilted her head upward, looking deeply into her eyes. "Are you afraid you're going to change your mind?"

She held her breath one last moment as she looked back at him. How could everything seem so simple now, when she had agonized so long and hard before? This man was nowhere near as handsome as her first suitor, it did not make her blood run hot in her veins just to look at him, yet there was in her feelings for him a kind of tenderness, a depth of affection that made even the touch of his hand sweeter than Running Deer's most passionate embrace. It would be good to share his bed with him, yes, but it would be good to sit beside him in the tepee, too, good to cook his meals for him and bear his children . . . and grow old and know that he would always be there. Taking his hand, she laid it gently on her breast.

"I am not going to change my mind."

Seven

When she woke the next morning, she found Fire-Wind tethered to a stake in front of her lodge. It was not an authentic Indian proposal. Little Bear had not sent his female relatives to her family bearing armloads of presents—nor was the sorrel truly his to give, for Brave Eagle had only lent it to him to use for a while—but Morning Star did not fail to understand the gesture. A soft smile touched her lips as she slipped outside and, untying the horse, brought it to pasture and mingled it with her father's herd.

All that remained for her then was to leave her parents' tepee for the last time. The Cheyennes had never believed in formal wedding traditions, and even the coming of the white man had not changed their customs. No priests intoned elaborate chants over the bowed heads of a young couple, no ritual vows were exchanged, no legal documents signed and registered with the local authorities. Morning Star, like many a bride before her, simply mounted one of her father's horses and rode off to the place where her new family was waiting to receive her.

Several days earlier, the chiefs had split the band into two groups, to ease competition for grazing land and the limited supply of firewood, and the place where Little Bear's mother had been assigned to set up her tepee was across a briskly flowing stream, already swollen with the first spring thaws. Icy water swirled around the horse's legs as he plunged into the water, and Morning Star tightened her hold on the reins to steady him. The black gelding was one of Brave Eagle's most prized possessions, and she had felt strange riding him away that morning, but she knew her father would never have it any other way. It was a matter of pride for a Cheyenne to be able to send his daughter to her bridegroom with at least as fine a mount as the one the young man had left tethered in front of his own tepee.

Not that it really mattered, Morning Star thought, smiling to herself as she urged the horse across the stream and onto the bank on the opposite side. The gift was only a token. Brave Eagle had gotten used to the gelding after all these years. He would no more do without him than he would want to see his daughter and her husband deprived of a strong young mount like Fire-Wind. Long before the spring wildflowers had died on the hillside, an excuse would be found to exchange gifts again, and the horses would once more find themselves tied in front of familiar tepees.

The area on the far side of the stream was flat and barren. Morning Star cast a casual eye over the desolate landscape, grateful that custom required the young couple to set up their tepee not with the man's family, but with the woman's. At least in the area where Brave Eagle was camped, scattered pines broke the rocky monotony of the slopes, and a gentle hollow offered shelter from the bitter winds that howled across the plains.

The women of Little Bear's family had gathered in his mother's tepee to wait for her arrival. At the first sign of her approach, they hurried out of the doorway to greet her. Morning Star caught sight of Corn Woman, her new mother-in-law, standing a little apart from the others, and in the quiet half smile on her features she sensed the timeless, uncomplaining sadness of a woman about to lose her only son forever. Lined up in an almost even row behind her were her three sisters, the eldest of whom was the mother of Morning Star's first suitor, Running Deer.

The older women maintained their dignity, but the younger ones, unable to control their enthusiasm, began to race toward the arriving bride, waving a blanket wildly over their heads. Among them, Morning Star recognized her favorite, Running Deer's youngest sister, Wades-in-the-Water.

"There you are, Morning Star," the girl cried out, greeting her from a distance. "You took so long, we thought you had decided not to come."

Wades-in-the-Water's laughter was infectious. Leaping down from her horse, Morning Star ran forward and met her in an impetuous embrace.

"Did you think I was going to drop everything and come running? It would never do to let my new husband think I am too eager! Besides, a bride needs time to make herself beautiful. You wouldn't want me to disgrace my new family."

"As if you ever could . . . Oh, do hurry!" Glancing over her shoulder, the girl urged the others forward. "Look how beautiful Morning Star is today! Have you ever seen a more beautiful bride?"

Her two sisters arrived just at that moment. The younger of them, a girl about Morning Star's own age, moved with surprising grace even though she was already heavy with her first child. The other, Singing Cloud, lagged behind with a decidedly sour look on her face.

"All brides are beautiful, Wades-in-the-Water. Haven't you learned that yet, foolish little girl? It's a law of nature."

Morning Star resisted a sharp retort as she turned. Wasn't that just like Singing Cloud? She couldn't even welcome a bride graciously! Still, it was too nice a day to quarrel.

"Thank you for coming to greet me, Singing Cloud. You and your sisters—and all your cousins, too. I will try and prove worthy of the warmth and generosity of my new family."

The other girls seemed to arrive all at once. The air was filled with shouts of laughter as they crowded around Morning Star, chattering gaily and calling out congratulations. After a few ebullient minutes, they threw down the blanket they had brought with them, and spread it out on the ground so she could scramble onto it. As soon as she was in place, they lifted her up, carrying her between them into the lodge where it would be their duty to prepare her for her new husband.

Once inside, Wades-in-the-Water waited until they had dropped Morning Star in a place of honor at the rear, then slipped close enough to whisper in her ear:

"Did you know that my grandmother, the wife of Blue Thunder, is furious with your bridegroom? She doesn't mind that Little Bear stole you away from Running Deer, mind you, for they're both her grandsons and she loves them equally, but she is wild with anger about the way he did it! She was counting on going with the other women to your mother's lodge when it was time to bring the betrothal gifts and leave Little Bear's horse tied outside. My grandmother absolutely dotes on things like that!"

That the words were at least mostly in fun became apparent a moment later when the old woman came into the tepee with Corn Woman and her three sisters and took her place next to the new bride. Wrinkled features broke out in a broad, toothless grin as she took a buffalo tongue brush in her own hands and stroked Morning Star's long, loose hair, then plaited it into thick braids on either side of her face. The younger women helped to dress her, coaxing her into a long cotton saque they had made themselves, decorated not with glass beads, as it would have been in grander days, but with little tufts of brightly colored fabric that somehow contrived to give it an even more festive air. All that was left then was to paint round red dots on her cheeks, and she was ready to be led back to her young husband, waiting across the stream.

The new lodge had already been erected by the time the party of women arrived. It was not as tall as the bridal tepees Morning Star remembered from when she was a little girl, nor did it have the same look of newness about it, for Buffalo Calf Woman had been forced to make it out of whatever scraps and pieces she could find, but still it was sturdy and serviceable, and she could not help feeling a lump of pride in her throat as she dismounted and looked up at it. This was the first thing that had ever been really hers, not a responsibility she shared with another woman, but something that was totally, completely her own!

But it was many hours before the wedding celebration finally ended and she had a chance to step inside the tepee and give it a closer look. It seemed to her, at that second glance, that the place was curiously empty. Her mother had taken great pains to arrange everything, decorating the liner with cheerful patterns and stacking pillows and piles of cooking utensils throughout, but still there was something missing. Perhaps, she thought with a surprising touch of sadness, it was only that no place would ever quite seem like home without Brave Eagle sitting cross-legged in front of the fire, puffing on his pipe, and Buffalo Calf Woman quietly sorting out wild herbs to flavor their evening meal. Even Wolf-Dog was not there, banished for that one special night to the new in-laws across the stream.

Little Bear, too, seemed to sense the strangeness, for he lingered outside longer than necessary, finding last-minute tasks to keep himself occupied, even after the fire was out and there was nothing left to do. Or maybe, she thought with a tremulous smile, it was not the strangeness that affected him at all. Maybe it was only that he, like she, had had a sudden glimpse of the long night hours that stretched out in front of them.

He appeared at last in the doorway, vaguely uneasy, hesitant, as if he were wondering whether he might not have wandered into the wrong tepee after all. Morning Star laughed a little uncertainly as she looked up from her place on the low fur pallet.

"Are you sure you want to be here, husband? You look for all the world like a man who wishes he could change his mind."

Nervousness showed in her voice, but it seemed to have a calming effect on him. The beginnings of a smile made his lips more familiar as he sat down and took both her hands in his.

"It is too late to change my mind, you silly child. We are already married."

"But not by the rituals you wanted."

There was a question there, somewhere, and he sensed it. It was true—he *had* wanted to be married in the white man's legal ceremony, but not for himself, only for her protection. And he had given up the idea when he saw how much it upset her.

"Haven't I already told you I was wrong to ask for that? When I agreed to live as you wanted, in the tribal way, under Indian law, I knew I was relinquishing my claims on the white man and his world. That was a promise I made to you."

"And you made it without regrets?"

Without regrets? What a way she had of getting at the heart of things. There were some regrets, he supposed—regrets for all those lonely years at the white man's mission school, years that now seemed utterly in vain. But when he looked at her and saw firelight shimmering in long auburn hair, all he could think was that she was beautiful . . . and that he would give up anything to be with her.

His arm was light around her shoulders, tender, an echo of the yearnings in his heart. Dark eyes searched her face in the faint light, trying to see what was going on inside her.

"Are you afraid of me, Morning Star? You do not need to be, you know. I promise, I will be gentle with you tonight."

Half a smile played on her lips as she looked up to meet his gaze. He had not answered her question, but that did not matter now. He no longer needed to. Just the feel of his arm around her was enough. Just the quivering whisper of his breath against her cheek.

"No, my love, I am not afraid. I could never be afraid of you."

She surprised him by taking his hand and laying it on her breast, not gently as she had before, but boldly, demandingly, with a freedom almost akin to wantonness. How sweet her hair smelled, tantalizing, clear and fresh like pine needles in mountain streams—far better than the perfumed soap he had once longed for. Perhaps all those years were not wasted after all, he thought, laughing a bit at himself. It would not have been right for a man to come to his young wife ignorant of the ways of love.

"I will make you happy tonight. When you feel my arms around you, there will be only tenderness in them, only caring . . . and, oh, my sweet, I will teach you to love me as I already love you."

His lips were soft, as he had promised, gently guiding her into the teasing passion of the first kiss she had ever known. Sighing, she coiled her arms around him, letting her body slip into the shared abandon of their embrace. The fire died away, the night air grew cold around them, but they did not notice, warm and safe as they were, huddled together in the folds of a thick buffalo robe.

A crash of thunder shook the sides of the tepee, jolting Morning Star out of the sweetness of her dreams. For a moment, muffled up to her chin in thick fur, she could not remember where she was or what she was doing there. Then, slowly, her eyes began to pick out familiar objects in the dim morning light—a new tepee liner patched out of old skins, the cooking utensils Buffalo Calf Woman had given her the day before, a rusted metal water bucket that once belonged to Little Bear's family—and she realized she was in her own lodge.

Sleepily, she pulled herself up on one elbow and glanced toward the doorway. Low, rumbling echoes of thunder still reverberated somewhere in the distance. An early spring storm? she wondered, puzzled. But the sky had been so blue yesterday, and even now the air was crisp and dry.

She turned toward Little Bear to ask what he thought, but to her surprise, she discovered she was alone. He must have been there only moments before, for the space beside her was warm to her touch, but there was no sign of him now. The first gnawing hints of anxiety began to tug at the back of her mind. Even if it was late in the morning, shouldn't her young husband have been there, lingering beside his new bride in the warmth of their marriage bed?

Wrapping the robe around her, she went over to the door, opening the flap a crack to peer outside. The air was cool, but the sky was clear and not a cloud could be seen. She was even more aware of the rumbling now, relentless as before— much too constant and unremitting for thunder. And it no longer seemed far away.

Gunfire!

The thought raced through Morning Star's body with a cutting force. Tossing aside the fur robe, she pulled on her clothes as fast as she could, tugging at them so roughly she tore the neck of her new dress. That's what the sound was— gunfire! And the first loud crash that woke her must have been the roar of the white man's cannon. Brushing aside the flap, she hurried outside.

In the open air, the sounds were clearer, not muted as they had been inside, but sharp and distinct, and Morning Star could pick out the terrible cracking of each individual shot. She could not be sure—they seemed to echo off the rocks all around her—but she had the sickening feeling they were coming from the camp across the stream.

Her heart pounded wildly against her chest as she raced between the tepees, heading toward a narrow ravine that led down to the banks of the creek. An eerie silence had fallen over the camp, contrasting dramatically with the savage sounds in the distance. Not a man was in sight, not even an old grandfather or a gawky teenaged boy, but women seemed to be everywhere, catching their children up in protective arms or piling their possessions in pathetic little heaps outside of open doorways. Across the square, a solitary figure hailed Morning Star with a wild waving of her arms.

"Oh, *na' go!*"

Morning Star hurried toward her mother, hoping desperately, unreasonably, for some word of comfort from those taut, grim lips. But as she drew near, she realized the worst had happened.

"It is the Blue Coats!" the woman explained tersely. "They were searching for a band of hostile Kiowas. When they could not find them, they surrounded the camp across the stream instead. The men have gone to see what they can do, but I fear they are already too late."

"The men?" Morning Star's breath caught painfully in her throat. "All the men? Little Bear, too?"

Buffalo Calf Woman did not waste time confirming what her daughter already knew.

"Your father says we must lead the other women to safe hiding places in the hills. If the soldiers learn there is another camp nearby, there is no telling what they will do. Brave Eagle says they will go mad with killing for a while, and we must do nothing to provoke them. When it is over, they will be quiet again, and the women and children can come out."

"No!" Morning Star knew her mother was right, but she could not bring herself to accept that terrible truth. "How can you ask me to leave my husband at a time like this? Little Bear has been away too long. What does he know of battles and fighting? I must be by his side in case he needs me. I will not hide like a coward in the hills!"

Without waiting for a reply, she dashed away from her mother, circling around one last tepee and into the rocky ravine. In her haste, she had come away without her moccasins, but she barely felt the sharp stones that cut her skin and dug deep into bare soles. All she knew was that, somehow, in all that madness, she had to find her husband and keep him from doing anything foolish.

But when she reached the stream, the sound of gunfire had already begun to diminish, erupting only sporadically in nerve-shattering bursts of violence. Morning Star hesitated for a moment on the bank, even more frightened by the sudden, unexpected silence than she had been by all the clamor that went before. Whatever had happened in that other camp, it was over now—or nearly over—but that did not make it any easier for her to plunge into the ice-cold water and force herself across.

She had nearly reached the opposite bank when a harsh

grunting noise caught her ear. Startled, she looked up to see a man on horseback not twenty paces from where she stood. Bright sunlight glinted off shiny bars on the chest of his blue uniform.

Reacting instinctively, she drew her arms tightly across her breast, as if to ward off the bullets that must surely come at any second. But instead of reaching for his gun, the man only raised his hand, motioning her back with broad, coarse gestures. Choking on her bitterness, she had no choice but to obey.

Crouching down helplessly on the rocky bank, just across from the place where the horseman had driven her back, she scanned that far shore with her eyes, searching for hints of the terrible slaughter that must have taken place. But the camp was too far away, and all she could make out was the vague outline of tepees against the sky. Here and there, mounted soldiers patrolled the bank, holding back all those who tried to cross. Farther away, other Blue Coats could be seen herding small clusters of women and children away from the direction of the camp.

Even more frightened now, Morning Star squinted into the glaring sunlight, trying desperately to find a face that was not there. All she could see was an elderly woman, standing by herself, dazed and motionless in the middle of the stream. The old grandmother who had dressed her hair only the day before—but how had she gotten there? None of her family seemed to be with her. A boy plunged into the water and, catching hold of her arm, pulled her safely to shore. Morning Star recognized one of Owl Woman's brood, a lad too young to have left the shelter of the hillside camp but too willful to stay behind with the women and children. Not far away, seated alone, her feet dangling forgotten in the edge of the stream, a pretty girl stared into the dark ripples.

Wades-in-the-Water!

Morning Star leaped up at the sight of her. In her anxiety over Little Bear, she had completely forgotten that her young kinswoman was in that other camp. Rushing to her side, she knelt down to catch her up in a grateful embrace. Not until she pulled back again did she get a look at the child's eyes, dazed and glassy—as lost as the eyes of the old woman in the stream.

"I was fetching water when it happened," she told Morning Star, her voice dull and heavy. "I tried to go back, but the gunshots got worse and worse. I was so frightened, I ran across the stream and hid behind the rocks. Singing Cloud is all right because our grandfather, Blue Thunder, wanted to visit the other camp and she had to go with him—and Running Deer, too, because all the braves were out on a hunting party. But, oh, Morning Star, I am so worried about my parents . . . and my middle sister and her unborn child.''

Morning Star sat down on the bank beside her, taking hold of her hand and letting the girl cling to her. She longed to do something, say something, to make it easier, but nothing came to mind. What words of comfort were there for this child—or for anyone else in that terrible place? All they could do now was wait. Wait and pray that the loved ones they could not see were safe somewhere on that other shore.

It was late afternoon by the time the soldiers finally drew away from the bank, and frightened, heartsick Cheyennes could at last begin crossing the stream to the other side. Even then, the sense of the enemy was strong, and Morning Star was keenly aware of watching eyes as she made her way across the desolate plain toward that lonely, silent circle of tepees.

The sight that greeted her eyes when she arrived was even more terrible than the appalling devastation she had imagined. If any of the Blue Coats had been killed or wounded, their comrades had already carried them away, but the bodies of dead and mutilated Indians seemed to have been strewn haphazardly across the earth, a mangled heap of bloodied torsos and grotesquely twisted arms and legs. There were no young men among the fallen, for none of the braves had been in the camp when the attack occurred, but there were more than enough old men to compensate. Old men and women, and little children, some too small even to walk.

Morning Star thought she had come to terms with violent death, for it was part of the duties of an Indian woman to go out onto the field after a battle and tend to the dead and wounded, but there was no way she could ever have hardened her heart against a sight like this. Everywhere she looked, the carnage was ghastly and complete. Skulls had been brutally bashed in, over and over again, long after the first violent blows had accomplished their purpose, and babies had been run through by the same lances that still jutted grotesquely out of their mother's breasts. Genitals had been cut away from some of the bodies, the men's to make tobacco pouches, if the white man's savage boasts could be believed, the women's to provide grisly ornaments for saddle horns.

Many of the dead were beyond recognition, but others were almost frighteningly identifiable, their dark eyes ironically lifelike in the pain and terror that seemed to scream out of them. Little Wades-in-the-Water would not need to worry about her parents anymore, Morning Star thought, and tried not to look down at them—they were beyond earthly cares now. Or about the sister who had come so close to giving birth to her child. All she could hope was that whoever told the girl would be kind enough to spare her the details. The woman had died quickly enough from a bullet that blasted away the side of her head, but some primitive savagery had prompted the white soldiers to tear the unborn baby out of her body and smash it again and again against the rocky earth.

Sickened and dazed, Morning Star wandered through the camp, sinking ankle deep into the earth, muddy with the rains of spring and the blood of her own people. By the time she finally reached the tepee where she had been dressed for her wedding feast and discovered the body of the woman who had been her mother-in-law only for a single day, she was too drained of emotion to be able to feel anything. The memories were there, she knew they were—the way Corn Woman had laughed at her childish pranks, the sadness they shared the day Little Bear went away, the bittersweet acceptance in those dark, gentle eyes when he left her tepee for the last time—but all the tears seemed to have dried up inside her and she could not even weep.

It was a moment before she spotted a mass of mangy yellow fur, half buried in the mud beside the lodge. Almost instinctively, she turned her head away, half pretending she had not seen it, as if somehow that could make it disappear. But when at last she forced herself to turn back again, the thing was still there.

Wolf-Dog. The one night in all those years when she had not let him sleep at the foot of her pallet. And it was the one night he had needed her!

Kneeling down beside him, she took his head in her hands and raised it out of the mud. He seemed so thin and fragile, nothing but bones under all that tangled fur. She could see it all as clearly as if she had been there when it happened. He must have heard the commotion and come racing out of the tepee, nipping and snarling at the horses' hooves. The soldiers could not have feared him—he was much too scrawny to menace anyone—but they had cut his throat all the same. They had cut his throat and ripped open his belly, spilling his bowels out onto the earth.

They did not even have the decency to shoot him cleanly.

At last the tears Morning Star had not been able to shed flowed freely down her cheeks. He had been so little when he came to her, all warm and wriggling in her arms. And he had been such a good friend. She could not even imagine carrying a water bucket back from the stream without Wolf-Dog loping eagerly ahead of her—or going into the forest to gather firewood or dig for roots. And they had not even shot him cleanly!

She found an old skin beside one of the tepees, and wrapping it around the dog, gathered him up in her arms. It surprised her to feel how light he was as she carried him back through the camp and across the stretch of plain that led to the stream. It had not occurred to her before how much of him was fur and how little substance.

Only one Blue Coat still stood on the bank as she approached. He looked up at the sound of her footsteps, but he did not try to move, as if he, too, were stunned by all that had happened around him. Morning Star paused for a moment, caught by something unexpected in his face. He was a young man, far too young for all the insignia on his uniform, but his eyes seemed old and haunted. Had he seen something white men were not supposed to see in the Indian camp that day? she wondered bitterly. Felt something white men were not supposed to feel? Ah, but what would he have felt if those had been his people, not strangers, lying there in the mud?

Dismissing the man from her thoughts, she turned back toward the creek, letting cool water wash away the blood and filth that caked her skin. The woods on the other side came almost to the shore, and she found a sturdy young pine and laid the dog in its branches, tucking the makeshift shroud tightly around him. She did not know if the *tasoom* of an animal was free to make the long journey up the Hanging Road into the heavens—she did not suppose it was—but somehow it was not as hard to leave him there as it would have been in the camp.

The men had already returned by the time Morning Star reached the sheltered hollow where they had pitched their tepees, but the relief she felt at finding her young husband among them vanished the instant she caught sight of the hard, grim look on his face. He was seated on Fire-Wind, a little apart from a group of mounted braves in the center of the clearing, but his eyes did not leave them for a second. One of the warriors, older than the others but still strong and hot-tempered, seemed to have taken charge, raising his voice in impassioned tones above the cries of the throng. As the men milled around, turning their mounts first this way, then that, Morning Star saw bold streaks of black and green and red painted on the faces of many of them. Not until Little Bear prodded his horse forward did she realize that he, like many of the others, had a gun slung across the front of his saddle.

It was only a rusty, single-action Springfield, a hopelessly outdated weapon, but the sight of it made her blood run cold. She had known that many of the men kept rifles and shotguns hidden among their possessions, burying them in the woods when it came time to make camp, but it had not occurred to her that her own husband might be among them. Anxiously, she hurried toward him.

"Little Bear . . .!"

The words died on her lips as he turned to face her. She had never seen his eyes like that before, brittle and guarded, as if somehow it pained him to look at her.

"I was the one who wanted to live in peace with the white man. Do you remember?" He sounded bitter and tired, far older than his years. " 'Let us learn his ways,' I said. 'Let us exist with him side by side in his world.' Well, I was wrong. We will never live in peace with the white man—because he will not let us."

Morning Star backed away slowly, hearing her own words on his lips and appalled by them. This was what she had asked for—what she had begged him to admit from the day he came home—yet now, on his lips, it sounded so futile. Fight the white men? But how could a handful of braves, armed only with primitive weapons, take on a regiment of soldiers?

Catching sight of her father standing alone in front of his tepee, she hurried to him for help.

"*Nihu*, we must stop him. We cannot let him do this."

"Cannot, my child?" His voice sounded low and strangely

unreal, as if he listened to her but did not truly hear what she was saying. "But I think we must. There is nothing we can do to change things now."

"But he knows nothing of fighting, *nihu*. I understand about the others. It is all right for them to go if they must— they know what they are doing. But how can Little Bear hold his own with them? We must keep him here."

Brave Eagle laid his hand on her arm, half comfortingly, half tense, as if to hold her back in case she decided to bolt forward. The young braves were already beginning to form into long lines, ready at any moment to ride out of camp.

"Let him go, daughter. There are things a man must do if he is to call himself a man."

A man? How empty that sounded, just a word, a label—yet there it was, all that fierce male pride, too strong and stubborn for a mere woman to fight. Yes, she would let him go, not because she wanted to, but because there was in what her father had said a truth too deep to be denied. She did not know why it should be so, she only knew it was.

"Oh, *nihu*—once you called yourself a man of peace. How could you let this happen?"

"I *am* a man of peace, but the white man is not. If our young men try and fight the Blue Coats, they will die. I know that. But if they do not, they will be slaughtered anyway. No, daughter, it is better this way. He must go."

"But to die like this? Senselessly?"

"All death is senseless if it comes before its time. If a man must die needlessly, let him at least die for something he believes in."

There was a quiet finality in his words. Morning Star did not speak again, but stood beside him, tall and motionless, watching in silence as the braves filed one by one out of the camp. Little Bear rode toward the front, as befitted the son of a chief, and Fire-Wind, sensing the honor, pranced with exaggerated gaiety, tossing his flame-red mane into the wind. Close behind them came Running Deer, the handsome youth Morning Star once thought would be her husband, and after him, a young cousin who always used to pull her braids, then a boy she had singled out in the Swing-Kicking Game because she knew she could always beat him.

All the young men of the tribe, she thought sadly. All the

handsome, foolish, bold, clumsy, gentle, arrogant, loving young men. And how many of them would ride back again?

The camp was strangely silent after the braves had gone. Morning Star spent the evening in her parents' tepee, helping her mother with dinner, as she had every night for as long as she could remember. But when the last scraps had been cleared away and the fire was no more than smoldering embers, it was time to return to her own lodge. There, for the first time in her life, she went to bed alone.

The next morning, Wades-in-the-Water woke her shortly after dawn.

"There is a man in the camp," she whispered, her eyes wide and frightened. "His name is Rafe Valero, and he says he is looking for a white woman who was stolen by the Indians."

II

The Moon
of Red Cherries

Eight

The white man's fingers dug into Morning Star's arm, bringing tears of pain to her eyes. She tried to pull away, but resistance only made him tense his grip, and she thought for a moment the bone would snap in two.

"Let go of me! You're hurting my arm. What right have you to hold me against my will?"

"Every right in the world." Jet-black eyes snapped with amusement as he looked down at her. "I have been paid handsomely by your father to bring you back—Miss Kristyn Ashley!"

The words seemed to echo in the stillness. Morning Star felt a tremor of fear run through her body as the sound died away and only the crackling of the fire filled the empty night. She could not make out the breathing of the other Cheyennes in the darkness, but she knew they were there, watching somewhere in the shadows. And she knew not a one of them would dare to help her!

"I—I am not this person you speak of. This Kristyn Ashley." She glared down resentfully at the scar on her arm. What a fool she was to let him intimidate her like that! Such marks could hardly be uncommon. "That is only the place where—where a coyote bit me when I was a little girl."

White teeth flashed suddenly against sun-bronzed skin.

"That is not the mark of a coyote. You are right, it did happen when you were a child, but it is a burn. From a scalding teakettle when you were four years old. And if you wanted to convince me you were really a blue-eyed half-breed, you shouldn't have spoken fluent English. They don't send girls to the mission school."

The cool triumph in his voice was enough to send a new

shiver down Morning Star's spine. His hands still gouged into her flesh, but she barely noticed the pain as she stood in the firelight and stared up at him. There was something commanding in that tall presence, a kind of raw masculine power, towering over her, making her more afraid than she had ever been in her life. This man did not care how much he hurt her. He simply did not care! He was only playing a game—and it amused him to think he was winning!

A sudden surge of anger mingled with her fear. How dare he insult her like that? It was one thing to do the job he had been paid for, and quite another to demean her in the process! Summoning all her strength, she twisted her arm free and pulled away from him.

"What if I refuse to go with you, white man? What are you going to do then?"

He did not try to grab her again, but leaned back casually, looping his thumbs through his belt. Something in the coolness of the gesture gave Morning Star the feeling he was actually enjoying her defiance.

"I don't think you will refuse. That would be a very foolish thing to do, and you don't look like a fool to me. Scruffy, yes, and definitely unwashed, but foolish? No, you'll do what you are told."

"*No!*" All the fury, all the fear, seemed to burst inside her, exploding out of her mouth in that one single word. "No! These are my people, whether you believe me or not. And this is my home! You can beat me with your fists if you want to, you can take out your whip and lash me the way you white men lash your horses, but you cannot force me to go with you!"

Whirling around, she darted away from him, racing with lightning swiftness into the darkness. The unexpected motion must have caught him off guard, for he did not pursue her right away, giving her a split second's start. That was all she needed. Slipping out of the circle of tepees, she ran lightly behind them, picking her way through terrain so familiar she did not need eyes to see.

Soft-soled moccasins fell noiselessly on the earth as she twisted in and out of the shadows, listening always for the telltale *slap-slap*, *slap-slap* of leather boots behind her. When she heard nothing, she paused briefly, straining her ears for the subtle sounds that were not there. It was hard to believe she had gotten away from him so easily, yet surely a white man could not move stealthily enough to keep her from hearing. Slowly, after what seemed an eternity, she let out her breath in a soft, audible sigh. He was not there.

Of course he wasn't! If she had not been so frightened, she would have known all along that he would never follow her. How could he when she knew the territory and he did not? Besides, hatred of the whites ran strong in the camp that night. He could not be sure she was not leading him into a trap! Laying her hand lightly on her breast, she felt her heartbeat begin to still at last. She might not be safe yet, but at least the danger was no longer immediate.

Turning back toward the tepees, she began to glide silently between them. She dared not return to her own lodge, it was far too dangerous. Nor could she try to find a hiding place in the hills, for she did not know where the man was and she could not risk stumbling on him in the darkness. But there was still one place she could go. Whenever she had had a problem in the past, whenever something had troubled her, she had always turned to Brave Eagle—and he had never failed her.

The ground was cold in front of her parents' lodge, but a soft glow seeped through the edges of the closed doorway telling her a fire had been laid inside. Morning Star hesitated for a moment, vaguely uneasy, though she could not for the life of her figure out why. It was almost as if the wind that whistled through the camp carried hints of foreboding on its icy wings and touched her heart with coldness.

Brushing aside the feeling, she pushed open the flap and stepped into the tepee.

The enclosed space seemed as warm as the night outside had been cold. The wind had driven smoke back through the opening at the top, and the air was thick and hazy. Morning Star could barely make out her mother's figure, hunched over a fire in the center, poking at it with the green willow stick in her hand. In the rear, her father was sitting absolutely motionless, his face so deep in shadows she could not see his eyes.

"Oh, *nihu!*" Relief flooded through her at the sight of him. "The white man has seen me. The one they call Rafe Valero. I managed to get away from him, but I know he is looking for me. You must help me."

Brave Eagle did not move, not even to turn his head so his

eyes would catch the firelight. The eerie wailing of the wind dominated the interior of the tepee, low and somehow menacing, reminding Morning Star once again of the strange uneasiness that had assailed her outside. What was going on? she asked herself, puzzled and suddenly tense all over again. Her father should have leaped to his feet at her first words, alarm spreading across strong, decisive features. As for her mother—well, even now her mother should be clasping her in warm, protective arms. Why were they behaving like this?

"*Nihu* . . . ?"

The wind picked up, drowning the word even as it escaped from her lips. Slowly, Brave Eagle turned toward her, raising his hand and patting the empty space on the pallet beside him.

"Come here, my child. Come sit beside me and let me talk to you."

His voice was muffled and heavy, adding to the alarm Morning Star already felt. Could something have happened she did not know about? Anxiously, she turned toward her mother, looking for reassurance, but Buffalo Calf Woman had busied herself with the fire and would not look at her. Reluctantly, she stepped over to the pallet and sat down gingerly on the edge.

She half expected Brave Eagle to reach out and draw her closer, but he did not.

"There are things it is hard for a father to say to his child, but I must say them now to you. I cannot do this thing you ask of me. I cannot help you escape from the white man."

"You . . . cannot?"

Morning Star heard the words, but she could not make herself believe them. Was this really her father, the man she had run through the darkness to find? The man who had always protected her from everything she feared?

"Oh, *nihu*, don't you love me anymore?"

Brave Eagle's face hardened, as if somehow, inadvertently, she had managed to touch him, but he made no effort to defend himself.

"Love has nothing to do with it, my daughter. Think what you are asking of us. The white man has already seen you. He knows you are in the camp. If we refuse to turn you over to him, he will take a terrible vengeance on us. You saw yesterday what the Blue Coats are capable of when they are angered."

"But that was yesterday, *nihu*. You said yourself the soldiers would go mad with killing for a while, then they would quiet down and things would be all right again. They will not want to attack us again so soon, especially if they think I am no longer in the camp. You could tell them I am willful and rebellious, and you have no control over me!"

A hint of emotion showed in his eyes, dark and vaguely troubled.

"You would defy me, my daughter?"

The question caught her off guard. Was he right? *Would* she defy him? She had always trusted his judgment before— but then she had always felt she could count on him.

"I would not want to, *nihu*."

"But you would?"

"Yes, I would."

She was aware of a quick moment of communication between the man on the pallet and the woman at the fire. Not so much a glance, more a flicker of motion, as if they already knew what they had to say to each other. There was a discomforting expression on her father's face as he turned back to her, a kind of sadness he had never let himself show openly before.

"We had hoped we would not have to tell you this. We thought you could go away with the white man and never need to know. But I see now we were wrong. We have had news of the war party that rode out of camp, and it is not good. They have already met the white man in battle, and they were badly defeated. Many of our finest young braves will not return."

He paused, looking long and searchingly at Morning Star.

"Among the fallen was your own husband, Little Bear."

Little Bear? How still the tepee seemed in the silence that followed those fateful words. Rising quietly from the pallet, Morning Star moved mechanically, without thinking, toward the open doorway. The wind had subsided; the soft feel of it was like a cool caress on her cheek.

Among the fallen, Brave Eagle had said. *Among the fallen.* But he really meant among the dead. Tears touched the inside of her eyelids. She could feel them lingering there, hot and moist, but they did not flow down her cheeks.

A funny word, *dead*. She knew it ought to mean some-thing—it always had before—but she could not make herself focus on it. How could Little Bear be dead when she had just learned to love him? How could their life together be over before it had really begun? Was it possible to wake up one morning, so eager to be a bride, and go to sleep the next night with the heaviness of death hanging over her?

Still silent, she looked back into the room, trying to make out her father's face, but his features seemed to shimmer in the haze of her tears. What was it he had said before? Something about going away with the white man? But why would she leave now when she needed her family more than ever?

Brave Eagle seemed to sense the unspoken question.

"I a man old man, my child. My eyes do not see what they used to. My arms are no longer the strongest in the tribe. It will be all I can manage in the years to come to provide meat and lodge poles for myself and my wife. How can I put food in another mouth as well?"

Morning Star could only stare at him for a moment, too hurt and confused to make sense out of what he was saying. Then slowly, she began to understand.

"Oh, *nihu*, you think I am going to be a burden if you take me back into your lodge. But I would never let that happen. I love you too much. If it is necessary, I—I could . . ." She choked on the words, but painful as they were, she knew she had to say them. This was her family. She would do anything—*anything*—to keep them safe. "I could—take another husband! Then there would be a son-in-law to care for you in your old age."

Brave Eagle shook his head sadly.

"If only it were that easy. Did you not hear the things I told you before? Many of our young warriors are already lost, more will be lost in the days to come. Where will you look for a husband then? Only old men will be left. And how can an old man provide for his wife and daughter, and the daugh-ters of his dead brothers as well?"

A cold chill seemed to creep into the tepee, almost blowing all the warmth away. Morning Star heard the words on her father's lips, but a deeper instinct warned her that they were not the words in his heart. The events of recent days had changed him bitterly. Yesterday, before he had seen the

devastation of that terrible massacre—before he had lost the
young man he called his son to the white man's bullets—he
would have wanted to draw his daughter close in times of
trouble. Yesterday he would have faced starvation gladly
rather than break up his family. Could it be that today, when
he looked at her, he did not see Morning Star at all, but only
a stranger with fair skin and pale blue eyes?

"Then I must go, *nihu*?"

"You must go."

Soft and final, there was no denying it. Morning Star
turned away in silence, her head held high, the tears in her
eyes still unshed. Years of living with the Cheyennes had
given her a deep sense of her own inner dignity. That, at
least, they could not take away from her.

Even outside, even alone in the bitter night, she did not
weep. There were feelings that ran too deep for tears, emotions that did not know how to express themselves. Someday,
she knew, she would cry for her young husband, but now her
heart was dead even to grief. The white soldiers had done
their work well in that sad camp across the stream. It was not
only women and children they had killed—it was the trust
that had been building for fourteen years between a father and
his daughter.

The night was quiet as she stole softly behind the tepees,
taking the long way around to the ravine that led out of camp.
So the white man had been right, after all. That stranger,
Rafe Valero. She *was* going to go with him, though not for
the reasons he had thought. Not because he was stronger than
she, and certainly not because she feared him, only because
there was no place else to go.

The moon was a disk of cool white in a deep blue sky.
Morning Star paused to look up at it. Funny, how much of
her life had been measured by the moons. The Moon When
the Wolves Run Together, and the world had seemed so
dazzling and clean, sparkling under its crystal cloak; and the
Moon of the Ponies Shedding, with spring wildflowers bursting out on the meadows and hillsides. The Moon When the
Plums Turn Ripe—how she had loved to watch the first hints
of color touch the green leaves on the trees—and then the
Moon of Frost in the Lodge, and the whole cycle had begun
again. Now she would count her days by the white man's
moons, and she did not even remember what they were called.

*   *   *

Little tongues of flame lapped at the edges of charred logs, then died away, leaving only the luminous glow of red embers. Buffalo Calf Woman held the green willow stick tightly in her hands, but she did not try to reach out and prod the fire into life again. She could not see Brave Eagle, deep in the shadows behind her, but the light sound of his breathing reminded her he was there.

Finally, the silence grew too much for her.

"Have we chosen wisely, my husband? It is a heavy thing we have done this night. My heart is troubled."

Brave Eagle left his pallet and, kneeling beside her, put an arm around her shoulders. The warmth of the fire touched her features, recalling the youthful softness of years gone by. She had been so beautiful when he first began to court her; she had brought such joy into his tepee. All he had ever wanted for the children he loved was that same contentment he had found with her.

"We chose the only path we could. We had to let the girl go. She belongs with her people now."

"But to tell her that Little Bear . . ."

"Would she have done what we asked if I had not? You saw the way she reacted. She was ready to follow her own instincts. Ready to . . ." He paused, an ironic smile touching his lips. "Ready to defy her own father."

Buffalo Calf Woman caught a hint of bewilderment in his voice, and even in her pain, it touched her. There were things it was hard for a strong man to admit.

"Sometimes, husband, it is good for a child to know her own will."

The words caught him off guard, and he looked at her in surprise. In the early years of their marriage, she would never have thought of contradicting him. But since the child had come to them, their lives had changed in subtle ways.

"She has been good for us," he admitted. "She has brought happiness into our hearts and laughter to our fireside. But we must not dwell on our loss now. We must remember the many years she was with us and be grateful for that."

"I know." The woman sighed softly as she gazed into the fire. "I know you are right. I *should* be grateful . . ."

"Still, it is hard to give her up. I know that. But we are giving her to a better life. Every year the whites find excuses to take more and more of our land, until soon there will be nothing left.

"Already it is whispered that they are going to drive us into the barren place they call Indian Territory, far to the south. Many will perish on that long march, and many more when we get there. With her own people, Morning Star will at least have food for her stomach and warm clothing to cover her body in the winter."

The woman drew away from him, rising to step over to the open doorway.

"I know what you say is true, but . . ."

She stared out into the darkness, broken only by the echoes of fires in front of other tepees. *She* was out there somewhere, the little girl she had raised from early childhood, and a mother's eyes could not pick her out.

". . . but, oh, it *is* hard."

The man did not intrude on her grief for a moment, but left her alone with the tears she needed to shed. It was a measure of the girl's influence over their lives that for the first time he wondered why it was that a woman could weep and a man could not. Finally he rose and, taking hold of her hand, as he had when she was a young girl, led her back to the half warmth of the fire.

Moonlight accented the jagged lines of a broken pine at the edge of the woods, not far from the place where the ravine opened onto the shore. The white man was waiting for her there, his tall, lean body resting with supple tension against the fallen trunk. Morning Star lingered unseen in the shadows and studied him with wary eyes. His coloring was striking in the darkness: his pale skin had lost its swarthy tan, and his smoldering eyes seemed to sink into deep black pits. The night was cold, but he wore only a cotton shirt, stretched taut over strong shoulders, and the muscles in his arms and chest seemed to ripple through the thin fabric.

He had not even bothered to look for her, Morning Star thought with a rush of bitterness. He had just waited, leaning nonchalantly against that old tree, as if he knew all along she would be there. As if there was no doubt in his mind she would come.

And, of course, she had. Swallowing her humiliation, she forced herself to step forward, slipping out of the protection

of the shadows. His eyes turned toward her, but he did not
move, watching her instead the way he might watch a wild
fawn, careful to make no quick motion for fear it would bolt
away.

Like a hunter, she thought miserably. Exactly like a hunter—
and she his prey! How smug he looked at that moment, how
condescending, as if he actually believed she was afraid of
him! She took another step forward, then held her ground,
meeting his eyes with a gaze as cold and unflinching as his.

The gesture seemed to surprise him, though not in the way
she had hoped. His lips did not quite move, but something
happened to his eyes, and she had the decidedly uncomfortable feeling he was laughing at her.

She could not help remembering the way those same mocking eyes had looked before, that first moment in the firelight.
He had been cool then, too, and arrogant—and so unnerv-
ingly sure of himself, it still made her shiver to think of it.
For a sharp, uncanny instant, she almost felt herself back
there again, crouching in the shadow of a tall tepee, her
breath catching in her throat as she waited for black, penetrating eyes to search her out in the darkness. He had known then
that she was there. He had not guessed, he had *known* . . .
and he knew she was too fascinated to tear her eyes away
from his face.

There *was* something magnetic about him, she had to
admit, some almost hypnotic power that commanded the
attention of men and women alike. She had felt it then, in the
compelling red glow of the fire; she felt it now, even more
strongly than ever. And she knew that he felt it, too. Felt it
and reveled in it—and used it to his advantage!

Was that why he had not plunged into the darkness after
her? Why he had been so sure she would come to him of her
own accord? Not because he sensed she had no other choice,
but because he was so sure of his own strength, his own
savage magnetism, that he believed she could not stay away?

It suddenly occurred to her that not the least unpleasant aspect
of the journey that lay ahead was the idea of making it in
Rafe Valero's company.

Nine

Kristyn Ashley . . .

Morning Star sat down on the ground, still cold with the last vestiges of winter even though the sun had been quite warm that day, and turned the name over and over in her mind. Kristyn . . . Ashley. How alien the words sounded, harsh and flat, not at all like the sweeping Cheyenne rhythm she had grown used to over the years. Could that really be her? That person with the strange-sounding name, so displeasing to her ears?

She glanced over at the place where Rafe was unloading the horses, moving back and forth between them and the campsite with long, easy strides. Dusk was falling rapidly, but there was still enough light to see him clearly. He moved like a woman, she thought, intrigued in spite of herself. Like a Cheyenne woman. Deft and efficient, with an economy of motion that tolerated no wasted energy.

And yet there was nothing womanly about him. A new awareness of him crept into her consciousness, a sense of him not as a white man at all, but simply as a man. His strong, lean body seemed to exude virility, even to eyes that had no desire to see it. His shirt was half open to the waist, offering glimpses of tangled black hair, and the same tight denim pants that showed every muscle in long, powerful thighs did nothing to conceal the ultimate proof of his manhood.

A man with the skills of a woman. The idea was so unexpected, Morning Star could not help being fascinated by it. Looking around the camp, she was forced to admit, albeit grudgingly, that even Buffalo Calf Woman could not have chosen a better site. The clear waters of a shallow creek trickled down from the hills, and tall cottonwoods offered both shelter and firewood, while a low bluff would protect them from rising night winds. A man would have to be very sure of his own masculinity, it seemed to her, to let himself succeed so well at a woman's task.

A shrill whinny broke the twilight stillness, drawing her attention back to the horses. In the dim light she could barely make out a dark mane tossing impatiently around features so proud that, even from a distance, they almost looked human. A fiery black stallion, skittish yet bold, so hard to handle only one man could ride him—that was exactly the mount she would have expected Rafe Valero to choose for himself. But the horse tethered beside him had come as a complete surprise to her. They had headed for a livery stable in the first town they had reached, Rafe being more than a little tired of carrying her behind him in the saddle, and she had watched him go inside with little interest, certain that he would save his money and bargain for some tired old nag that would barely carry her weight to the end of the journey. But when he came out again, he was leading a strong chestnut gelding, almost as tall as his own horse and, if not as spirited, at least lively enough to be fun to ride.

Certainly, the man was full of surprises; much as she disliked him, she could not deny that. Even now, he had managed to do the unexpected. Leaving the campfire he had just finished laying, he had gone over to the horse and was speaking in low, soothing tones as he ran a sure hand down that sleek neck. As long as he was with her, he was cold, almost brutal, treating her throughout the long day's ride with a forced civility that barely masked his rudeness, and it was easy to convince herself he was the most despicable man who had ever lived! But now, seeing him unguarded like this, without the wall of icy arrogance around him, she was aware of a kind of suppressed tenderness that was almost touching.

They were two of a kind, this man and his horse, so alike in their faults and their virtues. Willful, arrogant, only half tamed, yet strong, too, in the most unexpected ways, and fiercely independent, capable beneath that harsh pride of a depth of feeling only a few would ever see. What was he saying now, she wondered, his head bent so close to the horse that only the subtlest hint of low, vibrant tones reached her ears? What was he saying—and what would it be like to feel that same whisper of breath against her own neck?

As if he sensed her eyes on him, sensed perhaps the unwilling fascination she could not control, the man turned slowly to face her. There was no tenderness in his eyes now, not even the cool civility she had resented so much before, only a coarse boldness that sent cold shivers down her spine. How savage and male he seemed at that moment, stripping her naked and raping her with his eyes.

The thought threw her into a sudden, unreasonable panic. She was being foolish, of course—the man had made no overt threats, he had not even started toward her—but still she could not help it. The way he was looking at her . . . what was it he reminded her of? Not a fiery stallion, the way he had before, but a cat. A wild, marauding mountain cat, poised on the balls of his feet, every muscle coiled and tense, ready to spring.

"You—you stay away from me!"

The wrong move. She knew it the instant the words were out of her mouth. He *was* a wild cat, and wild cats had a nose to scent out fear.

"Stay away from you?" he drawled unpleasantly. "Why, madame, I was not aware that I had come anywhere near."

"No, not—not near exactly. Not . . ."

Not with his body, but with those terrible, insolent eyes of his! How could she have forgotten the way he had reacted before, that one time she had dared to let herself look at him? Amused, arrogant, insultingly sure of himself.

Agonizingly conscious of her fear, she tried to pull herself up, but her ankles betrayed her, twisting underneath her and throwing her back on the earth. He reached her almost at once, his tall body brooding over her, his grip like iron as he clutched her wrist and dragged her to her feet.

"So—you're not all ice and anger. I was beginning to think I had only imagined that smoldering fire in your eyes. Maybe this isn't going to be such a dull trip after all."

There was no mistaking the lewd insinuation in his tone. Brutal and unyielding, he pulled her roughly toward him, clutching both wrists now, forcing the full length of her body against his savage male strength. Trembling with fear, she tried to resist, but he was too strong for her. She could feel the man-hardness of him against her body, the warmth of his breath, tinged slightly with whiskey—the pressure of his hands digging into her arms, not painful as they should have been, but powerful, somehow provocative. Any minute now, any second, he would force that hard mouth down on hers, and she could do nothing to stop him!

"Is that why you brought me here? To treat me like—like an animal! You said my white father had paid you a great deal of money to find me? Did he also pay you to force your unwanted advances on me?"

"Your father?"

Gruffness could not quite conceal the surprise in his voice. He loosened his grip for a second, just long enough to let her wrench her arms free. Eyes flashing with fury, she stood and faced him. Had she stumbled on some vague remnant of conscience? Did even a ruffian like Rafe Valero draw the line at taking a man's money and betraying his trust?

"Yes, my father. Surely you——"

"Damn your father! This is strictly between you and me, sweetheart. No, of course your father didn't pay me to make advances to you. That was strictly my idea—and yours. Or wasn't that what your eyes were telling me when you looked at me just now?"

Shame flooded her body, mingling horribly with the fear that already surged through her veins. She *had* been looking at him—but not like *that*! Or if she had, she had never intended this to happen.

"You—you're wrong. I was just watching you! You set up a camp very well, you know. It amuses me to see a man doing woman's work."

"No." He seemed frighteningly close, closer than before, even though she could have sworn he had not moved. "You were watching me, all right, but that wasn't amusement I saw in your eyes. It was something else, and we both know it."

"That—that's ridiculous. You're the most disgusting, the most arrogant——"

"I *am* arrogant—but at least I am honest, which is more than I can say for you. Why all these protests? This sudden show of maidenly modesty? It hardly goes with those brazen eyes. Do you think I've forgotten how long you've lived among the savages? You've been with the Indians so long, you're a squaw yourself. And a squaw is only there to take care of her men."

"A *squaw*?"

Morning Star spat out the word disgustedly. Was that why

he was treating her like this? Not because she had dared to turn bold eyes on him, but because she dressed in deerskin and wore her hair in braids, and thus was beneath contempt? Why, would he have behaved exactly the same way no matter what she had done?

"That shows how much you know about us, white man. A Cheyenne woman may have a hard life, but at least she can count on her man to protect her. And no Indian would ever call his wife a 'squaw.' That is a demeaning word you whites like to use."

Red twilight burnished the tanned skin on his face, giving tight, twisted lips an almost savage look. But his voice, when he spoke, was strangely soft.

"A *woman*, then. Yes, that is a better word. Not a squaw, but a woman, sure of herself . . . and sure of her needs. You can tell me anything you like—and you might make me believe it—but you can't tell me you didn't want me when you looked at me like that."

He paused, dark, knowing eyes searing into her face.

"And you can't tell me you aren't going to enjoy this every bit as much as I am."

Horrified, she backed away, trying to block out words that sickened and fascinated all at the same time. He was more like a cat than ever, wild and predatory, scenting what he wanted—sure of his prey. Every slow, insinuating move of that sinewy body told her he wanted her, the way an animal hungered for a temporary mate, and in his unspeakable arrogance, he believed he could make her want him, too!

And something in her own body, some deep, primal, unnamed urge, warned her he might not be wrong.

"No, white man, *no*! I am not going to let you do this to me. I will kill you—or myself—before I allow it to happen."

The tide of anger seemed to burst inside her, and she began to run, stumbling on the rocky earth in her desperate need to get away. She knew she could never escape from him—he was faster than she, and stronger—but at least she would make him pay for his cruel triumph. She would prove to them both that her virtue was not his for the asking!

Footsteps pounded on the dirt behind her, sounding like thunder in her ears, and with one last, frantic flash of terror, she realized it would only be seconds before he was on her. Panic-stricken, she scanned the barren earth, looking for something, *anything* to use against him. All she could see was a few loose stones, and she stooped swiftly, catching up a pair of them, one in each hand. Taking careful aim at his groin, she hurled the first with brutal force.

He saw it coming and swerved to the side, but only just in time. A grunt of pain escaped his lips as a jagged edge of rock glanced off his thigh and clattered loudly to the earth. Morning Star raised the other stone apprehensively and she waited for him to come at her again.

But surprisingly he did not move. He only stood there, a few yards away from her, raw and masculine, his eyes blazing with a heat that did not look at all like anger.

"By God, what a fiery bitch! Where the hell did you learn to fight like that? A Spanish virgin couldn't defend her honor more fiercely!"

Taken off guard, Morning Star lowered the rock an inch or two, then raised it again. What was he up to? Was he really ready to give up so easily, or was this just another devious white trick?

"I don't know what this thing is. This—this Spanish virgin. But if you come near me again, I promise you will be sorry!"

White teeth flashed out in a quick smile.

"Don't worry, my dear, only a fool would tangle with a throwing arm like that. A fool or a madman, and I am neither. I don't know what the hell you're up to—if I were a swarthy-skinned brave, you'd spread your legs fast enough for me—but I'll be damned if I'm going to play your little game. I have too much regard for my manhood to give you another crack at me."

Morning Star could still feel her body trembling, even after he had gone, leaving her alone again. Alone and unexpectedly bereft. It was almost as if he had taken all the anger, all the fear, all the complex emotions he had aroused in her breast, and left nothing in their place to shore her up. The feeling confused and frightened her. Why was it that she felt so completely, horribly drained, so weak her legs would barely hold her up? Was it because of the violence of it all? The shattering suddenness of both his attack and his departure? Or was there something about this man, some force she could not name or explain, that had the power to sap her strength, leaving her strangely lost and empty when he had gone?

The moon rose slowly, drenching the earth in cool white

light, and the smell of coffee drifted on light breezes from the campfire, but Morning Star made no attempt to move. She knew Rafe had been telling her the truth—he would not try to force himself on her again—but still she was afraid. Not afraid of him, but of herself, afraid of this thing that had almost happened between them, and might happen yet if she did not find the strength to hold it back. One by one, bright pinpoints of light appeared above the horizon, decorating the night sky with starry brilliance, and a cold loneliness settled over the earth.

The same spring moon cast an impersonal glow over the Indian camp, now a full day's ride to the south. There, the evening seemed silent and strangely subdued. No open fires blazed in front of the tepees; no husky cries or peals of laughter broke the stillness. Only a solitary man stood in the shadow of one of the lodges, his ears straining into the darkness to pick up a sound he could sense but still not hear.

His instincts did not fail him. Only minutes later, the first hint of hoofbeats reached the camp, and soon the shadows began to swell with other figures, all waiting as tensely and unexpectedly as he had waited before. Behind him, a woman's face appeared in the doorway, hesitating a moment to look at him with questioning eyes, but he put out his hand and waved her back. What he had to do now was his responsibility, and his alone.

It had all seemed so clear yesterday, when he told the girl that she must leave them. He had felt strong then, and sure of himself. But now, standing alone in the darkness, waiting for a long line of braves to ride back into the camp, the right and wrong of it were all mixed up in his mind. It had seemed just as clear that day he sent the boy off, sent him to the white man's school where he had learned nothing that would help his people, and nothing that could make him happy. He had been wrong then. What if he was wrong now, too?

The warriors began to appear at the edge of the camp, moving not in one long, orderly line, as they had when they rode out, but straggling into the clearing, sometimes singly, sometimes two and three abreast. Most of them looked exhausted, and some were obviously hurt—he had not lied to the girl about that at least; there *had* been a battle, though he had not known it at the time—but the terrible violence of their anger still seemed to hang like a heavy pall over their heads. How many of them would still be there at dawn? he asked himself wearily. And how many would have ridden to fight again after one brief farewell to wives and sweethearts?

He waited until a single figure detached itself from the others and began to move toward the empty tepee beside his own. Slipping out of the shadows, he stepped forward.

"Little Bear . . ."

The rider turned slowly to face him. Brave Eagle saw the first flicker of doubt cross the young man's features as he looked down and saw not his wife, but his father-in-law waiting at the doorway of his lodge.

"*Nihu?*"

How like the girl he sounded at that moment. Naked hope in a single soft question, as if somehow an old man's love could set things right again.

"I am sorry, my son. The girl is not here. She has gone back to her own people."

"She has . . . gone?"

His voice sounded hollow, like a desert wind with no coolness or life in it. Brave Eagle was bitterly aware that there were other things that needed to be said—how could he add to Little Bear's bewilderment by letting him think his wife had left of her own accord?—but it was hard to force the words out of his lips. If only he could make the young man understand first.

"It is better this way, you must believe me. With her people, the girl can have a good life. What could we have offered her but hunger and sickness? Many of the braves who rode out with you did not come back tonight. How many moons will pass before we wait in vain for you? Is that what you want for your wife? Loneliness and suffering? We are Cheyennes. We must bear our fate with dignity. But the girl is white—she does not need to die with us."

Little Bear sat straight and rigid in the war saddle, his face impassive, his lips set in a taut line. The old man's words seemed to flood over him, touching but not penetrating, like water spilling off the feathers of a duck. He could feel nothing, think of nothing except that he had ridden like a madman half the afternoon and well into the night to be with her—and she was gone. Not a word, not a touch, not even a kiss—simply gone.

Digging his heels into the sorrel's flank, he urged the animal suddenly forward, galloping out of the camp in an impulsive fury that left a trail of dust floating in the moonlight behind him. He did not hear the old man's startled cries. He had no way of knowing that there were things he still needed to hear, nor would he have stopped if he had. Anger and pain filled every corner of his being, drowning out everything else in his heart.

The wind was a kindred force, cold and savage, whipping into his face and whistling through dark, short-cropped hair. Turning away from the stream, he headed up into the hills, hungering instinctively for broad, open vistas, for a place where he could feel as free as the galloping horse beneath him. By the time he finally reached the crest and reined in his mount, his hair was plastered against his neck and forehead, and sweat drenched his buckskin shirt, as if it were he, and not Fire-Wind, who had made that wild, impulsive charge up the hill.

Below him, the earth stretched out, silent and serene, bathed in deep blue shadows as far as the eye could see. The circle of tepees in its sheltered hollow seemed so small from that height, it was like a little girl's collection of miniatures, all laid out on the ground. No golden flames teased the darkness; no signs of motion were visible to give the setting an aura of reality.

She had left him.

Slowly, the words began to sink in to his consciousness. She had left him, this pretty, captivating creature who had filled his heart almost as long as he could remember. She had stood and watched him ride out of the camp, and she had looked for all the world as if she cared, but when he came back, she was gone.

He leaned back in the saddle, letting the wind blow damp hair away from his forehead. He had needed her desperately tonight. The brutality of the past two days had sickened him almost beyond belief. The battle against the Blue Coats, so brief yet so devastating, the swift retaliatory raids, with warriors acting like white men . . . he had not known which tormented him more. He only knew that he longed for the solace of warm, feminine arms, and the understanding of the one heart that had never failed him.

And she had not been there.

Waves of anger surged over his body, half drowning him in their bitter deluge. Raising the reins, he clasped them tightly in both of his hands. White men had robbed him of everything that mattered in his life. Land and sustenance, friends and family—even his dignity in those terrible years at the mission school. Now they had taken his wife as well. It was time they paid for what they had done.

Flicking the reins against the horse's neck, he guided him back down the hill, moving slowly this time, taking care not to press him too hard. His eyes were dry and clear as he cast one last look at the camp beneath him. He had been so naive that afternoon he rode away. He had not even known how to fight—but he knew now. Already he had the blood of one white man on his hands. He would have more before he was through.

. He cut into the ravine that led down toward the stream. When the other warriors gathered there shortly before dawn, they would find him waiting for them. Great Chief Man-Who-Lives-with-the-Wolves. It was funny, he had almost forgotten that silly name the day *she* had taunted him with it. Now it was the only dream he had left.

He did not look back as the ravine led him farther and farther away from the camp. Never would he look back again. There was no past for him now. No memories. Only the present—and the future.

And the future was red with blood.

The night sky was breathtakingly clear. Morning Star sat alone, leaning against the trunk of an old oak tree, and stared up at a shimmering cascade of stars that seemed to hang over the distant horizon. How achingly lovely everything seemed at that moment, and how strange to think that pain and suffering could exist in a world that held such beauty in it.

"The Hanging Road . . ."

The words lingered, half whispered, half spoken, on her lips. The Hanging Road, the path that warriors took to the place where buffalo still roamed in great herds and a man could feel like a man. Always before, even when her little brother had died, it seemed an abstract concept, distant and somehow detached from herself. But now, she was bitterly aware of every sparkling step on that long pathway to eternity, the pathway that was taking her own young warrior farther and farther away from her.

A soft footfall broke the stillness behind her. Looking up, Morning Star was startled to see Rafe standing over her, a steaming mug of coffee in his hand.

"Peace?" He held out the metal cup with a crooked half smile.

She hesitated briefly, remembering only too well that she had little cause to trust him. But his eyes did look sincere, and the aroma of coffee was too tempting to resist.

He waited until she had taken a sip of the warming liquid before speaking again.

"I was only half joking, you know, when I told you I wouldn't tangle with you again. Don't think I am afraid of that fiery temper of yours—God help me, I find it fascinating! But I am not some sort of barnyard animal, too unfeeling to follow any urges but my own. I have never forced a woman in my life, and I will not force you now, if this is truly against your will."

"If it is . . . *truly* . . . against my will?"

She could barely whisper the words. Was he thinking of the way she had looked at him before, she asked herself uneasily, or was he so depraved that he actually thought a woman enjoyed that kind of brutality?

She saw his lips move, an ironic smile perhaps, though she could not be sure.

"You have beautiful eyes, Kristyn Ashley. Did any of the young braves ever tell you that? Very beautiful—and very expressive. I thought I saw something in them tonight. It seems I was mistaken."

So that *was* what he was thinking? That she had brought this on herself by her shameless conduct. Yet, even in her confusion, the whole thing didn't make any sense. Surely not even a white man would attack every woman who dared to look at him. Unless . . .

"That's it, isn't it? That's why you behaved so crudely? Not because you thought I wanted you, but because you look on me as a savage, and you don't care what I want? You're just like every other white man. It doesn't matter whom you hurt—as long as it's an Indian!"

He looked startled for an instant, then began to laugh.

"More of that fascinating temper? Spare me, I beg you.

We do seem to butt our heads against each other's prejudices. You with your compulsive hatred of anything white, and me with my goddamn ignorance.''

"And why shouldn't I hate the whites?'' she retorted sharply. It amazed her sometimes, the way these people talked, as if they didn't have the vaguest notion what they had done! "They have broken every promise they ever made to us, they have stolen our land and killed our people . . .''

"Whites in general, yes. I offer no defense for us as a race. But surely there are individuals . . .''

"Individuals?'' She gave him a long, pointed look. "The only individuals I have ever seen did nothing to change my opinion.''

Rafe leaned back on his elbow, still laughing, though softly, almost to himself. There was more than fire and fury in this woman—there was a quick wit as well, and a stubborn pride that caught his fancy.

"Touché,'' he said lightly. Then catching the look on her face, he added: "That means, 'You got me,' and fairly, too! But if I am not a walking advertisement for my race, neither are the Indians I have met—and I admit there have been woefully few of them—exactly a credit to theirs. The men always seemed a shifty lot to me, and as for the women— well, the women were the sort that lead a man to only one conclusion. I daresay, without giving the matter much thought, I simply assumed the others were all the same.''

"Well, they aren't. Indian women, at least those who do not associate with the whites, are noted for their chastity, especially the Cheyennes. Do not judge us all by your de-based standards. After all, everyone knows that white women are easy and immoral.''

"Are they really?'' Black eyes glittered in the moonlight, mocking her in the most unsettling manner.

"Well, of course they are. Don't try to——''

"Ah, if only it were true,'' he broke in, speaking in a slow, teasing drawl. "There are some, of course, thank God—if it weren't for them, how would a man like me get through those long, lonely nights?—but alas, they are too few, and definitely too far between. Try and steal so much as a kiss from any of the others, and all a man gets is her father at the wrong end of a shotgun.''

He paused, waiting for her to join in his laughter, but she

either did not understand or was not about to give him the satisfaction. So she was going to make it hard on him, was she? Well, no doubt he deserved it.

"What I am trying to say, my dear Kristyn, and making a bad job of it, I grant you, is that I know I've behaved vilely toward you—and that is as close to an apology as you will ever hear from these lips. Damn it all, we seem to have gotten off to a rotten start with each other. What do you say we forget it all and try to be friends? We have a long trip ahead of us, you know." His lips twisted into a smile, as if tempting her to forget the other, darker emotions they had shown only a short time before.

"Is that possible, white man? Can you really be friends with an Indian? Or a woman?"

"I can try. It would be a hell of a lot easier, though, if you'd stop calling me 'white man' all the time. I have a name—Rafe. I wish you'd use it."

"And I have a name, too! Morning Star! But you keep on calling me Kristyn, even though you know I hate it."

He smiled again, subtly, even more distracting than before. How she wished he would let her stay angry with him! It was safer that way.

"Another mistake?" he said softly. "But I don't do it to be unkind. I call you Kristyn only because it is your name, and that is what you will hear when you get home. I thought it might be easier to get used to it now."

Easier? Perhaps in a way, but harder, too. Morning Star rose and moved a few steps away from him, trying not to concentrate on the deceptive softness she heard in his voice. She did not dare let herself think that his feeling for her might be genuine. She could hold him at arm's length if she did not mean anything to him, if his desire for her was purely physical. But how could she resist a man who cared?

She felt him move up behind her, warm and solid somewhere in the darkness, so close and still so far. He did not speak, but there was something comforting in his presence, and she realized she did not want him to go away.

"How pretty the stars are," she said impulsively. "Do you know what they look like to me? Like the mist of a waterfall on a hot afternoon, with every drop exploding in the sunlight."

"A liquid stream, spilling to the earth." How low his voice sounded, almost like a caress in her ear. "An appropriate image. Perhaps that is why we have always called it the Milky Way.''

"The Milky Way?'' To her surprise, Morning Star caught herself smiling. ''What a funny name.''

"Funny? Look over there. See those distant stars, merging into a soft white glow? Doesn't that look like milk to you?''

"Of course not. It looks like . . . like a thousand tiny torches in the sky.''

"No, torchlight should be yellow. The stars are clear and white. More like a thousand perfect diamonds.''

"Diamonds?'' Morning Star stumbled on the word. So much of the white man's language came back when she spoke it, but there were still things that continued to elude her. ''I don't think I know what they are, these diamonds.''

He laughed softly. ''A woman who does not know diamonds? Will wonders never cease? Ah, well, you will learn soon enough what they are—and when you do, God help the poor bastard who has to please you. Diamonds, my sweet little innocent, are small stones that look like shiny pieces of cut glass. Only some of them are worth a king's ransom.''

Morning Star drew her brows together in a puzzled frown. Some of the white man's customs were most peculiar.

"Indians have small stones, too. We use them to decorate our headbands and moccasins. But they are not worth all that much in trade, certainly not as much as a warrior or a chief. It seems strange that a stone could be that important to anyone.''

"Strange, indeed, but that is the way it is. I daresay you'll get used to it all too soon.''

Was he laughing at her again? Almost certainly, but this time, she hardly minded at all. When he talked like that, when he treated her like a person instead of an object of contempt, she was almost tempted to like him.

"Do you know what they are to us? Those stars you call the Milky Way? They are our Hanging Road.''

"A hanging road? What an interesting concept. Where does it go?''

"To the home of the spirit who lives in the sky, the one you call the Great Spirit. When someone dies, we hang his body high in the branches of a tree so his soul can climb up the stars into the heavens. Everyone goes there someday, even those who have done wrong on earth, for death is forgiving and eternity belongs to all."

"What a generous religion," Rafe commented dryly. "I wouldn't mention that to the white man's priests if I were you."

Lost in her own thoughts, Morning Star barely heard what he was saying. There was something disturbingly seductive in the sense of this man in the shadows behind her. Something that reminded her how lonely it had been before, sitting there all by herself and thinking of the past.

"*He* is there. My husband. On that Hanging Road."

"Your husband?"

The sharpness in his voice told her he was surprised.

"They did not tell you that? In the camp?"

"They said nothing to me. Not even that you were there, although I guessed it from the way they evaded my eyes. Certainly I did not know you were married. Or that your husband was dead. I am very sorry."

Pride held her head high as she turned to face him. If that was pity he was offering, she wanted no part of it. Not from a white man!

"He died fighting your people! He rode out with the other braves to avenge a savage attack on one of our camps. I hope he took many Blue Coats with him when he began his journey to the other side of the stars. And I don't care if you hate me for saying that!"

"Hate you? Good God, why should I? If I were you, I would say exactly the same thing, only I don't think I would have expressed it quite so politely. And if I were your young husband, I would have been every bit as hungry for revenge. I saw that camp after the soldiers had finished with it."

What was it she heard in his voice now? Not pity, surely— something else, a kind of quiet anger, as if he did indeed share her feelings. She recalled suddenly the Blue Coat she had seen on the banks of the stream that very day—a man with eyes nearly as haunted as her own—and for the first time, she wondered if they were truly so far apart, the white man and the Indian.

How like her own young warrior this man seemed when he spoke like that. Strong-willed, stubborn, almost to a fault, but open to compassion and great understanding. She and Little Bear had quarreled, too, sometimes bitterly, but when the fighting was over, they had always come together, closer than before.

"We grew up with each other," she said softly, more to herself than to him, "my husband and I. We shared everything from the time we were children. The same feelings, the same ideas, the same secret dreams of the heart."

She paused, looking up at the stars, so cold and unfeeling . . . and so very far away.

"It's funny, the things that come back to you when everything else is gone. I remember sitting on the ground one day—I couldn't have been more than eight or nine years old—and Little Bear was angry with me because I called him by a childhood nickname. He was going to be a great warrior chief, he told me, and warriors leave childish things behind. Man-Who-Lives-with-the-Wolves, that was the new name he would take for himself, and oh, how men would tremble with fear when they heard it. . . ."

Her voice trailed off, evaporating in memories too painful to cling to, and she realized suddenly that she had said more than she intended. It was dangerous, this way he had of moving from one thing to another, challenging her senses one minute, then lulling her into unexpected confidences the next. If she turned and looked at him now, she wondered, startled by the thought, would she see Rafe Valero at all, or would her eyes pick up only reflections of the two men who had touched her heart? Running Deer, dynamically handsome, with his strong physical appeal, and Little Bear, able to work himself into her most private thoughts and feelings . . . It seemed to her she could detect more than a little of both these men in one dark and threatening stranger.

Turning away, she began to walk back toward the fire.

"I am very tired, white man. I think I would like to sleep now."

Ten

"If I didn't know better, Kristyn Morning Star, I'd say you were lagging behind on purpose." Rafe's eyes were laughing as he turned to take in a slender figure, following several paces behind the powerful stride of his own strong stallion. "Or have you forgotten how to handle a horse already?"

The girl looked up, a little startled at the sound of his words. Kristyn Morning Star. It was a compromise on his part, she knew, and not a bad one perhaps, but she could not forget the disdain she had felt when her own young husband compromised his Indian identity that way. Was the same thing happening to her now? Had two weeks in the company of a white man, eating white food and speaking nothing but the white language, begun to draw her into a world she had never intended to accept? She did not feel at all like Kristyn Ashley, of course—not yet—but she didn't exactly feel like Morning Star either.

"What are they like?" she asked abruptly. "These friends of yours? The ones who are going to let us spend tonight in their house?"

"Oh, quite a decent sort, really. Luis is a blood cousin, on my father's side, but we've never held that against each other. His wife, Elena, is a charming woman. And don't worry—I understand they've given up eating little Indian girls for breakfast, so you'll be quite safe."

Morning Star wrinkled up her nose and tried to pretend she hadn't heard him. Was he teasing her again, or was he making fun of her ignorance? With a man like that, she could never be sure.

"They aren't going to—to look down their noses at me?"

"Look down their noses? Good God, what things you

135

come up with.'' In the days they had been together, Rafe had been amazed at the speed with which she had picked up English again—obviously she had a quick and curious mind— but she did seem to go in for the most colorful expressions. ''No, they are not going to 'look down their noses' at you. Why should they?''

''You said yourself I am nothing more than an 'unwashed savage.' Weren't those your exact words? That is why we are stopping at this house tonight, so you won't have to take an 'unwashed savage' back to my parents.''

Rafe tried not to laugh at the defiant set to her chin, though in fact, he did not quite succeed. What a contradictory creature she could be. So easy to hurt—and so determined not to let him see it!

''I was joking,'' he said quickly. ''Well . . . mostly joking.''

He held in his horse, waiting until she had drawn alongside him on the narrow dirt road. Then, thrusting out his hand, he caught hold of her reins and drew her toward him.

''I really can't take you back looking like this, you know. Try and imagine how your parents must feel, your mother especially. The last time she saw you, you were a pretty little girl with long red curls. It will be hard enough for her to accept you as an adult without having to put up with stained buckskin as well, and that foul-smelling grease you put on your hair. Anyway, I am looking forward to seeing what Elena makes out of you. I have a feeling it's going to be quite a treat.''

Morning Star tugged at the reins, pulling them out of his hands and flicking them against the horse's neck to start the animal down the path again. She knew Rafe was right—she *couldn't* be cruel enough to meet her mother like that—but something in his voice made her vaguely uneasy. His manner toward her had changed subtly in the past few days, evolving from mockery to teasing to a kind of open admiration that had an unsettling way of appealing to the femininity in her nature. It was not that she wanted to be attracted to him, she told herself miserably—indeed, she wanted nothing more than to cling to the attractions of the life she had left behind. But somehow, with each new mile that separated them from the Indian camp, that life seemed to be slipping farther and farther away from her, and she did not know how to hold on to it.

The road twisted through scattered clusters of elm and cottonwood, then opened onto a wide expanse of fields, still brown and barren before the first spring planting. The house stood by itself, a weathered gray building, with nothing but an occasional wooden fence to break the flatness of the land around it. If anyone was there to welcome them, Morning Star could see no sign of it. Sturdy shutters barricaded most of the upper windows, and even those on the ground floor had the vacant look of a house with all its draperies drawn.

Rafe reined in his horse beside the half-open gate.

"Would you say there's nobody home?" A wry grin twisted his lips as he glanced back at Morning Star. "I should have taken that into consideration, I suppose. With the children grown and married, there isn't much to keep an older couple here. Well, no harm done. I know where Luis keeps the key, and he won't mind if we borrow the place for a night or two. Tomorrow morning, we'll have to find a seamstress in town and——"

He broke off suddenly, turning back toward the house with a startled expression. Morning Star followed his gaze, just in time to see the door slide open and a young man appear on the threshold. For a moment, she thought the sunlight was playing tricks on her eyes. He was slightly shorter than Rafe, with a physique that had more leanness than power in it, but otherwise, he was an almost exact duplicate of the man seated beside her on his stallion.

Rafe recovered first. Leaping off his horse, he hurried toward the man and caught him up in a forceful embrace.

"¿Hola, Carlitos, que pasa? ¿Que estas haciendo? ¿Hay problema?"

The younger man answered with a peal of laughter, then let out a barrage of words that were no more comprehensible to Morning Star than the ones Rafe had just uttered. She was surprised to see that a young girl had followed him out of the house and was now standing a few steps behind the two men, watching their reunion with an amused look on her face. Morning Star was aware of a startling beauty, a kind of obvious flamboyance that the white men no doubt found more than a little intriguing. The girl was not tall, but the pride of her carriage gave an illusion of regal height, and her hair, thick and black, seemed to shimmer like a coronet in the bright sunshine.

Rafe, too, seemed surprised to see her. His brow tensed and his eyes narrowed in concentration, as if he did not quite know what to make of her. Then slowly, a look of recognition crossed his features.

"*¿Ysabelita?—¡no puedo ser! ¡La inocente, sencilla que siempre nos molestaba!*"

"*La misma.*" A faint half-smile touched the girl's lips, enigmatic and somehow secretive. "*¿Es sorpresa, amigo?*"

Sultry throatiness seemed to hang on each word, accenting a blatant sensuality unlike anything Morning Star had ever seen before. Fascinated in spite of herself, she prodded her horse forward, stopping just outside the gate to have a closer look at her.

The girl *was* beautiful, even another woman could not fail to see that. Hers was a provocative style, as dramatic and daring as the bold black and white of her appearance, and she obviously knew it. Pale, milky skin and snapping ebony eyes had been deliberately set off against the false innocence of soft white silk, elusively sweet as it flared over childishly slim hips, and the seductive sophistication of black lace, peeking out from the edges of an almost obscenely low neckline.

The girl's manner was no less bold than her appearance. She stood absolutely still for a moment, looking up at Rafe through coyly lowered lashes, then without the least bit of shame, she reached out and caught hold of his hands. The same throaty sound smoldered in her laughter as she raised them lightly, almost jestingly, to her lips.

That was too much for Morning Star. She did not care how immodestly white women behaved—after all, what was that girl to her, or any of the others for that matter?—but she did not see any reason why she should have to sit there and be subjected to it! Digging her heels into the horse's flanks, she turned through the gate, giving it a sharp kick as she passed to swing it shut again.

Rafe looked up at the sound, obviously surprised, and she realized with a twinge of annoyance that he had completely forgotten she was there! The first stirrings of an emotion she did not recognize began to rise in her breast, and she hated the way it seemed to catch in her throat making it harder than usual to breathe. Almost unconsciously, her eyes slipped back to the place where the dark beauty was standing, only a few feet away. If it had been that girl and not she whom Rafe had left behind, would he have forgotten so quickly?

"Ah, Kristyn!" Rafe said, a little too abruptly it seemed to her. "Where are my manners, speaking Spanish like that in front of you? I was so surprised to find these two waiting for us, I'm afraid I didn't think. This is my brother, Carlos." He extended a hand to draw the other man toward him. "My younger half-brother. The bastard of the family."

Then, catching her confused expression, he added:

"The son of an indiscreet father—and a lady who was not his wife."

A flush of embarrassment stole into Morning Star's cheeks, and she cast a sympathetic glance at the young man who looked so much like Rafe. But if Carlos felt any awkwardness at this open expression of his mother's shame, it did not show on his handsome, smiling features.

"What a pleasant surprise, *señorita.*" He acknowledged his brother's introduction with a low, surprisingly flattering bow. "I had known that Rafael was bringing a young woman with him, of course. I heard about the message he telegraphed to your father, and even though Luis and Elena are on a trip back east, I hoped he would stop here before taking you home. But I had not expected anyone quite so—attractive."

The words were warming, and even though she knew he would have said exactly the same thing no matter what she looked like, Morning Star could not help enjoying the gallantry in his manner. She did not have time to savor the compliment, however, for Rafe cut in quickly:

"And this captivating little minx—" he slipped an arm around the girl's waist—"is Ysabel, the orphaned daughter of one of my grandfather's oldest friends. We have looked after her ever since she was a small child. Would you believe she was just a little girl the last time I saw her? Now she is all grown up."

And grown up quite prettily, his eyes added, or so it seemed to Morning Star at least. It was almost disgusting the way they lingered on that softly feminine form, still enticingly girlish beneath the deliberately womanly lines of her dress. She could not help remembering the women he had told her about that first evening—the kind that helped a man through the long, lonely nights—and it occurred to her that Ysabel might very well be one of them.

Not that it mattered, of course! Rafe could do anything he wanted with his nights—she did not in the least care about that! Still, it was sickening to watch a woman cheapen herself that way.

Ysabel seemed to sense her thoughts, or at least catch the general drift of them, for she glanced up sharply, meeting Morning Star's eyes with a look that was remarkably shrewd for one so young. She held her gaze steady for a moment, then composed her face in a vaguely impish smile and turned back to Rafe.

"*¿Quien es tu amiga? Pensabe que teneás buen gusto. Le gustaba mujeres elegantes. ¿Como has cambrado!*"

Morning Star felt a slow, unwelcome warmth rise to her cheeks again. She did not need a knowledge of Spanish to understand the insults in the girl's tone, and she knew just what Ysabel saw when she looked at her. Exactly what any other white woman would see! An unwashed savage—wasn't that what Rafe had called her? An Indian with greasy braids and skin too tanned from years of exposure. What could be more contemptible?

To her surprise, Rafe threw the girl a sharp look.

"Speak English, Ysabel. You know it as well as I. Grandfather has always tended to your education. This young lady is Miss Kristyn Ashley." He softened his voice as he turned back to her, letting a hint of laughter creep into it. "She might not look like much right now, but I think she'll wash up quite nicely, don't you? She's been living with the Indians for a number of years, but you would do well to cultivate her acquaintance. I daresay she could teach you a thing or two."

"Me?" Ysabel's black eyes widened with astonishment. "How can you speak like that, Rafael, even in jest? I am not used to such—such crudity! You have been among the savages too long. You have forgotten how to treat a lady!"

Rafe seemed to enjoy the outburst.

"There's the Ysabelita I remember. A little Spanish spitfire—and proud as the devil himself! Do you still cause as much trouble as you did when you were a *niña*?"

"More," Carlos broke in, grinning. "Now that she's grown so beautiful, there's no controlling that hot temper of hers. It is even deadlier than ever."

"Heaven help us, then!" Rafe's eyes danced with amusement as he studied her in the sunlight. "But at least go easy on Kristyn. I told you, she has been living among the Indians for a long time. She's not used to women with minds of their own.''

Something in his voice caught Morning Star off guard, a kind of veiled irony that gave her the feeling he was making fun of both of them at the same time. Would she ever be able to figure out what was going on in that mind of his? A minute ago she had dared to hope he was irritated with Ysabel. Now he was looking at her with that same disgusting, frank admiration.

''I have absolutely no desire to impose on your friend, Rafe.'' Dismounting, she tied her horse to the fence and joined the others on the walkway. ''I am sure she is not the least bit interested in cultivating my acquaintance—or going easy on me, as you put it. If you will just be good enough to show me where I am to go . . .''

''Ah, but I'm afraid we must impose on her.'' Rafe put out a hand to hold her back. ''At least for a while. We want someone to make you into a lady of fashion, after all—and who better to ask than Ysabelita? Obviously, she has exquisite taste in clothes.''

''And a consuming passion for them,'' Carlos agreed with a laugh. ''No one spends more time on style than Ysabel, or knows more about it. You could not make a more perfect choice.''

Ysabel looked from one to the other, the confusion on her pretty face darkening as she realized what they were saying.

''But surely you can't mean . . . you want me to——''

''Why not?'' Rafe interjected. ''Carlos is right. You are the epitome of fashion. I can tell that much just by seeing you in one enchanting dress. I wouldn't be surprised if you could work wonders.''

''But not with . . .''

Ysabel seemed to choke on the words. Morning Star felt hot, angry eyes on her face, and she knew exactly what the girl wanted to say. Not with *that*! her tongue longed to lash out, but she didn't dare utter the words. Not with Rafe looking at her like that.

''Very well,'' she agreed reluctantly. ''I will do what you want, of course. Only . . .'' Her eyes drifted back to Morning Star. ''Only don't blame me if the results aren't what you want.''

Morning Star stiffened, but bit back the hot retorts on her tongue. She hated herself for letting the girl bully her that way, but anything she said would only set her off again. Besides, she had the uncomfortable feeling Ysabel might be right. What if she didn't "wash up nicely," as Rafe had put it?

But if he had any compunctions, he did not let them show.

"Do her hair like yours," he said calmly. "All twisted up on her head, with combs to hold it in place. I like it that way. And surely you can spare her a dress or two. If I know anything about young ladies, you haven't come without at least one trunk to keep you company. Kristyn is taller, but otherwise you seem to be much the same size. Organdy and lace, I think—softness would become her—and see if you can find something in sky blue. It ought to be devastating with those eyes."

Ysabel stood, silent and seething, hating him less for the things he was saying than the fact that she did not dare answer him back. Morning Star could almost see her draw in a long, deep breath, struggling to keep her temper. Then slowly, visibly, she let it out again.

"I never wear sky blue. *No me cae.* It is a color I despise."

Turning on her heels, she walked up the pathway and through the open door into the house. Morning Star hesitated, half hoping that Rafe or his brother would engage her in conversation, even for a moment, but when they did not, she was forced to swallow her pride and follow the girl inside.

The house was dark and cool, with a musty smell that seemed to hang in the air. The same heavy drapes that blocked out the sunlight muffled the sound of voices outside as Morning Star stepped into a shallow entry hall and closed the door behind her. Wide wooden planking, stained a deep brown hue, stretched across the floor, and the walls were a drab sand color. Small rectangular rugs, their bright stripes muted in the shadows, added welcome touches of green and gold to the setting.

Ahead of her, on a steep staircase along the side wall, Morning Star was acutely conscious of Ysabel's back, proud and rigid as she moved away from her. It seemed strange, all that controlled anger here inside the house. Out there, where Ysabel had wanted all the attention for herself, yes—but here? With no men around to watch her? Morning Star would have been less surprised if the girl had simply ignored her, treating her with the icy hauteur that seemed to have been bred into her bearing.

They had just reached the top of the stairs when Ysabel turned suddenly, whirling unexpectedly to face her. There was no ice in those black eyes now, no carefully groomed hauteur—only a kind of sulky, brooding challenge.

"You think you know Rafael, don't you? Well, you do not. I have known him longer than you, and I know what he likes. Oh, he might dally with someone like you—he is a strong man, and he has strong cravings—but only a woman with beauty will hold him. Beauty and elegance, that is what matters to him."

Morning Star caught at the railing, too surprised by the sudden attack to say anything for a moment. Dally, indeed! Was that why Ysabel was so angry with her? Because she wanted Rafe for herself and thought Morning Star had designs on him, too? But surely she couldn't believe there had been anything like *that* between them?

Or couldn't she? Morning Star ran a cool eye over the girl's face, noting the faint flush she had missed before, the almost feverish glint to her eye. Ysabel *did* think she and Rafe were lovers—and for some reason the thought frightened her.

"Your guardian may have seen to your education," she said sharply, "but you are still a fool. Anyone with eyes in their head could tell that I am not remotely interested in Rafe. And even if I were, I have too much pride to let myself be used like that!"

Ysabel did not reply, but turned her back pointedly, leading the way into a small room that opened onto the hall. It was, Morning Star decided, pausing on the threshold to look in at it, a sleeping chamber of some sort. A pair of narrow beds, jutting out from one of the walls, nearly filled the room, and frilly chintz curtains gave it a softly feminine feeling, as if it belonged to a young girl. Dresses and petticoats seemed to have been tossed everywhere, spilling in wild disarray over the colorful quilts and half obscuring a small dressing table set in the dormer window.

Morning Star watched, fascinated, as Ysabel picked up first one dress, then another, appraising it with thoughtful eyes before tossing it aside again. Now that she had seen beneath the Spanish beauty's cool, self-confident veneer, if only for a second, she no longer felt as intimidated as she had before. If anything, she thought, smiling to herself, the girl's consternation was amusing.

Poor Ysabel. The look on her face was almost laughable. She had chosen her frothy dresses and lovely, sophisticated ballgowns well—much too well for the task that had just been thrust upon her. Which one of them could she possibly give the young woman she obviously considered her rival? Not the white lawn with little pink flowers all over the skirt and ruffled lace on the sleeves. Anyone would look sweet and demure in that. Nor the shimmering yellow silk, slim of waist and daringly low in the bosom, so flashy it would be certain to draw every eye to its alluring folds. And certainly not that fashionable velvet riding habit, striking of line and utterly elegant—and exactly the color of the sky at noon.

At last, Ysabel settled on one, holding it up to the light as if to test her choice. In spite of herself, Morning Star felt her heart skip a beat as she studied it out of the corner of her eye, pretending she was not the least bit interested in the outcome. It seemed to her she had never seen anything quite so pretty in her life. The dress was surprisingly simple, but simplicity was its strength, emphasizing flaring lines and dramatic color. A wide scoop neck dipped low in front, and the sleeves looked as if they had been designed to cling to enticingly plump arms, then float away at the wrists. Velvet panels in the skirt echoed in deeper tones the gemlike clarity of a vermilion bodice.

"Yes, that should be perfect." Ysabel shifted her gaze to Morning Star, letting her lips turn up ever so slightly at the corners. "The color should be very interesting . . . with your hair."

Morning Star knitted her brow together, puzzled at the odd inflection in the other girl's voice, then dismissed it with a shrug. She had no way of knowing what was going on inside a head that was obviously as devious as it was pretty, nor did she truly care. Ysabel might have reasons of her own for giving her the dress, but it was still the loveliest dress she had ever seen, and for the first time she found herself actually looking forward to the final step in that transformation that had begun the night she was taken from the Indian camp.

The next hours were filled with activity. Soaking in a deep

metal tub, up to her chin in warm, sudsy water—what an odd experience, yet one that was not altogether unpleasant, and she found herself more than a little reluctant when the time came to climb out again and wrap herself in a soft, thick towel. The same water, subtly perfumed with the smell of soap, left a flowery scent in her hair, even after she had rinsed it several times and spread it out in the bright sunlight to dry.

How Little Bear would have loved it, she thought sadly, touched less by the memory of her young husband's closeness than the deeper sorrow she felt at feeling him drift away from her. He had begged her once to wash her hair just that way, and she, obstinate creature that she was, had refused. What capricious fate had brought her to this moment now, when he could not be there to share it with her?

Twilight had already begun to ease the world into a soft gray silence by the time, cleansed and gowned at last, her hair piled high on her head and fastened with a comb—*I like it that way*, Rafe had said—she was ready to sit down at the small vanity table and look into the mirror. Only then did Ysabel's words come back to her, complete with the veiled malice of their utterance.

An interesting color? The faintest hint of a smile caught at the corners of her lips. Yes, interesting indeed—though not, she suspected, the way Ysabel had intended.

The image in the mirror, faint and shimmering in dusky lamplight, smiled back at her. Ysabel's sullen features, trapped in the background, drifted in and out of the elusive reflection, but she was barely aware of them. Her eyes focused only on the girl in front of her, soft and somehow vulnerable, as if she sensed she was about to be judged. Lifting one hand, she ran her fingers along the cold glass, tracing the contours of a face that was all the more intriguing because it was so unfamiliar.

That is me, she thought wonderingly. That is really me!

Only this morning, it had felt strange to hear Rafe call her Kristyn Ashley and know that that person was her. Now it was even stranger to try and remember she had once been Morning Star. With a vague kind of sadness, more detached than penetrating, she realized that a part of her life was over, lost with her grease-stained braids and the shabby deerskin tunic Ysabel had taken out to burn in the yard.

The looking glass called her back to the present, catching old daydreams and turning them into new ones. Even with her ignorance of fashion, she knew that Ysabel had outwitted herself with her own cleverness, for the dress suited her superbly. Deep red-orange tones, vivid even in the lamplight, did not clash with auburn hair, but brought out echoes of flame in that fashionable coiffure. And skin that had seemed too dark only a moment before—how exotic it looked now, all bronzed and golden against the tantalizing glow of vermilion silk. She pursed her lips tentatively, shaping them into a kind of semipout that gave fascinating new dimensions to her face, then let them part of their own accord, as if to say, Come now, you knew all along, didn't you? You knew that this would be you.

Her gaze slipped downward, timidly, almost against her will, lured by the soft contours of a body that was already full and ripe. A slender waist, yes—as slender as Ysabel's, even without corsets to lace her in—but beneath that billowing skirt, her hips showed gently rounded curves, and firm young breasts strained the meager fabric of her bodice. Beauty and seductiveness were hers tonight, a smoldering sensuality ready to burst into flame like the fiery brilliance of her gown.

Was that the look she had seen in Ysabel's eyes? That sudden flash of fear at the top of the stairs? Yes, surely so, for even then the girl must have sensed what her mirror was telling her now. She *was* beautiful. Not just pretty, the way she had once hoped, but strikingly beautiful. Every bit as beautiful as Ysabel.

And as elegant.

Rising slowly, she turned to search out dark eyes in the half-light behind her.

"I think," she said softly, "I would like to go downstairs now." Without another word, she slipped out of the room and glided down the hallway.

She felt only a moment's doubt at the head of the staircase. Everything looked so different, now that night had fallen. Candles had been lighted in brackets on the wall, casting flickering shadows into the darkness, and an eerie luminescence seemed to drift up from somewhere far below.

Darkness behind her, and light ahead—the past and then

the future. She wondered if it was an omen. She had walked up those same steps only a few hours before, Morning Star, a young Indian girl, nervous and unsure of herself. The woman who walked down them now would be Kristyn Ashley.

Eleven

Kristyn fairly floated down the narrow staircase. For the first time in her life, she understood what it meant to be beautiful, and she was young enough—and inexperienced enough—to enjoy the sensation thoroughly. Yards of silk and velvet billowed around her, giving her the illusion that she was lighter than air, and her feet barely seemed to touch the ground.

She did not need a look of surprise or admiration in Rafe's eyes to tell her what kind of effect her dramatic entrance had created, but she received it anyway, and in spite of herself, she could not help warming to the flattering gaze. He had stepped forward quite nonchalantly, as if to greet her politely at the base of the stairs, then stopped, his lips parting slowly in an expression that had nothing to do with mere courtesy.

She paused a few steps from the bottom, allowing herself the faintest of smiles. Not too obvious, instinct warned her—it would never do to be obvious with a man like that. Just enough to give a hint of mockery to her features.

"So . . . do you still think I am an unwashed savage?"

The breathless confidence in her tone caught him off guard, in a way that frankly intrigued him. She had been so unexpectedly meek earlier that day when she followed Ysabel into the house, unassertive, almost timid in her mien. There was nothing timid about her now.

"Not unwashed at all. And not a savage either, though I'll wager you're dangerous enough for a whole passel of them."

And dammit, she *was* dangerous, too, the little *descarada*. What was there about a new hairdo and an elegant gown that had the power to change a woman so completely? Or was she just showing him the natural coquetry that existed in every female heart—and threatened to make a fool of any man who came too close? Once she had had occasion to remind him that he was there only at her father's bidding and not to make advances to the daughter of the man who had hired him. Now it was he who would have to remember that warning for himself.

Coolly, with an innate suavity he turned on and off at will, he offered her his arm.

Kristyn took it, still hiding a knowing smile as she let him lead her to the dining room at the rear of the house. What a fraud he was, this man who tried so hard to be gruff and crude, then lapsed into debonair good manners the minute he was confronted by a woman in a pretty dress. She could not help noticing that he, too, had changed for dinner, trading buckskin and blue denim for tight black pants and a flowing white shirt, the perfect foil for tanned skin and rugged male good looks.

What would he do if she dared to flirt with him, the way Ysabel had in the yard? Would he turn crude again, rebuffing her with that impossible rudeness of which he seemed so skilled a master? Or would he respond as he had with the Spanish girl, teasing one minute, scolding the next, but always interested, always captivated—always verging just on the edge of sensual assault with his eyes? It occurred to her it might be fun to find out.

And Carlos, too? Her eyes slipped toward the younger man, now standing at the edge of the hallway with a scowling Ysabel by his side. There was none of Rafe's surprise in the warm, appraising look he gave her, as if his opening words had not been mere gallantry after all. But Rafe's admiration *was* there—and a fascination all his own.

Yes, definitely with Carlos, too, she thought, laughing secretly to herself. She would flirt with both these men tonight, boldly and outrageously, enjoying a freedom she had never known before—and would never know again if her white parents turned out to be as strict and overbearing as she feared. She would tilt her head, just at that angle she had seen Ysabel do, and look up at them through lowered lashes—and make the sound of her laughter deep and sultry in her throat. And she did not care what they thought of her for doing it!

She was aware, as Ysabel passed her on her way into the dining room, of a low, seething hatred that seemed to hover in the air between them. Physically, it was subtle, no more than a sharp look, a quick intake of breath, but that was enough to warn her she had made an enemy that night. Not that she truly cared. Ysabel had been ready enough to be unkind to her when they first met, why should she feel guilty about turning the tables? Besides, she thought, throwing a last quick glance at her, the girl could hardly do anything to retaliate. Not when they would never see each other after tonight.

The dining room was as spare as the hallway she had first entered. The floor was the same wide, dark planking, the walls the same dusty tone of tan. A steaming iron stewpot on the massive, carved-wood sideboard spread an enticing aroma of meat and wild herbs through the room, and the rough trencher table in the middle had been set with earthenware plates and surprisingly delicate crystal glasses. The only illumination came from half a dozen candles in a crude wooden chandelier that dangled by a rope from the ceiling.

Rafe and Carlos sat at the ends of the table, leaving the two women to face each other with guarded hostility on either side. Ysabel seated herself first, flaring her skirt gracefully around her legs as she drew her chair forward. Kristyn watched closely, trying as best she could to imitate the studied elegance of that motion.

That she did not succeed was mirrored in the look of almost feline pleasure that crossed the other girl's pretty features. Ysabel had discovered her rival's weakness, and she was quick to exploit it!

Raising her fork, a sharp-pronged pewter utensil, she ran her fingertips lightly along the points.

"I don't suppose you have ever seen one of these," she said with exaggerated sweetness. "You'll learn how to use it, I imagine . . . in time. But don't worry if you can't manage it tonight—you can always eat with your hands, the way you're used to. I'm sure Rafe and Carlos will understand."

And wouldn't you love it if I did, Kristyn thought, meeting Ysabel's eyes with a veiled gaze of her own. Keeping the thought to herself, she made her voice as cool as the other girl's.

"I know perfectly well what a fork is. I lived with my white parents until I was six years old. I haven't forgotten everything they taught me."

"Oh?" One eyebrow went up slightly, just enough to create a faintly ironic effect. "Somehow . . . I thought you might have. It would be perfectly understandable of course, living with savages all this time."

Would it, indeed? Kristyn was tempted to raise an answering brow, but she held herself back. She wanted to beat Ysabel at her own game, but not with the same weapons. Let the other girl look catty and spiteful! She would show herself a perfect lady.

"We were not quite the savages you seem to think," she said demurely. "Indian manners may not be the same as yours, but that doesn't mean they are any less strict. We do not have forks, of course—we think them unnecessary—but we use sharp knives to cut our meat, and we have metal plates and cups from the trading post. If we are invited to a feast in someone else's lodge, we bring them with us, for Cheyennes do not expect their hosts to provide utensils for them. And we say grace, too, like the missionaries, only not with meaningless words, but by offering a bit of our meat to the fire or burying it in the ground."

"Do you hear that, Rafael?" Carlos turned with a laugh to his brother. "Even the Indians say grace." He had gone over to the sideboard with their plates; now he began to heap them with the stew he himself had prepared while the women were upstairs, bathing and dressing for the evening. "I am afraid you will find us somewhat more remiss, Señorita Ashley. If my grandfather were here, he would be furious, but away from that formidable influence, we tend to be scandalously lax."

He set hot plates in front of each of them, reminding Kristyn with the tempting odor of onions and wild thyme that she had not eaten since early morning. When he had finished, he placed a platter of biscuits in the center of the table and sat down to join them.

Kristyn glanced at him out of the corner of her eye. He was not as rugged as his older brother. His slender body did not show the same muscular power, and his features were more even, almost pretty in their classic regularity. Still, she sensed something of Rafe's confident masculinity in his bearing, and in the easy way he tended to dinner while two women simply sat there and watched him.

It was a strange world these white men had made for

themselves, she thought—but she did not find it was altogether unappealing.

"I am not used to sitting down with the men," she confessed. "Usually we wait for them to finish eating, then make do with the scraps that are left. And even between mealtimes, there are strict rules about where we may sit. The north side of the tepee is reserved for the men. Whenever a woman enters, she is expected to go to the left, keeping to her own place, always separate from the men."

"An interesting system," Rafe remarked dryly. "Most useful at times, I should think—but definitely not tonight."

He accented his words with a bold, vaguely teasing glance at the soft swell of her bosom, only half concealed in its filmy veil of fire-red silk. Kristyn tried to be angry with him—what an arrogant rogue he was, looking at a woman like that, without even trying to hide his thoughts!—but she could not quite manage the emotion. No Indian would dare do such a thing, but then, no Indian had ever made her feel like she felt now.

She picked up her fork, taking care to hold it the way Ysabel did, daintily between her fingers, and jabbed half-heartedly at one of the pieces of meat on her plate. Perhaps it was not going to be quite as easy as she thought, this business of flirting with a man like Rafe Valero. He seemed the sort who would want to play by his own rules.

"Why are we talking about me?" she asked, changing the subject. "The life I have led cannot be very interesting to you. Besides, your own experiences must be so much more fascinating. Do you know, in all the time we've been traveling together, you haven't told me anything about yourself. I don't even know where you're from."

Without waiting for an answer, she caught the meat on the tines of her fork and raised it to her mouth. Carlos had concocted a savory stew, simmering tough chunks of beef until they almost fell apart and adding various kinds of tinned vegetables. The meat proved easy to handle, much to Kristyn's relief, but peas and onions were balkier, sliding off the unfamiliar utensil, and she was forced to leave even tender morsels of carrot half submerged in the gravy on her plate.

Rafe obliged, turning the conversation comfortably around to himself.

"I come from a place you have never heard of, a small town far to the south called Santa Fe."

"Santa Fe?" He was right, she hadn't heard of it, but the name had a lilting sound as she rolled it out on her tongue.

"The words mean Holy Faith in our language—though God knows, there is little enough that is holy about the place. It can be a hell-hole at times, dry and dusty in the summer, and so hot sometimes you can barely move when the sun is out. There is a small settlement, a few *indios*, a few dirt-poor farmers, a few rich *hacendados*—nothing more. Just one town plaza with buildings the color of the earth and purple mountains off in the distance."

"Small, yes," Carlos agreed. "But we are a proud people. Don't let my brother's jesting fool you. We were under the Spanish flag for nearly two centuries before my *abuelo*, my grandfather and Rafael's, helped win it for the new republic of Mexico fifty years ago. We have only been a part of the United States half that long."

"And to hear Don Diego tell it," Rafe added, reaching for a biscuit in the center of the table, "he didn't *help* win the territory for Mexico, he did it single-handed. And lost it the same way!"

Kristyn cast an envious eye at the platter, still heaped high with mouth-watering biscuits, made in the white man's style, with plenty of baking powder to keep them light and fluffy. If Ysabel hadn't broken hers into little, ladylike pieces, dabbing each with a tiny pat of butter, she might have taken one herself and used it to sop up all the delicious gravy cooling on her plate.

"What is your grandfather like?" she asked, curious about an old man who had fought so hard for his country's freedom.

To her surprise, Rafe and Carlos both burst out laughing.

"Just like Rafael," Carlos said. "Proud, hot-tempered—and as stubborn as one of those purple mountains around the town."

Rafe did not deny it. "They call him El Valeroso, the courageous one, after the exploits of his youth. That is our family name now, and when I am home that is how I am called: Rafael Valeroso. Whatever Don Diego's real name was—and even I do not know it—he left it behind with the rest of his reputation on a dark stormy night when he fled his native Spain forever. But that is hardly unusual. The New

World is full of men who are running away from something in the Old.''

Kristyn narrowed her eyes, puzzled. There was affection in Rafe's voice when he talked of his grandfather, but there was something else, too. Brittle irony . . . almost mockery.

"And you think that was what your grandfather was doing? Running away? But from what?"

"The hangman, I daresay, or perhaps an irate husband. What do you think, Carlitos? Which was it?"

"Oh, an irate husband, no doubt. I fancy Don Diego was quite a firebrand in his day."

"Perhaps that is why he is so straitlaced now." Rafe turned to Kristyn with a sharp laugh. "You have never seen anyone as pious as El Valeroso. Or as unyielding."

"Rafael! What a thing to say!" Ysabel's lower lip jutted out in a sultry pout. "Your *abuelo* is the finest man who ever lived. He has always been very good to me, a poor little orphan girl."

And we have always been very close, her wheedling tone seemed to imply, so be careful how you treat me or I will make him very angry with you.

Rafe did not miss the insinuation in her tone, and it was clear he did not like it. Obviously, Kristyn thought, filing the information away—as if she would ever have any use for it!—here was a man who did not like being manipulated by women.

"Don Diego and I have never seen eye to eye," he said coldly. "You must have realized that, Ysabel, even as a child. I would have made my grandfather very unhappy if I had tried to stay in Santa Fe—and myself even more so. That is why I left. That . . . and other things."

"Other things?" In spite of herself, Kristyn was curious. This man frightened her sometimes, with his rough masculinity and all-consuming sense of self, but there were depths to him she longed to explore. How fascinating it would be to climb inside of him and see what really made him tick.

"My brother is very ambitious," Carlos explained. "He has grand dreams for himself."

"And why not? Don Diego carved an empire in New Mexico, and now he is one of the most powerful men in the territory. Why should I not do as much for myself somewhere else? My dreams—my visions—are no grander than his, and look how he succeeded!"

Passion turned his eyes to dark, blazing fire, and he raised his fork, waving it in the air to punctuate his words. The gesture did not look crude on him, but strong and forceful, as it would have on an Indian brave.

"I refuse to live in the past like El Valeroso. I live for the future, and I thrive on it! He believes in Mexico, he grieves for lost Mexican rule, but me . . . I believe in this brash new country that is swallowing up everything else with such voracious appetite. One day it will be the greatest country in the world, greater even than France or Spain, and I intend to be a part of it. Already I have begun. Let others waste their time searching for gold or raising cattle. I know where the real wealth lies: in the stores that supply the miners and the railroads that shuttle all that beef back and forth, and the land on which the towns will one day lie. A different kind of empire, perhaps, but one that will stretch from one end of Colorado to the other. And when it does, the name Valero will mean there what Valeroso does in Santa Fe."

Kristyn caught her breath at the sudden fervor in his tone. What kind of a man could throw himself into his dreams like that, to the exclusion of everything else?

"Then that is why you came to find me. Because you wanted my father's money to help with your plans."

He gave her a startled look, then began surprisingly to laugh.

"Good God, no! I play for higher stakes than that. Actually, I was bullied into it by a friend of your father's. A man who claimed I owed him a favor because he had helped me negotiate an important deal."

He leaned back in his chair, relaxing enough to raise a crystal wine glass to his lips.

"I didn't agree with him at the time—I told him it was a damn fool waste of money—but now . . ." He paused, staring moodily into the dark red wine. "Now I'm glad I gave in."

He raised his eyes, giving her the same look as before, bold, unashamedly insolent—only this time, his eyes were only half teasing. Yes, she thought with a shiver, she *had* been foolish to think she could flirt with a man like that. Playing with Rafe Valero would be like playing with fire.

It was almost a relief, a few minutes later, when Ysabel rose and, in a cloyingly sweet voice, announced that it was time for the ladies to retire to the other room.

Well, here is where the white world and the Indian one join company again, Kristyn thought, making a move to push back her chair. It is all right for the women to eat with the men, but after dinner they have to go back to their own place again, like Cheyenne women, all clustered together on the south side of the tepee.

But, surprisingly, Rafe did not seem to care.

"Stay if you like, Kristyn. This isn't a formal *banquete* in Santa Fe. There's no reason why a woman can't enjoy a cup of coffee with the men, or a glass of brandy for that matter."

What was he up to now? Kristyn wondered, studying his profile with a suspicious, sidelong glance. Was he trying to be kind, sparing her the hour or so that would surely have been an ordeal in Ysabel's catty presence? Or had he simply noticed how uncomfortable she was growing with him and thought it would be fun to toy with her for a while?

She would have refused had she not been so intensely aware of Ysabel hovering in the doorway behind her. Obviously, the girl wanted to get her away from the men— and that was reason enough to stay!

"I would like some coffee, thank you, but none of your brandy. I have already seen what the white man's liquor does to my people."

"And to a good number of mine," Rafe agreed complacently. "Whiskey is not a secret weapon we invented to use against our enemies, you know. White men are as susceptible to its temptations as Indians, and a damn sight too many have had their lives ruined by it. But there's a differenece between a man—or a woman—who gets falling-down drunk, and one who enjoys a taste of fine brandy after dinner."

A rustle of silk in the doorway reminded Kristyn that Ysabel had not yet left. She turned just in time to catch an unexpected look on the girl's face. Not angry at all, but peculiarly smug, almost elated, as if Kristyn had played right into her hands. As if she had only pretended all along to want her to leave, knowing that that would be like waving a red flag in front of an angry bull.

Why, she actually wants me to stay, Kristyn thought, confused. She deliberately tricked me into it. But why?

She did not have time to ponder the question for Rafe had already begun to pour the brandy out of a cut-glass decanter. Kristyn frowned slightly as she watched the amber liquid flowing into a squat, round glass, but she could not quite find the nerve to object. She had touched none of the wine at dinner, and no one had said anything, but this seemed different, more a ceremonial custom than a mere beverage. She waited until Rafe had pushed the glass across the table, then forced herself to pick it up and lift it to her lips. The strange, round shape seemed to hold in the aroma, sharp and startlingly pungent.

Holding her breath to keep the smell from assaulting her nostrils, she took a deep swallow.

"Pah!" Tears stung her eyes as she shoved the glass away. "That—that is the vilest thing I have ever tasted! No wonder the Indians call it *fire*-water!" Even now, the inside of her mouth was stinging, and she felt her stomach begin to burn with a slow, searing heat.

The men did not seem insulted, but laughed instead, as if they had expected exactly that reaction and did not mind at all. They chatted easily for a while, steering the conversation to innocuous subjects, like the weather in spring and conditions on the road ahead, then turned back to their own interests, lapsing into their native Spanish again.

Kristyn leaned back in her chair, feeling not at all neglected, but comfortably lazy, almost sleepy. She liked the sound of their language, softly mysterious, yet lilting, melodic, so different from the harsher sounds of English. The coffee was strong, the way she liked it, bitter in its sugary sweetness, and even the smell of brandy, now that it was no longer directly in her nostrils, had an almost tantalizing piquancy.

She took advantage of the respite to study their faces, so alike and yet so completely different. Carlos. Refined, almost delicate of feature, every inch the gentleman in looks and manner. But underneath it all, a kind of animal restlessness that showed in that sudden tilt of his head—and the way black eyes seemed to catch the candle flame and toss it back again.

And Rafe . . . yes, Rafe was the mirror image of this brother. Deeper voiced, rugged, almost unbearably crude when he chose, earthy in the way he looked at himself—and the way he regarded a woman. But sophisticated, too, subtly, as if he did not want it to show, and inherently elegant. A

man equally at home in a rough buckskin jacket and a flaw-
lessly tailored white silk shirt.

They had been deep in conversation for perhaps an hour
when Carlos turned toward her with an apologetic smile.

"*Perdone*, Señorita Ashley—a thousand pardons. I had
forgotten you do not speak our language. I was just telling
this scoundrel of a brother that I have ridden many hundreds
of miles to find him and bring him back with me."

Beneath the surface smoothness, Kristyn thought she caught
a note of strain in his voice, though she could not be sure.
Certainly, Rafe did not seem to take him seriously.

"Come, Carlos, you don't expect me to believe that, do
you? I think it was just an excuse to take a pretty girl for a
long ride . . . away from the strict supervision of Don Diego
and all the *dueñas* he must have hired to watch over her."

"Ah, Ysabelita!" Carlos raised his hands in protest, but
his eyes seemed to shine with laughter. "You think I brought
that little *descarada* with me? *Dios*, I would rather carry a
satchel full of live rattlesnakes! Ysabelita is a beauty—and I
admit I have tried to steal her from her chaperones many
times—but not on a trip like this. No, it is she who learned
where I was going and ran off after me. With a wagon and
eight trunks full of clothes!"

"And you could not send her back, of course."

"Not by herself. Don Diego would never forgive me. We
had heard rumors of hostile Indians in that area. And I did not
have time to go back with her. I had no choice but to bring
her along. I made her leave the wagon behind and most of the
trunks, but still I had to buy another horse to carry all her
finery!"

And you did not mind one bit, Kristyn thought, surprised
that the idea should annoy her so much. Even Rafe seemed
more charmed than irritated by the pretty *señorita*'s vagueries.

"You must have a fatal fascination for her, Carlitos."

"Either that," his brother agreed, laughing, "or she re-
members how handsome you looked when she was a little girl
and longed to see you again."

Rafe shrugged, dismissing Ysabel and her motives with a
casual abruptness that would have seemed surprising had not
the look on his face already changed from mild good humor
to dark, brooding concentration. Rising, he stepped over to
the window and stood looking out—at what? Something in

the moonlight outside, or only the brittle lines of his reflection on the glass?

"So, brother, you think you can persuade me to come back?"

Carlos drummed his fingers against the tabletop, then stopped, self-consciously.

"I think so, yes."

"Even when I told you the day I left that I would never come back? Not for anything in the world?"

"He needs you, Rafael." Carlos's voice was low and persuasive. "He is an old man, although he cannot bring himself to admit it. He can no longer defend himself against his enemies—and he cannot accept help from me. Never will he forget that I am the bastard offspring of his only son. Your own mother died in the convent where our father's indiscretions drove her—do you think Don Diego will ever forgive that? Or stop taking his anger out on me?"

Rafe laughed, a harsh, abrasive sound.

"No use, *hermanito*. I might weep for my grandfather's frailties, but not for the stubbornness that brings all these troubles down on his head. Besides, I relinquished my claims on Santa Fe and my inheritance long ago. What happens there is no concern of mine."

"There, perhaps—but what about Colorado?"

"Colorado?"

The word seemed to hang in the air. Carlos rose and stepped over to his brother, standing beside him at the window. Kristyn, watching from her place at the table, sensed that they had forgotten her, as completely as Ysabel had been forgotten a moment before.

"Admit it, Rafael. The holdings there are important to your plans. The mine, the land the railroad is to be built on—all that has been lost. Of course it would be dangerous to try to recover it. I have heard rumors that there are hired gunmen. . . ."

Carlos let his voice trail off, leaving an almost visible silence in its wake. Like a challenge, Kristyn thought—but a challenge to what?

Rafe turned slowly, warily, as if he understood what she had only sensed. There was something almost breathtakingly bold in that stunning male virility—no, not bold, but reckless, savagely, tamelessly reckless, like an animal scenting something on the night wind.

"Danger? You think I am afraid of danger?"

Like an animal, she thought again, half hypnotized by the look of him, the low intensity in his voice. Hungry, alert, but not afraid—no, never afraid, not a man like that.

Not afraid, but excited.

That was it, the savage thrill that made his body seem to vibrate with tension. *Danger.* The idea did not dismay him, as it might another man, it attracted him—and Carlos must have known it when he threw out that seemingly off-handed challenge. Nothing else could have persuaded him, not love, not loyalty for family, not even a feeling of responsibility. But danger, daring, the sense of pitting male strength against long odds and greater numbers—ah, yes, that would appeal to the Rafe Valeros of this world.

"I am sure you gentlemen must have many things to talk about," she said, rising. "If you will excuse me, I will go upstairs now."

Outside, in the hallway, she was surprised to find that she was shaking. What was there about this man that had the power to upset her so much? He meant nothing to her—he was only a stranger who had barged into her life and would leave again as abruptly as he had come—why, then, did she let him do this to her? Why, when she should have been revulsed by the violence she sensed in his nature, did she find herself fascinated instead?

She would have been even more upset had she realized how transparent she was. Rafe, watching her retreat, wrenched his lips into a half-ironic, half-irritated smile. A *descarada*, that's what he had called her, a brazen hussy—dammit, she was, too, but she was more, much more than that. He tried to concentrate on the coppery highlights in her hair, the soft female curves of a thoroughly ripe body, letting them call out to urges as uncomplicated as they were basic, but other sensations, other awarenesses, kept getting in the way. That stubborn pride of hers, carved out of fire and stone, just like his own . . . and the wildness in her heart, wonderfully savage, only half concealed beneath a fashionable gown and civilized, upswept coiffure. By God, the man that ripped that silk and velvet from her body and tore her hair out of its pins . . .

Angrily, he forced the thought out of his mind, turning back to the window and staring out at moonlit fields, half hidden in shadows in the distance. He had known many women in his life, beautiful, warm, uninhibited women— women who knew exactly what he was and asked nothing more of him than he was willing to give. Freedom and sensual pleasure, the two had always gone hand in hand for him, and they always would. He wanted no part of a woman who made more than temporary claims on his heart, no part of a woman who would ever try to touch his soul.

A woman like Kristyn Ashley?

Clenching his hand into a fist, he beat it against the sharp-edged windowsill to drive away the image of her. Blast it, he felt—violated! How could he let one woman, a woman he barely even knew, worm her way into his thoughts like this? There was something about her, some subtle, elusive quality— boldness coupled with vulnerability, perhaps, a challenge both to male recklessness and strong protective instincts—that made her almost fatally treacherous.

Damn, he would be glad when it was time to bring her home and get her out of his mind once and for all!

At the same moment, Kristyn, too, was trying to clear her mind of Rafe, and with little more success. She had been surprised, on entering the small bedroom she had expected to share with Ysabel, to find it empty, but her first feeling of puzzlement quickly gave way to relief. The last thing she needed right now was company, especially the company of someone like Ysabel, whose sharp, jealous eyes would be certain to detect more than she wanted to give away.

Eyeing the beds, she chose the one that seemed least cluttered. After clearing it of its burden of velvet, silk, and lace, she stripped to her chemise and prepared to climb into it. The mattress looked soft, unappealingly so after years of hard pallets on the ground, and she was tempted to pull off the quilts and make a more comfortable bed for herself on the floor. But the thought that Ysabel might return at any second held her back. She was not about to give someone like that an excuse to laugh at her!

The softness of the bed was not as distracting as she had expected, and she soon fell asleep, but it was a fitful, restless sleep, disturbed by dreams that constantly tugged at her consciousness, threatening to wake her. Pictures seemed to swirl around her in the darkness, faces that dared her to recognize them, then slipped away before she could make out their features. A woman—was that her mother? But the image was cool, like ice, and strangely aloof. And surely that man was not her father. No strength there. Laughter, yes, joviality perhaps—but no strength.

And feelings, too. Not just faces, but feelings. Coldness—oh, what coldness . . . and warmth! A slow, insidious warmth seemed to seep into her entire body, heating her blood, touching her in the strangest ways, making her tremble like— what? Like she had trembled on her wedding night?

Anxious now, frightened, trying to wake herself, but unable to, she scanned the feverish darkness, searching for the face of her young husband in that terrible, anonymous crowd, and knowing all the while he was not there. Dark eyes seemed to bore into her heart, but they were not *his* eyes. Not gentle at all. Laughing, mocking—daring! And, oh, those lips! She knew them well, too well for only a dream. Twisting scornfully, bestial in their cruelty, parting to suck her into the restless maelstrom of a kiss the likes of which she had never known.

Wrenching herself out of the dream, Kristyn sat up in bed, shivering painfully, cold in the sweat that rolled off her body. She was still alone, but the candle had half burned down, telling her it was late and a good part of the night had already passed. Jerking the covers off the too-soft mattress, she laid them out on the floor, the way she had longed to before, and slipped defiantly between them. She did not care who saw her now—or what they thought! She was not going to spend the night on that bed, swathed in softness like a white woman who had been pampered all her life.

And she was not going to dream of Rafe Valero again!

Twelve

Downstairs, in a small study off the main hallway, Ysabel sat huddled in the corner of a leather couch, listening to the lone *tick-tock, tick-tock, tick-tock* of the mantel clock. Two o'clock, two-fifteen almost, and still the men had not finished their brandy and made a move to retire.

Rising restlessly, catlike in her pent-up energy, she resisted the urge to pace back and forth, crossing instead to the desk and turning down the lamp that rested on its surface. The flame shrank into a thin band of gold, brilliant beneath the smoky glass shade, and brooding shadows seemed to steal around her, like secret conspirators in the darkness.

The room was masculine in look and smell, as if no woman ventured into it, even to sweep the wide-planked floor or brush away dust from the hundreds of volumes in book-shelves on the walls. The desk was dark and heavy, the couch and chairs no more than wide strips of cured brown hide stretched taut across sturdy wooden frames. The musty smell of drapes, too long closed, provided a subtle undertone for the predominant male odor of leather and tobacco.

She opened the door a crack, straining her ears in a vain attempt to pick up some kind of sound in the darkness outside. Soon, she knew, the men would scrape their chairs back from the table; soon their footsteps would echo in the hallway, telling her they were drawing near. And if she was right . . .

She shut the door noiselessly, leaning against it, suddenly conscious of a quickened pulse in her temples, a wild pounding of her heart against her chest. Ah, if she was right! It would be a gamble, of course, a bold, mad gamble, but *Santo Dios*! the very boldness of it was what made it so exhilarating.

The blood of the *conquistadors* flowed through her veins at that moment, hot Spanish blood, and she had the sudden insane feeling that even if things were different—even if it had all gone just as she planned—she would not change it now for all the world.

If she was right, if she had not miscalculated, those same footsteps she expected at any moment would separate somewhere in the hallway, and Carlos would go upstairs alone. Not for a man like Rafael those stifling rooms on the second floor, with beds too close together and frilly curtains at every window. No, a man like that would be drawn toward masculinity, toward the smell of tobacco and the feel of a narrow couch, hard beneath the hard strength of his body.

And when he was, he would find her waiting for him.

Rafael . . .

She sat down on the couch again, not in the corner, as she had before, but gingerly on the edge. Catching up a small throw pillow, she pressed it against her breast and hugged it unconsciously to her body. Rafael . . . She had been a child that day, eight years ago, when he left his grandfather's house for good, but she could still see every detail, remember every sensation, as if it had happened only yesterday. How handsome he had looked with the sun streaming down on him, a proud man, tall and straight-backed on his spirited black stallion. The very maleness of him had been a tangible physical force, too primitive for a nine-year-old to understand, but too potent for her to forget. He was wearing a wide-brimmed black hat, banded familiarly in silver, but he had pushed it back on his head, like a Texas cowboy, and the stark black of his shirt made him look mysterious and romantic to her eyes.

It was a picture of him she would always remember, firmly etched in her mind, yet changing subtly with her changing perception of herself and the new urges that had begun slowly to make themselves felt in her body. Black-clad, bold in the way he stood up to the fiery anger of El Valeroso, achingly graceful as he rode into a burst of sunlight and disappeared in the distance—what man could touch that memory in her heart?

And what man was meant to?

Irritably, she pulled the pillow away from her breast, dissatisfied with its softness, and sat upright again. Oh, she had dallied with a handsome young man here and there—why not? It was amusing to watch the way the blood rushed to their faces when she tilted her head, just so, and let long lashes flutter against pale cheeks. And, of course, if she was going to be completely honest about it, there *was* something definitely intriguing in the taste of a forbidden kiss, stolen right from under the watchful eyes of her *dueña*, or even the brush of a masculine hand, carelessly, as if by accident, against her arm. But always, with every one of them—every man and boy she had ever known—there was a sense of holding back, a feeling that all this was only a prelude, a rehearsal for the moment she would see Rafael again and all the dream-passion of those kisses would be real at last.

Yes, and that was exactly what would have happened, she thought bitterly, if it hadn't been for *her*!

Tossing the pillow across the room, she watched it bounce off the far wall and land with a soft thud on the floor. She had seen the way he looked at *her*, that *perversa*, all perfumed with the soap she had brought for herself and had to give away. *Por Dios*, what fools these men could be! Did he really think it meant anything, all that tangled red hair that kept defying its pins and flying around her face? Didn't he know that she—Ysabel—had more fire in her veins than a little slut like that would ever know? If only he had never seen her!

Well, there was no use crying about that, she reminded herself sharply. Leaning back, she let her head rest against the couch. He *had* seen her, and he had responded in the coarsest male way. How clever she had been, getting rid of that hussy after dinner; now she would have to see to the rest of it. If she let him go away with Kristyn—if she let him leave with no deep sense of herself, no commitment to her own tempestuous beauty—she was certain to lose him.

And if she lost him, she would forfeit all the dreams that had filled nearly half her life.

Letting her eyelids close, she focused on the elusive shadows she could feel but no longer see in the darkness around her. As if she were going to lose him! The thought was impossible—insane! After tonight, after she had teased his body with her passions, satiated his ego with the completeness of her surrender, how could he even look at another woman?

The night was seductive, lulling her from conscious thoughts into unconscious reveries. Slowly, her sense of the room around her began to ebb away, and she was aware only of the weight of her head, so heavy she could not hold it up any longer. Hard . . . the arm of the couch felt hard beneath her cheek, then not hard at all, but strangely numbing . . . and the blackness was complete.

She did not even know she had fallen asleep until a soft sound from somewhere nearby woke her with a start. Groggily, she looked up to see a muscular male form barely visible in the dim light of the doorway.

"Rafael?"

All the sleepiness was gone, abruptly, joltingly, but it was too late. Ysabel scrambled to her feet, running a fluttering hand over the wrinkles in her skirt, but her costume was hopelessly disheveled, and tousled curls kept tumbling onto her forehead. It did nothing for her shattered composure to realize that what had awakened her was the faintly mocking sound of his laughter.

"Why, Ysabelita, have you fallen asleep waiting for bedtime? Shall I pick you up in my arms and carry you upstairs, the way I did when you were a little girl?"

There it was again, that mockery! And in English, too! She hated it when he spoke English, as if he were denying his Spanish heritage, and with it, everything he had shared with her.

"I am not a little girl anymore, in case you hadn't noticed! You would not dare pick me up now. I am much too heavy for you."

Not a little girl? Rafe leaned casually against the doorframe assessing her with the sure instincts of a man who was accustomed to getting what he wanted. She looked, if only she knew it, exactly like a child at that moment. No, not quite a child—a child-woman. Still girlish enough to have the lure of forbidden fruit, but womanly enough to salve the conscience of the man who plucked it. Her breasts were small and youthfully high, her hips as slim as a boy's, but there was something about the way her hair half tumbled to her shoulders. Bedroom hair, that's what he called it, and bedroom eyes, not quite clear, yet saucy still, smoldering from somewhere deep within. And a bedroom mouth, full-lipped, pouty, begging to be kissed.

Dammit, what was he thinking of? he cursed himself irritably. He had been too conscious of another, riper beauty that evening, of full, womanly breasts, sun-darkened, yet tantalizingly white just at the edge of a daring décolletage, of touches of flame in shimmering auburn tresses and the promise of an even more brilliant fire in eyes that were bluer than he had ever seen. Now he was transferring those same feelings, those same urgent man-hungers to this girl in front of him, and he knew only too well where that would lead.

"You are more a child than you think if you believe it is possible to come into a man's room looking like that—and still go out again. I'll make you a bargain, *niña*, though God knows, you don't deserve it. I will try and remember what a child you are if you remember that I am a man."

His voice was low, but not gruff, as he had intended, raspy rather than rude. The barely veiled passion she sensed in those earthy tones was more for another woman than her own sulky earthiness, but Ysabel, misreading it, felt her confidence return. Boldly, she let her eyes run up and down his body, as he had done a moment before with her. She liked the way he wore his clothes, a clinging silk shirt, leaving not a muscle to the imagination, and pants so tight she knew instantly he was not totally oblivious to her charms.

"But I am *not* a child, Rafael. I know exactly what I am doing. And I have never for an instant forgotten that you are a man."

He followed her gaze. His laughter was crude and to the point.

"That, my dear, is a basic animal reaction. A mere conditioned reflex, having to do with the proximity of a woman. *Any* woman. Don't flatter yourself that it means anything."

"Oh, but I do, Rafael . . . or rather, you do the flattering for me. You are a very virile man, but even virility has its limitations. I cannot believe you would look at me quite like that if I were not at least a little pleasing to your eyes."

"Oh, I acknowledge that. You *are* pleasing to look at. A man would be a fool or a liar, or both, if he denied it. You're a damnably beautiful temptress. But unfortunately for me, you're also my grandfather's ward, a child who has been entrusted into our family's keeping. I haven't exactly been a saint in my dealings with women—and I hope to God I never will be!—but that is too much even for my free wheeling code of honor.

"A child again!" Her lower lip jutted out, full and sensual.

Damn her, she was pouting like that on purpose! She knew exactly what effect it had on him.

"Why do you keep on saying that? I have told you before—I am not a child!"

The nearness of her was a sore temptation. The soft texture of her hair, so close a single stride would be enough to bury his head in it. The smell of her perfume, heavy and exotic. It had been a long time since he had had a woman, too long. And all those days on the road with Kristyn . . .

"If you had any sense in that devious little head of yours, you'd clear out of here right now. If you don't . . ."

He left the words dangling, unspoken, but Ysabel saw only too well where they were leading. If you don't go, he was warning her, I will throw you on that couch and do to you the things a man does to a woman, and I won't give a damn how much I hurt you!

She was surprised to feel that she was trembling as she took a half step toward him.

"You think I am afraid—of you?"

"I think you're a fool if you're not."

And God help him, so was he! But things had gone too far now; he could no more pull back than she could let him go—and why should he try? It was not her he wanted. He wanted that soft, maddening, feminine, fiery creature lying alone in her bed upstairs with not a thought for him, wanted her suddenly, unreasonably, with every fiber of his being. But, hell, Kristyn was not available—and Ysabel was! She was his kind of woman, uncomplicated, uninhibited, sure of what she wanted and not afraid to take it. He would forget himself in her.

"Come here," he said gruffly.

Still trembling, she went to him, half timid now that the moment was actually here, half exhilarated to think she had won him. Impatient with her slowness, he pulled her roughly toward him.

There was a sudden urgency in his lips on hers, hard, demanding—a sudden, unexpected brutality in the arms that pinned her against his body with unyielding force. Tenderly, *tenderly*, she longed to beg, but there was no tenderness in the mouth that stopped her cries, no gentleness in the tongue that assaulted her clenched lips, forcing them apart, thoroughly, savagely scourging her mouth. Sickened, she wedged her hands against his chest, trying to push him back, beating at him with clenched fists when she failed. Then somehow—how had it happened? she wondered helplessly—she found her arms around his neck, and she was clinging desperately, passionately to the same male strength that had frightened her only a second before.

"Oh, Rafael . . . Rafael," she murmured hoarsely. *"Te adoro, mi vida."*

She felt his body stiffen, subtly, almost imperceptibly, and suddenly his hands were on her arms, pulling them down, forcing her away from him. She looked up to see dark eyes boring into her face, hard and strangely questioning. Oh, *Dios*, what had she done—what could she possibly have done? . . . And then she realized.

"You think I am like—them."

Like all the women who had flitted in and out of his life. Cheap and vulgar, content to toy with one man after another, collecting hearts like perfectly matched pearls to string up on display. Just like that slut upstairs, no doubt—like every other slut he had known!

"Oh, no, Rafael. There has been no one, *no one*, but you, I swear it. I have loved you as long as I can remember . . . and I have waited only for you."

She swayed against him, weakly, half swooning, waiting for him to catch her up in strong arms again. But still he held himself back—still he did not draw her into that savage embrace that left her all weak and shivery inside.

"So-o-o . . ." The sound was a low hiss between clenched teeth. "You have come to offer me your virgin purity. The sweetest gift a woman can make a man."

"Well, yes . . ." Why did it sound so—cynical when he said it? "You didn't think that—that I would do this with *anyone*?"

He laughed harshly. "Forgive me, my dear, if I thought just that. It was you who made the advances, remember? In my experience, that usually indicates a certain degree of practice."

"Oh-h-h, you—you . . ."

She broke off, driven to incoherence by his brittle sarcasm.

Indignation flashed out at him from dark eyes—and fairly so, he had to concede, squirming inwardly. What the devil had he been doing, concentrating only on his own needs, not even bothering to take a good look at her? He had had more than enough dealings with virgins in the past, sweet little innocents who thought all they had to do was lure a man into their bed and he would follow docilely to the altar, and he had never come close to falling in that trap before. What was there about tonight—the smell of spring in the air? the sense of Kristyn so close in her bed?—that had made him so blasted careless?

Well, the kindest thing he could do now was nip this affair right in the bud!

"See me again when you've had a little more experience, sweetheart. I don't have time to teach the facts of life to young virgins. And I sure as hell don't have the patience to play around with a little girl whose head is full of silly daydreams. Now if you were a real woman—but that's another story."

Shame rushed into Ysabel's cheeks, flaming them a vivid crimson, and her whole body felt hot with anger and self-disgust. How could she have thrown herself at a—a *beast* like that? A man with no scruples or conscience! Somehow, she did not know how, she managed to make it to the door and, flinging it open, staggered out into the cooler air of the hallway. The room behind her was silent; she could hear no sound as she leaned briefly against the wall, trying desperately to still the quickened beating of her heart, but she imagined she could hear him anyway, laughing softly in the shadows.

If you were a real woman . . . Oh, the man was a savage! An animal! No, worse than an animal. He *used* women, he took them and used them for his own ends, and if any little "inconvenience" came into the picture, anything like innocence, or God forbid! love, he couldn't be bothered. *If you were a real woman* . . . As if all it took to be a woman was sleeping with a man!

Anger took hold of her, a deep, unreasoning anger, all the more devastating because it was born of frustration and humiliation. So he wanted experience, did he, the bastard! Well, that was just what she was going to get—and with the one man who might be able to make him jealous!

She started up the stairway, taking no pains to conceal the sound of her footsteps. Carlos had always looked at her with ill-concealed longing in his eyes, a little like Rafael had looked for a moment tonight, only not so crudely of course. And Carlos would never be ungentlemanly enough to pack her off like that!

She paused only briefly outside the closed doorway to his room. The morality of what she was doing did not concern her overmuch. She might be using Carlos, the way his brother used women, but after all, Carlos was going to get something in return—something he wanted desperately. As for not loving him . . . well, love was a commodity that seemed in short demand these days.

Turning the knob, she pushed the door slowly inward.

Carlos was sitting up in bed, his back propped against a pile of white pillows. He wore no nightshirt, not even a thin *camisa*, and in spite of herself, Ysabel's eyes drifted toward his bare chest, lean and masculine under a tangled mat of dark hair. A single candle flickered on the bedside table, as if he had stayed up to read, but there was no sign of a book, and his eyes looked as if they had been fastened on the door even before she shoved it open.

Almost as if, she thought, shivering, he had known she was going to come. Almost as if he were waiting for her!

What was she doing here? she asked herself suddenly—and why, *why*, was he looking at her like that? Naked to the waist, and underneath—*por Dios*! she turned crimson to think of it—was he naked all the way down to his toes? Jumbled thoughts, confused and troubling, spilled over in her brain. For a moment, she was tempted to turn and run away, but she knew Carlos would see what she was doing and laugh at her. The sound of other laughter still echoed in her ears, *his* laughter, Rafael's, taunting, cruel. She could not bear it if another man laughed at her tonight.

Carlos saw the conflicting emotions she tried to hide, and while he smiled inside, he was careful not to let his amusement show. What a beguiling bundle of contradiction she was! Physically passionate, though she did not know it yet, brazen one minute, timid the next, utterly calculating and utterly vulnerable—and all wrapped up in as pretty a package as a man could ever want. So Rafael had rejected her, had he? Carlos had not missed the sound of voices in the small study downstairs, and he had known exactly what was going on. How long had she stayed with him?—five minutes? ten? —and then he had thrown her out, so humiliated she would do anything to erase the memory.

Well, that was all right for Rafael. Rafael wanted no softness in his life, no feminine entanglements to hold him back. But such ways were not for Carlos, they never had been. As long as he could remember, he had dreamed of only one kind of woman, a woman who would belong only to him, a wife who would lie beside him all night long, showering him with honeyed kisses when he woke her in the early half-lit hours of dawn.

And ever since he had noticed that Ysabel was beginning to grow up, those dreams had centered more and more around her.

He held out a gently tempting hand.

"Come, sit beside me, Ysabelita. Let me tell you how beautiful you are . . . and how much I have always wanted you."

Her head was still full of Rafael; he could see that, yet strangely, it did not disturb him. Perhaps because Rafael was a part of childish daydreams, and childhood was a world she was about to leave behind forever. After all, he reminded himself, what did a real flesh-and-blood man have to fear from the phantoms in a pretty girl's head. Once he had tapped that deep vein of passion, once he had taught her what a woman was meant to feel, surely she would have no need of fantasies.

The unexpected tenderness in his manner, a sharp contrast to the harsh brutality of Rafael's lust, caught Ysabel off guard, but far from reassuring her, it only added to her confusion, making her warier than before. More than ever, she longed to run away from him, but cowardice was a luxury she could not afford. Rafael must surely have heard her footsteps stopping at Carlos's door. Even now he would know what she was doing, and crude and male as he was, it would torment his body to think of the ecstacies he had given up. Yes, and his ego, too, when he realized how easily she had replaced him!

She felt dreamlike, unreal, as she forced herself to sit down on the edge of the bed, forced herself to ignore the feel of his hands undressing her, slowly, gently, as if somehow it made a difference whether he tore the pretty lace on her gown. There was something about his fingers—so soft where they touched her, yet hard-looking, masculine when they pulled away her dress and slipped the sheer chemise from her shoulders—something that frightened her, calling out to primitive instincts buried deep within her. Horrified, she realized his hand was on her breast, toying with her, caressing her, and her nipple was rising, hard and erect, beneath his touch.

No! She could not let this happen. Sick with anguish, Ysabel gathered all her strength to pull away from him. She had been prepared for the humiliating way he was going to use her—she would endure that gladly if it helped her win the man she loved!—but the shame, the utter degradation, of feeling her body respond was too much for her. No matter what it cost, she had to get away.

But he would not let her go. Trembling with shame and terror, she felt him tighten his hold, clutching her roughly, savagely, the way Rafael had before. Suddenly his mouth was on hers, stifling the protests she was too weak to make, daring her to fight her way free if she could! One minute she was struggling, terrified and desperate—the next she seemed to be melting into him, her body no longer resisting, but moving with the rhythm of his strong torso and long, lean limbs.

Feverishly, they sank into the softness of the mattress, she too caught up in compelling new sensations to realize what she was doing, he so wracked with his need for her he forgot even to be gentle. Their lovemaking was brutal, elemental, but it was exciting, too, even in its violence, and after that first stunning thrust of pain, more rapturous than anything she had ever dreamed.

Only afterward, lying in his arms, the lingering warmth of his body next to hers, did violence suddenly seem violation and rapture turn to remorse. Bitterly aware of what she had done, she turned her head away, weeping silently into her pillow.

Tender hands drew her back, tender lips—so soft now, so different—showered her brow and cheeks with kisses, but all the tenderness in the world could not make up for that terrible sick shame inside of her. She was as cheap as the cheapest whore on the streets—no, cheaper, for those women sold themselves only for money. She had actually *wanted* the things he did to her body.

"Oh, what would people think . . . if they knew?"

What would *Rafael* think?—that was what she was really saying, and Carlos knew it. He stiffened slightly as he looked down at her, and the thought crossed his mind that perhaps he ought to speak of it. But to talk about forbidden things, to bring them out in the open, would that not spoil what was between them now?

"Let them think what they will. Does it matter?"

"And you?" Troubled eyes searched his face through tear-moistened lashes. "What must *you* think of me?"

He kissed her again, lightly on the eyelids, tasting the salt of her tears on his mouth. She was in such pain, his poor sweet *niña*, and pain was the last thing he wanted for her now.

"I think you are very beautiful, *querida*—and very passionate. And I think I am beginning to want you again."

His hands played with her body, touching her intimately, caressing her in ways that warned her he was not teasing. Could it be happening again? she thought, miserably, desperately. She could not bear it if it was, and yet . . .

"But can you?" she murmured awkwardly. "Should you . . . ?"

Oh, why was she so ignorant of the ways of men? She didn't even know if it was possible, this thing he threatened her with.

"I can," he said, laughing as he drew her closer. "And I should, and I will."

She did not try to protest again, either to him or to herself, knowing, as he had known before, that she belonged to him, at least for the length of time his hands were on her body. He did not try to hurry her, but drew her slowly, tantalizingly along with him, teaching her with sensitive fingers and oh so loving lips how to respond to the wondrous new emotions in her breast. This time she was his partner, his co-conspirator, eager to help him lift her to the peaks of ecstasy, hungry to share her passions with him—rejoicing in that moment when sweet forgetfulness came at last, carrying them both away in a wild, tempestuous flood.

Is this what it is to be a woman? she wondered later, listening to the quiet night sounds in the darkness around her.

This wonderful, terrifying sense of being drawn outside herself until she could no longer even control her own body? How still the night sounded, still, yet remarkably full: the low wailing of the wind shaking the shutters, crickets somewhere in the fields, the quiet, even breathing of a man beside her in the bed.

How could this have happened to her? It seemed so plausible, so real, and yet so utterly impossible! She did not love this man—she was not even tempted to pretend she did. She loved Rafael, loved him to distraction, loved him so much sometimes it almost seemed like madness. How, then, could she find such sweetness in his brother's arms?

Thirteen

Confusion turned to bitterness the next morning as Ysabel stood in the yard and watched Rafe make the final arrangements with his brother before riding off with Kristyn.

"We'll meet in Dodge City then in a week and a half," he said brusquely. "Two at the most. But I warn you, *hermanito*, do not expect too much of me. I will go with you to Santa Fe, but I will stay only long enough to make that stubborn *viejo* listen to reason."

"As stubborn as his grandson, eh?" Carlos retorted, then added with a laugh: "A short time is all I ask. You need give no more."

"Well, Dodge City then."

Rafe swung into the saddle and touched his hand to the wide brim of his hat in a farewell salute.

And that was it! Ysabel thought, seething with anger and misery as she stood and watched them. Not one word for her, not one gesture, not even a casual glance in her direction! She might as well not have been alive for all he cared. What did it matter to her, this meeting in Dodge City in a week's time or two? She did not even know where Dodge City was—somewhere in Kansas, or was it Missouri?—and a week or two seemed eons away!

It was not as if he were angry with her. Quite the contrary, he had greeted the two of them that morning with a look so deliberately knowing it was downright insulting—and a bawdy wink at Carlos when he thought she wasn't looking.

Or had he known all along that she was? she asked herself irritably. She would not put it beyond him, humiliating her like that! Not for him the barbs of remorse, or even resentfulness—and what a *boba* she had been to expect

176

them! That colossal ego of his, that stubborn male pride, would never let him show jealousy for a woman who had walked away from him. As long as she lived, Ysabel was sure she would never forget that terrible expression on his face, so careless and cool, so ironically amused. Even now, the thought of it made her feel faint with shame.

And there *she* sat. The red-haired cat who had started it all! Calmly mounted by the gate on a strong chestnut gelding that was much too good for her. She had changed into more appropriate garb for riding astride, borrowing a pair of tight denim pants from Carlos, and a silk *camisa* with long, full sleeves and an annoying habit of clinging where it should have concealed. And any minute now, Rafe was going to ride off with her!

Damn her, Ysabel thought with a burst of hot, irrational hatred, this was all her fault! If it hadn't been for that bitch, she would have had time to develop her relationship with Rafael instead of bolting into it like a willful child. She would have been able to smile at him, tease him, flirt with him, all in that bold-shy way women were supposed to have with men. Then it would have been he who sought her out, he who pleaded not just for the favors of her body but the honor of her hand in marriage!

The force of her hatred, intense though it was, was completely lost on Kristyn, absorbed in her own thoughts across the yard. Even when the Spanish temptress flounced furiously into the house, slapping her feet loudly against the earthen path all the way, Kristyn barely even noticed she was there. More immediate problems had already begun to fill her mind, stirring her with a vague, unexpected uneasiness, and she realized, surprisingly, that she had given almost no thought to what would be waiting for her at the end of the long journey she had begun two weeks ago. Always before, that moment had seemed nebulous and distant, something that belonged far in the future. Now suddenly it occurred to her that she was no more than a day or two's ride from the place she was expected to call home.

A cold, unpleasant sweat made the reins slippery in her hands, and annoyed, she flicked them against the gelding's neck, following Rafe through the gate and out onto the road that had brought them here. She hated herself for being afraid, but no matter how she fought it, the emotion would not go away. As hard as she tried, she could not get them out of her mind, this elderly couple who had changed her life so drastically, yet she could not visualize them either, could not dredge up so much as a single feature or feeling to flesh them out in her memory. Would she even recognize them when she saw them, would she be able to accept them? Or more to the point, perhaps, would they accept her?

Kristyn had no illusions about the way she would appear to her parents, even in the prettiest of the dresses Rafe had forced Ysabel to give her. Her sun-bronzed skin would be too dark for them, her manners too crude by their standards, her eyes filled with a fire and independence that made a mockery of feminine propriety. Would they be able to forgive her for that, overlook it, love her in spite of it? Or would they only grieve all the more for the child they had lost long ago?

Her uneasiness stayed with her throughout the day. The countryside was flat and pretty, with a smell of water and spring wildflowers in the air, but for once she took no comfort in the beauties of nature. Nor did Rafe's presence offer any distractions. She cast an occasional glance at him, riding silently by her side, but the hard, withdrawn look on his face warned her he was in no mood for conversation, and she kept her thoughts to herself.

What is it like? she longed to ask him, this place you are taking me? He had told her a little about it, but that was in the early days of their journey, and she had been too angry to listen. Now she could only remember that he had said the town was called St. Anthony, at least it had been when she lived there, although it was later rechristened Minnearamis or Minneapolis, something like that, some funny name she would never get right! How ironic that both the town and she had been born with one name and then changed to another—only unlike her, the town was not going to be forced to switch back!

She could not resist another cautious, sidelong look at Rafe's stony profile. What a puzzling, infuriating man he could be! Last night she had seen an almost magnetic reckless-ness in his eyes, a sense of danger and daring that had fascinated her in spite of herself. But today those same eyes were so hard and emotionless, they might have been carved out of cold marble! Which was the real Rafe Valero, the man of passion or the man of ice? And why on earth should it matter to her?

They did not stop for the night at an open camp, as they had before, but hitched their horses to a rail in front of an inn just off the main road. At least there was something to be said for "civilized" attire, Kristyn thought with a wry smile. When she had dressed like a savage—and acted like one, no doubt, as far as he was concerned!—a campfire and a bedroll on the ground had been good enough for her. Now, even in denim pants and a mannish shirt, he felt obligated to treat her like a lady.

The exterior of the inn had a dubious look about it, as if it had seen better days, but inside it was cozy and not at all uninviting. A smallish room just off the entry hall served for both reception and dining, and it was there that Kristyn waited while Rafe saw to their rooms and stowed away their belongings. The rough wooden flooring was dark and unpolished, but fur rugs had been scattered across it, providing a touch of softness, and golden afternoon sunlight filtered through smoke-stained windows high in the walls. A fire was already blazing in the rugged stone fireplace that took up one entire end of the room.

Rafe returned after a few minutes and, seating himself on the hearth, he called out to the landlord for a whiskey and "a bottle of wine for the lady." Kristyn sat beside him and tucked her long legs under her, grateful for the unaccustomed freedom of her boyish garb. As if to make up for his earlier coldness, Rafe reverted to the charm he had shown the night before, treating her with an unusual, if slightly impersonal attentiveness and regaling her with stories of his travels, which turned out to be much more extensive than she had imagined. By the time dinner finally arrived, she was surprised to find she had managed to work up an appetite. No longer self-conscious, she plunged into a bowl of stewed chicken still clinging to the bone, finger food, and ate her biscuits the way Rafe did, dipping them into the rich, savory gravy or smearing them with fat dabs of homemade gooseberry jam.

The fire was warm on her back, and the ruby-red wine sweet and surprisingly warming in her stomach, and Kristyn felt a mellow glow begin to seep slowly into her veins, easing away the tensions of the day. Night seemed to creep up on her, catching her unawares, and she was already more than half asleep when she followed the landlady up the staircase that led to her room. The bed was narrow, the mattress lumpy and almost as soft as the one she had slept on the night before, but she barely noticed as she sank into it and closed her eyes.

The sun was already streaming into the room by the time she opened them again the next morning. She woke up abruptly, startled to find she had slept so late, and hurried over to the window, leaning out to get a breath of air. A narrow side street, muddy with spring rains and badly rutted, led from the inn to the main road, perhaps a quarter of a mile distant. It was a lazy morning, dusty and unseasonably warm, and she was about to pull her head back inside when she caught sight of Rafe just beneath the window, loading his belongings into a clumsy wooden farm wagon. Her chestnut gelding had been hitched to the front, together with a smaller, rather nondescript-looking gray. Rafe's saddle had been tossed in the back, and his own horse was tied on behind.

Even groggy with sleep, Kristyn realized instantly what was going on. No more comfortable pants for her, she thought, turning back toward the chair where she had flung her garments the night before. Obviously, Rafe expected to reach her parents' home sometime that day, and he wasn't going to bring her back looking like a boy!

A knock came at the door, followed almost immediately by a woman's voice. Kristyn threw a light quilt over her thin chemise before responding, even though she knew it could only be the landlady.

"Well, bless you, dearie," the woman twittered, chuckling as she entered the room. "The gentleman's jist sent me t' help ya dress. A sweet little gray gown, he tol' me, right there in yer bag. Nice an' modest."

Without waiting for a word of assent, she began to rummage through the saddlebag Rafe had left in Kristyn's room, pouncing on a bit of polished gray cotton and pulling it out with a triumphant "Aha!"

"Needs a bit o' pressin', but I reckon it'll do. I'll pile yer hair on top o' yer head, too, all purty an' fetchin'. My, won't ya look a pi'ture when ya see yer Ma and Pa agin."

Obviously, Kristyn thought, suppressing a twinge of anger, the woman had heard her story and found it irresistibly romantic. Still, in all fairness, she could hardly blame her. A child stolen by Indians and reunited with her parents—what could be more appealing to someone who did not have to live through it?

The woman proved a more willing dresser than Ysabel had been, but her hands were nowhere near as deft, and it was well over an hour before Kristyn was finally ready. Her mirror told her she did indeed "look a pi'ture," as the woman had promised, but it was a slightly jarring one. Dove gray became her, and white lace was chaste at her throat and wrists, but there was no disguising darkly exotic coloring and a wild, trapped look in sky-blue eyes.

Rafe greeted her matter-of-factly when she joined him outside a short time later, showing neither the scorn she had half expected nor the raw male approval he had offered the night before. Instead, he gave her a quick, appraising look, then touched his fingers to his hat as if to say, Yes, that will do, and helped her up onto the high seat of the wagon.

"It's not the most fashionable carriage in the world," he grinned. "But don't let these rough looks deceive you. It may not be elegant, but it's sturdy and strong. Besides, it's all they had at the livery stable!"

He was trying to make her laugh, Kristyn knew, but somehow his low-key attempt at pleasantry only added to the confusion she already felt. As always, this man seemed to have a knack for throwing her off balance, almost as if he was doing it on purpose. She had seen him in so many guises by this time—crude, sensual, mocking, teasing, sometimes even pitying—and still she did not know what to expect.

"I—I don't want to go back," she blurted out suddenly, hating herself for letting him see her weakness, but not able to keep the words from spilling out of her mouth. "Please, *please*, don't force me. You could let me out right here, just send me on my way. I promise I won't ask anything of you . . . only don't make me go back!"

She thought for sure he would laugh at her, but instead, he laid down the reins and turned toward her, taking hold of her hands in the most unexpectedly tender manner. If she had not known better, she thought guardedly, she would almost have believed the compassion in his eyes was real.

"Are you afraid, pretty Cristina? You don't need to be,

you know. Your parents are good people. They love you very much. I would never bring you back if that were not so.''

The gentle concern in his voice made her even more uneasy. Didn't he know how hard it was, trying to adjust to this new life? How could she come to terms with her feelings about him as well?

"Why do you call me Cristina, like—like . . .'' Like what? she wondered. Like some pet endearment he had made up just for her? ''. . . like you thought it was my name?''

Why indeed? Rafe asked himself wryly, careful not to voice the thought aloud. Because he was in some contrary way homesick for the natural lilt of a language he had left behind? Or because she had touched within him some unacknowledged hunger, as deep and elusive as the memories of his boyhood or the love he bore for the land of his birth?

"It *is* your name—in Spanish. Why? Don't you like it?''

"I do like it, very much—at least I like the way it sounds when you say it. Only you see . . . it isn't me! I am not Cristina, any more than I am really Kristyn, no matter how hard I pretend when I look at myself in a pretty dress in the mirror. But I am not Morning Star either. Not now. I am no one—no one at all!''

The quiet despair in her voice gave him a sudden, unaccustomed stab of conscience. He had been ready enough to drag her out of that filthy Cheyenne camp, why hadn't he taken a minute to wonder what she was going to feel like when he finally got her away? What her life would look like then from her own perspective?

Impulsively, he raised her hands, startling himself as much as her by the touch of his lips against her half-opened palms.

"Cristina *lucero del alba*,'' he said, trying to keep his voice light. "Beautiful Cristina with the morning starlight in your eyes. Haven't you learned yet that it doesn't matter what men call you? That has nothing to do with what you are inside. They can name you Kristyn or Fifi or Esmerelda, or even Jebediah for that matter, and it doesn't make one whit of difference! You are still you—that special, secret you inside your heart—and nothing will ever change that.''

The gesture was so unexpected Kristyn could still feel his mouth against her hands, even after he had released her and taken up the reins again, prodding the horses forward. The wagon wheels groaned their creaky protest, drowning out the morning sounds, and the plodding *clop-clop, clop-clop* of horses' hooves seemed to beat out a slow counter rhythm to the quickened racing of her heart. Folding her hands in her lap, she tried as best she could to look settled and demure, but she could not erase the warmth of his touch, could not keep her thumb from running back and forth over the spot where he had branded her with his kiss.

It was indeed a strange world she was entering, she thought, as she had so often since she began that fateful journey. A world where men and women could see each other without chaperones, and talk together without their elders listening in—and touch each other in ways that looked casual to the watching eyes, but in reality burned with unseen intimacy.

Yes, strange and confusing . . . yet not altogether unappealing.

She stole a glance at Rafe, quiet again, as he had been yesterday, every bit as unreadable, and for the first time she wondered what it would be like when he had taken her home and gone away and left her alone.

It was nearly dusk when they finally pulled up in front of a red brick house on one of the wide sweeping avenues that crisscrossed the twilight-hushed city. The building was substantial, solid, but almost stodgy in its unrelenting squareness. The bricks were still shiny, not yet mellowed by time and the elements, and the crisply white trim looked as if it had been pasted on at the last minute. Yellow flames leaped out of gas jets on either side of the bulky wooden doorway, casting an eerie glow in the hazy gray light.

The door opened even before the wagon could draw to a stop, as if the occupants inside had been peering through cracks in the thick draperies. A middle-aged woman stepped out onto the front stoop, followed seconds later by a man.

Her parents? Kristyn squinted into the shadowy light, searching for something familiar in either of those guarded faces, but try as she would, she could detect nothing. The man, who could have been anywhere from sixty to eighty, was somewhat shorter than average height and solidly built, like his house. Fawn-colored trousers and a well-cut brown waistcoat looked incongruously dapper on his rotund frame, and his ruddy cheeks were deeply creased, giving him a benign, almost jovial air. The woman, by contrast, was an inch or two taller, but thin to the point of emaciation and almost alarmingly brittle in appearance. Her features were unlined, but pale and ashen, and only the vaguest echoes of gold still showed in her thinning white hair. A fashionable satin gown, silvery blue in color and trimmed with girlish ruffles, only emphasized her age.

They did not try to come down the steps, but stayed where they were, staring at her almost as solemnly as she was staring at them. Kristyn shrank back in the wagon seat, feeling the same cold, uncomfortable sweat begin to coat her hands again, and half hoped they would go back inside, leaving her to slip away in the darkness. Anything, she thought miserably—any fate, no matter what—would be better than being left behind with these total strangers.

But Rafe, catching the mood she could not conceal, obviously had other plans for her. Reaching out suddenly, he caught hold of her arm in a tough, unrelenting grip. Before she could even gasp out in surprise, she felt herself being jerked up, set in motion by a sharp forward thrust that propelled her roughly out of the wagon and onto the pavement. Almost simultaneously, she heard the saddlebag containing her few possessions land with a clumsy thud beside her.

It all happened so quickly, she barely had time to think. Only when he was gone, only when nothing was left of him but the sound of hoofbeats fading in the distance, did she finally realize what Rafe had done. A sudden surge of bitterness welled up in her heart. How could he treat her like this? How could he barge into her life the way he had, tearing her away from everything she had ever known, pretending sometimes to be concerned and understanding, and then just ride off and leave her alone!

Her anger sustained her for a minute, rising around her like a protective shield, but she could not hold on to it, and all too soon it ebbed away, leaving her with nothing but that terrible debilitating fear, catching in her throat and threatening to choke her. Reluctantly, she forced herself to admit that Rafe was right. These people were her natural parents, and she was going to have to come to terms with them sooner or later. Putting it off would only make things harder. The best thing she could do now was march right up those steps and look them in the eye!

But when she turned and saw them, still standing in exactly

the same place, all her good resolves failed her. They looked so cold and emotionless, the woman especially, as if they were sorry now that they had made such a fuss and tried to get her back.

It was the man who finally broke the uncomfortable deadlock. Moving down the short flight of steps, he reached out casually to pick up her bag. His voice was as bluff as his appearance, and while it was not unkind, it was not reassuring either.

"There, there, you must be tired. Such a long journey, wasn't it? Why don't you come inside and rest?"

If he had stretched out his hands—if he had subjected her to a horribly embarrassing embrace, even a display of unmasculine tears—Kristyn might have been able to bear it. But he simply stood there, looking at her with that terrible, quiet expression on his face, and it was all she could do to keep from turning and running away.

"Very well," she said softly. "I will do as you say."

The room he led her into was an elaborately appointed parlor facing onto the main street. Although it was quite large, it seemed more cramped than spacious. Chairs, sofas, and tables had been fitted into every available corner, and the walls were almost completely covered by gilt-framed pictures and little shelves filled with bric-a-brac. Highly polished dark-wood floors peeked out around the edges of a thick carpet, dyed a deep shade of red that would have been restful to the eye had it not been splashed with a vivid abundance of the most astonishingly unlifelike flowers Kristyn had ever seen. Burgundy velvet draperies were not quite the same hue, but they blended nicely, subduing what would otherwise have been a garish room.

A sweet scent, flowery but somehow cloying, warned Kristyn that the woman had followed her into the room and was standing directly behind her. Turning, she was just in time to catch a startling expression in her eyes.

Why she's afraid, she thought. She's not cold at all, she's just afraid—every bit as much as I am. She must have wanted me back all this time. She must have prayed for this moment every day for years, and now that it's here, she's afraid!

Astrid Ashley caught the flicker of awareness in her daughter's eyes, and for a moment, she felt as if she had been exposed, left almost naked to that knowing gaze. She knew

only too well what she must look like: a rigid, aging woman,
too stiff to show her feelings, too embarrassed to catch her
own child up and clasp her in her arms. But she had never
been comfortable with spontaneous affection, not even when
Kristyn was a little girl—how could she begin now?

"You will not recognize this place, of course," she said,
speaking a little too quickly to cover her nervousness. "We
moved here two years ago from a smaller house on the other
side of town. That's where we lived after we left the farm.
Everything here is new."

She hesitated uncertainly, looking around at all the objects
that must seem so alien to her daughter.

"Benjamin always told me I should keep a few things from
the old days. Remember your roots, he would tell me, don't
cast everything away. But, oh, I did so want to forget! You
were too little to realize, but it was such a struggle then. We
never knew what was going to happen next or how we would
manage from day to day. And now . . . well, look at that."
She thrust out her hand toward a small blue-and-white vase
set on a round, marble-topped table against the wall. "That is
genuine Chinese, from the Ming Dynasty, which was a very
long time ago. Benjamin's business associate picked it up for
us at an auction in London. And that mirror over the mantel
is Louis the Fourteenth. Made in this country, of course, so it
is much nicer, but every line and detail is absolutely authentic.
Benjamin sent for it all the way from St. Louis."

She broke off abruptly, aware that her words must sound
like aimless prattle. Even as a child, Kristyn had been willful
and hard to fathom—now there was a defiant, half-tamed
look about her that made her almost bewilderingly hard to
deal with. Benjamin, sensing her confusion, stepped over to
her, patting her mutely on the arm, that way he had of letting
her know he was there if she needed him.

To Kristyn, watching the interplay between the older couple,
the gesture came as a silent rebuke. She knew she ought to
feel something for them, sympathy perhaps—pity!—but the
emotion was not there. All she could manage was a kind of
vague irritation. Why couldn't they just say what was in their
hearts and get it over with? Why couldn't they tell her they
loved her, if indeed they did, and were only behaving so
peculiarly because she looked like a stranger and that made

them afraid? If only they would do that, then maybe everything would be all right.

And yet, a nagging little voice in the back of her brain
insisted on reminding her, isn't that exactly what you are
doing? Aren't you standing there every bit as silent and
reticent as they? And every bit as afraid!

The thought annoyed her, and she brushed it impatiently
aside. What was she thinking of, letting these people get to
her like that? Why should she feel guilty? After all, it was
they who had brought her here, not she who had asked to
come. Let them make the first move!

Astrid recovered her composure after a moment, although
not without visible effort. Her bearing seemed stilted and
mechanical, less like a mother than an embarrassed hostess
determined to see to her guest's comfort no matter what.

"Why don't we sit down? I'm sure it would be much
nicer. That is, if you don't mind . . ." She stammered
awkwardly, dismay showing in her features. "I mean, if
you . . ."

Kristyn did not fail to catch her meaning. Like every other
white woman, she obviously thought that Indians were nothing but uncultivated savages, too ignorant to be capable of the
most rudimentary manners. Just like Ysabel, taunting her
with the fork!

"I know what a chair is," she snapped resentfully. "And I
know perfectly well how to use it—if I want to!"

Astrid flushed a deep shade of pink.

"Of course you do. I'm sorry, I—I didn't mean it that
way. Why don't you sit over here . . ." Her eyes widened as
she realized she had inadvertently laid her hand on the back
of a rocking chair, setting it in motion with a harsh creaking
sound. "Or perhaps you'd like that nice hard-backed chair
over there by the window."

Kristyn felt her resentment boil over into anger. So her
white mother thought she was too clumsy to handle the chair
with the funny round legs, did she? What did she think was
going to happen, that her daughter would tumble off the edge
and make a fool of herself?

"Well, it doesn't matter anyway. I don't like chairs!"

She flounced over to the fireplace, uncomfortably aware
that she must look a little like Ysabel had that morning when
she flounced in such a tizzy up the walkway to the house.

Plopping down on the floor, she crossed her legs defiantly in front of her, just like a boy!

Childish, she thought irritably—childish and ridiculous! But she tilted her chin up anyway, just to show them she did not care. The look that came over Astrid's face did nothing to make her feel any better. The woman did not have any fight in her: she just crumpled up, almost visibly, her eyes losing whatever light they had, her hands fluttering in helpless little motions at her sides. Then, looking as if she wanted to cry but had forgotten how, she turned and drifted wordlessly out of the room. The silence that followed her leaving was all the more uncomfortable because Kristyn knew she had brought it on herself.

Benjamin Ashley had stood quietly to one side all this time, watching the scene between his wife and daughter without comment. He had always been overly protective of Astrid, almost fatherly in the way he treated her; now, rather to his surprise, he realized he was beginning to feel those same urges toward the child he had not seen for fourteen years. She looked like a little wild creature at that moment, a bird with a broken wing caught in a trap, unable to fly away but pecking fiercely at anyone who came near. Where had she gotten all that fiery spirit? he wondered with an ironic half smile. Not from him, that was for sure, he had no spirit at all. And Astrid was all coolness and quiet endurance.

Going over to the girl, he squatted awkwardly on the floor beside her.

"Chairs aren't really such dreadful things, you know. I rather fancy you'll get used to them by and by."

Kristyn looked up guiltily, surprised to see not the reproach she had expected, but only a benign twinkle in his warm gray eyes.

"It isn't the chair . . ."

"I know," he said quietly. What a pretty young woman she had turned out to be. Rather like Astrid in the old days, only livelier, more vibrant. "I'm afraid this must all seem very strange to you. *We* must seem strange, your mother and I."

"No, not strange exactly, just—just . . ."

He patted her arm lightly, as if to let her know he understood.

"You must make allowances for your mother, my dear. She has not had an easy life, and that makes her defensive sometimes, holding in the feelings she cannot bring herself to express. You, for instance—do you know what she sees when she looks at you? She sees all the things she wants for you, material things, and she is desperately afraid she won't be able to get them for you."

He shifted his weight slowly, rocking back on his heels.

"Things haven't been bad since she married me—I wouldn't want you to think that. Oh, it was hard sometimes, but there was always food on the table and a roof over our heads. But in the years she was growing up, her life was more than uncommonly bitter. Her father was a penniless immigrant who died when she was very young; her mother had too many mouths to feed and neither the time nor the talent to do more than take in an occasional batch of laundry. Even now, even to this day, your mother sometimes wakes up whimpering in the middle of the night, dreaming that she is hungry again, and cold. Why do you think I worked so hard all these years, building up a business in town when I already had a perfectly good farm? I bought her first one house, then another, and filled them with enough possessions to drive away the specter of poverty, at least while the lights are on and she is awake."

He fell into a reflective silence, then to Kristyn's surprise began to chuckle softly.

"Not that I'm complaining, mind you." He laid his hand on his stomach, well rounded beneath the expensive brocade of his waistcoat. "It never hurt my feelings to be well fed. And if the truth were to be known, I enjoy possessions almost as much as Astrid. It's just that I would never have worked so hard to accumulate them."

He stood up, wincing a little as he straightened out his knees. Only a few years ago, he had still felt strong, capable of almost anything; now, age seemed to have caught up with him all of a sudden. Stretching out a hand, he coaxed her up beside him.

"Come along, my dear. There are some people I think you ought to meet."

"People?" The sharpness in her voice prompted a smile to his lips.

"Not real flesh-and-blood people. Don't be alarmed, I know you're not ready for that. These are recent photographs. And don't think I expect you to recognize the faces in them. People change a great deal in fourteen years."

He laid his hand on the mantelpiece, drawing her attention to a row of brownish tintypes in unmatched gold and silver frames.

"These are your half-brothers, my children by my first wife who died many years ago. The eldest is Richard—here he is with his wife and three boys. He is managing the family farm, but he has added so many acres I barely recognize it now. And here is young Benjamin, with his wife, Sarah, and their four little ones. There will be five soon, I have been told. He is in business with me at the store. And this pretty girl is your half-sister, Charlotte, who moved to Nebraska many years ago. Her youngest boy, Adam, had whooping cough last month and we were very worried about him, but he seems to be fine now."

Kristyn studied the pictures dutifully, knowing he expected it of her, but try as she would, she could not find anything familiar about any of them. She had just turned back to Benjamin to tell him so when something in his face stopped her.

"We don't have pictures of the others," he said softly. "The ones we lost. Photographs were not common in those days, and we couldn't afford to have their portraits done. Caroline was taken by an epidemic of scarlet fever, just after your fifth birthday, and Thomas of course, was killed in the Indian raid. So was your full brother, John—Astrid's oldest boy. She lost two of you that day."

He turned back to the mantelpiece, taking down the one picture he had not yet mentioned, the largest of the collection.

"But we do have this . . ."

Kristyn took the photo from him, looking down at it with mild interest. The face was that of a young man with intense eyes and hair that could have been either brown or dark red like her own. The frame, ornate with gold curlicues, seemed too heavy for features that appeared sensitive and somehow delicate.

"He is a very handsome young man," she said politely. "But I am afraid you are right. I don't recognize any of them."

"That was Joshua. You and he were near to the same age. You were always very close. So close your mother and I never knew from one morning to the next whether you were going to wake up bosom buddies—or mortal enemies!"

Taking the picture back from her, he returned it to its place on the mantel.

"We were very proud of him. He had read for the law, and they said he had a brilliant future ahead of him. But his health had been poor for many years, and he was not as strong as his friends, though he would never admit it. One day, he was showing off for them, trying to master a horse whose spirit was too much for him. He smashed almost every bone in his body when he was thrown. He lingered for a month—then we lost him, too."

Kristyn turned back to the picture, running her fingertips over the protective glass, trying to find with touch what her eyes had failed to detect. This was her own brother, someone she must have loved very much in a babyish way, and yet he meant nothing to her. Impulsively, she tipped the photo over, setting it on its face so she would not have to look at those dark eyes.

"I know what you are trying to say. You are telling me that you have all those other faces in those other frames—all those children and grandchildren—and she has no one. Only me."

"Well . . . in a way." He was surprised to realize how perceptive she was. Much more so than she looked, even with that wildness about her. "I don't know as I would have put it quite like that, but yes, that *is* what I am saying."

"But it isn't fair!" Why was he doing this to her, asking things she could not possibly give? "It isn't *me* she wants, don't you see that? I doubt if she will ever accept me as I am. She wants the little girl who was stolen from her, exactly the same, just a little bigger and a little older. Only that girl doesn't exist anymore! She wants my childhood back, all the years that were taken from her—and no one can give her that!"

"I know that, and so, I think, does Astrid, though I admit it doesn't always look that way. But knowing something, my dear child, and accepting it, are two different things."

"Then what . . ." Oh, why did he have to look at her like that? As if somehow this whole thing were her fault, as if she had chosen to come back of her own free will! "What do you want me to do?"

"I do not ask you to love your mother, Kristyn. Love is not a note that can be called in on demand. Nor do I expect you to understand the fears and torments that drive her. All I ask is that you try to be kind to her.''

He did not try to press her further, but left her alone after that, lost in thoughts and feelings she did not want. For the first time in her life, it seemed to her that approaching night was not an old friend, but an oppressor, hovering like a silent threat beyond the golden lamplight. Getting up restlessly, she wandered over to one of the windows. The velvet draperies had been tied back with tasseled cords, but sheer lace curtains still covered the panes, and she brushed them aside with her hand.

Outside, gas light cast a clearly defined circle of yellow on the ground, picking up even the tiniest marks in the pavement. But across the avenue, the tall oaks seemed strangely muted, no more than giant shadows that twisted and undulated in the first whisper of a rising night wind. Had Benjamin been right after all? Should she try to find some feeling in her heart for the woman who had given her birth? But how could feeling be forced where none existed?

She was about to turn away when her eyes picked up a flicker of motion somewhere in the shadows across the street. Pressing her nose against the glass, she peered out, surprised to catch hints of moving figures beneath the trees. Vague, mannish figures, perhaps eight or ten of them, all muffled up against the chill, and showing no inclination to move down the street or cluster in front of other windows. She stared at them curiously for a moment, wondering idly what sort of peculiar white customs they could be engaged in. Then, slowly, the truth began to dawn on her.

They had come to get a look at the savage!

Of course! What a fool she had been not to realize it sooner. They would have heard that Rafe was bringing her back. Obviously, they were consumed with curiosity to see this new creature, this primitive half-woman, half-beast in their midst. And they did not care if they hurt her feelings by gaping at her.

Or perhaps they simply thought she had no feelings to hurt.

She let out her breath slowly, staring in fascination at the mist that built up on the glass, momentarily obscuring the watchers from her view. Was this what Rafe had taken her out of the Indian camp and dragged her back to ''civilization'' to find? Nothing but ghoulish curiosity? Revulsion?

Unkindness?

She tugged at the tie that held back the drapes. *Try to be kind*, Benjamin had told her. *Just try to be kind*. But who would be kind to her?

With a soft, sighing sound, the draperies fell in thick folds over the windows, shutting her in with the lamplight, the gilded frames, and the big, strangely colored flowers on the carpet.

Fourteen

Astrid planned her daughter's introduction into local society with meticulous care, organizing one of the glittering teas for which she was justly renowned and inviting all the best people, but even she could not deny that the whole thing had turned out to be an absolute disaster!

She paused briefly just inside the doorway, extricating herself for a moment from her duties as hostess, and scanned the room with anxious eyes, trying to figure out what had gone wrong. Certainly the setting was everything that could be expected. Most of the furnishings had been stripped from the front parlor, revealing a room that was much larger than it seemed before, and the carpet had been rolled up and stored away in preparation for the dancing that would follow. A long table had been set up at one end. On it, a magnificent silver tea service, Astrid's pride and joy, shimmered against snowy damask, and fine china platters held dainty little rounds and diamonds of crustless white bread, spread with all manner of tasty delicacies. Even the gray aspect of a heavily clouded sky, faintly visible through wispy lace curtains, did not detract from the mood; indeed, the golden flicker of candles, set ablaze in a breathtakingly elaborate crystal chandelier, added an aura of romantic elegance to the room. Only the barest minimum of uncomfortable hard-backed chairs had been positioned along the walls, a none-too-subtle ploy to encourage the guests to move about and mingle.

Only the guests, unfortunately, were not cooperating. Instead of circulating freely, they had clustered together in groups of threes and fours, absolutely refusing to move from the spot, the hostess's ultimate nightmare. The sound of conversation was bright and brittle—too bright? she wondered—

and mellow music drifted in from a small orchestra hidden away in a screened alcove. But to Astrid, sharply tuned to the finer shadings of society, it was only too obvious that things were not going well at all.

As for the guest of honor . . .

Astrid's eyes were drawn almost unwittingly toward the place where her daughter stood alone, staring silently out of the window, a cup of tea cooling half forgotten in her hands. Honestly, the girl could be hopelessly exasperating at times! Of course it wasn't easy for her—heaven knows, the better elements of society were not exactly rushing up to greet her with open arms—but then, she hadn't done anything to ease the situation herself. Every time Astrid had tried to help her, coaxing one of the bolder of the young gentlemen to go over and engage her in conversation, she had seen Kristyn turn toward him with a vague half-smile and a few succinct words that, even from that distance, were clearly some form or other of "Please go away and leave me alone."

And the young gentleman, of course, had been too happy to oblige!

It was not as if the girl had not attracted a certain degree of attention, and not all of it unfavorable, at least not from the men! There was something distinctly unsettling in her earthiness, a kind of simmering expression in those dusky blue eyes, darkly trapped in absurdly long lashes, a pouty fullness to the lips that looked as if they knew secrets that should only be whispered in the darkness. As for her figure . . . !

Ah, that figure—it made Astrid flush uncomfortably even to think of it. Kristyn had inherited her height from her, but the soft curves of her hips, the ripe womanly swell of firm young breasts, the oh-so sinuous way her long legs moved when she walked—those were all her own. The dress she was wearing was one of Astrid's own choosing, a girlishly virginal white lawn, dotted with dainty yellow flowers, but seeing her daughter in it now, she realized she had made a mistake. Far from subduing Kristyn's sultry beauty, the gown only accented it, making her look not childlike at all, but even more of a woman, not sweet and sophisticated, but wild and strangely, provocatively primitive.

Well, at least it was better than that gray traveling dress she had arrived in! Falsely modest, with its high neck and long sleeves, and all the time cut to emphasize every sensual curve in a body that was already eye-catching enough as it was. Or that other gown, that dreadful vermilion silk that that man Rafe Valero had insisted on bringing along with the rest of her meager belongings, though where he had gotten it, Astrid could not imagine. It would have been much better suited to a Spanish dancer, or a gambling hall hostess!

That man! The mere thought of him made her cringe with revulsion. She had seen Rafe Valero for what he was the instant he pulled up in front of the house, a hired mercenary, crude and prone to violence, ruggedly virile in a coarse male way, sure of what he wanted—and not afraid to take it! It had disgusted her to receive him the next day in her parlor. She had known Benjamin was right, of course—they owed it to the man to invite him into their house when he came to collect his pay—but still, it appalled her to see his boots on her carpet, his lean, hard body lounging insolently on one of her best chairs. And the way Kristyn had looked at him when she came downstairs . . . !

Hurriedly, she blocked the thought out of her mind, unable to bear the memory of her daughter's face, eager, almost wistful, as she came into the parlor and saw him sitting there. What was it he had called her, some absurd Spanish name—Cristina *lucero del alba*, something like that—and her eyes lit up at the sound. Well, at least, Astrid had thought then, taking comfort where she could, the man would be leaving soon. At least Kristyn would not see him again.

Only, much to her consternation, Rafe Valero had not gone at all. Quite unexpectedly, he had announced that he was planning on staying for a week or two, and even had the effrontery to set himself up at the Hadley House. No doubt it amused him to pretend he was a gentleman! He had business that needed to be settled, he claimed—as if a man like that ever had any *legitimate* business! No, if he was hanging around, it could only be for one reason. Because he, too, had noticed that sultry, smoky expression in her daughter's eyes every time she looked at him.

And Kristyn? Was she deliberately encouraging him?

The thought Astrid had been blocking out pushed its way into her consciousness, too persistent now to be ignored. They had been alone together, Kristyn and that man, alone in the long days it had taken him to bring her there, and alone in dark nights spent in some secluded forest glade. It was hard to imagine that Valero would have had any compunctions about the way he treated her. And she . . . ?

Bitterly, Astrid realized she must face the worst. The girl had been raised by savages, nurtured in a code that must be abhorrent to every decent, God-fearing woman. Would it really be surprising if she had accepted those raw urges of the flesh as something inevitable, natural? Why, even now, standing there so docilely by the window, mightn't she be thinking of him, thinking of the things that had gone on between them . . .

Well, that at least she could put a stop to! Casting her eye about, she sighted a plump figure, incongruously clad in a frothy lavender silk gown. Eliza Shepherd was an exceptionally garrulous young lady, rather too pushy for Astrid's taste, but those two traits were exactly what she was looking for now. Eliza would not be the least bit timid about approaching a stranger, and once cornered, Kristyn would have no time to think about anything else.

As it happened, Kristyn's thoughts were indeed centered on Rafe Valero at that moment, but had she been able to peek into her daughter's mind, Astrid would not have been nearly as alarmed as she expected. There was nothing erotic in the bittersweet reverie that held the girl captive as she stared out at the silent avenue, darkened by scattered showers; nothing even vaguely reminiscent of the strong man-woman feelings that had sometimes sprung up between her and this man; only a dull, unexpected sense of her own aloneness now that he was not there. It was not that she had forgotten the disturbing magnetism he exerted over her, the volatile animosity that had masked her early attraction, even the unexpectedly tender feel of his lips for a brief second against her palms—it was just that those feelings, those sensations no longer seemed as important as they once had. Far more compelling now was the sudden startling realization that, much as she had once despised him, Rafe Valero was the only person among all the whites she had met, with the possible exception of her father that first night, who had even tried to talk to her, tried to understand what she was feeling. The one, unlikely person she dared to think of in any way as her friend.

She set the teacup down on the windowsill, frowning at the party sounds behind her, intruding on her thoughts. She hated the way Astrid served her tea, weak and almost devoid of color, not at all like Cook made it for her when she sneaked down into the kitchen, the only room in which she felt comfortable in the entire house.

If only she had been allowed to invite Rafe that afternoon, she thought restlessly. At least then she would have had someone to talk to. But Astrid had been adamant.

"I will not have that man in my house, Benjamin," she had said angrily when she thought Kristyn was out of earshot. "He is nothing but an adventurer and a ruffian! I don't know why you insist on letting him spend time with your own daughter!"

Benjamin had tried, rather half-heartedly it seemed to Kristyn, to reason with her.

"We can hardly refuse the man entrance to our house, my dear. After all, we do owe it to him that we have the girl back at all."

"For which he has been richly paid," Astrid reminded him sharply. "Oh, I know we can't slam the door in his face, much as I wish we could, but surely we don't have to entertain him with our friends! Oh, Benjamin, what will people think if they see him with Kristyn? He does have an insultingly familiar manner, you know. Her position is already much too precarious—something like that could ruin her forever."

And that, Kristyn thought, sighing as she turned from the window, was undoubtedly that. She had already noticed that whenever Astrid made up her mind, Benjamin did nothing to change it. She, too, had been surprised when Rafe elected to stay in town, even more so than her mother for she knew how anxious he was to rejoin his brother, and in her more optimistic moments, she even dared to hope it might be because of her. But what good was that going to do her if she never got to see him?

The sigh deepened as she caught sight of a small mountain of pale purple silk heading her way. Eliza Shepherd—she looked even more formidable now than she had when Kristyn had met her briefly an hour before. Although the other girl could not have been much older than she, no more than a year or two at most, she already had the bosom and imperious bearing of a dowager three times her age.

"So there you are," she said, her smallish black eyes reflecting the sheen of jet beads around her neck. "All by

yourself in the corner like some sad little wallflower. Tell
me, are we really that offensive, or are you just bored to
tears?''

Well, at least she was candid, Kristyn had to give her that.
Not that it made the prospect of her company any more
appealing.

''I haven't as yet developed a taste for this kind of
gathering,'' she demured, politely.

''Really? I wasn't aware that social parties were an acquired taste.''

Kristyn noticed that Eliza had brought two of the small tea
sandwiches with her, holding them daintily between her thumb
and forefinger, one in each hand, and she found herself
wondering, irrepressibly, just how many of them it would
take to maintain her girth.

''I suppose it is all a matter of what you are used to.''

''Yes, I daresay it is.'' How peculiarly her eyes shone, as
if she were about to say something exciting but had not got
around to it yet. ''Society is very important to us, of course.
But perhaps to the—uh, *primitive* races——''

''If by primitive,'' Kristyn cut in, her patience wearing
thin, ''you mean the Cheyennes, I think you have been
misinformed. Social gatherings are important to Indians, too,
only they are much livelier—and much more fun! I get the
feeling everyone here stayed up half the night just trying to
think of the most trivial, pointless things to say.''

She was rewarded with a surprised expression, but Eliza
did not try to pick up the challenge. And after all, how could
she? Kristyn thought with a grin—she had just been following
her example! Say the most outrageous things in a sweet tone
of voice, and it seemed to be perfectly acceptable.

''Well, yes . . . You really should try one of these
sandwiches.'' Eliza formed pink lips into a perfect *O*, pop-
ping a round of bread into it. ''Such lovely delicacies. Your
mother is quite famous for her teas. The refreshments are
always superb.''

Kristyn's eyes narrowed as she glanced down at the remaining sandwich, another little circle smeared with sweet butter
and flecked with sprigs of something green. They were English,
Astrid had told her with a note of pride in her usually
restrained voice, and very sophisticated. Everyone was serv-

ing them nowadays. It did not, Kristyn decided, say much for
the English.

"I'm afraid I have not acquired a taste for those either."

"No? You are probably used to something more—basic?"
At last Kristyn recognized the look in her eyes—it was
curiosity, frank and unabashed. "Something like—buffalo
meat? Tell me, is it true what they say? Do Indians really tear
meat off the bones with their bare hands?"

For an instant, Kristyn was too startled to do anything but
stare. Even for Eliza, the comment seemed exceptionally
rude. She was not sure whether she wanted to burst into
laughter or reach out and slap the smug look off her face!

"Of course we don't tear the meat from the bones with our
hands. We gnaw at it like an animal, especially if we get it
raw, the way we like it. And we only eat buffalo as a last
resort. Actually, we prefer dog."

She could not have said what prompted her to come out
with such a thing, but the effect was eminently satisfying.

"D-dog? You eat—dog?" Eliza's voice was so quavery
Kristyn could hardly keep from laughing.

"Certainly dog. Why should that shock you? You white
people are all alike. You'd eat a friendly little chicken any
day of the week, or a lamb with sad, melting eyes, but the
idea of dog turns your stomach." She was not about to let
Eliza know that she was every bit as squeamish herself, no
doubt because of her attachment to her own pet. Still, she
wouldn't be surprised if white children felt the same way
about the lambs and chickens they had raised.

"But, surely . . . You must be jesting! Even Indians couldn't
be so—so disgusting!"

"Disgusting?" Kristyn put all the sweetness she could
back in her voice. "But dog meat is not disgusting at all.
Why, it is considered a great delicacy. Oh, not recently, of
course. We've been so poor we had nothing but mongrels,
and everyone knows how tough and stringy they are. We
especially miss the fluffy little dogs. You know, the kind
ladies hold on their laps. We used to get two or three a week
from passing wagon trains. The white ones with pink noses
are the best."

"Pink noses?"

Eliza's own nose quivered, as if in sympathy, and suddenly
Kristyn found herself wearying of the game she herself had

begun. With a barely murmured apology, she turned her back and began to thread her way through chattering groups of guests toward the tea table. What was it about that woman that offended her so much, her lack of understanding or her gullibility? If that was all she had to look forward to from white society, she had a feeling she was going to be very unhappy in her parents' home.

She paused beside the table, picking up one of the sandwiches and studying it with a dubious eye. It was much like the one Eliza had just consumed except that it had something red next to the something green.

"Dog, eh?" a masculine voice said suddenly in her ear. "That's a good one. Bet that biddy is up swooning in one of the bedrooms right now. She has a pampered lapdog herself. Little beast is even fatter than she is."

The young man who seemed to have materialized out of nowhere was tall and rather handsome in a bloodless way, although his studied good looks were too self-conscious for Kristyn's taste. She vaguely remembered his name, Alden Something-or-Other, she thought—or was it Something-or-Other Alden?

"I am sure Eliza Shepherd is stronger than she lets on. And at any rate, it was hardly my intention to throw her into a swoon."

"Maybe not, but you did all the same. Or at the very least you drove her to her smelling salts! That was quite a story you handed her." He leaned closer, the sour stench of his breath warning Kristyn that he had been imbibing something stronger than the sherry Benjamin was handing out to the gentlemen in his study.

"Do you always eavesdrop on other people's conversation, Mr. Alden?"

If she expected to pique him, she was quickly disillusioned. The slightly intoxicated grin on his face merely broadened into what looked to her like a decidedly offensive leer.

"It isn't eavesdropping at a party. As a matter of fact, it's considered quite *de rigueur*. Anyone who doesn't know what's going on is definitely out of things. But back to the dog meat—now, that intrigues me. How do you prepare the animal? Just slice it open and spill its guts out on the ground?"

Kristyn felt the color drain from her face as, unbidden, a glimpse of mangled yellow fur, half buried in the mud, came back to her. She could only suppose the young man thought he was wonderfully witty, but it was all she could do to choke back the obvious retort that, in her experience, it was white men who treated dogs with grim brutality.

"Indians dress their meat just the way you people do with chickens, Mr. Alden—right after you wring their necks with your bare hands! And no, they don't waste the bowels; they utilize every part of every animal they kill. The Cheyennes are very poor people. They occasionally allow themselves the luxury of a pet, but that is rare, especially in these troubled times. For the most part, they take whatever meat they can get and are grateful for it. Perhaps when you have a little more experience in the ways of the world, you will understand that simply because others do not share your customs they are not automatically barbarians!"

"Bravo!"

A soft clapping of hands greeted Kristyn's outburst, and half jumping at the sound, she turned to find a slender man of perhaps fifty or a little older standing behind her. Asa Martens had been a frequent visitor in her parents' home, and while he referred to himself as a "business associate" of father's, the quiet authority in his bearing reminded her that the relationship between the two men was not an equal one.

"Well, Alden!" he said crisply. "It's about time someone put you in your place. And quite tidily, too, I am delighted to say. Perhaps in the future, you will mind your manners a little more, especially in someone else's home. I can't imagine what you think you were doing, talking to a lady that way."

Alden reddened, but whatever hot retorts rose to his lips died away when he got a better look at the expression on Asa Martens' face. His pale-colored eyes fairly seethed with hatred as he sidled away, casting a last backward glance over his shoulder, but it was an emotion directed totally at Kristyn, as if even in his thoughts he was afraid to defy the older man.

Kristyn turned her attention back to her unexpected benefactor and found rather to her surprise that he was studying her with quite a puzzling look.

"I suppose I must thank you, Mr. Martens, for rescuing me from my own bad temper."

"Not at all, my dear. Not at all. As a matter of fact, I'm afraid I was indulging in that same rudeness you accused young Alden of—eavesdropping." His voice sounded warm and genial, like a kindly old uncle trying to put her at ease, but he was still staring at her in that strange way, setting her teeth somehow on edge, though she could not have said why.

"That's very kind of you, but I fear the rudeness was mine—at least I am sure my mother will think so. The man is, after all, a guest in our house. He is entitled to a certain courtesy."

"He is entitled to nothing." Martens surprised her with the sudden hardness in his tone. "And I think you know it beneath that veneer of politeness you are suddenly affecting. Come, come, Miss Ashley, I much preferred you honest and outspoken. That young blackguard abused your father's hospitality shamelessly, and he got exactly what he deserved. I for one have no intention of apologizing to him. I hope you don't either."

In spite of herself, Kristyn felt her eyes being drawn toward the man, half out of curiosity, half out of something that felt strangely like trepidation. He was almost blandly modest in appearance, no taller than she and slightly built, his very dark hair at odds with the lined, grayish aspect of his face, and his vested brown suit unpretentiously if expensively cut. Still, there was something about him, some vague indefinable quality she could not quite put her finger on, that gave him the air of a man who was used to being in command. Martens was, Rafe had told her in one of the few moments Astrid had allowed them alone in her parlor, a railroad magnate, busy with the task of spreading iron rails across the continents, and amassing a fortune for himself in the bargain. It was through his patronage—through the arbitrary purchase of supplies from one place rather than another—that Benjamin's store had prospered. It gave Kristyn an uncomfortable feeling to realize she was in the presence of a man who had literally made her father, and could ruin him again with a snap of his fingers.

Martens seemed to pick up on her thoughts, for he changed moods abruptly, breaking into a light, almost boyish smile.

"Don't you think you had better do something about that poor *hors d'oeuvre*? There isn't going to be anything left of it if you keep pinching it between your fingers like that."

Kristyn looked down, surprised to find the tea sandwich still in her hand.

"I suppose I should. I had completely forgotten it. I was just trying to work myself up to——" She broke off abruptly, realizing what she must sound like, but Martens only laughed.

"It isn't very appealing, is it? That's one of the reasons most men have to be dragged to affairs like this. There's nothing on that whole table you can sink your teeth into. But I'm told your mother takes great pride in her teas, so I try to do my part to keep from hurting her feelings."

He smiled faintly as Kristyn took the hint and bit off a chunk of soft, butter-daubed bread, trying to eat daintily, as she had seen the others do. Obviously, she disliked the taste of it, and just as obviously, she was determined not to let him see it! What a fascinating creature she was. He did not think he had ever seen eyes quite so blue—or so luminous. And that defiant lilt to her chin! Asa Martens had always admired proud women; it was his weakness in dealing with the fairer sex, and he recognized in this one particular woman something he had never seen in any other.

"You're not at all what I had expected," he said impulsively.

"No?" Kristyn watched him warily, conscious, as she had been before, of the fact that his eyes seemed to be fixed like magnets on her face. It suddenly occurred to her that he had presented himself in the front parlor at one time or another nearly every day since she had arrived, even though she could have sworn her father's business was not all that important to him. "What did you expect to find, Mr. Martens, that first day you came to call? A snarling savage with filthy garments and even coarser manners?"

"Well . . . perhaps."

Good God, what fire the girl had when she thought she was cornered and had to fight. It intrigued him to watch her. She was so young, she still had so much to learn—but ah, what rewards would be waiting for the man with the patience to teach her!

"In a way you are," he went on. "Not filthy or coarse, but quite wonderfully savage, especially when you snarl. And yet there is something about you, some kind of inbred dignity that makes you more than a match for any lady with a title and a string of family castles. I have always thought the most devastating kind of woman was one who was half a perfect lady—and half a perfect whore! Now I am beginning to wonder if half a tameless savage wouldn't be more exciting."

The unmistakable innuendo in his words caught Kristyn off guard, leaving her speechless for a minute. Surely, even a man as important as Asa Martens should not be permitted to speak to her so—so coarsely. Or should he? How she wished she knew more about the white man's customs.

And how she wished he would stop looking at her like that. Like—like what? she wondered, trying to figure out when she had felt like that before. Like those other, anonymous men had looked at her from across the street the night of her arrival? The sudden, wildly ridiculous thought crossed her mind that he might actually have been there, gawking with the others, but she dismissed it almost as quickly as it came. Asa Martens was a powerful man: he would never have to stand on the outside, looking in. Still, there was no denying the way he made her feel, like an animal being exhibited in a cage.

"Oh, how I wish my parents had never brought me here!" she blurted out, not stopping to think what she was saying. "They could not have been crueller if they set out to do it on purpose. Didn't they realize no one would ever be able to forget my past? Or treat me like a normal woman?"

"But my dear . . ." Martens sounded genuinely shocked. "Of course you are a normal woman, and you will lead a normal life in time, I promise you. If I hadn't sincerely believed that, I would never have helped your parents find you."

"You *helped* my parents?" Kristyn was too surprised for an instant to remember to be wary. Rafe had said something about a friend of her father's, but in the flurry of her homecoming, she had completely forgotten.

"Yes, certainly—someone had to. The last man they hired to search for you was a polite, scholarly young man. I have nothing against him personally, but going through all the right channels and asking all the right questions doesn't come up with the right answers. I've known Valero for a long time. He has nerves of steel and an almost uncanny daring—and not a scruple in the world. In short, my kind of man, not your father's. And just the sort for the job."

Something in his voice, something in the way he was regarding her out of the corner of his eye without seeming to, set off a responsive alarm in Kristyn. There was more to his words than met the ear, but what could it be? Was he testing her for some reason? Throwing out Rafe's name to see how she would react?

Well, if he was, he wasn't going to get anything out of her. She was not about to give Asa Martens the satisfaction of knowing that there was anything at all she liked about the man he had hand-picked to track her down.

"He certainly has a lack of scruples," she agreed. "And a lack of manners as well! As far as I am concerned, Rafe Valero is an absolute boor, without any redeeming qualities, and I resent the fact that you sent him after me almost as much as I resent being brought back against my will!"

The minute the words were out of her mouth, she realized she had spoken too sharply. Martens seemed to sense it, too, for he eyed her suspiciously, then relaxed, apparently satisfied, for the moment at least.

"Valero is the kind of man who either fills a woman with revulsion or fascinates her. In your case, I had feared it might be the latter. I am happy to find it is not so."

Happy to find that she didn't like Rafe? An odd choice of words, Kristyn thought. And an odd look in his eyes, too, strangely proprietary, almost as if he thought she belonged to him.

A powerful man. The words came back to haunt her. Powerful and unscrupulous? Young troublemakers like Alden backed down from him, and even an arrogant, independent Rafe Valero was there to do him "favors." A man like that would always get what he wanted, one way or another—if what he wanted was a woman, would it bother him that he was old enough to be her father and the idea disgusted her completely?

"You must excuse me, Mr. Martens. It—it really is very hot in here. I think I would like to go outside for a breath of fresh air."

The slow smile that twisted up the corners of his lips told her she had made a mistake, giving him just the opening he was looking for.

"Then you must allow me to escort you, Miss Ashley. How could I permit a beautiful young woman to wander alone in the streets and still call myself a gentleman?"

Kristyn was spared the consequences of her own carelessness by a sudden commotion that broke out at the far end of the room, near the door that led to her father's study. Much to her surprise, she saw that it centered around Alden. He seemed to have come in from someplace outside for his shoulders were damp and little beads of moisture clung to his fair hair. His face was even redder than it had been when Asa Martens confronted him earlier, and he was waving a sheet of newsprint in his upraised fist.

"Those damned savages are at it again," he bellowed out, making sure his words carried across the room. "Beggin' your pardon, ladies, but there's no other way to describe the bastards. I got this sheet off the boy that calls out the news on the corner. A whole band of filthy cowards crept up on a farmhouse not more'n a few hundred miles from here. Bludgeoned five innocent people to death, and took the scalps of every one of them. And the youngest was a babe at the breast!"

Kristyn gasped aloud as she realized the audacity of what he was doing. He might not be able to get back at Asa Martens for the way he had been humiliated before, but clearly she was fair game! That he was succeeding was only too apparent from the sly, sidelong glances everyone threw her way as they edged over toward the corner where he was already beginning to gather a crowd.

"When did it happen?" one of the men called out.

"A few days ago. It took a while for the news to get here. A rotten, sneaky thing, that's what I call it! Those farmers never have more'n a shotgun or two to defend themselves. It would have been a regular slaughter!"

"I'll be damned if I know why the Army lets 'em get away with it," an older man chimed in. "Why don't they break out the militia, that's what I want to know? If I were younger, I'd be the first to sign up."

A pink-cheeked youth agreed: "I'm tempted to go myself. If my father didn't need me in his business, by God, I'd do it!"

"We've taken enough from these damned savages," Alden went on, flushed with his triumph. "It's time we fought back! Not a one of us will ever be safe as long as there's an Indian left alive. Let's round 'em up and shoot 'em, every last man, woman, and child, and be done with 'em once and for all!"

The murmuring of approval that shivered through the crowd chilled Kristyn to the bone, reminding her once again, if

indeed she needed reminding, how deeply hatred of the Indians ran in these people—and just how untenable her own
position among them was.

The sound of raised voices had drawn Benjamin from his
study, and Kristyn saw him standing in the doorway, taking
in everything with a quick glance—the ruddy color of Alden's
face, the newspaper in his hand, the answering gleam in the
eyes of all too many of the watching guests. Then, with a
quiet forcefulness as effective as it was surprising, he went
over to the young man and uttered a few obviously telling
words in his ear. Kristyn could not hear what he said, only
the cool, even tones of his voice, but whatever it was, Alden
seemed to lose all of his bluster. When Asa Martens stepped
forward a second later, he gave up completely, throwing the
newspaper down on the ground with a muffled oath and
stomping disgustedly out of the room.

Kristyn stayed where she was, her eyes on the fallen paper,
as the guests began to disperse again, breaking back, some
with mildly shamed faces, others still belligerent, into the
little groups that had occupied them before. The bold letters
running in a black banner across the top of the newspaper
seemed to laugh out at her, taunting her not only with past
loyalties but present ignorance as well. How degrading to
realize that of all the people in the room, she was the only
one who could not read the thing—and she was the only one
who was truly affected by it!

A silence in the hallway just outside the parlor told her that
Alden had already taken his leave, so—hungry for a few
moments of solitude—she stepped out and found her cloak on
the peg where she always kept it. She had only been making
excuses before, when she told Asa Martens she needed a
breath of fresh air; but now pretense had become reality, and
suddenly the house seemed so stifling, she did not think she
could breathe if she stayed. There was nothing for her in that
terrible party-festooned room—nothing now, and nothing ever!
How could her parents ask her to spend the rest of her life
among people who would always be looking at her with
morbid curiosity in their eyes. Always wondering if she, too,
had dipped her hands in blood—if she, like so many of her
own people, had a secret string of scalps hanging somewhere
in her room?

She pulled the cloak tightly around her, huddling into the

soft fur lining as she threw open the door and let in a cold draft. Raising the hood to shield her face, she stepped out into the faint drizzle that was still falling on the street.

Kristyn made a pretty picture as she scurried down the street, her dark green cloak blowing out in the wind around her, but Astrid was not even tempted to smile as she stood in the silent hallway and watched her through one of the long, lace-curtained windows. She had seen her daughter slip out of the parlor a moment before, and had guessed, even before Kristyn herself was aware of it, where she was going.

Not that she blamed the girl for running away. God knows, only years of training herself to remain cool and reserved had kept her from doing exactly the same thing when she saw what that despicable young wretch was up to. The viper! She had only invited Alden in the first place because his parents were too prominent to ignore and she had not wanted to incur his animosity for her daughter; now she would see to it that he never set foot in her house again, not for any reason, and she didn't care if she damaged herself socially in the process! Why, if it had not been for Benjamin . . . !

She realized suddenly that she was clutching the curtain, and she released it, letting sheer lace fall back over the window, softening stark shadows on the now-empty street. Benjamin. In all the years they had been together, all the years she had thought she knew absolutely everything about this man, he was still capable of surprising her. He could be so mild and genial at times, he absolutely infuriated her, never fighting for his rights, always taking the easy, the gracious way out—yet this afternoon he had not hesitated to stand up for his daughter, showing a strength and subtle authority she had seen in him only a few times before, and that many years ago. It occurred to her, perhaps for the first time in her married life, that for all his surface weaknesses, somehow Benjamin was always there when she needed him.

If only it had not been such an empty gesture! She ran her hand unconsciously down the window, barely feeling the crisp edges of freshly laundered lace beneath her fingertips. Benjamin might be able to shame people into silence for a moment, but after all, it was the Aldens and the Eliza Shepherds—the rich, the successful, the socially prominent— who really ran the town. It was they who would decide

Kristyn's fate in the long run. Unless the girl had someone far more powerful than Benjamin and Astrid Ashley to shield her, nothing was going to prevent Alden and Eliza from going home and tearing her apart with the sharp, frighteningly witty rapier-edges of their tongues.

Astrid was so wrapped up in her thoughts she did not hear the sound of footsteps behind her, and the light touch of a hand on her shoulder made her jump with nervousness. A minute ago, she had thought she longed for her husband's company. Now, turning and seeing him, she was filled with a sudden, unaccountable anger.

"She has gone to him, Benjamin! She didn't say anything— she just took her cloak off the peg and went outside—but I know! She has gone to that—that adventurer!"

Benjamin nodded abstractedly. He, too, had seen Kristyn flee from the parlor, and although he remained behind a moment or two to smooth things over, he had been almost as worried as his wife.

"There, there, my dear." He tried to keep his voice soothing as he patted her absent-mindedly on the arm. "Perhaps it's not as bad as all that. Rough as he is, I don't think Valero is the sort to take advantage of a woman when she is distraught. Even if honor didn't prevent him, he would hardly want to bring all that trouble down on his head. Besides, they say he comes from quite a decent family—somewhere to the south, I hear—and his manners are gentlemanly enough when he chooses. Perhaps we should have given in to Kristyn's pleadings and invited him after all. I suspect his presence would have defused the situation."

"Invited him *here*? Oh, Benjamin, how can you be so—so . . ." Astrid stammered awkwardly, struggling to find the words. "So naive! The man *is* an adventurer! What does he care about honor, or trouble either, for that matter? All he sees is the way Kristyn looks at him—her eyes are so transparent, even when she is trying to hide her feelings—and his male ego thrives on it! He is only playing with her, dallying with her, and when he is bored, he'll walk away and leave her with a broken heart! Yes, and a broken reputation, too. Maybe he has already! Oh, God, I can't bear to think of it . . ."

She bit down on her lower lip, clamping it so tightly between her teeth that the flesh turned white. Benjamin watched her, sensing her fear, feeling it, but unable to do anything about it.

"I don't think things have gone that far, my dear. I may be an old fuddy-duddy at times, but I am not all that naive, and I must admit the thought had occurred to me. But I have been watching the girl very closely these past few days, and it seems to me she has a peculiarly innocent air about her. No, I really don't think *that* has happened."

"And if it has. . .?"

So much fear in her voice, so much pain—it tore him apart to hear it.

"If it has, it will soon be over, and we must try not to blame her too much for things that are not her fault. As you said, the man is an adventurer. He will not stay here long, no matter what, and when he leaves, Kristyn will not go with him."

Such sensible words, Astrid thought miserably. Sensible and reasonable—if they referred to someone else's daughter! How hard it was to take that same cool, detached logic and apply it to her own child.

"Oh, if only we could protect her, Benjamin. If only we were powerful enough to stop those vicious gossips once and for all—or rich enough to thumb our noses in their faces!"

Rich enough . . . Benjamin turned away, letting his eyes scan the hallway, filled with all the possessions he had bought her. Money, it always came back to money with Astrid—only this time he had the feeling she was right. They wouldn't have a problem now, if only they could just "thumb their noses" at the world. He had done well enough in his day, making more money than he had ever expected to see, but most of it had gone into houses and furnishings, silks and soirees, and there was precious little left even to provide for Astrid in her declining years. How could he ensure his daughter's future after he was gone?

Dammit, sometimes he hated that hall! Golden oak banisters polished until they shone; velvet-flecked red wallpaper, so expensive everyone knew exactly what it cost; the little imported sidetable, the only European object in the house that had actually come from Europe—what did all that mean if he could not even take care of his own daughter?

"So, it all comes down to the same thing in the end."

He said the words dully, without expression. Ever since he

had come out there, he had been avoiding them. Just as he knew she had been waiting—*hoping* for him to say them.

"Don't you see, Benjamin? It's the only way. If Kristyn had a husband, a man strong enough to protect her . . ."

"A husband, yes!" Of course a husband. That wasn't even debatable. If a young woman's father couldn't provide for her, then a marriage had to be arranged. "But surely we don't have to push her into this match you want, even if it does look desirable from our point of view. We could introduce her to more young men, perhaps send her back East to school."

"She is too old to go to school. And you saw today how the young men reacted to her. Oh, they are polite enough for the most part, I grant you, but they have to be pushed to go over to her, and they can hardly wait to get away again! Strangeness is too intimidating to youth. Kristyn's beauty might capture a young man's eyes, but it will never win his heart."

She turned away, conscious of the sound of raindrops beginning to beat a harsh tattoo against the pane.

"It might have been different, Benjamin, if we had found her sooner, while she was still a child, untouched—unsullied. But no one will look at her that way now, especially if they find out about that Indian 'husband' of hers. All they will think—all they *can* think—is that she was living in the squalor of a tepee, bedded down with some unspeakable savage."

Benjamin stared at his wife in mild surprise. Astrid had never even alluded to the affairs of their *own* marriage bed, secretly, almost apologetically conducted under cover of darkness, and it shocked him a little to hear such things on her lips. Plainly, she was more distressed by her daughter's plight than he had understood.

"Are you sure?" he murmured heavily. "This is really what you want?"

"We have to do it, Benjamin. We *have* to! At least this way we will know she is safe."

Safe? Yes, he could not argue with that. The girl would be safe—but would she be happy?

And would it matter if she wasn't? The thought surprised him, unaccustomed as he was to questioning things he had always taken for granted. Youthful happiness—it did have a way of slipping through your fingers just when you thought you had gotten hold of it at last. Perhaps contentment was better, the kind of contentment that came from years well spent and daydreams gracefully surrendered to the exigencies of reality.

He studied his wife's features in the waning light, trying to remember what she had looked like when he first saw her. Had she ever really loved him? He had doubted it then, and he doubted it now. She had been so young when he married her, barely seventeen, and he already well into middle age, a widower with children almost as old as she. But it had been a love match of sorts, for he had loved her, deeply, with the love of the aging for youth and beauty, and she had been grateful to him. Somehow, over the years that uneven love-gratitude balance had ripened into genuine affection and a need for each other. Perhaps if Kristyn was lucky . . .

"But we don't have to rush into things. After all, there's plenty of time."

"Oh, Benjamin . . ."

She left the thought unspoken, but he winced at it anyway. Oh, Benjamin, indeed! Yes, he *was* getting old. His health was good, always had been, but then one never knew. If he didn't arrange for his daughter's future now, he might not have another chance, and Astrid would never be able to manage things without him.

The light was almost gone now, and he could barely see her face. She had had so little savor in her life, no childhood laughter, no girlish romances to set her heart aflutter, no one great passion—if he could at least spare some measure of anguish in her later years, how could he deny her that?

And perhaps, after all, things would not work out so badly for Kristyn.

"Very well, my dear. I am sure you are right. I will tell her myself when she gets back."

Fifteen

"Oh, Rafe, it was so—so ridiculous, it was almost funny!" Kristyn stood straight-backed beside the second-floor window, staring down at the carriages that had begun to crowd the street again now that the rain had finally ended. "All those people just standing around with little cups balanced on saucers in their hands, nibbling bread and butter and listening to violins they couldn't even see! Is that what white people call fun?"

Rafe suppressed a grin as he lounged back against a small writing table, the only piece of furniture in the room except for a single bed and a chair. How piquantly waiflike she looked, with her hair damp and curling where the wind had driven rain under her hood, and her cheeks bright with color.

"If it's so funny, why don't I see you laughing?"

"Well, it's hard to laugh when everyone is pretending you're as invisible as the violins! At least, *almost* everyone."

A light shudder trembled through her body, drawing Rafe's eyes automatically, almost involuntarily, down from her face toward the softly curving lines of a frankly female form. When she had appeared at his door minutes before, his first instinct had been to turn her around and send her packing— little girls with full, kissable lips and protective fathers were Poison with a capital *P*—but a soft, pleading look in huge, misty eyes had stopped him, and against his better judgment, he had compromised, leaving the door a few inches ajar and inviting her inside. Now it had swung shut again, caught in the drafts that swept through the hallway, and Rafe found himself wondering wryly what Benjamin Ashley would say if he knew his precious daughter was alone with a man of shady repute in his hotel room.

"But not quite everyone?" he prompted, getting the conversation back on track again.

"No. Some of them seemed to see me all too clearly—especially the men. The worst was that dreadful friend of yours. That Asa Martens!"

"Asa? Now what on earth could he have done to get you so outraged?"

The words were mostly tongue in cheek. Rafe knew perfectly well what Martens had done. The poor devil had come back quite besotted from his first look at Benjamin Ashley's daughter, glimpsed through the window of the man's house when he had gone to make a courtesy call and suddenly lost his nerve. Imagine, Asa Martens losing his nerve! Since then he had been making strange noises about wanting to have the girl, *having* to have her, even if it meant doing the honorable thing. And he a lifelong bachelor at that! Ah, well, the older they got, the harder it seemed to hit them.

"He didn't exactly *do* anything," Kristyn admitted. "It was the way he looked at me—as if I were standing there in nothing but my chemise! Other men do that, too—it seems to be a 'civilized' trait—and it can be downright infuriating at times—but Asa Martens? Oh, Rafe, that man is old enough to be my father!"

"Poor bastard," Rafe said, feeling an unexpected twinge of sympathy for Asa Martens. The little witch *was* a beauty, and spirited too, even if she was the last woman in the world a man ought to consider settling down with. "Dare I surmise you haven't given him any encouragement?"

The cool sarcasm in his drawled tones made Kristyn bristle with annoyance. Really, Rafe could be so exasperating! Every time she dared to think he was her friend, every time she thought she was actually getting close to him, he would start to laugh at her or raise an ironic brow right in her face.

"You're awfully quick to take his side, aren't you? Pity he isn't as ready to stand up for you."

"No?"

There it was again, that mocking brow, forming itself into a deliberate question mark.

"No. He said you were utterly reckless, and didn't have a scruple in the world!"

Rafe only laughed, white teeth flashing suddenly against dark skin.

"Coming from a man like Asa Martens, that's a compliment."

"A compliment?" Kristyn stared at him in amazement. What was there about these white men, taking words that would have made an Indian fighting mad and turning them around with an inflection of the voice? "Was he telling the truth then? Are you really as unscrupulous as all that?"

He gave her a long, amused look.

"Asa Martens and I are in business together, my sweet little innocent, and business is always unscrupulous. He owns a railroad; I own land along the route that would be most profitable for him—we have simply gotten together to help each other out. If our methods don't always please the bankers and entrepreneurs who have other ideas about where the tracks should run . . . Well, that is their concern. But don't worry, I'm not quite as hard-hearted as I sound. I'd screw some rich bastard out of every last penny he'd put into a devious deal, or even an honest one, and I wouldn't lose a night's sleep over it, but I'll be damned if I'll squeeze the lifeblood out of dirt-poor farmers, eking a bare subsistence from the soil. That's where Asa and I part company."

His words frankly confused Kristyn, and she turned back to the window, trying to make sense out of all this talk of scruples and methods. When an Indian wanted to steal a horse from another tribe, he just went out and stole it. He didn't talk of business and deals, and try to make it sound like something it wasn't.

"Why are people so cruel, Rafe?"

His shoulders stiffened slightly at her words; then he relaxed and began to laugh softly.

"Ah, you're talking about the party again."

Kristyn nodded. "Why did they treat me like that? I didn't do anything to them. I just stood there very quietly, trying as hard as I could to be polite, and I didn't do a thing to provoke them." The memory of Eliza Shepherd made her flush a little guiltily as she recalled the look on her face when she had made up that preposterous story about white dogs with pink noses. "Well, maybe once or twice, but only when I couldn't help myself!"

Rafe's rugged features twisted into a ready grin. No, he couldn't imagine the hot-tempered vixen who had hurled rocks at him with such deadly aim meekly putting up with the eyes of boorish males, or the tongues of catty females. And, hell, would he want her to?

"Did it ever occur to you, my dear Kristyn, that some of those people might not have intended to be cruel? Don't judge us all by one or two rotten apples. How many of them do you suppose even realized you would notice their 'sidelong glances'? They probably thought they were being very subtle and surreptitious."

He spoke evenly, patiently, as one did with a small child, and when she turned to face him again, he half expected her eyes to be moody and indignant, the way they always were when she thought he was putting her down. But rather to his surprise he saw that they were dancing with suppressed laughter.

"Now you are going to give me one of those lectures of yours," she teased. "All about how I should try and be more tolerant and understanding. Do you know how I can tell? Because you call me Kristyn when you're serious and Cristina when you're teasing."

He could not help admiring her. What a sly minx she was, always giving him what he least expected. Did she know, he wondered, irrelevantly, how scandalous it was, coming to a man's hotel room like this?

"Am I really so easy to read? Say no, my pet—it's damaging to the male psyche to have women see right through you. But lecture or no, I think you have to understand that very few of the people who hurt you at the party were even aware of the fact. We do have a habit, you know, of seeing things from our own perspective, not the other person's point of view."

"But that's not fair!"

"Isn't it?" His eyes were mocking again, but gently now, almost provocatively. "I think it's only human nature. And after all, isn't that what you were doing, too?"

"How can you say that? I never set out to hurt any of those people, the way they did with me."

"Of course not. I didn't mean that. But you were looking at things from your point of view, not theirs." Almost unconsciously, his eyes crept down to the sheet of newsprint beside him on the desk, the same hastily put-out extra that Alden had obtained on the street corner. He had been appalled when Kristyn told him how people had reacted to it at the party, but he had understood, too.

"They are afraid, my dear—deeply and genuinely afraid. And not without cause. I had just started to read that confounded article when you came in, and I tell you quite frankly it was enough to make the hair stand up on the back of my neck. The victims were not soldiers or scoundrels, they were simply unarmed farmers. They had done nothing to provoke an Indian attack."

"But that was hundreds of miles from here!" Sometimes she hated him when he talked like that. Like a white man! Why did he have to make everything sound so one-sided? "How can people be afraid of something that happened so far away?"

"This atrocity, perhaps," he admitted. "But others have been nearer. There's hardly a family in the entire community that didn't lose something—property, relatives, friends—in the bitter Indian wars. How do you think your own parents felt when they came home to find their daughter missing and their sons lying dead in their own blood? That kind of thing makes people afraid."

"But the Indians are afraid, too! You think you understand us, only you don't. You came into our camp after the Blue Coats had been there, and all you saw were the bodies of strangers strewn across the ground. I saw my husband's mother, the sister of a friend, the dog I had raised from a puppy. Fear? Pah!" She spat out the word with disgust. "What were they afraid of? A girl with a cudgel or a rooting stick? Or maybe an old woman? A poor scrawny excuse for a dog?"

Her voice broke, and she turned her head away, too proud to let him see the tears that had already begun to moisten long, dark lashes. She had not realized how much it would still hurt, just thinking about that day, much less trying to speak of it.

Rafe leaned back uncomfortably against the edge of the writing table, cursing himself for bringing the subject up and not at all sure what he could have done to avoid it. The newspaper nagged at the corner of his eye and he picked it up, rolling it impatiently in his hands and tapping it against his knee.

Let the girl go, he had told the old Cheyenne, squatting in the dirt in front of his tepee. How long ago was it now, four weeks? five? *Let her go and she will have a better life.*

Damn, what an ass he had been. A better life, sure! With people who hated and distrusted her? Who didn't give a damn what she was really like inside? As long as there was one person left alive who remembered the Indian raids, what kind of life would Kristyn ever have in the white man's world?

He glanced up, surprised to see that she had turned and was watching him again. He was conscious of the tears she did not want him to see; conscious, too, that he was trying not to notice them. He thought at first that her gaze was fixed on him. Then he saw that she was looking downward, staring almost hypnotically at the newspaper in his hand.

"Oh, hell!" He unrolled the thing and glowered at it. He *had* brought the subject up—and all he could do now was see it through. "Here! You might as well have a look at it. It doesn't make a very pretty reading, but maybe it will help you understand."

Kristyn caught the paper deftly enough, but she could not keep herself from panicking as she turned it toward the light and tried, ridiculously, to pretend she was reading it. Of all the things that had happened to her, somehow this, the tacit admission of her own ignorance, was the most humiliating. But no matter how she struggled, no matter how hard she tried to make sense out of that vast jumble of letters, she could not seem to make them come together. The headline was not too hard. FAM-I-LY, she sounded out the first word—yes, that was it, family. FAMILY OF FIVE . . . but she could not get any farther.

Swallowing her pride, she forced herself to lower the newspaper and look up at him.

"I—I can't read."

"You can't . . . ?" He looked dumbfounded for a moment, then to her chagrin burst out laughing. "I had forgotten how young you were when you were taken. Of course you couldn't read yet."

"I was six years old!" she retorted hotly. How she loathed him when he acted patronizing like that! "I could read very well. I even taught my husband when we were little. And I can make out the first words in the headline—FAMILY OF FIVE. I just can't figure out what comes next."

Rafe left the desk and came over to stand beside her. Taking the paper out of her hand, he ran a quick eye across the headline.

"That's a tough one," he conceded with a grimace. "In more ways than one. It says massacred. FAMILY OF FIVE MASSA-CRED BY—INDIANS."

In reality, the headline read MASSACRED BY SAVAGES, but Rafe did not feel compelled to repeat it exactly. Not when she was looking at him with those wide, questioning eyes. He glanced hastily through the article, reading ahead as he summarized it for her.

"It seems the five of them were just sitting down to dinner when the attack occurred." No point going over that patheti-cally scant menu: bread, fried potatoes flavored with bacon-grease, weak coffee watered down from the morning—the reporter had probably made it up anyway. "There was a young couple and their three children, the eldest seven years old. By the time the neighbors found them the next day, the house and barn were smoking ashes, and the spring crops had been crudely hacked with a scythe and trampled to the earth. They think it was the work of a renegade band of . . ."

His eyes raced ahead, scanning the paragraphs he had not had time to read before. The authorities had reason to believe, the paper told him, that the raid was the work of a particu-larly violent warrior chieftain just beginning to be known.

Man-Who-Lives-with-the-Wolves.

The words seemed to leap out at him from the paper. Kristyn's husband. The young brave who had led the attack, the man who perpetrated that senseless violence, was Kristyn's husband!

Let the girl go, he had said so glibly. *Let her go,* and obviously the old man—or whatever old man had control over her destiny—had taken him at his word. They knew she would not leave her husband, of course. They had had her long enough to know how stubborn and willful she was, so they did the only thing they could. They lied to her and told her he was dead.

Impulsively, he wadded up the paper and threw it brusquely on the bed.

"Well, it's all over anyway. There's no point worrying about it now."

"But it isn't over, Rafe—not for me. Those people were killed by Cheyennes, weren't they? That's what you were going to say when you stopped. They were killed by a band of renegade Cheyennes."

Her eyes seemed to echo the question, challenging him, daring him to answer, but looking at them, all he could remember was the soft mistiness in their depths that night she first told him about her husband. She had loved the man, loved him with a kind of commitment Rafe could sense, if not truly understand, and he knew as sure as he knew she was standing there hurting in front of him that she would want to know he was alive.

But would he really be doing her a favor to tell her? She would have to go back if he did. Loyalty alone would demand that, if not love, and what would she find when she got there? A warrior who had already set his feet on the path from which there was no retreat—a man whose only destiny could be a bullet or the gallows. She had already grieved once for her young husband's death. What would it accomplish to go through all that pain again?

"No," he said abruptly. "The article didn't say anything about Cheyennes, or any other tribe for that matter. It just said a renegade band of Indians."

The sudden sharpness in his voice confused Kristyn, and she drew a little bit away from him, feeling cold and empty inside. Even Rafe, she thought miserably—even the one man who seemed to understand—could not read an article like that and look her in the eye.

"You are just like all the others! Oh, you pretend to be kind sometimes, you even force yourself to smile at me, but deep down inside you think I am just like those brutal warriors, and you despise me for it."

"Despise you?" Anger mingled with the surprise in his tone. Wasn't that just like a woman, so wrapped up in herself she didn't know what a man was all about? Reaching out impetuously, he caught her shoulders in rough male hands and drew her toward him. "Despise you, you little idiot? Are these the eyes of a man who despises you?"

His voice was light, half teasing, but there was no teasing in those dark, enigmatic eyes. Kristyn could only stand there, mesmerized by the suddenness of his move, looking up at him through quivering lashes. She was acutely conscious of everything about him: the way his hands felt on her arms, the warmth of his body so close to hers, the unfamiliar male smell of him.

"Sometimes," she murmured breathily, "I think you look at me the way Asa Martens does."

He laughed harshly.

"I'm beginning to understand the much-maligned Asa. Of course the man looks at you, my dear—how could he help it? You are a damnably beautiful woman."

And blast her, she knew it, too, the little she-devil! Rafe tightened his hold on her shoulders, tempted suddenly, irrationally, to hurt her—to thrust her forcefully away from him. His desire for her surprised him, throbbing in his groin with a familiar masculine hunger, making him feel for a moment as if he were drowning in the sultry perfume that wafted up from the heat of her body.

What was there about this woman that made him want her, even against his will? Against his better judgment? Not her beauty alone. He had known many women as beautiful as she—no, more beautiful if he were to analyze them feature by feature. But never had he seen eyes like hers before, innocent one instant, knowing the next, trusting, provocative, sad, tender, yearning—sensual. Or lips that could smile so sweetly, so girlishly, then part with all the wanton expectation of a woman of the world. Someone ought to show her what happened to little girls who played with a man's feelings. Someone ought to kiss her the way she was asking to be kissed!

Kristyn felt herself begin to tremble as he drew her roughly against his body, all hardness and sinewy muscle, challenging the softness of her own flesh. This was not the man she had come to find, she thought helplessly, the man whose comfort she had sought. This was a stranger, savage and threatening, and suddenly she was afraid of him. Naked passion mocked her from his eyes—a raw, primitive hunger, as akin to rage as desire. His breath felt hot on her face, his lips were parted, taunting, and she realized almost at the same moment he did that he was going to kiss her.

Cries of protest turned to weak moans, stifled by the hard pressure of his mouth. Anguished, she tried to free herself, but his arms held her, locked in the relentless vise of his embrace. His lips were brutal, his tongue insolent, assaulting the privacy of her mouth the way he longed to assault her body, and to her horror, she felt some deep primitive instinct in her own flesh begin to respond, urging her to cling to him even as she struggled to pull away. Terrified, she realized that he had sensed her changing mood, and manlike, it had made him bolder. His hand slipped down from her shoulder, pulling away the sheer fabric of her dress, groping arrogantly, uninvited, for her breast and finding it.

Desperately, Kristyn tried to wrench herself away, tried to focus on the treacherous shame of her own sudden reactions, but somehow, there was no strength in her. This man knew her body too well, knew it no doubt from all the other women he had used and discarded, and he played on her responses, manipulating her with his hands and mouth until she no longer even tried to resist. All she could feel now was the sensory impact of him—the rough demands of male fingers on her breast; the way strong, lean muscles seemed to surround and envelop her; the hard, arrogant thrust of his erection against her belly—and dimly she realized that this had been building between them from the first moment she had looked out of the shadows and seen him in the firelight.

A sudden flash of white lightning burst through the room, accenting the blackness of Rafe's eyes as he looked down at her, giving his lips a wry, almost cruel twist. Agitated as she was, Kristyn barely noticed the crash of thunder that followed, or even the heavy rush of raindrops against the window just inches away, but the forces of nature seemed to have a dramatic effect on Rafe. His whole face changed, taking on a brittle, self-mocking aspect, and he let her slip coolly, almost carelessly, out of his arms.

"And that, my dear, is what little girls can expect when they come to a man's hotel room. Now, if you're smart, you'll hike up that frilly skirt and run out of here as fast as your feet will carry you. Unless, of course, you're curious to see what comes next."

"Curious?"

For an instant, Kristyn could only stand there and gape at him. Curious! Was that all it was to him? A game? Some kind of egotistical male bet with himself to see how quickly he could break down her resistance? And, oh, God, she had let him win easily, hadn't she?

Sick with shame and resentment, she began to stumble toward the door, clumsily, unthinking, not even stopping to remember that he had pulled her bodice off her shoulder and her breast was still half exposed. She did not know how her fur-lined cloak got around her body, she only knew that suddenly it was there and he was standing beside her, pressing a crisp new bill into her hand to pay for a hired carriage.

"And don't ever kiss a man like that. Not unless you mean it."

The sound of his laughter echoed in her ears as she raced down the stairway and through the half-filled lobby, already beginning to bustle with the fashionably dressed men and women who had gathered for the cocktail hour. An anemic-looking clerk half rose from his chair at the sight of her, then settled back to his habitual lethargy, his briefly suspicious eye reassured by the stylish lines of her coiffure and her obviously expensive cloak. The management did not object to a gentleman entertaining a lady caller in his room—as long as she was the sort who did not make the other ladies nervous!

Outside, Kristyn found a carriage waiting by the door, and after giving the coachman her father's address, she sank gratefully into the cushions, her heart pounding so loudly she was certain everyone in the street would be able to hear it. The rain seemed to come and go, sometimes letting up almost entirely, sometimes pelting down so heavily she could not see out of the glassed-in window.

Oh, why had she gone there? she berated herself bitterly. And why, *why*, had she let him do this to her? He didn't want her, he had made that clear; he would never have let her go if he did. And yet—she knew if he were there at that moment, if he opened his arms and let her come, sobbing, into them, she could not keep it from beginning all over again.

What a naive child she had been before she met him! She had thought she knew what love was; she had even thought she had experienced it herself, in different ways, first with Running Deer, then with the young brave she had eventually married. Only love was more than the quickening of the senses that had drawn her toward her first suitor, more even than the tender feelings she had shared with her husband. Love was a total, all-consuming passion, an emotion that captured your heart and your body—yes, and your soul, too—sweeping you away, whether you wanted it or not. An emotion she now realized she could experience only with one man.

And that was a man who would never want her!

The rain pounded dismally on twilit streets, accentuating

the gray bleakness that seemed to hang over Kristyn's heart. How bitter to realize that she truly cared for Rafe at almost the same moment she realized she must lose him. Soon his business in town would be over—and honesty compelled her to admit now that only business held him there—and she would never see him again. She let her head fall back against the window, cold from the rain outside, and tried not to feel anything but the jolting of the carriage as the wheels creaked slowly, drawing her closer and closer to home.

Benjamin was waiting for her in the entry hall when she returned, standing just inside the doorway to the silent parlor. The look on his face, ashen and somehow older, reminded Kristyn guiltily of the terrible worry her parents must have gone through when she bolted impulsively out of the house. Panicking for a moment, she realized what she must look like. Her hair—would he believe those stray curls were the effect of the wind? And what if he tried to get her to take off her cloak? Her dress was badly disheveled, still hanging half-on, half-off her shoulder, and the creamy whiteness of her breast would tell him all too clearly what had gone on between her and Rafe.

"I—I'm sorry," she murmured hastily. "I didn't mean to run away like that. It's just that I—I wanted to take a walk."

If he noticed that her cloak was only slightly damp despite the heavy periodic rain, he said nothing about it. Indeed, his eyes did not even seem to focus, as if he could not quite bring himself to look at her, and Kristyn felt the first vague stirrings of apprehension tug at her heart.

"No, child, I am the one who is sorry," he said quietly. "This afternoon was unpardonable. Your mother and I should have realized what would happen. It's just that she wanted so much for everything to work out, and I . . . well, I always seem to have a blind spot when it comes to Astrid. But it will not happen again, I promise you. We have settled on a much better way to arrange your future."

"To—*arrange* my future?" Kristyn felt the chill deepen in her heart. Something in the way he said the words gave them a faintly ominous sound—or was it the fact that he still couldn't seem to look her in the eye?

"You must trust me to do what is right, Kristyn. I know it may seem hard sometimes, but I am older than you and I know what is best. I have been approached by someone—a good man, very substantial—and he has asked me for your hand. We have given the matter a great deal of thought, your mother and I, and we have decided you should be married.''

Married.

The word sounded strange, almost unreal in her ears. *Married?* Of all the things he could have said, that was the one she least expected. Who in that entire town would want to marry her? And how could she give herself to any man now that she had just realized where her heart truly lay?

Dismay was written on her features as she stared at her father. Could he do this to her? Did a white man have that kind of control over his daughter that he could tell her, Arrange your future this way, Marry the man I have chosen, and she would not have the right to say yes or no?

And if he did, what kind of man would he choose?

''Who . . .'' She choked on the words, having trouble forcing them out. ''Who is this man who wants me?''

He looked up at last, meeting her gaze with eyes that were veiled and unreadable.

''Asa Martens.''

Sixteen

It was, Rafe had decided, coldly assessing the situation, time to get out of there.

His saddlebags were spread out on the bed, and he had already begun to roll up shirts and spare pairs of pants, stuffing them inside with no particular attempt at order. He had only stayed in the first place because he felt responsible. Not that any of this was his fault, but there it was—he had brought the girl here, and he could not forget the way she looked when he dumped her on her parents' doorstep, wide-eyed and frightened, like a small child being sent to live with strangers.

So he had stayed—and what the hell had it gotten them, either himself or her? He could have been in Dodge by now. Dammit, he *should* have been there! Carlos would have been expecting him days ago; by now he must be pacing the floor of his hotel room, alternately impatient or worried. As for that sly little baggage he had brought along with him—well, Rafe would be willing to bet his brother was having the devil of a time keeping her out of mischief in that bawdy hellhole.

Sly little baggage, yes, that was the term for Ysabel. The corners of his mouth turned up slightly as he stowed the last of his belongings into the saddlebags and closed them securely. Carlos would have his hands full with that one. Maybe he should have taken her up on her offer that night she came to his room and threw herself into his arms. He would have saved his brother a hell of a lot of grief, and he wouldn't have all those unsatisfied male hungers clouding his judgment now!

The rain beat down on the window, hardening into hail-stones that tapped a brittle tattoo on the glass. If it hadn't been for the weather, he asked himself wryly, if it hadn't been for the lightning, the crash of thunder that seemed to shake the entire room, would he have come to his senses when he did? Always before he had been so cool-headed with women, taking the ones he wanted, turning his back on the ones who spelled trouble. What was getting into him now? By God, he was almost as dotty as old Asa Martens, panting after forbidden fruit, just because it was forbidden—only he was damned if he was going to offer up his freedom in the process! Give him a man's life any day, open ranges with the feel of wildness in the wind and a rough wooden cabin at the end of the day. No nagging wife for him, thank you, no whining children always underfoot, no domesticity, sweet or otherwise—he'd stick with his own kind of woman.

Not that Kristyn was such a far cry from what he was looking for. He picked up the saddlebags and slung them over his shoulder. What a lascivious creature she had turned out suddenly, quite unexpectedly, to be. Against his will, Rafe felt himself begin to grow hard again, teased by the memory of the way she had let her thighs press against him, the way her lips had softened under his. She *was* his kind of woman— she just didn't know it yet. Perhaps in a year or two, when she had learned not to be afraid of her own passions, when she had already taken her first lover . . .

Dammit, it *was* time to get out of there. He tossed the saddlebags in a heap by the door, irritated with where his thoughts were taking him. Next thing he'd be telling himself that it wouldn't be so bad, having a pretty woman in a frilly apron waiting for him at the end of a long day. That it would be worth whatever it cost to be the first—the *only*—man to know the fiery passions just beginning to awaken in that deliciously female breast.

He had just turned back to the window, checking out the rain and hoping it would let up before morning, when suddenly the door burst open. Startled, he looked around to see Kristyn standing on the threshold. The lamplight in the hall was brighter than the room, and backlit, her hair seemed to float around her face like dark red flames.

His first thought, perversely, irrationally, was—She couldn't stay away from me any more than I can keep myself from her! Then he got a look at her face, wild-eyed, frenzied, almost desperate, and his body went stiff with alarm.

"Damn!"

He was not even aware that he spoke the word aloud as he hurried over to her. Her cloak was nearly saturated, her face so wet he could not tell if those were tears or raindrops shining on her lashes. What a bastard he had been, what a confounded ass, sending her out alone so close to dusk! If anything had happened to her—if anyone had hurt her . . .

But her first words dispelled that fear.

"Oh, Rafe, my—my father . . ."

Had some ill befallen Benjamin, then? An accident? A heart attack? But no, the anguish Rafe saw in her face was too real, too intense, for that. Kristyn did not know her father that well yet; she had not formed the kind of ties that would make her so distraught. Whatever had occurred, it had to be something far more personal.

Then slowly, the irony of it began to dawn on him.

He had wondered what Benjamin Ashley would do if he knew his daughter was alone in a hotel room with a man of shady repute. Well, now he had his answer. He would do his damnedest to marry her off to someone else!

"So Asa has made his move, has he?"

Kristyn stood in the doorway, watching the cool, sardonic amusement on his face, and for a moment she was too dazed to make any sense out of it. What was he saying? And why was he looking at her like that? She had run madly through the storm, desperate to tell him what had happened, and here he was, acting like it was no surprise at all.

As, no doubt, it wasn't!

"You knew all along, didn't you?" Her voice was dull, catching in her throat. "You knew that Asa Martens wanted to marry me and my father was going to agree."

Oh, how could she have been so stupid! She knew Rafe did not care about her—hadn't he made that plain enough?—and still she didn't have the sense to stay away from him. She had not even known she was coming there. She had just raced blindly through the streets, letting her feet carry her where they would, and traitors that they were, they had brought her right to him!

And he, true to form, had been only too ready to make light of her!

Choking on her humiliation, she spun away from him, not even seeing where she was going as she plunged through the doorway and out into the hall. All she wanted now was to get away from him, to hide from the terrible, shaming realization that she had made a fool of herself for the second time that day.

Then suddenly his arms were around her, drawing her back into the room, pushing the door shut behind her. Suddenly, her wet cloak seemed to be spread out on the chair, and she was sitting beside him on the bed, leaning her head against his shoulder, forgetting completely that only a second before she had hated him and wanted nothing so much as to hate him for the rest of her life!

The feel of his body was surprisingly sweet against hers, gentle now, not hard and demanding as it had been before, and she let herself give in to her emotions, daring to trust him, even against all reason. His lips touched her forehead lightly, barely perceptibly, covering her brow and hair with surprisingly tender kisses, and she realized suddenly, elatedly, that all that mocking coldness was only a facade. He did care for her! He couldn't bring himself to admit it, but he cared. And he wanted her, just as she wanted him!

She pulled away slowly, an unconsciously seductive smile playing on her lips as a half-formed plan began to take shape in her mind. She still did not know if her father had the right to force her to marry against her will, but she was not afraid of him anymore. Rafe was stronger than Benjamin Ashley, and Rafe would never let him do that to her.

Not when he learned that she wanted to belong to him.

Oh, he might not want to marry her. She was wise enough in the ways of the white man's world by now to realize that her background hardly qualified her as a wife, and besides, men like Rafe seemed to show more than a typical aversion for matrimony. But marriage did not truly matter to her. All she wanted was to follow this man when he rode away, stay with him wherever he went, share the cravings of his body as she felt sure he would share the longings of her heart. What, after all, would be the greater shame: living openly with a man she adored, or legally with one she despised?

And if he did not love her, at least not right away—well that did not matter either. Surely she had love enough in her heart for both of them.

She raised her hand slowly to the lace-trimmed neck of her

dress, holding it there for the space of a single heartbeat. Then she eased the fabric off her shoulder.

The naked emotion that flashed through his eyes told her that Rafe had not misread the gesture, and she did not need words to know that he had begun to desire her again. She thought for an instant he was going to reach out and rip the dress off her body, but when he moved, it was only to catch hold of her hand.

"I am not a marrying man, Cristina," he warned her, his voice low in his throat.

Cristina. She knew then that she had won, even before he was aware of it himself.

"Yes, I know that."

"God help us both, I am too much of a man not to respond to you—and too little of a gentleman to worry about the niceties. If you slip that pretty dress off your body, I will take you right here on this bed, without stopping to wonder if you really mean it. And don't think I'll feel guilty enough to ask you to marry me in the morning."

She drew her hand back and, rising, stood beside the bed.

"Maybe," she whispered huskily, "I am not a marrying woman."

She fumbled with the fastenings of her dress, but only briefly, tugging them loose with fingers that trembled not from fear or doubt but from the longing she knew they both shared. The lacy gown slipped easily from her body, landing with a soft, rustling sound on the floor. Stepping out of it, she kicked it aside with her foot. No stiff corset laced her in; her waist was slim enough, her bosom high and firm without it. Only the thin fabric of her chemise veiled her from his gaze.

She knew, almost instinctively, what she looked like to him at that moment; yet instinct was not necessary, for she could see herself mirrored in the feverish darkness of his eyes. Tall; slender, but not too slender; her long legs coming together in a triangular shadow beneath that filmy whiteness; her breasts a perfect outline, slightly darker in the center where erect nipples teased the sheer fabric. Then she raised her hand again, and with a few deft movements, even that veil was gone.

A cold draft chilled the air, but Rafe's eyes were hot and searing on her body, warming every inch of skin they caressed.

An answering heat seemed to surge through her veins, burning her breasts, her belly, her limbs, catching on fire in that sweet, secret spot between her thighs where she longed to feel his strength. She held herself away from him one last second, conscious that he had not yet reached out to her, that she could still change her mind if she was afraid. But his needs had become her needs, his longings her longings, and even had her mind been clear enough to counsel caution, her body would not tolerate retreat. Slowly, achingly, she opened her arms and went to him.

A low moan escaped his lips as he buried his head in the ripe softness of her bosom. Rough male cheeks rasped her tender skin, a male mouth, hard and hungry, opened to suck her greedily inside. He was demanding now, brutal as he had been once before, but this time Kristyn did not resist. This time she was a willing, eager captive to the crushing weight that pushed her backward, pinning her against the yielding mattress. Wanton hands—could they be her own?—tugged at his clothes, helping to rip them off, joining her own nakedness to the raw masculine power of his flesh.

They needed no tender words, no sweet caresses to arouse them; their passion was abrupt and savage, all the more exciting for its savagery. Kristyn thrilled to the hard muscles in his chest and shoulders, the lean hardness of his thighs as he forced them between her legs, urging them apart. He hurt her when he entered her, for her body was almost new to lovemaking, but the pain was fleeting, over almost before it began, and soon she found herself sweeping along on tides so swift and turbulent she could think of nothing, feel nothing, but her need for the sweet fulfillment that broke in her body at last, leaving her weak and shivering in its wake.

Afterward, lying beside him, their arms still twined around each other, it seemed to Kristyn that her heart would never stop pounding wildly against her chest. How gentle he was, how wonderfully, unexpectedly tender, now that his passion was spent and he could hold her lightly in his arms, reminding her with his hands and lips of the sweet ecstasy they had shared. What joy to wake up next to this man every morning and feel the mingled strength and gentleness of him beside her on the bed!

"Oh, Rafe, it's going to be so perfect when you take me away with you," she murmured dreamily, forgetting in the haze of contentment that she had not yet shared her secret plans with him. "We will be so happy with each other, won't we?"

Even when he pulled away, propping himself up on one elbow to gaze down at her, she did not realize what she had said, or stop to think how he might have taken it. Only when she looked up and saw the faintly ironical curve to his lips did she begin to be alarmed.

"I did warn you, my dear," he said dryly. "I am not about to let myself be hauled up in front of a preacher."

So that was it! Kristyn almost smiled at his words. How funny he was, how transparent, when he defended his male independence like that.

"Is that what you are afraid of? That I am going to try to bully you into marrying me? But I told you I wouldn't, and I meant it. You don't have to make me any promises. All I want you to do is take me away with you when you leave this place—and keep me as long as I please you."

Her pulse quickened, and she arched closer, waiting for the sound of male laughter deep in his throat, the feel of his willing surrender as he drew her tight against his body again. But to her surprise, he only pulled farther away, looking down at her with eyes that were distinctly amused.

"Did you really think I was planning to take you with me, Cristina? Or were you only sure you could convince me once I had tasted your seductive charms? Either way, I'm afraid you're going to be disappointed."

For a moment Kristyn could only stare at him, stunned.

"But—but, Rafe . . ." How could he talk to her like that? So cool and mocking, as if she were nothing at all to him? Surely he didn't mean what he was saying. He couldn't! "After what we have been to each other . . . after the way I felt in your arms . . ."

"And you think that's all it takes?" His lips curled up in an insulting grin. "Fire a man up to a fever pitch, slake his passions in your soft, yielding flesh, and he'll be putty in your hands forever! Ah, but it doesn't work that way, or there wouldn't be a bachelor left in the world. There are men who can accept a woman's favors, quite comfortably, and not feel a qualm in the morning. I thought I had made that perfectly clear before you began that delightfully uninhibited striptease of yours."

Oh, how it hurt, the laughter in his voice! Kristyn lay alone on the bed, feeling waves of humiliation flood over her as she watched him walk over to the window and stare out into the night. He was a monster, a beast, using her like that, with no concern for her feelings—and yet, heaven help her, she could not hate him the way she should! After all, he *had* warned her, and she had chosen to ignore him. Chosen instead to pretend that somehow, miraculously, everything would be all right after one breathtaking night of love.

His body looked lean and hard in the lamplight, stirring unwanted feelings in her breast, and Kristyn found herself wondering suddenly, bitterly, what would hurt most in years to come—the memory of the way he had laughed at her tonight . . . or the realization that she would never feel those strong, masculine arms around her again.

"Oh, please . . . please, don't leave me. I will do anything you want, *be* anything you want . . ."

Her voice caught, and she broke off, sensing that pleading would only annoy him. Still, it was true. She *would* do anything to keep from losing him. How could she let this man go without a fight?

"A willing slave?" she teased, forcing a new lightness into her tone. "What more can any man ask? If I promise to cook for you, clean for you, greet you always with a sweet temper— well, almost always—and never, never make any demands on you, then will you take me with you?"

Rafe stood silently beside the window, still looking outward. Nothing in the erect set of his shoulders betrayed the fact that he had heard the tears in her voice, or that they had angered him. What was it about women that always made them challenge a man with weapons he could not use?

The rain began to slacken again, and shadowy figures scurried along the street below, their heads bent against the biting wind. It gave him a certain perverse satisfaction to imagine the shock in their eyes if one of them should happen to look up and see him standing in the lighted window, completely naked and visible from the waist up. No doubt the management would have something to say about that in the morning!

Take her with him? The idea was surprisingly tempting, now that it had taken hold in his mind. It could be damned lonely on the road. Days of empty land with not another human being in sight. And even the towns he came to—well hell, one whore started to look like another after a while. There was no real excitement in that; there hadn't been since the days when he was an adolescent and sex had still been new to him. But with a woman like Kristyn beside him, sharing the same blanket roll, pressing her soft feminine warmth against him in the long, cold nights . . .

In spite of himself, he felt his body begin to respond, giving in to the strong male urges that had always been a dominant part of his makeup. Lucky the windowsill was so high, he thought with a wry twist of his lips. A few inches lower and the management would be pounding on the door right now, probably with a policeman in tow.

Yes, the idea was a tempting one. He could almost see the look on Carlitos' face when he rode into Dodge with Kristyn at his side. Surprised, dubious—faintly disapproving. And Ysabel? By God, it would almost be worth it just to see the fire flashing out of that comely little witch's eyes!

And, after all, why not?

He turned back toward the bed. Kristyn's hair had come loose, spilling around her on the sheets, and he was struck by the astonishing pinkness of her: soft pale breasts and belly reflecting the deeper firetones of her tresses. She was lying to him, of course—she *would* make demands, would even press, woman-like, for marriage sooner or later—but when she did, he would tire of her, and then it would be easy to let her go, salving his conscience with money and freeing his body at last from this obsessive need for her.

He was not even aware that he had started toward her until he felt his toe brush against something soft and, startled, he glanced down to see the wadded-up newspaper on the floor beside the bed. Why not, indeed? The answer had been there all the time, lying at his feet, if only he had had the sense to see it. Sooner or later, Kristyn was going to figure out how to read those half familiar letters, and when she did, when she learned the name of that young renegade chieftain, she was certain to remember how he had faltered halfway through the article today. He understood enough of her heart by now to realize that she would never forgive him if she learned he had taken her away knowing her husband was still alive.

No, better to let her go now while they could still part friends.

"Stay here where you belong, pretty Christina. I have too far to go to take a woman with me. And you would be a fool to come, even if I asked you."

Kristyn's heart sank at the low-pitched finality in his tone. A minute ago, when he had come toward her, she dared to let herself hope. But then he had stopped, half a room away, and all she could see now was distance in his eyes.

"Then I—I have to do as my father says? I have to marry—*him*?"

"You have to marry someone, my dear. You are a woman, and like it or not, a woman cannot get along in this world without the protection of a man. Unless, of course, she has the qualifications to be a schoolmarm—which you haven't—or can sing like an angel and go on the stage. A man does not necessarily mean a husband, of course, but if I were you, I would give serious consideration to the thought that husbands tend to be more reliable than lovers."

"Oh, but Rafe . . . *Asa Martens*!"

Rafe laughed disconcertingly.

"You say it like he was an adder snake. Asa is not a bad man, in his own way, and I think he would be kind to you. You could do far worse." He paused, his eyes turning positively wicked as he looked down at her. "Or are you afraid he won't know how to tap the raging passions in that shamelessly wanton body? Don't worry—if he doesn't, I predict you'll cuckold him within the month."

Bright patches of red showed in her cheeks as she turned away, trying not to hear the lewd insinuation in his tone, trying desperately not to see how his eyes ran insolently all the way from her head down to the tips of her toes.

"You make it sound so—so cold."

"It is cold, or at least it ought to be. Marriage is a business for women, just like ranching and railroading for men. Don't let a moment of hot passion tempt you into a lifetime of regret. Besides—" he grinned maddeningly— "Asa is out of town a great deal, and you can have as many lovers as you like. If you're lucky, maybe he'll die young and leave you a very rich widow."

Kristyn turned away, burying her head in the pillow. She recognized in his barbed wit a not-unkind attempt to tease her out of her misery, but she hated it all the same. Bitterly, she forced herself to acknowledge that he was right. She *was* going to have to take a husband. No doubt that was what Benjamin had been trying to tell her, too, in his own way, with his gruff voice and downcast eyes—that there were realities in the world no one could change for her. And if she had to marry a man she did not love, surely Asa Martens would do as well as any other.

But to commit herself to him forever, to give away all her hopes of true happiness with only one brief hour of memories to sustain her—no, that she could not do.

She raised her eyes, soft and misty like a foggy morning. If Rafe would give her only this one night of himself, she was going to experience it to the fullest.

"Come back to me, my love. I want you beside me on the bed."

He took a step toward her, almost automatically, as if he had not quite realized what she said.

"Cristina . . ."

She reached up, laying her fingers lightly on his lips. So many things she longed to say, so many words of love, but now was not the time. One wrong move, and she would lose even these last precious minutes with him.

"How am I to attract these lovers you predict for me if you will not teach me how to love a man?"

He hesitated briefly, as if his mind were saying no even as his body cried out *yes*! Then, surrendering to the stronger of the impulses, he sat on the edge of the bed and gazed down at her.

"If I teach you anything, beautiful Cristina, it will not be how to love a man, but how to make a man love you. You are a passionate, sensual woman, even if you are only beginning to realize that now. There will always be pleasure for the man you look upon with favor. Never be afraid of demanding pleasure from him in return."

His hands were achingly tender as he tangled them in her hair, spreading the long strands out like a dark, flowing river on the bed. For the first time in his life, he wished he were skilled with a brush and oils—he would have liked to capture the color and form of her at that moment and keep it with him forever. Shimmering hair, dark brown in the shadows, dancing with flames in the lamplight; cream-hued skin, faintly tinged with warm flesh tones where the sun had never touched it, deeper, almost golden on her face and throat and arms;

blue eyes, so dazzling they looked unreal. What palette could hold all those subtle, vibrant shadings? What brush could capture the silken texture of her tresses, the softness of her skin, the almost perfect roundness of her breasts?

"Portrait of a Wanton," that was what he would call it—yet even had he the skill, would he dare to attempt his masterpiece? It was not Kristyn's features, which could indeed be transferred to canvas, that made her such a striking beauty, but rather the turbulent mercurial spirit just beneath that pretty surface. No painting could do justice to eyes that were like quicksilver, changing from softness to brooding passion, then back again, all in the space of a single second. Or catch that faint hint of a quiver on full, parted lips.

Leaning forward, he brushed his mouth gently against her cheek.

A light tremor ran through Kristyn's body as she sensed the subdued intensity of his touch. Reaching up with her hands, she tried to hold on to him, to draw him even closer, but he slipped away, leaving her with nothing but the elusive memory of rough male whiskers against her fingertips.

Everything about him was rough and male. Kristyn lay silently on the bed, letting her eyes take in all the rugged masculinity of his body. His leanness was deceptive, for she could see the strong, rippling muscles in his chest and shoulders clearly now. But his waist was slender, his hips even slimmer than they had looked in tight denim pants. Black hair tangled across his chest, accenting sheer virility, then narrowed to a thin line running down his stomach toward . . .

Catching her breath, Kristyn let her eyes follow, lingering at last on the ultimate proof of his maleness, swollen and hard in his renewed need for her. She had never been bold enough to look openly at that part of a man before—her young husband had not encouraged it on their first, their *only* night of marriage—and she was startled to see now how big, how threatening, he seemed. And yet, that very largeness, that very threat, was capable of giving her the most excruciating pleasure.

She raised her hand tentatively, daring to touch him.

A quick, responsive intake of breath told her that the light touch of her fingers had excited him. But to her surprise, he took her hand and drew it gently away.

"What an impatient little girl you are. So you think *that* is the instrument of all your pleasure, do you? Well, my sweet, you are wrong."

Kristyn squirmed uncomfortably. His words so exactly mirrored her thoughts of a moment before.

"But that *is* the instrument of my pleasure, Rafe—you know it is! You are only teasing me."

"No, you adorable child, it is not. You want a lesson in love? Well, you shall have it. This is the instrument you are longing for." He raised his hand to his brow. "And this." Then his lips. "And this, and this—and this. My entire body, from my head to my toes, is there to please you. Just as your entire body was created to receive pleasure. Not just that sweet, warm temptation between your legs."

He half raised her from the pillows, twisting her body around in powerful arms, then coaxing her back, face downward, on the bed. All the while his lips toyed with her, planting light kisses on her hair, her cheeks, her ears.

"But, Rafe . . ."

"Shhhh, darling, stop struggling so. You said you wanted this, remember? Now relax and let me give it to you."

"But what—what are you doing?"

His hands seemed to be playing strange games with her, not touching her the way she expected at all, but caressing her shoulders, running lightly down her arms, massaging the tension out of every weary muscle. Not erotic, not overtly so, but somehow intensely personal.

"I am teaching you what it is to be a woman. And reminding myself what it means to be a man."

His fingers were soft, but provocative—so provocative Kristyn thought she could hardly bear it. How could her skin tingle so when he was barely touching it? How could the feel of him be so sensual against her shoulders, the back of her neck—and ah, what sweetness when his mouth followed, teasing her with lips and tongue.

"Oh, Rafe . . ."

"No, sweet, hush. No words. Just close your eyes and lie there . . . and let yourself feel."

Downward, slowly downward, his hands savored every inch, knowing her and teaching her to know herself. Her back, how smooth it was beneath his caressing fingertips; her buttocks were gently rounded, trembling slightly as he explored them with unembarrassed intimacy. Even her legs seemed to burn with the heat of his sweet assault, her calves, her ankles, the very tips of her toes.

The slowness of his movements was a temptation and an agony both, giving excitement and withholding it all at the same time, and Kristyn could barely contain herself when at last he turned her over, gazing down at her with dark passion in his eyes. Oh, the feel of his hands now, hard against the softness of her breast, the tantalizing moisture of his tongue playing with a nipple that seemed to leap up to meet it. All her body was his now: her belly, her hips, her thighs, wet with longing for him. Then at last—at last!—his fingers touched her where she longed to be touched, challenging, provoking, moving suddenly in the most unexpected ways.

"Oh-h-h . . ."

She could not believe the way he made her feel, shameless and seared with longing.

"You—you mustn't do that."

"Mustn't I?" Laughter mingled with passion in those dark eyes now. "Why not?"

"Because it's—it's . . ." Oh, how could she make him understand? Before, their lovemaking had been impulsive, unplanned. Now suddenly it seemed so premeditated. "Because it's—sinful!"

"Sinful?" His voice was muffled with amusement. "How quick you are to pick up the follies of our culture. Sin, my sweet child, is a commodity that belongs to the devil, not to a mature man and woman who genuinely, caringly, want to give pleasure to each other."

He drew her closer, one hand resting with deceptive lightness on the small of her back, the other still tormenting her with provocative impudence.

"Ah, Cristina, Cristina, don't you know yet that your body was made for love? There is no shame in that. Sensuality is as much a part of your nature as the need to draw air into your lungs. You can no more deny it than you can deny me now."

In his husky, whispered tones, Kristyn sensed the truth, and no longer could she resist the sweet yearnings that ebbed and swelled in response to his skillful fingers. She did not know if he was right about sin, she did not even know for sure what the devil was—she only knew that her body loved him at that moment, craved him, would not have let her draw away even had she had the will to try. Perfection was within her grasp, and she reached for it, catching it suddenly, almost unexpectedly, clinging to it for one brief moment before it slipped away. His arms were like a cradle then, holding her, rocking her, easing away the aching emptiness as she drifted back to reality again.

"So that is what you meant," she said softly, finding her voice at last, "when you said you were going to teach me about my body—and yours."

"That is part of what I meant."

He leaned over her, his weight half resting on her. She could feel his desire now, see it in the dark eyes that ravished her flesh, and to her surprise, she began to respond. It had not occurred to her that she could want him again so soon. Was that what it meant to be a woman? Not the tender yearnings she had first tasted on her wedding night, not even the savage culmination she had known with Rafe, but this terrible, consuming hunger that would never be completely slaked.

Her arms twisted around him, even without her knowing it. Her heart cried out for the sweetness of his touch. If this was to be their only time together, if this was all she would ever know of him, she did not want to spend it being taught anything else. She wanted what she had already learned—the power of him strong and hard inside her.

"What—" she barely dared whisper the words—"what are you going to do now?"

For a second, only a second, his eyes seemed to laugh again.

"I am going to love you—the way you were meant to be loved."

Seventeen

The next morning Kristyn sat alone in the front parlor, waiting for Asa Martens to make the call they both knew was only a formality. White morning light gave the room a stark look, washing out its vibrant colors and showing up dull patches where the carpet had started to wear thin.

She had told her father the night before that she was ready to do his bidding, or rather she had told him early that morning, for the first hints of gray had already begun to lighten the sky by the time she slipped back into the house. Benjamin had not been waiting up for her, as she had feared, but he must have been lying awake in his room, for no sooner had she closed the door softly behind her than she saw him coming down the stairs, hastily knotting the sash of a dark burgundy dressing gown around his ample waist. One look at her flushed cheeks had been enough to tell him what had happened, if indeed he had any doubts by that late hour, but he did not say anything, nor did Kristyn try to confide in him. The years of separation, all the bonds that had never developed between them, made them shy with each other, unable to speak of things that touched the heart.

"I have made up my mind," was all she had said. "I am willing to marry Asa Martens if you think I should."

Now all that remained was the proposal itself: a mere formality—a polite query on his part, a polite response on hers, and it would all be over. Kristyn raised her eyes from the silver tea service Astrid had arranged artfully on a low table in front of her and took in every detail of the room: the cluttered furnishings, the heavy velvet draperies, the line of photographs on the mantelpiece. She had not liked the parlor when she first saw it, and she had not changed her opinion in the intervening time, but now that she was about to leave it for another home, she was surprised to find herself feeling something akin to affection even for the overgaudy flowers on the carpet. How much easier it was to cling to the familiar than venture into the unknown!

The sound of voices in the hallway warned her that her suitor had arrived, and she sat absolutely still, a tight feeling constricting her throat as she listened. She knew she was being silly. Nothing was going to happen that day. Nothing of substance. Martens would simply say what he had come to say, hear what he had come to hear, then he would go away and leave her alone again. Why then was her heart pounding so violently against her chest? Her head so light she felt as if she must surely swoon?

Then the voices faded away and only the sound of a clock ticking somewhere in another room broke the stillness. Suddenly, Kristyn realized that Martens was standing in the doorway, staring in at her. She had not raised her eyes, but she knew he was there. She could sense it.

It was all she could do to force herself to look up.

Yes, he was there, just where she had known he would be, on the threshold, gazing inward. There was something unexpected in his bearing, something subdued, almost—uncertain? But why should Asa Martens be uncertain? Surely Benjamin had told him he was not going to be refused. Otherwise, why would he have come?

Yet that same uncertainty was there as he took a step forward, then hesitated. His voice, when he spoke, seemed thinner than usual.

"What a pleasure to see sunlight streaming through the windows. I had begun to think it was going to rain forever, but here it is, quite lovely again."

In spite of herself, Kristyn almost smiled. Of course, the weather! How predictable these white people were. Whenever they didn't know what else to say, they always talked about the weather. Not anything important, like how the smell of moisture in the air might affect wild game, but always the obvious—whether it was raining or whether the sun was shining.

"Yes, it is quite lovely, isn't it?"

"I think spring has finally arrived. I must say it took its time this year, but the air is definitely balmy."

"It does seem nicer than usual. I hope you are right. I am ready for spring."

She leaned forward, placing one of the dainty china cups on a saucer and drawing it toward her. Really, Asa Martens did look strange, standing in front of her like that. If she had not known he was a powerful railroad magnate, she might have taken him for a humble farmer or a small shopkeeper in town. He had dressed in a surprisingly formal black suit, tailored in the latest fashion, but neither black nor fashion became him, and she sensed he knew it.

"May I offer you a cup of tea, Mr. Martens?" she said, surprised to find herself taking charge of the conversation. "There are some little cakes, too, if you like, although I'm afraid there still isn't anything to sink your teeth into."

He smiled appreciatively, stepping forward and resting his hands against the back of one of the chairs.

"Just tea, please. That will be fine. I see you're not going to let me live down that rude remark about your mother's table." He wished, just for once, Astrid had given up her slavish devotion to style and served something more palatable in her drawing room. He could have used a strong cup of coffee, preferably with a shot of brandy in it.

"Do you take it with milk, Mr. Martens?"

"Thank you, no."

"Sugar then?"

"No, nothing. You will find when you know me better, Miss Ashley, that I am a plain man with very simple tastes."

A plain man . . . He was ironically aware as he reached out to take the cup from her hand, just how aptly he had described himself. He *was* plain, although he was not used to having people see him that way. Money and power had long since colored his appearance in the eyes of others, and he dared hope it was that way with this woman, too.

Still, there was something in her eyes as she looked up and saw him hovering behind the chair. Something that made him wonder if he had not underestimated her.

"Are you waiting for me to ask you to sit down, Mr. Martens? You have me at a disadvantage, you know. I have noticed that white men get up when a woman enters the room, but women remain seated in the presence of men. Is that because it gives you a sense of power, looking down on us?"

"Looking down on you? What an extraordinary notion!" Almost in spite of himself, Martens was intrigued. A moment ago, when he first entered the room, he could have sworn she was frightened. Now she was showing a quite astonishing will of her own. "But that is supposed to be good manners. Of course, I must wait for you to ask me to be seated—and of course, I will do so now since you have requested it. If your mother caught me behaving any other way, she would run me clean out of the house."

He seated himself on a chair, balancing the saucer gingerly on one knee as he watched her pour out another dose of the weak amber liquid for herself, moving as deftly and gracefully as if she had been serving tea all her life. By God, he had to give Astrid credit—she might have her foolish vanities, but she had certainly worked wonders with the girl, and in an amazingly short time at that. He could still remember the way Kristyn had looked that first night when he had glimpsed her secretly, furtively, through lamplit windowpanes. Restless and trapped, like a wild animal snared in a cage . . . yet even then so beautiful, so strikingly, breathtakingly beautiful.

"You look very lovely this morning. But then, you always do. That gown is particularly becoming. I like what the color does to your eyes."

"Thank you. I am told it is azure."

"Yes, azure . . . well, I daresay it is. I don't know much about colors or fashions. I only know what I like, and I like the way that looks on you. It is very flattering."

"So my mother tells me. She chose the color especially for me."

Chose more than the color, I'll warrant! he thought, watching the way the silken fabric clung to her body as she moved. Surprising Astrid. So lacking in judgment when it came to her own clothes, yet absolutely, intuitively right about her daughter's. She knew just how much bosom to show and how much to keep hidden away. Ordinarily, Martens had no liking for these new-fangled bustles, much preferring the frothy femininity of an old-fashioned crinoline, but something about the way the soft folds caressed Kristyn's hips . . .

"Your mother has superb taste. I must remember to compliment her."

What a cool look she gave him, so utterly self-contained.

"She will like that, I am sure."

Yes, cool, even as she leaned forward, exposing tantalizingly deep cleavage for a brief instant to his hungry eyes. Cool now—but not cool later. Not when he finally had the right to come to her room and strip away those pretty garments layer by tantalizing layer, drawing her into his arms. There was no doubt in his mind that a deep vein of passion ran through her exquisitely sensual body. Any fool with eyes in his head could see that. A vein that had already been tapped, more than likely. That story about an Indian "husband" was a painfully transparent device, an attempt on her parents' part to explain away the notorious permissiveness of the primitive society in which she had lived. Then, of course, there were those nights with Valero on the road. The man *did* have a way with women, even the ones who disliked him.

Perhaps *especially* the ones who disliked him! Hatred, after all, was very close to passion.

Well, if other men had already awakened her taste for the physical side of love, so much the better for him. It would make things that much easier on their wedding night. Asa Martens had long since discovered that skill as a lover was more than a match for virile good looks in the boudoir, and he had carefully developed his talents in that direction, not because he gave a damn about pleasing the ladies with whom he lay, but because he liked to feel the ultimate power of his domination over them. He would be utterly sure of himself when he went to Kristyn, as he had been with every other woman in his adult life.

Oh, she might think she would be able to hold herself back from him—she might actually believe she could stay aloof, the way she was doing now—but he knew better. In the end, whether she willed it or not, this beautiful woman was going to surrender completely, totally, to him, writhing beneath the assault of his body. And he was going to luxuriate in it as he never had before!

He laid a tentative hand on her arm, testing her reaction, then drew back as he felt a slight shudder pass through her body. There was no point in pushing her unnecessarily now. Time enough for all that later.

"I hope you have had a chance to see something of our city since you arrived," he said, adroitly maneuvering the conversation onto neutral ground. "It is quite exceptionally beautiful, I think, especially along the river."

"No, not really. It's been raining off and on since I got here. And, of course, my father has been busy with his business, and my mother doesn't approve of ladies going out unescorted, even in a closed carriage."

"Well, we shall have to remedy that, now that the fine weather is here. It would be a pity not to be acquainted with the city in which you live."

"Yes, a pity . . ."

Kristyn set her cup down on the table and went over to the window, trying not quite as subtly as she had hoped to discourage any further intimacies. He, too, laid down his cup and followed, but he did not try to touch her again.

"I hope you will allow me to call for you in my carriage one afternoon, with your mother as chaperone, of course. Those of us who helped build the city take a great pride in it. It would be my pleasure to be able to show it to you."

He continued to chat casually for a while, talking of things that probably did not interest him any more than they did her, but while Kristyn listened with half an ear, making all the appropriate responses, she did not truly hear what he was saying. Her mind seemed to be racing off in a dozen different directions at once, trying to sort out what was happening to her—and why she had this terrible sinking feeling in the pit of her stomach.

It was not a bad marriage he was offering her. No matter how she resisted, she could not claim that. Not bad, at least, from a practical point of view. Rafe had almost certainly been right—Asa Martens *would* be kind to her, and more than unusually generous. If marriage really was a business for women, and she suspected, realistically, that it was, then why was every impulse, every nerve in her body screaming out for her to rebel?

She looked over at him, surprised in the stark light of the window to see how old he looked, surprised, too, that that should make a difference. If love did not enter into the relationship, what could physical beauty, or the lack thereof, possibly matter? He had played the perfect gentleman with her that morning, showing her an unexpected, almost diffident, formality, and she realized suddenly that he was a little in awe of her. Perhaps because she was considered beautiful by the white man's standards—perhaps only because she looked so young to his eyes.

A diffident formality? The idea caught her fancy, and for a moment she had the ridiculous feeling she was going to break out in giggles. It wasn't funny—no one could possibly think it was funny!—but there it was, she wanted to laugh all the same. How silly they would have sounded had someone been there to hear, saying "Miss Ashley this," and "Mr. Martens that," as if they were the most casual of acquaintances. They would probably keep on calling each other "Miss" and "Mr." until the day of their marriage—and even then they would say "Kristyn" and "Asa" in those same formal tones!

Except, of course, in bed.

The thought made her feel cold all over, and suddenly she no longer wanted to laugh. No, there would be no formality in their bedchamber—and no perfect, gentlemanly behavior either! Asa Martens was not the kind of man who would accept a woman lying placidly beneath him, giving of her body but not her heart, her passions. She had not failed to see the way he looked at her before, and she knew only too well the demands he was going to make on her! It might be within his character to allow her her dignity during the daytime, but not at night. Oh, never at night!

She was so lost in her thoughts, she almost missed the words when they finally came. He uttered them coolly, matter-of-factly, with nothing in his inflection to set them off from the small talk that had come before.

"I believe you know why I am here."

"I . . ." Oh, why did her heart stop beating like that? "Yes, I know."

"You are willing?"

And that was it! Just, you are willing? No words of wooing, no pretty promises of love—just, you are willing? and the whole thing was at an end. Bitterly, Kristyn realized that flowery ardor was the one thing that was beyond Asa Martens. Money he could offer her, position, the passion she did not want—but never if she accepted him would she know one moment of romance in her life.

"I—I think you must speak to my father about that, sir."

Martens looked surprised.

"But I already have, Miss Ashley. I thought you knew that. He has given his consent—if you agree."

If she agreed! As if anyone cared whether she agreed or not!

"Well then, if my father has given his consent," she said softly, "it seems to be settled, doesn't it?"

Coward! her heart cried out as she remained those last minutes in the parlor, saying very little, but smiling and nodding courteously until he had taken his leave. Coward! it repeated later when she passed Benjamin at the foot of the stairs and murmured something about having a headache and wanting to spend the rest of the day in her room. She had not lied, not to either of them—her words to Martens, after all, had been deliberately ambiguous—but she knew very well that her unwanted suitor had gone away satisfied, believing he had a bride.

And her father had assumed that his daughter's future was settled.

The scent of sachet was strong as she opened the door to her room and stepped inside. It was a comfortable chamber, solidly but rather plainly furnished, quite at variance with the clutter in the rest of the house, and she had the feeling that Benjamin had taken a hand in decorating it for her. A four-poster bed, softly feminine with a rose-sprigged white cover and curtains, was set against one wall, and beside it, a small washstand held a ewer and basin, seemingly always filled with warm or at least tepid water. There was a dark-wood bureau with a mirror above it on the opposite wall, a pair of chintz-covered chairs, a colorful rag rug on the floor—nothing more. The window was open and lacy curtains fluttered slightly in the breeze.

Asa Martens. She sat down on the edge of the bed, trying not to remember him, trying not to see the image of his face the way he had looked when he said good-bye, and she realized again, as she had in the parlor, that her life would be unspeakably empty if she married him. If he were a different man, perhaps—if there could ever be any true rapport between them . . .

Sighing, she picked up a pillow and pressed it unconsciously to her breast. She might have been able to overlook the rigid formality of Asa Martens' manner, she might have learned to forget his age in time—she might even have managed to endure the indignity of his unwelcome weight sweating and grunting above her in bed. But to give up all hope of romance in her life? All the pretty dreams that had filled her heart these many years? How could she live without her dreams?

Oh, Rafe, Rafe, she thought miserably, clinging to the pillow, holding it tighter against her body. How could he have done this to her? How could he have taught her to hunger for romance in one sweet, beautiful night of love, and then just gone off and left her again. If only he were here now, if only he were beside her, things would be so different.

But he was *not* there, she reminded herself coldly. He was not there now, and he would never be there again, no matter how she might long for him. Whatever she was going to make of the rest of her life, she was going to have to do it without him.

That same thought continued to trouble her heart throughout the long day that followed. She saw the worried look on the face of the young serving girl who brought a tray with soup and a crusty loaf of bread to her room, and she tried to smile, but she could not quite succeed. Nor could she manage to work up an appetite for the hearty broth, even though it was thick with the tender vegetables and tasty morsels of chicken Cook knew she loved.

No doubt, the servants were all gathered around the kitchen table at that very moment, clucking over her headache and speculating as to what had brought it on. And probably with devastating accuracy, too! Kristyn had already noticed that very little went unobserved in that unique kitchen-world at the back of the house, and she had absolutely no doubt that everyone there knew exactly what had happened in the parlor that morning—and just how she felt about it!

But the one thing they could not know was the thing she had just decided herself. She was not going to marry Asa Martens.

Only if she didn't, if she refused, what was she going to do?

Pushing the bowl of soup away, barely touched, she rose and began to walk restlessly around the room. When she told her parents what she had decided, how could she stay in their house? Surely her father would press her to go through with the marriage, especially after the position she had put him in, pretending to accept Martens that morning. And even if he didn't, what would she have to look forward to? More of Astrid's teas, with all the eligible young men in town being paraded one after another in front of her? No, that she could not bear!

Afternoon sunlight streamed into the room, streaking the dark floor with gold. Kristyn slipped over to the window and gazed down at a quiet garden, just beginning to burst into flower. What was it Rafe had told her before? A woman has to have the protection of a man, unless she can teach school, of course, or sing like an angel and go on the stage.

Well, she could do neither, heaven knows. But she did have other skills—skills she could certainly put to advantage! She could ride as well as any white man, and hunt or fish better than most of them, too. And if she could carve a straight arrow out of an ash bough and build campfires and erect tepees, what was to keep her from putting up a split-rail fence, or even a log cabin in the middle of the forest? This was still a new, growing land. There had to be a place in it for any man—or woman!—who was not afraid of strained muscles and dirty hands.

And if there was not . . .?

The thought was fleeting, vanishing as quickly as it had come. If there was not, did it truly matter? One way or another, she could not stay here.

The decision, once made, filled her with a sudden burst of energy, and she rummaged through the storeroom at the end of the hall until she found a small carpetbag, just the size she could carry comfortably. What to put in it was another matter. Never before had she possessed more clothes than she could cram into a single bag, and it was surprisingly painful to have to choose what to bring and what to leave behind. It had not occurred to her that owning things could be such a burden.

So many pretty dresses. Kristyn pulled them out one by one, her feminine heart unable to resist a stab of regret as she studied the graceful lines and soft, rich colors. For all that they must have been bitterly disappointed in her, Benjamin and Astrid had been remarkably generous. The sweetly child-like white lawn her mother had chosen for the tea—how could she possibly leave that behind when it was the very dress she had worn to go to Rafe? Or the exquisite peach-toned satin ballgown, so smooth to the touch, almost iridescent, changing colors in the changing lights. She had never gotten to wear it, but she had tried it on once, just after it was finished, and the beguiling image in her mirror had told her

that only the stigma of her background kept all the young
swains from flocking around her. How heart-wrenching never
to put it on again. And her favorite, a deep forest-green
velvet, cut surprisingly low in front, sweeping out in a flowing train in back . . .

Perhaps, she thought with a wry half-smile, it was just as
well she was leaving. She seemed to be growing remarkably
attached to all the possessions that were so much a part of the
white man's world.

In the end, she narrowed her choice down to three dresses,
two to pack and one to wear when she left. She donned the
heaviest of them, a serviceable beige cotton with a high neck
and little buttons running all the way down the front. It was
not especially becoming, she thought, frowning a little as she
tossed a quick glance into the mirror, but it was simple and
inconspicuous, and that was what counted. The other two went
into the bag: a crisp blue-checked gingham with a round,
ruffled neck, and a less practical afternoon dress, made of
lawn like her tea gown, but not so elaborate, pale blue
patterned with deeper blue and white forget-me-nots. On
impulse, she tossed in a pair of white dancing slippers as
well, not because she thought she would need them, but
simply because she could not bear to leave everything pretty
behind.

The time, which had seemed to rush by so quickly while
she was packing, began to drag interminably, and it seemed
forever before twilight slipped into darkness and the house
was silent at last. Kristyn did not know what time it was,
perhaps midnight, perhaps closer to one o'clock, when she
finally picked up the valise and began to tiptoe down the
stairs, moving carefully so the steps would not creak under
her feet.

The door to the parlor was open and, while it was empty, a
single lamp was still lighted, casting a faint, eerie glow out
into the entry hall. Kristyn paused briefly, the carpetbag still
in her hand, and stared in at the familiar furnishings she
would never see again. On the mantelpiece, the row of faces,
captured forever in brown-tinted immobility, seemed to stare
at her in silent accusation. For the first time since she had
planned her hasty escape, she remembered how long Benjamin and Astrid Ashley had searched for their lost daughter,

and she felt a moment's qualm, wondering how they would react when they woke up in the morning and found her gone.

Not that she was deserting them, of course, she reminded herself, soothing her conscience. After all, they had not expected her to go on living in their house. They had assumed she was going to be married and they would lose her anyway. Besides, she was going to write them letters, lots and lots of letters, just as soon as she learned how, and perhaps even send them a photograph so she could join all the others on the mantel. Then she would be just like Charlotte, the half-sister who had gone away all those years ago to live with her husband in Nebraska.

No, not quite like Charlotte, she thought with a funny little catch in her throat. They had had Charlotte for a long time, and they had loved her deeply—she must have left a terrible void in their lives when she went away. But with her . . .

With her, it would not hurt so much. They would worry about her, of course, they might even feel guilty for not having loved her more, but somewhere deep in their hearts they would be relieved that she was gone and they did not have to deal with her anymore.

She took her cloak down from the peg and slipped out into the darkness. Was she running away, she wondered, pausing to cast a last backward glance at the house, now only a bulky shadow against the moonlit sky—or was she running toward a better life? Only time would tell.

III

The Moon
When the Plums
Turn Ripe

Eighteen

"How on earth do you find anything in here?" Kristyn shook her head as she stared in amazement into the back of the old Conestoga wagon. "I don't think I've ever seen so many things crammed together in one small space in my life."

Luke Perkins grinned good-naturedly. "It ain't exactly tidy," he admitted. "But then my Pa always told me, if you can't find something, it probably wasn't worth lookin' for in the first place."

Kristyn could not help laughing. Luke might look like a buffoon, with his bulky body and broad, moon-shaped face, but there was something surprisingly comforting about him. When she had left her parents' home, nearly a week ago, she had been filled as much with hope as apprehension, but two days of begging for food at isolated farmhouses and sleeping on the ground had taught her how hard it was to make her way in the white man's world without the white man's gold jingling in her pockets. By the time she caught sight of the Yankee Peddler and his gaily colored wagon, she had been at her wit's end, not knowing what to do next. When he had offered to share his lunch with her, she had been grateful; when he agreed to let her travel with him, it seemed the answer to a prayer.

"Well, sure," he had said, as she broached the subject. "I could use the company—and maybe you could help me sell my wares. I've noticed it never hurts to have a pretty face around."

If there were any ulterior motives beneath his seemingly straight-forward offer, Kristyn had not sensed them. Quite the contrary, Luke had made a point of treating her with exaggerated courtesy. Every evening when supper was over and he had helped her rinse off their plates and cups, he would take his blanket roll and, abandoning the warmth of the fire, leave her to sleep alone under the wagon.

Plainly, Kristyn thought, appearances were not what they seemed in the white man's world. In her mother's elegant salon, she had met men with velvet collars on their coats, and gold watches and expensive silk cravats, and not a one of them had been as gentlemanly as coarsely dressed, rough mannered Luke.

And the last thing she wanted was to take advantage of his courtesy without giving anything in return.

"I don't care what you tell me, Luke Perkins," she said, pulling items out of the wagon and stacking them on the ground. "I know very well it bothers you when you can't find things. You lose sales that way, and you can't afford it. Besides, it's time I started pulling my weight around here. I'm going to get this wagon so well organized you won't recognize it."

Rather to her surprise, Kristyn discovered that the task was not tiresome at all. If anything, she was actually intrigued.

It had never occurred to her that a woman could have so many things for her kitchen. Huge iron cauldrons had been designed to hang on hooks directly inside the fireplace, where they could be used to heat bath water or hold soups and stews that often simmered for days, releasing pungent odors into the air. Tin cups and plates contrasted sharply with pretty patterned chinaware, packed in sturdy wooden crates, and all the table utensils had been arranged in sets, with the handles on the knives matching the forks and spoons. Rough wooden piggins came in a variety of sizes, some big enough to hold an entire winter's supply of flour or rice, others so light that, even filled with water, a woman could easily carry them back from the well. Tins of preserved foodstuffs were unexpectedly colorful, with pictures of yellow and green vegetables or little silvery fish called sardines, and big glass jars held wonderfully aromatic supplies of cinnamon and nutmeg.

But it was not merely the concerns of the kitchen that formed the typical peddler's stock in trade. Luke carried farming implements as well, hoes and shovels, scythes and plow irons, and all the things a woman might want for sewing—papers of pins, cards of horn buttons, bolts of serviceable calico and gingham, bed ticking in a variety of colors, shirting, gaily hued ribbons, and soft velveteen for party frocks. There was shaving soap for the men, and dolls with pretty wax faces for little girls, clocks and jew's harps, shoes from New England and pure linen tablecloths—in short, anything and everything a person could possibly need or want, or even dream of owning.

How spoiled they were, these women who lived in their permanent houses, made of wood and brick and sod. If an Indian broke her sewing awl, she had to make a new one for herself, carving it, painstakingly out of a piece of bone. All a white woman had to do was save up a few small coins and wait for the Yankee Peddler to come.

Kristyn had saved the most interesting for last, and the sun was already beginning to set by the time she turned her attention to a small pile of books on the ground. Luke had taken an old metal bucket down to the stream, and she was alone in the fading light.

Books! So ordinary looking, with plain hard covers and bold black letters, yet how her blood stirred to look at them! Of all the advantages she might or might not have lost in her childhood, this was the only one she regretted.

"What are these like?" she asked shyly when Luke returned. "Have you read them?"

"Me?" Luke set the bucket down so hard water slopped over the side. "Oh, pshaw, no! Those are *McGuffey's Readers*, the whole lot of 'em, four in all. I reckon every kid gets his share of 'em, sooner or later, except me. I didn't never take too kindly to 'em."

"You mean you can't read?" Kristyn asked. "Or write?"

"I can write my name well enough. And I can make out one o' them public notices on the walls in town if I set my mind to it, though I don't try too often. Seems as though there's always someone around to read it to me. Anyhow, it makes 'em feel good, seein' how much smarter they are than me."

Kristyn stared at him in amazement. If Luke felt the slightest embarrassment at having to admit he could not read, it didn't show. Yet she could not help remembering the pitying look on Rafe's face when she had confessed that very ignorance to him.

Rafe.

The thought of him wrenched at her heart, and she realized

bitterly that the pain she felt now was at least partly of her
own making. Why—*why?*—had she made such a fool of
herself over him? For a woman to give her heart to a man
who did not love her was bad enough, but to give her body as
well? How, in years to come, was she going to live with the
knowledge of what she had done? Or with the added loneliness that would always be hers, having once allowed herself
the sweetness of a passion she would never know again?

And yet, if she had to do it all over—if somehow she could
go back and relive that fateful night—would she change it?
Would she give up the bittersweet joy of those few brief
hours for all the peace of mind in the world?

Kristyn was so absorbed in her thoughts that she had almost
forgotten the books in her hands. Glancing down, she was
vaguely surprised to see them.

"Do you suppose I could borrow these? I—I can't read
either, and I'd like to learn. I'll be very careful of them."

Luke made no effort to conceal his surprise. To a young
man who had spent most of his life running away from
schooling, the idea that someone might voluntarily open a
book seemed utterly incomprehensible.

"Well, sure, take 'em if you want. I can't see what use
you'll make of readin', but if you've got your heart set on it,
why then, it's all right with me. Keep 'em if you like."

A light, half-smile played on Kristyn's lips as she looked
down at the books. She would not keep them, of course—
Luke was much too generous for his own good—but at least
she would be able to use them for a while. Somewhere in
those crisp white pages, somewhere in the symbols she had
once understood, was a whole new world, just waiting to be
discovered. A world that Rafe already knew, and one day she
would share.

The next morning, when Kristyn climbed up beside Luke
on the high seat of the wagon, she already had the first of
McGuffey's Readers open on her lap. To her delight, the
half-remembered symbols started to make sense almost at
once, and by mid-morning they had already begun to shape
themselves, almost automatically, into identifiable groups of
syllables and words. The problem that had plagued her young
husband when he first learned to read—the natural, primitive
urge to treat letters as pictures, turning them every which way
in his imagination—did not trouble her, for written language

was a part of her heritage and she was comfortable with the concept. Within a few days, she found herself reading, slowly of course, and so haltingly she did not even try to whisper the words aloud when Luke was around, but reading nonetheless. And a few days after that, she had written her first letter to her parents.

It was not exactly the polished missive she had hoped for. In fact, it looked remarkably childlike, with scrawled block letters and a vocabulary limited to the frustrating simplicity of McGuffey's early primers, but it was a first attempt, and in spite of all the obvious flaws, Kristyn could not help taking a certain pride in it. The next day when she handed it to Luke, asking him to see that it was safely posted, she had the satisfying feeling of having paid her obligations. Once Benjamin and Astrid knew she was all right, they would at least feel a little bit easier in their minds when they thought of her.

It was a hot day. The sun seemed to reflect off the parched earth, and even the rising wind had no coolness in it. Kristyn adjusted the strings of her sunbonnet, glad now that Luke had insisted on giving it to her out of his diminishing stock. She had felt a little foolish at first, covering her hair and face like a white woman afraid of the sun, but on a day like this, she had to admit it made sense.

She cast a sidelong glance at Luke, beside her on the wagon seat. His features had a vacant look, as they often did when he was driving, stoical, somehow old beyond his years. For the first time it occurred to her, rather to her surprise, that in all the days they had been traveling together, she had never once asked him about himself.

"Why do they call you a Yankee peddler? Is that because you are a Yankee?"

"Me? A Yankee?" Luke looked away from the road long enough to throw her a peculiar glance. "No, ma'am, I'm a southerner through and through. Well, south Nebraska, that is, but my heart has always been with them poor rebels. I don't have no use for slaveholdin', mind you—I wouldn't keep none myself, even if I had the money for it—but it burns me to see one man tell another what he can do. It just don't seem right."

Kristyn studied him skeptically out of the corner of her eye. With Luke, she could never tell whether he was teasing or not. The war between the North and South had had little effect on her, but she had already learned that white men could come to blows over it, even though it had ended a decade before.

"But if you aren't a Yankee," she persisted, "why do they call you a *Yankee* Peddler?"

"Well, shucks, they have to call us something, and I reckon that's as good as anything else. Peddlers whistle 'Yankee Doodle' when they come into a town so folks'll hear 'em and know they're there. Even when it's pourin' rain and the danged horses are stuck so deep in the mud it don't look as if they'll ever get out, we're still s'posed to whistle."

"And *you* do that?" Kristyn was skeptical. She had heard Luke whistle, but it didn't sound like "Yankee Doodle" to her.

"Me? No ma'am. You ain't never going to catch Luke Perkins whistlin' no song with the word Yankee in it. Generally I just stick to 'Dixie.' "

"Goodness, not in the North I hope." Kristyn tried not to laugh, but she couldn't help it. "People get awfully touchy about things like that."

"They might," Luke agreed complacently, "if they knew what I was up to. But I ain't never been able to carry a tune, singin' or whistlin'. I just pucker up my lips, and whatever wants to come out . . . well, I just let it come. It seems to me folks hear what they expect, and from a peddler, they expect 'Yankee Doodle.' Only I hear 'Dixie,' so we're all of us happy at the same time."

Kristyn could not suppress a grin. Dear, whimsical Luke—he always seemed able to make her laugh, even when she was tired or feeling glum. She was grateful, of course, for the food he shared with her and the shelter of his wagon, but she would have given it all up for that wonderful, soul-easing gift of laughter.

The winds picked up early in the afternoon, blowing broadside against the wagon with such force they threatened to topple it over. When Luke pulled the horses up beside a briskly flowing stream, announcing that it was time to give up the struggle and make camp for the day, Kristyn was only too ready to scramble down from the hard seat and stretch out her cramped muscles.

The shade was surprisingly cool beneath the cottonwoods, but in the distance, the air was still so hot it shimmered visibly. Kristyn wandered over to the edge of the grove while Luke unloaded the wagon, and stared out at mile upon mile of brown grasses, blowing in the dry winds.

"Where are we?" she called over her shoulder. "Is this Nebraska?"

"Not hardly." Luke's round face broke into a grin. "Nebraska's right pretty country, leastaways, that's what my Ma always tells me. Whenever you see anythin' as flat as this, you know right away you're in Kansas."

"Kansas?" The name tugged at Kristyn's memory, but she couldn't quite place it.

"Nothing here but dirt and wheat, and railroad tracks, of course. This is the end of the line. They're gonna add onto it one o' these days, but for now, if those hot-headed Texans want to get their cattle to market, they have to load them onto cars in Abilene or Dodge City."

Dodge City! Kristyn's heart gave a funny little jump. So that was why the name Kansas had sounded so familiar.

"Is that where we're going? To Dodge?"

If Luke caught the hint of wistfulness in her voice, he did not respond.

"I should say not. That place is rough enough for a man—I wouldn't take no lady there. Dodge is two days' walk to the south, and I aim to keep it that way. Besides, they got plenty o' stores there. What would they want with the likes o' me?"

Kristyn fell silent after that, but Luke, absorbed in the task of unhitching the horses, did not notice how distracted she had become. Even when she picked up the carpetbag she had brought from her parents' house and began to carry it down to the stream, it did not occur to him to wonder if something was wrong. It had been a hard, tiring day, and Luke, ever conscious of the relative fragility of the female sex, did not find it surprising that she was in no mood for conversation.

When Kristyn reached the stream, she found the air almost pleasant. The sunlight reflecting off the water had a crisp feel to it, and tall clumps of scattered shrubbery offered protection against the dusty winds. Choosing a secluded spot, she stripped off her sweat-stained dress, then her petticoats and chemise, and, wading naked into the water, began to wash them out until they had regained some semblance of their original brightness. Only when she had finished and they were lying on the stony bank to dry, did she allow herself the luxury of taking down her hair and easing her overheated body into the stream. Gentle ripples splashed her skin as she sank neck deep into the welcome coolness, letting the weariness of the day drift away from her aching muscles.

She tried to keep her mind blank as she leaned back, half floating on the buoyant current—tried not to let herself think or remember—but the pull of the past was too strong, and old feelings, old sensations, began to creep into her heart. Sighing, she surrendered, letting them sweep over her like the cool water that cleansed her skin and drew long tresses out in the ripples behind her.

Dodge City. Luke's words, but it was Rafe's voice she heard, as if he were whispering in her ear. Dodge City, two days' walk to the south. And that was where he had planned to meet his brother.

The water lapped softly against her limbs, teasing her with gentle caresses, not cooling now, as it had been before, but strangely warming, reminding her poignantly, cruelly, of the raging heat that had spread through her veins when *he* had touched her. Helpless to resist, she felt her body swell with yearning for the tender fulfillment that would never be hers again. Oh, how could she have imagined she would be able to forget Rafe? How could she have dreamed she would free herself of him? He had become a part of her that night, an extension of her flesh, a deep, irrevocable instinct that could never be denied. Her mind might forget him, if she willed it hard enough, but not her heart. Or her body.

Slowly, almost without being aware of it, she moved her hands, resting them lightly on her breasts, trying timidly to evoke the feelings he had once aroused in her, and failing utterly. It was not the touch of hands on her breast for which she hungered—it was the touch of *his* hands. Not the cool kiss of rushing water on her ferverish flesh, but the hot impertinence of his mouth, bold and challenging, ravishing her over and over with the sheer force of his male virility.

The sun was searing as she lay naked on the smooth rocks beside the stream, drying first her skin, then her long, loose hair. Not until dusk had begun to fall, touching the earth with the first chill of evening, did she rouse herself and prepare reluctantly to return to the campsite where Luke was waiting. The dress she had washed was not quite dry and, leaving it where it was, she dipped into her bag, searching for the plain beige cotton.

She had just caught hold of it when her eye fell on a glimpse of sheer pastel, patterned with little flowers in various shades of blue and white. Tugging it out impulsively, she rejoiced in the soft interplay of colors in that elusive light. Suddenly she could not bear the idea of dressing like a dowdy matron again, plain in sun-faded calico and prim long sleeves. She was not a matron, after all: she was a young girl, with a young girl's need for gaiety and prettiness.

She was not sorry, once she had given in to the impulse and put on the festive gown, for even without a mirror she knew she looked enchanting. Yards and yards of frothy lawn billowed out around her, catching the evening breezes with a softly seductive femininity. The sleeves were short, and the bodice dipped low in front, clinging to the curves of her bosom with a frankness that belied the coy modesty of a row of lacy ruffles along the neckline.

Perhaps, after all, that was what was wrong with her! Not an aching loneliness for the lover she had left behind, but simply a girlish need to revel in the delights of her own youthfulness again. A need to feel young and pretty . . . and desirable.

Laughing out loud, she began to run through the dry grasses toward the camp, leaving her bag forgotten on the ground behind her. She could hardly wait to see the look on Luke's face when he caught sight of her frilly gown and realized how happy it had made her. Luke had been the soul of patience with her, as affectionate and kindly as a big brother. Surely he would want to share her high spirits now.

It was almost dark by the time she reached the wagon. Luke had gathered together a pile of firewood, and as she approached he was in the process of throwing a log on the leaping yellow flames. He paused, the wood poised in midair, as he saw her running toward him, emerging dreamlike out of the enveloping darkness.

It seemed to him, in that moment, that he had never seen anything quite so bewitching. The moonlight had paled her soft blue gown, turning it into an ethereal shimmering white, and her body seemed to sway unconsciously, moving with a soft sensuality. The reflected glow of firelight blazed in long red hair, floating with careless abandon over her shoulders.

Pretty girls had always made Luke vaguely uncomfortable. Whenever he spied them lounging on verandas in town, or passed them on the street, so close he could hear the rustle of taffeta petticoats and catch a whiff of flowery perfume, they seemed to him as cold as the night—and as untouchable as stars in the distant heavens. Suddenly here was Kristyn, pretty, provocative Kristyn, running not away from him as he might have expected, but toward him, her hair blowing in the wind, her full lips parted in anticipation.

For a moment he was bewildered, too dull of thought to sort it all out in his mind. Then slowly, he began to remember things, little things he had not noticed before—the way she had fallen silent just after they made camp, the strange distant look on her face as she turned away from him.

Could it be she had begun to have feelings for him? Luke's heart leaped up as he stumbled on what seemed to him an indisputable truth. Yes, obviously, that was the reason for her exceptional behavior. Sometime that day, perhaps just that afternoon, she had grown aware of him, and womanlike, she had not been able to admit it, even to herself. That was what she must have been doing all that time, lying there in the stream. She had been thinking of him and making up her mind.

The physical sensations evoked in Luke's body by the thought of Kristyn lying naked in the water seemed to him at once both natural and utterly incredible. He had possessed women before, but always, those brief, embarrassed acts had been a compromise, less satisfying than disappointing. The women he had really yearned for, the pretty, nameless women on their verandas, had never noticed him, and he had had to settle for the ones he did not want.

But now there was Kristyn, and Kristyn would not disappoint him.

He would marry her, of course. Luke had never thought much about marriage, one way or the other, but he had noticed that women set great store by such things, and he would never willingly deny this pretty girl anything she desired. Yes, certainly he *would* marry her—tomorrow, if she wanted—but tonight . . .

Luke made no effort to conceal the look of longing on his features, and Kristyn, coming into the clearing, saw instantly what he was thinking. Her first reaction was one of dismay, her second, anger with herself for her thoughtless folly. She had been so wrapped up in her own feelings, her own needs, she had completely forgotten that he had feelings, too. A big brother, indeed! That was what she wanted Luke to be, not what he wanted for himself. What man ever wanted to play big brother to a woman, when they were traveling together day after day, and sleeping so close at night they could almost hear each other breathe when the wind was still.

"I—I thought it would be fun to dress up for a change," she said lamely. "I think everyone ought to do something . . . well, something unexpected once in a while. It makes things more fun."

Luke hardly seemed to hear her stammered rationale.

"It's a real pretty dress," he said, his eyes glowing. "You don't have to make excuses for wearin' it."

"I'm not making excuses. I just like to . . . oh, to be spontaneous every now and then. Don't you?"

"It's real pretty. You can wear it any time you want."

He doesn't believe me, Kristyn thought helplessly. He doesn't believe me—and how can I blame him?

For just a moment, she saw herself as he must have seen her, running toward him, her eyes alight with eagerness, her gown low-necked and seductive, her hair flowing down her back like a bride come to her husband on their wedding night. What on earth had she expected?

"I am sorry," she said softly. "I was telling the truth before. I only wore the gown because I wanted to look pretty for a change. I—I think I had better go and put on something else."

Hating herself for her ineptness, Kristyn turned away and wandered back to the banks of the stream, moving slowly this time, with none of the eagerness that had marked her steps before. She was bitterly aware of Luke's eyes following her in the darkness, and she knew, without glancing back, that they were dull with bewilderment and disbelief.

Moonlight played on the silent creek, bouncing shafts of brightness off the water and giving life to flickering blue shadows on the banks. Even here, Kristyn could still feel Luke's eyes—huge, wide eyes, confused, rejected . . . hurt. Tucking her skirt around her, she sat down on the bristly grasses and pulled her traveling bag closer so she could lean against it in the darkness.

How could she have been so clumsy? So thoughtless? Luke had never been anything but kind to her, and how had she repaid him? By playing games, unintentionally perhaps, but cruelly, letting him think for one exhilarating instant that she wanted him, then spurning him with an abruptness that must have left his head reeling. She had hurt him, hurt him badly, and there was nothing in the world she could do to set things right again.

And the worst of it was, she thought miserably, her actions had made it impossible for them to maintain their friendship. Luke had been her one companion in the long days since she had left her parents' home, the only person she could turn to for help, and now she could not even consider traveling on with him. Oh, he might act as if nothing were amiss in the morning—he would be embarrassed and as eager as she to pretend nothing had happened—but there was no denying that he had begun to look at her in a different way, and things would never be the same between them.

No, she could not stay now. Like it or not, she was going to have to pack her pretty dress away in her bag again and strike off on her own. Perhaps she would try to find Abilene, wherever that might be—at least it had a pretty sounding name. Or maybe Dodge City, since it seemed to be closer. Two days' walk to the south, Luke had said.

Dodge City?

Kristyn's lips twisted upward in a faintly ironical smile. Was she really leaving Luke because she had to? she asked herself with a burst of objectivity. Was she leaving because her clumsiness had made it untenable for her to stay, or was there some instinct deep in her heart that made her long to follow Rafe?

Not, of course, that she thought he would still be in Dodge. He and Carlos had been much too anxious to reach their grandfather in Santa Fe to linger there. Nor would it have done her any good if he were, for he had made it clear that his interest in her was purely physical and he had no intention of letting their brief dalliance ripen into anything lasting.

Still, there *was* something perversely comforting in the idea of going someplace where he had been. Of moving closer to him, instead of farther and farther away.

Nineteen

A hellhole. That was how men referred to Dodge, and it seemed to Kristyn an accurate description.

She stood at the edge of Front Street, letting her eyes drift with a kind of revolted fascination down the wide, rutted thoroughfare that cut the town in two. It was early afternoon, the peak of a searing summer day, but despite the debilitating heat, hard-faced Texans prodded their horses at a good clip down the street. Men in dusty broadcloth jackets paraded along the boardwalks, the heels of their boots clicking sharply as they passed open swinging doorways, leading into saloons and stores where almost anything could be purchased, from rot-gut whiskey and rounds of ammunition to lace for parlor curtains and bone china made out of bleached buffalo skulls. Rough plank benches had been propped up against the walkways, and massive barrels of stagnant water, dark brown with scum, studded the street at haphazard intervals, mute testimony to the fires that frequently broke out in ramshackle wooden structures.

Dodge City had grown quickly, perhaps too quickly for its own good, changing in less than a decade from a sleepy Kansas village to a major railway terminus. The cattle pens that dominated the area were located on the outskirts of town, but their presence was felt even here on Front Street, where the low milling of the animals rumbled faintly beneath the sound of tinny music drifting through paper-thin walls. Even on a windless day, the smell of the pens was subtly pervasive, mingling with sweat and leather, dust and horses, urine and sour liquor, to create a stench that was as much a characteristic of Dodge as the wide-open gambling halls and sudden sporadic bursts of aimless gunfire.

"Try your luck, ladies and gentlemen." Doc Hammer's sing-song voice broke into Kristyn's thoughts. "One dollar. I ask you, is that much? One small dollar? This could be your lucky day."

Turning away from the dusty street, Kristyn watched as the man who had been her employer for a week began to work his special magic on the crowd. Doc had found her the afternoon she arrived in Dodge, hungry and exhausted, and in a canny combination of charity and good business sense, he had made her part of his act. No matter how many times she saw him go into his routine, she never ceased to wonder at the way he managed to manipulate people into doing what he wanted.

"You, sir . . . !" Doc pointed a deft finger at a passing Texan, a young man with a faded brown shirt and a dirty red bandanna. "You look like a gambling man. One slim dollar to try your luck? And who's to say it's all luck? Is the hand quicker than the eye, sir—or is the eye quicker than the hand? Why, a sharp man could clean me out in less than a hour. And show himself a regular devil in front of the ladies."

Kristyn saw the boy's eyes drop toward the shells Doc was sliding temptingly back and forth across a smooth-topped table, and she knew he had chosen his mark well. Any minute now, the lad would look up and he would see all the glittering items in that glass-enclosed case behind the table. What green youth could resist the lure of shining silver goblets, so new looking they never seemed to lose their luster? Or rings set with diamonds, or silver belt buckles, silver spoons, handsome pearl-handled revolvers, even a solid gold hunting watch, the kind a man would be proud to own?

Sure enough, the boy's hand dipped into his pocket, and as a dollar appeared on the table, the shells began to move again, faster and faster, spinning across the slick surface so dizzyingly it almost looked as if the game were legitimate. But when they came to rest at last, the shell the boy chose was empty, as Kristyn had known it would be. The dollar transferred itself into Doc's pocket, and his attention strayed back to the crowd.

"Just call me Doc Hammer," he called out jovially. "Everyone does." Leaning forward, he winked a rakish eye at a tired-looking woman in a bleached-out gingham dress. "What's my real name, you ask? Percy, madam. Percy Bysshe

Hammer. My mother was a hopeless romantic. Now, I ask you, who would take a man called Percy seriously? No, madam—just call me Doc. You see before you a traveling dentist, like that other famous gunslinger, Doc Halliday.''

Kristyn, who had already learned that Doc's real name was John Hammersmith, found it all she could do to suppress a giggle. Not only was he no dentist, he was no gunslinger either. But she had to admit he wore the image well, and it seemed to have an effect on the crowd.

Doc waited only long enough for the laughter to die down, then launched into his attack again.

"You sir . . . !" He singled out another Texan, an older man this time, dressed like the first, but with a lined, leathery face. "Are you bold enough to wager a dollar or two? A mere pittance, sir—barely a fifth of what the Marshal will fine you if he catches you north of the Deadline with that gun in your boot.''

The cowpoke, knowing full well he had nothing in his boot but his foot, grinned appreciatively, enjoying his moment as a desperado enough to toss a silver dollar onto the table. Doc let one hand rest on the shells, as he had before, but this time he raised the other, giving the corner of his moustache a tug.

Kristyn, recognizing her signal, pushed her way up from the rear of the crowd and leaned over the table, as if to get a closer look. Doc had not called on her before because the other man had been young and easy to handle. This one was considerably older and had a shrewd look about him.

Her movement did not go unnoticed. Doc had fitted her out in a simple calico dress, but he had chosen a soft shade of blue that accented her eyes, and the neckline was just low enough to make sure no red-blooded male would be watching a con man's hands while she was anywhere in sight.

"It's a matter of distracting the eye, my dear,'' he had told Kristyn that first day he began to train her. "If one man doesn't see what another is doing, who's to know what happened? It's really quite simple—just distract the eye.''

Simple indeed, Kristyn had to agree as she watched Doc tuck the ball under one of the shells and begin to shuffle them around with almost hypnotic dexterity. Simple, but not much of a way for a grown man—or a grown woman either—to make a living. She knew she ought to be grateful. There weren't many occupations a decent woman could aspire to in that bawdy frontier town, but still, it was discouraging, watching cowboy after cowboy plunk down his money and walk away with nothing to show for it. Even on those rare occasions when business was slow and Doc was trying to attract a crowd, Kristyn noticed he never parted with anything but one of the silver cups that didn't tarnish or a gold-and-diamond ring, which he replaced later with another gold-and-diamond ring from a large sack in his saddlebag.

"Sorry, cowboy, looks like fortune decided not to smile on you." Doc's voice was smooth as he palmed the silver dollar, sliding it deftly into his pocket. "Maybe the hand *is* quicker than the eye. Why don't you come back tomorrow? Your luck might be better then."

The cowboy grinned, shrugging off his loss with good humor. That was one of the smartest things about Doc, Kristyn conceded with grudging admiration. Not only did he know how to pick his suckers, he knew just how long to play them—and when to let go.

"I never press a man to bet again if he doesn't want to," he had told her once. "And I never let him go away losing more than he can afford. That's why I play the same town for longer than a day or two at a time—and I never have to hightail it out at full gallop in the middle of the night."

But even the best-run games had their limit, and Doc, with the innate caution of a successful gambler, seemed to know when he had reached his. Anyone else might have laughed off the string of churlish comments that came his way that second week in Dodge, or put down an occasional surly loser as part of the breaks. But Doc, with his nose for trouble, knew that word was getting around. He played the territory one more day, testing it out, then told Kristyn it was time for him to pack up and move on.

"Once they start comparing notes, it's all over. A dollar here doesn't mean much to them, or a dollar there, but when they add it all up, they get mad as hell. I'm a fast hand with a gun, but I don't aim to pull it unless I have to . . . and only a fool puts himself in a position where he has to."

Kristyn nodded abstractedly. She had seen Doc in action enough times to imagine the righteous anger of men who stopped enjoying his game and started thinking about what he was doing. He was right, it *was* time for him to get out of there. And it was time for her to try to find something better to do with her life.

"I've been thinking of leaving Dodge myself," she said impulsively. "Maybe heading west."

Doc had been stowing the last of his gear in the wagon. Now he paused to throw her a sharp look.

"Do you have someplace to go?"

"Oh, yes," Kristyn said, not meeting his gaze. "I have friends I can go to in—in Santa Fe. I was just waiting until I could save up enough money to get there."

Doc closed the case he had finished packing and swung it onto the wagon. He did not mind admitting her words came as a relief. He liked this pretty girl, with her stunning looks and spirited, independent ways, and he had not relished the idea of leaving her behind. If he hadn't had another pretty, spirited woman waiting for him in Abilene . . .

"Well, that's a load off my mind, I can tell you. I would have been worried about you, all by yourself in a place like this. It's a rough trip to Santa Fe, train part of the way, then coach or horseback from there, but it's better than trying to stay in this godforsaken place. Dodge can be hell for a woman, even with a man to look after her. But alone . . ."

Kristyn cut him off with a quick laugh.

"Don't worry, Doc. I'm leaving. Tomorrow probably, or the next day at the latest."

She had meant the words when she said them, but later, sitting alone in her room in the only respectable boarding house in town with nothing but flickering lamplight to keep her company, she wondered what on earth had prompted her to utter them with such bravado. The idea of starting again, of heading someplace new, had seemed wonderfully appealing when it came to her. Now, all she could think of was the sharp look on Doc's face when she had blurted it out.

Do you have someplace to go, he had said.

Oh, yes, she had lied.

But that, of course, was precisely what she did *not* have. There was no place she could go, no friends to take her in when she got there . . . absolutely no one she could turn to for help.

No one but Rafe.

Kristyn closed her eyes, leaning back in her seat and letting an uncharacteristic wave of futility sweep over her. Rafe, the

one man who would be able to help her . . . and the one man
she could not go to. He had made it so clear, that last dawn
when they said good-bye, that he did not expect to see her
again. He would not appreciate her coming after him now.
Oh, he might take her in, out of pity, or a vague sense of
guilt, but pity and guilt were the last things she wanted from
him. Somehow, she did not know how, but *somehow*, she
had to find a way to stay where she was and make a life for
herself.

But remaining in Dodge was not going to be easy, as she
found out the next day when she wandered up one street and
down another, searching for something she could do to earn
her keep. She had a little money set aside, but the boarding
house where she was staying was expensive, and she knew it
would not last for long.

What was it Rafe had told her before? *A woman can make
her living two ways in the West, by learning to read so she
can teach school, or having the voice of an angel.* Obviously,
he had not been referring to Dodge. There *were* two kinds of
working women here, and the first was indeed the sort who
could sing, if not angelically, at least passably well. But the
other . . .

Kristyn broke off the thought with a little shudder. The
other was definitely not a schoolmarm.

She was almost ready to give up when Art Barstow, the
owner of the Lucky Lady Saloon on the south side of Front
Street, came to her with another kind of proposition. It was
not particularly appealing, but common sense warned her she
had to listen.

"I'm not asking you to be a saloon girl, Kris," he assured
her, lapsing into the easy familiarity that was so common in
Dodge. "I know you'd never go for anything like that.
You've got too much class. But dealing at the gaming tables
is not the same at all."

"Dealing?" Kristyn knotted her brow in a puzzled frown.
"At the gaming tables? But Art, I wouldn't have the vaguest
notion how to go about it. I don't think I've even *seen* a
gaming table."

Art chuckled.

"Sure you have. And if you can handle Doc Hammer's
game, you can handle mine. I watched you, some of those
slow times when he was teaching you to play the shells

yourself. You've got good hands, and you're fast. Once you get the feel of a deck, you'll do just fine.''

"But why would you want me?''

"Because you're the prettiest woman I've seen in a long time, and you've got a fresh look about you. Beatty and Kelley got themselves a cute little piano player, a pink-cheeked girl from New York City, to sit in the window of the Alhambra and pull in the customers. I need someone like that, too. Not for the bar, but for the back room. I figure a fiery-haired faro dealer would just about do the trick.''

"Oh, I don't know . . .'' Kristyn stared at him helplessly. It made sense when he said it, but . . . "Art, your bar is south of the Deadline.''

"Aw, come on, Kris,'' Art protested, grinning. "Don't turn snobbish on me now. The wrong side of the tracks isn't as bad as all that.''

"Isn't it?'' Kristyn was not so sure. The railroad tracks that ran down the center of Front Street—the Deadline, as the locals called it—divided the town in more ways than one. North of the line, a compromise had been reached with the citizens who wanted a law-abiding community, and there respectability reigned, or at least a veneer of it. Any man who strapped on his guns when he went for a stroll on that side of town could expect to tangle with the Marshal, a solemn-faced, mustachioed man with the unlikely name of Wyatt Earp. But south of the line, the wide-open lawlessness of earlier days still prevailed. In that no-man's land, it was said, a cowboy could break all the commandments in a single night and wake up the next morning with anything from a severe hangover to a case of lead poisoning. Assuming, of course, he woke up at all.

And that was the place Art Barstow wanted her to work!

Or more to the point, Kristyn reminded herself, trying to be realistic, that was the place she was going to have to work if she wanted to stay in Dodge.

The large back room of the Lucky Lady was already thick with smoke, even though it was early in the evening. From somewhere in the front came the tinkling tones of a piano, interspersed with raucous bursts of male laughter, telling Kristyn that the long polished-wood bar was doing a rousing business as usual. But here in the gaming room, which offered not only poker tables and wheels of fortune, but lively stage shows as well, and even livelier dancing that sometimes went on until dawn, it was still relatively quiet. The candles in the footlights were dark, and the stage was barely a shadow at one end of the hall. A poker game was in progress and had been since the day before, but for the most part, the customers who had already gathered were content to pause occasionally in front of one of the wheels, or wander around the room with glasses of whiskey in their hands.

A row of private boxes ran along the side walls, not gilded, as they might have been in a fancier establishment back East, but plain and unpainted, like so many packing crates propped up on stilts. In these "cages," the saloon girls had begun to appear, their pallid skin and garish make-up dulled by the smoky haze until they almost looked pretty. It had come as a surprise to Kristyn that the women who worked in the dance halls did not adorn themselves in satins and silks, but wore instead the same cheap ginghams and cotton prints that could be seen on the street. They looked tired, as they always did at that hour, and most of them lounged indolently on padded chairs that had been provided for the comfort of the men. Occasionally, one would lean over the railing, calling out greetings or bawdy comments to a favorite customer as he passed.

Kristyn lay down her cards for a moment, leaning on the table as she shifted her weight from one foot to the other. She had been delighted by the eye-catching gown Art Barstow ordered for her, a shimmering flame-colored satin calculated to bring out the fire in her hair, but she absolutely loathed the high-heeled slippers that went with it! Why any white woman would willingly put on shoes that pinched her toes and threw her weight forward just so she could be as tall as a man was utterly beyond her. She had thought, when she started this job, that her greatest problem would be the rough behavior of the men; now she was beginning to realize that nothing was quite so daunting as the prospect of spending hour after endless hour on her feet.

There was only one man at her table that early in the evening, the same young Texan Doc had once swindled out of a dollar of his hard-earned wages. Here at least, Kristyn thought, he would get a better break. Art might not run the most honest game in town, but he didn't run the crookedest one either. If the odds always favored the house, there was at least an element of luck left, and a man could sometimes walk out with his pockets heavier than when he came in.

Rather to her surprise, Kristyn found that she enjoyed the game Art had hired her to deal. It was known as faro, because one of the cards in the French deck, where the game had originated, called to mind the pharaohs who once ruled ancient Egypt. In the West, it was played with an ordinary pack, and Kristyn, accustomed to tasks that required manual dexterity, had no difficulty learning to shuffle the cards the way Art taught her or to flip them over with a dramatic flourish. The bets were placed directly on the tabletop, where a painted layout of thirteen cards, all depicted in spades, contrasted starkly with the green felt background.

"Howdy, Kris. Slow night tonight?"

Kristyn looked up to see Ham Lynch standing in front of her. He was a tall, big-boned man, usually taciturn, but somehow more talkative when he paused at her table.

"Howdy, Ham. No, I don't think so. It's just early. Things will liven up later." Kristyn smiled to herself as she picked up the deck and began to shuffle. Ham might prefer the action at the pocker table, but he always found the time to stop and throw a few dollars her way.

She had just finished shuffling and was ready to recommence the game when she became aware suddenly that a hush had fallen over the room. The evening had been quiet before, but there had been a steady undercurrent of masculine voices, accented by the rhythmic clatter of cards and poker chips, balls and wheels. Now the stillness was so intense it was almost eerie.

More curious than apprehensive, Kristyn looked up.

A man she had never seen before was standing just inside the swinging door that led to the bar. He was not tall, but the dull gold lamplight distorted his figure, elongating sinewy limbs until he loomed up larger than life. His garb was the stark black and white affected by gunslingers and lawmen alike. Straight black pants fitted snugly over lean thighs, and a loose white shirt flowed from his shoulders. His eyes were dark and brooding in the shadow of his hat, and a pair of deadly-looking pistols rested in a black leather holster, low on his hips.

"Who . . . ?"

Kristyn formed the word with her lips as she turned back to Ham, but to her surprise, he had slipped away and was now seated with his cronies at the poker table. Only the young Texan was still there, and it was he who answered in a hushed whisper.

"Billy Collins."

Billy Collins? Fascinated in spite of herself, Kristyn turned to stare at the man. She had heard many tales of violence and lawlessness since she arrived in Dodge, but none as savage or chilling as the exploits of that notorious outlaw. Billy Collins was as mean as a rattlesnake, Art Barstow once told her, and twice as dangerous, for he didn't give warning when he struck! Once, it was said, he had emptied a pair of six-shooters into a man, shooting him slowly, one bullet at a time, moving closer and closer to the heart until his victim died of pain, or fright—or both.

The man lingered for a moment in the doorway, obviously aware of the sensation he was creating. Then slowly, his eyes began to move, taking in the gamblers at their tables, the saloon girls in rough wooden cages halfway up to the ceiling. They stopped when they reached Kristyn.

A faint shiver ran through her body as she felt the impact of those cold eyes running frankly up and down her scantily clad form, making her feel suddenly naked, as if in his insolence, he had the power to strip the pretty satin gown from her body.

Billy seemed to sense her discomfort. His lips turned up just slightly at the corners, warning Kristyn that the idea amused him. He stood where he was a few seconds longer, then began to saunter toward her table.

The young Texan backed away, leaving Kristyn alone. She threw a nervous glance toward the place where the poker players were seated a few yards away, but they had turned back to their cards again, glowering at them with a single-mindedness that shut her out. Only one of the men was looking her way, and that was an old muleskinner who stared up with such dull eyes she was sure he was too drunk to see. His twitch, a stout stick with a leather loop fastened to the end, had been propped against the back of his chair.

Billy stopped in front of her table, leaning against the edge of it to fix her with the same blatant gaze that had unnerved her before. Now that she could see him clearly, she realized that his eyes were not dark at all, but a luminous cornflower blue. A single flaxen curl peeked out from under his hat, spilling onto his forehead.

He did not speak, but took a wad of bills out of his pocket and tossed one of them carelessly onto an oversized facsimile of the ace of spades. Trying to look cooler than she felt, Kristyn forced herself to pick up the deck and deal it again.

Billy lost, but he hardly seemed to notice. Peeling off another bill, he placed it on the same painted rectangle.

"A woman dealer? At the Lucky Lady?"

His voice was unexpectedly deep, softened by hints of the South. Kristyn caught the note of sarcasm he made no effort to disguise, and she felt herself bristle with indignation.

"Why not? Do you think a woman's only place is up there in those ridiculous cages where you men can stroll back and forth and check her out? If a girl at a piano is good enough to draw customers into the front of a saloon, surely she can lure them to the gaming tables as well. Besides, it gets rough sometimes in back rooms south of the Deadline. A woman can keep peace better than a man."

"What? Not just pretty but spirited, too?" Billy raised a slow, deliberate brow. "An enticing combination—almost as enticing as that bit of feminine logic you just threw at me."

"You don't believe me?" Kristyn tossed her head, determined not to let him intimidate her again. "I suppose you think saloonkeepers should hire fancy gunslingers for their tables, with even fancier reputations! Well, a man like that attracts crowds all right, but he attracts trouble, too. Every hot-headed kid with a gun on his hip and too much liquor in his gut has to test out that famous timing. A woman doesn't provoke fights like that. After all, how much glory is there, drawing on a woman?"

The brow went up again, half an inch higher.

"No, ma'am—I wouldn't feel any glory myself, drawing on a woman. Not drawing *my gun* . . . that is."

The lewd insinuation in his tone left nothing to the imagination, and flushing, Kristyn realized how foolish she had been, trying to bait him with words.

Cautiously, she steered the conversation to safer grounds.

"Are you a gambler, Mr. Collins?"

"The name's Billy, ma'am," he drawled coolly, tossing

another crumpled greenback on the table. "And no, I'm no gambler. I only like sure things."

Sure things. Kristyn shuddered slightly as she flipped over another card and raked in his cash. Sure things—and he had been looking at her when he said it!

"Well, that lets out prospecting, doesn't it? How about bounty hunting? Is that your game?"

"No, ma'am."

"You're a train robber, then?" Kristyn met his eyes with a steady gaze of her own. "No? Well then—a horse thief?"

She had thrown the words out carelessly, intending them as a jest, but to her surprise, he responded. Grinning slowly, he raised his hand, touching it to the brim of his hat.

A horse thief! Kristyn felt cold all over. Even in a rough-and-tumble cowtown like Dodge, a horse thief was the lowest of the low, the kind of outlaw other outlaws despised. A man like that, was a man who might well be capable of anything!

Kristyn lowered her eyes, aware suddenly that her hands had begun to tremble, and she braced them tensely against the table. Whatever else Billy Collins might be, he was plainly a bully, and bullies had a sixth sense when it came to scenting fear in others.

The gesture came too late. Her hands *had* trembled visibly, and he had not failed to see. Taking advantage of her confusion, he leaned forward, catching her wrists in a strong grip and pulling her toward him.

"What do you say we get out of this place? There's nothing here to amuse a pretty girl like you. Why don't you let me take you someplace nice and—uh, quiet. Where we can . . . talk?"

Kristyn froze, panicking. Someplace quiet, he had said. Only there was no place quieter at that moment than the back room of the Lucky Lady—unless it was one of the private cubicles Art Barstow maintained upstairs for the saloon girls. And talk was hardly what Billy had in mind.

She cast a quick, sidelong glance at the poker table, but the men were still concentrating on their cards, seemingly so absorbed in the game they had no time for anything else. Only the old muleskinner was still watching her, and he had begun to shake so badly, he had knocked his twitch down on the floor. Terrified, Kristyn realized she might as well have been completely alone in that room. Billy Collins could throw her over his shoulder if he wanted, carrying her kicking and screaming upstairs, and not a one of those men would so much as look up from his cards!

Slowly, she forced her eyes upward, countering Billy's arrogant gaze. If she was going to get away from him, she was going to have to do it herself.

"You are hurting my wrist, Mr. Collins," she snapped icily. "Is this your way of wooing a woman? Taking her by force because you cannot win her with words?"

The barb seemed to amuse him, but he released his hold, and Kristyn drew her hands back, letting them rest on the pack of cards. She was painfully aware that his eyes had not left her for a second, their lascivious frankness warning her that the victory she had just won was only a temporary one. Anxiously, she scanned the room one last time, catching sight of the muleskinner's twitch where it lay a few feet away.

If only she dared to pick it up! It was not much of a weapon, but it was better than nothing. Only Billy was certain to see what she was doing, and he was just fast enough to stop her. Unless . . .

It's a matter of distracting the eye, my dear.

Doc's words came back to her, suddenly, unbidden. *Distract the eye*, he had said, and the ploy worked wonderfully for a simple game of chance. Would it be as effective for a more dangerous game as well?

Not giving herself time to think, Kristyn drew her hands to her breast, clutching the cards for a second. Then with a seemingly involuntary gesture, she sent them spilling to the ground.

Billy straightened up abruptly, startled by the sound. His eyes followed the cards as they slid across the floor, but he made no move to pick them up, and Kristyn, her heart beating suddenly faster, dared to hope she was going to succeed. Not for a man like Billy Collins the show of gallantry that would have been almost automatic for anyone else. His macho image of himself would never let him grovel on the floor at a woman's feet.

And it was that very machismo that was going to prove his undoing!

Bending down, Kristyn began to pick up the cards, taking care to lean forward so he would be treated to an alluring glimpse of softly feminine cleavage. *Distract the eye*, Doc had said, and Billy was indeed distracted. His eyes were hers now, captive to her beauty and his own male lust, and he did not see her hand reach out, as if to clutch at a card that had slid just beyond her grasp.

Only it was not the ace of spades that met her groping fingers. It was the hard, smooth handle of the muleskinner's twitch!

Leaping up, Kristyn whirled to face her adversary, her eyes blazing with anger and defiance. Too late, he realized she had tricked him, but there was nothing he could do. He tried to raise his arms, but she was too fast for him. Thrusting the twitch forward, she slipped the leather noose over his head, tightening it as a skinner might tighten it around the neck of a bad-tempered mule.

Billy's hands jerked up, clawing at the leather thong, but he could not get his fingers around it, nor could he stop the searing pain that choked off his breath and gouged into his throat. For one brief moment of almost superhuman effort, he managed to hold his balance. Then, with a rasping grunt of defeat, he toppled to the floor.

Kristyn followed the downward motion of his body, dropping to one knee beside him. The noose was still tight in her hands, a deadly reminder that he was in her power and she could do with him as she chose. Then, with a sudden, disdainful gesture, she let it go and rose dramatically to her feet.

There! Let him try and force himself on her again! She had beaten him soundly, and in front of half the town at that. His pride would never let him come near her again.

But as he struggled to his feet, pulling the twitch away from his neck and hurling it savagely across the room, Kristyn felt her initial triumph ebb into a sudden sense of foreboding. There was, in those piercing blue eyes, none of the hot anger she had expected, none of the surly resentment of the bully bested at last—only a controlled coldness that was more frightening than anything she could have imagined. She had meant to make an ally of that fierce pride of his; now she realized she had dealt it a mortal blow.

And Billy Collins was not the sort of man to give up his pride.

He stood where he was for a moment, fixing her with that same unfathomable look that sent tremors of fear up and

down her spine. Then, to her amazement, he slung his hands
on his hips, leaned back—and began to laugh!

"By God, if you were a man you would be dead now."

Waves of relief flooded over Kristyn, making her feel
giddy with excitement. She had won—she had actually won!
—and just when she was sure everything was lost.

"If I were a man, Mr. Collins," she retorted tartly, "I
wouldn't have needed to defend myself."

Billy's answering laughter was so easy and good-natured it
surprised her. No one had seen fit to mention that the infamous outlaw had a sense of humor, yet obviously he did, and
obviously, he was not the bully she had taken him for. A
bully would never have had the perspective to laugh at himself,
nor would a bully's ego ever allow him to respect the person
who had beaten him.

And respect her Billy did—that was clear from the unre-
strained look in his eyes as he stood halfway across the room
and stared at her. Somehow, Kristyn thought, amazed and a
little bewildered, her boldness had won her an admirer.

An admirer and a friend.

It occurred to her that, in a place like Dodge, where
violence was a way of life and strength was law, at least
south of the Deadline, a man like Billy Collins might be a
good friend to have.

Twenty

Billy Collins' friendship was a mixed blessing, as Kristyn was to discover in the days that followed their tempestuous meeting. There was no denying that she felt safer now, protected as much by his reputation as by his actual presence, but with that safety came a frustrating sense of isolation. What man in Dodge—or what woman, for that matter?—wanted to associate with the known companion of a notorious gunslinger?

Sighing audibly, Kristyn ran her hand across her forehead, brushing stray curls back from skin that prickled with sweat. Although it was not yet mid-morning, the sun was already scorching, and for the first time since she had arrived, Front Street lay half deserted in the shimmering heat. A handful of men skittered along the boardwalk, heading for F.I. Zimmerman's on the north side of the street or Wright and Beverley's at the corner of Bridge, but the road itself was almost eerily empty. Only a pair of anonymous forms could be seen, cutting across the railroad tracks at the far end, while a lone cowpoke steered his spiritless steed past the hitching post in front of the Long Branch.

The door to Zimmerman's swung open, and a familiar figure emerged, pausing beneath the massive red wooden gun that proclaimed the store's chief stock in trade. Catching sight of him, Kristyn hiked up her skirts and hurried impulsively across the street.

"Ham! Ham Lynch."

Lynch turned abruptly, the look of surprise on his features changing to a distracted scowl. Ever since that night at the Lucky Lady, Kristyn noticed he had been aloof with her, but this was the first time he greeted her with out-and-out brusqueness.

"Well, what is it, Kris? What do you want? I'm in a hurry."

"I won't take a minute of your time, Ham." Kristyn snapped the words more sharply than she had intended. "I was just curious. Why is everything so quiet? What's going on?"

"Going on?" Lynch's face remained expressionless, but his eyes did not meet hers. "Why, nothing as far as I know. What gave you an idea like that?"

"Oh, come on, Ham. There haven't been more than a dozen people out on the street all morning. It's almost as if everyone were . . . well, as if they were *afraid* to come out."

"Afraid? Hell, Kris, it's hot out here! It's got to be well over a hundred degrees in the shade. Only a fool would come out in heat like this. If you had any sense, you'd be inside with the others."

Kristyn bit her tongue as Lynch turned on his heel and walked pointedly away from her. The man was right, it *was* hot—but it had been just as hot yesterday, and the street had been swarming with people. Something *was* going on, no matter how Ham protested, and neither he nor anyone else was going to tell her about it!

Not, of course, that she blamed them. Kristyn leaned against a convenient hitching post. After all, everyone in town linked her name with that of Billy Collins—and Billy was a dangerous, volatile man.

"Did you really do those terrible things," she had asked him once when she worked up her nerve. "The things they say about you?"

Billy responded with a laugh. "I don't know. What do they say?"

"They say you emptied two six-shooters full of lead into a man, killing him inch by inch. Were they . . . exaggerating?"

"No," he had replied, fixing her with a cool, even look. "They were not exaggerating."

"But . . . why?"

"Why, indeed?" He had spoken the words quietly, but there was a kind of hardness in his voice. "Maybe because I've got a mean streak running through me, the way everyone says. Only so did Stark, the man I shot, so don't waste your tears on him. He killed a boy I knew, a green kid whose only fault was that he looked up to me as some sort of hero. Stark got him all liquored up and goaded him into drawing first so the law couldn't touch him. Afterward, he bought drinks for everyone at the Silver Spur . . . and they all sat around and laughed about it.''

He paused for a moment, staring off into the distance.

''I might have shot him clean—if he hadn't laughed about it. That boy was a friend of mine. No one messes with a friend of Billy Collins and lives to tell about it.''

No, Kristyn thought, shivering in spite of the heat, she couldn't blame all those people who shied away from her. She, too, was a friend of Billy Collins, and any offense against her, real or imagined, would meet with harsh justice at his hands.

A sudden flurry of motion erupted on the previously quiet street, and Kristyn was startled to see the cowpoke spur his dusty horse into action, trotting briskly around the corner and onto Bridge. Even before he had disappeared, the two men at the far end dove with alarming abruptness into a shallow ditch along the railroad tracks.

Reacting instinctively, Kristyn leaped onto the boardwalk, ducking into the shadows beneath a low awning that ran the length of Beatty and Kelley's storefront. Common sense warned her to scurry inside, but she could not resist one last impulse to look around.

As she turned, she spotted a man standing alone in the center of the dirt roadway. His legs were slightly spread apart, his shoulders taut and squared, giving him the look of a wary animal, ready to spring. His arms hung loosely at his sides; his hands were only inches from the twin holsters that held his guns.

Wyatt Earp. Kristyn had never met the Marshal of Dodge, but like everyone in town, she knew him by sight, and like them, she was aware of his reputation. Almost the instant she spied him, she realized what was happening. For days, the saloons had been filled with rumors that disgruntled Texans, embittered by his rigid law enforcement north of the Deadline, had put a price on the lawman's head. Five hundred dollars, some said, a thousand, others whispered, enjoying the exaggeration. But whatever the dollar amount, it was going to draw out every man daring enough, or desperate enough, to try to collect it.

And one of them was about to try now.

Kristyn pressed deeper into the shadows, staring out in fascination at the Marshal. He was not, she thought, vaguely disappointed, a particularly imposing figure. He was neither large nor powerfully built, and his plain, dark suit made him look like a ordinary businessman. His pants cuffs were dusty, as were the points of boots that peeked out from beneath them, and his jacket was open, showing a pair of holstered guns, one on each hip. Only the glint of his badge gave him an air of authority. That, and the way his jaw seemed to tighten under a full moustache, as hard, flinty eyes gazed straight ahead, shifting neither right nor left.

A sudden alertness seemed to come into his body, not a movement exactly, but a subtle tensing of the muscles, and even as she turned, Kristyn knew what she was going to see: another man, poised in much the same stance at the opposite end of the street. But what she had not expected was a glimpse of intense blue eyes, or a thatch of blond hair showing under the brim of a black hat.

Billy! A shock of recognition wrenched through her. Of course it was Billy! Who else could it have been? That was why Ham Lynch looked at her so strangely before, and that was why everyone had been avoiding her these last few days! They knew only too well what she herself should have guessed. An ego like Billy Collins' would never be able to resist the challenge the Texans had thrown out. Nor could his fingers resist the itching temptation of that handsome reward.

He looked almost touchingly boyish, standing by himself at the end of the street. Boyish and debonair, with his thumbs hooked through his gunbelt and his head cocked slightly to one side, like an adolescent not yet aware of his own vulnerability.

If only she *had* guessed, she thought unhappily. A day or two ago, even an hour or two ago, she might have prevented this senseless tragedy. Now, these two proud men were standing face to face in full view of everyone in town, and neither of them would be able to back down.

They stood for a moment, sizing each other up with steady eyes. Then, slowly they began to move forward, each starting at the same time. Every muscle in their bodies was taut, every nerve alert. The street was absolutely still, the only sound the crunching of their boots against the gritty earth.

Then they stopped, a few yards away from each other, and all that was left was the silence. No sound could be detected, no movement, no expression—only a kind of savage tension that seemed to snap through the air between them.

It was Billy who finally broke the silence.

"I've been looking for you, Earp."

"Well, you've found me."

The man was cool, Kristyn had to admit, admiring him against her will. Totally, unbelievably cool. If he felt any fear, any fear at all, he did not show it.

Nor, for that matter, did Billy. Not a muscle twitched, not an eyelid blinked as his hand flashed out, reaching for the butt of his gun.

Horrified, Kristyn realized he was not going to try to goad the other man into drawing first. The act he was about to commit would be murder, pure and simple, and he did not care who knew it!

Everything happened so swiftly after that, she could not sort it out in her mind. She did not see Earp's hand move, though she knew it must have, for suddenly his gun was out, glistening in the sunlight as he matched Billy in a deadly race of speed and skill. A deafening explosion shattered the stillness, a single gunshot perhaps, or two occurring simultaneously, she could not tell which, and a cloud of blue-gray smoke erupted in the air around them.

Sickened, yet unable to tear her eyes away, Kristyn squinted tensely, trying to make out those two erect figures, sure that at any moment one or the other of them was going to topple into the dust. Only as the haze began to clear did she notice the details she had missed before: a flash of metallic brightness in the dirt at Billy's feet; the way he clutched his upper arm with one hand; the blood that had begun to seep through his fingers, staining the pristine whiteness of his shirt. It was another second before her numbed mind could grasp the truth.

Earp had not shot to kill!

Stunned, Kristyn stared at the lawman, trying to figure out what was going on in his head. Art Barstow had told her that the Marshal of Dodge took his job seriously, and his job was to prevent bloodshed, not add to it by cutting new notches in his gun. She had not believed him at the time. It seemed to her incredible that any man could stand in the center of the street and let another man take potshots at him without trying to stop him once and for all.

Yet obviously, he could.

Kristyn turned to scan Billy's face. If he was at all surprised, she could see no trace of it in his features. He looked even cooler than he had before, as if the whole thing were nothing more than a joke. When he moved, it was only to touch his fingers to the brim of his hat, tipping it in a reckless show of gallantry. Then, with a quick grin, he turned and sauntered cockily down the street and around the corner.

Kristyn stared after him in disbelief. Could that be all there was to it? Not the savage violence she had expected. Not the grim finality. Only one brief moment of confrontation, one shattering burst of gunfire . . . and the Marshal of Dodge had earned his keep for one more day.

The street that had been so hushed before now bristled with noise and activity. Every door seemed to swing open at the same time, and men and women poured out into the dusty sunlight, all talking at once, all shouting over one another in an attempt to sort out what they had glimpsed from behind drawn curtains and closed shutters. Kristyn's knees felt weak, and her legs were shaking so badly she could hardly stand. Locating a nearby bench, she sank onto it.

What was there about these men of the West? Was life only a game to them? A deadly game to be won or lost with the draw of a pistol? What motivated the Wyatt Earps, the seasoned gamblers turned lawmen, who set themselves up again and again as targets for other men? Or the Billy Collinses, always on the lookout for a reward or a reputation?

But, of course, she reminded herself grimly, it was a different game for Billy. After all, courting a bullet in the arm was not quite the same as risking one in the chest.

Still, Billy did have style. Even angry as she was, Kristyn could not deny that. Billy had a flamboyance all his own, an insouciant charm that was disarmingly appealing. Any man who could grin at his own defeat, a man who actually tipped his hat to the enemy who had bested him, was not one to be easily dismissed.

She had been sitting on the bench for some time before it occurred to Kristyn to wonder what was going to happen to

Billy now, or to be alarmed for him. Before today, he had existed in Dodge on a combination of boldness and bluster, and because everyone was afraid of him, the pose had worked. But now, the townsmen had seen his weakness, his vulnerability, and they would circle around him like a flock of vultures around a wounded mountain lion.

And with his arm out of commission, he would not be able to defend himself.

Not that he deserved any help! Kristyn shook her head, tossing back the curls that had spilled onto her forehead, sticking in the dusty heat. Billy had made his own bed, it would serve him right if she let him lie on it! Still, he had been good to her. For that alone, she owed him a debt of gratitude.

Besides, in his own way, Billy had been her friend. How could she live with herself if she turned her back on a friend?

Billy sat on a rock ledge, high on a hillside at the edge of town, ignoring the throbbing pain in his arm as he stared down at the flatlands below.

Like little ants, he thought contemptuously, watching the swarming figures that had begun to fill the streets of Dodge again. Little ants, all scurrying around, all absorbed in their own self-importance, heading in every direction at once and not going anyplace at all. Except, inevitably, up here.

He glanced around with a grim sense of satisfaction. He had always had a secret fondness for the rugged promontory northwest of town, and today the bleakness of the place seemed especially suited to his mood. The earth was almost defiantly barren, a combination of gypsum, rock, and clay, supporting nothing but scattered clumps of buffalo grass and soapweed. But its loneliness was a loneliness that was close to the clouds, its wildness the wildness of nature, stark and uncompromising.

Boot Hill.

Billy liked the name. He always had. It added, for him, a touch of whimsy to what might otherwise have seemed a grisly business. Some said it came from the fact that the men who were carried up there still had their boots on; others claimed it was because they were laid to rest with nothing but a saddle blanket for a winding sheet and their boots propped under their heads as a pillow. But one way or the other, Boot

Hill was still the last home for everyone without friends or finances—for vagrants and thieves alike, penniless cowhands down on their luck, and hanged killers . . . and poker players who found themselves at the wrong end of a six-shooter with no more aces up their sleeve.

Billy let his eyes wander, taking in the weathered gray boards that marked the individual graves. These were his kind of people. "John Hall, Died of Lead Poisoning." "Jake Lerner, Hanged Legally." "Billy Bates, Shot One Night by Mistake." Some day he would join that outcast crew, whether on this rocky tor or another, and he would have no regrets for a life spent exactly as he wanted. For now, he would sit there and enjoy their silent company.

The plains below were unusually quiet, with virtually no movement beyond the outskirts of town. Only a solitary figure could be seen, weaving slowly through waist-high grasses toward the base of the hill. Billy shielded his eyes with his hand, squinting into the glaring sunlight, then relaxed as he recognized that gracefully swaying form.

Pretty Kris. How well the little minx knew him! She had guessed where he was, and no doubt she knew why he had come, too! She had seen enough of his macabre humor these past days to realize how irresistible the lure of Boot Hill would be on a morning like this. She would be hopping mad, of course, but she was too stubborn—and too hot-willed—to let that stand in her way.

Pretty, pretty Kris. Almost unconsciously, his tongue flicked across his lips, moistening the coating of dust that had settled there. It fascinated him, the way she moved, so free and loose, as if no one had told her that ladies were supposed to hold their bodies just so and walk with coy mincing steps. There was a delightfully basic quality about her, a kind of uncomplicated naturalness that seemed more animal than human, like a half-tamed kitten, or a timid doe about to dart across the fields.

He remembered suddenly the way she had looked that first time he saw her. What a surprise she had been, utterly enchanting, even in the absurd satin gown Art Barstow had procured for her. She had seemed almost innocent then, naive enough not to realize that the dress was garish and cheap, a mere parody of prettiness rather than pretty itself.

And yet, beneath that beguiling innocence, even then,

Billy had sensed a smoldering sexuality that drew his eyes toward her, and held them there. He had wanted her at that moment, wanted her as much as any woman he had ever seen. He wanted her still.

What a bitch she had been that night. What a fiery, hot-tempered, infuriating, absolutely glorious bitch! She had known just how to put him in his place—blast her!—and she knew how to keep him there. That devious feminine brain told her that she had made a fool of him in public once, and his pride would never let him show interest in her again. At least not where men could see—and laugh.

But on a deserted hilltop?

Billy's eyes drifted toward the place where she had already begun to work her way up the rocky path. Did she realize, he wondered, that when she reached the top they would be absolutely alone for the first time since they had met? Down below, in the town, he had been afraid of the laughter of other men. Who would laugh at him here?

Perhaps this was not going to be such a bad day after all.

Kristyn, unaware of Billy's eyes on her, continued up the steep path, stopping occasionally to catch her breath. When at last she reached the edge of the graveyard, she paused for a moment, studying the hardened mounds of earth with frank distaste.

What was it that made the white man bury his dead in holes in the ground, where their souls would be trapped forever? Indians had more respect for those who passed before. Even a Cheyenne criminal fared better, for sinners were not segregated in death, and the *tasoom* of every man save he who committed suicide was free to begin the long journey up the Hanging Road into the heavens.

She was surprised to catch sight of a bouquet of half-dried wildflowers in front of a marker with no name on it. The gesture touched her, but it seemed odd, too, out of keeping in a desolate spot where only drifters and criminals were laid to rest.

And yet, she reminded herself ironically, if things had gone differently—if Wyatt Earp's bullet had found Billy's heart instead of his gun arm—wouldn't she be carrying a handful of flowers up that same hillside now?

"Hah-hah!" a loud voice cried out suddenly.

Kristyn whirled around just in time to see a lean figure

looming up like a ghost from behind one of the gravestones. For an instant, she felt faint from shock and horror. Then she recognized a mop of unruly yellow hair—and the most impudent blue eyes she had ever seen!

"I suppose I should have said, 'Boo!' " Billy grinned, a self-satisfied smirk giving his face a puckish look. "That's what a real ghost would have done. He would have cried out, 'Booooooo!' in deep, sepulchral tones. But you've known me long enough to realize I never do anything I'm supposed to."

Kristyn was too stunned at first to do anything but gape at him. She did not know if she wanted to throw her arms around him with relief—or scream at him for the idiotic way he was behaving!

She decided on the latter.

"Billy Collins, you are—you are a damn fool! Has anyone ever told you that?"

"Of course!" Billy's grin broadened as he plopped down irreverently on a mound of earth. "All the time. In fact, my mother used to say that to me. 'Billy Collins, you are a damn fool,' she would say—or words to that effect."

Kristyn tried to cling to her anger, but as always with Billy, she did not succeed. Giving up, she sat down beside him, tucking her skirts around her.

"Did she really? Well, I'm not surprised. It must have been very aggravating, having a son like you. I wouldn't blame her if she yelled at you every minute of the time."

"Actually, she didn't." Billy was still smiling, but there was a subtle edge to his voice. "And she never called me a fool either. It would have been better if she had. I don't think I heard twenty words out of her all the time I was growing up. She was too busy trying to stay out of my father's way so he wouldn't beat her. We used to huddle in the darkness, my sister and I, listening to the sounds. We knew she was trying to keep from screaming so we wouldn't hear."

"Are you serious?" Kristyn eyed him skeptically. She knew that men could be cruel to their wives, but among Indians wife-beating was rare, tolerated neither by the woman nor the tribe. "You mean your father actually *hit* your mother? And no one stopped him? Oh, Billy, I can't believe that!"

"Well, believe it or not, it's the truth. He used to pommel her face until it looked like raw meat. I think he took a special pleasure in hitting her where it would show. Maybe he liked to look at his handiwork. When he wasn't beating her, he was beating me. He'd take me out in the shed and whip me with a leather belt until there was hardly any skin left on my back. If you're a good girl, I'll take off all my clothes and show you my scars.''

He twisted his features into a rakish leer. Then, catching the look on Kristyn's face, he relented.

''Hey . . .'' Reaching out with one hand, he tucked his finger under her chin. ''You didn't think a fellow got to be the meanest bastard in Dodge all by himself, did you?''

He uttered the words lightly, with nothing in his voice or his eyes to echo their haunting darkness, and for an instant, Kristyn half dared to hope he was joking. But something in his manner told her he was not.

''Come on, let's have a look at that arm,'' she said, eager to change the subject. ''The blood is already beginning to congeal—and just look at that! Why, you haven't even had the sense to cut away your shirt. It's sure to get infected if you leave it like that.''

Ripping the sleeve lengthwise, she tore the fabric, tugging at it as gently as she could, but making sure she removed every bit of fraying thread from the wound. Billy winced when she first touched him, but he held his arm steady, and after that one brief, involuntary movement, he made no further show of pain or weakness.

''Well, it's not as bad as it could have been,'' she said, completing the examination with probing fingers. ''The bullet cut deep, but it didn't damage the bone. If you can just keep it clean, it will be all right in a week or two. I'll gather some wild herbs to dress it later—that will help the healing process and cut down the danger of infection—but right now, all I can do is bandage it.''

Removing her petticoat, she tore the filmy white cotton into neat, even strips, which she wound expertly around his arm. Billy watched in silence, fascinated by the deft efficiency of those long, sun-bronzed fingers.

''You're full of surprises, aren't you?'' he asked, when she had nearly finished. ''Remind me never to underestimate you again—and never to get involved in a gunfight without you! Where did you learn to bind a wound like that?''

''It's my——'' Kristyn caught herself just in time. My

Indian background, she had started to say, but Billy did not know about her past, and she had no desire to speak of it now. "It's my upbringing. I wasn't raised in the city. I grew up in the woods, far from doctors and hospitals, or any kind of medication for that matter, except what we could gather ourselves in the fields. I learned how to take care of all sorts of emergencies—including gunshot wounds. Now, just hold still a minute longer and let me wrap this around one more time . . . there, I'm almost done."

She leaned closer, tying the last ends together, her body so near to his he could smell the fragrance of her hair in his nostrils. Surprised, Billy realized he had nearly forgotten the wave of longing that had swept through his loins as he watched her climbing slowly, sensuously, up the hill. Now abruptly, it returned, more intense than ever, reminding him once again how much he wanted this woman.

Taking hold of her hand, he drew it away from his arm, laying it lightly, almost teasingly, against his cheek.

"I was watching you before," he said, his voice strangely low in his throat. "You were looking at the flowers on that pathetic grave, and I know what was going on in your mind. You were thinking of me."

Kristyn looked up with troubled eyes. She was keenly aware of the male roughness of his cheek beneath her hand, and she longed to draw it back. But she was aware too of something unexpectedly lonely in his expression.

"Yes, I was thinking of you."

"If that were me," he said only half teasing, "if I were lying under that ugly marker instead of some poor anonymous bastard, would you bring me wildflowers? Would you grieve for me?"

"You don't deserve it, God knows. But yes, I would bring flowers. And yes, I would grieve."

"Don't you think that's rather illogical?" Billy laughed, twisting her hand around until suddenly her palm was against his lips. "Why do something for me then, when it wouldn't make any difference? I can think of something you could do right now, while I'm still around to appreciate it."

Kristyn's heart sank at the undisguised insinuation in his tone. Belatedly, she realized her first instinct had been right—she should not have let him touch her, however lightly.

"Why, Billy Collins," she said, pulling her hand away

with a teasing lightness she did not feel. "I would have thought you'd learned your lesson the first time. Didn't I teach you what happens when you force your attentions on a woman who doesn't want them?"

Almost to her surprise, the ploy worked. Billy stared at her in silence for a moment, then his features took on a look of grudging admiration.

Blast the little she-devil, she still knew how to handle him! Until that moment, he had thought he was only afraid of making a fool of himself in front of the other men in town. Now he realized the humiliation would be the same, whether anyone was there to see it or not.

"All right, I won't force my filthy lust on you, at least not for the time being. But I'm not going to stop wooing you, and I will win in the end, you know. Maybe after you help me get out of this place."

"Help you, indeed!" Kristyn retorted, laughing. "What makes you think I have anything like that in mind?"

"You wouldn't be here if you didn't. And not only are you going to help me—you're going to come away with me when you do!"

"Now that's too much!" Kristyn's eyes widened in astonishment. "I suppose I will help you. I can hardly leave you here to fend for yourself. But I am most certainly not going to go away with you."

"Think about it, Kris." Billy's voice was cool and even. "It isn't so farfetched. You'll have to bring some of my things from town. I can hardly make my getaway in a bloody shirt with one sleeve torn out of it—I'd stick out like a sore thumb. Even then, I doubt if I could make it on my own. Too many men have a score to settle with me. They'll all be on my trail by nightfall. I wouldn't be able to get anywhere near the livery stable, and neither would you. And if I try and get on a train in some hick Kansas town, word is going to get back so fast, it'll make the Pony Express look slow. But if a young couple were to wait on the railroad platform, a nice, clean-cut couple—well, who would think anything of that? Besides . . ."

He paused, giving Kristyn a mildly disturbed look. He was beginning to be sorry he had involved her in this, though not sorry enough to change his mind and let her go.

"Besides, I'm afraid you don't have a choice. If you fetch

my things for me, someone is bound to find out, and you can hardly hang around Dodge after that. There is too much bitterness against me, too much anger. If I get away now—if they can't take it out on me—then it's all going to come down on your head."

Kristyn remained thoughtful for a moment, mulling over his words. A faint breeze had picked up, bringing with it not the coolness she would have welcomed, but a renewed wave of oppressive heat. Bitterly, she realized Billy was right. If life had been hard for her before he came along, it was going to be pure hell after he left.

"But—where are you going?"

"I don't know. Maybe West. West is a good direction for a gunman."

"West? Toward Santa Fe?"

Billy heard the catch in her voice, but he was careful not to comment on it. So she had reasons of her own for wanting to go West, did she? Well, that was all right with him. He wouldn't take her anywhere near Santa Fe, of course—he wasn't going to risk losing her—but she didn't have to know that now.

"Well, sure, Santa Fe. If you like."

Kristyn moved a few feet away from him, grateful when he did not try to follow. Massive fields of waving yellow grasses seemed to stretch all the way to the setting sun. Santa Fe. Why did her heart insist on beating fast like that whenever she heard the name? Santa Fe. It was not as if she expected to see Rafe there, not as if she even *wanted* to see him. Not after the finality of their parting. And certainly he did not want to see her!

But Billy had been right. There was no escaping that. She could not hope to stay in Dodge, not with the things that had happened today. And if she had to move on anyway . . . well, why not toward Santa Fe?

"All right," she said softly. "I'll come with you, but just long enough to get you away from here. After that, we split up and go our separate ways."

Twenty-one

"Grasshoppers! Look at 'em! All over the place. Thick as blades of grass."

The boy loped down the narrow train aisle, calling out his announcement again and again in high-pitched tones. When he reached the slatted wooden bench where Kristyn was seated, he stopped to point excitedly at the window beside her.

"Look out there, missus. There are thousands of 'em, all over. Bet you've never seen anythin' like it in your life."

Kristyn resisted the impulse to smile. Young Jeremiah Clayter was much too grown-up for a twelve-year-old. It was good to see him acting like a boy for once.

"Yes, they're . . ." She paused, searching for the right word. "They're *fascinating!*"

And, in truth, they were. Moistening a handkerchief with spit, she rubbed a clear space in the dust and coal smoke that coated the window. The ground outside rippled with movement, as masses of tiny bodies swarmed and hopped all over the earth. Even to the rear, where the train tracks curved out in a wide, sweeping arc, not a glint of metal could be detected beneath that mat of grayish green.

"Like the plagues of ancient Egypt."

Kristyn looked up to see Billy standing beside her. His bandaged arm was stiff beneath a loose-fitting jacket, but he moved well enough to keep anyone from noticing. Propping one foot up on the bench opposite her, he leaned toward the window.

"The plagues of ancient Egypt?" she asked, puzzled. "What on earth are those? All I know about Egypt is that they had rulers called Pharaohs, like the card game."

"Well, they had plagues, too, and plenty of them. The locusts were the eighth, I think, or were they the ninth? After all these years, I get them mixed up."

"Locusts?" Kristyn frowned. "But what do locusts have to do with these insects? I thought they were grasshoppers."

Billy laughed, glancing back at her with a look that was half amused, half entranced. The more he saw of this woman, the more intrigued he was. Sometimes, she seemed so sharp and knowing, her quick mind left him far behind. Other times, she was as ignorant as a little girl. He had agreed readily enough to her terms when they began their journey. They would go their own separate ways, he had promised, when they were far enough from Dodge to be safe, but he had known even then he was lying.

Still, this was hardly the moment to press the matter.

"The plagues are a Bible story," he explained. "From the Book of Exodus. When the pharaoh refused to let Moses deliver the Israelites from bondage in Egypt, the Lord visited a succession of plagues on the land. I've forgotten most of them by now, but I do remember that the waters of the Nile turned into blood—that impressed me greatly as a boy—and locusts, or grasshoppers, as we call them today, infested the entire country. Even then, pharaoh would not relent, and in the end, every Egyptian firstborn was struck down, from the child of the ruler himself to that of his lowliest handmaiden."

"Struck down?" Kristyn stared at him in horror. "You mean *killed*?" Every new glimpse she had of this harsh religion the white man practiced only served to remind her how far removed it was from the simpler faith of her childhood. "I don't think I like the Bible if it has stories like that in it."

Billy looked startled, then began to laugh again.

"It's easy to see you weren't raised on the Bible."

"No. No, I wasn't."

"Well, I was." Billy took his foot down and leaned his lank body against the window frame. "And you can see the good it did me! My father was very strict about the Sabbath. No frivolity on Sundays. No work. No liquor. Only the trouble was, he was even meaner when he was sober."

As always, when he spoke of his past, Billy's voice was light, almost brittle—and as always, Kristyn was taken aback. The words were as bitter as any she had ever heard, yet here he was, actually laughing, as if somehow the whole thing hadn't mattered at all.

Covering her confusion, she turned back to the scene outside.

"Is that why we've stopped here? Because of the grasshoppers on the track?"

"You bet!" young Jeremiah chimed in, crowding next to them at the window. "They're all over the place. I went up front to see. The fireman says they don't have enough sense to get out o' the way when the train comes. They just lie there and get squished all over the tracks. The wheels'd slide right off if we tried to go on."

"Jeremiah, that'll be enough!"

The words were so sharp, they stopped the boy instantly. None of them had seen Zeke Clayter approach, but he was there now, standing in the aisle, a tall, dour man with dark hair, clumsily cut, and an ill-fitting black suit.

"Aw, Pa——"

"I said, that'll be enough! Go and fetch your Ma a drink of water from the cooler at the back."

Jeremiah flushed a deep beet red, but did not try to protest. Clayter waited until he had made his way down to the end of the car, then he turned to Kristyn with a scowl.

"The boy is fanciful enough as it is," he said sharply. "Don't you go encouragin' him."

Kristyn's cheeks burned, but she bit back the angry retort that rose to her lips. Even when Clayter turned away, following his son to the rear of the car without so much as another word, she did not have the heart to pick a fight with him. His back was rigid, his shoulders taut, as if he were afraid to let them relax, and she knew he had seen enough trouble in his life to break a lesser man.

"Zeke didn't mean what he said," a new voice added apologetically. "At least not the way it sounded. He's just worried right now."

The words so exactly mirrored what Kristyn was thinking, she almost believed she had imagined them. But as she turned, she saw that Elizabeth Clayter, a small, frail woman with thinning grayish hair, had come to join her on the bench.

"I know that," Kristyn replied. "I understand how he feels—and I didn't take any offense, believe me."

"Things have been real hard for us these last few years," Elizabeth explained. "It seemed like we could never get two pennies to rub together, and whenever things started to work out—well, something always came along to set us back. Only this time . . .''

Her voice trailed off, but Kristyn knew what she was thinking. Once Elizabeth had gotten over her initial shyness, she proved as talkative as her husband was taciturn, and Kristyn had quickly learned that this was the first time she had been back to see her family in the fifteen years she had been married.

"This time,'' she prompted gently, "you hoped it would be different.''

"It *did* look as if things were finally turning around,'' Elizabeth conceded. "We got some real good seed wheat from the Mennonites. Zeke says he's never seen anything like it before. The rust doesn't touch it, and it doesn't even mind the drought. Last year, we had our best harvest ever, and this year was shaping up even better. But now . . .'' She turned her head slightly, glancing toward the window. "Now I just don't know.''

Kristyn followed her gaze.

"Are you really that worried about the grasshoppers?'' Certainly she had never seen so many insects in one place in her life, but they hardly seemed capable of doing any real damage.

"They could clean us out in less than a day, Zeke says. We could lose our whole harvest, even our seed for next year. That's why he was so mad when Jeremiah got excited about them. The boy doesn't understand how dangerous they are.''

"Well, there's no point fussing about things that haven't happened yet,'' Kristyn put in, secretly siding with the youth. "Even if they *are* a real threat, and I'm not at all convinced of that, there's no reason to believe they're anywhere near your property.''

"I don't know.'' Elizabeth sounded skeptical. "There are an awful lot of them . . . and we're real near here.''

"You are?'' Kristyn glanced back at her surprised. "I hadn't realized you were so close. Where is your land?''

"About ten miles away, I reckon. Maybe not that far.''

"Ten miles! Why then, you're almost there.''

"We get off at the next station. Zeke's brother, Zeb, is

supposed to come and pick us up in the wagon. If we hadn't stopped here, we'd be home by now."

Home! Kristyn caught the longing in Elizabeth's voice, overriding her tension, and she understood it instantly. Home— the end of that long, uncomfortable journey! A chance to get out of the stifling cage in which they had been confined, day after tedious day.

Kristyn let her eyes drift with distaste around the car that had begun to seem like a prison to her. At one end, a squat coal-burning stove had been banked for the day, but the embers of last night's fire still radiated heat, and sooty windows had been shut against the swarming grasshoppers, making the air almost unbearably fetid. A group of men in filthy flannel shirts were clustered in the corner, eyeing everyone who passed and spitting out tobacco juice until the floor was shiny and slick. The smell of kerosene was sharp and pervasive. Kerosene and coal smoke, and too many people crowded into too small a place.

"Maybe your brother-in-law will figure out what happened and come to rescue you," she said, trying not to sound jealous. "At least then you won't have to spend another night in this place."

And it was the nights, she thought later, when Jeremiah had brought the water to his mother and they had wandered back to their own seats, that were the hardest. The long, hot days were bad enough, but when dusk fell and kerosene lanterns were lighted on the walls, the dreariness became almost intolerable. Occasionally they stopped for supper at a railroad-operated buffet, where surprisingly substantial, if not very tasty, plates of food were available for twenty-five cents, but for the most part, they clustered around the coal stove, taking turns preparing their own meals. When they had finished, it was time to take out a number of long, flat boards and lay them lengthwise between the benches to form sleeping platforms for a fortunate few. A variety of bedding was spread on top of them: thick, fluffy featherbeds or threadbare quilts, bug-infested mattresses, even old overcoats that had seen better days.

Well, at least she had one of the plank-beds. And an "immigrant mattress," too, a flat bag stuffed with lumpy straw, which they had purchased from someone at the station for $1.25, and would resell for the same amount when they reached the end of the line. Billy slept in a blanket roll on the floor.

It was not that she was truly jealous of Elizabeth, Kristyn thought, trying to curb the feeling of rebelliousness that surged through her breast. She liked the older woman and wished her nothing but good, and she honestly hoped that Zeke's brother *would* come and pick them up. But, oh, wouldn't it be heaven to get out of that place herself! To wake up, just for one morning, without the smell of sweat in her nostrils, and the taste of smoke and cinders in her mouth!

Kristyn was to get her wish, although not quite the way she had imagined. Early in the afternoon, the grasshoppers had finally thinned out and the train had chugged forward again, only to stop a few miles farther on, brought to a halt by a mechanical breakdown. The Clayters shouldered their bags and tramped across the fields, and Kristyn and Billy brought out their blankets and laid them a short distance apart in the tall grasses beside the tracks.

But when she woke in the morning, Kristyn was aware not of the refreshing coolness of the air, but of a strange, disturbing sound that pulled her fretfully out of sleep. Still groggy, she lay back and listened, trying to figure out what it could be. Not the sweet bird call she had expected, that was for sure—not even the vaguely eerie whistle the wind sometimes gave as it passed through the leaves. This was a steady, constant beat, a kind of *chomp-chomp, chomp-chomp, chomp-chomp* that hammered in her ears until it seemed to echo all around her.

Chomp-chomp, chomp-chomp, chomp-chomp. Like the jaws of some predatory animal, she thought, shivering. Like something eating its way across the earth!

Snapping to attention, she sat up. Her skin had begun to crawl, but she could see nothing to justify her alarm. The sky was clear, but surprisingly dark, with a faint greenish cast to it, and the air was almost deathly still. Off to the east, she could see black clouds gathering on the horizon.

Billy was already up, standing several yards away, staring off at something in the distance. The uneasiness Kristyn had felt before seemed even more intense now, and she hurried toward him.

"What is it?" she cried out. "A tornado?"

Billy glanced back, a strange, half-excited look on his face.

"A tornado? No, rather a different act of God, I'd say. Or perhaps I should call it an 'ungodly act.' The grasshoppers are moving."

"The grasshoppers?"

Kristyn followed his gaze, unable for a moment to believe that that pervasive sound she heard could be coming from such tiny creatures. But as she looked, she saw that what she had taken for a broad, grassy meadow was in reality a vast sheet of grasshoppers, stretching perhaps a quarter of a mile across the earth.

Their progress was both dramatic and appalling. In front of them, farmers' fields burgeoned with grain, and tall, stately cottonwoods stretched leafy branches into the heavens. Behind them, only the grotesque skeletons of trees, denuded even of their bark, jutted out of raw, brown earth.

And those dark clouds she had seen, blowing in from the east? Horrified, Kristyn turned to gape at them again. They were not clouds at all, but other insect armies, drifting toward them from the horizon.

"Oh, Billy, the Clayters."

Billy spun around. "My God, I had forgotten about them. Their farm is just over that hill. Come on!"

Without waiting for her reaction, Billy began to race across the fields, clearing ruts and prairie-dog holes with nimble leaps. Kristyn followed as best she could, but her long skirts hampered her, and he was already out of sight as she approached the rise of the hill.

She was gasping painfully by the time she rounded the crest and peered down into the valley below. The Clayter house stood by itself, a weathered, gray building in the center of a small, dusty clearing. Beyond it, splashes of color turned the landscape into a green-and-gold patchwork of irrigation ditches and neatly fenced fields.

They were all right! Kristyn almost shouted out loud with relief. The Clayters were all right—for the time being at least!

Hiking her skirts up, she hurried down the hill, heading for a field behind the barn where she had spotted Billy talking to Zeke Clayter and another tall, dark-haired man. As she drew nearer, she saw that the men had hitched a pair of farmhorses to a plow, and a number of tools, spades and picks for the most part, lay scattered on the ground. On the far side of the barn, Elizabeth and Jeremiah were gouging a furrow at the edge of what seemed to be a field of new wheat.

"What on earth are you doing?" she called out. "The grasshoppers are just over that hill! They could be here any minute. Why are you plowing fields at a time like this?"

To her surprise, the man behind the plow started to laugh.

"Not plowin', missus. We're aimin' to clear a break around some of the fields. It's the only way we might be able to stop them ornery little critters."

That must be Zeb Clayter, Kristyn thought. Zeke's brother.

"A break? You mean a strip of barren land? But what good will that do? They'll just hop over. Or *fly*, for heaven's sake!"

"The breaks aren't to stop the grasshoppers." Billy tossed her a sharp look. "They're to keep the fire from spreading to the crops on the other side."

"What fire? Billy, there's no fire around here."

"No, but there will be when the grasshoppers arrive. As soon as we spot the first of them, we're going to set a torch to the area around the fields we want to save. The flames ought to keep them from getting through on the ground, and if we're lucky, the smoke will discourage them in the air."

"But, Billy . . ." Kristyn glanced around dubiously. "The land is so arid here. There's nothing to burn except . . ."

"Except the rest of the crops," he agreed grimly.

"There's no point gettin' greedy," Zeb Clayter broke in. "If we try to save everything, we'll lose it all for sure. The corn can go, and most of the grain too, over there on the hillside. If we can just save the Mennonite wheat, we'll be all right. At least enough for seed for next year."

"Might as well just get down on our knees," his brother countered gloomily, "and pray to the Lord for deliverance. It's a far sight easier, and it'll do more good."

"Zeke Clayter, you know as well as I do, the good Lord isn't going to lift a finger to help us if we haven't got the gumption to help ourselves. Now, are you goin' to pick up that shovel an' get to work, or aren't you?"

"Amen!" Billy heaved a pick and shovel onto his shoulder. "I'm all for prayer, Clayter, if you think it will work, but you can pray while you're digging. Your brother can manage this section with the plow. You go on over and help your wife and boy. I'll take the other end of the same field, and we'll meet each other in the middle.''

Kristyn watched as the men burst simultaneously into action. Zeb prodded his horses forward again, and Zeke and Billy, both with picks on their shoulders, sprinted across the fields. Kristyn stared after them for a moment, then chose one of the lighter shovels and hoisted it over her shoulder, the way she had seen the others do.

Billy looked up at her approach. With a terse nod of his head, he indicated a far corner of the field. Kristyn saw instantly what he was telling her. If she started at that point and worked back toward him, they would reach each other just about the same time Zeke and his family had finished clearing the other end.

The sun was already high in the sky, and as the morning progressed, beads of perspiration dripped down Kristyn's forehead. The ground felt brutally hard beneath her shovel, not dry and dusty, the way it looked, but dry and caked, as if the uncompromising extremes of climate had weathered it to a solid concrete. A hot wind picked up, gusting occasionally, then dying away to a feeble whisper. Almost instinctively, Kristyn tilted her face upward, gauging the speed and direction against her skin.

From the east, she thought, with a catch in her throat. From the east, where even now, dark clouds were massing in the sky!

Sinking her shovel fiercely into the earth, she redoubled her efforts. Her hands were blistered almost raw, her dress so drenched it clung to her legs, but somehow she managed to keep going until she had crossed that final stretch of land that separated her from Billy.

He finished at the same time and leaned, exhausted, against the handle of his spade. He had given up any pretense of concealing his wound and was in his shirtsleeves, with the outline of a bandage showing clearly on his arm. A thin trickle of blood seeped through the fabric, and Kristyn could see he was in pain.

She started to cry out, then stopped, knowing he would bristle at her fussing.

''Where did you learn so much about farming?'' she asked

instead, recalling suddenly that it was he who had taken charge, almost from the moment they arrived.

Billy swung around with a start, then relaxed.

"I was raised on a farm. Didn't I tell you that? I was expected to earn my keep at an early age. Actually, I was glad to do it. As long as I was good at my chores, my father couldn't afford to break every bone in my body."

"Billy!" Kristyn was so tired, she couldn't even pretend to be patient. "Honestly, the way you talk sometimes, I don't know what to think! Did your father really beat you? Or do you just say that because it makes a good story?"

"So little faith . . . I'm shocked! Billy Collins has been accused of many things—and just between you and me, he's guilty of most of them—but no one has ever called him a liar. No, if I tell you my father beat me, rest assured he did."

Something in his tone, the sheer lack of emphasis perhaps, warned Kristyn he was telling the truth.

"What about your sister?" she asked. "You said once that you had a sister. Did he beat her, too?"

"No." Billy's face changed subtly, stiffening almost imperceptibly. For the first time, something seemed to stir in his eyes. "No, he didn't beat her. My sister, you see, was very beautiful. He had—uh, shall we say, *other plans* for her. He used to———"

He broke off abruptly, studying Kristyn with a piercing look.

"Well, enough of that. You have a vivid imagination . . . you can figure out for yourself what he did to her. I was younger than she, no more than seven or eight when it started. I used to lie in the other room, listening to her crying, *pleading* with that bastard! I felt so goddamn helpless because I couldn't do anything!"

"Oh, Billy, how terrible."

"I stood it as long as I could. Then, when I was twelve, I cleared out."

"You mean you ran away?"

"Yes, I ran away."

"But your sister, Billy!" Kristyn stared at him, aghast. She knew he loved his sister—she had glimpsed it in his eyes when he spoke of her—and yet he had deserted her. "How could you have gone away like that and left her alone? With him?"

"Oh, she ran away, too . . . in her own way. She went down to the millpond one morning when my father was busy and couldn't keep track of her. They didn't find her for several days, she was buried so deep in mud at the bottom. She had tied a stone around her neck, the way you do to drown an unwanted kitten."

He turned away for an instant, lost, Kristyn assumed, in his own dark thoughts. But when he looked back, his lips were twisted into that wry half-smile she knew so well.

"I've often thought she was the smart one. People always said my sister got the brains in the family."

If Kristyn had not been so exhausted, she would gladly have throttled Billy at that moment. There it was again, that same infuriating flippancy!

But she did not have time to say anything, for just at that moment, she caught sight of Zeke Clayter heading toward them. He had almost reached them when suddenly he stopped, gaping at the ground near Kristyn's feet with a look of horror on his face.

Glancing downward, Kristyn was startled to see a small green form wriggling on the earth in front of her.

A grasshopper! She was stunned to see how small it looked, how harmless, all by itself on the ground.

Billy spotted the insect at almost the same time and, raising his foot, he stomped down on it, grinding it beneath the heel of his boot. A second grasshopper followed an instant later, then another and yet another until they seemed to be landing everywhere at once, hopping and writhing all over the earth.

Bewildered and horrified, Kristyn stared helplessly around her. Only a minute before, there had not been a grasshopper in sight. Now the ground was almost solid with them.

"Get up to the house," Billy told her brusquely. "Make sure all the doors and windows are shut. Stuff paper and rags in the cracks. I doubt if it will do any good, but at least you can try."

Kristyn reacted without question, obeying more from instinct than conscious will. Even as she raced toward the house, she scented smoke in her nostrils, and she knew that Zeke and his brother had already set fire to their precious crops in a desperate attempt to salvage at least something from that terrible devastation.

When she reached the house, she realized she was too late.

Through the glass-paned window, she could see Elizabeth battling vainly against hordes of insects that had already penetrated the structure.

Grasshoppers seemed to be everywhere in that small room. They covered the floor like a solid, squirming carpet and hopped onto windowsills and furnishings, playing havoc with cabinets and tables alike, with chairs and threadbare couches, even the clumsy wooden chandelier that dangled from a leather thong in the center of the ceiling. Elizabeth had a broom in her hands, which she was using to swat at them, but all her frenzied energy accomplished little, for every time she crushed a dozen of them against the floor, a hundred others swarmed in to take their place.

Fascinated in spite of herself, Kristyn stood there and gaped at them. Everything seemed to be fodder for those voracious jaws. Small scatter rugs on the floor showed holes where they had been partially chewed away, and white lace curtains were beginning to disappear from the windows. Chairs had lost their upholstered covers, and even the wooden legs and smoothly waxed tops on the tables were pitted with the scars of tiny teeth.

Elizabeth had fought valiantly, jamming the cracks around the doors and windows with bits of paper and old rags, as Billy had suggested. But far from deterring the hungry locusts, the stuffing material actually seemed to attract them, giving them one more thing to gnaw on. They were eating their way into the house!

Bitterly, Kristyn realized there was no point staying where she was. She dared not open the door to go in to Elizabeth. Besides, there was nothing she could do for her. At least, if she went back to the men in the fields, she might be of some use.

As she began to head down the path, she was appalled to see how rapidly the grasshoppers had multiplied. Everywhere she looked, she saw evidence of their amazing capacity to destroy. The trees along the road were already leafless, their branches bent and cracking under the weight of thousands of writhing bodies. Behind the house, Elizabeth's kitchen garden, so neat and green a short time before, was nothing but naked earth, pocked with even rows of holes where onions and other bulbs had been.

Puffs of thick black smoke rose from various sections of

the fields, and here and there, Kristyn could see patches of flame flashing red-gold against the blackish haze, but generally the fires had been slow in taking hold. The grain burned readily enough, but the corn was still too green, and alarming gaps showed in the protective ring around the Mennonite wheat.

Kristyn made her way through the wall of smoke, pausing for a moment to get her bearings. Billy had positioned himself just inside one of the irrigation ditches with a flat-bladed spade in his hands. Even through the cracking flames, she could hear the ringing sound of it as he brought it down with indiscriminating fury on stray grasshoppers and wind-blown sparks alike. His sleeve was red with blood, but there was no sign that he even knew it, he was so caught up in the fierce anger that seemed to consume his entire being.

Anger against what? Kristyn wondered fleetingly. Against the grasshoppers that came on the wind? The fire they had started themselves? Or against that haunting darkness in his own soul?

A piece of sacking lay next to the ditch, and dipping it hastily into the tepid water, Kristyn brought it down again and again on the wriggling bodies that seemed to be all around her. There were so many of them, she thought helplessly. Even with the fires, there were so many!

The wind seemed to grow hotter, picking up the blazing heat of the fire and swirling it brutally around her. Kristyn's entire body ached, and she had the terrible feeling that any minute, any second, she would simply throw down that water-drenched sack and fall to the earth, too exhausted to fight on. The clouds on the eastern horizon drifted nearer, looming dark and nebulous behind the heavy smoke, no more than a mile away at most.

If they came closer, even a little bit closer, all the fires and all the smoke in the world couldn't save them.

Even as the thought crossed Kristyn's mind, the black haze suddenly grew thicker, and she could no longer see the encroaching clouds with her eyes. The air seemed strangely, unnaturally dark, an eerie effect, almost as if the sun had vanished from the earth. Lowering the sack, she gazed around her with an uneasy sense of foreboding. It had never occurred to her that smoke might turn so dense she would not be able to see even a foot ahead of her.

Only slowly did it occur to her that what she was witnessing was not smoke at all, but quite another phenomenon. The grasshoppers, moving as with a single will, had begun to lift off the ground, filling the air so thickly they blocked out all the light.

Stunned, Kristyn realized that the unexpected had happened. The grasshoppers were abandoning the wheat and the corn as abruptly and inexplicably as they had come to it.

Had their scheme worked then? Kristyn stood motionless, too numb to think or even feel as she stared after that retreating army with dull bewilderment. Had the fires driven them off?

It was a moment before her mind began to clear, and she became aware once again of the hot breath of the wind, blowing not from the east, as it had before, but from the north. That was it! she realized suddenly. The wind! Just as it had once borne the grasshoppers toward them, now it had changed course, carrying them off to fields in the south. It was not the fires that had saved them. Not the carefully laid plans of men, but a whim of nature. A capricious change of the winds they could neither control nor predict.

Letting go of the heavy sacking, Kristyn sank wearily to the ground. A few grasshoppers had remained behind, and these she swatted at with half-hearted gestures whenever they came too close, but for the most part, all that remained of the invaders was a mass of carcasses, lying mangled in the fields, floating like green scum on the irrigation canals.

It was late in the afternoon before Kristyn finally found the strength to get up and, wandering off by herself, she surveyed the extent of the damage. Some of the outlying fields had been virtually untouched, and a surprising amount of corn was still intact, but every place else she looked, she saw nothing but smoke rising from charred patches of earth, or wide swathes of barren land with naked trees jutting out of absolute nothingness, eerie winter silhouettes against a hot summer sky.

Even the barn, standing alone on a flat stretch of land behind the house, had not escaped. The heavy double doors were standing open, and as Kristyn stepped inside, she was aware of a strange emptiness in that gloomy interior. Only wisps of straw still showed on the floor where haybins had once stood, and the remains of leather harnesses, half gnawed away, dangled from rusty hooks on the walls.

The two plow horses Kristyn had seen before had been unhitched and stood now in their stalls. Even from across the room she could see that they were wild-eyed and restless as they tossed their manes into the flickering shadows and pawed at the earthen floor with their hooves. Going over to them, she stretched out her hand and began to speak in quiet, soothing tones.

It saddened her to think that Zeke would have to sell them, or one of them at least, probably the gray, for the other looked strong enough to pull the plow alone. He would not get one tenth of what the animal was worth, for money was going to be tight everywhere now, with other farms hit even worse than the Clayters', but at least he might get enough for potatoes and salt pork to see his family through the winter.

For the first time, it occurred to her that these people, like the other farmers in the area, with their small plots of earth and their solid, secure-looking houses, were not wealthy at all, but poor. Desperately, unspeakably poor . . . as poor and wretched as the Indians in the days after their land had been taken from them and the buffalo had disappeared forever.

The thought was unsettling. Until that moment, Kristyn had assumed that poverty and despair were limited to the world in which she had been raised. Now she realized that whites, too, could suffer deprivation and hunger, even starvation. How naive she had been, that day she left her parents' home, to believe she would be able to make a life for herself with nothing more than hope and goodwill.

And how naive, later, to think she could hold onto her pride and not turn to the one man who might help her!

Santa Fe, Kristyn leaned against the rough wooden slats, letting her mind drift off in directions she had not expected. Santa Fe—she had been heading there all the time, if only she had not been too stubborn to admit it. Heading toward a town she had never seen . . . and a man she could not forget.

Well, there would be no more foolish denials now, no more false pride. Tomorrow morning, before anyone was up, she would steal back to the train and gather together what few possessions she could carry with her. Billy was safe now—he could not pretend he needed her any longer—and there was nothing she could do for the Clayters. It was time to move on.

And moving on meant Santa Fe.

Whether he wanted to or not, Rafe would have to help her. Surely, after what they had shared together, he owed her that much.

Twenty-Two

The same hot sun that scorched the Kansas fields blazed even more intensely to the west, parching the yellow earth until it was as lined and wrinkled as an old man's face. A solitary Indian stood on the crest of a steep hill, staring down at arid plains and dried-out streambeds. His horse stood beside him, a strong red sorrel with lean, coltish legs and a pride of bearing that matched his master's.

"Man-Who-Lives-with-the-Wolves."

The Indian spoke the words aloud, liking the way they sounded on his tongue. "I am Man-Who-Lives-with-the-Wolves," he had told the young soldier—just before he killed him.

Man-Who-Lives-with-the-Wolves. It seemed to him a fitting name for a young chieftain who had struck terror into so many hearts in that desolate countryside. To his braves, he might still be Little Bear, but whenever the white men wrote articles in their newspapers or gathered together in public meetings, they called him by his new name. And they trembled when they uttered it.

The horse moved restlessly beside him, shaking out his fiery mane in the sunlight. Almost automatically, the man reached up to catch hold of the reins. That sudden, unexpected flash of red stirred bittersweet memories deep in his subconscious. *She* had had red hair, too, dark red hair that shimmered in the firelight—silky, sweet-smelling hair, like pine boughs in the spring, or rippling crystal streams.

The thought angered him, and he brushed it impatiently aside. Tightening his grip on the reins, he steadied the sorrel and swung into the saddle. He had not allowed himself to think of his young wife for many weeks now. He had promised himself he would never think of her again. There was too much that was still soft inside him, too much that yearned for the aching sweetness he had known but one night in her arms. Softness was his enemy. now, tears a weakness he could not afford.

Shifting his weight in the saddle, he glanced to the side, staring down at the empty plains. He was keenly conscious that there was one thing he had yet to do, one last act to be performed before this day, in many ways the most painful of his life, was finally over.

The emptiness of the earth below seemed both a cry and a rebuke, reminding him that he, like the other men of his tribe, had failed to hold on to what was theirs. Once—was it really such a short time ago?—a great circle of tepees would have added splashes of color to that stark yellow-ochre setting, and voices and laughter would have drifted up from the flatlands to temper the lonely howling of the wind. But the tepees were gone, the voices stilled. He had not heard the sound of laughter for many weeks.

Everything was empty. Everything finished, in a way few men his age had been called upon to understand. It was not the extermination of one small band of Indians he was wit- nessing but the annihilation of an entire way of life. The blood would go on—as long as there was an earth, there would be men who went by the name of Cheyenne—but those few survivors would be herded onto reservations, where they would eat the white man's food and live by the white man's rules, until everything that was truly Indian had died away inside of them.

Releasing the reins, Little Bear slung his rifle across the front of his saddle, letting his hands rest on the hot metal. He liked the feel of it beneath his palms. It was a good weapon, a 73 Springfield carbine, better than the old Civil War musket he had been using before.

It had belonged to the young soldier, the one he had killed that morning. He had found it lying beside the body when he paused to stare down at that awkward form sprawled out in the dirt. Only a handful of details still remained in his memory: the surprising crispness of the man's blue uniform, and the yellow facing that marked him as a horse soldier; the unblistered softness of his hands; the way his eyes stayed open, gray and gaping in death.

He had been surprised, as he bent over that still figure, to discover that the soldier was younger than he had seemed, barely more than a boy. The thought had left him unmoved. Once he might have felt pity for a youngster like that, caught up in battles he could not understand. Now there was no pity left in his heart.

Indian boys were dying, too, boys much younger than this one, and old men with gray hair, who had earned the right to live out their days in peace. He would not grieve for their murderers.

The sun was already low in the sky, a ball of glowing orange nestling among the crowns of distant hills, by the time Little Bear finally gave up his lonely vigil and prodded his mount slowly down the slopes. He was even more aware now of the thing that still lay ahead, and he dreaded it, but he knew he could put it off no longer. The path was steep and rocky, but he held the reins loosely, trusting Fire-Wind to find the way without guidance from human hands.

The weeks that had followed the massacre in that ill-fated camp across the creek had been hard ones for the Cheyennes. Little Bear had not been there to share his people's suffering, for once away from the tribe, he had vowed never to return, but he had learned of their plight from the young men who came to join his renegade band in the hills. And each new retelling of what had become an all-too-familiar story made his blood run hot all over again.

Far from being shamed by their cowardly actions, the white men had actually used that infamous attack, and the retaliatory raids it provoked, as an excuse to force the Indians farther and farther from the sweeping plains and mineral-rich mountains that had once been theirs. One by one, the soldiers had rounded up individual bands, and herding them together like domesticated animals, they had begun to drive them toward the place they called Indian Territory, far to the south. Those who resisted could expect no mercy, for once the order had been given, it was announced that any Indian who tried to remain in the villages, or hide out in ravines on the barren hillsides, would be considered hostile and therefore dangerous. Even a wide-eyed toddler or a toothless old woman could be shot on sight.

Not that the ones who gave in would fare much better, Little Bear reminded himself grimly. They might not fall beneath the white man's thundering cannon, but many would die on that long forced march, and even those who survived would find themselves struggling for existence on a sterile strip of land so arid it could not support even their most basic needs. The white man had made promises, of course, as he had many times before, guaranteeing foodstuffs and agricultural tools, but as before, the promises would not be kept. There would be no meat there for the belly, no tobacco for an old man's pipe, no sugar to sweeten the bitter taste of coffee. There would be no plows to break the soil, no hoes, no seeds to sow . . . nothing but dust and a few loaves of the white man's moldy bread.

Secretly, Little Bear had been relieved when a distant cousin, a boy of fourteen, had come to tell him that Brave Eagle and his wife would not be leaving with the others, but planned to stay in the hills and fight. He had no one else now, no kin close enough to call family, and he needed to feel pride in them, as he needed to feel it in himself. Somehow, in some small way, it helped to make up for the pretty young wife who had not had the courage to stand by her husband.

"They will die for their defiance," he had told the boy. "But they will die breathing the air of freedom. It is not right that a man should shrivel up and waste away in the dust of a place his heart cannot recognize."

The boy had nodded solemnly, trying to pretend he was old enough to understand.

"They had to leave everything behind when they fled. The lodge poles Brave Eagle cut for himself—you know how proud he was of them, they were the straightest in the village—and the tepee covers with the medicine symbols painted on them, all their cooking utensils . . . even the buffalo robes that would have kept them warm in the winter. They could take nothing but the clothing on their backs and a few parfleches filled with nuts and dried fruit."

Little Bear had studied the boy calmly. "Those are only possessions. A man can leave his possessions behind without regret. But not his spirit, or his independence."

"Brave Eagle even had to give up his black gelding," the boy went on. "The rocky slopes are too rugged for a horse, and there is no grass or sweet clover for grazing. One of the other men shot his mount and made a stew of the meat for his wife and children, but Brave Eagle would not consider such a thing. 'This horse has been with me for many years,' he told us. 'He is no longer an animal in my eyes, but a friend. I will not kill a friend to sustain my own poor life a few days longer.' So he took the horse down to the plains on a clear, moonlit midnight and let him go. He said the gelding seemed to understand, for he did not circle around and come back, as he always had before, but galloped off into the darkness.''

And into some white man's corral! Little Bear thought bitterly, turning away so the boy would not see the emotion in his eyes. It was a strange thing that Brave Eagle had done, a courageous gesture in a way, but distinctly uncharacteristic of the people among whom he had passed his entire life.

"I would never have done that," he said, his voice low and intense. "Nor would any of the warriors who ride with me. I would see Fire-Wind dead before I would turn him loose on the plains where a white man could find him."

But then, there had always been a touch of gentleness about Brave Eagle, a quality strangely alien to an Indian way of life. Little Bear had sometimes wondered if it came from the alien child he had taken into his tepee. Or perhaps there was simply a kind of wisdom, a quiet acceptance, that came to some men with age.

And that, he reminded himself, tightening his hold on the reins, was something he would never know. Wisdom had always come hard to him, and age was a thing he would never experience.

The path leveled off, giving way to flatlands that stretched out from the base of the hill. Little Bear turned his horse into the setting sun and made his way toward the rocky crevices where the women were hiding. Even now, Buffalo Calf Woman would be among them, crouching with the others, searching the dimming landscape for some trace of the men who would not be coming back.

She would know, of course, the minute she saw him riding toward her. She would know, but she would come down anyway, not because there was any reason for it, but simply because it was a thing that was expected of her. And he would speak the words he had come to say, because they, too, were expected, and today was not a day to break with formality or tradition.

The battle that had taken place earlier had been a savage one, with heavy casualties on both sides. He had not been there to see the beginning, for he had been camped with his men in a shallow ravine, but the instant he heard the gunshots, he realized what had happened. A platoon of soldiers, out on routine patrol, had ventured too close to the place where the women and children were hiding, and the men, in a desperate attempt to divert them, had circled around to attack from the opposite side.

The men! The thought made Little Bear's blood boil with anger. There had not been a warrior among them, not a single strong young brave, only old men, past the days of their fighting, and boy-children, some barely twelve or thirteen. Because they had no horses, they had taken their stand on foot, armed with a handful of old bows and a few of the white man's outdated weapons. It must have been a simple matter for the Blue Coats to form their mounts into a long line, raise their rifles to their shoulders—and shoot them down where they stood!

Little Bear only regretted that he had not been close enough to see the looks on the soldiers' faces when they had heard the sound of approaching hoofbeats and turned to see a band of whooping savages charging down from the hills. Not the old men they had thought they were fighting, not the little boys who were no match for them, but wild, raging renegades, half crazed by the massacre that they had just witnessed. The soldiers had broken ranks immediately, wheeling around in every direction at once, making of themselves for one brief moment an inviting target. The main body of survivors managed to get away, but a few straggled behind and were caught by pursuing Indians. Those few were not treated gently.

It was only afterward, when an unnatural hush had fallen over the scene, broken only by the pawing of horses and the muffled groans of the dying, that Little Bear realized for the first time how completely his world had been destroyed by this never-ending invasion of Blue Coats and seekers after gold. First his earthly goods had been taken from him, then the customs and rituals that had once formed the structure of his existence . . . soon there would not even be old friends with whom he could share the memories.

He stood a little apart from the others, surveying the bodies strewn across the earth with an unspeakable sense of loneliness and loss. There, beside the trickling waters of a half-empty stream, lay Blue Thunder, one of the great chiefs of his boyhood. Blue Thunder! The old man's eyes were so dim, it was a wonder he could see to use the weapon that was still clutched in his hand. And there, not far to one side, was a boy he was shocked to recognize as one of Owl Woman's brood. The lad was big for his age, making him look older than he was, but Little Bear knew he could not have been more than ten. What had the others been thinking of, letting a child like that come with them today?

And over there, across the stream . . .

Little Bear turned his head to the side, aware of the taste of bile rising to his mouth. That still form he had glimpsed just briefly, lying broken on the ground, was like an open wound, raw and bleeding, in his heart. He was glad now he had killed the young boy-soldier. Glad that no white man had known mercy at his hands.

It was dusk by the time he finally reached the jagged slopes where the women had secreted themselves. A half-moon had begun to spill eerie white light over the earth, and he was aware of unseen eyes, watching him from high in the crevices above. He remained where he was, a solitary horseman, silhouetted against the twilight sky, until at last his own eyes picked out a shadowy flicker of movement in the rocks. Buffalo Calf Woman was coming down.

He did not try to speak until she came to a stop in front of him. Even then, he held himself erect for a moment before bending down to let his eyes touch hers.

"You know what I have come to tell you."

"Yes," she replied quietly. "I know."

"He died a warrior's death, cleanly, as he would have wanted it—and with honor. Never in the living of his life did he know one moment of shame. There was no disgrace in his parting from it."

Buffalo Calf Woman inclined her head slightly.

"Yes," she repeated softly. "His body might have lived if we had gone to the white man's reservation, but his heart would have died there. And his soul. It is better this way."

"Even now, he is beginning his journey up the Hanging Road, *na'go*." Little Bear used the Cheyenne word, *mother*, for in his need to cling to what was left of his past, he had forgotten she was no blood kin to him. "I took his body from where he fell and laid him to rest in the branches of a tall pine. It is a good place, *na'go*, green and cool, fitting for a great chief like Brave Eagle. You would be proud if you could see it."

The words were a lie, but the woman did not seem to sense it, or perhaps she had not been listening. Trees were sparse in that rocky region, and those that rose out of the sandy soil where the slaughter had taken place, were scarcely more than shrubs. Little Bear had been bitterly aware of his own inadequacy as he chose the best of an unlikely lot and, wrapping Brave Eagle's body in his own blanket, he had lashed it securely to the sturdiest of those low-hanging branches. It was not the burial place he would have liked, but it was the best he could do.

And perhaps, after all, it did not matter. Surely the *tasoom* of a man as valiant as Brave Eagle would soar into the heavens on the first white shaft of starlight. Would it make any difference then what happened to the poor shell of a body he had left behind?

Buffalo Calf Woman did not speak again, but remained where she was, staring at him for a long time in silence, yet not seeming to see him at all. At last she turned away and, still without words, began to climb up the rocks again. Little Bear sat on his horse, watching as she half disappeared into the shadows of the hillside. Her back was bent, and she moved with an unsteady gait, like an old woman who could barely walk by herself.

He knew at that moment that she was going to die. He had sensed it before, just as she turned away; now he was sure. He had seen that look too many times before, that resignation in the eyes of other old people, that sudden weariness of limb and heart. And always, when it came, their time was measured in hours and days.

He would not leave her until then. That, at least, he could do, though he sensed she would not know he was there. He would not leave her, but she would die anyway. And when she did, he would ride off alone.

Twenty-Three

The city of Santa Fe lay quiet and drowsy in the noonday sun. The sound of church bells echoed in Kristyn's ears as she guided her horse through the half-deserted side streets. In the background, stately purple mountains soared high into the heavens, but here on the outskirts of town, the man-made structures with their low lines and mud walls seemed to cling to the earth. Squat brown hovels closed in on both sides of the dust-brown lanes, their squalor and drabness mocking the majesty of the distant peaks.

What if Rafe was furious when he saw her?

Kristyn jerked the reins back, bringing the horse to a startled stop. What if he was even angrier than she had imagined? What if he took one look at her, standing on his threshold, and told her to get out and never come back again?

Squirming uncomfortably in the saddle, Kristyn had to admit she could not blame him if he did. Rafe had been completely honest with her, right from the start, telling her he wanted her for one night, and one only, with no strings attached, no commitments for the future. She was not going to make any romantic demands on him, of course—all she wanted was his help in establishing a new life for herself—but he would not know that. Could she really be surprised if he slammed the door in her face?

The horse stirred impatiently, half turning his head, and Kristyn caught herself with a little laugh. Plainly, the animal's instincts were truer than her own. It was idiotic, sitting here in the middle of the road, wondering what Rafe was going to do . . . and how she would react if she saw only rejection in his eyes! There was only one way to find out.

Leaning forward, she flicked the reins lightly against the horse's neck.

"All right, Pharaoh. Come on, boy . . . let's go."

She smiled to herself as the horse moved slowly forward. Pharaoh. The name was like a secret joke, reminding her both of the gaming tables where she had gotten her stake and the plague of locusts that made the animal available at a reasonable price. She had known, that morning two weeks ago when she had roused Zeke Clayter out of bed in the half-light of early dawn, that he would part with the horse for almost any sum, but she had offered as much as she could afford anyway. Clayter had accepted gratefully.

"He doesn't look like much," he had told her apologetically. "But he's got a good heart. He'll get you where you're going."

As it turned out, the gray proved to be a better bargain than either Clayter or Kristyn had anticipated. Once away from the drudgery of the plow, he had shown himself to be a surprisingly frisky mount. A walk was less a walk with him than a spirited prance, and a gallop seemed almost a caper as he cut across the sandy desert plains, leaving feathery trails of dust behind his flying hooves.

Perhaps it's an omen, Kristyn thought, daring to let herself hope. Perhaps things are not going to go so badly after all. If Pharaoh can be happy, then so can I—here in Santa Fe!

The narrow street on which she had been riding gave way suddenly to a large plaza, which dominated the center of town. Kristyn tugged at the reins again, holding Pharaoh back for a moment as she stared around her with curious eyes.

The same low, drab buildings that lined the outlying lanes also delineated the four sides of the square, only here they were fronted with covered portals, forming graceless verandas around the perimeter of the plaza. Only in one place was the flat-roofed monotony broken, and that was in the far corner, where the primitive lines of a typically Spanish church rose out of the surrounding mud and adobe. Scraggly trees cast meager spots of shade along the inner edges of a wide dirt avenue, effectively setting off the center of the square. Almost exactly in the middle, Kristyn saw a tall pole, empty now, but designed to hold the gaudy red-white-and-blue flag of the United States on ceremonial occasions.

The plaza was obviously a popular gathering place, for

unlike the side streets, it was filled with people. Despite the cooling mountain breezes, an air of indolence hung over the scene. Everywhere she looked, Kristyn saw dark-skinned men and women with jet-black hair and even blacker eyes, lounging on benches and stools, or sprawled out on the ground with their backs against the trunks of convenient trees. Even the sounds had a lazy feel to them: the slightly off-key tones of a fiddle, coming from one corner; the jingling of a guitar somewhere farther off; a soft undercurrent of conversation, punctuated by subdued bursts of laughter.

Across the square, not far from the church, a long table had been set up, with a faded cloth cover. Tall bottles made of some sort of painted pottery were scattered across the top, and here and there, a cracked cup could be seen, half filled with cold coffee, or a platter heaped with pieces of fruit or sweet bean cake.

Only one of the crude wooden stools beside the table was occupied, by a young woman with long, loose hair. A gaily patterned purplish red skirt flared out around her ankles, trailing carelessly in the dust, and her blouse was full and flowing, its low, round neck exposing nearly all of her ample bosom. But if there was anything scandalous or overtly sexual about her costume, Kristyn could detect no trace of it in the expression of the man who had paused to speak with her. He, too, was dressed simply, in rough white cotton pants and a long-sleeved cotton shirt, but a brightly striped *sarape* over one shoulder gave him a jaunty dash of color.

The lethargy of the siesta hour extended even to the children, who had drawn a little away from the adults to play quietly by themselves in the shade. They were, for the most part, naked, with nothing but dust coating their lean brown bodies, although a few wore tattered shirts, barely reaching to their waists, or other garments, so ragged they were nothing more than strings and shreds. A thin layer of straw was scattered on the ground, and on this, a dozen or so chickens roosted fretfully, while pigeons fluttered past, swooping down occasionally to peck at odd crumbs they had missed, or stray kernels of corn.

Fascinated, Kristyn looked around the square, taking in every detail of that setting, so completely different from anything she had experienced before. In the shadows of one of the portals, the peasant women, the *rancheras,* had set up a makeshift market, with a sampling of local produce displayed in eye-catching abundance.

Lacking groundcloths, the women had covered the pavement with their *rebozos,* and against this backdrop, their wares were placed in surprisingly artistic array. Beside a tall pyramid of shiny red apples, so brilliantly polished they gleamed, Kristyn spied a basket of fuzzy-skinned peaches, their soft tones contrasting dramatically with the brilliant crimson of freshly picked plums. Next to them, plump summer melons, barely ripe, dwarfed the succulent sweetness of tiny purple grapes. Vegetables, too, had their part in that vivid tableau: strange-looking peppers, long and green, and that green corn the Spanish called *mais verde;* squashes, in an amazing variety of sizes and shapes, and firm little onions, wrapped up in their crinkly brown skins.

A spicy smell piqued Kristyn's nostrils, and glancing around, she spotted an open fire at the opposite end of the plaza. A heavy metal cauldron had been placed on the glowing coals, and an old man poked solemnly at something inside with a long, rough stick. Curious, Kristyn prodded Pharaoh forward, eager to get a look at what he was concocting. It seemed, on closer examination, to be a stew of some kind, composed of small chunks of meat and seasoned with the piquant *chiles verdes* that the Southwestern Indians used in so much of their cooking.

A crowd had begun to gather around the man, and people were offering him small coins in exchange for a portion of that savory stew wrapped up in a flat round of bread, so thin it almost looked like parchment. The smell was unbearably tempting now that Kristyn was nearer, and it was all she could do to keep from dipping into her pocket and searching for what little change she had left.

But that, she reminded herself firmly, was just putting things off! Attractive as the smell of the stew might be, she was even more attracted to the idea of postponing her meeting with Rafe, and that was the one thing she dared not do! If she did, she might lose her nerve altogether.

"Here you, boy!" She picked out a ragged urchin from a group of older children lounging at the edge of the plaza. "*Niño!*"

The boy looked up, but he made no attempt to rise or come

toward her. He seemed to be about ten or twelve, though he was so scrawny Kristyn could not tell for sure.

"*Señora, me llamás?*"

"*Hablas inglés, niño?*" Kristyn had picked up a few words of Spanish in the short time she had been in the territory, but she was none too sure of them. Besides, she had already learned that the children, more curious than their elders, often managed a surprising amount of English. "*Un pocito?*"

But the boy shook his head. "*No, señora—no inglés. Nomás, hablo español.*"

"I speak, lady," a new voice chimed in. "I speak good. What you want?"

Kristyn turned to see a second boy, younger and even more ragged than the first. His eyes were bright and aggressive, but he seemed more eager than knowing, and she had the feeling he had just exhausted his entire English vocabulary.

"I am looking for a man," she said, speaking slowly and distinctly. "A friend. His name is Rafe Valero. Do you know him?"

The boy's eyes were glued on her face, but not a flicker of recognition showed in them, and Kristyn realized her instinct had been right. If she was going to get through to him, she would to have to do it with her own faulty Spanish.

"He lives with his grandfather, *Son abuelo*. A very important man, *comprende? Muy importante*. You must know him. His name is Don Diego El Valeroso."

"El Valeroso?"

The words burst out of the boy's mouth, echoed by the other lad, who had leaped to his feet and come over to join them. Kristyn almost laughed aloud as she looked down at those two bright faces. What a ninny she had been, trying to communicate in a language she did not know when all she needed was that one name—El Valeroso.

"*Sí*. El Valeroso. You know him?"

Both boys began to speak at once, letting out a torrent of Spanish so rapid and explosive Kristyn could not make out a word of it. After a minute, the first boy, the older one, broke off, shrugging his shoulders with a surprised, almost apologetic look.

"*Pero, señora . . .*" He threw up his hands. "*El Valeroso es un gran hombre. Un hidalgo. Es uno de los ricos.*"

Los ricos? In spite of herself, Kristyn had to smile. She did not need a knowledge of Spanish to know what the boy was saying, or what he was thinking for that matter! When she had left Kansas, she had been clean and fresh-looking in a pair of fawn-toned britches purloined from Billy's luggage and a dark brown shirt that set off her exotic coloring. But two weeks on dusty roads had dulled everything, even her shimmering red hair, to a muddy beige.

"So, *niños,* you think I will be out of place with the *ricos,* do you? You think I am one of the *pobres,* eh?"

The younger boy did not seem to understand, but the older lad caught on.

"*Sí,*" he agreed, flashing an impudent grin. "*Eres uno de los pobres—con yo y mi amigo.*"

Kristyn, unable to resist, grinned back at him. Something in the boy's spirit appealed to her, reminding her a little of herself at that age.

"I'll show you how poor I am, *niño.*" Reaching into her pocket, she took out a coin and flipped it up in the air. "How would you like to have this?"

The boy's eyes followed the coin with a greedy glint. Kristyn let him contemplate it for a minute, then slipped it pointedly back in her pocket.

"Where is the house of Don Diego? *La casa de Don Diego? Donde está?*"

The boy studied her solemnly for a few seconds. Then with a brusque nod of his head, he spun around and darted across the square, sending pigeons fluttering out of his way as he ran. Kristyn took up her reins and began to follow, heading for the spot where he had just disappeared between two long, low buildings.

The streets in which she found herself were much like those narrow lanes on the other side of the city, quiet shadowy places that offered a sharp contrast to the sleepy activity of the square. If anything, the buildings seemed to crowd the road even tighter here, and Kristyn's eyes were drawn toward them as she rode past. They were all constructed in the same manner, with adobe walls two or three feet thick, plastered over with a coating of mud and straw. The roofs were nothing more than hard mud plates laid over pine beams which jutted out of the sides of the building. Here and there, a cluster of dried red *chiles* dangled from the end of one of them, adding a welcome touch of color to that otherwise drab setting.

"*Señora!*"

A sharp voice drew her attention back to the end of the street, and she was startled to see that the boy had come to a stop and was urging her on with an impatient wave of his arm.

Kristyn felt her heart begin to beat faster, and a funny dry taste came into her mouth. If the boy had stopped like that, it could mean only one thing. They had reached their destination.

For an instant, she was tempted to turn around and ride off again. It was so foolish, this thing she had come to do. Rafe could not possibly want her there. He would be bitterly angry when he saw her, and rightly so! What kind of hospitality could she expect from him?

Still, she reminded herself, touching her heels to the horse's flanks, she had come this far, she might as well go on. Perhaps Rafe would prove kinder than she had expected, more charitable. And if he didn't—well she could hardly be any worse off than she was now!

The street ended abruptly at the corner, opening onto a sweeping vista of mountains and fields, capped by a breathtakingly blue sky. Kristyn reined in her horse, so startled by the sheer loveliness she could only sit and stare at it. The distant mountains had an almost crystalline quality, soft purple tones shimmering in the crisp air, and below them, fields of summer squash and waist-high corn, irrigated by melting snows, seemed to stretch on forever. Vast flocks of sheep milled lazily over the hillsides, their tinkling bells blending into a subtle melody that floated on the breeze.

"*Ahí está, señora,*" the boy cried out, pointing excitedly toward a high adobe wall. "*La casa de Don Diego. Es muy grande, sí?*"

"*Sí,*" Kristyn agreed weakly, feeling that dry taste in her mouth again. "*Muy grande.*"

Grand, indeed! Far grander than anything she had envisioned, even in her wildest fantasies. The wall itself was not prepossessing, for it had been constructed of the same mud brick as everything else in the area, but the size of it, the scope, was unexpectedly intimidating. This was not a mere *casa* Don Diego had erected for himself, not a house at all, but a fortress, a palace set like a separate kingdom on its own private hilltop. Fields terraced the slopes around it and sheep seemed to be everywhere, herded by old men with long sticks and dogs that yapped at their heels.

A private kingdom. The thought sent a faint tremor down Kristyn's spine. A kingdom where El Valeroso was absolute monarch—and Rafe his crown prince!

A sound behind her drew her out of herself and, looking around, she saw that the boy was watching her intently. Remembering her promise, she took the coin out of her pocket and tossed it at him. Catching it deftly, he whirled around and flew down the street.

Kristyn waited until he was out of sight, then glanced back at the hill again. She was surprised how much the light had changed, even in the brief moment she had been turned away. The afternoon was latening, and the sun had already eased into a deep gold, playing on aged adobe until it seemed to glow from within. How pretty it looked, she thought. Pretty . . . and untouchable. What was she going to find when she breached that mysterious fortress? What kind of welcome awaited her there?

Ysabel sat alone in a small enclosed garden at the back of the house. The sun slanted obliquely on high, drab walls, warming them with splashes of yellow, and roses the color of a twilight sky spilled lushly over curved trellises, their muted tones accenting the brighter red of geraniums set in glazed pots along the tiled paths. A tiered fountain in one corner cast a glittering spray into the sunlight, and the subtle melody of splashing water mingled with the sound of sheep bells, drifting in from the fields beyond.

The serenity of the setting was lost on Ysabel. She was aware, with the canny instinct of a spoiled young woman, that she made an enchanting picture, dressed in lacy white in the midst of that shimmering profusion of color, but the thought of her own prettiness, usually so satisfying, was not enough to lift her spirits today. What good was it, looking absolutely beguiling, if not so much as a single man was there to admire her? Men, after all, were a woman's natural prey, and there was not a one of them strong enough to resist if only the woman knew how to make herself enchanting in his eyes.

The way *she* had. Unconsciously, Ysabel's lips twisted

into a pout. *She*, that woman, that—that *descarada* Rafe had
picked up in an Indian camp on the plains!

A flash of vermilion silk rustled, unwanted, in her memory,
and she found herself focusing on a tall, gently swaying
form, trapped in candlelight at the head of a low flight of
stairs. Yes, *descarada*, the perfect word for her! She was
indeed a hussy, so shameless it filled Ysabel with disgust to
think of her. How she had flaunted that flaming hair, tossing
it boldly as she descended. And how wantonly she had arranged the neck of her dress—Ysabel's own gown!—pulling
it low to expose pale skin where the sun had never touched it.

And Rafael—oh, Rafael had not taken his eyes off her!

Ysabel sat up irritably, tucking her legs under her. Rafael,
typical male that he was, had been so taken in by that blatant
display of sexuality, he had not even tried to resist. And even
Carlos . . .

Ysabel broke off with a distracted frown. Pulling her legs
out from under her, she got up and began to wander down the
tiled path, scowling as she caught sight of an empty doorway
at the side of the garden. It was time for her afternoon
chocolate, well past time in fact, and that lazy girl, Rosa, was
nowhere to be seen!

It was not that she felt the least bit guilty about Carlos.
That was not why it made her uncomfortable to think of him.
After all, Carlos *was* a man, and even in her limited experience,
she had already figured out that men considered it amusing to
dally with women, then drop them when they had had enough!
It would serve one of them right if a pretty girl turned the
tables on him for a change!

Nor did she have any qualms about the act she had performed with Carlos in the candlelit shadows of his room that
first night, or any of the nights that had followed. Ysabel had
been raised by the tenets of a strict religious code, but she
had learned at an early age that what was required of her was
unyielding obedience not understanding, lip service not love,
and these she was willing in varying degrees to give. Faithful
attendance at the mass had never been a hardship, for she
enjoyed the color and moodiness of the service, and even
daily recitations of the rosary with the sonorous tones of a
padre nuestro or an *ave maria* repeated over and over stirred
a romantic chord in her soul. But the deeper implications of
her faith continued to elude her, and she for her part contin-

ued not to pursue them or even to think of them overmuch. When it came to something she had her heart set on, there was not a rule of God—or man—that could hold her back.

And what her heart was set on now was the only man she had ever loved!

The sound of water spilling over the top of the fountain caught Ysabel's attention and, turning, she stared at the ripples that seemed to dance across the surface. It was so hard, these days, to think of Rafael . . . and so utterly impossible not to! She had been absolutely certain when she had waited for him in that dusty Kansas town that the instant he saw her he would throw open his arms and beg her to come to him.

But his eyes, at that first meeting, had been maddeningly cool. Cool and almost mocking.

"Well, Ysabelita, have you stayed behind with Carlos because you wanted to greet me, or do you have other reasons for being here? Can it be you have forgotten your schoolgirl crush on me already? What a fickle little heart you have, *muchacha*."

Muchacha? Even now the memory rankled.

"I am not a little girl, Rafael! Don't you ever dare call me *muchacha* again! And how can you say I have forgotten you? You know I would never do that!"

Far from being chastened, he had only grinned. "Of course you would—and you have. We men are not quite the fools you take us for . . . nor are most of us stone deaf. Do you seriously think I didn't hear where your footsteps went that night when you left me? Or the sounds that came from the room directly above mine?"

"But—but Rafael!" Ysabel had been so stunned she began to stammer. "That—that's not fair. You're twisting things all around. You know you are! Everything I've done, it—it was all for you!"

"Was it, *niña?*"

"It was, Rafael. It was! Don't you remember? You told me you wanted me to be more experienced. To be more—more of a woman!"

"And that is what you are doing with my brother?" How strange those dark eyes had seemed, searching her face, making her feel hot and cold at the same time. "Learning to be a woman? I think, my sweet, you have a ways to go, and I think my brother is going to have his hands full with you. God help the poor devil if he thinks he can tame that fiery temper. Or win your willful little heart.''

Oh, how it still hurt, just to think of it! Ysabel swayed toward the fountain, reaching out to steady herself as she fought against the memory, trying to drive it from her heart. It seemed to her everything had changed that afternoon, not just her relationship with Rafael, but even those new and distinctly flattering attentions she had begun to receive from his brother.

She was not sure why things had gone sour with Carlos after that day; she only knew that somehow they had. Perhaps he had overheard her conversation with Rafael, though she did not see how he could have. Or perhaps he simply saw the hunger in her eyes when his brother rode into town and guessed her guilty secret. She still caught him looking at her sometimes, quite strangely, the way a man looked at something he wanted and couldn't have, but he had not tried to come to her again. And he had not left his door open for her to come to him.

Turning away from the fountain, Ysabel stared at the long, brooding shadows that had begun to stretch across the garden. Not that she minded the idea of losing Carlos. After all, she did not love him. She did not even want him, not really! But sometimes, just *sometimes*, on a hot, languid afternoon, she found herself remembering other afternoons in his arms, and she could not keep her body from yearning for the feel of hands that had the power to draw her out of herself, the touch of lips that made her forget, for one sweet moment, everything else in the world. And sometimes at night, just as she drifted into sleep, she would feel herself begin to dream . . . and those first tentative dreams would not be of Rafael. They would be of the man who had taught her to love.

''Rosa!''

Whirling around, she glowered at the doorway. Where was that foolish girl anyway? If she had a cup of chocolate now, she would be relishing its warm, delicious sweetness, faintly tinged with cinnamon, and not drifting off into unwanted thoughts.

''Rosa . . .!''

The girl appeared abruptly, looking flustered and out of breath, as if she had had to run to answer her mistress' call.

Her hands dangled empty at her sides, and Ysabel, her Spanish temper roused, was about to scold her for forgetting the chocolate when her eyes picked out a motion in the shadows behind her. The rebuke died on her lips as she watched a slender woman slip out of the interior of the house.

It was Kristyn Ashley!

Without even being aware of it, Ysabel's hand slipped upward, resting on the throbbing pulse at the base of her throat. Kristyn Ashley! The very person she had been thinking of a moment before. That same sultry temptress who had worked her wiles on Rafael in the past—and who might well do it again if she didn't somehow find a way to get her out of there!

Ysabel's consternation showed plainly on her face, but Kristyn was so absorbed in her own thoughts, she did not notice. In all the times she had imagined that moment of arrival, this was the one possibility that had not occurred to her, and yet she knew it should have. Rafe had made it clear that the girl was his grandfather's ward and had been raised in his house. She should have known that Ysabel would still be there, and that she would have been using these intervening weeks in an attempt to ingratiate herself with the man she obviously wanted!

The two women eyed each other for a moment. Then Ysabel turned her head, flashing an irritated glance at the servant.

"*Rosa, tienes la boca abierto como uno pescado, no quiero que nada venga en el járdin, entiendes? Quiero estar solo con esta—señorita!*"

She waited just long enough to make sure her order was obeyed, then whirled around again, challenging Kristyn with snapping eyes.

"I don't know where you learned your manners, Señorita Ashley. Probably in that savage camp you came from. But here among civilized people it is customary to announce your intentions in advance when you plan to visit someone's home. And never would you come dressed like that! The only decent thing you can do is leave right now before anyone has a chance to see you!"

Her words had exactly the opposite effect, shocking Kristyn not into embarrassment, but out of the stunned immobility into which she had fallen. She had been uncomfortable at the idea of seeing Rafe again, but that was because she cared about him and did not know how he was going to react. She did not care one whit about Ysabel, and she was not about to let herself be intimidated!

"I am sorry my manners don't meet with your approval," she said with a deliberately exaggerated sweetness. "But I find it hard to believe 'civilized people' are not capable of spontaneous hospitality, especially after the warm welcome I have seen many travelers receive from total strangers. As for my garb, I admit it is none too glamorous, but I can't imagine I look any worse than other wayfarers on the road."

Ysabel flushed a deep pink, hating the sound of Kristyn's voice almost as much as she hated her presence. More than ever, she sensed her as an enemy to be reckoned with, and she knew she had to dispose of her quickly.

"I'm sure I don't know about the other 'wayfarers,' nor do I care to. I have never consorted with such people in my life. I know only that my guardian, El Valeroso, is a dignified and proper man, and he would be shocked by your appearance. I suggest you leave now, before he comes and finds you here. I have sent Rosa to fetch him."

"Have you really?" Kristyn asked quietly. She had caught only a word or two of that fiery spate of Spanish, but she could have sworn the girl had told her maid to keep everyone away.

"Yes, of course I have. He will be here any minute now. I have told you so already. And in that case, I think you should——"

"In that case," Kristyn interrupted firmly, "I should stay right here and meet him. Actually, I'm looking forward to it. Rafe has told me a great deal about Don Diego, and so has Carlos. It will be a pleasure to make his acquaintance."

"You would not say that," Ysabel snapped, "if you knew him as I do! Oh, I know what you think. You think because you are pretty in a vulgar sort of way you can twist any man you like around your fingers. Only this time you are wrong! Never has El Valeroso allowed a woman to come into his house garbed as you are now. I cannot think how he is going to react when he sees you in trousers! And dusty ones at that!"

Her voice had a brittle edge, and Kristyn, catching it, felt her confidence begin to return.

"Well, then," she said coolly, "I'll just have to take my chances, won't I?" Turning away, she strolled down the path, stopping to stare with feigned preoccupation at a trailing spray of blood-red roses. All right, Ysabel had promised Don Diego. Let her produce him!

Ysabel stared after her with undisguised resentment. What a bitch she was, what a *perversa* . . . so sure of what was going to happen when Don Diego saw her there. And the worst of it was, she was right! Don Diego might be an old man, but he was a man nonetheless, as hot-blooded in his own way as his grandsons were in theirs, and she could imagine only too well how he was going to respond to his first glimpse of that earthy sensuality.

And after all, there was something about the woman. Grudgingly, Ysabel let her eyes take in that deceptively slender figure. It did nothing for her already sullen disposition to be forced to admit that Kristyn Ashley did indeed possess a certain raw appeal. She was covered with dust from head to foot, her masculine clothing was outrageous, wisps of hair stood out of her coiffure in the most untidy manner—and yet far from making her look repulsive, that very roughness actually added to her effect. There was in her style a kind of wildness, vaguely reminiscent of uncharted forests, thick with pine and tangled with undergrowth—a wildness calculated to stir whatever it was that was adventurous and unfettered in men.

Just the sort of wildness that would appeal to Rafael!

"What do you want?" she asked suddenly, unable to bear the silence any longer. "Why did you come here? Rafael told us your father had found a rich husband for you. Don't tell me the man changed his mind already?"

Kristyn turned slowly, staring at her in mild surprise.

"No, Ysabel," she said, letting a faint smile play with the corners of her lips. "He didn't change his mind. Quite the contrary. It was I who decided I didn't want to marry him."

"Well, then, what happened? Did your parents throw you out? Oh, but of course they did! What a disappointment you must have been. Is that why you are here? Because you want money?"

"Money?" The smile lingered on Kristyn's lips. "No, I haven't come for money. At least . . ." She faltered briefly. She *had* come for money, of course, but she was not asking for charity. Only the chance to earn a living for herself. ". . . at least, not the way you mean it."

"Oh. . .?" Ysabel's eyes narrowed. "Forgive me if I find that difficult to believe. But don't worry. I'm not going to make things hard for you. I suppose it's not your fault, the way you behave. I know you haven't had an easy life. Besides, Don Diego has been very generous with me—I can afford to help you. I have a little money set aside. Not much, but enough to buy a stagecoach ticket any place you want to go. I'll give it all to you if you get out of here before anyone sees you."

"You'll give me *all* your money?" Kristyn gave her a slow, inquiring look. "Why would you do that for me, Ysabel?"

"I told you. My guardian is a proper old man. I want to spare him the embarrassment of receiving someone like you in his home."

"Oh . . .?"

Kristyn pursed her lips around the word, mimicking Ysabel's tone of a moment before. So . . . the girl was afraid of her. That was why she had tried to buy her off! And if she was afraid, there could only be one reason for it.

Perhaps, after all, Rafe was not quite as indifferent as he seemed. Perhaps he was sorry he had let her go, and Ysabel was aware of it!

"Now," she said quietly, "it's my turn not to believe *you*. I don't think you're worried about your guardian at all, Ysabel. I think you're worried about yourself."

"Myself? But that's . . ."

Whatever protests the girl had been about to make died on her lips as a familiar voice interrupted from somewhere inside the house.

"Ysabelita!"

Both women froze in position, Ysabel so tense she was unable to move, Kristyn paling until she was certain every hint of color had drained from her face.

What is happening to me? she thought helplessly. Why am I reacting like this? I haven't even seen him yet—I've only heard the sound of his voice—and I'm trembling so badly I can barely stand.

Approaching footsteps echoed on a tiled floor, just beyond the open doorway, and Kristyn, her heart thumping wildly against her chest, realized suddenly that she could not bear to face this man she had come so far to see. Reacting from some unnamed instinct, she slipped hastily behind a flower-laden trellis and watched, unseen, as Rafe entered the garden.

"Ah, there you are!" He paused in the doorway, his dark eyes laughing as they sought out Ysabel. "What is this Rosa tells me, that you want to be left alone? You always crave admiring eyes around you, *muchacha*, especially when you have taken care to dress so fetchingly."

Ysabel did not respond, not even to bristle at his use of the word *muchacha*, but she had managed to compose her features and Rafe did not seem to notice anything. Kristyn, watching from her vantage point, stared out at him with troubled eyes.

How handsome he looked. How utterly, impossibly handsome! Waves of longing surged through her body, reminding her bitterly how much she had once loved this man . . . and how hopeless that one-sided passion had been. The flair of Spanish styling suited him, showing off a body that was lithe and muscular. A flowing white silk shirt clung to broad shoulders, and tight black pants and high leather boots looked as if they had been molded onto his thighs and calves. The only color in his costume came from a brilliant crimson sash at his waist, giving him a rakish air, like a gypsy prince or a pirate on the high seas.

Why, *why*, had she ever thought she was strong enough to come here? A rush of tears stung her eyes, and she hated herself suddenly for the weakness—the foolishness!—that had brought her to that spot. She should have known that whatever help Rafe might offer her would never compensate for the pain that would be hers when she saw him again. Or the agonizing realization that her love for him, far from being muted by time and reason, was still a keen, aching force in her heart.

But she *had* come, she reminded herself, ironically aware that the situation in which she found herself was one of her own making. She had come to his home, she had hidden herself behind a trellis in his garden, and any minute now, any second, he was certain to turn around and catch her there. If she wanted to keep from making a total fool of herself, she was going to have to step out and face him.

Taking a deep breath, she forced herself out of the shadows.

Rafe's eyes widened at the sight of her; and in that split second of recognition, a whole gamut of emotions showed in his face. Shock first, then doubt . . . then disbelief. And then, incredibly, the one thing Kristyn had not dared to hope!

Rafe was glad to see her!

She was too stunned for an instant to react. Then suddenly, a giddy sense of excitement swept over her, and she realized that all her fears had been groundless. He might try to deny it—he almost certainly *would* try to deny it—but she had seen that flash of brightness in his eyes, that moment of eagerness, and she knew he cared.

What a fraud he was! Her lips curled into a secret smile, and it was all she could do to keep from puncturing his masculine ego by laughing aloud. What a transparent, foolish, absolutely endearing fraud! He had reset his features already, veiling his eyes with a faintly mocking expression, but all that self-protectiveness came too late. He had given himself away—and she had not failed to see it!

He wanted her. He might bluster all he chose, he might protest to his heart's content, but she knew the truth and he would never fool her again. He wanted her. As much as she wanted him.

Stretching out her hands, she took a step forward.

"Why, Rafe," she said softly, "aren't you glad to see me?"

Twenty-Four

There had always been an air of formality about Don Diego, even when he was young. Now, in age, his back seemed so rigid, his shoulders so set and squared, he looked as if he had been chiseled out of marble. But for all the unyielding stiffness that set him apart from his peers, he was still an exceptionally handsome man. Sharply molded cheekbones dominated a face that was essentially aristocratic, and generations of proud inbreeding showed in a long aquiline nose and strong, jutting chin. His hair, although pure white by now, was thick and wavy, sweeping back from his brow to form a striking frame for shrewd black eyes.

He was especially aware of his own strengths and weaknesses that morning as he paused in the doorway of the spacious *sala* and looked in at two young people absorbed in conversation in front of the cold stone hearth. There was much in this favorite grandson that reminded him, physically at least, of himself. Rafael had the same sharp nose, the same high, wide forehead, the same touch of squareness to his jaw. But his eyes were his own, softer somehow, capable of an openness he himself had never acquired. And there was a casual look about him that was alien to the old man's temperament.

They were so much more natural, he thought, frowning slightly—this younger generation. It seemed to him incredible that Rafael could be comfortable slouching there like that, his legs stretched out in front of him, his boots propped up on the hearth like a cowboy. As for the girl, she had an almost gamine quality about her, perched as she was on the edge of her chair, her feet tucked under her like a small child. Her face was lively and animated as she tilted it slightly to the side, giving Don Diego a clear view of her features.

Ah, what a surprise she had turned out to be, that little one! The old don lingered in the doorway, letting his eyes take her in with a frank show of appreciation. He had kept a full staff of dressmakers busy day and night for half a week preparing a hasty wardrobe for her, but the results had been well worth the effort. The white silk blouse she was wearing now was simple and loose, reminiscent of the *rancheras* on the plaza in town, and while it was not quite so low in the neck, it did nothing to conceal the ripe lines of a body that was already more womanly than girlish. A flame-red cotton skirt spilled out around her, its wide ruffled hem showing an edging of lacy petticoats and just the barest sliver of ankle. Don Diego was past the age of dallying with women himself—he had in his declining years neither the patience to build a serious relationship nor the youthful curiosity for a shallow one—but his eyes were still sharp, and he had the ability to appreciate beauty when he saw it.

As did his grandson, he thought, smiling to himself at the intent look on the younger man's face. Ever since the girl had arrived, Rafael had gone out of his way to appear aloof in her presence, treating her with exaggerated politeness. But for all his posturing, he always seemed to find an excuse to spend a few minutes alone with her in the middle of the day, and those few minutes were getting longer all the time. Obviously, much as he tried to deny it, especially to himself, he was deeply, almost compulsively, attracted to her.

That attraction had been apparent from the first afternoon, when Rafael had sent one of the servants to summon him to the garden.

"We have an unexpected visitor, grandfather," he had said, his voice just bluff enough to rouse the old man's suspicions. "With your permission, I have offered her our hospitality. May I present—Señorita Cristina Lucifero."

The girl had looked vaguely surprised, as if something in the words surprised her, but she recovered quickly, looking up at Don Diego with the bluest eyes he had ever seen.

"I am very grateful to you for receiving me so graciously in your home."

"Señorita Lucifero." Don Diego had taken her hands, conscious as he bent over them of a feminine softness that stirred half-dormant memories. "Rafael introduced you in English, so I assume you do not speak our language. I must tell you then that *lucifero* is, for us, that last bright star that sometimes shows in the morning sky."

"Cristina is kin to the morning star, grandfather." Rafe smiled slightly as if the idea amused him. "Señorita Lucifero. I think it an appropriate name for her, don't you?"

Privately, Don Diego had agreed. There was something in those lustrous eyes that brought back the morning of his own youth, when he, too, had worshiped beauty, as young men did today, and nothing had seemed beyond him. But because he was of another generation, and because it would never have occurred to him to treat a woman with anything but gallantry, he had said only those polite words a Spanish gentleman always uttered when a visitor appeared at his door.

"*Mi casa es su casa, señorita.* Any friend of my grandson, Rafael, will always be a welcome guest in my home."

"Actually, grandfather, Cristina is not my friend at all. She is the daughter of a friend. Her father once asked me to look after her, and I did not feel I could refuse. I suppose, under those circumstances, I could hardly throw her out on the street now."

His voice had risen slightly, punctuating the sentence with a subtle question mark, and Don Diego, ever alert to a delicate nuance, had realized instantly what was going on in his mind. Rafael, faced with feelings he was having difficulty controlling, was only too ready to hear his grandfather dispute his offer of hospitality.

But that was the last thing the old man had been prepared to do.

"Not appropriate at all," he had agreed dryly. "Friends deserve better than that. If you promised to look after the girl, then of course you will do so."

And perhaps, he thought, standing unseen in the doorway of the *sala,* that impetuous decision had been the right one after all. He had often worried about his grandson. The physical graces came too easily to Rafael, and that, together with a kind of innate arrogance that seemed to intrigue the opposite sex, had had an almost magnetic effect on women. He had had too much from them, too, too soon, and he was spoiled. A woman who wanted to hold him would have to be not merely beautiful but quick of mind as well, witty and warm, fiery enough to captivate, sweet enough to charm, innocent in her heart, yet earthy and exciting to the physical

senses—in short, the embodiment of all the variety and sensual
pleasures a man like Rafael would never leave behind. Once
Don Diego had hoped that that woman might be his own
ward, Ysabel, but of late, he had grown increasingly disen-
chanted with the child. She was too self-centered for his
grandson, too coy . . . too predictable. Now Cristina, on the
other hand . . .

Yes, there was a woman who might prove a match for that
young devil! And did it really matter which one he chose,
Cristina or Ysabelita, so long as he settled down and began to
live as a man should, with roots in one spot and commitments
for the future?

"What an enchanting picture you make," he said, stepping
into the room. "I must commission an artist to paint you just
like that. You look quite charming in front of the hearth . . .
together."

The girl did not fail to catch his emphasis, and she flushed
a fetching shade of pink, as he had suspected she would. He
did not for a moment doubt that she, too, had been aware of
his grandson's confusion of late, and she was quite capable of
using it to suit her own ends, the sly little *zorra!* Rafael might
think he was in charge of his own destiny, but he, Don
Diego, would not have bet an American penny on it.

"I am sorry if I startled you, my dear," he said with a
distinct twinkle in his eye. "Perhaps I should have cleared
my throat discreetly in the doorway."

"Oh, Don Diego, of course not." The girl's voice sounded
slightly breathless. "You didn't startle me, not really. It's
just that we—well, we didn't see you standing there."

"Ah, that is the trouble with growing old. Young people
never seem to see you. They are always too engrossed in
concerns of their own. Why, you and that young grandson of
mine were so caught up in each other just now, I felt quite
guilty intruding."

The girl's flush deepened, as he had intended, but Rafael,
young scoundrel that he was, took the teasing in stride.

"Not at all, grandfather. Quite the contrary, your timing
was excellent." He had already arisen, and was now edging
toward the door. "As a matter of fact, I was on the point of
leaving myself. There are some papers I want to look over in
your study."

Don Diego was not about to let him go so easily. "You

needn't be in such a hurry, sir. Why must you rush off the minute I come into the room? Surely the papers can wait. They waited long enough while you were off on your own, gallivanting around the countryside. Now I ask you, *señorita*—" he glanced toward Kristyn— "does it seem reasonable to you that a young man should come all this way to see his aging grandfather and then refuse to spend time with him?"

"I am not refusing to spend time with you." Rafe's back stiffened until he looked more like his grandfather than ever. "And I did not come back just to see you. I came because you led me to believe your affairs were in disorder, although now that I am here, I see that Carlos has managed everything quite capably. But since you have me, don't be too stubborn to let me do what I came for."

"Stubborn? You dare to call *me* stubborn, boy?" Black eyes snapped with sudden spirit. "*I* am stubborn, you say? But who is more stubborn than you? Surely it is not so much, what I have asked? A few minutes out of your busy day? Is that more than you can give?"

Rafe's jaw tightened, as if he were about to rebel. Then, with a careless, almost amused shrug, he caught himself. Sinking back into his chair, he thrust his legs out in front of him.

"Very well, grandfather."

Fascinated in spite of herself, Kristyn watched as these two strong-willed men deliberately faced each other down. Never in the world of her childhood had she heard a young man address his elders so freely, nor would any respected chief have tolerated it if he had! Yet, far from being embarrassed by their unseemly conduct, Rafe and his grandfather actually seemed to take a perverse pleasure in their sparring.

"I was just admiring this room, Don Diego," she said, taking the conversation into her own hands. "If you had come in a minute earlier, you would have heard me telling Rafe how lovely it is."

The old man's face eased almost immediately, and his eyes took on a new sparkle, telling Kristyn he saw what she was doing.

"Thank you, my dear. I must admit to a certain partiality for this room myself. It has always been my favorite, except perhaps for my study. I took a hand in decorating it. As a matter of fact, I chose all the furnishings."

"Did you indeed?" Kristyn glanced around curiously. "I should have guessed. There is something about it that is very much in keeping with your own style. It looks like you."

And it did, too, she thought, with a smile. Like Don Diego himself, the room was too formal to be completely comfortable, yet there was something dramatic about it, an unusual touch of color here and there, a deviation of line, that gave it a flair all its own. Thick adobe walls had been whitewashed, then covered with brightly patterned red chintz to a height of six feet so that even the tallest man could lean against it without soiling his shoulder, and the floor, composed of tamped-down clay, was so slick and glossy it looked like tile. A large carpet with wide, bright stripes dominated one end of the room, while smaller, less obtrusive rugs, woven in earth tones, formed focal points for groupings of chairs and low tables on the other side. Sanctuary benches and chests of various sizes were ranged along the walls, with a particularly striking wooden cabinet decorated in primitive designs beside the outer door.

"So you think it looks like me?" Don Diego chuckled. "Well, perhaps you are right. That rug over there, the large one, is my special pride. I had it sent from Guadalajara, which is not unusual, but it was made to my specifications. You will not find colors like that any place else. Most of the other rugs were woven here, by our own Maria, one of the Indian servants, who is quite a skilled weaver. The furniture, too, is a mingling of styles. The *trastero*, for example, that cabinet by the door, is especially interesting. The designs are Indian, executed in mineral paint, but the form is definitely Mexican."

"As you may have noticed," Rafe cut in, "Grandfather has a penchant for anything Mexican. He doesn't mind if there are a few Indian patterns on it, just as long as the essence is right."

"Well, and why not?" Don Diego's eyes had begun to flash again. "What is wrong with Mexican craftsmanship? Or Mexican style? I suppose you would like to see the floor covered with Brussels carpet, the way that fool Vargas has done in his Europeanized castle on the other side of town. Or do you fancy a Queen Anne tilt-top table in the corner, with a silver service set for afternoon tea?''

"Of course not. Queen Anne furnishings would look ridiculous in this room, as would Louis the Fourteenth or Empire . . . or heaven help us, rococo! But a few classic American pieces would fit in nicely. And they would add to the comfort of the place.''

"Ah, yes, comfort!" Don Diego's voice was heavy with sarcasm. "I was wondering when you were going to get around to that. Is it really the lack of comfort you object to in this room? Or is it the fact that you don't like anything that reminds you of Mexico?''

"That's not fair, Grandfather. I love Mexico very much, though you find that hard to believe. My background is Mexican, my heritage—just as yours is Spanish. I will never turn my back on the traditions of my past, or forget them in my heart. But tradition is not the only thing that counts. Progress is important, too.''

"Progress, bah!" The old man spat out the word. "I know what you mean by progress! You mean that you would like to see this entire territory turned over to the United States.''

"I already have seen it, Grandfather! New Mexico belongs to the Americans. It has for more than twenty-five years. Don't you think it's about time you finally admitted it?''

"Being in physical possession of the land, sir, and putting your stamp on it are two different matters. Or do you think in your arrogance that the mere passage of time makes things right?''

"I think it makes them real, whether they are right or not. Besides, the majority of people here like being part of the United States. Life is better for us under the Americans. There are more choices, more possibilities. And yes, I do think that is right!''

The outburst, expected though it was, infuriated Don Diego, so much so that he could not answer. Ashen with anger, he turned his back and stared at the cold stones that fronted the fireplace.

Kristyn shook her head in amazement. "Honestly, the two of you! I can't believe how fast you go from a guarded truce to positively violent eruptions. Don't you feel childish sometimes?" Lowering her eyes, she softened them to a teasing, flirtatious expression as she waited for the old man to cool down and turn back again. "I do beg your pardon, Don Diego. I know I am only a guest in your home, and I am sure my outspoken comments must sound impudent. But really, I can't help wondering why you and Rafe keep bringing up subjects that will only make you quarrel."

"She has us there, Grandfather." Rafe leaned back in his chair, laughing softly. Almost against his will, he found his eyes seeking out Kristyn, and liking what he saw. How well the little vixen handled the old man! First she reminded him, however subtly, that he had behaved abominably in front of a guest. Then she looked up at him with eyes that would melt an iceberg. "I am afraid our hospitality leaves something to be desired. Between the two of us, we make exceptionally bad hosts."

Don Diego tried to look stern, but his sense of humor got the best of him.

"We agree then . . . at last. I think it is the first time since you came home." He turned toward Kristyn. "I am afraid it is I who should beg your pardon, my dear. You are right—we *have* been behaving childishly. Rafael and I have a habit of reducing each other to the same age. That age, I suspect, is about five-and-a-half."

Kristyn could not resist the laughter in his eyes.

"Five-and-a-half can be quite charming, even in a man who is supposed to be grown up. But it does seem silly to quarrel about the same things over and over, especially when there are more interesting subjects to discuss. Why, do you know, Don Diego, in the entire week I've been here, you've hardly told me a thing about yourself. There are all sorts of questions I'd love to ask . . . unless you find my curiosity unseemly."

"Unseemly?" Don Diego settled his lean frame into the nearest chair and studied Kristyn with a frank, almost rakish look. She really was astonishingly lovely, this girl who had set her cap for his grandson, and he was just old enough not to be afraid of letting his admiration show. "There is very little that is unseemly in a pretty woman, especially curiosity. Nothing makes a man feel quite so masculine as to have a fetching creature pry into the most private details of his life with breathless fascination."

For all the teasing in his tone, Kristyn could not help feeling flattered by the way he was looking at her. It suddenly occurred to her that "fetching creatures" must indeed have once hung quite breathlessly on his every word.

"What were you like when you were a young man?" she asked impulsively. "When you were Rafe's age, or even younger? Say, when you were twenty-one?"

"Ah, my dear child!" Don Diego threw up his hands. "What a lot you ask of an old man's memory. When I was twenty-one? Do you have any idea how long ago that was? No, no, don't try to guess, I would rather you didn't succeed. Suffice it to say, it was a long time indeed. I don't think I could remember that far back even if I tried."

"I find that hard to believe. You might call yourself an old man, Don Diego, but your mind is sharp, and I doubt there is anything you couldn't remember if you wanted to. All right, then, if you won't tell me, I'll guess. Rafe said that your heritage was Spanish, so I assume you grew up in Spain."

"Yes, yes, naturally. My family had a beautiful villa—I think it would have pleased you very much—not far from the capital. There was no Republic of Mexico then. All the New World territories were still part of the Spanish Empire, and many an adventurous young nobleman of that era was tempted to seek his fortune here."

"To seek his fortune?" Kristyn pressed impishly. "Or to run away from his fate? Rafe told me once that most of the young men who came to the Americas were fleeing either the hangman or an irate husband . . . especially the ones who changed their names."

A slight sound, like a quick intake of breath, came from Rafe's direction, and Kristyn was afraid for an instant she had gone too far. But Don Diego only looked amused.

"Did you call yourself impudent a moment ago? Most assuredly you are, and yet, heaven help me, I find your candor disarming. I would have called out a man for just those words, but with you . . ." He broke off, catching himself with a laugh. "Or perhaps I wouldn't. The older I get, the more I find I admire spirit in a man almost as much as I do in a woman."

And that, Kristyn thought, suppressing a smile, is why you are so partial to your grandson. Rafe has the same spirit you do, and the same outspoken way of saying what he thinks.

But aloud she only said: "You are not going to answer my question, Don Diego?"

"Do I need to?" His eyes sparkled. "I was under the impression I already had. But perhaps you are looking for a definite yes or no."

"No, not a yes or a no. You are right, I already have the answer to that part of my question. I know you *were* running away from something. But which was it? The hangman or the husband?"

"Which do you think? You have a quick wit and sharp eyes. Surely you have formed some conclusions about me in the days you have been here. Can you not work it out for yourself?"

Kristyn, enjoying the unexpected challenge, took a moment to study him in silence.

"It could have been either," she said at last. "I can see you as a highwayman, dressed in blood-red velvet and riding a horse the color of midnight. Or perhaps a rebel fleeing from soldiers of the crown. Still, I prefer the idea that there was a woman involved in it. There is something quite romantic about you, though you do your best to hide it. Yes, definitely, I think there was a woman!"

Little crinkly lines formed in the flesh around his eyes. "What an astute young lady. So my secret is finally out, after all these years. Yes, of course there was a woman. A beautiful, gentle woman."

"And you loved her?"

"Certainly, I loved her. What a question! I told you, I was young then, and young men always fall in love with the objects of their admiration. It is only as we grow older that we temper our passions. You will discover that one day yourself . . . or perhaps, if you are fortunate, you will not. Perhaps you will have more courage, more spirit, than I."

A kind of softness had crept into his voice, a vague, remotely sad tone that piqued Kristyn's curiosity. It was almost like watching the past come to life again, right in front of her eyes.

"Didn't she return your love? Is that why you never married her? Or . . ." She hesitated, remembering the jesting words she had used to start the conversation. "That's it, isn't it? She was already married!"

Don Diego did not answer at once, but fell into a deep,

introspective silence. Out of the corner of her eye Kristyn was conscious of Rafe, rigid and motionless in the chair beside her, and she knew he was listening to things he had not heard before.

"Yes," the old man acknowledged at last. "She *was* married. But she was married to a brute of a man, an animal who abused her physically and mentally. Every minute of her life with him was a living hell. You would have to have seen her to understand. Luisa was a very beautiful woman, but even her beauty was fragile, and a part of that gentle spirit had already been broken when I met her. I fancied then that I could persuade her to leave him, even though she was deeply religious, and perhaps, had things been different, I might have succeeded. But you see, there was a child, a little girl of six, and coming away with me would have meant leaving her with that monster."

"So there was nothing you could do but become secret lovers."

"Secret lovers? What a lot of romantic nonsense you young girls cram into your heads! You think we were star-crossed lovers, meeting breathlessly in the shadows of some warm, secluded garden? No, I am sorry to disillusion you, but it did not happen that way. We loved each other, but we were not lovers. We belonged to a different generation, Luisa and I. We had different values. Never would I have considered behaving so dishonorably—or bringing shame on the woman I loved."

"Come now, Grandfather." Rafe broke into the conversation for the first time. "That you were not lovers I might believe. But that you never even considered it . . .?"

"You doubt my word, sir?" Don Diego's voice bristled. "I suppose you think everyone has the standards of an alleycat, like you and your generation. Do you honestly believe I would have thrown my honor to the wind and gone to Luisa, had she allowed it?"

"If you loved the woman . . . yes, that is exactly what I believe."

Anger crackled in the old man's eyes for a moment. Then, to Kristyn's surprise, his face eased and those same deep lines appeared at the corners of his eyes again.

"All right, all right, have it your way if you must! Yes, of course; I would have gone to her—and the devil take the consequences! I was besotted with the woman. Absolutely besotted. I would have done anything, given up anything, even my precious honor, to lie beside her for a single night."

"The lady, I take it, did not feel the same way?"

"Luisa? No." Don Diego's expression mellowed subtly at the memory. "Luisa had honor enough for both of us. She had taken a sacred vow in front of God and his priest, and she could not forget that. At least, that's what I told myself at the time. In the years that followed, I must confess to wondering sometimes if it was really religious feelings that kept her from me, or if she was afraid. Or . . ."

He broke off for an instant, glancing with a bemused half smile at Kristyn.

"Or perhaps she just didn't love me enough."

Rising from his chair, he wandered over to the window, where afternoon sunlight filtered through the rippled panes. His back, from behind, looked almost unnaturally straight, but there was a slight stoop to his shoulders.

"How long ago it seems now. You see what you have started, my dear. I feel like I am cleaning out an old attic, filled with trunks of things I have half forgotten. Everything I pull out, I say to myself: Did I wear this once, did I play with it as a child—or did it belong to someone else? Do I really remember it, or do I only think I do? Does it even exist at all?

"Ah, but I am rambling, aren't I? You must forgive me. Old people do that. It is an annoying habit."

Something in the lonely aspect of his profile, silhouetted against the window, touched Kristyn, and moving from her chair, she went over to stand beside him. Afternoon shadows had lengthened across the courtyard, dulling the dark red tiles to a soft brownish hue.

"So that is why you left Spain, because you could not have the woman you wanted."

"Is it? Well, yes, perhaps in a way that is right. But it might be more accurate, after all, to say that I was running from the hangman. Or from a raging father and two powerful brothers. Before I left Spain, I challenged Luisa's husband to a duel—and I defeated him."

"You . . . defeated him?" Kristyn's eyes widened with horror. "You mean you *killed* him?"

"He was a better shot than I," Don Diego retorted sharply. "I did not take advantage of him. It was a fair fight, and honorable—as honorable as that sort of business ever is. Luisa came to me the night before and begged me to take back my challenge, but I was too proud and angry to listen. I think, even these many years later, she was more afraid for me than for him, although she need not have been. His hand was impetuous; mine was steady and cool. I did not regret my actions then. I have never regretted them since. Whatever it cost me, I at least had the satisfaction of knowing he would never raise his whip to a woman again.''

"But Luisa? She did not come away with you?''

"No, Luisa never understood. She hated the man, but she was bound to him, too, and I think she felt responsible for his death. She might have been able to forgive me for what *I* had done, but she could not forgive me the part I forced her to play in it. The next day, she took the child and found shelter in the convent.''

"And you never saw her again?''

"Never. She died there seven years later. Almost immediately after the duel, I came to America and married a woman I thought could make me forget my first love. It was, of course, a mistake. Love is not something you leave behind, and pain has a way of scarring the heart. My young wife never complained, but I know she must have felt I cheated her out of the passion I was no longer able to give. When she died giving birth to my only son, I never married again.''

Kristyn turned away, staring through the window again. The garden outside was still, with no breeze to rustle the leaves on the tall shade trees.

"What about the child?'' she asked softly. "What happened to her?''

"The child?'' Don Diego's voice was brittle enough to draw Kristyn's eyes back to him.

"Luisa's child. The one she took into the convent with her.''

"Ah, yes, the child. Of course you would ask about her. She was thirteen when her mother died. The nuns kept her a few years longer—for a generous compensation, of course. I sometimes think the good sisters are not quite as gentle-hearted as the women they shelter. When the time came for her to leave, she had no place to go so I sent her passage money to come to America. She was nineteen when she arrived, and very frightened, I suspect, though I did not realize it at the time. She was exquisitely beautiful, like her mother, but she had been raised in piety and sorrow, and she lacked that gift some women have of being able to make a man laugh. It was easy enough finding a husband for her— she had many suitors in those early days—but keeping him was another matter. Some men cannot seem to live without laughter.''

He started slowly toward the door, stopping to throw one last glance over his shoulder.

"Her name," he said cryptically, "was Catalina."

Then, without another word, he disappeared into the shadows of the hallway. Kristyn stared after him with puzzled eyes. For the life of her, she could not imagine what significance the name of Luisa's daughter could have after all these years, and yet obviously it seemed important to the old man. Turning, she started to ask Rafe, but one look at his face was enough to tell her there were still aspects of the story she had not heard.

Going over to him, she knelt down beside his chair, laying her hand lightly on his arm.

"Rafe?"

He glanced down at her, looking startled for a second, as if he had forgotten she was there. Then, catching sight of the expression on her face, he began to laugh, a soft, ironic sound.

"Catalina was my mother's name."

Twenty-Five

Long after Rafe had gone, Kristyn stood alone at the window and stared out into the quiet courtyard garden. The air was still breezeless, and even though the hour was late, the sun was bright enough to shimmer hotly on green-gold foliage and high adobe walls.

It was funny, the way everything suddenly seemed to come together. All the puzzles that had confused her before, the attitudes and feelings she had not been able to understand, were now almost startlingly clear. Don Diego's insistence on making a clean break with his past, the passion with which he had thrown himself into revolutions in his adopted homeland, his bitter rejection of Carlos and the ignominy of his birth—all this could be explained by the love he once bore a beautiful woman and the guilt he felt for his part in her daughter's pain. Even the obsessive partiality he had always shown for Rafe made sense now that she knew the younger man was not merely his grandson but Luisa's as well, the grandson they might have shared together had things worked out differently.

What was even funnier was the way Rafe had reacted. Leaning forward, Kristyn let her brow rest against the windowpane as her thoughts drifted back to the expression she had seen just for an instant in his eyes. Not surprise at all, not even curiosity. Only a kind of brooding intensity, black and strangely haunted.

Had he been so shocked by the story he had heard? Not that she could blame him, of course, yet that alone hardly accounted for his reaction. What else then? Had he been touched by his grandfather's pain, sharing manlike in feelings Kristyn could only guess at? Had he felt a surge of male protectiveness for the fragile grandmother he had never known? Or had he perhaps, just *perhaps*, caught a glimpse of that same indescribable sadness that stirred her own soul at the thought of all those empty years spent without love?

The idea was so startling, it took Kristyn's breath away. Had he, like she, said to himself: What a waste! What a terrible, foolish, unnecessary waste! And if he had, if the true significance of his grandfather's story had gotten through to him, then surely he must have been applying it to himself.

To himself . . . and to her!

She felt her heart begin to thump wildly as she turned back into the room. *Love is not something you leave behind,* Don Diego had said—and oh, hadn't she had cause these last lonely weeks to know how true that was? Could it be that Rafe, too, was beginning to learn that bitter lesson? He had been so cool with her, so maddeningly aloof after that one brief moment when he let his guard down, she had almost despaired of coaxing him into showing his passion again. Yet here he had sat, no more than an hour ago, looking for all the world as if he had seen into his own future and realized for the first time how desolate a man's life could be if he turned his back on love.

But the whole thing was so silly! Sparks of rebelliousness ignited in Kristyn's heart, making her angry and astonished all at the same time. It was amazing the way a man could turn things around in his head, and for no good reason at all! She was no Luisa, bound by marriage vows to another man—their love was not doomed from the start. Only one thing was keeping them apart, and that was pride! Rafe's stubborn, willful pride! He had to know by now that she wasn't going to threaten his precious masculine independence by trying to press him into marriage, and still he——

Kristyn broke off the thought, startled suddenly by the one thing she had not seen before. What if Rafe *didn't* know? It seemed incredible, but there it was. She had tried to tell him how she felt, but what if he hadn't believed her?

And after all, would that be so extraordinary? Rafe had no knowledge of the Indian world in which she had been raised. How could he know that for her the pomp and ceremony of the white man's nuptials did not matter, not so long as love was there?

Almost without thinking, Kristyn hurried out of the room

and cut across the garden, a sudden new plan taking shape in her mind. Tonight of all nights, after what he had heard, Rafe was going to be open, vulnerable. If she could only get him alone, even for a few minutes, she knew she would be able to catch him off guard again. Surely then he would admit, this time in words, that he loved her and needed her.

She spent the rest of the day alone in her room, spreading the prettiest of her new outfits out on the bed and choosing among them. Tonight was going to be the most important night of her life and she had to look lovelier than ever before. When it came time for dinner, she told Rosa demurely that she had a headache—*Tengo un dolor de cabeza*—and begged a tray in her room. She dared not sit across from Rafe at the table, knowing that a word, a look, a gesture, might give away the flurry of hopes in her heart. This way, when he saw her he would be surprised, unwary.

By the time she ventured outside, the gardens were almost dark, illuminated more by moonlight than the occasional torches that had been set along the paths. She was wearing a lightweight silk blouse, dyed pale blue to match her eyes and set off by the deeper blue of a ruffled velvet skirt. Daringly, she had opted to wear nothing underneath, sensing that the natural litheness of her body would be more provocative to a man like Rafe than all the artifice in the world.

"Tonight . . ." she thought breathlessly as she hurried along the paths that led away from the women's quarters. "Tonight, Rafe will tell me he loves me—and oh, I know he will be speaking the truth. Tonight I will lie in his arms and everything will be all right."

She found him, surprisingly, not in Don Diego's study, or even in the small candlelit library off the main *sala*, but in the quiet garden where Ysabel had received her the afternoon she arrived.

Perhaps it's a sign, she thought hopefully. Yes, surely it was! A sign that everything was going to be all right! This was the place she had first seen Rafe when she came to Santa Fe, and it was the place where his eyes had revealed the longing in his heart! What better place for him to confess his love at last?

She started toward him, then hesitated, shivering slightly even though the night was warm. For just a second, a brief dizzying second, she dared to ask herself what would happen if she failed, and she knew she could not bear the answer. He looked so darkly handsome, lost in thought like that, with the moonlight playing on bronzed skin and jet-black hair, and those deep, moody eyes drowned in shadow. It would tear her apart if he turned around and saw her . . . and told her he did not want her.

But that was not going to happen!

Kristyn pushed the treacherous thought to the back of her mind, just where it belonged! She loved Rafe, and he loved her! She knew he did, even if he could not say the words! It was absolutely unthinkable that they might spend the rest of their lives apart simply because neither of them had had the courage to go to the other.

"How solitary you look," she said softly as she slipped out of the shadows. "If I didn't know better, I'd say you were hiding. This is the one place in the whole house where no one is likely to come."

Rafe turned, but his eyes were veiled, as they had been too often of late, and try as she would, Kristyn could detect nothing of that flash of ardor she had half expected.

"Kristyn . . . I must say I am surprised. What are you doing here?"

Kristyn—The word caught her off guard, sending out warning signals her mind did not want to acknowledge. He had not called her Kristyn for a long time, certainly not since she had come to Santa Fe.

"Kristyn, indeed! Why, what a way to greet me. Have you forgotten how much I like it when you call me Cristina, or are you doing it on purpose? Really, Rafe . . ." She made her voice low and deliberately flirtatious. "If you treat me so coldly, I'm going to feel unwelcome here."

"Well, perhaps you are."

Amusement edged his tone, but there was enough of a serious undercurrent to make Kristyn distinctly uneasy. Somehow, she did not know how, but somehow, she had lost control of the conversation, and she could not figure out how to get it back.

"Rafe . . .! What a thing to say!"

"Rude, I grant you," he agreed, laughing, "but not undeserved. Did it ever enter your pretty head that a man who seeks out the 'one place in the whole house' where he is likely to be alone, might be doing it for just that reason—

because he *wants* to be alone? And speaking of rude, I notice you didn't answer my question. As a matter of fact, you maneuvered your way quite adroitly around it. What *are* you doing here? I thought you had such a headache you couldn't come to dinner."

"Well, no I—I . . ." Kristyn broke off, stammering awkwardly. Things were not going at all the way she had planned. "I didn't have a headache at all. I just didn't feel like going to dinner. Maybe Rosa misunderstood me. It's hard, getting through to the servants when you only speak a few words of Spanish. As for what I am doing here . . . maybe, like you, I needed some air. Maybe I wanted to go for a walk."

"And you just happened to come this direction?" It seemed to Kristyn that his brow went up, just slightly, a faintly mocking gesture that made her vaguely uncomfortable until she realized what he was thinking.

So that was it! She was so relieved she almost laughed out loud. That was why he had seemed so cold and stiff when he saw her! He assumed she had come there looking for him, and just like a man—even though it was what he wanted himself—he could not bear the idea that someone else was doing the chasing.

"Well, of course I just happened to come this way. What did you think, that I was looking for you? Come now, this is the last place in the house anyone would expect to find you. You don't seriously believe I combed every inch of the grounds specifically searching for you?"

"Actually," he said, his brow going up again, quite noticeably this time, "the thought never crossed my mind . . . until now. You do have a way of putting ideas into a man's head."

Kristyn felt her cheeks begin to burn, not so much because she had been caught in a lie, but because it was her own foolish protests that had trapped her.

"All right," she admitted, "I *was* looking for you. But only because I knew you didn't really want to be alone, no matter what you say. Not on a night like tonight."

"Oh . . . and what makes tonight so unique, pray tell, that I cannot bear to be without company?"

"Oh, Rafe, honestly!" Kristyn could hardly believe how exasperating he was. He had to know she could see right through him, yet still he insisted on making her spell it out.

"I don't think there's a stubborner man on the face of the earth! Why can't you tell me the truth? Does it embarrass your masculine pride to admit that even a strong, tough man can sometimes feel tender and confused?"

"The truth?" To Kristyn's consternation, he seemed irritatingly sure of himself. "And just what 'truths' would you have me tell? Assuming, of course, I could manage to keep that, uh, masculine pride of mine under control?"

The laughter in his voice was almost insultingly undisguised now, and Kristyn hated him for it. But if she turned away—if she stomped off in a huff the way she longed to—how was she going to get through that arrogant facade?

"You could tell me you love me," she blurted out. "You do, you know, even if you won't admit it—and oh, my dearest, I love you, too!" With that impulsive declaration, all the carefully rehearsed phrases, all the things she had been so sure she was going to say, vanished from her mind, and words began to spill out of her lips. "I saw the way you looked this afternoon, when your grandfather finished his story. So much love . . . all gone to waste. Oh, Rafe, imagine! Their whole lives were ruined, and all because they didn't have the courage to acknowledge their love. That's what you were thinking, too, wasn't it? Only you were applying those thoughts to yourself. You were finally beginning to realize how precious it is, this passion of ours. And how empty your life is going to be if you deny it!"

She paused breathlessly, waiting for him to pick up the challenge, but the brightness she searched for in his eyes did not materialize. Instead, he looked almost casual as he strode over to a nearby bench and sat down, propping one knee up beside him.

"Remind me never to underestimate the devious twists of the feminine brain. How is it that a woman can look at a man who has been successful by any other standard, by measure of wealth or influence or renown, and still say, His life was ruined because he could not have that pretty girl he wanted when he was young? A man, now, looks at things from a different angle. I won't deny that my grandfather's life was marked by his ill-fated love, but I find it difficult to imagine that he has spent the rest of his life dwelling on his loss. Quite the contrary, I suspect whole seconds sometimes go by, minutes even, when the name 'Luisa' does not pop into his mind. As for applying those thoughts to my relationship with you . . ."

He broke off, grinning.

"Do you really think it's 'masculine pride' at play here, or a healthy dose of female ego?"

"Ego?" Kristyn was so astonished, the word came out of her mouth in a squeak. "You think it's ego that makes me say you love me? That's ridiculous. I say it because you told me so yourself—even if you didn't mean to!"

"*I* told you? Indeed, you take my breath away. Forgive me if the occasion has slipped my mind. Or was I talking in my sleep?"

"You weren't asleep—you were wide awake! And you didn't tell me in so many words. You said it with your eyes. It was that first afternoon when you came into the garden and saw me. For just a second, you were so surprised you couldn't put on that sarcastic mask you usually wear. And in that second, like it or not, I saw the truth. You *were* glad to see me!"

"The truth again," he drawled, looking even more amused. "How it does have a way of cropping up . . . and in the oddest places, at that. Don't you think it's dangerous, my dear child, to make sweeping generalizations about a man's heart from a mere second's glimpse at 'the truth' in his eyes? Of course I was glad to see you! You are a pretty, provocative, altogether perverse creature—in short, exactly the type to appeal to a man of my rather debauched tastes. But . . ." He drew out the word as his eyes played up and down her figure, assessing her boldly in the moonlight. ". . . as I have had cause to point out in the past, you do have a propensity for confusing very different passions. Lust is a perfectly palatable emotion, not at all unsatisfactory in its place, but it is not love, and it never will be."

Caught off guard, Kristyn dropped her eyes, suddenly very conscious that she was wearing nothing underneath her blouse.

"I am not as good with words as you are," she murmured, sitting beside him on the bench. "I could never spar with you and hope to win. But I do know that what you say is not true. Not for us. You cannot take desire and love and disassociate them so completely. Oh, I know you want me—*that way*. And I—I—"

She faltered, a guilty flush painting her cheeks at the thought of the indiscretion she was about to commit. But she cared enough—hungered enough—to risk anything, even humiliation, to win him.

"I want you, too, even if it is shameful for a woman to speak those words aloud. Only there's more than just *wanting*, Rafe. For both of us. I can feel it, I *sense* it, when we are together."

"You do sense it, Kristyn," he said, his voice unexpectedly gentle. "But you sense it because you long for it, not because it is real. Because for some reason, you want to be my Luisa."

"*No!*" Kristyn shook her head so emphatically dark red curls tumbled onto her shoulders. Hadn't he been listening at all? "I *don't* want to be your Luisa! A phantom of lost love for you to mourn in your old age! Besides, I'm not like Luisa at all. I'm not married to someone else, and even if I were, I wouldn't let that get in my way! I love you so much I don't care about anything else."

"Don't you?" Rafe leaned back, his eyes taking on a strange, hooded look. "But I think you do, my dear. I think you care deeply, even if you don't realize it. Loyalty is very much a part of your nature. Believe me, for all my flippant talk of 'prettiness' and 'perversity,' I have noticed that, and it is one of the qualities I find most appealing in you. I cannot imagine your ever intentionally being unfaithful to your husband."

"Even if he was a brute?" she asked incredulously. "The kind who abused his wife mentally and physically?"

"No . . . perhaps not a brute like that." Rafe's lips twisted at the corners, an ironic expression that gave his face an oddly lopsided look. "But every man is not deliberately cruel. And the fierce loyalty of some women for their husbands can be frightening to behold."

The brittleness in his voice puzzled Kristyn, and for a moment she could only stare at him as she tried to figure out what was going on inside his mind. Then suddenly she understood.

Of course! What a fool she had been not to realize before. There was one subject absolutely guaranteed to set Rafe off—and she had brought it up herself.

"Even the word sends cold shivers down your spine, doesn't

it?'' she said, smiling indulgently. "Marriage, with a capital *M*. The ultimate threat to a bachelor's sense of self. Only, oh, Rafe—it's so silly! Of all the women you've ever known, I'm the least likely to lure you to the altar. Don't you see? I was raised in a different culture, one in which the concept of marriage as it is practiced by the white man is virtually unknown. When a Cheyenne man and woman want to join their lives, all they do is build a lodge and move in with each other. There are no elaborate ceremonies, no papers to be filled out and filed with the authorities. For us, love is simpler . . . and less pretentious. What is important is not the ritual itself but the commitment. Not the vows we speak in front of others but the promises we make in the privacy of our own hearts.''

She fell silent, her eyes lingering lovingly on his face as she watched expectantly for that first hint of tender laughter, telling her he finally realized how she felt. But to her surprise, he seemed to withdraw even deeper into himself. Rising, he took a few steps away and stared abstractedly into the darkness.

"I am afraid,'' he said, his voice sounding muffled as it drifted back to her, "that you have come to the wrong conclusions again. The word *marriage,* I assure you, holds no terrors for a man who is certain he will not fall into that trap. No, it is those other words I find so disconcerting on your lips. *Commitment* . . . and *promises.*''

He turned back slowly, his face not quite the mask it had been before but not truly readable either.

"I have made no promises, Kristyn, to you or any other woman—and I am not about to start now. Perhaps someday, when my life is more settled, I will be ready for that kind of involvement, although, to be honest, the older I get, the more I am inclined to doubt it. I have always been a bit of a loner, even when I was a boy, and the passing years only seem to accentuate that trait. All I want from a woman—and all I am willing to give—is a night or two of uncomplicated passion. Now, can you look me in the eye and tell me, quite seriously, that that is really what you have in mind?''

"No,'' Kristyn whispered, choking on the word. No, that was not at all what she had in mind. Only something inside of her would not let her believe that that was what he wanted either. She *could* not believe it. It would hurt too much if she did.

"I don't mean to be cruel," he said, sitting beside her again and leaning slightly forward. "I only want to be frank. And fair. I *do* care about you . . . very much. I was wrong to insult your intelligence by trying to pretend I don't. If I didn't have deeper feelings than desire, I would bundle you off to bed right now, enjoy you thoroughly, and wake up in the morning without a twinge of conscience, knowing I had been completely open about the business. But I do care, and because of that—because I don't just *want* you, I like you as well, and respect you—I will not treat you shabbily. That is not how a man behaves toward a woman he respects."

Kristyn turned away, aware of the sting of tears against her eyelids.

"Then you can't have respected me much before," she whispered miserably. "You did lie beside me once, you know. And you made it very clear that it was only for one night."

"Damn it," he muttered hoarsely. "I *am* a man, and you, God help me, are an extremely beautiful woman. Yes, I gave into temptation, but do try to remember, sweet, that that very delightful temptation was partly of your own making. I am not saying I'm sorry, mind you—no man with blood in his veins would regret a night like that—but I'm not particularly proud of it either. You were confused then, and vulnerable. I'll always have the feeling that I took advantage of you, and hurt you perhaps, a bit more than I was aware."

The gentleness in his voice coaxed the tears from Kristyn's eyes, and they ran in little rivulets down her cheeks. Before, when he had tried to bottle up his feelings, as if they did not exist, it had been easy to convince herself that he was lying, as much to himself as to her. Only now, he admitted he *did* care—just not enough.

"Oh, what a terrible fool you must think me."

"No, not a fool at all." He sensed her tears even before he touched his hand to her face and eased it toward him. There was something about a woman's pain that had a distinctly unsettling effect on him, especially when he could not disassociate himself from its cause. "What I do think is that you are a very pretty girl, and I am an unspeakable cad, not worth a single one of those tears."

Kristyn tried to smile, but even to please him she could not manage it.

"I still feel like a fool," she murmured awkwardly.

"Well, you shouldn't. Don't be so hard on yourself. You're a very young woman—flirting *should* come as naturally to you as breathing. We've been selfish, keeping you cooped up in the house because we've been too busy to socialize. You need to be surrounded by gaiety and laughter. By friends your own age. I'll tell you what! Don Antonio Vargas is holding a *fiesta* the day after tomorrow. It promises to be the liveliest event of the season, and I'll wager every handsome young *cabellero* in the territory will be there. We had not planned to attend, but I think now we will. When you see how popular you are—and how all the men are drawn to you, like flies to honey—you won't have time to moon over me."

"But I don't want other men," Kristyn protested unhappily. "I don't think I ever will again. I only want——"

"Shhhh!" He laid his fingers on her lips. "Leave the words unsaid . . . and let me leave them unheard. Ah, pretty, pretty Cristina, why must you try so hard to entice me to taste forbidden fruit again? Don't you know I will hate myself if I use you that way? And you will never forgive me."

Cristina. Everything else vanished in the wake of that single word, slipping like an unconscious endearment from his lips. Cristina. She was suddenly, intensely conscious of the closeness of him, the body heat, as she knew he must be conscious of her warmth, and she had the heady sensation that any second now, he was going to draw her into his arms and bruise her lips with the kiss from which neither of them could retreat. And if he did, if he carried her off to his bed and made love to her, surely his passions would not be satiated in a single night . . . or two, or three!

"How can you say you would be using me? If I want you, my darling, as you want me, that is not using. It is sharing."

"It is," he admitted hoarsely "*if* you want me. But I wonder, right now, if you know what you want."

"Oh, I do, Rafe, I do!"

"You *think* you do, I'll grant you that, and what you think you want is me. But ask yourself this one question, my dear. 'Do I really want this man, with all his flaws, all his very obvious reluctance to offer any kind of commitment, or do I just want *a* man, any man, to admire and flirt with me?' "

"That's not fair!" Kristyn tried not to rise to the bait, but she could not help herself. "You make me sound so—so

shallow! Do you really think I'm the kind of woman who
would profess love for a man one day and forget him the
next?''

''No?'' He drew back a little. ''Ah well, a natural mistake.
After all, you have been known to do that in the past.''

''*I* . . . have?'' Kristyn stumbled on the words, feeling
suddenly cautious, apprehensive, though she was not sure
why.

''Most assuredly. Or didn't you profess love for your
Indian husband. Certainly you forgot him quickly enough.''

If he had reached out and struck her across the face, he
couldn't have hurt her any more. Recoiling as from a physical
blow, Kristyn jumped up and moved almost compulsively
down the path, anxious to put space between herself and this
man she had only wanted to be close to before. The sting of
that caustic quip cut all the deeper because somewhere in her
heart she suspected he was right.

''My—my husband?''

''You sound confused.'' His voice was cold in the darkness behind her. ''Don't tell me he's slipped your mind? I'm
afraid I can't do much to refresh your memory. All I know
about him is his name. What was it now? Man Who-Lives-
with-the-Foxes?''

''Wolves,'' she corrected automatically, staring sightlessly
at the dark wall. ''His name was Man-Who-Lives-with-the-
Wolves. At least, that's what he planned to call himself when
he was a little boy.'' How it hurt, the way he was treating her
now. So scornfully, as if he had no use for her at all! How
could she ever have thought she could come to him and win
his love? ''I never tried to deny my husband . . . and I
haven't forgotten him, no matter what you think! We grew up
together; we had too many memories in common, too many
hopes and dreams, ever to forget. I don't pretend our love
was the same fiery passion I once knew with you, but I like
to think that one day it would have grown into that. But he is
dead now, and all the remembering in the world—all the
mourning—will not bring him back.''

Her voice drifted off, leaving nothing but the empty sound of
the wind to fill the night. Rafe did not speak as he slipped up
behind her, nor did he touch her, waiting instead until she turned
of her own accord. When she did, she was surprised to see
that his eyes were not hard at all, but soft and compassionate.

"It is all right to forget, Cristina. You *should* forget—don't blame yourself for that. Only try to understand. As you once learned to forget him, so now it is time to forget me and get on with your life." He leaned forward, letting his lips brush lightly, impulsively, against her cheek, then turned away, as if embarrassed by his own tenderness, and strode out of the garden.

Gone! Kristyn stood alone in the darkness and stared helplessly after him. Just like that, he was gone . . . and nothing had worked out the way she had planned! A tumult of half-formed thoughts whirled through her brain, pulling her this way and that until she was so confused she did not know what she felt anymore. That Rafe did not love her, that he could *never* love her, was pain enough—but, oh, the manner of his rejection! How would she ever be able to face him again, remembering that sarcastic twist to his lips when he had taunted her about her dead husband? The biting edge she had heard in his voice as he uttered those terrible, cruel words?

And yet—and *yet*—there had been gentleness, too. A look of something almost like yearning in those dark eyes just before he left her. An unexpected softness in the lips that grazed against her cheek.

Raising her hand, Kristyn let it rest on the side of her face, remembering with little tremors of emotion the way his mouth had felt, so hot for one brief moment, searing like a brand into her skin.

He does care for me! she thought, daring to hope again. And not just as a friend, no matter what he claims. He could not have looked at me like that, *touched* me like that, if he didn't!

And there had been that other moment, too. That moment just before, when she had been so sure he was going to take her into his arms. She hadn't been imagining that—she knew she hadn't! He *did* want her. If he hadn't chosen just that time to——

Kristyn caught herself abruptly, realizing where her thoughts were taking her. If Rafe hadn't chosen that time to bring up her young husband, she would be in his arms right now, and nothing on earth could stop them from giving themselves, freely, joyously to each other.

And that, of course, was precisely why he had done it! If

he had tried to reason with her, if he had explained his arguments coolly and logically, she would have found an answer to everything he said, and sooner or later, she would have broken through his resistance. By deliberately hurting her—by forcing her to withdraw into thoughts and pains of her own—he had accomplished the thing he set out to do. He had made *her* pull away from him.

He *was* afraid of commitment. Stunned, Kristyn pondered this astonishing new discovery, her head reeling with the implications. He had told her as much, of course, but she had not understood, thinking that he dreaded the embarrassment—or the annoyance!—of having to fend off unwelcome demands from her. Now, suddenly, she realized that that was not it at all. What he really feared was the commitment his own heart had begun, unbidden, to make.

A secret smile played on her lips as she turned toward the fountain, staring at the water that cascaded over its double tiers. For the first time, she was aware of the sultry perfume on the night breezes, the exquisite beauty of soft, velvety roses, their multihued reds and pinks only half muted by shadows.

They were so funny sometimes, these white men who played at love, approaching it obliquely from every angle but straight on. Courtship, for them, was a game, as intricate and complex as the game of war they fought on so many battle-fields in so many different places. Dimly, Kristyn realized that she herself had just engaged in such a battle; even more dimly, she sensed she had lost. But that thought held no terror, for like a good general, she had learned from her defeat. She had seen the enemy's strength, but she had seen his weakness, too. And that weakness could be turned to her advantage.

Rafe had eluded her tonight, but there was still tomorrow . . . and all the tomorrows after that. He could not hide behind arrogance and a quick wit forever.

Kristyn was so caught up in her thoughts she did not notice a ghostly figure slip out of the shadows and watch, black-eyed and intent, as she returned to the house. But Ysabel, who had been lurking in the darkness long enough to hear every word of that passionate dialogue, did not fail to notice a single thing about Kristyn, including the secret half-smile on her lips.

Bitch! Sultry Spanish features contorted into a spiteful grimace. *Perversa!* It was positively disgusting the way she threw herself at Rafael, with no restraint at all. No sense of shame! Completely forgetting another night when she, too, had hurled herself into that same man's arms, she concentrated on her rival's despicable conduct.

So she had been right about the slut all along! A hot current stabbed through Ysabel's body, making her blood boil in her veins. She and Rafael *had* been lovers—and that was why she was here! To lay claim on him again!

And judging from that smug smile on her features, she thought she was going to succeed!

Tension knotted up in Ysabel's stomach, lying there like a ball until she thought she was going to be sick. For the life of her, she could not figure out what men saw in a woman like that. A sultry glance, a blatantly vulgar way of moving, a promise of easy sexuality? Surely no male over the age of fourteen could mistake those for lasting virtues. And yet, fools that they were, they seemed to! Even Rafael had obviously surrendered once to that *descarada*'s coarse charms, and he was showing every sign of doing so again, this time perhaps with disastrous results. Oh, he had said no to her tonight, but he had said it with his lips; his body, leaning subtly forward, had sent another message . . . and that message was *yes!*

That he would live to regret his weakness if he gave in, that he would come to hate himself for being trapped and her for trapping him, offered cold comfort. The trap would of course include marriage. Ysabel, well acquainted from personal experience with the twists of the female mind, knew perfectly well that, despite her protests, Miss Kristyn Ashley had only one goal—to become part of the powerful El Valeroso family. And in that rigidly religious environment, a man once trapped was trapped forever. Even had it been socially acceptable, Don Diego would never countenance the idea of divorce, and Ysabel sensed that Rafael, for all his assertions of independence, would be unlikely to go against his grandfather's wishes.

Nor, she thought, frowning, would the unexpectedly puritanical streak in his own nature allow him to rectify things when he came to his senses and realized what he had done. He might go his own separate way, as men often did, but he would never make that final, formal break, nor would he follow in his father's footsteps, forming an unholy if ecstatic alliance with someone more to his taste.

And at that point, Ysabel reminded herself, miserable and frustrated, she would lose him forever.

But that had not happened yet!

Clenching her hands into fists, she dug her nails so deeply into her palms she drew blood. Furiously, her mind began to work, sorting through the things she had just overheard, desperate to find something—*anything*—she could use against her rival.

The Indian husband Rafe had mentioned . . .?

She focused on the thought, turning it over in her mind. Husband, indeed! Why, the *perversa* herself had admitted that Indians had no marriage rituals. They simply "moved in with each other." And she could well imagine what they did, too, in their filthy, squalid tepees! She could hardly wait to see how Don Diego was going to react to that bit of information. And to the knowledge that the girl he was so fond of, far from being contrite, had continued her immoral ways when she re-entered the white world, going wantonly to the bed of at least one other man—his own grandson!

Of course, she would have to be careful how she used that little detail.

Scowling abstractedly, Ysabel pondered the idea. Don Diego, prudish as he was, might well be disgusted enough to order the girl out of his house, but he might go the other direction, too, and demand that Rafael marry her now that he had ruined her! Yes, she would have to think things over very long and very hard before she made up her mind how she was going to play this, the strongest card in her hand.

But one thing, at least, was clear. Ysabel tilted her chin upward, taking an unconscious stance in the moonlight. She had loved Rafael too long, she had devoted too many of her dreams to him, to let someone else walk away with him now!

Somehow, she did not know how, but somehow, she had to get him out of the clutches of that slut and win him for herself.

Twenty-Six

Kristyn could not suppress an impish feeling of satisfaction as the carriage wheels jolted over the rough dirt road toward Antonio Vargas' estate. Opposite her, squeezed in next to a plump *dueña,* the pampered *princesa* of the El Valeroso household was scowling at passing trees and clumps of sand with a face as dark and lowering as a thundercloud. Ordinarily, Ysabel would have been excited at the idea of attending the most glittering *fiesta* of the season, especially since she had spent the last three weeks wheedling Don Diego to allow her to come. But because she knew the concession had not been made for her, and because she was not accustomed to sharing her carriage with another young woman, especially one who was at least as pretty as she, the afternoon had lost its savor and she was thoroughly out of sorts.

Not that her jealousy was totally misplaced, Kristyn thought, running her fingers surreptitiously over the crisp taffeta folds of her skirt. She could not help knowing she looked especially striking in the new gown Don Diego had had made up expressly for the occasion.

It was the color of the dress, an almost pure scarlet with shimmering hints of something deeper, that particularly suited Kristyn's earthy beauty, highlighting auburn curls and mellowing her tanned skin to an exotic, tawny hue. Riding in the open carriage, she looked like a picture painted by some frontier artist, with the basque of her gown stretched across a slender ribcage and firm young breasts, and her ruffled sleeves blowing in the wind. The combs in her hair were high and elaborately carved, but they had been crafted out of simple tortoise shell, and with a sure instinct, she had refused Don Diego's offer of the exquisite ruby necklace that once belonged to his wife, sensing the sparkle and luster of those rich stones would detract from her own natural fire. The only jewels she would accept were a pair of heavy gold rings, now glittering saucily in her ears.

Perhaps it was just as well that they were arriving late. Kristyn flared her skirt out around her, grateful that Don Diego had not been able to find a suitable *dueña* for her on such short notice, and thus no stout matronly body was crowded next to hers in the carriage. Had they planned to arrive earlier for the picnic that had been promised on an open, grassy field, they would have been garbed more simply, in full cotton blouses and brightly colored skirts, with their evening wear packed away to be donned at the appropriate moment.

But because Don Diego had agreed only to attend the *barbacoa* and the ball that would follow, they had come dressed for the night's festivities, and Kristyn, despite her disappointment at having missed the other activities, could not help hoping that her arrival in that flattering red dress would create at least enough of an impact to justify those pouts and scowls on Ysabel's lips.

Ahead of the carriage, the three El Valeroso men escorted their women like an honor guard, Don Diego in the center, a few paces ahead of the others, his two grandsons flanking him on either side. Centuries of Spanish influence, muted only subtly by contact with Mexican and American soil, showed in the instinctive pride of their bearing and the arrogance with which they handled their horses, flicking the reins lightly, almost disdainfully, in hands held high above the animals' necks. Unlike their northern cousins, these white men of hotter climes asserted their masculinity with boldness not restraint, and the male of the species was as colorful as the female.

From Don Diego's wine-red *chaqueta* to the purer claret and forest green of Carlos' more youthful costume, to Rafe's starkly dashing black, set off at the waist by a crimson crushed-silk sash, they made an eye-catching sight. The horses were as gaily caparisoned as the men who mounted them, and as hot-blooded, and flashes of silver caught the sunlight as they pranced impatiently, shaking their manes in the wind.

The road curved sharply, causing the carriage to lurch from side to side, and Kristyn, laughing, sank deeper into her seat, feeling the first tingles of anticipation as she realized they must be nearing the Vargas estate.

Perhaps Rafe had been right. Not that she was going to forget him simply because there were other men to flirt with. That she would never do. But, oh, it would be good to have fun and enjoy herself again! After all, she *was* young, and what young girl did not need to hear laughter from time to time? Or feel her feet tapping against the floor to the beat of music she could not resist?

And perhaps, just perhaps, she would prove to be as popular as Rafe had promised and all the young *caballeros* would be lined up to teach her the *fandangos* and sweet, romantic waltzes she longed to learn. The image caught her fancy and she began to smile, not noticing that Ysabel, who had been regarding her closely, was looking more vexed then before. Some traits were universal, crossing the boundary from the Indian culture to the white man's northern cities to the·volatile Spanish settlements in the south. And one of the first things she had learned, coming of age in the Cheyenne world, was that there was nothing quite so intriguing to a man—even one as arrogant and sure of himself as Rafe—as the sight of a woman surrounded by other men.

The carriage rounded one last hill, and Kristyn felt her excitement mount as Don Antonio Vargas' estate came into view. Leaning over the side, she stretched out as far as she could to get a better look.

It was not nearly as impressive as Don Diego's elaborate *hacienda,* for it was nestled in the midst of disappointingly flat plains, but the very size of it was enough to tell her that Vargas must be numbered among the great *hidalgos* of the area. The fields around it burgeoned with well-tended crops, and on distant slopes, utterly oblivious to the noisy comings and goings of the humans beneath them, sheep grazed lazily on sparse clumps of grass or lay down to take a *siesta* in the late afternoon sun.

As they approached the high wall that enclosed the estate, Kristyn saw that the massive wooden gates had been flung open, and the area directly outside was a flurry of motion and color. That they were not the only latecomers quickly became apparent for another carriage appeared almost simultaneously on a road that veered off to the west, and a group of young men, bold-eyed and laughing, had just reined in to dismount at the gate. Music vibrated in the air as melodies drifted over the wall from various sections of the *hacienda*, where strolling bands of performers paused to tempt the revelers with rollicking fiddles or the jingling tones of a guitar.

Don Antonio greeted them as their carriage rolled to a stop just opposite a tall oak in the center of the entry court. He was a plump man with thinning black hair and black eyes that seemed to dance in a round, jovial face. As Kristyn gave him her hand and let him help her from the carriage, she was surprised to note that he was wearing a dark vested suit, impeccably tailored, but somehow out of keeping with his swarthy Spanish appearance.

Glancing around, she saw that a number of the other men, too, seemed to have a penchant for things American, and she sensed that only deference to his grandfather's iron will had kept Rafe from adopting the same style himself. The women, for the most part, were still clad in the lightweight cotton dresses they had been wearing since early morning, but a few had changed into elaborate ballgowns, and the effect they created as they flitted back and forth, calling out greetings to newcomers and catching up on the latest gossip, was one of colorful dissonance. Every shade, every style, seemed to be represented in that gathering: vivid primary hues and soft, muted pastels; sheer lawn and rich wintry velvet; wide, ruffled skirts and prim little artificial roses, made of China silk; white lace *mantillas* and pencil-slim satin, draped over bustles like pictures in fashion magazines from the East.

No sooner had they alighted than the coachman, cracking his whip sharply in the air, prodded his pair of lively bays toward the entry gate. Some of the guests, those who had come considerable distances and would be staying a week or two before returning, bedded their horses down in the stables, but closer neighbors like Don Diego were content to find a spot of shade in the surrounding fields where the animals could be unhitched and allowed to graze. The proud stallions the men had ridden would be tethered closer to the gate, remaining there at least until sundown, their backs still bearing the weight of brightly striped blankets and silver-ornamented saddles. As long as even a trace of light was left in the sky, every male over the age of puberty and not yet in his dotage knew that one last, spontaneous bet might still be made—one final challenge to his skill or his horse's speed—and no man with Spanish blood in his veins wanted to be left out of the action.

A heavy aroma of *piñon* smoke hovered in the air, mingling with the smell of slowly cooking beef and hot red *chiles*. The courtyard seemed even more bustling now that Kristyn was on the ground, not viewing it from the carriage, and she pulled a little away from the others to stare around her in fascination.

A pair of elderly matrons, dressed in black silk, had cornered Don Diego and were carrying on an animated conversation at one side of the yard, while children scurried underfoot, chasing each other in games of tag and hide-and-seek. Small brown-skinned boys had been set the task of controlling the dogs, and now and then one of them would pick up a stick and hurl it in the direction of an offending cur, but the canny beasts paid no attention as they yapped ferociously at the heel of every passing leather boot. Pretty girls with laughing black eyes locked their arms around each other's waists and bent their heads together, whispering the same secrets they had whispered a week or two ago at the last *barbacoa* or grand *fiesta*.

As Kristyn turned, first one way, then the other, to take in the activity around her, she became aware that a man was standing a little apart from everyone else, staring at her with a frankly curious look on sharply handsome features. Glancing up, she found herself mesmerized by bold ebony eyes, their scrutiny so open and undisguised, it was not flattering at all, but almost deliberately insulting. He was older than he seemed at first glance, perhaps forty-five, perhaps fifty, but his skin was unlined, and thick black hair showed only a splash of white at the temples. Although he was not as tall as Rafe, he carried himself in much the same manner, with the air of a man used to being in command, and Kristyn sensed he was not the sort who would be kind to anyone who defied him or failed to carry out his orders.

Blushing suddenly, she lowered her eyes, realizing that she had been staring at him much too freely, and a man like that would no doubt consider such behavior an open invitation. Her heart caught in her throat as he began to move toward her. Then to her relief she saw that he was not looking at her, but at Rafe who had left the friends he had been greeting and was now standing behind her.

"*Pues Don Rafael,*" he said, pausing a few paces away. "*Dicen que estabas en Santa Fe, no lo creo. Pues regresaste, eh?*"

"Yes, I am back," Rafe replied, switching to English. "Though why you find that hard to believe, I can't imagine. Didn't you expect me to come?"

"No, actually I didn't." The stranger lifted his brow slightly, as if the idea amused him. Like Rafe, he managed the switch in languages easily, speaking with only the slightest hint of an accent. "Frankly, if anyone had said to me, 'Where do you think young Valeroso will show up next?' the last place I would have named is here."

"Well, then, you'd have been wrong. I am here. And I intend to stay until I've accomplished what I came for."

An unexpected hardness in his voice caught Kristyn's ear, and she stared at him in puzzlement. When he first began to speak in English, she assumed it was out of consideration for her. Now, detecting no other sign of courtesy in his manner, she wondered vaguely if he had done so because he wanted her to know he disliked the other man.

Still, that didn't make sense. That these two might feel animosity toward each other was not unreasonable, but this hardly seemed the place to settle their differences. Surely, even among the whites, one man would not abuse another's hospitality by quarreling with a guest in his home.

"Why, Rafe," she said, deciding impulsively to defuse the situation, "aren't you going to introduce me? I am eager to meet your friends. But I must warn you, *señor* . . ." She turned a little hesitantly toward the stranger, hoping her graciousness now would make him forget the unseemly way she had behaved before. ". . . there are so many people here, I think by the end of the evening I will not know who is who or what name goes with what person."

The man obliged with a nod of his head, a casual gesture, but one that somehow had the effect of a courtly bow.

"I find that very easy to understand, *señorita*." His eyes were still playing with her, but coolly now, almost jokingly, as if that insulting quality she sensed before had been a mistake. "But let me assure you, the problem will not affect anyone else, at least none of the male guests. No man who has looked upon so lovely a woman could forget who she is."

The words were no more than exaggerated gallantry, but they seemed to have a grating effect on Rafe. Scowling, he took a step forward, then hesitated, holding himself back with visible effort.

"May I present Señor Ricardo Cuervo, my dear? You seem to have caught his fancy, but I don't suppose I should wonder at that. Señor Cuervo has always been notorious for enjoying pretty women—even when he had a wife of his own languishing at home. Now that he is a widower, I daresay he considers his manners acceptable. But you are wrong if you think he is my friend. Or my grandfather's."

"Ah, *señorita* . . .!" Cuervo turned to Kristyn with a disarming smile. "What shall we do with this young man? He always was a hothead, even years ago. I see time has not changed him."

"No it hasn't," Rafe interjected sharply. "And it's not going to. You've had things much too easy around here, Cuervo. There has been no one to stand up to you, only an old man and a very young one. Now that I am back, I think you'll find things different."

"Perhaps, *amigo*," Cuervo hissed the words softly through his teeth. "Perhaps. But is this the time to discuss it? I think we must be boring this beautiful young lady." Glancing toward Kristyn, he let her know, with his eyes again, that the words were not an empty compliment. But this time he took care not to make the gesture threatening. "It seems that Rafael is ready to present me to you, *señorita,* but not you to me. Ah, well, no matter. I do not need an introduction to know who you are. Everyone is talking of the lovely Cristina Lucifero who is staying in the house of El Valeroso. I have heard it said that your beauty, like your name, is the dazzling perfection of the morning star. Now I know that that is not an exaggeration."

He bowed again, as if to emphasize his words. In spite of herself, Kristyn could not help being intrigued by the man. Before, when he had wanted to insult her, she had felt almost ravished by that same intense gaze. Now, quite obviously, he intended exactly the opposite—and he was succeeding every bit as well.

"I, too, have heard rumors, Señor Cuervo," she said, injecting an amused tone into her voice. "I have heard that the men of New Mexico are capable of outrageous flattery. That also is not an exaggeration."

"Enough, *señorita*," he protested laughing. "Enough! If you must best me with words, at least don't call me '*Señor* Cuervo.' I insist on being 'Ricardo.' And I hope you will not let your opinion of me be colored by Rafael's hostility. I would be saddened beyond words to think that an old family quarrel might deprive me of the pleasure of knowing such a beautiful young woman."

Kristyn, who was beginning to enjoy the repartee, was about to respond much as she had before when a subtle intake of breath in her ear told her that Rafe had been listening intently to what they were saying, and he did not like what he heard! It occurred to her that it might be fun to see how he would react if she carried that casual flirtation one step farther.

"I, too, hope not, *señor*." She lowered her eyes, as if in confusion, letting long lashes flutter against her cheeks. "Ah, excuse me—Ricardo. It would be an equal sadness for me to be deprived of the company of so gallant a gentleman."

"Well, then, we are in agreement?"

Kristyn looked up to see dark eyes probing her face, not teasingly, as she had expected, but challenging her in ways that were vaguely disturbing. For just an instant, she was sorry she had started the whole business, but it was too late to go back now.

"We are in agreement." Extending her hand, she waited, a little uncomfortably, for him to bend over it.

"*Señorita . . .*"

His lips were strangely hot against her skin, impertinent, reminding her of the way his eyes had made her feel before, and she sensed that he was deliberately holding her hand a second longer than propriety allowed. But when he released her, a mask of politeness had come over his features, and only good breeding showed in the casual way he bowed, first to her, then to Rafe, as he said good-bye and sauntered slowly across the court toward an exit on the other side.

Kristyn found her eyes following his retreating form, and with a little shiver, she realized that Ricardo Cuervo was not a man to be taken lightly. Obviously, he was used to manipulating people, women at least, and if she was any indication, he was a master at it. Just when she had wanted to hate him, he made her like him with his laughter and his flattery—and then when she had wanted to like him, he twisted everything around and made her feel cheap and degraded!

Turning back to Rafe, she was surprised to see that he, too, had been watching Cuervo walk away. And in that moment, his face was as black and glowering as she had ever seen it.

"Dare I assume," she said dryly, "that you do not like Señor Cuervo?"

"And you, I suppose, find him exactly to your taste." He threw her a sharp look. "God only knows why that surprises me. I should have realized that type would appeal to you."

The raw emotion in his voice puzzled Kristyn, and for an instant, she could only stare at him in amazement. No matter what his differences with Cuervo, surely it was unreasonable to expect her to snub the man. Or to object to a harmless flirtation.

"That type? How dreadful you make him sound, and quite unfairly, too. Señor Cuervo is a very attractive man, Rafe. Even you, with your arrogance, will have to admit that."

"Oh, I'll admit it all right. At least I'll admit that the man has a certain degree of physical attractiveness, which seems to be all that matters to you. You see a man who excites your senses and you can't take your eyes off him, can you?"

"Oh, come, Rafe!" Kristyn could hardly keep her lips from turning up at the corners. He was jealous. That was why he was behaving like this. He was actually jealous! He had told her right out he did not want her himself, but let her look at another man and he turned positively surly! "Now you're making *me* sound dreadful, and just as unfairly, too. If you saw a girl whose looks you liked—one that 'excited your senses'—you'd practically rape her with your eyes. And you wouldn't feel the least bit guilty either! Why is it different when I do it? Why can't a woman be accorded the same privileges as a man?"

The irrefutable logic of her words was hardly calculated to improve the temper of a man unused to losing arguments, especially with a woman.

"Well, then, look all you want . . . just don't let my grandfather catch you. I suppose you were taken in by that story about some old family quarrel. Family quarrel, hell! It's a quarrel, all right—though I'd hardly call that a strong enough word!—but it doesn't involve Cuervo's family, and it doesn't go back for generations. Do you remember I told you once that someone was trying to steal my grandfather's land? Well, that someone is Ricardo Cuervo.''

''Is it really?'' Kristyn's eyes drifted toward the place where she had first seen the man. Yes, she could imagine he might be capable of almost anything. There had been something fascinating about him—even when she distrusted him most, she felt the pull of that inexplicable magnetism—but there had been something sinister, too, beneath the easy charm he turned on and off. ''He doesn't seem to have succeeded. I mean, if your grandfather has lost any land, it doesn't show. He must have hundreds and hundreds of acres left.''

''Thousands and thousands,'' Rafe corrected. ''And no, he hasn't succeeded, not here in Santa Fe. Carlos, despite his youth, has managed to stop him quite nicely, and I have no doubt he'll continue to do so in the future. But he did get his hands on some land in Colorado, including a valuable silver mine.''

''Colorado?'' At last Kristyn was beginning to understand. ''That's what you and Carlos were talking about the night he came up north to ask you to go back with him. I could have sworn at the time you weren't going to do it. Then he said that one word—Colorado—and all of a sudden everything changed. Is that why you dislike Ricardo Cuervo? Because you want the Colorado land for yourself and he has managed to get it?''

''Damn the Colorado land!'' Rafe said, almost shouting. He didn't know why it bothered him, but somehow, perversely, it did. ''I don't care about the mine, or any of the rest of the property. I intend to get it back, but only because the idea of losing it is eating away at my grandfather's pride. I don't want it—or need it—myself. As for you, my dear . . .'' He turned searching eyes on her face, seeing in those sultry features exactly what Cuervo must have seen a moment ago and hating himself for beginning to respond. ''You would be well advised not to dally with a man like that. He might be attractive, but he can be dangerous, too. Very dangerous. Do you know what happens to a foolish little moth when she gets too close to the candle flame? She gets her pretty wings burned.''

''Does she?'' Kristyn ran her tongue over her lips. ''I think perhaps you shouldn't have used quite those words, Rafe. Don't you know that nothing intrigues a woman as much as a 'dangerous' man?''

"Let me put it another way, then. Ricardo Cuervo is calculating and unscrupulous, and I don't want you to have anything to do with him. Not now, not ever! Is that clear?''

"No, it is not!" Kristyn's head snapped up, her eyes flashing with blue fire. "I am neither your servant nor your wife, Rafe Valero! You can't order me around. Besides, didn't you tell me yourself that you're not interested in me? What business is it of yours what I choose to do? If I decide I want Ricardo Cuervo, or any other man, I'm going to go after him. And there's not a thing you can do about it!''

Tossing her head, she flounced away from him, moving with unerring instinct toward that one destination certain to annoy him, the pathway Ricardo Cuervo had followed a minute before. Rafe was suddenly conscious of the childish way she had thrown back her shoulders, the little girl tilt to her head as she stared straight ahead, pretending she did not know he was watching, and for reasons he would have been hard-pressed to explain, these essentially innocent touches affected him even more than the seductive sway of her hips or the smoldering fire that burned in dark red sunlit tresses. A feeling of tightness swelled in his chest, and he realized with a surge of self-anger that, as always with this woman, he could not keep from rising to the bait.

Dammit! He shoved his hands into his pockets and leaned against a nearby wall. He had never let a woman get under his skin before, and plenty of them had tried. Women as beautiful as this one, yes, and as passionate, too! But not a one of them had that uncanny knack of always seeming to answer him back, giving as good as she got every time. And not a one had been able to turn around and walk away—and make him follow with his eyes.

Unbidden, the memory of that one night they had spent together came back to him, sensory impressions only partially muted by time. The feel of her hands, timid at first, then bold, as she dared to explore his flesh. The yielding pliancy of her body beneath him. The intoxicating perfume of thick, silken hair spilling across the pillow. The soft, involuntary cry that slipped out of her lips when at last they surrendered to each other.

How many men had she been with since then? The thought cut like a knife in his gut. More than one, that was for sure. There was that itinerant peddler she had traveled with. A boy, she said, and none too bright, but no doubt he had had a pretty face—and the physical capacities of a man. And then, of course, there was Billy Collins. *Nothing intrigues a woman more than a 'dangerous' man*—and they didn't come more dangerous than that.

Damn! he thought again, casting his eyes around the courtyard in a vain attempt to find something to distract his attention. Sexual jealousy was new to him: the sensations sweeping his body were strange and unfamiliar, though he recognized dimly what they must be. Always before, he had taken women on their own terms, as he expected them to do with him. If a woman wanted to claim fidelity, true or not, that was fine, so long as she understood he wasn't making any promises in return. And if she wanted to go to the bed of another man, a dozen other men—well, so much the better. He liked a woman to be free and experienced, and not inclined to cling to him.

But with Cristina . . . Dammit, with Cristina he wanted it all, every part of her, every secret, every longing, exclusively for him. With Cristina, he wanted the illusion that she was his woman, completely, totally his, for the rest of his life.

And illusion was exactly what it would be. He had known, right from the beginning, what she was. And every time she took up with another peddler, another Billy Collins—every time she let her eyes exchange bold glances with a man like Ricardo Cuervo—she proved that he was right. Hell, she wasn't interested in those pretty commitments she claimed to want. She was the kind of woman who liked the challenge of a man, the excitement of forcing from his lips those words he had vowed never to utter, the triumph of proving her mastery over him. That done, she would probably walk out on him and try her wiles someplace else. Even if she didn't, even if she stuck around long enough to lure him into marriage, she would never really be his.

Especially if she stuck around for marriage, he thought with a bitter laugh. He had seen it happen all too often. A woman with a taste for other men before her wedding day was a woman with the same taste afterward, and God pity her poor fool of a husband then.

Well, that wasn't going to happen to him. Rafe pushed away from the wall and strode forward, determined to join the *fiesta* and forget everything else. He had always been too smart to fall into that kind of trap, and he wasn't about to do it now. She was right—the men she saw *were* none of his business. She could go with anyone she wanted, lie beside anyone she chose. He did not give a damn if she took on every handsome *caballero* at the ball.

Only not Ricardo Cuervo.

That same burning pain tore at his gut again. Anyone else—*anyone*—and he would let her go and say good riddance. But not the one man who was his sworn enemy.

He would kill her before he would see her in the arms of a man like that.

Twenty-Seven

Kristyn sat alone on a stone bench in one of the estate gardens, grateful for a few minutes' respite from the frenzied activity of the *fiesta*. The sun had already begun to set, but there was still enough light to see a stylized arrangement of flowers set in pots all around her. From nearby, the strains of a violin filled the air, lively still, but softer, less raucous now that twilight was here.

So far, the *fiesta* had more than lived up to her expectations. From the minute she stepped out of the carriage, she had found herself flattered and fought over by one young man after another, none of whom seemed the least bit reluctant to abandon the familiar *señoritas* he had known since birth to ask her for a stroll around the grounds.

If there was one shadow over the afternoon it was that Rafe, after that brief outburst of jealousy, had seemed almost oblivious to her popularity, acting instead as if he were so intrigued with every other woman he had completely forgotten she was there.

Still, for all that studied aloofness, Kristyn thought, smiling at the memory, he never seemed to be too far away, behaving for all the world like a man who could not bear to let her out of his sight for more than a few minutes at a time. Surely before the evening was over, he was going to let his true feelings show again. In the meantime, she had been content to allow some of the young men to show her around the grounds.

The Vargas *hacienda* was large and spaciously arranged, and Don Antonio, famed throughout the territory for his hospitality, had thrown open every section of the grounds. The barbecue pits themselves were located behind the serving quarters where the odor of piñon and mesquite would be less likely to annoy the revelers, and ordinarily no one ventured near. But Kristyn, as curious to learn about the inner workings of the *fiesta* as she was to enjoy the strolling musicians and gaily colored decorations, had insisted on being taken there.

The area around the pits was as busy and bustling as the entry court. Great joints of meat, which had been threaded onto metal skewers, were roasting over a series of long trenches, filled with glowing red embers. Surprisingly enough, for all those sheep on the hillside, lamb and mutton were rarely seen on the table, especially when a man like Don Antonio entertained his friends, and the smell that piqued Kristyn's nostrils was that of beef fat sizzling on the coals. Men in white shirts and trousers, streaked with sweat and smoke, crouched at each end of the long spits, turning them by hand, while others braved the heat even closer to paint the meat with liberal coatings of a thick paste made from ground red chili peppers. When each joint was roasted to perfection, crisp on the outside, with barely a trace of pink in the middle, it was carved up and heaped onto huge platters.

The *tortillas,* those tasty rounds of corn bread that accompanied every New Mexican meal, were prepared elsewhere, in the kitchen courtyards that opened off the main cooking area. Here the women prevailed, and except for an occasional small boy who had to be shooed out from underfoot, not a male could be seen.

The corn, which had been soaked in unslaked lime until it was soft enough for the hulls to be removed, had been brought outside in what looked like large metal washtubs. The women scooped out handfuls of the grain, throwing them onto large, hollowed stones on the ground. Then, dropping to their knees, they rubbed a second, smaller stone back and forth over the corn, wetting it occasionally until the entire mass was ground into a thick, malleable paste. When they had prepared it to their satisfaction, they slid the finished mixture out on a long, flat board and began the tedious process all over again.

While these women were working, others were busy greasing metal plates that had been placed over the fire. As the *masa* was prepared, they took it from the boards and formed it into two-inch balls, which they flattened out to a paper thinness. These they laid on the hot cooking surface, flipping them from one side to the other until they were brown and faintly blistered in appearance. When an entire plateful had been prepared, it was covered with a crisply pressed napkin and hurried, still steaming, to one of the many tables that had been scattered throughout the grounds.

These tables were the most colorful part of the *fiesta,* and almost from the moment she caught sight of them, Kristyn had been fascinated by their gaudy splendor. Arranged in groups of three and four, with a sprinkling of stools and chairs around them, they had been spread with vividly striped cloths, their reds and golds and greens echoing the brightness of paper lanterns strung out on lines above them. An almost unbelievable quantity of food supplemented the hearty slices of beef and freshly made *tortillas:* platters of relish, and rice cooked with chunks of tomato to give it color and flavor; dark *frijoles,* Mexican-style beans mashed into a paste, and summer squash prepared with corn and green *chiles;* thin, cool slices of melon and tiny purple grapes, so sugar sweet they teased the tongue. Huge copper kettles, simmering over open fires, held savory *caldillos,* made of almost everything imaginable, from bite-sized chunks of beef and chicken to onions and chili peppers, chick peas and sweet corn, tomatoes and turnips, squash and apples, all seasoned with herbs that had been grown in the kitchen gardens.

Still, for all the color and excitement, Kristyn thought, leaning back against the ivy-covered wall, the *fiesta* was exhausting, too, and it was good to have a minute to relax by herself. No girl could fail to feel at least a little excited by the way the men had been pursuing her all afternoon, and indeed, she was grateful for their flattery. But already she had begun to notice a certain sameness, even in their compliments, and she was beginning to have the rather guilty feeling that, by the end of the evening, she would long for nothing so much as a chance to get away from them and find somebody, one of the older men perhaps, like Don Dicgo, who would be willing to sit down and talk with her, for a few minutes at least, as if she were a reasonably intelligent being with a brain or two in her head!

A sound of male voices, coming from nearby, broke into her thoughts, and Kristyn tilted her head, trying to make out whether they were raised in dispute or raucous cheers. Just at that moment, a serving boy cut through the garden, making a detour on his way to the barbecue pits with an empty platter in his hands. Curious, Kristyn stopped him.

"What is all that noise? *El ruido. Que es? Que pasa?*"

"*La palea de gallo,*" the boy replied, then added with a grin, "The cockfight, *señorita.* We all speak English here in the house of Don Antonio. You should go and see it. It is very exciting. Another day, I too would stay and watch, for my master is very lenient, but today—¡Ay!—today there is so much to do."

A cockfight? Kristyn turned back toward the sound. Almost in spite of herself, she felt her interest mounting. Carlos had told her that the cockfights which would be staged spontaneously throughout the day were considered by many to be the highlights of the *fiesta,* and even Ysabel, who had been sulking moodily at the dinner table when he said it, had looked up to agree. That the confrontation would be a brutal one, Kristyn had no doubt, but in the very brutality of nature there was sometimes a kind of primal excitement, like the terrible sense of awe that came from watching lightning strike the earth, or two strong stags lock horns on a distant plain. Not wanting to be left out, she jumped up and began to follow the sounds.

When she arrived at the small courtyard where the fight was in progress, Kristyn saw that it was overflowing with people, men for the most part, but a few of the women, too, their jeweled fingers clutching bills and coins as they raised their voices in hoarse cheers or howls of derision. Caught up in the confusion, she elbowed through the crowd, jockeying for a position from which she could see the action. The minute she did, she realized she was gazing at something quite different from the savagely thrilling spectacle she had expected.

A ring had been scratched out in the center of the court, and here the cocks had been set, one pitted against the other, spurred on not by their will to fight but the prodding of the gamblers. They were feisty little birds, Kristyn thought, saddened. They put on a good show, pecking gamely at each other with swift thrusts, but for all their outward ferocity, it was apparent that the quarrel they were engaged in was not one of their own making. Horrified, she watched, unable to tear her eyes away as they went at each other again and again, drawing blood until their dusty feathers oozed red in places.

Only when it finally became apparent that one of the birds had won and the other was about to die did Kristyn pull back at last, letting the crowd of men close in in front of her. As she slipped away, returning to her stone bench in that nearby garden, the boisterous sound of their voices followed her, and she realized, sickened, that they were still making bets.

How disgusting they are! she thought with a flash of anger. All those men, prodding animals to tear each other apart for no better reason than their own amusement. Where was the excitement in that? The sport? White men might call their culture civilized, but every day she spent among them she found new evidence that they were at least as barbaric as the "savages" among whom she had been raised.

"So . . ." A soft voice broke into her thoughts. "You do not like our cockfights, I see."

Glancing around, Kristyn saw that Carlos had slipped up from behind and was watching her with laughter in his eyes. Ordinarily, she would have taken his teasing in stride, but after what she had just seen, she could not contain her feelings.

"I hate it!" she blurted out. "It is not exciting at all—it is appalling! What kind of man would want to kill like that, just for the fun of it?"

"Most kinds, I suspect." Carlos looked vaguely amused. "It seems to be in the nature of man to flirt with cruelty. Women respond differently, at least to cockfights. Although, as you may have noticed, there are exceptions. I thought you might be among them, or at least that you would not mind so much. Surely, living with the Indians, you must have seen many animals die."

"Yes, of course," Kristyn admitted impatiently. "But not that way! When an Indian kills, it's for necessity, not entertainment. Every part of an animal is put to good use, the flesh, the skin, the hooves—even the horns. Nor is such an act committed without conscious admiration for the animal's beauty . . . and sadness for that which is gone forever. An Indian understands, as you white men seem to have forgotten, that all of life is diminished by the loss of a single living creature."

"A pretty philosophy. But I wonder, is it realistic?"

"I think," Kristyn replied, aware now that the cheering had diminished and one of the cocks was dead, "that sadness is always real to an Indian."

"Perhaps," Carlos conceded, smiling as he sat on the bench beside her. "But perhaps you will think better of us if I tell you that the cock will be thrown into the cooking pot, and eaten and enjoyed, even if the stew is a little tough. Still, I must admit our love of gambling does bring out the worst in us. Sometimes I think there are those who would be willing to pit two men against each other in a fight to the death if they could wager on the outcome."

Indians love gambling, too, Kristyn thought—but that doesn't make them throw two birds into a ring to peck each other to death!

"Don't you think," she ventured, "that that might be carrying gambling too far?"

"Carrying it too far? But of course," Carlos replied, throwing back his head with an easy laugh. Then, seeing her puzzled expression, he added: "That is part of being Spanish. Excesses are as natural to us as the air we breathe. Wait until you see one of our horse races. If a man wagers half his fortune on a gaming cock, imagine what he will do for his favorite stallion! I had hoped we would see a few this afternoon, but perhaps it is for the best that we don't. El Valeroso himself, despite his years, is very vain about his horsemanship, and I have no doubt he would insist on joining the field, if for no other reason than to impress his pretty houseguest. And if Grandfather competed, then of course Rafael would have to compete, too. They would ride only against each other, those two, leaving everyone else in the dust as they strained their skill and their horses' endurance to the limit."

"Are you serious? Or are you only making it up so I will forget about the cockfight? I know Rafe and his grandfather have to be on the opposite side of everything they do, but can that extend to horseraces as well?"

"It can . . . and it does."

"Are they always so competitive? Do they always battle everything out with each other?"

"Always. There is only one man on the face of this earth more stubborn than El Valeroso, and that is his eldest grandson. They seem to have a need to test themselves against each other, though to be honest, I have never been able to figure out whether each is trying to prove his own strength . . . or the other's."

"I don't know . . ." Kristyn turned away. "It all seems so strange. Sometimes—just sometimes—I almost think I'm getting to know him. Then—well, then, I realize what a stranger he really is."

Carlos paused, regarding her profile in the fading light. Then softly, very softly, he said:

"Are you in love with my brother, Cristina?"

The question caught Kristyn off guard. "In love? With Rafe? Well, no I—no, of course not! It's just that I—I—"

Carlos interrupted with a gentle laugh.

"You don't need to protest so much. I'm sorry if I embarrassed you. I didn't mean to. I think it must be the Spanish in me again—a good quality this time—that makes me think of passion as something to be shouted from the rooftops. But if it troubles you, you need not answer. In truth, I know already. I think I have known all along."

"You . . . have?" Kristyn felt the warmth rise to her cheeks. "But if you knew, then the others must have, too." And they must have been laughing all this time. Not unkindly, of course—they were not unkind people—but with that unconscious condescension that would make it almost impossible for her to face them again.

"I don't know about the others," Carlos said, laying a reassuring hand on hers. "I can only speak for myself. And, yes—for myself—I did know. I think I suspected that first night when you came down the stairs and your eyes met Rafael's. Later, when you came to Santa Fe, I should have been sure, but by that time, you see . . ." He paused, studying her intently as if searching for something he could find in her face. "Shall I make a confession, _amorcita?_ By that time, I did not want to believe that you cared for my brother, or that he returned your feelings, because I had begun to hope I might court you myself."

"_You_ wanted to court me?" Kristyn glanced up, troubled. Then, seeing the smile on his lips, she realized what he was doing. "Oh, Carlos, why do you say things like that? You almost had me believing you. Here I thought you were serious and you were only trying to flatter me, like every other man I have met today."

"But I _am_ serious," he said, still smiling, not just with his

mouth but his eyes as well. "Very serious. I do enjoy flattering the pretty *señoritas*, I admit to that, but they always
know when I am doing it. And they know when I am
serious."

"But—you can't be being serious now. I mean, why would
you want to court me?"

"Why?" He laughed softly. "Are you turning modest on
me all of a sudden? Don't. Insincerity doesn't become you.
You are a very beautiful woman, and I think you know it, a
little too well perhaps, judging from the number of hearts you
have collected this afternoon. Of course, I was serious when I
said I wanted to court you. I would want to still if I didn't
believe you had already chosen my brother."

Kristyn glanced down awkwardly, feeling somehow embarrassed, not sure what she was expected to say or do.

"But I always thought . . . well, I thought that—that you
and Ysabel . . ."

"Did you?" His voice sounded strangely far away. "Well—
another confession, then—so did I. Once. But it seems that
was not meant to be. I think perhaps I have dreamed about
her too long. She was such a pretty little girl, an enchanting
creature. It was easy to convince myself she would be even
more enchanting when she grew up. And in a way she is. She
can be maddeningly provocative when she wants—and maddeningly exciting to look at. But that's just the problem. She
has only grown up on the outside. Underneath, she is still a
little girl, and I think she always will be. I don't want a little
girl. I want a woman . . . like you, Cristina."

Kristyn caught the subtle deepening in his tone, and she
sensed, in spite of everything he had said, that he was not
quite ready to give up. All she had to do was utter one
encouraging word, throw him one wistful glance, and he
would take her in his arms and make all the sweet promises
she had ever longed to hear. Bitterly, she cursed the fates for
having crossed her path with that of the one man who had the
power to turn her heart against all others.

"I wish I could care about you the way you want me to,
Carlos. It would be so much easier. But—don't you see?—I
can't. No matter how I want to, I can't! My heart is not my
own any more, to direct or to control. I am—oh, my dear, I
am so sorry."

"No, don't be sorry." He was smiling again, gently as

before, with no sign that she had hurt him. "Sorry is a word that should never be used for love. I do not regret my feelings for you. They have enriched my life. And you, I think, no matter how you protest, do not regret loving my brother. Shall I give you a bit of advice?"

He leaned forward, tightening his hold on her hand for just an instant before he released it.

"Do not be afraid of love . . . and do not let it slip away from you. Rafael can be very taciturn sometimes, not at all Spanish in the way he hides his feelings. It may be that he will always be too proud to come to you. Go to him, then— you cannot both be proud. If you want his love, reach out for it. And cling to it as hard as you can."

Reach out for love.

Carlos' words still haunted her later as she wandered alone through twilit paths that led from one enclosed garden into another. *Reach out,* he had told her . . . but, oh, wasn't that what she had been doing all along? How could she reach out any more than she already had? She had thrown herself into his arms, she had told him in so many words that she was willing to share his bed without benefit of marriage, and where had that gotten her? Yes, and she had spent the whole afternoon throwing herself at other men, too! But far from erupting in a jealous fit, the way she had hoped, he seemed quite content to keep an eye on her from a distance—and squire other girls around on his arm!

Twilight deepened moodily into darkness, and candles set aglow in paper lanterns cast a spell of color and shimmering light over the earth. Other guests, too, had chosen that time for a quiet stroll, but their indistinct forms were half enveloped in shadow, and Kristyn, only vaguely aware of an occasional soft laugh or rustling whisper of taffeta, almost had the feeling she was alone. The sound of distant music seemed to swell in the night around her, making her ache with its plaintive beauty.

Somehow, she thought, *somehow* I have to make Rafe want me again. I can't give up now. Carlos was right. If I don't reach out to him, we'll never have any kind of life together. And life without Rafe would be too empty to bear!

A shadowy figure materialized out of nowhere on the path in front of her, and Kristyn, not ready to give up her solitude, was about to turn and slip away when she sensed something familiar in the man's bearing. Something she recognized in the way he held his head, cocked just slightly to the side on a long neck.

Ricardo Cuervo. A tremor of revulsion ran through her body as she recalled their earlier meeting. Cuervo might be a man with a taste for pretty women, as Rafe had implied, but quite plainly he was a man who enjoyed humiliating them, too! She took a step backward, anxious to get away, but even as she did, a new, unexpected thought leaped into her head.

Rafe had not so much as glanced her way when she went off to survey the grounds with two of the handsomest young men at the *fiesta*, one on each arm, but when she had dared to flirt with Cuervo, he turned almost livid with rage! Supposing, just supposing, he were to come along right now and find her with him?

The plan was just bold enough to work. Bold . . . and almost foolproof! If Rafe *did* come—and she was sure he would—if he saw her with the only man capable of reducing him to seething jealousy, how could he keep up that aloof facade?

Impetuously, she stepped onto the path, extending her hands as she moved forward.

"Señor Cuervo . . ."

The man turned at the sound of her voice, his mouth curling just slightly at the corners.

"Señorita Cristina. What a delightful surprise."

Bending over her hands, he brushed them with polite, impersonal lips. But he did not release his hold as he straightened again, and his eyes—those same dark eyes that had scourged her before—ran up and down her body with an oddly knowing leer. For an instant, Kristyn longed to pull away again. Only the thought that Rafe might be watching at that very moment held her back.

"Why Señor Cuervo," she said, forcing a note of teasing into her voice. "You disappoint me. All that gallant flattery earlier, and here we meet only by chance. I thought you meant those pretty things you said, but no, an entire afternoon has passed and I have not so much as seen you."

"Ah, but *I* have seen you, my dear." Still holding her hands, he drew her pointedly to the side of the path where the shadows were deeper, the sense of aloneness more intense.

"You were cutting your teeth on the hearts of half the men in the territory, most of them good looking and all of them younger than I. Do you wonder that I didn't venture over to join that assemblage? But now it is you who disappoint me. Did I not ask you before to call me Ricardo?"

"As you wish—Ricardo." Kristyn felt her heart begin to thump against her chest, though she knew she was being foolish. The garden was filled with people. What could happen to her here? "Did you really notice me this afternoon? When I thought you were nowhere around?"

He laughed, a guttural sound, deep in his throat.

"Oh, I noticed—and I saw exactly what you were doing."

"You saw . . . ?" Kristyn flushed guiltily. "Oh . . . you mean what you said before. That I was cutting my teeth on all those hearts. Do you really think it unkind to flirt with more than one man at a time?"

"I don't think you *were* flirting. At least not with them. Just like you're not flirting with me. You are using me to try to make young Rafael jealous."

"I—I don't know what you mean," Kristyn stammered awkwardly, unable to meet his eyes. He was right, she *had* been using him—and no matter how she felt about him, it was a dirty trick.

Yet, surprisingly, he seemed amused.

"I think you know perfectly well what I mean. But don't think you have offended me. Quite the contrary, I have always been fascinated by the wiles of a woman, especially one as beautiful as you. I am delighted—and flattered—that you have chosen me to play your little game. Only . . ."

He drew her closer, so close she was intensely conscious of the warmth of him, the maleness, against her in the shadows.

". . . if you want to make the man jealous, don't you think you should provoke him with more than an innocent walk in the garden?"

Before she realized what was happening, he had pulled her abruptly off the path, forcing her into the shadows of a rose-draped arbor. The nearness of him was almost animal now, raw and frightening as he caught her roughly in his arms.

"Señor Cuervo . . .!" She tried to squirm away, tried to protest, but he clamped his hand across her mouth, choking off her breath.

"Hush!" She was more conscious than ever of his body, conscious of that hard, threatening proof of his desire pressing up against her. "Why do you insist on struggling? If you want to make your lover jealous, this is the way to do it. Besides, you might find that you like it. Then we can both forget young Rafael."

He took his hand away, but before she could react, he followed it with his mouth, bruising her lips, savagely, crudely. There was no tenderness in that forceful kiss, no softness, only a kind of primitive violence that was terrifying and strangely compelling at the same time. Unwanted, thoughts of Rafe came back to her, potent memories—the way *his* lips had felt, as demanding as this sometimes, as arrogant, the way *his* body seemed to overpower her—and for a moment all she could feel was an aching hunger to be close to him again.

Realizing suddenly where her thoughts were taking her, she broke away from them, but it was too late. For one brief, shameful second, she had let her body sway against this foul beast of a man, and he had not failed to sense it.

Horrified, she wedged her hands against his chest, trying to push him back, but he was too strong for her, and she realized, frightened, that mere force alone would never free her from his grasp. She had been so sure when she accosted him, so foolishly sure that she would be safe with all those people around her. Now she knew that safety was an illusion. No one would come to her rescue if they did not know she was there, and with Cuervo's mouth fitted like a gag over hers, how could she call out for help?

Then, just as she was sure she would never get away, she felt the man relax his hold, letting go so abruptly she almost stumbled. Stunned, she looked up, half expecting him to say something, do something that would tell her what had happened. But to her surprise she saw that his eyes were focused on something behind her. There was a cool, distinctly amused look on his face.

"I think, my dear, you have gotten your wish. Although I wonder if it isn't more than you bargained for."

Puzzled, Kristyn turned to see a tall figure silhouetted in the red glow of a lantern on the far side of the path. Waves of relief flooded through her as she took a step forward.

"Oh, Rafe, I was so . . ."

Even before the words were out, they died on her lips, ebbing away as she caught sight of his features. I was so frightened, she had started to say, but now, seeing the way he was looking at her, she was more frightened than ever.

"Rafe . . .?"

He did not answer, but moved toward her, his body tense, coiled. Half hypnotized, she watched his hand spring suddenly upward, felt the sharp sting of a blow across the side of her face.

"Tramp!"

With a little cry, Kristyn recoiled from the slap, smarting not so much from physical pain as from the force of that cruel accusation. For a second, she was too shocked to understand. Then bitterly she realized what he was thinking, and she knew she had no one but herself to blame. She had been trying to get away from Cuervo when he arrived, but he had not seen that. He had seen only that she was in the arms of a man he hated, and all her terror, all her frantic struggles, had seemed to him no more than a clumsy attempt to writhe even closer.

Cuervo had been right. She *had* gotten more than she bargained for—and there was not a thing she could do about it! What could she possibly say? This isn't the way it looks, Rafe? Well, yes, I *was* flirting, but I never meant things to go this far? I was only trying to make you jealous? Each excuse she thought of sounded even lamer than the last. She would not have believed them herself if she were in his place.

A sharp pain surged through her body as he reached out and grabbed her wrist where Cuervo had already bruised it. Biting her lip to keep from crying out, Kristyn allowed him to drag her through the garden toward the main house where the noise of the *fiesta* was still loud and boisterous. If only he had left her where she was, she thought miserably. If only he had been content with that one angry slap. She would rather be alone with Cuervo—she would rather suffer his ugly advances again and again than have to face Rafe wherever he was taking her and see that look of accusation in his eyes.

Why—oh, *why*—had she given in to her foolish impulse? She knew how Rafe felt about Cuervo, knew how much he hated him. Surely if she had taken a minute, a *second*, to think things through, she would have realized that the sight of her with that man would trigger reactions she could not control. And then to let him catch her in his arms, with his lips on hers . . .

Oh, now, for certain, he would hate her forever! Tears of bitterness rose to her eyes, but she choked them back, dimly aware that there were people around them. Rafe had slowed to a normal pace, but he was still gripping her arm, steering her roughly through that milling throng toward the main gate. Now he would never want her again. To him, she was nothing but a cheap little tramp, the kind of woman who went with any man, no matter how despicable, and he would never forgive her for that. She had come close, so close, to winning him, and then she had ruined it all.

Almost before she realized it, they were at the gate, and then they were through it, finding themselves in an area that seemed strangely subdued after the raucous liveliness of the party.

Rafe stepped up his pace, stopping only when he reached the place where his horse was tethered. Releasing Kristyn, he unhitched the reins, barely glancing back at her as he flicked them over the animal's neck. She longed to call out to him, asking what he was doing—why he had brought her there—but his face was so harsh in the moonlight, her mouth turned dry inside and she could not speak. For just an instant, when he turned his back, fitting his boot into the stirrup, she had the sudden, insane urge to hitch up her skirts and try, somehow, to run away from him, heading back toward the lights and crowds of the *fiesta*.

But the urge lasted only a second. Then Rafe was beside her again, staring grimly down from the saddle, his hand demanding as he extended it to her. Barely aware of what she was doing, Kristyn obeyed. She was afraid now, inexplicably afraid, to ride off with him, but she was even more afraid to defy him. His hand was hard as he drew her up to the saddle in front of him; his arms were like iron, crushing her against him, not with the passion she had dreamed of night after empty night, but a kind of savage anger that vibrated through his body. He waited only a second, then touched his spurs to his mount, plunging recklessly into the night.

The lights of the *fiesta* faded on the horizon, dissolving into a moon-drenched darkness that seemed to close in around them, and Kristyn could hear nothing anymore, not even the last spirited echoes of a faraway *fandango*. Her body began to tremble, softly, like the quivering of a leaf in the wind. She was all alone with Rafe now, completely alone in that silent desert, and in his present rage, he was a man who might be capable of . . . of what? Of murder?

Shutting her eyes, she leaned back, feeling the warmth of him behind her, the rapid beating of his heart. Angry as he was, hating her the way he did right now, what was to prevent him from reining in his horse and forcing her down on the sand where he could . . .

She snapped her eyes open, pushing the thought away. Rafe was angry—but he wasn't a killer! Surely even he would not want to see her punished so savagely for one foolish indiscretion! It was just the darkness that was getting on her nerves, making her imagine things. The darkness, and that terrible strained silence between them.

"Where are you taking me?" she said at last.

She sensed a tightening in those arms around her, a slight, almost involuntary movement.

"It's not where I'm taking you that matters. I haven't decided that yet myself. It's what I'm going to do when we get there."

A long, slow shudder passed through Kristyn's body at the words she had half expected but dreaded to hear.

"And what—what *are* you going to do?"

"What I should have done a long time ago."

Twenty-Eight

The night wind stung Kristyn's cheeks, pulling her long hair out of its combs and blowing it back against Rafe's chest as they rode through the darkness. She was intensely conscious of the feel of him, strong and hard in the saddle behind her, a potent, unsettling force, reminding her almost as much of the passion they had once shared as the desperate fear she felt now.

What I should have done a long time ago . . .

The words echoed in her ears, disturbing somehow, ominous, though she did not know why. *Before,* he had had no reason to harm her, certainly not to kill her—yet she could swear she had sensed violence in those muffled tones. A savage physical violence that made her shudder to think of it.

Oh, why is this happening? she asked herself miserably. Why is there all this anger between us? Why did I provoke him so stupidly when all I wanted was to love him—and to let him love me?

She had no idea how long they rode like that, silently through the darkness. She only knew it seemed forever before a shadow on the horizon materialized into the vague outline of a high-walled *hacienda,* and she realized he was taking her back to his grandfather's estate. She sat rigidly in front of him in the saddle, not daring to speak or even move as they mounted the hill and rode through a half-open gate, heading for the stableyard in the rear. Drawing the horse to a stop, Rafe allowed her to slide to the ground, then dismounted himself and tossed the reins to a sleepy-eyed groom.

Kristyn waited until the lad had taken the horse away before she dared at last to look up at Rafe, silent and stiff beside her in the darkness. If she had had any hope, however faint, that the ride had cooled his raging temper, it was dashed almost instantly. His eyes were as black and brooding as ever. And as unforgiving.

"Oh, Rafe, if only I could make you understand."

"Understand?" She had never heard his voice so cold and controlled. "I should think everything is quite clear. I understand perfectly."

"But you don't!" How could he, when she had made such a mess of things? How could he even guess she had only flirted with Cuervo to make him jealous?

"Ah, but I do, my dear. You are hardly the first slut I have run across, and you won't be the last. I know exactly what you're looking for—and I intend to see that you get it."

Grabbing her by the arm, he steered her roughly through the maze of paths that led deep into the estate. Flashes of alarm went off in her mind, making her feel cold all over. Something in his voice, his words, warned her she should be afraid, but she could not make herself focus on it.

Even when they came to her room, pausing in front of the door, she still could not understand what he was doing—or what he wanted of her. Glancing up hesitantly, she waited for him to speak, but he only nodded curtly in the direction of the doorway.

Too numb even to know what she was doing, Kristyn stepped into the room, her heart pounding so wildly she was sure he must hear it. A single candle had been lighted, anticipating her return much later in the evening, and its flickering rays illuminated familiar furnishings: a massive, carved-oak bureau, its gaily painted patterns softened with age; the small, dark-framed mirror above it; the candle itself, on a long table, tapering and white against a whitewashed wall. And in the center, dominating everything, a wide bed, meant for two, satin-covered . . . seeming to glow in the shadows.

Almost in spite of herself, Kristyn's eyes were drawn toward it. Suddenly, she felt cold again, and she knew she was afraid. Afraid of things she was only beginning to understand.

"Rafe . . ."

The appeal died on her lips as she turned and caught sight of his features. He had stepped into the room, kicking the door half-shut behind him. Now he stood just inside the threshold, staring at her with a look that sent shivers down her spine.

Slowly, deliberately, he raised his arms, taking off his jacket and tossing it on a chair behind him. Terrified, Kristyn thought for an instant he intended to beat her, working out his rage on her helpless body. But a second later, his hands slipped down to the blood-red sash at his waist, and as she watched him unwind it, she realized at last the terrible, frightening truth her heart had been too timid to accept.

He *was* planning a violent fate for her—she had not been wrong about that—but it was not the violence of murder he had in mind, or even a brutal beating. It was that savage violence men had used from the beginning of time to subject women to their will, enslaving them with passions that were only degrading when neither love nor tenderness were there to give them meaning.

Rafe caught the look of recognition on her face, and his lips tightened ironically. Taking his time, he finished unwinding the sash, then threw it over on top of his jacket. Looking back at her, he said gruffly,

"Take off your clothes!"

His brusqueness stunned her.

"What?" she said numbly.

"You heard me. I said, take off your clothes."

Kristyn closed her eyes, swaying weakly. Why—*why*—was he doing this to her? Didn't he know she would give herself to him willingly, *gladly*, if only he offered one word of tenderness?

"I know you're angry," she whispered miserably, hating herself for the foolishness that had aroused all this savage jealousy, "and perhaps you're right. But don't you see . . . I can't do what you ask. Not like this. I just can't."

"You *can't?*" His voice was muffled, taking on hints of something she could not understand. "Or you won't? Before you answer, I suggest you recall that delightful striptease you performed for me once before. You and I both know you're capable of removing your clothes in front of a man . . . if you want to. If you don't, I'm capable of ripping them off."

Trembling, Kristyn realized he was not bluffing. He *would* tear her clothes off if she tried to defy him—and he would not be gentle about it. Her hands were shaking as she raised them to the neck of her dress.

The tight basque resisted her efforts and she struggled with the unfamiliar fastenings, trying not to panic at the thought of what would happen if she did not succeed. Then, at last, she felt it give way, and she dropped it with a faint rustling sound around her ankles. She was standing before him now clad only in a sheer linen chemise and lacy pantalettes.

His lips parted slightly, and in the dark mirror of his eyes Kristyn saw what she must look like, her hair floating sensuously around a slender throat and soft white shoulders, her flimsy undergarments translucent in the candlelight. A slow shudder passed through her as her eyes sank downward, drawn hypnotically by that hard swelling in his groin, straining the taut fabric of his trousers. In spite of herself, she felt an answering warmth begin to burn between her own thighs.

"Take the rest of it off," he said, his voice deep and husky. "I want to see if your body writhes as seductively against me as it did for Ricardo Cuervo. Only I don't want anything in the way. I like my women free—and natural."

Kristyn's hands slipped upward, answering his command. Even as that last veil fell from her quivering flesh, she saw him rise, moving sinuously, with the lithe grace of an animal. Every nerve tensed as she waited for him to close the terrifyingly short gap between her helpless body and his savage male will.

He did not fail to see her reaction and it seemed to anger him. Striding forward, he caught her in his arms, pressing her against him. His breath was hot on her cheek, his mouth only inches from her own.

"I'm not a rapist, sweetheart, tempting as that notion is right now. I'm not going to take you by force. I'm going to take you because you want me."

"No," she murmured weakly, sensing that her body had begun to cling to him, despising herself for it. "Oh, no, no—no."

"No?" A guttural laugh rose from somewhere deep in his throat. "So many no's, all in a row, and what you are really saying is . . . yes."

Suddenly his mouth was no longer inches away, but there, where she longed to feel it, and even as she tried to struggle, her lips parted, hungry for the taste of him, as hungry as he was for her. She willed her arms to push him away, disdaining that rough embrace, but instead she found that they were around him, and her hands were clutching at his shirt, trying to claw through to the flesh beneath.

Sensing her acquiescence, Rafe urged her yielding body backward, forcing her down onto that pile of ruffles and lace on the floor. Kristyn heard the sound of ripping fabric, and she knew he was tearing his own clothes away, or perhaps she was doing it for him as her hands reached out, eager to touch him, hold him, guide him deeply, throbbingly into herself.

Then there was nothing but Rafe, nothing but the hard male feel of him inside her, angry, pulsating, challenging. All else forgotten, Kristyn let herself follow the lead he had set, her hips surging upward again and again to meet those potent downward thrusts. Nothing mattered now, not even the pain he had caused her. All that existed was the sweet familiar yearning that swelled in her body, straining almost beyond endurance, bursting at last in a thousand tiny explosions that tore her apart even as they healed, making her feel whole and alive again for the first time since they had become lovers so many weeks before.

"Oh, Rafe," she cried out. "Oh, my darling . . . my love."

If he had taken her in his arms then, if he had cradled her, soothed, caressed, she would gladly have forgiven everything that came before, rejoicing instinctively in the closeness she longed to feel. But when he rose instead and moved away, stepping over to the table where the candle still flickered, she felt her mind begin to take over, recalling everything that had happened. Sick with shame, she turned her head to the side, letting bitter tears drench the sea of taffeta around her.

"How could you do this to me?" she cried out irrationally, hating him not for what he had done, but for the way her own treasonous body had responded. "How could you behave so vilely?"

"How could *I* behave so vilely?" His voice had an amused edge, and she sensed without looking that he was laughing at her. "It seems to me you are the one who was caught in the garden in someone else's arms. And kissing him quite passionately, too."

"That's not what I meant!" Kristyn looked up, her eyes wary as she studied him in the faint yellow light. Now that his passions were spent, he no longer seemed angry. "I wasn't talking about a kiss, which is perfectly harmless, and you know it! You *did* treat me vilely. What you did was—it was hateful!''

"Hateful?" To her discomfort, his lips twisted up at the corners. "Ah, and here I thought this was what you wanted from me all along."

"*This?* Oh, Rafe . . ." Embarrassed, Kristyn felt the tears begin to slide out of her eyes again. How could he misunderstand her so cruelly? "I never asked for anything like *this*. I wanted to share something special with you. Something beautiful. I didn't want to be taken on the floor like—like some sort of animal in the barnyard!"

She half expected him to laugh, but his eyes looked guarded, almost wounded.

"I know that," he said gruffly. "You are a woman, and as such, you need all those pretty, romantic illusions women crave. I *did* behave unspeakably, though not for possessing you—which you, my sweet, wanted as much as I—and certainly not for performing the act on the floor! But I knew you craved tenderness as much as sexual pleasure, and it was wrong of me to punish you by withholding it."

He smiled faintly as he brought the candle over and squatted beside her on the floor.

"And that, my dear, is as close to an apology as you are ever going to hear from these lips, so make the most of it while you can."

An apology? Kristyn eyed him cautiously. When he treated her like this, when he was gentle and loving, she longed to trust him, even though she knew he was capable of hurting her again.

"You are a selfish beast," she said, trying to scold, but hearing only a lover's teasing in her tone. "You are selfish and cruel . . . and I don't know why I don't hate you!"

Rafe laughed. "I'm afraid that's something you're going to have to get used to. The male of the species, my dear child, *is* selfish and he is cruel . . . yes, and he can be an animal at times. Or perhaps," he added with a wry half smile, "I like to think he is because that's the way I am."

He set the candle down, fascinated by the way its penetrating shadows seemed to caress her body, cupping full, ripe breasts the way his hands had cupped them before, accenting the pallor of her thighs, so milky white they seemed more porcelain than real . . . veiling the dark, mysterious triangle between them, at once his delight and his despair. The shimmering red of her ruined party gown formed a soft frame around her, reflecting the coppery fire in her hair, the feverish flush of her cheeks, and he realized, hating himself for his lack of control, that he had already grown hard for her again.

What was there about this woman that robbed him so completely of all reason? That fierce, pulsating hunger swelled in his groin. Why was it that he couldn't make himself forget her, the way he always had with women before? Passion was a game to him—a game he was used to winning. Now for the first time he sensed he was about to lose.

Why, of all the women he had known, did it have to be this one who had the power to enflame his senses until he could think of nothing else . . . dream of nothing else? And why, dammit, did she have to be the one woman in the world he could never completely possess?

"What are you, *querida?*" he said, half whispering. "A she-devil—or a witch?"

"A witch?" Kristyn looked up, puzzled. The words were harsh, yet there was no harshness in his voice.

"A witch," he repeated, laughing softly. "*Bruja*, my people would say. Yes, I think you must be, for you have cast a spell on me."

Kristyn caught her breath, hearing in that throaty passion the deeper, truer feelings she barely dared to recognize.

"Sometimes," she murmured, confused, "I don't know what you want me to think. First you tell me you don't love me—then you say I've cast a spell on you. How am I supposed to know which is true?"

"Perhaps they both are." He smiled for a moment, then turned serious again. "I don't say I love you, Cristina—not the way you want to be loved. But God help me, I do care much more than I ever intended."

His eyes were veiled and secretive as he studied her in the candlelight. Then suddenly, impulsively, he caught her up in his arms and carried her over to the bed.

"Did I rob you of tenderness before, *querida?* Well, then, I must give it back to you. All that your heart desires."

He laid her down on the satin coverlet and turned away, moving across the room. Kristyn closed her eyes, conscious of the sensuous feel of the spread beneath her naked flesh as

she waited for him to come back and draw her once again
into his arms. When he did not, she propped herself up on
one elbow and glanced around the room. To her surprise, she
saw that he had paused beside her dressing table and was
searching methodically through her perfume bottles, unstop-
ping them one by one and holding them up to his nose.

"What are earth are you doing?"

He turned toward her, a small vial in his hand glowing
amber in the candlelight.

"I had a feeling that somewhere in all those perfumes my
grandfather chose for you, I'd find one that didn't remind me
of every sloe-eyed Spanish beauty in Santa Fe. This one
now—" he held the bottle a little higher— "is just your style.
The subtle sweetness of wildflowers, with a touch of rainforests
at dawn."

Kristyn, who was not quite sure what a rainforest was,
wrinkled her brow quizzically.

"I still don't understand. What are you planning to do with
it?"

Rafe sat down on the edge of the bed.

"I am planning to show you, my sweet, that the male
animal can, on occasion, be capable of something akin to
sensitivity, though we manage to keep it under wraps most of
the time."

"But perfume, Rafe?" Kristyn squirmed slightly, enjoying
the flattering caress of his eyes. "What does perfume have to
do with sensitivity?"

He did not answer, but reached out instead, resting his
hand on her forehead.

"You are flushed, my dear. Are you coming down with a
fever—or is it thoughts of passion that set your blood boiling?"
He pulled his hand back, touching her now only with dark,
impudent eyes. "The latter, if I am any judge—and I think I
am. It would be unfair of me, would it not, to set up such a
burning in your flesh and not cool you down again?"

"With that?" Kristyn tapped the bottle with her fingers,
beginning to understand what he had in mind.

"It is an age-old remedy, or so I've been told. I remember
once when I was a young boy I had a raging fever and the
doctors despaired for my life. It was a hot summer's night
then, too—or perhaps it only seems that way in my memory.
My mother was on her knees in the chapel they say, praying

for my recovery, and who knows, perhaps her prayers did save me. But it was my father who sat up with me the entire night, rubbing perfume on my chest and brow to cool the fever, and it is his gentleness I will always remember."

Loosening the stopper, he poured a little of the pale gold liquid onto his palms. A scent of fields and forests wafted through the air, reminding Kristyn of another night, spent with a stranger on the banks of a swollen spring stream—a night when new and frightening emotions were just beginning to take hold in her heart.

"Your father sounds like a very kind man," she said softly.

"My father was a weak man, in many ways perhaps a coward. When life got too hard for him—correction, when it got too unpleasant—he simply ran away and left the rest of us to take the consequences. But for all his glaring faults, and I would be the last to deny them, he was not without his virtues. He was a man capable of great warmth, when he was allowed to express it spontaneously . . . and great tenderness." He paused, giving Kristyn an unexpectedly rakish grin. "Let's hope I've inherited at least a little from him."

"A little of what?" she teased. "His warmth? Or his weakness?"

"You be the judge . . . when I am through."

His hands felt strong as he pushed her back into the softness of the pillows —achingly strong, yet achingly gentle, too. Kristyn yielded, unprotesting, not quite sure what he was going to do, knowing only that she dared not break the spell by questioning him now. Lightly, so lightly she could barely feel it, he began to rub the sweet-scented moisture into her skin, beginning with her brow, now indeed as feverish as he had claimed, moving slowly to her cheeks, her neck, her shoulders, pausing only occasionally as he replenished his supply of perfume from the bottle.

The softness of his hands was an illusion that did not last. As Kristyn felt him work his way slowly down her body, lingering on the quickening pulse at the base of her throat, she sensed a new, probing urgency in fingers that had only teased before. Easing toward her breasts, he played for a moment with hardened nipples, then left them to explore her belly, her buttocks, her thighs, offering everywhere not the coolness he had promised but a searing heat that burned into her flesh. Flowery sweetness rose to her nostrils, clinging, erotic, accenting the raw, driving need that surged through her veins.

The door had blown partly open, letting a gentle night breeze into the room, but even where it touched her perfume-drenched skin, Kristyn felt only smoldering heat, reminding her that only one power on earth could quell the raging fire in her body. Every part of her belonged to him now, every inch of her flesh was his for the asking—and demanding as he was, he did not fail to ask. His fingers grew more daring, massaging her closed thighs, slipping between them, stroking, caressing, half teasing, half tantalizing.

Soft moans escaped her lips, little animal sounds that would have embarrassed her had she had the awareness left to recognize them. Rafe replaced the stopper in the bottle and set it on the bedside table as he paused for a moment to stare down at her. In the completeness of that sweet surrender he sensed a defeat that would be his as well. To give the sort of pleasure he had in mind was one thing when he was about to ask for favors in return, or even to give it because it titillated his ego to satisfy a lusty woman. But to give simply for the sake of giving . . .? That implied things he had never meant to feel, emotions he had assumed he was strong enough to resist.

Gently, so gently it sent a little tremor through Kristyn's body—he drew her thighs apart. Lowering his head, he laid it between them, kissing her, very lightly, just at the edge of those soft, moist curls. Then slowly he moved closer, following the boldness of his hands with lips that were even bolder.

For just a second—a short, instinctive second—Kristyn tried to resist, sensing that she was already too much in his power. But as his fingers had swayed her before, so his lips did now, his tongue, drawing her to new heights, new raptures. Her legs twined unconsciously around his neck, her fingers tangled in his hair, drawing him tighter and tighter against her, writhing forward—always forward—to meet the searching motions of his tongue.

There was nothing he could not do to her, she realized helplessly—nothing he could not make her feel, this man who held her so completely in his thrall she could not call her soul her own. Then even that thought was gone and she was drowning in the mindless flood of sensations that made her for one brief moment his and his alone.

Only afterward, when he was finished with her, did she feel the welcome coolness of the air against sweat-glistening skin, and she collapsed back onto the pillows, weak and satiated in the wake of a passion that seemed strangely new yet sweetly familiar all at the same time. How many things there were that a man could share with a woman, she thought, marveling at the way he had managed to manipulate her, not just with his hands, but with his mouth as well. It was so exciting to be young, to be learning about love for the first time . . . and oh, to learn from a man like that!

Looking up languidly, she saw that he was sitting on the edge of the bed again, gazing down at her. She was conscious now of his unslaked desire, reminding her, a little uncomfortably, that he had given satisfaction but taken nothing for himself.

"I thought you told me men were selfish," she said softly. "And cruel."

"So they are." He bent forward, laughing lightly as his lips grazed her cheek. "But I also told you that they are capable of sensitivity." He touched the other cheek then, and then her chin, her neck, her shoulders, accenting his words. "And generosity—and warmth . . . and restraint."

"And what about women?" she teased. "Are they capable of restraint, too?"

"Sometimes."

"And sensitivity?"

"Sometimes."

"And . . . selfishness?"

He grinned. "Sometimes."

"Like now?" She let her eyes drop boldly to his erection, hard and dark against the gleaming white of the coverlet. "When all I do is lie here and take what I want from you?"

Rafe shook his head, trying not altogether successfully to keep his eyes cool and amused. There was a new womanliness about her, a kind of earthy sensuality that was almost disconcerting.

"No—it is never selfish to let someone give to you."

He drew her into his arms then, lying beside her on the bed and holding her in an achingly tender embrace. Soon, Kristyn knew, he would offer her the sweet passion they could share together, but for now he seemed content to cling to her, as she clung to him, loving without words . . . without demands.

They were so engrossed in each other they did not hear the faint sound of a footfall just outside. Then suddenly a voice boomed through the darkness.

"*Que diablos pasa?*"

Horrified, Kristyn looked up to see a tall, white-haired figure standing in the doorway.

"Don Diego!"

Sick with embarrassment, she clutched the satin coverlet, pulling it up over her breasts to cover her nakedness. Too late she realized what she had done. Don Diego had treated her with kindness when she came to his home—he had every right to expect her to comport herself properly under his roof. What must he think of her now?

But to her surprise the old man did not look at her. All of his wrath seemed to be directed at his grandson, now seated, naked and not the least bit contrite, on the edge of the bed.

"*Que diablos esta pasendo, hombre, no tienes orgullo? Esto es comportamiento de un adolescente menos un hombre . . .*"

Rafe listened for a minute, then held up his hand to stop that seemingly endless torrent of Spanish.

"*Ya, abuelo, ya,*" he protested. "*Ya, basta!*"

"*Me dices, ya basta? Desgraciado, despues de mancha mi casa, con tu conducta.*"

"I said, enough," Rafe interjected, his voice taking on a sharp note. "And I meant *enough!*" He picked up his pants from the floor and pulled them on, but made no further concessions to propriety. "You can hardly tell me that I have defiled *your* home when you insist on claiming it is my home, too. And don't you think it would be better if we spoke English? After all, it hardly seems polite to talk of things that concern Cristina when she can't understand what we are saying."

"Polite?" Don Diego snapped out the word. "You speak to me of polite, sir?" He took a step forward, his hands clenched at his sides, and for an instant Kristyn was afraid he was going to strike the younger man.

But if Rafe had any qualms, he did not let them show.

"Of course I do, Grandfather," he said coolly. "I have always spoken my mind, and you know damn well I'm going to keep on doing it. And while we're on the subject of manners, has it ever occurred to you that, even in your own home, common courtesy dictates knocking on a door before you come barging through it?''

Kristyn gasped, certain now that Rafe had gone too far. But his grandfather seemed to take his impudence in stride.

''If you wanted privacy,'' he said, raising one brow the way Rafe did when he wanted to be sarcastic, ''you might have had the sense to lock the door. Or at least to close it. I returned early because I couldn't find Cristina anywhere at the *fiesta*. I was afraid she might have taken ill and not wanted to spoil my evening by informing me. When I saw the light in her room, I naturally came to see if she was all right. I did not expect to find—*this!*''

''*This?*'' Rafe paced angrily to the door, staring out into the darkness before whirling to face the old don again. ''You speak of *this* as if it were some unnatural, disgusting thing. Lovemaking is not disgusting, Grandfather. What Cristina and I have enjoyed tonight—by *mutual* choice—is exactly what you yourself would have done with your precious Luisa if she had allowed it!''

The color drained from Don Diego's face.

''You dare to equate my love for Luisa with what has gone on here? I am not blaming the girl, mind you—I know she is young and impressionable—but you, sir? You have behaved despicably! And you dare to justify your actions now by claiming I would have done the same thing? You know very well the circumstances were different!''

''Different, sir?'' Rafe parroted the old man's tone. ''Ah, you mean that you are you and I am I—and somehow different sets of standards apply to the two of us.''

''I mean that Luisa was not free! If she had been, do you think I would have taken her to bed without taking her to the altar, too? Apparently your mind doesn't work that way. Unless, of course . . .''

He paused, giving Rafe a long, shrewd look.

''. . . unless you are telling me that you plan to marry the girl and this is only a somewhat—uh, premature celebration of your nuptials.''

Now it was Kristyn's turn to feel the color ebb out of her face, and she knew she looked as pale as Don Diego had before. Marriage? The one forbidden subject certain to make

Rafe angry again. And yet, if it bothered him now, he gave no sign of it as he stood calmly in the doorway.

"Is that what you think, Grandfather?" His mouth twitched just slightly at the corner. "That I should marry her?"

Marriage again. Just for a second Kristyn felt as if her heart had stopped beating, and she realized bitterly that she had let herself dare to hope. But one look at the mockery in Rafe's expression was enough to warn her she was being foolish. Plainly, he was baiting the old man. Tell me no, those dark eyes challenged—and I will have the license to do exactly what I want. Tell me yes, and I will turn so stubborn no power on earth can force me to obey!

But Don Diego was not about to fall into the trap.

"I think you have acted shamefully, bringing disgrace upon yourself and upon the house of El Valeroso," he said, parrying the question. "You were entrusted by a friend with the care of his daughter, and you have abused that trust. I know, of course, what a man of honor would do, and I think you do too. But then—" up went his brow again, a touch of lightness Kristyn had not expected— "it occurs to me that you and I have not always seen eye to eye."

The change in mood was not lost on Rafe. He hesitated a minute, then broke into a boyish grin.

"You're right, Grandfather—we don't always see eye to eye." With that he turned and walked out of the room.

Twenty-Nine

The air outside was cool and crisp, tinged with the peculiar dryness of the desert. Rafe paused at the edge of the garden, looping his thumbs through the waistband of his trousers and staring up at an impersonal moon drifting across the blue-black sky.

Marry the girl, the old man had as good as said. Marry her—and, blast him, was he right?

I know, of course, what a man of honor would do.

A man of honor, hell! Rafe jerked his thumbs free and began to pace back and forth on the tiled path, moving from one side of the garden to the other. The old fox knew exactly what he was doing! It was not honor that would tempt any man to marry a pretty hussy like Cristina—he doubted if men had ever been lured to the altar by such obscure sentiments, for all that the poets liked to sing about it. Certainly it was not honor that had surged through his loins that night he looked up and saw Cristina standing at the top of a candlelit staircase. No, and it wasn't honor that had motivated his grandfather either, all those years ago when he gazed at the lovely Luisa!

Dammit, he couldn't remember when he had felt like this!

Turning on his heel, he began to pace down the path again, conscious of the thudding of his bare feet on the cold tiles. Confusion had never been part of his nature. He had always been sure of himself, decisive. Only tonight he was as confused and muddle-headed as a fourteen-year-old.

Fourteen—or was it fifteen?

He paused, caught up suddenly in memories he would have sworn he had forgotten. Teresa. Where had it come from, that picture of her, so clear in his mind? Beautiful, brown-

411

eyed, vixenish Teresita, his own phantom from the past—his own sweet little Luisa.

Only not so sweet, he thought wryly. Not sweet at all, though he hadn't known it at the time. All he had known then, all he had seen, was the beauty of one perfect afternoon, the excitement of a passion that came at a time when he was old enough to feel the yearnings of the flesh and young enough to believe in romance. And in the capacity of a beautiful woman to love.

Memory, unleashed, came flooding back. Teresa, pretty mischievous Teresa, escaping the watchful eye of her *dueña* on a hot summer's afternoon. Teresa, finding a place for them in the underbrush because he did not know where to go; pulling the combs out of her long, dark hair to let it spill free and sensuous down her back. Teresa, slipping the dress off her slender body without a trace of self-consciousness; taking his hands and placing them on her breasts, as she lay beside him in the prickly grasses. Teresa, the first to teach him the secrets of love.

He had not been the first with her, but he had not known that then, nor would he have cared if he had. He knew only that he loved her with all the passion in a fourteen-year-old heart, and he would have given anything, sacrificed anything, even his life, to be with her again. He had thought, ingenuously, that she felt the same way about him. He had just assumed it—until the day Ricardo Cuervo's handsome young nephew came back from the university in Madrid and he had never seen her alone again.

Ricardo Cuervo. The wind picked up, biting against his naked chest. Was that why he had always hated the man? Not for the petty cruelty that lay just beneath that suave exterior, not even for the grief he had caused Don Diego, but simply because he was the uncle of a young man who once robbed him of his illusions?

Perhaps. And yet, in the long run, it had mattered so little. He turned around, staring idly at vague forms in the darkness. He had been hurt, but at that age, the hurt had affected his ego more than anything, and by the time the fickle Teresa had tired of Cuervo's nephew and cast him aside, he had already forgotten how much he loved her. His heart had been so resilient then, when he was young. It had healed so quickly. Would it heal as quickly now?

A rustling sound in the corner caught his ear and, turning, he saw a black cat lurking in the shadows. It seemed to have found something, a mouse perhaps, or only a dead leaf, for it batted out with a swift paw, then stood absolutely still, staring straight ahead with enormous jade-green eyes.

What would it be like if he married her?

The thought caught Rafe by surprise, sneaking up on him in that one moment when he had let his guard down. What *would* it be like, marriage? That act of setting down roots, of belonging to someone specific, of knowing every morning when you rode off just where you were going to return that night? He had always been vaguely contemptuous of men who needed that kind of security. He had considered himself too strong, too self-contained, to require—or accept—routine in his life. Now, for the first time, he was not sure.

A sign of age? A sign that he was getting weak, and soft?

And yet, there was more to it than that. Glancing up at the moon again, he imagined a face in that scarred surface, faintly mocking as it looked down at him.

What would it be like to come home and see her waiting for him in the doorway of his own house? A simple image, yet one that was somehow compelling. To lie beside her every night in the darkness, not just to make love but to know she was there. To watch her body thicken with the child—*his* child—growing inside her. To feel age creeping up on them, so slowly they would not know it was there. Or care.

A tempting picture. For all his fierce independence, Rafe could not deny that. Tempting and seductive, like a woman in a sheer, clinging gown, holding out her arms to him. He might almost give in if . . .

If.

The word had a coldness about it, as cold as the wind, and as biting. I would have married my Luisa, El Valeroso had told him, *if* she had been free. He had meant that *if* only for himself, thinking of his own past, but it was as appropriate for his grandson today as it had ever been for him. Luisa had not been free when he wanted her. Cristina was not free now.

Man-Who-Lives-with-the-Wolves.

Damn that absurd name! Rafe's jaw jutted out unconsciously. It was so ridiculously childish, so adolescent—so exactly the kind of name he would have chosen himself under similar circumstances. Blast it, he didn't want to feel anything for the man! He didn't want to identify with him. He certainly didn't want to like him! How the devil could he think about stealing his wife if he liked the poor bastard?

And Cristina?

The thought was a sobering one, more real than other, abstract considerations. What would Cristina do if, against all reason, he gave in to his grandfather's demands and claimed her as his wife? How was she going to feel when one day she learned the truth and realized he had lied to her? For all her passion, all her lusty fire, there was a streak of conservatism in her, part of what appealed so strongly to the old man, no doubt. Conservatism and loyalty. What would happen if he married her . . . and she found out?

And what was going to happen if he *didn't* marry her?

The thought hit him harder than he had expected, chilling the blood that ran through his veins. If he did marry her, there was no guarantee she would ever find out. And even if she did, she might be able to understand. But if he didn't marry her . . .? Dammit, if he didn't, he knew exactly what to expect!

A dull, heavy feeling landed like a fist in the pit of his stomach. Never, as long as he lived, would he forget the way he had felt, standing in the shadows, watching a slender, supple body writhe in Ricardo Cuervo's embrace. Nothing, not even the loss of his first love, had brought that same acute physical sensation, that sickening awareness not only of his jealousy but of his helplessness.

He had not been totally unaware of what was going on. He had been watching Kristyn throughout the afternoon, and he had been in the garden long enough to see what happened. He knew it had begun as a harmless flirtation, and by the time he rushed in to rescue her, he had sensed that she was struggling to free herself. But he also sensed—as he knew Cuervo had, too, damn the man!—that single moment when she almost surrendered. Next time, he told himself bitterly, the moment would be longer, and then longer, until she could not resist any more and even a swine like Cuervo could have her.

Disgust welled up inside him. No, dammit, he could not permit that! At all costs, he had to keep it from happening! He would see her dead before he would let her go to Cuervo's bed, or any other man's, for that matter! Yesterday, perhaps, he could have lived with the idea, even this morning, but not now, not after he had felt her one more time in his arms. Now, right or wrong, reasonable or foolish—sane or insane— she was his, and his alone.

The cat lunged forward, a black streak in the midnight blackness of the gardens. Rafe turned to follow it with his eyes, but the animal was too swift, and he could not pick out where it had gone. What amazing creatures they were, these cats. Fat and furry in the sunlight, looking for all the world as if they could not move to save their lives. Yet, come night, they turned as sleek as jungle beasts, primitive again in the darkness. Predatory.

Rather like a man, Rafe thought. Snoozing off his lunch in the midday heat, too lazy to move, but like the cats, coming alive to his basic instincts at night, catering to the primitive just beneath the surface . . . reminding himself that he, too, was not so far removed from the jungle.

And forgetting to close the door in his eagerness!

A shadow seemed to pass across the face of the moon, but when he looked up, Rafe could see nothing. Even if he wanted to, he wondered, would he be able to pull it off? Everything he had ever worked for, everything he had accomplished in the years since he had struck out on his own, was in Colorado. But if he tried to take her there, into Cheyenne country, how long was it going to be before someone mentioned the uprisings? Or before she saw something about them in the papers, those English-language papers she was reading with more and more ease every day?

No, he could not take her to Colorado. But here . . . well, here he might just get away with it.

Only, could he give all that up? A last surge of rebellion flooded through his heart, one last angry attempt to hold on to what was his. Colorado was his Santa Fe, the dream that had captured his imagination, even as the New World had once held out its golden lure to a younger El Valeroso. Colorado was where he was going to build his own empire, as his grandfather had once done here. It was his future.

He looked around the garden, trying to remember when each tree had been planted, each bench put in place, or whether they had always been there, as long as he could remember. He had strong feelings about Santa Fe; he always had. It was the land of his birth, the territory of his childhood, and he loved the *haciendas* with their low adobe walls, just as he loved the cool, purple mountains in the distance. But here, life had a sameness about it. Here, the challenges were challenges that had been conquered long ago. Here, the empire he was a part of would never be an empire he had forged. Could he give up his dreams for one woman, no matter how beautiful? He wanted her—God help him, he could admit that now—he wanted her desperately. But he wanted his future, too.

He turned toward the door, still open, with the golden glow of candlelight seeping out into the darkness. He knew they must be waiting for him, waiting silently, not trying to speak, just waiting. Instinct told him that the time had come to go back, but he did not know what he was going to say.

He paused briefly in the doorway, taking advantage of the fact they still had not seen him to look in at them. His grandfather was standing on the far side of the room, his back stiff as always, his face slightly turned away. Kristyn was exactly where he had left her, seated alone in the center of the bed, looking like a little girl with the coverlet pulled up to her chin to hide her embarrassment.

Then, as if sensing his presence, she tilted her head up, turning her eyes on his face.

The instant Rafe saw those eyes—wide, dusky blue eyes with beads of moisture glittering on the dark lashes—he knew he had lost. He who could stand up against anything, floods and bullets, cattle stampedes and outlaw attacks, even the wrath of El Valeroso, was about to be defeated by a woman's tears.

"All right, grandfather," he said gruffly. "You win. Decorate the chapel and call out the priest. I'm ready to give up my freedom."

Thirty

Buffalo Calf Woman died on the third day of her stay on that rocky hillside overlooking an endless stretch of empty plains. Early in the morning, Little Bear had risen to find her sitting quietly on a large flat rock, staring into the east, where even at that moment a ball of fire was beginning to peek over the edge of the horizon. When he returned in the evening, carrying a thin blanket to guard her against the chill of twilight, he found her still there, her face still turned toward the east.

He had sensed, even before he approached, that she was dead. He sensed it again as he reached out to lay his hand on her arm, but he reached out anyway, half from habit, half because something inside him wanted to prolong that final moment of acceptance. He was no stranger to death or to the ways of dying—he had encountered them often enough on other hillsides, other plains—but still it was a shock to touch her and find her cold and unresponsive.

Where was it now, all that nurturing warmth he remembered so vividly? Was it an intrinsic part of her, like the laughter in her eyes, the skill in her sewing fingers, the thoughts in her heart? Would she take it with her when she began her long journey up the Hanging Road toward that land where others were waiting? Or was it, like her body, something that must be left behind? Something that would vanish forever from the earth, as the Indian himself was vanishing . . . and the Indian way of life?

It occurred to him, surprisingly, that she had not sung her death song, for he would have heard it farther down on the slopes where he had been keeping his quiet vigil. Had the end crept up on her so stealthily she had had no time for that one last ritual, that final, tangible proof of an Indian's dignity? Or had she simply not tried, sensing in the new, bewildering world around her a place where old ways, old traditions, no longer held any comfort?

Questions, he thought. So many questions—and none with an answer. Always before, death had been, for him, a part of life, as natural as birth or coming to manhood or growing old. It made him uncomfortable to think that he was questioning it now.

Bending down, he shook out the blanket and laid it over her shoulders, not for any reason, but simply because that was what he had come there to do. He thought at first that he would take her up in his arms and carry her off to the place he had chosen for her burial, but then, realizing the futility of the gesture, he decided to leave her where she was, still facing east, so she could greet the rising sun one last time.

In the old days, he would never have defied the spirits and the will of the tribe by postponing that simple rite, for everyone knew that the *tasoom* could become disoriented in those first hours after death, and it might try and snatch the soul of some living being, particularly a vulnerable child, to keep it company on the long, lonely journey up the Hanging Road. But there was no one here to be afraid, no healthy children to protect—no reason why she should not be left alone to say her last good-byes to the earth in privacy.

He buried her the next morning shortly after dawn under the pinkish gold rays of the morning sun she had loved so much. He remembered, not altogether logically, the way she had insisted on facing the doorway of her tepee to the east. Cheyenne doorways were always oriented in that direction, yet it seemed to him she had been especially emphatic about it. "We do not want the hot afternoon sun streaming into the lodge," she would say, smiling a soft half-smile. "The sun in the afternoon is not pleasant. But the morning sun is always welcome."

Would it be welcome today?

Questions again. He caught himself with a start, forcing his thoughts back to the task at hand. He was growing fanciful in these lonely hours on an empty hillside. That was not like him, not like him at all.

There were no trees on the upper slopes, so he could not lay her in the highest branches as he would have liked, but an abundance of loose rocks provided material for a bier. He worked swiftly, forming the stones into an even rectangle, taking special care as he piled them one on top of the other, not because neatness mattered, but because somehow it made him feel better. Perhaps it was simply the Indian in him, responding to a natural world where everything was ordered and in its place. Or perhaps, despite all his efforts, there was something left of that little boy in mission school, spending hour after endless hour making perfect corners on his bed.

When he had finished, he gouged what loose soil he could out of the sterile earth, smoothing it on top of the bier to soften the sharp edges of the rocks. Only then did he pick her up, surprised at the lightness of her, like feathers in his arms, and set her gently on the platform he had made. For the last time he took the blanket and laid it over her, tucking it in so the frayed edges would not show.

He was aware of one brief moment of helpless anger as he stepped back and looked at her. They had taken so much, these white men who swarmed like insects over the earth. Buffalo Calf Woman had been the wife of a great chief. She should have been laid out by wailing red-eyed women, her long black hair plaited with ropes of otter fur, her deerskin robe trimmed with the brightly colored beads and porcupine quills she had worked with her own hands. Beside her on the bier, a selection of her tools should have been set out in neat array, for just as a man expected to take his weapons and shield on that last journey, so a woman was intended to be buried with her rooting stick and sewing awl, her stone scraper and paintbrushes, perhaps even her treasured elkhorn flesher, handed down from generation to generation. Of her remaining possessions, some should have been given to her daughters, had any survived her, the rest passed out among the friends and female relatives who had gathered to mourn her.

But here there were no friends, no relatives, no tools to be given away or buried beside her. Most of her friends were already dead, and what few utensils she still possessed in troubled times had had to be left behind on that flight into the hills.

They could take nothing with them, the young cousin had reported. *Nothing.* He had not understood then what the word meant. He understood now. To have nothing during your lifetime was bearable, for as long as there was life a man, or a woman, could hope to find something better. But to have nothing to carry with you into eternity was to be a pauper forever.

The sun had barely begun to float above the faraway hills when Little Bear finished his task and glanced briefly down into the valley below. The lower slopes of the hill showed touches of color beside trickling mountain streams, but beyond, where the open plains stretched out to the horizon, the earth was brown and parched. It almost seemed, he thought sadly, as if everything were dying. As if the entire world and not just his part of it were passing beyond his reach.

Once such thoughts would have made him bitter. Now he was only tired. Too tired to care about anything—even about *her*.

He drew his forearm across his brow, wiping away the coating of dust that streaked his skin. What had made him think of her now? Today of all days? What had brought her back to his mind?

It was strange, the way time changed everything. He had hated her so much that night she left, hated her with a corroding passion that ate away at his heart. Now, standing alone on a desolate hillside with nothing but death around him, he could almost understand why she had run.

It was not the dying itself that was so painful, it was the way of the dying. Death in battle, one swift blow of the lance—a man could accept that. Or death at the end of a long life with happy memories, the sound of grandchildren playing around the tepee. But here, everything seemed to be shriveling up, browning like the parched earth, turning to dust and blowing away with the winds. Could he blame her for running from that?

He cast one last glance at the silent bier behind him. The pain of this moment, the final parting from everything familiar in a life that had once been full and rich—no, he could not expect her to share that with him. There was, it seemed to him, a threshold of suffering beyond which the heart could not endure. Buffalo Calf Woman had reached hers the day she lost her husband, and she had found a barren patch of earth and sat down and waited to die. Perhaps Morning Star, too, had reached her own threshold on the night she left him.

Was it really her leaving that hurt so much?

More questions. Little Bear moved slowly away from the

bier, following the steep path that led to the top of the hill.
Was it her leaving that hurt? Or was it the fact that she
seemed to take with her everything that had been good and
pure in his life?

He paused for a moment at the edge of the path, caught up
in feelings he had never pondered before. Was it really
Morning Star he had missed when she was gone, Morning
Star he wanted, as she was now? Or did he want the girl he
had learned to love so many years ago? The pretty young
bride who came to him for a single night? Was it reality he
wanted—or memory?

No, he did not hate her anymore. There was no hate left in
him, no feelings at all . . . not now. All his feelings belonged
to the past, and the past would not come again.

He set his feet back on the path, continuing his upward
climb. Reality . . . or memory? Was there really a choice? If
she were to come to him now, if somehow the hurts between
them could be healed, would he want her beside him? Would
he want to watch her grow thinner and thinner, as Buffalo
Calf Woman had, until he could count every bone in her
body? Would he want to build a stone bier for her, one day
before her time, in the rocky clefts of some other treeless
hillside? *That* was reality. The memories were prettier.

The path grew steadily steeper as it approached the top,
and he was sweating profusely when he finally climbed out
onto a wide ledge and let his eyes take in the sweeping vista
around him. Spreading his legs apart, his hands on his hips,
he tilted his face up to defy the sun and the wind. Buffalo
Calf Woman had not sung her death song before she died. He
would perform that last service for her.

"It is a good day to die.
All the things of our life are here,
All that is left of our people are here.
It is a good day to die."

His voice was soft as he began. Then, slowly, as he sang, it
grew stronger, echoing off the rocks around him, ringing out
in the valley below.

"All that is left of our people are here.
Cheyennes, it is a good day to die."

The wind gusted across the hilltop; the air was a breath of coolness against his skin. It seemed to him strange that it should be that way. The closer a man climbed to the sun, the cooler it got. Would it be like that, he wondered, when it was his turn to climb the Hanging Road into the heavens? Would he feel coolness then? Welcome coolness after the heat of life? Would he be too high to smell the wildflowers in the fields?

Soon now he would know. So soon.

Thirty-One

The wedding, which took place shortly after that impetuous nonproposal, was simple and private. Kristyn stood beside Rafe in the El Valeroso family chapel, feeling strangely small next to his rugged masculinity, as she listened to the priest intone the unfamiliar words that bound her to him forever. Candlelight glowed soft and golden, filtered by the thick lace veil that covered her eyes, and a heavy scent of roses and incense gave a dreamlike aura to the setting.

Then, suddenly, the dream was over, and Rafe was lifting the veil, touching her lips with a surprisingly gentle kiss, claiming her as his for the rest of his life.

The chapel seemed unexpectedly bright as Kristyn turned to smile tentatively at the small group that had gathered to watch her join her life to Rafe's. Reflections of tiny yellow flames flickered in the massive gold altar, wide enough to fill one entire end of the room, and carved wooden saints peered out of shadowy niches in the walls, their benign features overpowered by the effect of a large, painted crucifix.

Everything is so different, she thought, surprised by the sudden pain that tugged at the corners of her heart. Different from the gaiety and easy camaraderie of an Indian nuptial. Even the faces that surrounded her were only vaguely familiar. Don Diego, Carlos, pretty Ysabel, her lips forced into a wooden smile, a handful of servants, beaming, proud to have been included in their master's affairs—this was not the family she loved so dearly. Not the comfortable old friends with whom she longed to share this day.

But the sadness was fleeting, passing as quickly as it had come. What did it matter who was there as long as Rafe was at her side? What difference did it make whether she could understand the words of the ceremony when it was *his* hand the priest slipped into hers?

The celebration that followed the ceremony was as boisterous and jubilant as the rite itself had been restrained. Don Diego, typically, had insisted that his grandson redeem Kristyn's fallen virtue as soon as the priest could be summoned, but the fact that he had had less than a week to prepare the festivities did not diminish them in the least. Even as the small wedding party moved out of the chapel, Kristyn could hear the first guests arriving amid a flurry of hoofbeats and jangling harnesses. Tonight, the *fiesta* would begin with a gay *fandango*. Tomorrow the revelers would enjoy picnics on the lawn and bullfights in the fields outside the *hacienda* walls.

"Sometimes the festivities last three or four days," Rafe told her later when they had managed to find a quiet corner of the garden where they could be alone. "Everyone with Spanish blood in his veins loves a celebration. Especially a wedding."

"Three or four days?" Kristyn had changed out of her stiffly elaborate gown and was now garbed in the same pale blue blouse she had once worn to tempt him, mated this time with an elegant skirt, satin and velvet, striped in shades of blue and silver and white. "I love a party, too. But my goodness, isn't that excessive?"

"Not at all. It's a matter of pride with the great *hacendados*. They always have to outdo each other, throwing the wildest *fiestas* they can afford to celebrate the weddings of their children."

"But—three days?" Kristyn eyed him skeptically. "I've seen the way you Spaniards throw yourselves into everything you do, from riding horses to betting on cockfights to—well, to eating dinner, for heaven's sake! But three days? Honestly, Rafe, I should think people would drop from exhaustion!"

He laughed. "They do—eventually. And when that happens, I promise you, they're happy to pile into their carriages and sleep on each other's shoulders all the way home. But until then, the party goes on, and it's a weak man caught napping because he can't keep up with the rest." He leaned against a low adobe wall, grinning raffishly in the moonlight. "Of course, that means most marriages aren't consummated until three days after the ceremony, and by that time the poor groom is so exhausted he can't do anything about it."

Kristyn caught the underlying sensuality in his teasing, and her body began to stir with the familiar feelings he always roused in her. He looked so handsome tonight, darkly handsome in tight black *calzoneras*, fitting over lean, strong thighs, and a flaring scarlet shirt that accented his exciting, almost flamboyant style.

"Then it is fortunate, isn't it, love," she said, looking up through faintly quivering lashes, "that we consummated our marriage *before* the ceremony."

The earthiness of her tone evoked a physical response in Rafe, reminding him that his grandfather had watched him like a hawk these past days, not only seeing to it he had no further opportunites to molest his *novia*, but keeping him away from other temptations as well in the form of several pretty maid servants who would have been delighted to ease his week of waiting. Laying none-too-gentle hands on Kristyn's shoulders, he pulled her impulsively toward him, burying his face in thick curls that spilled onto the nape of her neck.

"If you think I'm going to wait three more days to make you mine again, you don't know the first thing about the man you married." His hands slipped downward, boldly teasing her breasts through the sheer fabric of her bodice, touching her so intimately he brought a startled cry to her lips.

"Oh. . . ! Rafe, I—I don't . . ." She tried to pull away, knowing she should not encourage him, but it was hard when his hands made her feel like that. "Really—this isn't——"

"I want you, Cristina," he interrupted, his voice deep and muffled. "God help me, I want you as much as I ever have, and I've waited long enough. You set my blood on fire, you little witch—and well you know it! You set my blood on fire, and then you ally yourself with my grandfather, forcing me to play the gentleman until everything is nice and legal. Well, dammit, it's legal now! You *are* my wife! I'm not going to wait even one more day to feel myself inside you again."

Rough hands grasped the neck of her blouse, pulling it away from her shoulders, sliding it down her arms until her breasts were exposed. Tremors of excitement shivered through Kristyn's body as he bent down, sucking her nipple into his mouth, harshly, demandingly.

"But . . ." she protested weakly. "You shouldn't. You know you shouldn't. Not here."

His lips left her nipple for a moment. His eyes were laughing as they turned up to hers.

"Why not, my sweet? We are married, you know. It would be the first time our coupling was legitimate."

"But even if we *are* married . . . Well, we can't . . . Oh, I don't know. You get me so confused." Kristyn felt herself begin to blush. "I mean—not *here*. This is the garden! Why, anyone could come by and see us! It's positively scandalous the way you behave sometimes."

"Scandalous?" Rafe laughed. Where the devil had she come up with that? A few months in the white man's world and already she had learned a damn sight too much. "What is really scandalous, my pet, is not the way *I* am behaving. Lusty males are supposed to show a healthy passion for the females they fancy. What is scandalous is that you, a proper young wife, adore it when I do."

He gave her breast a little pinch, as if to accent his words, but rather to his own surprise, he did not try to press her. Her eyes were too soft as she looked up, trusting even in her confusion, and he had the illogical feeling that he ought to protect her even from himself. He eased her breasts back into their silken casing, fluffing up the ruffles around her neck.

"Very well, sweet wife. It shall be as you wish. I will let you go—for now."

For now. Kristyn saw the way his eyes had begun to caress her again, and she knew what he was really saying. *I will let you go . . . but not for long.* Rafe was a man of immediate appetites, needs he was used to satisfying at his own whim. He would never wait three days to take her to his bed again.

And what really *was* scandalous, she thought, feeling a little giddy as she took his arm and moved onto the lighted pathway, was that she did not want him to. Something in her, some deep, indefinable need of her own, made her as shamelessly attracted to him as he was to her.

As they stepped out into the large central courtyard, they found the area surprisingly quiet. Only a few shadowy couples strolled along the paths, their murmuring voices like soft whispers on the wind. Lanterns had been strung out on long lines between the trees, subtle shades of red, casting a rich glow over blood-red roses that climbed the trellises and walls. The smell of summer was in the air, touched by pungent hints of pine and wildflowers.

"Everything is so beautiful here," Kristyn said, still holding on to Rafe's arm as she paused to gaze around her. "I don't think I've ever been so happy anywhere in my life. Do you think—I mean, would it be possible for us to stay here? At least for a little while?"

Rafe gave her a quizzical look.

"Of course—until I can make other arrangements. Grandfather has been very generous, setting aside space where we can have privacy. But no man wants to live indefinitely in a house that——"

"Oh, no," Kristyn cut in. "I didn't mean here in this house. I meant here in Santa Fe. I know how eager you are to get to Colorado, and I will follow, my love, wherever you take me. But I had hoped——"

She was surprised to feel him lay his fingers on her lips.

"We aren't going to Colorado, Cristina. I'm sorry, I hadn't realized you thought that or I would have said something sooner. We are going to make our home right here. In Santa Fe."

"In Santa Fe? I don't understand. I thought you planned to go to Colorado. Didn't you tell me that was always your dream?"

"It was—but it was a young man's dream. That's all well and good for a callow lad with his whole life ahead and nothing to tie him down. But you forget I'm a married man now. I have obligations. Commitments. I think, in light of that, it is time to leave youthful dreams behind. Even dreams of Colorado."

"Oh, but Rafe . . ." Kristyn faltered. There was something in his voice, something empty, almost sad, that made her realize how much his grandfather had been asking him to give up when he issued that self-righteous ultimatum. "I thought—well, I just assumed we'd be going to Colorado right away."

He smiled, but the gesture seemed forced.

"*We* are not going there at all, at least, not in the foreseeable future. *I* am going, but only briefly. And I am not taking you with me."

"You are going? By yourself? Why?"

"I told you, my dear—or have you forgotten? I hope not. I thought I married a woman with a few wits behind her pretty face. There is still a matter of some property Ricardo Cuervo stole from my grandfather, and the El Valeroso pride will never be intact until it is recovered. I think I owe the old man that much, don't you?''

"Of course. But why can't I come, too? I could help you.''

"Help me? Or distract me? No, you little vixen, you'd have me in some hotel room, making love all day long and forgetting what I'd come for. If you really want to help, be a good girl and stay right here. There, you'd only be in the way.''

In the way? The words sounded reasonable, but a subtle sharpness in his tone warned her there was more to it than he was saying. Was he really afraid she'd distract him? Or was he worried about her safety?

She looked up, trying to find a clue in his face, but there was nothing. He was as handsome as ever, breathtakingly so—but sometimes it seemed to her he was as much a stranger now as he had been that night she first saw him.

"You've never told me exactly what happened in Colorado," she said, keeping her voice light and casual. "I know El Valeroso owned land there and lost it to Ricardo Cuervo, but that's all.''

"That's all there is to it." Rafe turned away, staring abstractedly at the far side of the courtyard. "It's a simple story, actually. Cuervo managed to gain title to some land of my grandfather's, particularly a valuable silver mine. There was nothing very clever in the way he went about it. He simply got a local official to falsify the records, and now, of course, the man swears nothing is amiss. Unfortunately, that sort of thing happens all too frequently.''

"But a public official, Rafe!" Kristyn was aghast. "That man is in a position of trust. How could he do anything so—so despicable?" She knew she should not be shocked. She had already had ample opportunity to see the way white men dealt with each other, but still, it was hard to believe. A Cheyenne might steal from his enemies, but to steal from another Cheyenne would be unthinkable. And to lie about it in the process! Such a man would be an outcast from the tribe forever. "How did Cuervo convince him? Offer him money?''

"No, I don't think the man did it for cash. I daresay that was part of the bargain, but I doubt if it was the deciding factor. The real story is a bit more sordid. There was a brief indiscretion—a lady who as it turns out was not a lady at all, a few letters that should never have been written—and now the poor son-of-a-bitch is quaking in his boots for fear his wife will find out. Or his wife's very influential family, which by the way is how he got the job in the first place. Cuervo has those letters in his possession, and as long as he hangs on to them, he owns the man. He can do anything he wants with him. But if I can get my hands on them . . ."

Kristyn felt a sudden chill, as if the temperature had dropped.

"If you get them, then *you* will own him."

Rafe laughed, harshly. "You make me sound like an axe-murderer, my dear. I am not going to force the man to do anything except be scrupulously honest, which incidentally I don't think will be a hardship. He's not a bad man, really. He's just gotten himself in a corner and doesn't know how to get out. I think he does genuinely care about his wife, in his own fashion. He's probably as worried about hurting her as he is about losing his position and prestige. So you see, if I get those letters, it will work out to everyone's advantage. Except, of course, Ricardo Cuervo's."

He uttered the last words slowly, drawing them out. Kristyn was more aware than ever now of the cold.

"It all sounds . . . dangerous."

"Dangerous?" Rafe's teeth flashed in the darkness, not so much a grin as a wolflike leer. "This kind of mission can be dangerous, of course—but only if I let it. Do you really think I'm as daring as all that? Don't forget, I have reason to be cautious now. Men are never quite so reckless when they have pretty wives to come home to."

He tilted his head slightly, letting the moonlight play on his profile. For just an instant, Kristyn had a glimpse of that very recklessness he was trying to deny.

Daring, he had said? But daring had been a part of his life for years and he thrived on it. Why else would he have ridden alone into an Indian camp at night, relying only on his senses to protect him? It occurred to her suddenly that the mission he was about to embark on might be his last great adventure, his last chance to live the kind of life he truly enjoyed before settling down to the routine that society and his grandfather demanded of him.

"Do you have any regrets?" she asked softly. "About the

things you're giving up? Are you sorry your grandfather bullied you into marrying me?''

"Bullied me?" He threw her a sharp, unreadable look. "No one bullies me, my sweet, if I don't want them to. Besides . . ." His voice took on teasing hints of laughter. ". . . how could I regret having a beautiful, captivating, sensuous wife, whom incidentally I adore—even if she is too inhibited to let me throw her on the ground and have my way with her right now!''

The lightness in his mood was infectious, and Kristyn, laughing, felt her doubts slip away. What a silly goose she was—what a ninny to worry so much about nothing! Of course there were adjustments Rafe was going to have to make. But as long as he cared about her and she cared about him, everything would work out in the end.

They spent a happy quarter of an hour wandering through the gardens with their arms entwined around each other's waists, talking of nothing in particular and feeling wonderfully— *scandalously*, Kristyn thought, relishing the word— like the lovers they were. Whether that casual intimacy would have continued, or whether it was only the prelude to another appeal to her senses, she would never know, for one of the servants came scurrying up, interrupting with profuse apologies to tell Rafe that his grandfather wanted to see him.

"I am sorry, *querida*." Rafe grinned ruefully. "You see what kind of family you have married into. Business cannot wait—even on a man's wedding night.''

Kristyn smiled, turning her cheek up for a chaste farewell kiss. It made her a little sad, of course, to think of being parted from her new husband, even briefly, but she could hardly object. Not when it was Don Diego himself who had been the instrument of all this happiness. Besides, Rafe's absence gave her an opportunity to see something of the elaborate celebration that had been prepared in her honor.

Every room in the *hacienda*, with the exception of the sleeping chambers, had been opened for the occasion, and light flooded out of doorway after doorway, tempting Kristyn to peek inside. In one room, she saw that chairs had been arranged in a small, intimate circle to encourage conversation; in another, a guitarist played quietly in the corner. In still another, an eye-catching spread had been laid out on long, hardwood tables, not merely the Mexican *quesos* and *dulces* she had expected, but champagne as well, oysters too, and pieces of chicken fried in some kind of batter, for Don Diego, no matter what his personal preferences, was too generous not to cater to the tastes of his guests.

The Spanish penchant for gambling was apparent, for a least a half dozen of the larger rooms had been set aside for that activity. Kristyn paused briefly in the doorway of one of them, drawn toward it by the sound of laughter and bawdy shouts.

The room was so thick with smoke it was a minute or two before she could make out details with any degree of clarity. The sound of the place—spinning wheels, coins jingling on felt-topped tables—brought back memories of her days in Dodge, but the drama she sensed here, the color, the vibrancy, was uniquely Spanish.

Most of the action centered around a monte table in one corner, where a flashily dressed woman kept the game moving at a lively pace. Opposite her, an old man in a wine-red *chaqueta*, as gaudily embellished with gold as any young dandy, followed the movements of her fingers with shrewd black eyes. For all his age, he held his whiskey well, and it seemed to Kristyn he enjoyed his anger when he lost almost as much as the excitement of winning. An attractive young girl, her sharp features a youthful mirror of his, leaned over the table beside him. A slender brown *cigarito* dangled out of startlingly red lips as she, too, hung on every turn of the card, laughing boldly when it went her way, cursing like a man when it didn't.

A burst of music filled the night, and Kristyn slipped back into the courtyard where she could hear it better. It seemed to be coming from the grand *sala*, where even at that moment the dancing was about to begin. Her heart quickened at the prospect, and she joined the other young people who were hurrying toward the sound.

The room in which the dancing was to take place had been so transformed she barely recognized it. Every piece of furniture had been removed, and the rugs taken up from the floor, leaving only mud tones to echo the adobe ceiling and smoky cedar rafters. The only color came from the red-patterned fabric that ran shoulder-high along the walls, but color was hardly necessary, for the dancers, who had begun to form into two long lines in the center, were as gay and gaudy as a flock of tropical birds.

The young *caballeros*, lined up on one side, were dressed in deep, rich hues, jewel-like in clarity; their partners, facing them, had chosen softer tones to complement sultry, dark-haired femininity. Here, as in the gaming rooms, *cigaritos* were in vogue, not only among the males, but among the women dancers as well, and an acrid odor of tobacco and burning kerosene mingled with the sweetness of perfume to make the air heavy and stifling.

A stout, black-gowned matron at the side of the room pulled a small pouch out of the *reticulo* she carried at her waist and, spreading a portion of tobacco on a dried cornhusk, rolled it deftly into a long, slender cylinder. Watching, Kristyn could not help being intrigued. She did not care for the custom herself—the smell of tobacco would be forever associated for her with grave masculine discussions and pipes passed around an open campfire at night—but it fascinated her to think it was allowed. When she first came to Santa Fe, she had thought these Spanish women with their sharp-eyed *dueñas* and countless rosaries on cold chapel floors must surely lead rigid, inhibited lives. It came as a surprise to realize that they enjoyed some quite extraordinary freedoms too.

The musicians paused briefly, then picked up their instruments again. Kristyn watched, fascinated, as the first of the dancers began to move. A pretty girl in lacy gold with a *cigarito* clenched between her teeth and a young man in burgundy and black came skipping out of opposite corners, whirling around in the center of the floor, teasing but not touching as they circled each other, then flew back to their places again.

Why, I could do that! Kristyn thought with a rush of excitement. It's simple and it's fun, and I could do it every bit as well as they!

A second couple appeared almost before the first had finished their steps. The girl looked sweetly feminine in a rose satin ballgown. The man was in stark blue with no trim save the green insignia that marked him as a mounted rifleman.

Cold fingers clutched at Kristyn's heart as she caught sight of that hated uniform, and it was all she could do to force herself to remain standing in the doorway. She knew she was being silly. Now that New Mexico was an American territory,

these soldiers from the fort were going to insinuate themselves into alliances with prominent local families, and she
would have to meet them sooner or later, whether in someone
else's home or her own. Still she did not think, as long as she
lived, she would ever be able to look at that blue uniform
without experiencing a sick feeling in the pit of her stomach.

She had not recognized the man's lithe partner at first.
Now, glancing back, she was surprised to see that it was
Ysabel. The simple mint-green frock she had worn to the
ceremony had been exchanged for an elegant ballgown, so
tightly cinched at the waist it was a wonder she could breathe.
Tiers of wide ruffles ran down the skirt, flaring out when she
turned to show an occasional glimpse of shapely white ankles.

Poor Ysabel! Kristyn tried not to laugh, but she could not
help herself. It must have been infuriating to have to stand in
the chapel and watch another woman exchange vows with the
man she had tried to win for herself. Now she was little better
than a guest in her own home, not the center of attention
anymore, but only one of many who would raise their glasses
throughout the evening in a toast to someone else. The way
she was dancing, with total abandon, Kristyn sensed she was
trying to forget—and not succeeding.

Her eyes drifted back to the young soldier, and in spite of
herself, she almost felt sorry for him. He was barely more than
a boy, with downy cheeks and hair the color of bleached-out
straw. His natural gawkiness showed in every step, all the
more so because he was trying to impress the exotic beauty with
whom he had been paired. Obviously, he was quite taken
with the lovely Ysabel—and just as obviously, she did not
even know he was there.

Kristyn felt someone at her side and, looking around, she
saw that Carlos had come into the room. She flashed him a
smile of greeting, and he smiled back.

"If there was ever a lovelier bride in Santa Fe," he said
gallantly, "I have not seen her. Or a lovelier woman, for that
matter. You outshine every beauty here tonight—including
that sly little minx, Ysabelita, in her new red gown."

"It isn't red, Carlos," Kristyn teased, enjoying the light-
hearted repartee. "It's rose. And Ysabel looks very pretty
tonight. I think you are either being kind because you want to
make me feel good—or you are an incorrigible flirt who has
to flatter every woman in sight."

Carlos laughed. "I am neither, my dearest Cristina. I had hoped by now you knew that. I told you once exactly how I felt about you. I was not lying then, or exaggerating. If I were a flatterer, I would be forcing those same unwelcome attentions on you now. But because I am not, I tell you only how happy I am—since I could not win you for myself—that my brother has captured your heart. I hope he appreciates you, *amorcita.*"

"Sometimes I wonder."

Kristyn had intended the words lightly, almost flippantly, but a certain sharpness in her voice gave her away. Carlos, catching the sound, threw her a curious look.

"Don't tell me you are having qualms already? Even before the wedding champagne has ceased to flow."

"No, not qualms—not exactly." Kristyn had not meant to confide in him, but when he was kind like that, understanding, it was hard to resist. "Oh, Carlos, sometimes I wonder if he really loves me."

"If he loves you?" Carlos stared at her, startled for a moment. Then, seeing the confused look on her face, he began to laugh. "But my dear girl, how can you question that? The man has married you."

"Yes—but only because his grandfather ordered him to!"

The words were out of her mouth before she realized she was going to say them; then it was too late to call them back. She had never spoken them before—she had not even allowed herself to think them—but now that they were concrete in her mind, she realized that this was one aspect of her relationship with her new husband she was going to have to face. Rafe *had* asked her to marry him, but only after his grandfather insisted. And even then, he had not really asked—he had simply acceded to the inevitable.

"Ah, my poor, foolish little girl." Carlos shook his head bemusedly. Sometimes, in his preoccupation with all that earthly sensuality, he forgot how young she was. "You're going to torture yourself if you think things like that. Haven't you learned yet that no one can force my brother to do anything he doesn't want to, even our grandfather? Rafael would never agree to marry any woman unless he was certain, deep in his heart, that he was capable of loving her."

"I know he *cares* for me, Carlos. At least he . . ." Kristyn faltered, unable to find the words she needed. How could she talk even with someone as sympathetic as Carlos about the passions that bound her to her husband? "I know he is fond of me," she added lamely. "But is that love? He never says it . . . he never tells me . . ."

"Rafael is not a man who expresses his feelings, but that doesn't mean they don't exist." Carlos leaned forward, looking deeply into her eyes as if to emphasize what he was saying. "He would never have stood with you before the altar tonight, he would never have made the promises he did, if he believed he could not keep them. Nor would I have stood by and watched. I care too much for you—and him—to allow that to happen. You must learn to trust your husband, Cristina. Trust his love for you . . . and yours for him."

The music swelled suddenly, rising to a dramatic climax, then broke off again, and the sound of laughter and shuffling feet filled the room as young men scurried off to capture new partners of their choice. Kristyn, glancing toward the dancers, caught a glimpse of the young Blue Coat's face, ashen with disappointment when he could not coax the lovely Ysabel even to look his way.

Almost in spite of herself, she started to laugh. Carlos was right, she *was* behaving like a foolish little girl. Why, she was every bit as childish as that boy soldier who could not bear to lose his pretty partner. Only she, unlike he, had no cause to be unhappy. Rafe had married her. She was his wife now, and she would be his wife until the end of her days. Any other woman would have been beside herself with ecstasy instead of fretting over imagined ills.

"Come, Carlos." She whirled around, holding out her hands. "You are my brother now. You have been my brother for fully three hours, and what have you done in all that time except give brotherly advice? That is fine in its place, I suppose, but what I really want is for you to teach me how to do these marvelous dances. I am dying to learn."

Carlos, catching the gaiety in her mood, swept her a gallant bow, then offered his arm and led her out to that double line of dancers forming again in the center of the room. If he had any hesitation in pairing off with her, any fear that she might embarrass him with her awkward inexperience, he did not let it show but played the part of the young cavalier with perfect grace.

The second dance, like the one that had opened the evening's entertainment, was a reel, and while it was somewhat different, there was still enough similarity for Kristyn to follow it easily. The music was light and lilting, the steps simple, and she found herself executing the lively patterns as deftly and gracefully as if she had been doing them all her life. She had always loved to dance, loved the way the beat of the drums worked into her bones and her feet seemed to fly, barely touching the earth. There were no drums here, only marimbas and guitars, and the earth was a tamped-down floor beneath the soles of satin slippers, but the feeling was no less exciting. There was something inside her—a hunger for freedom perhaps, a need to feel the wind blowing wild once again in her hair—that reveled in the music and the movement, and forgetting everything else, she threw herself into the exhilaration of the dance.

Oh, what fun it was! What fun to be young and a bride— and dance her wedding night away! She felt almost dizzy as she whirled from one young man to another, flirting sometimes with her eyes, sometimes her lips, exulting in those seductive Spanish rhythms, and knowing all the while her husband would be there to claim her in the end and draw her into the safety of his arms.

The dance came to a close, the partners facing each other once again, and Kristyn, flushed and out of breath, swept Carlos a low, graceful curtsy. Raising her head, she started to smile, but her eyes fell on a tall figure standing in the doorway, and the expression froze on her face.

Rafe.

For an instant, she remained absolutely motionless, her knees still bent, her skirts billowing out around her. Rafe. She could not help remembering how jealous he had been, insanely jealous, that night he caught her in the garden with Ricardo Cuervo. She had not been flirting as outrageously with these young men, of course, but she *had* been flirting. How was he going to take it?

But when at last she dared to look up, she saw only an indulgent, vaguely amused smile on his face. His eyes held a kind of quiet pride.

Why, he *likes* to see me dancing, she thought. He even likes to see me flirting—as long as he's sure I'm teasing. And he loves it when other men look at me and he knows they are envying him.

Perhaps his jealousy was not quite as insane, as irrational, as she had imagined. He *could* be violent if he saw her with another man—there was no getting away from that—but it was not a violence that erupted totally without provocation.

Going over to him, she tucked her arm through his.

"Did you see me dancing, husband?" she asked breathlessly. "Did I look like I'd never done those steps before, or did you think I was good?"

Rafe smiled. "You were very good—and very tantalizing. It stirred my blood to watch you."

"Then come and dance with me—*please*. Oh, Rafe, it would be such fun. Only I don't want to do a reel with you. I want you to teach me one of those slow, sensuous waltzes."

"Later." He drew his arm around her, pressing her suggestively against his body. "Right now, I have other plans for you. I thought we might go for a walk in the garden first . . ."

"Oh, but Rafe . . ." Kristyn pulled back, a little coyly. When he looked at her like that—when he talked like that, his voice deep and husky—it was hard even to remember what she was thinking. "I was so looking forward to dancing with you, especially tonight. Besides, you said you thought I was good. Don't you want to dance with me?"

"We have our whole lives to dance, *querida*. Couldn't you be patient, just once, and humor me?"

"But we have our whole lives to walk in the garden, too."

"True," he agreed, laughing. "But a walk is what I want, and when you get to know me better, you'll find that I am a man who is used to having his way. Come, let me lure you out on those secluded paths—let me find a dark, shadowy corner someplace where I can tell you how much I adore you."

Kristyn felt her heart begin to beat faster. She did want to dance with him—truly she did—but she wanted that shadowy corner, too.

"I think, husband," she said throatily, "that adoration is not quite what you have in mind."

"Ah, but it is, my sweet." He leaned down, teasing her with a soft whisper. "Adoration of a very physical kind."

Kristyn was not even aware of moving, but somehow they seemed to be in the garden, away from the noise, the brashness of the music, the yellow light that spilled out of windows and open doorways. The corner he took her to, just off the central courtyard, was as dark as he had promised, but it was not altogether secluded, and she was aware of other figures moving back and forth in other shadows. But if Rafe saw them, he managed to block them out of his mind.

"Ah, Cristina, Cristina." He caught her in his arms and drew her toward him. "Why must you torture me so?" She could feel his hands, searching, demanding, as he ran them up and down her back. "You know you set my blood on fire. You always have."

"Oh, Rafe—we can't . . . *You* can't . . . you mustn't—"

"Mustn't I?" His voice was mocking, his eyes half laughing, half smoldering as he eased back to look at her. "And why not?"

"Because—because if you do, I won't be able to stop you!"

She turned away, confused. His hands gripped her shoulders, slipping downward, cupping her breasts beneath the flimsy silk blouse.

"Shhh, darling, don't fight me so!" His voice was hoarse in her ear, his hands burning brands against her breasts. "We'll go back to your room—to that same bed where we enjoyed each other so much before. And this time I promise I'll remember to shut the door."

"But . . ." Oh, how hard it was to resist him. Hard when he knew just what to do with his hands, just how to inflame her senses. "What if someone notices we're gone? What if they miss us?"

"Then they'll miss us, that's all. Dammit, Cristina, I want you. I want you like hell."

But do you love me? her heart cried out in one last burst of reason. He said he wanted her—he told her he adored her— but were those things the same as love? It was funny, the way the word never seemed to come into their conversations.

Funny, too, she thought, how little it really mattered. Feeling her body surrender even before her mind, she let herself turn back, sinking wantonly into his embrace. He could love her, he could merely want her, it made no difference now. Because, God help her, *she* wanted him—and she could not let him go.

"Oh, yes, Rafe," she whispered, lost in raptures she could no longer control. "Yes, my darling, yes . . . yes."

She swayed, half swooning, against him, knowing that

strong arms would tighten around her, sweeping her forcefully up from the ground. There were no eyes watching from
the darkness now, no smiling young couples who stepped
tactfully into the shadows as he carried her with long strides
across the garden. There was only one man, one woman . . .
and a moment of perfect ecstacy that would soon be theirs.

Thirty-Two

But eyes *were* watching as the lovers left the garden, black eyes that peered through the intricate latticework of a nearby arbor. Ysabel had been careful to remain hidden throughout that brief confrontation, but she had not failed to hear every word Rafe said to his new bride—or to see the way his hands had toyed with her body.

The bitch!

Ysabel stepped out on the pathway, trapped in the red glow of a paper lantern. She could not even wait the decent interval decorum demanded, that *desgraciada*. Nor had she handled the thing discreetly, slipping off by herself as if to repair her toilette, while her bridegroom stole stealthily through back ways to join her. No, she had to do it openly, letting him carry her off in his arms like some prize of war so everyone would see them and know exactly where they were going!

In contrast to the turmoil inside her, the garden seemed almost unnaturally serene, with couples strolling here and there along the pathways. A young man clad in blue stood by himself in the light of an open doorway. The lovesick soldier she had danced with earlier, Ysabel realized with contempt, that pop-eyed clod who had practically drooled over her. Across the yard, a girl in a lacy white *mantilla* laughed softly as she tilted her face upward, flirting with the two young men who were hovering over her.

The Vargas twins. Ysabel's brow knitted into a distracted scowl. Don Antonio's sons, dark-complected, handsome, so alike sometimes even their parents couldn't tell them apart. Ordinarily they paid court to no one but her, and she guarded their attentions with jealous zeal. But tonight, caught up as she was in her own thoughts, she had paid them no more than the scantest heed, and it occurred to her now with a faint twinge that they seemed to be managing quite nicely without her.

She took a step toward that little group, then stopped abruptly. The boys would be glad to see her, of course—they always were—but they were much too polite to abandon the pretty companion who had been occupying their attention for heaven knows how long. The most she could hope for was an awkward *ménage à quatre*—and tonight of all nights that was the last thing she wanted!

The only alternative, she reminded herself, casting her eyes around the courtyard, was the young soldier still standing by the doorway. Not that she was the least bit interested in his boorish company—any other time she would have snubbed him completely—but she could not bear the idea that one of the Vargas boys might look up and see her standing all alone with not so much as a single man on her arm. She would rather die than look like some poor little wallflower while that *perversa* was off wallowing in the joys of her marriage bed with Rafael!

No, she was going to flirt with every young man in sight. She was going to gather a dozen of them around her, a hundred, before the evening was over, and this boy would do as well as any for a start.

She played the game perfectly, as she always did when masculine feelings were involved. Making sure no one else saw her, she took a step forward, lingering just long enough for him to spot her, then slipped back into the shadowy arbor. Long ago, she had learned that one essential rule of courtship— always let the man come to you. Even the prettiest face, the most provocative figure, lost its zest if a girl seemed too eager, too willing.

The gambit worked, as she had known it would.

"Señorita Ysabel?" The boy peeked uncertainly around the corner. "Is that you? I thought so, but I didn't dare to hope."

Ysabel puckered her features into a vaguely confused expression, as if she could not quite place who he was. Then a flicker of recognition lit up her eyes.

"Why, it's my young captain from the dance. I am flattered that you would remember me, *señor*. You looked so

handsome in your blue uniform—and you were such a good
dancer. I'm surprised the other girls let you get away.''

"Not captain, ma'am." The boy stammered slightly, blushing his pleasure. "I'm just a lieutenant. And I'm not much of
a dancer at all—not usually. I must just have looked good,
dancing with someone as pretty as you."

"Well—lieutenant then." Ysabel barely managed to conceal her impatience behind a carefully composed smile. He
seemed more like a puppy than ever with those huge watery
eyes. Still, there was no one else around, and at all costs she
did not want to be alone. "I'm afraid you'll find me boring
after all those other girls. I'm still very young, you see. I
have so little experience with men. I don't know what I'm
supposed to say when you tell me I'm pretty—even though I
know you're only doing it to be polite."

"Oh, Miss Ysabel—*señorita*." The boy took a step toward
her, fascinated by the way she suddenly turned shy, such a
contrast to that self-possessed young lady on the dance floor.
Not only was she dazzling, she was innocent, too. "I wasn't
being polite. I meant every word I said. You're the prettiest
girl I've ever seen—I swear you are."

"You shouldn't say such things, lieutenant." Ysabel pursed
her lips into a fetching pout. "And I shouldn't permit it.
Indeed, I shouldn't permit you to be here at all, not without
my *dueña* to watch over me." She eased back into the
shadows as if she were afraid of being too close, sensing,
correctly, that he would follow. "I must confess I would
never have behaved so boldly except I seem to be quite giddy
tonight. This is the first time my guardian has let me sample
the champagne and the bubbles have gone to my head."

The boy stared at her with gaping eyes, unable to believe
his luck. She *was* innocent, but it was the kind of innocence
that cried out to be awakened. He had heard barracks talk
about girls like this, naive little virgins who didn't know what
was happening, but he had never run across one before.

He moved a little closer, feeling suddenly strong, masterful.
Maybe if he played his cards right . . .

"*Señorita*, do you suppose . . . would it be all right if I
kissed you? Just one little kiss. You look so pretty, I can't
help myself."

Her eyes turned soft as she gazed up at him.

"Oh, I—I don't know. You see, I . . ." Lowering dark

lashes, she fluttered them against her cheeks. "I've never . . . kissed a boy before."

There was just a hint of breathiness in her voice, a quiver of confusion, and for an instant, the soldier was almost touched by her inexperience. Maybe it wasn't right, what he was planning on doing. After all, she really *was* young. But then, she was awfully pretty, too, and obviously ripe for the plucking. If he didn't rouse those latent passions tonight, someone else was going to do it tomorrow.

"There, there, *señorita*. Don't you worry your pretty little head about it. I'll be real gentle, this being your first time and all."

A slight shiver ran through the girl's body as he put his arms around her and, mistaking it for passion, he clamped his mouth down on hers, making a faint sucking sound. Ysabel responded with new tremors, not desire at all, but deep shudders of revulsion.

He slobbers! she thought, stiffening in that awkward embrace. As if everything about him isn't disgusting enough, he slobbers! His mouth opened, and she felt the hardness of his teeth against her clenched lips, making her feel for a second as if she was going to swoon. There was no sensitivity in him, no caring for her needs, her feelings—her reactions. All of this was just for him!

Well, let him do what he wanted now! The nausea that had overwhelmed her before turned suddenly into a surge of anger. Let him be as vile and disgusting as he chose—she would have her revenge in the end! All thought of that little coterie of men she had planned on gathering around her vanished as a new, infinitely more appealing idea took form in her mind. What if she let this boy work himself into a frenzy over her? Why, she might even allow him to pull down her dress and fondle her breasts—nothing seemed to excite a man as quickly as that. Then, when he had lost control, when he was sure he was going to get everything he wanted, she would pull away! Yes, and give him a swift kick in the balls while she screamed out her lungs for help!

Let's see how smug and slobbery he was then! *Por Dios*, it would serve him right. Don Diego hated the Americans enough as it was. If she cried rape, the boy would be lucky to escape with his life.

And it would be exactly what he deserved! Exactly what

they all deserved, those men who used woman and played with them, and didn't give a damn how they felt. Men like Rafe—and Carlos!

Ysabel wedged her hands against the boy's chest, pushing him a little more roughly than she had intended. Catching her breath, she struggled to regain her composure. She would have a chance to work out all her anger soon enough—and stir up a fuss that would make Kristyn's wedding feast pale by comparison! Now she had to pretend she actually enjoyed the feel of that disgusting mouth on hers.

"You—you must let me go, *señor*," she murmured confusedly. "I don't know what I am about, letting you treat me like this. I must beg a moment to catch my breath."

"Aw, come on, honey. You liked it—you know you did. Let's go over to that bench, right over there, and do it some more."

"No! I—I . . ." Ysabel felt her whole body begin to tremble. She was going to go through with her plan—she was determined to go through with it!—but she needed a few minutes before she let that clod touch her again. "I couldn't possibly sit there. It's much too—too dirty. I would ruin my pretty party dress."

The bench was anything but dirty, having recently been sanded and covered with a new coat of paint, but the boy did not notice. He stared at it dully for a few seconds, and then, to Ysabel's amazement, reached in his pocket and pulled out a folded-up newspaper. Opening it, he began to spread it over the bench.

A newspaper! In spite of everything, Ysabel felt an almost irresistible urge to giggle. The fool—the absolute fool! If she would not sit on a neatly painted surface, what made him think she would soil her skirts with filthy newsprint?

"It is so hot in here, *señor*," she said, raising a fluttering hand to her face. "I'm not sure I can stay if it continues like this. Perhaps you would be good enough to get me a cool drink. A nice fruit punch."

"A fruit punch?" The boy's face was a mirror of surprise and dismay. "You want me to get you . . . a fruit punch?"

"Ah, yes—I do." Ysabel's eyes flickered with a sudden spark of mischief. "With perhaps a little brandy in it. Only not too much, mind you. I wouldn't want to get giddy again."

The boy relented almost instantly, his mouth opening as if to protest, then closing it again abruptly. Women could be so contradictory sometimes; he had never known what to make of them. But then she did look flushed—and after all, she was a sweet little thing. Besides, a glass of punch might do her good. Just look how a few sips of champagne had affected her, and brandy was much stronger.

"All right, honey. I'll get you some punch if it'll make you feel better. But don't you go away, hear? I'll be right back."

Ysabel watched with distaste as he bobbed across the yard, bouncing up and down in his eagerness to doctor up a glass of punch and bring it back to her. Just like a jackrabbit, she thought contemptuously. She'd be willing to bet it would take him an extra five minutes to search for the largest goblet in the house. And it would be filled more with brandy, too, than sweetened fruit juice.

Well, that was all right with her. She could use a good stiff drink about now. And as the young lieutenant would learn to his regret, she could hold her liquor as well as any man.

She stepped out of the arbor, forgetting for the moment that she had planned on keeping herself hidden away, and began to pace restlessly down the narrow paths. Only when she had gone too far to retreat did she realize that someone else was there, a man who had been standing quietly beside a stone bench in one of the darker corners. A little gasp slipped out of her lips as she recognized Carlos' profile in the moonlight.

He caught the sound, and turning toward her, he raised his brows, more ironic than questioning.

"Ah, Ysabelita . . . a nice night for a stroll in the garden, is it not? Should I say I'm surprised to see you, all by yourself in the darkness? Or should I be honest and say I'm not surprised at all?"

An angry flush burned Ysabel's cheeks. There was no mistaking the sarcasm in his tone, and no pretending she did not know what it meant. Obviously, Carlos had been standing there for more than a minute or two. He had seen her kiss that ugly fish of a soldier—and he had been laughing all the time!

"So you have taken to spying now, have you, Carlos? Really, I thought you had better manners than that."

"Ah, well, now you know I have not." He put one foot up

on the bench, leaning forward to peer into her face. "But then, you are hardly in a position to talk. If I was spying, it was at least inadvertent. You seem to have hidden yourself in the arbor for just that purpose."

"Me . . . spying?" Ysabel's eyes narrowed. Why on earth would he accuse her of something like that when it was she whose privacy had been invaded? Unless, of course . . .

Unless he didn't know the soldier had been there! Unless it was something very different he had just witnessed. Something that had caught his attention so completely he hadn't noticed anything else!

"That *perversa* again!" She stamped her foot like a little girl. "That's what you were watching! You saw Rafael carry that slut out of the garden, and you couldn't take your eyes off them. It tore you apart, didn't it? You were wild with jealousy, because you want her for yourself!"

"Do I?" He looked maddeningly calm about the whole thing.

"Of course you do! You have all along—right from the time you first saw her. And you made it very obvious, too. You're a fool if you think everyone doesn't know!"

She had expected him to be angry, but instead he only laughed.

"My dear child, Cristina is a very beautiful woman. Surely you can't blame a man if his blood stirs at the sight of someone like that."

Ysabel glared at him furiously.

"Once your blood stirred when you looked at *me*, Carlos! Or have you forgotten all those hours you spent in my bed?"

"Once," he replied calmly, "I thought I could make you love me. Now I know better. You are too caught up in daydreams of my brother. And the saddest part of it is, Rafael is not even real to you. He is only a fantasy you have had since you were a little girl. Ah, well . . ." He broke off with a smile. "Perhaps I shouldn't judge you so harshly. In a way, I've been doing the same thing, all these years I've watched you grow up and become prettier every day. I saw only the woman I wanted you to be, not the pampered child you are. Now my eyes are open. I see everything clearly at last."

His voice was touched with a quiet finality, making Ysabel feel as if something cold had settled over her heart. Never before had Carlos looked at her like that—so detached, without even a trace of longing.

"Then . . . you don't want me anymore?" She was surprised to feel tears rush to her eyes. "Because of . . . *her*?"

"No, *niña*," he said gently. "Not because of her. Because of *him*. You are so much in love with Rafael, or with your dreams of him, you have no room in your heart for me."

He reached out, touching her face, tilting it toward him until he could see the tears flowing down her cheeks. What a sly little monkey she was, he thought, responding to that feminine softness in spite of himself. Just when he was sure he was getting her out of his system, she managed to find some new way to make him remember how much he had always wanted her.

He drew his hand back, laughing a little at his own reactions. Just as Ysabel could not stop wanting Rafael, so he could not stop wanting her, no matter how attracted he might be to someone else. They were, it seemed, equally unrealistic about giving up their dreams.

"If I took you tonight," he said softly, "it would not be me you would come to, not me you would see when you closed your eyes—it would not even be me you would feel inside you. It would be my brother."

Ysabel sensed that moment of drawing away, and suddenly, without understanding why, she was afraid. She had never wanted Carlos, not *truly*, yet he had always been there for her, something solid and secure in her life. Now, for the first time, that stability was gone. Somewhere in the past days, weeks, just as she had come to depend on him, she had lost him. And she would never have him back again.

And it was not fair!

Anger surged in her heart, swelling her breast with a familiar, thwarted pain. It was not fair at all! She did not care what he said, it was not her feelings for Rafael that bothered him—it was his own feelings for that red-headed hussy!

"You only want *her*!" she cried out miserably. "You don't care about me anymore. You can't even see me. All you can see is her!"

Carlos was silent for a moment, giving away nothing with his eyes. Then very quietly he said:

"No, *querida*, you are wrong. I do not expect you to

believe that, but it is so." Turning away, he began to walk down the quiet path, leaving her alone in the darkness.

Ysabel stared after him, so blinded by tears she could barely make out his form in the shimmering glow of the lanterns. She longed to call after him, longed to beg him to stay with her, but as before, she was afraid. She had already endured enough that night. She could not bear it if he rejected her again.

That slut! All her anger, all her pain, turned suddenly outward, directed against the woman who was responsible for her misery. That bitch! If she had not come here, none of this would have happened. If it were not for her, Ysabel could have had Carlos with a snap of her fingers . . . yes, and Rafael, too, if she wanted! How she hated her! If she had her here now, she would tear every one of those exotic auburn curls out by the roots! She would scratch her face with sharp fingernails until nothing was left but long, bleeding gashes!

The bitterness welled up inside her, stifling her until she could hardly breathe. Whirling back toward the arbor, she caught sight of the newspaper the young lieutenant had spread out on the bench. Rushing over impulsively, she jerked it up, ready to crumple it up in her hands.

That stupid boy! The whole world was stupid. She could not bear it! Any minute now, he would come back, and when he did, he would find a very different girl from the one he had left, no longer interested in dallying for any reason with him. Even the thought of revenging herself for that awful, slobbering kiss held no appeal. No revenge would ever be sweet—nothing would have any savor—unless the vengeance was on Kristyn herself.

She glanced down with contempt at the sheet of newsprint in her hands. English! But of course it was English. The foolish boy spoke no more than a few words of Spanish, and she doubted if he could read it at all. He must have carried the paper all the way from wherever he was posted last. Kansas, no doubt, or perhaps Colorado.

She was about to screw it up and toss it into the dirt when her eye caught a headline on the front page:

MURDEROUS CHEYENNES TERRORIZE SETTLERS.

Cheyennes again! Ysabel stared down at the article with revulsion. Cheyennes. The very tribe that had stolen young

Kristyn Ashley and raised her to womanhood. She would
have thought a savage background like that would repel men
of taste and breeding. Instead, the promise of wildness seemed
to draw them like a magnet.

Disgusted, she let her eyes run down the page.

Marauding savages, emboldened by a temporary short-
age of manpower at Fort Avery, have set out on a deliberate campaign of terror and murder that threatens to decimate
our peaceful landscape. In the past week alone, three
heinous attacks have been reported. Four people have been
killed, including a defenseless woman and two young girl-
children. The attacks are attributed to a renegade band
of Cheyennes under the leadership of a new chieftain,
Man-Who-Lives-with-the-Wolves. When last seen, they
were——

Ysabel stopped abruptly, her eyes drawn back to the words
she had just finished.

Man-Who-Lives-with-the-Wolves. . . ?

Lowering the paper, she let old memories creep in on her,
bringing her back to the shadows of another garden, another
moonlit night. They had talked of a young Indian then,
Kristyn and Rafael. A young husband who belonged to her
past. A brave who called himself Man-Who-Lives-with-the-
Wolves.

Coincidence? Hardly, Ysabel thought, half closing her eyes
against the lanternlight. All the Indians she had heard of were
called funny things like Dull Knife or Black Kettle or Roman
Nose. If Kristyn's husband really was known as Man-Who-
Lives-with-the-Wolves—and why would she make up something like that?—it had to be the same person.

And quite plainly he was alive!

Ysabel snapped her eyes open, the first traces of a smile
forming on her lips. At last she had found what she was
looking for. A weapon to use against the woman who had
robbed her of her happiness.

Moving away from the arbor, she made her way into a
quieter section of the *hacienda*. How she wished she could
remember every detail of that conversation. What was it that
had given her the impression the man was dead? Something
Kristyn had said, or Rafael—or something one or the other

had implied? If only she knew whether Kristyn had deliberately lied to trap Rafael into marrying her.

Not that it really mattered. Even if he did know the truth, it
was obvious that El Valeroso did not, and the discovery was
certain to send him into fits of rage. An Indian marriage
might not be enforceable in white society, but the old don had
a strong sense of what was right and what was not. A woman
abandoning a living husband to take deceitful vows with
another man would not sit well with him. At the very least,
disclosure would cause trouble for Kristyn. At most . . .

At most, it would destroy her!

Vague plans began to catch hold in Ysabel's mind, and she
let herself play with them, enjoying her thoughts for the first
time that evening as she sat quietly in a small private garden
near the women's quarters. She could not hope to get Rafael
for herself—not now that he was bound by laws of God and
man to another—but at least she would have her revenge on
the *perversa* who had stolen him from her.

She did not know how long she had to wait, perhaps
an hour, perhaps two, before Kristyn finally reappeared,
looking almost ethereal as she glided down that secluded
pathway. Her face, as she paused beneath the light of a
solitary lantern, was soft and dreamlike, filled with sweet
feminine mysteries, as new as the moment, as old as a
woman's soul.

Whatever last qualms Ysabel may have felt vanished at that
moment. All her pent-up frustrations, all the deep unsatisfied
hungers of her own body, burst in a flood of hatred and envy.
Slipping up behind Kristyn, she pitched her voice low and
insinuating.

"I see you couldn't wait to sample the joys of the marriage
bed. Or is that the way those savages raised you—to couple
yourself with a man whenever the fancy strikes?"

Kristyn spun around, starting a little as she caught sight of
Ysabel in the shadows behind her. A dozen angry retorts
leaped into her mind, then she let them go. She was much too
happy tonight, too pleased with herself and her new life to be
upset by anyone.

"Rafe is my husband, Ysabel," she said softly. "There is
nothing I would deny him. Nothing that is within my power
to give."

"My, what a pretty speech." Ysabel leveled her eyes on

her rival's face. "You make youself sound so unselfish. Are you planning on being that accommodating for your Indian husband as well? Or do you find it convenient to forget all about him now that you have landed a man of wealth?"

The words caught Kristyn off guard, confusing her for a moment.

"I don't understand what you mean. I do have an Indian husband, at least I *did*, but he is dead now. I would never have married Rafe if he weren't."

The quiet conviction in her voice set Ysabel's anger off again. The bitch was good—she had to admit that. If she hadn't known better herself, she would have sworn she was telling the truth.

"Here!" She thrust the paper into Kristyn's hands. "See for yourself. You and Rafael may think you've fooled everyone, but let me assure you, you haven't. Your husband is no more dead that you are! He is very much alive, and he seems to be making quite a name for himself! I wonder what El Valeroso is going to say when he finds out."

More puzzled than apprehensive, Kristyn took the paper, staring down at bold, black letters that seemed to leap off the page.

MURDEROUS CHEYENNES . . .

The phrase made her wince. Why did they have to put it like that, murderous Cheyennes, as if every Indian was a bloodthirsty savage. And *terrorize*? They had so much to say about the white man's terror. Didn't it occur to them that Indians were afraid, too? Her eyes slipped downward, picking out some of the words with difficulty, skimming over the ones she did not know.

When at last she reached the words Ysabel had intended her to find, she felt her body go cold with shock.

". . . under the leadership of a new chieftain, Man-Who-Lives-with-the-Wolves."

For a moment she stood absolutely still, staring down at the paper, too dazed to sort things out in her mind. It can't be! she kept telling herself over and over. It can't! Yet even then, somewhere deep inside, she knew that it could.

Things began to come back to her, little things she had almost forgotten. The look on Buffalo Calf Woman's face that last night, half turned away from her, staring into the fire. And the anguish in Brave Eagle's eyes. She had thought then it was the anguish of a man who had to tell his daughter her husband was dead. Now she realized it was the even more complex pain of a man forced to lie when honesty was the virtue he had prized above all others.

"I—I didn't know. I had no idea . . ."

Ysabel, watching her reaction, saw instantly that she was telling the truth, and for the first time, she dared to contemplate the one thing that had not occurred to her. Kristyn *hadn't* known her young husband was alive—and for some reason the knowledge hurt her. Could she actually have feelings for the man? Could she care about that savage to whom they had bred her?

"Well, maybe you didn't know," she conceded, groping for something to say, some new plan of attack. "But Rafael did. And he made quite a point of keeping it from El Valeroso."

She could not for the life of her have said what prompted her to throw out those words, but they had a dramatic effect on Kristyn.

"No! No, Rafe *didn't* know! You're wrong about that. He couldn't have known! Rafe would never do anything so—so cruel to me!"

"Wouldn't he?" Ysabel could barely keep the excitement out of her voice. Somehow, inadvertently, she had stumbled on the way to get back at her rival! "Of course, he knew about it. He even mentioned it to me once. How do you think I learned all this in the first place? I would never have known you were married if he hadn't told me. Or that your Indian husband chose such a silly name for himself when he was a boy."

All the color drained out of Kristyn's face. She longed to deny what the other girl was saying, longed to tell her she was lying, but she knew she could not. She *had* told Rafe— and no one but Rafe—about her husband. Ysabel could have learned those details only from him.

Uncalled for, the image of a northern hotel room slipped into her mind. A window overlooking the street, a bed beside it, not yet shared between them, a newspaper lying open on the desk. He had started to read it to her. Then he had stopped, a strange, closed look coming into his face.

"Even if he did know," she said defensively, "that doesn't mean anything. If he kept secrets, it was because he loved me. He couldn't bear, even then, to think of losing me, so . . ."

"You really believe that?" Ysabel laughed contemptuously. "If you do, you're more of a fool than you look. You can't seriously think Rafael married you because he *loved* you. Rafael, who could have had his choice of any of the women—the cultured, educated well-bred women—of Santa Fe! He would never have considered you if El Valeroso hadn't required it! Make no mistakes, Rafael *does* care about his inheritance. No matter how he protests, he wants that land in Colorado, and he wants it badly enough to do anything for it. If he is ready to risk his life to recover it from Ricardo Cuervo, do you really think he'd balk at saddling himself with a woman he doesn't want?"

"But Rafe *does* want me!" Kristyn retorted, stung by the words that so exactly mirrored her own secret fears. "I just had proof of that, as you yourself pointed out a minute ago."

"Oh, he does *want* you—on one level." Ysabel's laughter was brittle now, triumphant. "But I wouldn't let that go to my head if I were you. Rafael wants every woman he sees. He is a lusty man, and perfectly capable of using any woman who's stupid enough to give herself to him. That doesn't mean he wants to marry them."

The barb struck home, as sharp as a slap in the face. Kristyn recoiled from it, feeling so weak for an instant she was not sure her legs would hold her up. It was as if the whole world had come toppling down around her and there was no way she could stop it, nothing she could hang on to in that terrible avalanche. All that was left was the quiet dignity she had learned from the Indians, and she wrapped it around her like a protective mantle as she faced Ysabel one last time.

"I wonder if you really believe that," she said with as much coolness as she could muster. "Or are you only saying it because you *want* to believe it? At any rate, I trust you'll understand if I don't stay and listen any longer." Without waiting for a reply, she turned and began to make her way, not toward the lights and noise of the party as she had intended before, but back to the silent room she had just left.

Once there, her carefully cultivated composure abandoned her, and tears spilled out of her eyes. Throwing herself on the bed—that same bed where she had lain in *his* arms such a short time ago—she let herself sob out all the pain and bitterness in her heart.

Everything Ysabel had said in the garden was true! She had

spoken out of malice—all those thrusts and jabs had been no more than vicious shots in the dark—but she had hit on the truth all the same. Rafe didn't care for her. He never had, not really. All he cared about was satisfying the cravings of his body and holding onto his grandfather's fortune—and not necessarily in that order.

Oh, he does want you—on one level.

The words cut like a knife into her heart. *On one level.* What a fool she had been. It was she who had thrown herself at him, she who prompted him once to call her a tramp. How could she hope to have his respect, his *love*, if she had done nothing to earn it?

But, oh, she had wanted to believe that he loved.

Her tears spent at last, Kristyn sat up on the bed, gazing dully around the room. Beside her, the newspaper lay crumpled on the coverlet, and she began to run her hands back and forth across it, unconsciously smoothing it out. She had wanted to believe because she had needed it so much. Carlos had said, *My brother loves you*, and she had said to herself, *Carlos must be right. Carlos knows him better than anyone in the world.*

Only Carlos did not know him. He did not know him at all. Carlos had looked at his brother with eyes every bit as naive as hers. Now he, too, was going to be disillusioned.

And all because of this!

Bitterly, she stared down at the newspaper. Half the words in that article were words she could not even make out. But the ones she could read had been enough to shatter her life.

"A renegade band . . . under the leadership of . . . Man-Who-Lives-with-the-Wolves."

Only Man-Who-Lives-with-the-Wolves was not Man-Who-Lives-with-the-Wolves at all. He was Little Bear.

Little Bear . . .

Kristyn looked at the paper, seeing it with new eyes, feeling for the first time the sensations that had not penetrated her consciousness before. Little Bear. Picking up the paper, she folded it in half, then in half again, not even aware of what she was doing. Little Bear was alive. Her husband was alive.

Turning numbly toward the window, she focused on a shaft of blue-white light that ran across the floor. She had been so concerned with herself before, so wrapped up in her own hurt, her own anger, she had lost touch with the reality of what was happening. Now, even through the anguish, things were becoming clear at last.

It did not matter whether Rafe had lied to her or not—it did not matter whether he loved her. Even if he could explain what he had done, even if things could be set right between them, she would not be able to stay with him. Her husband was alive—her *real* husband—and her first duty was to him.

She rose, moving stiffly over to the vanity where she pulled out a sheet of paper and the quill she had been using to practice her writing. She was bitterly aware, as she scrawled out a few hasty sentences, of how few words she knew how to spell, but she sensed that that did not truly matter now. Even had she possessed the most extensive vocabulary in the world, she still could not have described the pain in her heart.

Propping the note up against the mirror where Rafe would be certain to find it when he came to look for her, she wandered over to the window, staring sightlessly through the glass. It was strange, how far away the music seemed, as if it belonged to another world.

IV
The Moon of Changing Seasons

Thirty-Three

After a week of constant traveling, the swaying motion of the stagecoach had worked its way into Kristyn's body until it almost seemed a part of her. At least, she thought wearily, turning to look through the mud-spattered window, the scenery of Colorado was more hospitable than those unrelenting sand tones of New Mexico.

Not that the same could be said about the coach in which she was riding! Turning back, she studied the drab russet interior with distaste. It was just past dawn, and candles set in lamps with patterned wire shades cast angular shadows on the walls and seats.

"Not very purty, is it?" a rasping voice said. Glancing around, Kristyn saw that one of her two fellow passengers, a man named William Beatty, was staring at her from the opposite seat.

"No, not particularly, but then I guess you can't expect a stagecoach to be anything but utilitarian."

"Not here you can't." The drawling roughness of the man's speech was out of keeping with a tailored black suit and stiffly starched white collar. "They keep the good coaches for the ends o' the line so folks'll see 'em an' think they're runnin' things better'n they are. They use Concord coaches out o' St Louis—they come all the way from Concord, New Hampshire—an' a better vehicle I ain't never seen. They don't change you to these celerity coaches till you get away from the main towns."

"Well, yes," Kristyn conceded, "I suppose that might be true." Much as she disliked the man's chronic carping, she could not help suspecting he was right. When she had fled from Santa Fe, leaving hastily with the first morning light, not daring to risk a confrontation with Rafe after he found her note, she had pulled out in a canary-colored Butterfield coach with heavy wheels and broad tire irons. But not half a day out of the city she had been transferred to a smaller vehicle, much like the one in which she was traveling now.

"Of course it's true. They don't care nothin' for your comfort, them bastards—pardon me, ma'am—that run the line. They pack us in tight as they can. And when it's crowded, they put passengers on the roof, even if the sun is blazin' hot or it's pourin' rain. All they care about is their fares, and the hell—aw, shoot, ma'am, the heck!—with us."

Kristyn rested her head against the back of the seat, only half listening to what the man was saying. The way he was carrying on, anyone would think he was suffering, yet he looked as neat and immaculate as he had two days ago when he climbed into the coach. Something about him was almost anachronistic, as if he had stepped out of another era. Perhaps it was the way his collar held his neck so rigid, like somebody's grandfather in an old family portrait. Or perhaps it was simply his habit, in the midst of all that roughness, of apologizing for cussing in front of a lady.

"Well, then, Mr. Beatty," she said, "it's fortunate this isn't a popular run. There are just three of us here, which means we all have plenty of space. And of course the seats make into three beds at night, so we don't have to take turns sleeping."

She let her eyes drift toward the third passenger, a portly gentleman snoring quietly in the corner. He was a Canadian, a man she knew only as Mr. Braunstein, and while he was jovial enough, if a bit rakish, when awake, he seemed to spend most of his time dozing. With a little sigh, she turned back to the window, trying none too subtly to put an end to a conversation that was beginning to wear on her nerves.

The scenery, so pleasing only a few minutes before, had begun to take on a stark, almost primitive air. Huge clusters of jagged gray rock jutted out of the earth, pressing in so tightly on both sides of the road the coach almost brushed them as it passed. The grimness of the setting seemed to have affected the driver's mood, for Kristyn could hear the sharp sound of his whip cracking through the air, punctuated by an occasional "Heee-yah!" as if he were anxious to get out of there and back onto grassy plains again.

Well, at least here the road was comparatively smooth. Kristyn leaned forward, catching glimpses of the clearly marked pathway as it wound through groupings of rock ahead. The most unpleasant aspect of the journey so far had been the dreadful corduroy roads over which they traveled on flatter terrain. Whoever first thought of laying logs crosswise over highways must have hated humans and animals alike, for the things seemed deliberately devised to jostle passengers' insides even as they threatened the legs of the horses.

Oh, if only this wearying journey were over! Kristyn thought. She felt as if she had been riding forever in closed coaches with brown leather curtains half screening the windows and only an occasional chance to get out and stretch her legs. Sometimes it seemed as if she were never going to reach her destination!

And when she did, what then?

The question was a jarring one, nagging at the back of her mind, as it had with increasing frequency these last days. When she left Santa Fe, she had worried primarily about the difficulties she might encounter trying to find her young husband. Now, the closer she came to that goal, the more she began asking herself what was going to happen when she did.

How would Little Bear react when he saw her? Had they even told him why she left? When she explained, would he forgive her—or was his heart already hardened against her? Could he accept her again?

And more to the point, could she accept him?

She leaned back against the hard, leather-covered cushions, trying to sort out the thoughts that had begun to swirl through her brain. How *was* she going to feel when she came face to face with Little Bear? Could she love him again, as she had loved him once? Or would her heart be filled only with regrets? With memories of the lover she had lost?

Oh, Rafe . . .

Waves of helpless resignation swept over her, taunting her with feelings she was powerless to control. Sometimes, when she thought about what he had done, how he had used her, she almost hated him as he deserved. But other times, like now, all she could remember was the way his eyes looked when he was laughing at her, the way his lips could mock one minute, tease the next, and she wondered if she was only playing games with herself, only pretending that somehow she could leave her need for him behind.

And yet she had to. No matter how hard it seemed—how *impossible*—she had to! She was going to her husband now. Things were going to be difficult enough between them as it was. She could not bring memories of someone else into that already too-tenuous relationship.

"Heee-yah!"

The driver's voice cut sharply into Kristyn's thoughts. Once again she heard his whip snap as the horse surged forward, jolting her against the back of the seat. Opposite her, Beatty squinted out of the window.

"Dangerous territory around here," he muttered ominously. "I wouldn't be surprised if that fellow sensed something out there. That's probably why he's hightailin' it like this. They got noses like a wild fox, them cowboy drivers."

"*Something* out there?" Kristyn felt a faint chill run down her spine. "You mean there could be . . . Indians?"

"Maybe. Then again, maybe not. There's more to worry about in them hills than just Injuns. This is outlaw country."

"Outlaws? Here?" Kristyn glanced skeptically through the window. "That's hard to believe. I mean, it's so barren. What would outlaws want in a place like this?"

"Don't fool yourself. It only looks barren. There are plenty o' towns within a day's ride, and plenty o' banks, too, if that's what they're after. But most likely, they'd want the coach. Wells Fargo bolts the strongbox under the seat, but that don't stop 'em. They just take the whole blasted wagon and bring it someplace where they can smash it apart. Seems to me, I heard tell that the Collins gang was working this area, and a meaner crew you'd never hope to meet."

"*Billy* Collins?" Kristyn could not keep a gasp of surprise out of her voice. Beatty, hearing it, threw her a sharp look.

"You know Billy Collins?"

"N-no," Kristyn stammered. "No . . . of course not." She couldn't help wondering how Beatty's attitude would change if he learned she had been the companion of a notorious outlaw. "I don't *know* him, but naturally I've heard of him. I think everyone has."

"Yeah, especially the women." Beatty lapsed into his habitual ill-temper. "He sounds romantic to you, don't he? A real glamour boy. Well, let me tell you, there ain't nothing——"

He broke off in midsentence as a loud, explosive sound reverberated in the rocks around them. A gunshot? Kristyn pressed her face against the glazed windows, trying to make out some hint of movement in that craggy landscape, but nothing caught her eye.

A second report followed the first—definitely gunfire now—and then another, until the air seemed to be filled with noise. The terrified horses bolted forward, and the carriage lurched violently from side to side.

Clutching at the seat, Kristyn held on as tightly as she could. Across from her, the two men were doing the same thing, Braunstein still half-dazed with sleep, too groggy for a second to realize what was happening.

Something is out there, Beatty had said, and God help them, he was right. But which of those two menaces had actually materialized, Indians—or outlaws? And which did she fear most?

The outlaws? Kristyn's heart caught in her throat at the thought. Outlaws were notorious for the barbaric way they sometimes treated women. And if this band really *was* headed by Billy Collins. . . ! She shuddered to think how angry he must have been that morning he woke up in that Kansas farmhouse and found her gone.

But if it was Indians . . .

"Injuns," Beatty called out, putting an end to her speculation. "Back there, behind us. I caught a glimpse of 'em when we turned. I don't think there are a dozen, but that's more'n we can handle. Especially if they got the driver."

"If they . . . *got* the driver?"

Kristyn looked from one of those hard faces to the other, a sudden tightness swelling in her chest. Braunstein, wide awake now, was at the window, a six-shooter balanced in his hands. Beatty had opened his coat to expose a pair of pistols, one on each hip, but he had made no move to draw them.

"I'm going to climb up there," he said grimly. "If the driver's all right, I can ride shotgun for him. If not, I'll grab the reins and try to get the horses under control. If I can't outrun the red bastards, I'll pull up to a clump o' rock and we'll take a stand there. We can't hold 'em off long—there aren't enough o' us—but they don't know that. Maybe they'll leave us alone, especially if we cut the horses loose. That's likely all they want, unless . . ."

He turned back to the window, leaving the rest of the thought unspoken. Kristyn, watching tensely, filled it in for him. *Unless that's the band of marauders I've been reading about,* he had started to say. *The renegade band that has more than horse-thieving on their minds. The band of vengeance led by Man-Who-Lives-with-the-Wolves.*

"Careful, Beatty."

Braunstein's voice was tense. Beatty nodded curtly, then kicked out one of the windows with a swift thrust of his boot. He hesitated only a second, turning one last time to Kristyn.

"When the coach stops, wait till I call out, then run like hell for the rocks. If you don't hear anything, get under the seat—and for God's sake, stay there! If they're only after the horses, they may not look inside."

And if they aren't. . . ? Kristyn thought, shivering. But she did not voice the words aloud. The answer was already clear. Taut and silent, she watched as Beatty eased his lean body through the window and hoisted himself onto the roof.

When she glanced back into the interior, she saw that Braunstein was at the other window.

Moving decisively, he brought his gun butt down on the glass, then braced the barrel against the open ledge and sighted down it. Kristyn watched warily, certain that at any moment he was going to start shooting. But as the seconds passed and nothing happened, she realized that for some reason he was holding his fire.

Because of me? she asked herself tensely. He might only be saving ammunition, of course, but somehow she doubted it. If he were alone in that coach, she had the feeling he would have sent off at least a shot or two, hoping to drive the attackers away. But because she was there, because he had a woman's safety to consider, he could not risk drawing fire.

Sensing that she was in the way where she was, Kristyn slid down to the floor, wedging herself partway under the seat. Braunstein would be more comfortable with her there, more likely to do whatever he had to to protect them. Besides, there was something oddly sheltering in the shadowy darkness beneath the seat, almost making her feel she was safely hidden even when she knew she was not.

What if that *is* Little Bear out there? she thought helplessly. What if that was her young husband shooting at her now?

Had she come so close only to lose him this way? Only to be gunned down by a bullet from his own weapon?

The terror of that savage attack lasted no more than a few minutes, but to Kristyn, cringing beneath the shallow seat, it seemed forever. She had thought, listening to the thunder of hoofbeats in her ears, the groaning of wagon wheels strained to their limit, that nothing in the world could ever be quite so terrifying. Yet, a second later, when she felt the coach grind to a stop and the sounds suddenly ceased, she realized the fear had only begun.

Had Beatty reined in the horses of his own accord—or had one of the savages overtaken them and forced them to a stop? Crouching tensely in the shadows, Kristyn waited for the call he had promised—the call that would tell her to run. After one sheer second of agonized suspense, she realized it was not going to come.

Looking up, she saw that Braunstein, too, had been waiting. He had one hand poised on the door, as if to push it open; the other was clenched around his gun. She half expected to see him draw back, taking a second to formulate new plans in his mind, but to her surprise, he did exactly the opposite. Even as she watched, he thrust open the door and leaped out, his gun blazing recklessly in his hand.

A hero—or a fool? Kristyn hunched deeper into the corner, her heart seeming to explode as she listened to the sickening burst of gunfire that greeted his flamboyant gesture. Had he intended it as a bold diversion, drawing the Indians away from the carriage in a gallant attempt to protect her? Or had he only been choosing the moment of his own death, goading his attackers into shooting him cleanly, not prolonging the act with torture? Dully, she realized she would never know. Perhaps he had not even known himself. What man could guess how he was going to react when he came face to face with death? And who had the right to judge him afterward?

The silence that followed Braunstein's spontaneous recklessness was total and eerie, and Kristyn could almost hear the wild, frenzied beating of her own heart. Then, slowly, she became aware of other noises—the shuffling of horses, an occasional soft snort, harsh guttural murmurs, too low to be distinct—and she realized they were closing in.

Terrified, she strained her ears to listen, praying that Beatty had been right, that they *were* only interested in the horses, and sensing more and more with each passing second that they were not.

That was not a band of young braves out there, whooping and jubilant after a successful raid. These were hardened warriors. They would not be satisfied until every strip of leather had been torn from the frame, and the coach was a heap of ashes smoldering in the road.

And if that was going to happen, Kristyn warned herself grimly—if they were going to find her anyway—then the worst thing she could do was try to hide. If she was going to have to face them it was better to do it at her own time. And on her own terms.

She felt the sweat pouring down her forehead, stinging her eyes, but she forced herself to ignore it as she rested one hand against the door. If she could only manage to take them by surprise, she might have a chance. She had lived with Indians long enough to understand that warriors respected boldness. They were intrigued by it. Now that the shooting was over, a flashy enough move might just buy her a minute's time.

And a minute was all she needed to speak to them in their own language!

Reacting impulsively, not giving herself time to think, she pushed the door open, slamming it against the side of the coach as she jumped out and landed on the ground.

As she had hoped, the brusqueness of the gesture startled them, and they made no overt moves against her. All eyes turned in her direction, and one or two of the younger braves raised their rifles from the fronts of their saddles, but they made no attempt to brace them against their shoulders.

Sensing the importance of the moment, Kristyn stood absolutely still, not letting her eyes falter as she looked up at them. There seemed to be no more than half a dozen, eight or ten at most, but she could not be sure, for some were out of the range of her vision. Their arms and chests were dyed a vivid red, their faces so heavy with paint that, even if they were her husband's band, youths she had played with from early childhood, she could not have recognized them.

Everything was deathly quiet. No movement was visible except the occasional tightening of a hand on a gun. Out of the corner of her eye, Kristyn could see a black-suited form crumpled up on the earth, as twisted and gawky in death as William Beatty had been trim and supple in life. Braunstein was nowhere in sight, but a trail of crimson led behind a pile of rocks, telling her he had fought with surprising ferocity for his life.

The bulk of the warriors seemed to have gathered over to the left, and Kristyn turned slowly toward them, fighting the nausea that welled up inside her. These were her people. She had been raised among them—she knew how they were going to react. If she showed her weakness, her fear, it would all be over.

"Who is your leader?" she called out, speaking first in Cheyenne, then when they did not respond, in fluent Dakota.

They seemed to understand, but still they hesitated, throwing sidelong glances at each other. Finally one of them prodded his horse a few paces forward.

For just a second, something in that lean hard body seemed familiar, and Kristyn's heart leaped to her throat. But as he drew nearer, she realized she had been foolish, even for an instant, to think he might be her husband. This man was half a head taller than Little Bear and his shoulders were broader, although his body was spare almost to the point of gauntness.

She waited until he had drawn to a stop a few yards away.

"I am a Cheyenne," she told him, pitching her voice loud enough so the others could hear. "I am dressed like a white woman, but I am an Indian like you. My father is Brave Eagle. You may have heard of him. He is one of the Council of Forty-four. My husband is Little Bear, the warrior who is known as Man-Who-Lives-with-the-Wolves."

Reaching up boldly, she tore the combs out of her hair, shaking it loose. Even if these men were not Little Bear's band, they must surely have heard of him. Perhaps they had also heard of the flame-haired woman who had once been his wife.

The gesture accomplished what her words had not. Hints of movement stirred around her, hoarse whispers broke the silence, and she knew she had their attention.

Only the leader, still seated on his horse in front of her, failed to react. His eyes were skeptical as he studied her. His lips twisted faintly into a frown.

"You are the wife of Man-Who-Lives-with-the-Wolves?"

For all the brittle mockery in his tone, Kristyn recognized that rough voice instantly, and floods of relief surged through her.

"Oh, Running Deer. . . !" She could hardly believe it.
This *was* her husband's band. She was going to be safe!
"Running Deer! Don't you recognize me? It is I—Morning
Star."

She had expected him to respond, but to her surprise, his
scowl deepened as he looked down at her. Then slowly he
shook his head.

"No. You may have been Morning Star once, but you are
not Morning Star anymore. I look at you and I do not see a
Cheyenne. I see only a white woman."

His words took all the warmth out of Kristyn's body. If
even Running Deer, the friend of her childhood, the suitor of
her courting days, could not accept her, how must the others
feel? Terrified, she realized that her position was every bit as
tenuous as before.

A faint sound came from somewhere behind her, and
Running Deer, glancing sharply in that direction, began to
back his horse slowly away from her. Almost at once, Kristyn
realized what was happening.

The leader of the band—the *real* leader—had been somewhere else when she first appeared. That was why there had
been so much confusion in answer to her question. Now he
was back and the others were moving away to give him
space.

Even before she turned, she knew what she was going to
see.

Little Bear was seated on Fire-Wind, a short distance away
from the stage. He was clad not in rawhide breeches, like the
others, but a simple loin cloth, dividing the blood-red dye on
his chest from the bronzed tones of lean, hard legs. His hair
had grown since she had seen him last, falling almost to his
shoulders, knotted back with a cowboy's red bandanna into
which he had stuck an eagle feather. Kristyn could not help
remembering, incongruously, the way his mother used to put
a turkey feather in his headband when he was a little boy—
and how funny it had made him look.

She took a step forward, then faltered.

"Little Bear. . . ?"

He raised a hand to silence her, and frightened, she obeyed.

"My name is not Little Bear," he said, his voice so hard
and changed it was only half familiar. "I will not permit you

to call me that. If you must speak, you will say Man-Who-Lives-with-the-Wolves.''

"Well . . . Man-Who-Lives-with-the-Wolves, then.'' Kristyn tried unsuccessfully to inject a note of lightness into her tone. "I was with you when you chose that name, do you remember? And when you chose the name for Fire-Wind, too. Oh, please . . .'' She could not believe how much it hurt, looking up at this man she no longer even knew, seated on the horse she had won for them both so many years ago. "Please don't be angry with me. I didn't leave you by choice—you must believe that! I thought you were dead. That's what they told me, Brave Eagle and Buffalo Calf Woman. They said you were dead and I could no longer stay with them.''

If her words had any effect, they did not show on his face. He simply sat there, staring down at her with eyes she could not read. Then finally, he inclined his head slightly forward.

"Yes, that may be. I had thought the night I returned from the raid that Brave Eagle had something he wanted to say. But I was too angry to stay and hear his words and I never saw him again. It must have lain heavy on his heart in his last moments to know he did not speak them.''

"In his . . . last moments?'' Kristyn stared up at him in horror. "You mean . . . he is dead? My father—Brave Eagle—is *dead*?''

"No. Your father is a white man. I do not know if he lives or not. *My* father—the brother of my blood father, the man who took care of me after he was gone—is dead. Buffalo Calf Woman survived him for many days, but she did not speak of you then. Her mind was back in the old days, when she and Brave Eagle were young, and she was waiting only to join him again. I did not leave until the time came to bury her.''

"Oh, no . . .'' The words slipped softly out of Kristyn's lips.

Buffalo Calf Woman gone, too? Numb with pain, she turned her head to the side. Brave Eagle dead, Buffalo Calf Woman—everyone she had loved, everything she had known in her childhood, lost to her forever.

"You must believe me, Little Bear,'' she whispered hoarsely, clinging to what little she had left. "You must! I didn't betray you. I didn't leave of my own free will.''

"I believe only one thing.'' His voice was like a cold blade

cutting through her. "I believe you are no longer one of us.
Running Deer was right—he spoke for us all. We look at you
and we do not see a Cheyenne. We see a white woman."

He leaned forward, his eyes piercing, his hand reaching
toward the rifle on his saddle.

"Do you know what we do with a white woman when we
find her?"

Kristyn felt her body begin to tremble, and she could
almost taste the fear in her mouth. His hand was on his gun
now, raising it as he spoke. What have I done? she asked
herself helplessly. What have I done? She had been so
frightened, back there on the road in that runaway stage,
frightened that her husband might kill her accidentally with
his own bullet. Now she realized he was capable of commit-
ting that same act deliberately.

She was tempted for a moment to cry out, to beg this man
who had once loved her to spare her life, but reason warned her
she would be wasting her breath. Slowly, deliberately, she
forced herself to look up, leveling steady eyes on his face. Whatever she did now, whatever pleas she made, would have no
effect on him. Groveling would only demean her all the more.

Little Bear studied her in silence for a moment, his hands
still holding the gun. Then his lips turned upward, a cold
smile, not at all reassuring.

"I could kill you," he said. "And perhaps I should. You
mean nothing to me—I do not care what happens to you. But
for the love I bore Brave Eagle and Buffalo Calf Woman, I
am going to let you go. You are free to take one of the horses
and leave."

Kristyn hesitated, staring up at him, trapped by that strange,
impenetrable look in his eyes. It would be so easy to do what
he said, so easy to unhitch one of the horses, to take one of
the canteens of water and ride off without a backward look.

Only something in her would not let her do it.

Dully, she stood there, looking back at him, trying—and
failing—to understand what it was, some deep natural instinct
perhaps, a sense of loyalty, that would not let her forget
promises made long ago. She might look like a white woman,
but there was still enough of the Cheyenne left in her to make
it impossible to break her word.

"No," she said quietly. "I cannot do that. I have come to
be your wife again, and that is what I am going to do."

Thirty-Four

Cristina . . .

Rafe glowered abstractedly through the dingy window-panes of his second-story hotel room, trying without success to get the elusive image of misty blue eyes and dark red hair out of his mind. An early morning rain had fallen briefly, darkening the weathered storefronts and dilapidated boardwalks, and turning the main street of the typical Colorado mining town into oozing brown mud.

Damn, it hurt! Rafe doubled his hand into a fist, hating himself for the sharp pain that cut through his body every time he thought of her. He had known all along what she was. He had told himself often enough she was a flirt, a tease, the kind of woman who enjoyed the challenge of a man and wanted no part of him when she had won. And yet, when it happened he had been surprised. Surprised, hell! He had gone numb with shock and disbelief.

Turning back into the room, he stared at the sagging mattress and graying linen on the bed. His first reaction that morning had been one of total incredulity. He had simply refused to look at the truth. Ysabel had stood in front of him, her face white, her lips suddenly trembling as she blurted out the fact that his bride had run off, and he had called her a lying little cat.

"You've always hated Cristina," he had told her. "You'd make up anything to hurt her." But then El Valeroso himself had come into the room with that absurdly awkward note. Not a word about how she felt—why she was doing this to him. Just a few scrawled lines saying she was leaving because she could not be his wife. Within hours, he had discovered she had boarded a stage, heading north.

471

Heading for Colorado?

Rafe jammed his hand angrily against the window ledge. He didn't care where she was now, the bitch! She could be right here in town or a thousand miles away, it made no difference. Hell, the farther the better! If he had her here, he'd only want one thing—to wrap his hands around that pretty white throat and squeeze until there was no life left in her.

And no woman, no matter how beautiful—or how treacherous—was worth a rendezvous with the hangman.

Glancing back at the window, Rafe saw that the streets were beginning to fill with people. They were the usual for that sort of place, the flotsam and jetsam of humanity that floated into a mining town on the first waves of prosperity and drifted out again when fortunes began to wane.

He opened the window and leaned out, trying to separate the men who were going someplace from the ones who were simply moving. It was not hard. They all wore the same uniform, the same blue denim overalls, the same plaid shirts with a cowboy's bandanna around their necks, but something in their faces set one group apart from the other. There was a look the losers had about them, the look of men who left a mining camp too soon or came too late, the look of prospectors turned into drifters with nothing to warm them on a winter's night but glasses of whiskey cadged from strangers and stories about the one big strike that had slipped through their fingers.

Silver City. Rafe's lips twisted into a wry half-smile as he caught sight of the sign over the general store. Silver City. It had been a ridiculously pretentious label that day more than a decade ago when he first rode into town, a green kid consolidating his grandfather's holdings with an eye toward expanding the family empire. There had been no silver then, no lucky strikes, no more than a name and a dream that had never materialized.

Rafe pulled himself back into the room, trapped for a moment halfway between the past and the present. He *had* been young then, and terribly inexperienced, but he had been in control of his life. What kind of control did he have now?

His anger swelled again, a renewed sense of bitterness as he thought of all those pretty vows she had uttered—just before she walked out on him! Cristina, with the wistful eyes of a little girl, the full teasing lips of a courtesan . . . and a heart carved out of stone! She had abandoned herself in his arms that night, she had twined her long limbs around his body, heated his blood with her sighs and kisses, but she hadn't given a damn about him. Not really. She hadn't taken him as a lover, not even as a man—only as an object. A virile male body to quell the insatiable lusts of her flesh.

Like all those objects in his own past, he thought ironically, all the women without names, without even faces in his memory. The ones he had not approached as women at all, but as warm, pulsating bodies to relieve his compelling man-needs. Now she had done the same thing to him, and she had done it with a vengeance.

Who was she with today? Ricardo Cuervo?

The thought was like a hard fist, catching him in the chest. Irrational? Not necessarily. She *had* been struggling in Cuervo's arms the night he caught her, but how long was she planning to keep up that little game? He could not forget that she had fought him once, too, that first night on the banks of the stream, fought him like the wildcat she was! But she had come to him soon enough, opening her arms—and her legs— all her inhibitions gone. Was that what she had in mind for Cuervo, too? A lusty rendezvous in some . . .

"Dammit, Valero, you're a fool!"

Rafe peeled off his shirt and threw it impatiently on the bed, standing half-naked in the stagnant air in front of the open window. He *was* a fool to let her get to him like this, a fool to keep dwelling on her perfidy. He had to get her out of his mind, and the best way to do that was to concentrate on the task at hand.

Pulling a clean shirt out of his saddlebag, he began to put it on, casting a quick eye at the mirror as he did. It was badly rumpled, but it was nearly new and it would pass for business attire in the casual atmosphere of Silver City. Dark blue plaid was standard enough for that part of the world, but the color was striking with his jet black hair, and the superb tailoring made his body look lean and lithe. Almost as an afterthought, he knotted a light blue bandanna with a nonchalant flair around his neck.

He was already sorting out various alternatives in his mind as he ran one last comb through his hair. It shouldn't be hard to find an excuse to get into the mine. He could pass himself off as a writer, perhaps, a journalist doing a piece on local lore. No, that was too obvious—too conspicuous. Everybody would have their eyes on him. A mining engineer then, representing some syndicate back East, scouting out investments. Cuervo would never consider selling of course, not while the mine was producing at a peak, but he would like the idea that someone else wanted what he had. Besides, even if he was suspicious, it would be too late to do anything by the time word got back to Santa Fe.

Rafe was ready in five minutes. The raucous noise of a downstairs bar filled the stairwell as he descended quickly to the ground floor. It was still early and the stores would not open for at least an hour, but the saloon was already in full swing. Or perhaps, Rafe thought, casting a glance at the swinging doors on the side of the narrow entry hall, it had never closed the night before. Hurrying past it, he headed toward the main doorway and out onto the street.

Silver City had been a quiet town before the coming of prosperity changed its image of itself, and hints of an older grace still showed in places. A substantial woodframe building, once a hotel, now a combination saloon and courthouse, dominated the far end of the street, and a few comfortable, neatly painted houses nestled in the surrounding foothills. For the most part, however, the place had the temporary, ramshackle air of a town that had grown quickly from nowhere and knew, once the ore was gone, the mine shut down, it was going back to nowhere again. Flimsy, one-story buildings lined both sides of the main street, fronted by tawdry two-story facades with glassless openings cut to simulate upper windows. Cheap pine siding was warped and gray, and the boardwalks had rotted away until they were barely passable in places.

Rafe quickened his pace, heading for the outskirts of the town, an area that was, if possible, even uglier than the last time he had seen it. Tent City, some called it; Shanty Town, others said; and both descriptions were accurate. Like every makeshift community in the West, whether constructed to service miners or railroad crews, Silver's city of tents was designed to last only as long as the boom.

Hand-painted placards, most of them crooked, half misspelled, appeared on every side, proclaiming the activities that were the area's only *raison d'être*. "Elmer's Barber Shop," one read in bold orange letters, "10¢ a shave." "The Golden Nugget Gaming Hall," another proclaimed, although the "hall" was nothing but a gray-colored tent, made as much from old blankets as canvas. "Ma Appleby's Boarding House, Hot Home-Cooked Meals" had a distinctly unappetizing look about it, but "Scissors Ground and Sharpened Here, Hunting Knives, Needles," was surprisingly trim and neat. Down at the far end, "Bailey Eldon, Best Dam Smithy in Town," stood side by side with "Eldorado Bath House—Where Else Can You Get a Tub for Two Bits? LADIES Available on Request."

The road opened up after it passed through Shanty Town, dipping down into a shallow valley, then rising up again on the opposite side. There it forked off, one trail winding up a steep slope toward the entrance to the mine.

Rafe paused for a minute at the base of the hill, glancing up at the wooden building that fronted the operation, searching in vain for any signs of life. Had he come too early? When he was running the mine, crews had worked around the clock and the office was never closed. But perhaps Cuervo had other ideas.

"Here you—boy!"

Rafe jerked out his hand, beckoning to a lad of about sixteen who was lounging on the opposite side of the road. The boy glanced up, but he did not seem inclined to move.

"You want me, mister?"

"Yeah. You know if the mine office is open this early?"

"The Folly?" The boy shot him a quizzical look. "Sure. Old Gamper, he's the foreman, he don't never shut the place down. Gets every drop o' blood out o' his workers, and then some. Just try an' set down on the job, and you'll feel the bite o' his whip, that's for sure."

"Thanks."

Rafe caught himself grinning as he turned away. He'd be willing to bet the boy had worked for Gamper himself, and he wouldn't be surprised it he had tasted the bite of that whip more than once.

So they still called the place the Folly, did they? He had always liked the name. It was his own private joke. Valero's Folly—that's what the oldtimers had called his first claim, shaking their heads at anyone who traded in a choice piece of grazing land by the river for a played-out pile of rock. And

Valero's Folly was the name that had gone on the official papers when his first strike came in and ore was pouring out of the shafts. Cuervo had changed it, of course, when he seized control, but obviously the old title had stuck, at least as far as the townspeople were concerned.

Well, so much the better. If Cuervo and his foreman were unpopular in Silver City, and if the old days still held a certain appeal, that could only make things easier. Rafe wasn't worried about being recognized in the office—Cuervo would have brought in his own staff—but some of the miners were oldtimers. If one of them caught sight of him, he'd prefer to think the man didn't feel any particular loyalty for his new boss.

Rafe made his way up the slopes in half an hour, walking easily. The place had changed since he had last seen it. The paint, once neatly tended, was peeling away, and doors and windows hung crooked on their hinges. Old boards and strips of weathered brown paper replaced some of the panes. Others showed nothing but gaping holes.

Obviously, he thought, disgusted, Cuervo was planning to get everything he could out of the mine without putting anything back into it. And if things were bad outside, where everyone could see, he hated to think what they must be like in the pits. Conditions down there couldn't be very pleasant. Or very safe.

He found the foreman's office just right of the entrance, where his own office had been. The room was so different he barely recognized it. A long railing ran down the center, separating the business area from what seemed to be a waiting room, with uncomfortable-looking wooden benches along the walls. A carved-oak desk stood by itself in one corner; a smaller one, the one Rafe himself had used, was centered on the opposite wall.

Both of the desks were empty, but a young man was seated at a table in the middle of the work area, scowling through wire-rimmed glasses at a pile of papers in front of him. A clerk, Rafe thought. And not much of one, judging by the way he was fumbling with those papers.

"Boss man around?" he asked, leaning casually against the railing.

The young man glanced up.

"No, sir. Mr. Cuervo arrived very late last night. We don't expect him here for at least an hour or two."

"Cuervo?" Rafe could not keep a note of sharpness out of his voice. The clerk, hearing it, gave him a surprisingly shrewd glance.

"Mr. Cuervo is the owner of the mine."

"I know that, boy." Rafe snapped out the words, eager to regain his credibility. "Mr. Ricardo Cuervo of Santa Fe—Richard, they call him here. But I—uh, hadn't expected to find him in today. I thought he wasn't going to be here until Wednesday or Thursday. Did I get my signals crossed?"

It wasn't a particularly good line, but the boy fell for it.

"Well, to tell the truth, sir—" he threw Rafe a perplexed look, like an owl caught in the sunlight—"we hadn't known he was coming at all. He just showed up last night, all of a sudden. I don't know anything more than that. But I can take a message if you like."

"A message?"

Rafe ran a quick eye around the room, taking in every detail. Nothing particularly noteworthy there. The desks, a beat-up old armchair, a pair of tall wooden files, a standard-model black safe, set up rather too ostentatiously beside a window on the back wall.

"No, no message, thanks. Cuervo and I are . . . old friends. I'll catch up with him in town."

Rafe's mind was reeling as he left the office and made his way back down the pathway toward the main road. Cuervo was here, in Silver City—and he had obviously come on impulse, not even taking time to let his crew know he was on the way! That could only mean one thing. He knew what Rafe was up to, or he guessed.

And if he had come running like that. . . ?

Rafe felt his pulse quicken as the possibilities narrowed down. Cuervo would never have come there, not as fast as he did, if he wasn't afraid Rafe might find what he was looking for. The letters *were* in Silver City. Somehow—dammit, somehow!—he had to find them before Cuervo could get to them and spirit them away again.

Well, one thing was certain. They weren't in that old safe in the office. The thing was much too obvious, too blatantly displayed. Plainly it was a ruse, and a poor one at that.

No, the letters were someplace else. Someplace clever, or

they wouldn't have remained hidden all this time . . . but not so clever that Cuervo felt comfortable about them.

The road ahead was blocked by a team of mules being driven up the hill by a surly old skinner with a sharp whip and an even sharper tongue. The poor devils! Rafe thought, giving them a quick glance as he left the path and began to cut through stubbly undergrowth toward town. He had no fondness for mules—God knows they were as ill-tempered as their trainers—but he hated to think of any animal being shut up in airless shafts with no more than the light of a miner's candle for the rest of its life.

When he was in charge, he had tried to treat them humanely, working them only during their productive years and putting them out to pasture when they were old. But by that time they had gone blind from so many years in the darkness. Everything frightened them—the wind, the snow, the rain, claps of thunder, even the dramatic changes in temperature from day to night—and not a few had gone mad and had to be destroyed.

They had grown used to their prisons! They were so used to the shackles that bound them, they could not survive without them.

How many men did the same damn thing? Cursed the darkness, railed against it—but when the chance came, they were afraid to grope their way out. By God, he would never be like that! He would not succumb to the fears and despairs that chained men to their fate like dumb animals. He would fight with every ounce of strength in his body!

He had almost reached the bottom of the hill when he caught sight of a man who had positioned himself on his horse almost directly in the center of the road. The rising sun was behind him, silhouetting his slender form and casting his face into shadow, but Rafe recognized him immediately.

Carlos.

His first reaction was one of anger. Damn him, he had told him to stay in Santa Fe! What business did he have, following him? For an instant he was tempted to turn around, knowing his brother had not spotted him, but the impulse died quickly, replaced by cold reason. Carlos was capable of sitting there all day, and any minute now, Cuervo might come riding down that road. The last thing Rafe wanted was to tip his hand by forcing a confrontation.

Holding in his temper, he pushed his way through the

undergrowth, waiting until he had almost reached his brother to call out.

"What the devil are you doing here, Carlos? Didn't I tell you to stay in Santa Fe?"

If the younger man was intimidated, he did not show it. Leaping gracefully from his horse, he whirled around with a grin.

"I'm a big boy now, Rafael. I don't always do what I am told. Besides, is that any way to greet your brother? You always used to be glad to see me, even if we'd only been separated a short time. Aren't you glad to see me now?"

"I'm not glad to have you jeopardize my plans like this. Damn it, Carlos, this isn't a game. Don't you realize what I am trying to do here is dangerous? I don't need——"

"It's more dangerous than you think," Carlos cut in, his voice turning serious. "Shortly after you left Santa Fe, Cuervo disappeared, too. They put out some crazy story about his visiting family in Mexico, but it's too much of a coincidence for me. I think he got wind of where you were going. Maybe he bribed one of the servants. At any rate, I'm sure he's headed this way."

"He is," Rafe replied curtly. "Or rather he *was*. He arrived last night. I heard about it a few minutes ago."

"And you're still determined to go through with this wild scheme of yours?" Carlos stared at him, aghast. "You've always had a reckless streak in you, Rafael, but this time you go too far. It's one thing to prowl around the place when Cuervo isn't here, but it would be insane to try now. Can't you take a little time to think things through? To come up with a sensible plan?"

"There is no time, Carlos. Time is all on Cuervo's side. You know that. But . . ." Rafe broke into a sudden, unexpected grin. ". . . you're right about one thing. I *have* always been reckless, and I'm not about to change at this late date. I've never been afraid of danger before. Do you think I'm afraid of it now?"

Carlos eyed him steadily, seeing behind that sudden fire in his eyes a brashness that was distinctly unsettling. There was a hard quality about him that he had never seen before, a kind of cold determination, like a gunfighter about to set himself up against long odds.

"What about your wife?" he said softly. "What about Cristina?"

Cristina . . . Rafe stiffened at the sound of her name. He had known Carlos was going to say it, he had expected it from the minute he saw him, but he was not prepared to deal with the emotional responses it evoked. The pain was too fresh. Too raw.

"I have no wife," he said coldly. "I will allow no man to speak that name in my hearing. Not even you, Carlos."

"Rafael! Will you listen to yourself?" Carlos fairly exploded in exasperation. "You sound like El Valeroso now. 'I have no son.' That is what he always said about our father. 'I have *no son!*' Hasn't it occurred to you, *hermano*, that the girl might have had reasons for what she did? Cristina is not frivolous. She would not run away with no cause at all. Aren't you even curious? Don't you want to know if she is all right? Don't you care?"

"I have never been of a curious nature. You know that. As for caring——"

"You have *always* been curious! You could never stand it if there was something you didn't know. Yes, and you've always been caring, too—though you go to great lengths to hide it, as if love were something to be ashamed of. I cannot believe you don't care now. Cristina is your wife——"

"*No!*" Rafe's eyes burned with hot, angry flames. "I do *not* care, and nothing you can say is going to change that! *I have no wife.* I told you that before. I'm not going to tell you again."

Stubborn! Carlos thought, shaking his head at the rigid, unbending posture his brother had assumed. As stubborn as their grandfather, but there was no point bringing it up. That would only make him more determined than ever.

"Very well," he said quietly. He had always looked up to his older brother, practically worshiping him from the time he was a small child, but even then he had known that once Rafael set his will to something, there was no getting him to turn back. "I will not speak of her again if that is the way you want it. But I'm not going back to Santa Fe. If you won't let me help you sort out your life, at least I can keep you out of trouble."

"The devil you can. You *are* going back. I have——"

"No, I am not, and you can't force me. As I see it, you

have two choices. You can either let me come with you—or I can go back to your hotel and sit in the lobby and wait. Of course, Cuervo may come along and see me, but that's a chance we'll have to take, won't we?''

Rafe glared at him hotly for a second, angry retorts rising to his lips. Then suddenly, his mouth began to turn up at the corners. What the hell! Carlos was proving to have some of the El Valeroso stubbornness after all.

"Do you know, *hermanito*,'' he said, grinning in spite of himself, "I think there is a little of our grandfather in yòu, too. All right, stay if you must. But I warn you, it *is* going to be dangerous.''

"Dangerous?'' Carlos laughed, tossing his head back with a bravado Rafe recognized at once. Just like himself, in those days when he had been old enough to recognize fear—and young enough not to be able to admit it. "You think *I* am afraid of danger? Me? The youngest of the Valeroso blood? No, *hermano*, I am not just heir to Don Diego's iron will. I've picked up a little of your recklessness as well.''

"Have you indeed?'' Rafe studied his brother's profile in the white morning light. "Well, let's hope it serves you better than it has me.''

It suddenly occurred to him just how dangerous it was, this scheme that was beginning to take shape in his brain. He did not mind for himself—his life had little meaning now—but he was going to care very much if anything happened to his brother.

Thirty-Five

Kristyn perched miserably on a shallow outcropping of rock, her legs crossed boylike beneath the rumpled gray of her skirt. The gully Little Bear had taken her to after they left the burning stagecoach was well-protected from the winding road, half a mile distant, but it was also sheltered from the breeze, and beads of sweat had begun to run down her neck, saturating her lacy collar.

"Couldn't we go higher in the hills?" she asked tentatively. Little Bear had left her alone when he went off to tend to the horses, but he was back now, standing in the entrance to the ravine with his back to her. "I should think we'd be safer up there. Besides, it would be much cooler."

"Cooler?" He turned toward her with a scowl. "Is that what matters to you? Your own physical comfort? You've lived with the whites so long you've forgotten what it is to be an Indian. You should have taken the canteen and horse when I offered them to you. You don't belong here with us."

Kristyn's heart sank. Everything she had done that morning, everything she said, only seemed to anger him all the more.

"I'm sorry," she said softly. "I didn't mean to complain. I'm sure you have reasons for wanting to be here. It just seemed to me we'd be as well off if we went higher up. Anyway, it would be better for the horses."

"The horses are fine where they are. You forget, I've been tending to them all these months while you were living in the white man's houses. I know what I'm doing. We've been camping here for several days and we've already found the best place for the horses."

He glanced back through the narrow entrance, looking not so much *at* something, Kristyn sensed, as away from her. She had hoped when they separated from the rest of the band that he was planning to sit down and talk things out with her; but as the minutes passed and he made no effort to do so, she forced herself to admit it was not going to happen. Any chance they still had for a reconciliation, any overtures, would have to come from her.

Determined to try at least one more time, she rose and went over to him.

"Must we quarrel like this, husband? I know I was wrong to leave, even though I thought you were dead. I should have waited to be sure. But the instant I learned the truth, I came to find you. Doesn't that prove my good faith?"

"It proves nothing," he said, his voice cold as he continued to stare into the distance. "*Why* you insisted on coming with me this morning when I did not want you—*why* you are here now—is of no importance. Whatever the reason, it is not going to work between us. You and I do not belong together anymore."

"Oh, Little Bear . . ." Kristyn was so upset she forgot that that name was forbidden. "You can't mean what you are saying. You loved me once. Surely you can't have forgotten those feelings in so short a time. I know I could be your wife again if only you'd let me."

He threw her a sidelong glance. "What kind of wife? A Cheyenne wife? Or the sort of woman a white man has?"

The question hit Kristyn like a slap in the face. "What difference does it make? Why are you doing this? Putting labels on everything? White this and Cheyenne that. A wife is a wife, no matter what. She is someone who shares a man's heart, his dreams . . . his life."

"And you want to share *my* life?" Cold eyes seemed to bore through her. "Do you even know what my life is? Don't be so ready to make promises you might not be able to keep."

"But I *can* keep them! I know I can. Or at least—I *think* I can. And I have to try."

"Do you want to know what *I* think?" Little Bear paced restlessly down the ravine, then whirled to face her again. "I think you're playing games with yourself, and you're going to be very sorry when you find out where they lead. You *don't* know what my life is, just as you don't know what it is to be an Indian anymore. You will never be a Cheyenne again—and you will never be my wife."

Kristyn took a step back, recoiling from words that were harsh but hard to refute. She did not need the dark mirror of his eyes to tell her what she looked like at that moment. A fashionable lady in a dove-gray traveling dress, a little wrinkled, but expensively tailored, with silver filigree buttons running up the front and imported Belgian lace at her throat. Her hair was still loose, hanging down her back, but it was perfumed and silky, not dry with the alkali of the prairie, and her skin had begun to bleach out after weeks of wearing a sunbonnet or man-tailored cowboy hat whenever she went outside.

"I know I don't look like an Indian. But that's just because of the way I'm dressed. If I were wearing different clothes——"

"Clothes?" He snorted contemptuously. "You think it's clothes that matter? I could put a Cheyenne woman in a dress like that and people would laugh. On you, it does not look funny at all."

"That's not fair, Little Bear. I've been wearing clothes like this for several months—I've learned to carry them properly. I probably looked silly, too, the first time I put them on." She was vaguely aware that she was lying. She had not looked gawky or out of place that first night in Ysabel's vermilion silk gown, but she could hardly admit that to him. "And don't forget—I can wear Cheyenne clothes, too. I did for many years. They looked right on me then."

"And you think they would again?" His eyes narrowed as he leveled them on her, making no effort to hide his skepticism. "Just because they did once? Well . . . we shall see."

He strode forcefully down the ravine, heading toward the place where he had tethered the horses. Kristyn, left behind, could only watch helplessly as he disappeared behind the craggy gray rocks. He seemed so angry, so unreachable—was there nothing left of the gentle young man she had come so far to find?

She had half expected him to return with one of the horses he had cut from the stage, ordering her to mount and ride off someplace where he would never have to see her again. But when he did reappear, all he had with him was a small bundle tucked under one arm.

"Here!" He tossed it roughly on the ground at her feet.

"You think you can become a Cheyenne again? As easily as this? Here is your chance to prove it."

Curious, Kristyn hunkered down, unwrapping the bundle. The first thing she pulled out was a pair of man's denim pants, smallish and almost incredibly dirty. Next came a buckskin shirt, Indian in origin, but as disgusting as the trousers, with none of the beadwork left intact. A pair of boy's leather boots completed the ensemble, scuffed and worn, yet still sturdy and reasonably serviceable.

At first Kristyn could only stare at them.

"You want me to put them on?" It was all she could do to force her eyes up. "These—*filthy* things?" Was he trying to make her prove she was a Cheyenne? Or did he only want to humiliate her?

The look on his face, grim and hard, was all the answer she needed.

"They belonged to Gray Fox. You remember, Owl Woman's oldest son. He was killed in a raid a week ago. We did not bury him in his clothing. We never bury anyone in their clothes now. We cannot afford the waste."

Kristyn looked down again, shuddering in revulsion. A dead boy's pants, a dead boy's shirt—that was what he wanted her to wear! He *did* want to humiliate her, and she had no choice but to let him do it. If she tried to defy him now, she might as well turn around and walk away.

Clutching the clothing against her breast, she slipped behind a nearby boulder, feeling a little foolish at the modesty that would not allow her to disrobe in front of her own husband, but unable to force herself all the same. She undressed quickly, sensing that any further show of reluctance would irritate him more. To her surprise the trousers fit passably well, if a bit snugly, and after an initial moment of distaste, she found herself adjusting to them. The tunic proved harder to accept, and she held her breath as she tugged it over her head, trying not to notice the stench in her nostrils.

Was this how she had dressed when she lived with the Indians? How she had smelled, with no perfumed soap to rinse away the sweat and grime? No giggling maids to pour buckets of bathwater into an enormous copper tub? Was this what Rafe had seen—what he had scented—that first night by the stream?

Blocking the thought out of her mind, she turned her

attention to her hair, working it deftly into two long plaits. No doubt there were reasons for the way her lover had treated her—reasons why he could not love or even respect her—but there was no point dwelling on that now. Rafe was no longer a part of her life. She had to learn to forget him.

She was quiet and subdued when she stepped out from behind the rock. Her seductive beauty was muted by the drab loose tunic, and her hair hung in dark-red braids on either side of her face, but she still did not look like a Cheyenne, and she knew it the instant she saw the expression on Little Bear's face. He had given her one last test, one last chance to prove herself—and she had failed.

She braced herself for biting words, but to her relief, he only turned away, busying himself with the task of setting up camp. Grateful for his reticence, Kristyn vowed not to utter another word unless he asked her a direct question—and not to do anything further to annoy him. If only they could make it through the next few hours without quarreling, perhaps things would work out after all.

She spent the rest of the day trying with some success to prove she had not forgotten how to do the chores required of every Cheyenne woman. None of the other warriors appeared throughout the afternoon and Kristyn had the feeling that they were camped on the higher slopes where she herself had wanted to go, but caution prompted her to keep the thought to herself. Instead, she concentrated on gathering enough firewood and water to last them until morning.

Pine was abundant in that area, with fallen boughs scattered everywhere, but even though Kristyn was tempted by the pungent, resinous scent, she did not try to gather them, knowing from experience that they would give off smoke and sparks. Ideally she would have liked to find a clump of willows, for willow with the bark peeled off burned wonderfully well, or perhaps a stand of chokecherries or aspen. But since these were not available, she settled for a few scraps of scrub oak which she carried back and stacked in the ravine.

Water proved easier to find, for even though it had been a dry year, icy mountain streams still held a little of last year's melting snows, and Kristyn quickly found a place to fill their two canteens. Just as she finished and was about to straighten up, she was surprised to catch sight of a trail of thick black smoke drifting upward from somewhere just beyond the rise of the hill. Too thick for an Indian, she thought, puzzled, and much too black—yet it had to be coming from the rest of their band, camped just where she had assumed, higher in the hills.

She had intended to speak to Little Bear about it when he returned to the ravine, for she could not believe he would tolerate such carelessness, but by the time she got back, he was already there. To her embarrassment, he had built the fire himself instead of waiting for her, and was now coaxing it into leaping red flames. All thoughts vanished from her mind as she hastened to take over the woman's work he had begun. Moving deftly, she skinned and dressed the rabbit he had brought back with him, then grilled it over the fire, waiting Indian fashion until he had eaten his fill before she picked over the pieces that remained.

Only when they had both finished and the scraps and bones had been buried so they would not attract wild animals did she recall the subject she had planned to bring up before. Dusk had long since darkened into night, and Little Bear's face looked softer somehow, more approachable in the last rays of the dying fire.

"I saw smoke this afternoon," she said tentatively. "While I was at the stream. Is that where Running Deer and the others are? Up in the hills?"

Little Bear gave her an unexpectedly sharp look.

"You saw smoke in the hills? Campfire—or wildfire?"

"Campfire," Kristyn replied, confused by his tone. "That *is* where the others are, isn't it?"

Little Bear did not reply at once. Rising, he moved away from the fire, his head tilting slightly upward as he scanned the darkness with his eyes.

"The others are in another ravine, just east of here."

"Then who . . ." Kristyn let her voice trail off as she stepped over to him.

"Probably outlaws." He sounded brittle, almost amused. "We aren't the only ones who hide from the white man's wrath tonight. They chase others as well as us."

"Outlaws? Not Billy Collins and his gang?"

"Probably. If it is, they won't cause trouble. They know where we are, and we know where they are. We stay out of each other's way."

He turned back toward the fire, but Kristyn remained where

she was a moment longer, staring up at the shadowy hills. Darkness hid the smoke from her eyes, but she had the eerie feeling that it was still there.

Billy Collins. Only this morning it had frightened her to hear his name—now the thought that he might be someplace nearby was almost comforting. How far she had come in those few short hours. How desperately far to hunger for the protection of a man who might well have come to hate her.

When at last she turned back, she saw that the fire had died away and the embers were only vague touches of red in the blackness. Little Bear, faintly illuminated in the moonlight, had just opened a neatly folded blanket and was spreading it out a few yards away.

One blanket?

Kristyn stood absolutely still, wondering why that should shock her so much. The warriors were poor, they had almost no possessions—which of them was likely to own more than a single blanket? Of course Little Bear had only one, and of course he was laying it on the ground now. Dinner was over, the fire was out, and the time had come to go to bed.

A kind of numbness spread over her body. She had known from the beginning, right from the time she left Santa Fe, that this moment was coming, but now that it was here, she was not sure she was ready to face it. For one terrible, agonizing second, she was tempted to run, although reason reminded her that flight was not necessary. Little Bear had made a point of telling her she was free to leave any time she wanted. All she had to do was turn around and walk away, and he would not even look up to see her go.

Only if she did, she would never be able to come back.

Taking a long, slow breath, she began to move toward him. Only when she had reached the opposite side of the blanket did she stop, and then only to crouch down and help smooth it out on the ground.

Little Bear did not look up until they had finished.

"So," he said softly, "you are still determined to be a good Cheyenne wife."

Was that mockery she heard in his tone? Or amusement? She did not know. She knew only it was cutting and bitter.

"I am determined to be a good wife to you."

He did not speak again, but lay back on the blanket, propping himself up on one elbow to stare at her in the moonlight. He's not going to help me, Kristyn thought, panicking. He's not going to help me at all. He's just going to lie there and look at me—and laugh if I do something wrong!

Slowly, she drew herself to her feet. The air had turned chill, and every nerve in her body seemed to be tingling. She was intensely aware that there was one minute of choice still left, one last second in which to change her mind.

Or *was* there a choice?

The thought startled her, but she realized the instant it crossed her mind that it had been inevitable all the time. In reality, there were no options open to her. She had burned her bridges when she left Santa Fe; she could not go back there. What else was left but this uncomfortable alliance she had chosen herself?

Raising her arms, she slipped the tunic over her head, not even noticing this time the way it smelled. It was funny how much she had hated the thing before. Now all she wanted was to clutch it to her body and she knew she could not.

The wind picked up, penetrating even that sheltered ravine. How cold it was, cold against her bare breasts, making her feel her nakedness even more. Her skin—did he notice how pale it was, blue-white in the moonlight? And her nipples, rigid from the chill—did they excite him the way they had once excited another man?

Take off your clothes.

Oh, God . . . Rafe's voice. Harsh, angry, but hoarse with desire. Rafe! She had hated him at that moment, hated him bitterly, and yet—oh, it set her blood on fire even now to think of it—she had wanted him, too. Would she ever be able to love this man who lay silently before her as she had once loved *him*? Would she be able to desire him?

She was trembling as she touched her hand to the waistband of those tight trousers, loosening them and tugging them off. Cold, yes. The moonlight was cold and his eyes were cold . . . and there was nothing but coldness in her heart. Moving stiffly, automatically, she forced herself to kneel beside him on the blanket.

"I am your wife," she whispered huskily. "Do with me as you will."

He seemed to hesitate, trapped, as she was trapped, in emotions he could not understand. What was he feeling?

Loathing for her? For the white-woman smell of her next to
him on the blanket? Or self-loathing for the weakness of the
flesh no strong man could control?

Whatever it was, it seemed to pass, for suddenly he reached
out, pulling her down beside him.

A sickening sensation surged through her, a terrible, sinking feeling, like falling into a bottomless pit. She could feel
him against her, feel the heat of his breath, the man-roughness
of his cheeks. Any second now, she was sure he would kiss
her, sure she would feel the brutality of his mouth closing in
on hers, and there was nothing she could do to stop it.

Oh, Rafe, she thought miserably,—why can't it be your
arms around me now? Why can't it be your savage strength
crushing my body?

The thought was a bitter surrender, bringing with it the
poignant realization that no matter what he did to her, no
matter how he used her, there was only one man in the world
she would ever truly want. Floods of faintness swept over
her, mercifully dulling her senses, and she prayed that she
would swoon before she felt that terrible male hardness violat-
ing her body.

But the act she feared did not come.

Stunned, Kristyn lay back on the blanket, trying to make her
mind focus on what was happening. She had been so conscious of the weight of him before, heavy and oppressive on
top of her. Now all she could feel was the cold night air
touching her quivering flesh.

Slowly, more than a little apprehensive, she forced herself
to look up. He was standing a short distance away, his rigid
back only a faint outline as he stared off into the darkness. At
first, still numb with shock, she could not understand what he
was doing. Then she realized, and shame burned through her
body.

He did not want her. Even on that basic, primitive level,
the only level on which Rafe had ever accepted her, he did
not want her! He had tried to force himself, he had pressed
his body against hers in all the twisted postures of lovemaking,
but it had refused to function. He had not been able to make
himself harden for her!

She had failed even in that. Miserably, Kristyn turned her
head to the side, burying it in the rough wool of the blanket.
Totally, utterly—in every way!—she had failed to please this

man who had once loved her. Tears spilled out of her eyes,
dampening the coarsely woven fabric. She was not aware of
the exact moment he slipped away, for he moved so stealthily
she could not hear, but she sensed the emptiness he had left
behind and she knew she was alone.

Alone . . . The word had such a final sound. Little Bear
would not want her with him, not after tonight, and Rafe
would hardly take her back, even if she were ready to swallow her pride and return to him. She was alone, absolutely
alone, with no place to go, no one who would ever want her
again. Trapped in her own bitterness, she lay shivering in the
darkness, waiting in vain for sleep to come.

The moon was barely visible, half veiled by clouds that
grew denser every minute. Little Bear sat on a rocky ledge,
far above the barren ravine where he had left his young wife,
and stared up at the night sky with dark, impassive eyes.

She thought he did not want her.

The realization came as a surprise, for he had not sensed it
at the time, but looking back, he knew it was the only logical
possibility. He could see once again, as he had in that last
brief glance, the tears of her wounded spirit, and he understood now what she had been thinking. She was saying to
herself, *He does not want me.*

And yet, ironically, he *had* wanted her. The very moment
he had drawn back was the exact moment in which his body
had yielded, stiffening and throbbing in response to her seductive femininity. He had turned away—he smiled a little at the
childishness of the gesture—not only to hide the secrets of his
body, but those of his heart as well.

He shifted his weight, drawing one knee up and resting his
chin against it. So much of his life had been bound up with
this woman. So many of his memories were of her, so many
of the dreams that lay dormant but not quite dead beneath the
festering hatred in his heart.

Memories. Would he ever forget her helplessness that first
night? Her tears? The sudden bouts of shyness that prompted
her to bury her head in thick buffalo robes? And her eyes—
those magically, breathtakingly blue eyes. Even then they had
called out to something deep inside him, some instinctive
yearning to see and understand the mysteries of the world
beyond his own small village.

Memories. The wind whipping through her hair the day she first rode Fire-Wind; the glowing triumph on her face when she realized she had shown up every boy in the family! The night he learned his father was dead and she had sat across from him in the tepee, silently sharing his pain. The way her lips curled up in scorn when he dared to suggest she learn the white man's alphabet again, yet even then so naturally coquettish he knew he would be able to deny her nothing. Those same lips, parted just slightly the one time he came to her, tilting upward to accept his eager kiss.

That was the last time he had been with a woman. The other braves considered it their right to use the females who fell into their hands, humiliating them first, killing them afterward, and because he understood, he did not forbid it. But for himself, he never shared in those brutal passions. It was not that he did not want to. His body felt the same driving need as theirs when he looked down at a white woman in the dirt with her skirts flung up over her head, but his mind had never been able to accept the ugliness of the act. His mind, and that intangible something the missionaries had taught him to call his soul.

Perhaps, he thought, stretching his legs out on the ground in front of him, that was what had happened tonight. His body had been filled with those same hungers, but something in his mind, his heart—his soul—had rebelled.

He had wanted her, and yet it was not *her* he wanted at all, not the pretty woman who lay docile and rigid in his arms. He had wanted the little girl who first stirred manlike feelings of protectiveness in his heart, the breathless maiden who trusted him enough to let him touch her breasts beneath the buffalo robe, the sweetly sensuous bride who gave his troubled life the only moments of perfection he had ever known. He wanted the past with all its pains and joys and flaws, and if he could not have that, he would take nothing at all.

He got up and moved over to the edge of the embankment, staring down at the pine groves brooding on the lower slopes. It had been on a night like tonight, a hill like this, when he first realized that the world, *his* world, was coming to an end. He had stood alone then, too, recalling as he was now, the strange, haunted look on Brave Eagle's face when he had told the young warrior his wife was gone.

He had misread the look then, but he did not misread now.

The pain he had seen in those dark eyes was not the pain of regret or disillusionment—it was the pain of loving too much. They had given her up, the man and woman who had raised her—they had given up the one thing that added savor to their lives—and they had done it because they loved her.

Would he have understood if they had been able to tell him that night? Would he have sat with them beside the fire and talked calmly of the matter, agreeing in the end that they had done the right thing?

Somehow, he doubted it. He remembered the young man he had been then, idealistic, impulsive, ready to trust in life, and he doubted it. He had been too young, too full of romantic daydreams, to accept a loss like that so easily. He would have been sure that everything would be all right if only he could keep her at his side.

He would have been sure—and he would have been wrong.

Dense clouds drifted across the moon, darkening the earth, intensifying the silence. Because they had loved the girl, Brave Eagle and his wife had found the words to make her leave. And if *he* loved her—if there was anything left of the gentler emotions that once touched him, any reverence for the memories that had come to him tonight—he, too, would send her away. She did not belong here, not in a dying world with dying men driven by hate. She belonged in a world that held a future.

It would be hard, he knew, to find the way. Hard not only because she was clever enough to see what he was doing, but because something in his heart, like that something in his body, longed to lie beside her again, feeling the warmth of her next to him, listening to the sound of the wind rustling through the leaves around them.

The ground felt cold as he sat down again, surrendering for those last hours of the night to memories of other days, other emotions. He had not thought good thoughts for so long, he had not felt even the echoes of tenderness in his heart, and he knew he never would again. There was, in him, a bittersweet sense of both the ridiculousness of the world and the beauty of it, the continuity and the inevitability, and he leaned back on the unyielding earth, letting himself experience the last softness he would ever know.

*   *   *

Kristyn was waiting for him when he came back to the camp shortly before dawn. She was dressed in the clothes he had told her to wear, but she had taken her long braids and wound them around her head, tying them in place with strips of fabric torn from her dress, and she knew she looked more like a white woman than ever.

She started to rise when she saw him, then hesitated, squatting down again to poke at the ashes of yesterday's fire, even though they had long since gone out. She heard him come over, crouching beside her, but she could not bring herself to look up.

It was left to Little Bear to break the silence.

"Are you still determined to prove you are a Cheyenne?"

She glanced up, startled by the words she had not expected. Something in his features made her more uneasy than ever. If he had been angry, she could have dealt with that, contemptuous, coldly withdrawn. But all she could see was a kind of quiet weariness.

"Yes, of course," she replied softly. "If you will let me."

"You understand it is not going to be easy."

"Yes, I understand."

"How quickly you answer, without even thinking." His lips turned up just slightly at the corners, not mocking as she had expected, but gentle, almost pitying.

"Very well, if you are certain. Go and get your horse ready. You will be riding with us today."

"Riding . . . with you?"

The first hints of apprehension tugged at Kristyn's heart, though she could not have said why. There was nothing ominous in those words, nothing forbidding, and yet . . .

"I told you," he reminded her quietly, "the way we have chosen for ourselves is not easy. If you are going to share it with us, then you must share . . . *everything*."

"Everything?" The emphasis in his voice was frighteningly clear, but Kristyn, shivering in that first dawn chill, tried one last time to deny it. "I—I don't understand what you mean."

His eyes turned hard.

"Yes, you do—you know perfectly well what I mean."

And, oh, she *did* know! Kristyn felt so weak suddenly she was afraid she was going to faint. It was monstrous, this thing he expected of her. Unthinkable. It went against everything she cared about, everything she believed in.

And yet, God help her, it was not unreasonable. Not really. If she did want to be his wife, if she wanted to share his life, then she *was* going to have to share it completely. She was going to have to prove that she could not only garb herself in buckskin and do her hair up in braids, she could be a Cheyenne in her heart as well.

"Very well," she said, her voice dull and expressionless. "I will go with you."

Thirty-Six

They rode out of the ravine an hour later, a dozen lean, dark-skinned braves and one woman, formed into a silent column. The sun had just eased over the horizon, and it lay on top of distant hills, shimmering and red, hinting at showers later in the day.

This can't be happening, Kristyn thought numbly. It can't! The whole thing had to be a dream, a terrible nightmare from which she would awaken at any minute to find her body drenched in sweat and her mind clear at last. It couldn't be real.

And yet it was.

Kristyn forced her eyes straight ahead as they passed out of the ravine onto narrow forest paths. It *was* real, and there was no way she could pretend it wasn't. She had known the minute Little Bear ordered her to ride with them exactly what he had in mind. And she had known how it was going to feel.

Every detail of that last agonizing hour was vivid in her memory. Little Bear had not spoken again but had gone to the place where he kept the horses and, gathering together his gear, he had set off in search of an icy mountain pool. Not wanting to be left behind, Kristyn had followed, lingering a short distance away as he knelt on a frayed square of buckskin and began his sacred preparations.

First he had taken dried, ground-up puccoon root out of a small leather sack and mixed it with water in a tin cup from the white man's trading post. When he had worked it into a thick red paste, he smeared it on his chest and shoulders, rubbing it into his skin until he looked as if he had been saturated with the blood of his enemies. Then he mixed the remaining pigments, decorating his face with the symbols that would proclaim to friend and foe alike who he was.

Kristyn watched, intrigued in spite of herself, as he took up a heavy brush fashioned from a buffalo tail and drew a blue-black circle around his face, filling it in with yellowish pigment. Against this backdrop, he scrawled out the simple pictures Cheyenne warriors had used from the beginning of time. Five dots below the left eye. That meant he had been born near the water and still, in his heart, considered it his home. Next a crow's foot across his forehead, marking him as a man who dwelled in the forest. Then at last the lines she had both expected and dreaded—bold red lines from his eyes to the lobes of his ears, three red lines on his chin.

The lines that meant war.

Kristyn raised her hand abruptly, trying to block the image out of her mind as she daubed at beads of perspiration on her forehead. She hated herself for being there, hated the cowardice that made her ride tight-lipped and silent in that grim procession, but she was bitterly aware that she had no alternatives. Not if she wanted to remain with her husband.

If only it was the Blue Coats they were after! The thought gave her a fleeting moment of hope. If it was the Blue Coats, she would not mind so much. There was something about the sight of a uniform that made the whole business more impersonal, turning a man from an individual with hopes and feelings into a hated soldier. If it was the Blue Coats, she could close her eyes and think of that camp across the stream and she would not be so afraid of the shrieks of the attackers or the shrill screams of the dying.

But as she followed the warriors around one last looping trail and looked down into a secluded valley, she realized with sinking heart that even that small comfort was to be denied her. One glance at the trim little farmhouse set in the midst of carefully tended fields was enough to tell her how cruelly her husband had planned her initiation into the ways of Cheyenne warfare. If he had deliberately set out to find the harshest way possible to test her loyalty, he could not have done any better.

The house had been built of simple planking. Like most of the structures in the area, it had not gone untouched by the severe climate, but the residents had made an effort to maintain it, and it showed a touching pride of ownership. The exterior sported a fresh coat of paint, crisp white with an even crisper green trim, and the windows had been washed and polished until they gleamed. A white picket fence ran around the front yard, closing it in, and jaunty rows of pansies tilted their whimsical faces up to the sun.

Oh, please, Kristyn thought, her stomach turning with alarm—*please* don't let this happen. She did not know which god she was praying to, the stern white god she had learned to know in that quiet chapel in Santa Fe or the more colorful gods of her Indian childhood. She only knew she could not bear what was about to happen.

The warriors had already dismounted and even now they were moving stealthily along the shallow ridge, scouting out positions for themselves. Kristyn, catching the disapproving glances that one of them sent her way, hastily followed their lead, slipping off her own horse and handing it over to one of the younger braves. By the time she turned back again they were already in place, some squatting behind rocks and shrubbery, others stretching out full length in the tall grasses.

Kristyn hesitated. Then, spotting a wall of solid gray stone that jutted out of the earth, she slipped impulsively behind it. She was not sure she wanted to be that close—it terrified her to think of what she might see—but whatever it was, it could not be as brutal and agonizing as the things she would imagine, crouched by herself in the background with the noise of slaughter all around her.

It was still early in the morning and the house looked like it was only half awake. Lacy curtains fluttered in the windows and a dusty red chicken scampered across the porch, cackling self-importantly as it flapped its wings in the sunlight. Then, as Kristyn watched, the door opened and a woman stuck her head out, glancing toward the barn.

She was so young.

The thought caught in Kristyn's throat, making it hard to breath. She was so very young—no older than Kristyn herself. Her body looked slender and delicate in a gingham dress, half a size too big, and her hair, tucked into a neat bun at the nape of her neck, was a deep reddish-brown.

Sick with despair, Kristyn turned her head to the side, filled with loathing for whatever part she was about to play in that shameful business.

It's not as if I could do anything about it! she thought

unhappily. It was much too late to warn the people inside the house. It would mean almost certain death to try! Yet the mere fact of being there, of watching without protest—didn't that give her a share in the guilt? Wasn't she as responsible in her own way as the men who wielded the guns?

A slight sound from somewhere behind caught her ear, and welcoming the distraction, Kristyn turned to see that the horses had been tethered a short distance away. One of them, a spirited filly, was tossing her mane playfully into the wind, making little snorting noises as she did.

What carelessness!

A wave of anger swept over Kristyn, and she seized on it gratefully, using it to drive everything else out of her mind. Why, those horses would be right in the line of fire if someone got out of the house and made a run for it! She could not imagine who had tied them there, but she knew what Little Bear would say. Glad to have found something useful to do, she slipped out of her hiding place and crept stealthily toward the fallen log where he had taken his stand.

"The horses, Little Bear," she called out in an undertone as she squeezed in beside him. "Someone left them just over there. Within range of the guns."

Little Bear had been checking his rifle when she approached. Now he lowered it to throw her an impatient look.

"*Out* of gun range," he corrected. "And if things go my way, they'll stay out of range. At any rate, that's where I want them. I picked the place myself."

"*You* picked it?" Kristyn gaped at him in shock. "But your own horse is among them! Fire-Wind! And what do you mean, *if* things go your way? You know perfectly well you can't count on that. Oh, Little Bear, couldn't we take them farther down the hill? Then, no matter what happens, they're certain to be out of range."

"Out of sight, too," he reminded her, raising his gun to examine it one last time. "Don't forget, Billy Collins has been working this area, and working it thoroughly, too. I'm not about to turn my horses over to him."

"But that's—that's *illogical*!" If she hadn't been so frightened, Kristyn would have been tempted to laugh. "Why, Billy isn't . . ." She caught herself just in time, recalling suddenly that Little Bear knew nothing about her friendship with the famous outlaw. "Billy Collins is not likely to be anywhere near this place. There are no towns here, no stage routes—why, it isn't even on the way to someplace else. The chances against his just happening by are astronomical. But if someone breaks out of that house——"

"Also unlikely, as I'm sure you've figured out by now. But if they do, they do, that's all. It's a risk I'm ready to take. I'll lose every horse in the crossfire if I have to. But I'll be damned if I'll let a white man ride away on a one of them!"

"A white man?" Kristyn was so discouraged she could have cried. "Is that what this is about? Not what's best for the animals? Just a guarantee that no one with the wrong color skin will ever get a hold of them! Are you so steeped in hate, you would let a horse—your *own* horse—die before you'd see a white man on its back?"

Little Bear raised his head, his eyes unnaturally dark against the yellow mask of his face.

"No white man will ever come near my horse. Once you would have known that. Now you're so far removed from the ways of a Cheyenne, you have forgotten how to understand. You have lost all feeling for the old days. A man's horse is a part of him. What he wants for himself, he wants for his mount—and for myself, I would choose death over dishonor. Yes, and I choose it for Fire-Wind, too!"

"You can't mean that!" The rebuke had struck home, bringing tears to Kristyn's eyes, but she was determined not to let him see. She *did* remember the old days, but a part of what she remembered was how much she had loved her horse. "If you really cared for Fire-Wind—if he meant anything to you at all—you would never say that. You wouldn't even think it!"

"Wouldn't I? I was right about you, you know. You *have* forgotten. Caring for a horse—or a person for that matter—doesn't always mean doing the easy thing. If Fire-Wind broke his leg and I had to destroy him, would you commend me for putting him out of his pain? Someday, perhaps you will learn that there is more than one kind of pain in the world. The day before I die, I promise you this—I will take Fire-Wind out and shoot him with my own hand."

"Oh, Little Bear . . ." Kristyn leaned forward, resting her cheek against the rough log. "You're not even being rational. That doesn't make sense. How can you say what you are going to do the day before you die? You live wildly, dangerously—you could die at any time. You aren't going to know about it in advance.''

He studied her steadily for a long, silent moment.

"I will know," he said at last. Then, without another word, he turned back to his gun, propping it up on the log and squinting down the barrel.

Fascinated, Kristyn watched. Was he really as sure as he sounded? she wondered. Perhaps. She had lived with the Indians long enough to know there were mysteries in the human spirit that went beyond her comprehension. How many times had she seen an old person sit down and sing his death song only to die within hours. Perhaps it would be that way for Little Bear, too.

Only if it was, would there still be so much anger in his heart he would want everything he had loved to die with him?

She did not have time to ponder the question, for suddenly Little Bear's head snapped up and his body stiffened as he focused on something in the yard. Following his gaze, Kristyn saw that the woman had opened the door again. A man was coming toward her from the direction of the barn with a milk pail in one hand. The weight of it threw him off balance, and he walked clumsily, lurching a little to one side.

Oh, no, she thought. No—it can't be starting! Not yet!

But the words had barely flashed across her mind when she heard a gunshot, and she knew that it had. The man did not have time to realize what was happening. The bullet caught him in the chest, jerking him backward as if he had been pulled on invisible strings. Then he toppled to the earth, the milk splashing out in a pool around him before it sank into the soil.

In the split second before she turned away, Kristyn saw the woman move, her arms stretching out as she started forward. Hands clutched at her from behind, dragging her into the house.

Stay there! Kristyn pleaded, the words shaped but silent on her lips. Stay! Don't go out again—there's nothing you can do! But even as she thought it, she sensed the woman's dilemma, and her heart bled for her. If that were Rafe out there, if that were the man she loved lying dead or dying in the dirt, could any power on earth have kept her from going to him?

A volley of gunfire flared out briefly, most of it coming from the hills, but a few answering shots echoed from inside the house. The silence that followed was broken only by the loud clucking of the chicken on the porch, a ludicrous sound, almost comical in the midst of all that violence. Then a gun snapped again, and even the chicken was still.

Kristyn huddled against the log, conscious of the feel of rotting wood, the smell of decay in her nostrils. Why was it, she wondered, that she minded so much that the chicken was dead? It would only have been killed anyway to go into the stewing pot. A dog started to bark, a small frightened *yap-yap, yap-yap, yap-yap,* faintly muffled, as if it came from inside the barn.

At least she was not expected to fight with the men. Kristyn crouched beside Little Bear in the shelter of the fallen log and thought how grateful she was that ammunition was scarce and he had not trusted her with a gun. That humiliation, at least, would not be hers. She would not take a direct part in this disgusting spectacle.

And it was disgusting! These people had done nothing to deserve their fates. They were innocent, as innocent as Corn Woman that morning in the camp across the stream. As innocent as the unborn babe in the belly of Wades-in-the-Water's pregnant sister. Kristyn tried not to remember the look on the woman's face, that brief moment she had seen her in the doorway, but she could not drive it out of her mind. She had looked so pretty, so youthful, so full of eagerness for the day that lay ahead.

It was all so pointless! Where was it going to end if things like this kept happening? Wrongs had been committed on both sides, terrible evils by whites against the Indians, equally terrible ones by Indians in the name of retribution. All that anger and bitterness, and innocent people were dying every day!

The gunfire continued, but only sporadically, and Kristyn sensed that the defenders inside the house were as short on ammunition as their attackers. That they had returned fire so quickly told her they kept their weapons loaded and ready at hand, but if they had had a sure supply of ammunition, they would have gone on the offensive, blazing out with explosive fury. As it was, they were cautious, firing only when they caught a hint of movement in the rocky hills surrounding them.

Little Bear's body tensed suddenly, and Kristyn sensed that something had happened. Glancing over, she saw that he had lowered his gun and was staring at the fields beyond the house. Half curious, half frightened, she raised her head above the log and peered down into the shallow valley.

At first she could make out nothing. The fighting was still going on, but half-heartedly now, as if everyone had agreed to a respite, and what little action there was seemed to be centered on the side of the house that faced the barn. Only when she turned to the opposite side, where cornfields came within a few feet of the whitewashed fence, did she realize what was happening.

All she saw was a flicker of motion, barely noticeable, but the instant her eyes picked it out, she knew what it was. One of the braves had washed the warpaint from his body and was weaving through the cornstalks toward the house. The dark skin on his chest and shoulders provided an almost perfect camouflage, and Kristyn would not even have noticed him had she not caught occasional flashes of golden-red, like bursts of reflected sunlight.

Only that was not sunlight she saw! He was carrying a flaming torch in his hand.

He lingered for a second at the edge of the cornfield, then leaped boldly out into the open. All Kristyn needed was one glimpse of those sharply chiseled features to recognize her old suitor, Running Deer. He had always had a quality of bravado about him, and now he seemed almost defiantly reckless. In spite of herself, she could not help thrilling to the sight of him, a tall man, dynamic, daring to stand alone with a torch in his hand in full view of every window on that side of the house.

The tension lasted for the space of a heartbeat. Then, raising his torch in the air, Running Deer whirled it with savage force at a pile of dried branches and refuse in a corner of the yard. With a whoop of triumph, he dove back into the fields, burying his half-naked body in the anonymous yellow-brown of the corn.

Unable to tear her eyes away, Kristyn stared with horror at the torch. For one second, one brief second, it flickered feebly. Then, with a dazzling burst of light it took hold, and flames leaped into the air, blistering the paint on the side of the house.

Shadows flitted past the windows, curtains moved with no pretense at secrecy now, and Kristyn, watching from her vantage point, could almost feel the frenzy of those people inside as they gathered everything they could to fight the fire—buckets of water, milk, old blankets to beat it back, thick winter coats. But their efforts were to no avail. Within seconds, hot tongues of flame ate through the window frames, cracking the glass with their heat. Within minutes, the entire structure was a blazing inferno, and the terrified defenders had been driven out into the open.

They came out in a small group, huddled together. It seemed to Kristyn there were three of them, perhaps four, but the smoke was so thick, she could not be sure. The warriors had begun deserting their battle stations, knives clenched in their teeth as they raced down the hill and threw themselves into that inky haze.

Only periodically did the smoke swirl away, offering isolated details to Kristyn's horrified gaze. An old man, his hair white but his spirit undaunted, raised his hand to one of the younger braves, trying to club him with the butt of his gun, but the smoke grew heavy again and she could not see what happened. A young boy, no more than a teenager, broke off from the others, running toward the barn—toward shelter? she wondered. She saw one of the braves go after him, but everything else was lost. Then suddenly, as if from nowhere, a small terrier scurried into sight, yapping frantically at sounds and smells he could not understand.

"Oh, no—not the dog, too!"

The words were out of Kristyn's mouth before she realized she had uttered them. She knew they were foolish, frivolous—how could anyone fret about a dog when human lives were being sacrificed?—but she could not help herself. It seemed a symbol of everything that was evil in what the warriors were doing. That they might choose to kill one white man for what another had done was something she could half understand, remembering her own emotions that morning in the camp across the stream. But did their pent-up hatred extend to the white man's pets as well?

As if in answer, one of the braves spun around suddenly, catching sight of the terrier. The noise seemed to irritate him, or perhaps he was keyed up from that charge down the hill. Raising his tomahawk, he whirled it around his head, then hurled it at the dog. Kristyn's heart stopped beating for the second it took that deadly missive to soar through the air, then started again as she saw it slice into the dirt a few inches from the animal. With a yelp of terror, he turned tail and ran whimpering for the hills.

The brief drama had engrossed Kristyn's attention so completely she had not seen or heard anything else. Now, turning back toward the smoldering ruins of the house, she saw that the smoke had begun to clear and the quick, savage battle was over. The old man had lost his fight with the warrior, and he was lying on the ground with nothing but redness where thick white hair had once grown. A short distance away, the boy was curled up in an almost fetal position, looking even younger than he had before.

It was a moment before Kristyn realized that the woman's body was not among the others. Casting her eyes around the yard, she saw that one of the younger braves, a youth she could not recognize beneath sweat-streaked warpaint, had dragged her over to the side of the barn. She was struggling desperately, fighting with almost unnatural strength to free herself, but it was not the expression of fear on her features that sent a chill down Kristyn's spine. It was the look on the face of the man who held her.

"Oh, my God, he's going to—to . . ."

She caught her breath, unable even to whisper that terrible word. Rape. Ugly at any time, brutal—now it seemed doubly inhumane. The woman had already endured enough. Did she have to suffer this final degradation as well?

Anguished, Kristyn turned to Little Bear, ready to beg for his help. But the plea died on her lips the instant she caught sight of him. He had laid down his rifle and had a pistol grasped in one hand, a knife blade between his teeth, as he stared down at the barnyard with the hardest eyes she had ever seen.

He knows! she thought helplessly. He knows exactly what that man is going to do. He knows because he's seen it before!

And if he hadn't done anything to stop it then, he wasn't going to stop it now.

Her eyes were drawn back toward the spot where the

woman, surprisingly, was still holding off her attacker. For just an instant she seemed to get away, twisting out of his grasp and running a few steps toward the road. But with a loud "Hah!" he reached out and caught her, dragging her back so violently her bodice was torn away, exposing small, barely formed young breasts.

That savage grunt carried across the yard, and the others began to circle around, moving warily, like wolves closing in for the kill. Shivering, Kristyn realized that the woman could expect no mercy from any of them. All they could see were soft, pale breasts, filling them not with pity for her girlishness, but only a lust that was tied in with the blood of battle and the need of warriors to prove their virility. Her hair had come loose, tumbling thick, auburn-red to her waist, and her eyes—oh, why did they have to be blue?—were wide and frightened.

Why, that might be me, Kristyn thought, mesmerized by the woman's coloring, her extreme youthfulness. That might be me down there, terrified, not knowing what to do!

Suddenly all her fear, her disgust, exploded in a burst of anger. What was she thinking of, letting this happen? She had been a coward before. She had stood by, watching everything that took place, telling herself there was nothing she could do. But she would stand by no longer! She would not be a witness to this!

Glancing back at Little Bear, her eye fell on his rifle, a foot or two away on the ground. Horrified, she realized there was one way she could help the woman.

It was not what she would have chosen, God knows—it was the last thing she wanted—but there was nothing else she could do. Gripping the gun, she began to draw it toward her, moving stealthily so Little Bear would not see what she was doing.

By the time she had it in her hand and turned back to the barn, the woman was already on the ground, her gingham skirt torn away from convulsively twitching legs. Choking back her nausea, Kristyn braced the gun against the log and sighted down the barrel, aiming at that pale, childlike bosom.

There was no way she could save the woman's life. Even were she an expert marksman, she could not take on the entire band. One way or another, she was going to die. But at least she could die quickly.

Kristyn's hand felt numb as she forced her finger to tighten around the trigger. Taking a long, deep breath, she willed herself to squeeze—and found she could not move!

Oh, why is it so hard? she asked herself desperately. Why? I have to do this thing. I have to! Why can't I find the strength?

Then, suddenly, hands came down on top of hers, wrenching the gun out of her grasp, and she realized the chance was gone.

Coward! she cursed herself furiously. To watch a family being slaughtered was one thing when their salvation was not in her power. But to do nothing to ease a dying woman in her last moment of pain? How could she live with that?

Sick with shame, she looked up, expecting to see angry eyes blazing down at her. But to her surprise, Little Bear had turned away, concentrating his gaze once again on that ugly scene in the barnyard. But this time, instead of watching impassively, he raised his rifle to his shoulder and fired.

The sound exploded in Kristyn's ears. Her whole body went limp, and she clasped her hands over her face, trembling as much with anguish as relief now that the deed was done. She was bitterly aware of the feminine weakness of tears, pouring down her cheeks, and she knew Little Bear must despise her for it, but she could not find the strength to resist. So much had happened today, so many emotions had raced turbulently through her breast, she did not even know how she felt anymore.

At least the dog had gotten away.

The thought surprised her, leaping unexpectedly into her mind. It was idiotic, thinking of something like that, trying to find comfort in a situation where no comfort existed. But idiotic or not, there it was—she had to have something positive, something hopeful, to cling to. At least the woman had not suffered any more than she had to, and the dog had gotten away.

Kristyn buried her head deeper in her hands, conscious of Little Bear beside her. What would he say if he knew what she was thinking? Compassion for a white man's dog? No doubt it would be one more sin in his eyes.

But a dog, after all, was just a dog. Could he be expected to recognize color in the hand that fed him? No, she could not hate one small terrier just because he begged for scraps in the barn of a white man instead of outside an Indian teepee. All she could hope was that he would not be too bewildered when he slunk back out of the woods at dinner time and found only smoking ruins where the house had once stood and no one there to feed him.

It was several minutes before she finally looked up. When she did, she saw that Little Bear was still there, squatting beside her in the dirt. There was in his eyes none of the contempt she had expected, only a kind of gentleness—a little pitying, a little sad.

"You knew all along, didn't you?"

The remark might have been enigmatic to anyone else, but he seemed to understand.

"Yes," he said quietly. "I knew."

They needed no words between them at that moment, just as once, before time had slipped away from them, they were sometimes so close each seemed to sense what the other was thinking. He had known that morning when he ordered her to come with him how she was going to react. But he had known, too, that she did not yet understand these things for herself.

"I guess I am not as much of a Cheyenne as I thought."

He did not reply, but turned instead to his gun, absorbing himself in the task of cleaning it with a filthy rag he had taken from his pack. When at last he glanced up, it was almost as an afterthought.

"I offered you a canteen and a horse once. You should have taken them then. I suggest you do so now."

He did not wait for her answer; indeed, he did not seem to expect one as he involved himself again with his gun. Kristyn, watching in silence, sensed that he had seen the faint quiver in her lips, seen, too, the pain and embarrassment behind it, and she was grateful to him for understanding that she would welcome privacy to slip away unseen. They had already said everything they had to say, felt everything there was to feel—their true good-byes to each other had come long ago. Further words between them now, further looks, whether of pity or reproach, could only add to the hurt they both felt.

Little Bear had been right. Kristyn headed toward the spot where the horses were still tethered. Fire-Wind whimpered a greeting, but she resisted the impulse to throw her arms around his neck and bury her head in that thick red mane.

Like the man who now rode him, this horse belonged to her past. She had to let go of them both.

He had been so very right. She was a white woman now, not just white in the way she dressed or the fashionable pallor of her skin, but white in the way she looked at things, the way she felt and responded. It was more than a few months of sleeping on clean linen sheets and eating off of china plates with silver knives and spoons that separated her from her past; it was a sense of having come home again to a world she had left for a while but never completely abandoned in her heart.

She did not think like a Cheyenne anymore. She could see what was happening to the people who had once been her people, and her heart ached for them, but she no longer had the urge to throw herself into that terrible maelstrom and drown with them. She would always deplore the cruel, inhumane things that whites had done to the Indians. She would never think of that sad little camp across the stream without feeling sick with disgust—only she would be just as sick when she thought of today! She could not bring herself to hate every white man for what a few had done, any more than she could hate every brave for the anguish of that one woman in the dust. There was simply no hate left in her. She had seen too much, suffered too much, for that.

And yet . . .

She hesitated, throwing one last backward glance over her shoulder. Little Bear was still where she had left him, still engrossed in his gun, as if he had forgotten she was there.

And yet, there was something in her that was Cheyenne, too. Some secret part of her heart that would not let her slip away so easily. Would she always grieve, she wondered, when she heard the wind howling through the trees at night? When she caught the scent of pine, fresh and pungent in the air? Or would she forget in time the wildness of her youth, the freedom of a world that was gone forever, and learn to sleep comfortably in sturdy brick houses with doors that locked behind her and windows that could be shut at night?

Thirty-Seven

The sky was overcast, but the rains that had been threatening off and on all afternoon did not materialize, and as Kristyn rode slowly down the curving main street of a small mountain town, her horse's hooves left a film of dust behind her.

She had no idea what the place was called. And in truth, she thought, wrinkling her nose slightly with distaste, I don't think I care! She would have to take shelter there tonight, but she was going to be only too happy to clear out in the morning. Everywhere she looked, paint was peeling off of weathered grayish buildings, and the only people visible were a handful of ruffians lounging indolently on dilapidated boardwalks.

Well, maybe it's just as well, she reminded herself as she dismounted and threw her reins over a convenient hitching post. Dressed as she was in faded denims and a sweaty Indian tunic, she would be much too conspicuous anyplace else. Here she would blend in with the crowd.

She hesitated for a moment, glancing up and down the narrow street. What little cash she had brought with her had been lost with her luggage at the stage, and she knew she was at a disadvantage, arriving in a strange town without a cent in her pockets. She might be able to coax a kindhearted stablekeeper to let her burrow into a pile of straw for the night, but finding a meal was going to be something else again.

She had not made up her mind what to do when a rasping voice broke into her thoughts.

"Hey, girlie, what are you, an Injun or something?"

Looking around, Kristyn saw a man sitting on the edge of

the low wooden walkway. He was about fifty, perhaps older, with grizzled side whiskers obscuring part of his face.

"Are you addressing me?" She made her voice cool and imperious, determined to discourage any further contact. "Because if you are, sir, I have to warn you, I am not used to being accosted by strangers on the street."

"Sir, is it?" He broke into a broad grin, showing a partial set of browning teeth. "Hoo-ey! Will ya look at that? Dressed like a piece o' trash an' it talks like a duchess. I ain't never seen an Injun that was royal before."

"I never claimed to be royal," Kristyn snapped. It had been a long, hot ride, and she had gone through as much as she could handle for one day. "And if you think I'm an Indian, then you must be colorblind. When have you seen an Indian with red hair—or blue eyes?"

"Hell, ain't it a spitfire? Hey, Jake, c'mere!" He gestured broadly to a man across the way. "A red-headed bitch with a red-headed temper! Always wanted me a woman like that!"

"You always wanted a woman, period," the man called Jake replied as he came over to squint at Kristyn with pale gray eyes. He was younger than the other man and well built, but his clothes were filthy and there was a noticeable odor about him. "I ain't never heard it said Will Gatley was particular when it came to females, red-headed or otherwise. Still—" he let his gaze slide down Kristyn's body— "looks like you might've got yourself one now. Mebbe we both have."

Kristyn took a step backward, recoiling from eyes that had an unpleasant knack of seeming to see right through her clothing. Sensing that further conversation, even a cutting retort, would only encourage him, she turned and strode down the street, trying to look as if she knew where she was going. If this was what every man in town was like, she was going to wish she had foraged for roots on the hillside and spent the night under a blanket of pine needles!

But Jake was not so easily discouraged. As Kristyn hurried along, she was uncomfortably aware of footsteps behind her, almost exactly matching her own. She had just crossed a narrow side street when he sprinted forward, throwing himself in front of her.

"Now where are you goin', little lady?" He grinned.

"That ain't polite, walkin' away when someone's talkin' to you."

Kristyn tried to get past him, but he sidestepped adroitly, cutting her off. The gesture was almost deliberately menacing, and she felt herself begin to grow frightened, even though it was broad daylight and the street was filled with people.

"I wasn't trying to be polite!" she retorted, tossing her head defiantly. "As for where I'm going, that's none of your business! Now if you will step aside and let me——"

"I ain't gonna do that, an' we both know it." His voice hardened as he leaned closer, the smell of him distinct now in her nostrils. "You look right purty when your eyes snap like that. I think me an' old Will are gonna have a real good time. An' don't you worry none, we ain't as poor as we look. You be nice to us, we'll make it worth your while."

Kristyn gasped. Could this man really think that every woman alone on the street was up for sale, and all he had to do was fix the price? Suddenly, she could not bear to look at him any longer, and she began to retrace her steps.

She had gone only a short distance when she saw Will Gatley standing in the center of the boardwalk just ahead of her, a knowing leer spreading across his features. Disgusted, she turned into the side street, eager to be quit of them both.

She realized her mistake instantly, for the narrow lane in which she found herself was shadowy and deserted, but it was too late to turn back. Even without glancing over her shoulder she knew that Jake had begun to follow her, and she forced herself to keep moving, stumbling awkwardly in her haste.

Then suddenly the pathway twisted around a corner, and to Kristyn's horror she saw it deadend in a large, cluttered storage yard. Sturdy wooden planks fenced it in, much too high to climb, and the only opening was the one through which she had just come.

Whirling around, she saw that Jake was already standing in the entrance, his feet slightly apart, as if to brace himself in case she tried to run. His upper lip was raised, giving a glimpse of long, slightly pointed teeth, and Kristyn sensed he was laughing.

He knew this was going to happen! she thought suddenly. That's why he picked that particular place to stop me. He knew I would only have one way to run. And that's why he said those awful things! So I would react just the way I did!

He had set a trap. And like a fool, she had walked into it!

"You don't want to do this," she whispered hoarsely. "Please—there must be plenty of women who are willing. Please—*please*—don't hurt me."

The wrong move! She knew it the instant the words were out of her mouth. His eyes seemed to glisten, his nostrils flared slightly. Like an animal! she thought, horrified. And like an animal, he had scented her fear!

She wanted to scream, but suddenly she was afraid. She could not help remembering the ruffians she had seen on the street, men as crude as this one. If she called out, would her cries bring help, or only more bestial male lusts to abuse her flesh?

Jake seemed to sense her hesitance and, sure of himself now, he accepted it as acquiescence.

"That's right, little lady, you got the idea. No sense kickin' up a fuss. I'm going to do what I want anyhow. Might as well relax and enjoy it."

"Me, too, Jake," a second voice wheezed. Sickened, Kristyn saw that Gatley had moved in behind the other man, his breath coming in short gasps. "Don't forget about me. I get my share, too."

He's panting! she thought, disgusted. He's actually panting! Her skin crawled as he moved closer, stopping only when Jake thrust out a warning hand.

"You stay back, Gatley. She's mine first. After I'm finished, you can do anything that feeble little brain o' yours can imagine. Hell, I wouldn't worry none. Looks to me like there's plenty o' meat on them bones for both of us."

The remark seemed to amuse Gatley for he began to laugh, an odd, snorting sound that came out of his nose. Anger mingled suddenly with Kristyn's revulsion, releasing her from the blind panic that had held her immobile. So they thought they could use her, did they, like some creature with no sensitivities or feelings of her own! Well, they might be stronger than she—the battle might be two against one—but she was going to put up a fight!

"The first one of you that comes near me," she said in low, telling tones, "I'll kill him!"

"Well, now, ain't you the feisty one?" Jake clicked his

tongue against the roof of his mouth, but he did not try to move closer. "Shit, that's all right with me. A little spice always makes the meat taste better, don't it, Will? Tell you what we're going to do." He turned toward the older man. "You get behind her and grab her arms. Grab 'em real tight, you hear? You hold her for me, and I'll do the same for you. If there's any fight left in her when I'm through."

Kristyn caught her breath, daring for the first time since she had stumbled into that dismal alleyway to hope.

"You don't think you're man enough to hold me yourself?" she taunted boldly.

He looked angry for a second, then started slowly to grin.

"I'm man enough to do what I have to . . . and that's all that counts. Go on, Will—grab her!"

It worked! Kristyn felt a quick surge of triumph, but she was careful not to let it show as Gatley circled warily around her. She had fallen into Jake's trap before. Now he was falling into hers. If he had approached her himself, she would have been no match for his lean, wiry strength. But Will Gatley was older and out of shape.

She made no overt moves, standing still instead, trembling just slightly as he closed in behind her. Only when she felt him catch her arms, pinning her against his chest, did she raise her foot and, with one fluid motion, jab the heel of her boot into his kneecap.

A howl of pain burst out of his lips, and Kristyn felt the pressure on her arms release. Squirming free, she twisted toward the man, her hand sliding downward, searching for the butt of his pistol, whipping it out of his holster. Now, if she was just fast enough . . .

But as she whirled to face Jake, she saw that he had responded with terrifying speed. Even before she could raise the gun, strong fingers tightened around her wrist, twisting, wrenching, until the weapon flew from her grasp. His face reddened, contorting as much from anger as lust, and he doubled his hand into a fist, ramming it with sadistic force against the side of her head.

Reeling from the blow, Kristyn staggered dizzily, too numb with pain and faintness to hold her balance. This can't be happening to me, she thought as she felt herself sink help- lessly to the ground. It can't be! Reacting instinctively, forgetting everything else in that sudden rush of fear, she opened her mouth at last and began to scream.

Oh, please, someone hear me, she thought desperately. Please, *someone*—come and help before it's too late!

Calloused fingers clamped down on her mouth, choking off her breath, and Jake fell heavily on top of her, tugging at her tunic, working it up around her neck. She could feel the coarseness of his shirt against her flesh, feel him pawing her breasts, ripping the front of her pants open,—touching her.

Strange little sounds caught her ears, whimpers of fear, so soft and indistinct she did not even recognize them as her own. Then suddenly there was something else, another noise, one she could not place. But Jake seemed to know what it was, or sense it at least, for he pulled away abruptly, leaving her alone, trembling, on the ground.

All she could do was lie there, feeling the freedom of her body from that oppressive weight, knowing that somehow, miraculously, he was gone and the terrible nightmare was over.

Only slowly did she realize someone else was there, watching from nearby, looking down at her.

Apprehensively, she raised her eyes.

A soft gasp escaped her lips as she caught sight of a solitary man in the entrance of the yard, tall, broad-shouldered, lean-hipped, with a thick head of jet-black hair.

Rafe. . . ?

For just a second she dared to hope that he had followed her from Santa Fe, that she had been wrong about him all the time and he *did* care enough to come after her. But one look at those hard eyes, glittering like black fire in the darkness, was enough to warn her that whatever feelings he still had for her after she ran away had nothing to do with love.

Suddenly she was conscious of the way she must look to him, sprawled out in the dirt. Awkwardly, she made an attempt to adjust her clothing.

"I—I didn't expect to see you here," she murmured weakly.

"Obviously." He leaned against the fence, his thumbs looped through his gunbelt. "Though why it should surprise you to wander into Silver City and find me here, I don't know. I did mention I was coming—that last night we were together. Or did you mean," he added, drawling the words out with deliberately insulting sarcasm, "that you were surprised to find me *here*, in this alley. I hope I didn't interrupt anything—uh, amusing."

His words washed over her, making Kristyn feel as if she were drowning. What was he talking about? Silver City? The name did not sound even remotely familiar. And why was he being so harsh? He had been angry with her in the past, savagely angry sometimes, but never had he accused her of anything like this.

"How can you even suggest I find this amusing? You heard me scream—that's why you came! And you saw me trying to push that brute off my body. I didn't invite him to try to rape me, for heaven's sake!"

"You invite rape without even knowing it, sweetheart. There's something dangerous about you, a smoldering sensuality that men are bound to notice, whether you realize it or not. Besides, I might ask you what you were doing alone with those two men in a deserted alley if you didn't have this in mind."

"Oh!" Kristyn could hardly believe he was saying these things. She had never seen anything like that crazy jealousy of his, flaring up at the most preposterous moments. "You can accuse me of anything you like, Rafe Valero—and you probably will!—but even you can't claim I would go with men like that by choice! They were repulsive!"

"Yes, and you like them young and handsome, don't you?" He took a step toward her, then stopped. "Or perhaps . . . not so young."

He stood where he was, staring down at her, forcing himself to admit the bitter truth he had sensed the instant he saw her. There was only one reason why she could have come to Silver City, and it wasn't to see him!

"I seem to have a propensity for finding you with other men. Last time you were struggling against the 'unwanted' advances of Ricardo Cuervo."

Cuervo again! Kristyn thought with a rush of helplessness. Why was it that every time they quarreled, it always came back to Cuervo, even when it was totally illogical?

"Yes, I was with Cuervo then—and I *was* fighting."

"So you say. But you'll forgive me if I find that hard to swallow. I can't help remembering an occasion when you fought me off, too. Yet only a short time later, there you were in my hotel room, taking off your clothes in one of the most provocative stripteases I've ever seen."

He paused, his eyes biting into her flesh.

"Is that what you had planned for Cuervo, too, the lucky devil? A little struggle to whet the appetite, and then—ah, sweet submission."

A dozen angry retorts rose to Kristyn's lips, but suddenly she was too tired, too discouraged, to argue any more. How could anyone reason with such unreasoning rage?

"Is that what you really think of me? That I am capable of such mindless, indiscriminate lust?"

"Frankly, I try not to think about it. What I *do* think, if you are really interested, is that I was a fool to marry you, strong-willed grandfather or no. Although . . ." He laughed harshly. ". . . I daresay even Don Diego is sorry now he pushed us on each other. Your running away created quite a stir, as I'm sure you can imagine. The El Valeroso name will never be the same again. Or the family pride."

The family pride. Kristyn let heavy lids close over her eyes. Was that why he was so angry? Not because he was jealous, but because his pride, family and personal, was on the line. If she could have sneaked away quietly, he probably would have been relieved, glad to be rid of her once and for all. But because she had done it publicly, he was raging like a wounded bull.

Well, she had her pride, too! There was a limit to how many times she could let him abuse her and not stand up for herself! She could never make him love her, she could not even keep him from hurting her—but she could keep him from knowing it! She could make him believe she didn't care any more than he did!

"All right, I admit it! I'm tired of pretending to be something I'm not! Of course there have been other lovers. I *do* have an insatiable hunger for men, as you keep on reminding me. But you, of all people, are hardly in a position to judge. You have had other women, I have had other men—yes, and I'll continue to have them, too, and enjoy them thoroughly! Why is it that such behavior on your part is perfectly acceptable because you are a man, yet when I do it, it makes me a trollop or a whore?

"Besides," she added wickedly, "you're the one who

awakened all these passions in my body. How can you object when I go out and do what you yourself taught me?''

Rafe's face hardened into a mask, but inside, his stomach was churning, and he had the feeling he wanted to be sick. Angry more with himself than her, he realized that until that moment he had actually hoped, irrationally, that the whole thing was a mistake. That there was some reason other than the one his mind told him for why she had left. Now he had the words from her own lips.

"Well . . . we know where we stand, don't we? At least you're being honest. I suppose I should give you something for that."

Kristyn sat up, clumsily rearranging her tunic. She hated herself for the childish burst of temper that had made her lie to him, but pride would not let her take it back. She could not bear to have him see how deeply he had hurt her.

"Please, go away and leave me alone. Haven't we done enough to each other as it is? Couldn't you just let me be?"

"Nothing would give me greater pleasure, my dear. Unfortunately, I can't permit myself that luxury right now. You see, I happen to have other plans for you."

"Other plans?" Something in his voice sent a cold chill down her spine. "What—what do you mean, other plans?"

Rafe's eyes burned as he looked down at her.

"I've imagined this little scene more than once the last few days. Seeing you again. And all I wanted was to put my hands around that soft white throat and squeeze until there was no life left it in."

"You wanted to *kill* me?" Kristyn began to tremble, and she realized she was afraid, not so much of the words themselves as of the primitive anger that vibrated through him when he uttered them. "You can't mean what you're saying. That—that's insane! What kind of satisfaction——"

"I can mean it. And I assure you, the satisfaction would be intense. But you can stop shivering. I have no intention of carrying through on the threat—at least not for now. Now, I need you."

Kristyn pulled the tunic tighter around her.

"You need me? But I—I don't understand. What can I possibly do for you?"

"Don't you think that's a little overly naive? We are, after all, in Silver City. Doesn't that call anything to mind?"

"N-no . . ." Kristyn shook her head slowly. Rafe had mentioned Colorado often enough, but he had never said anything about a specific city. "No, it really doesn't."

"Let me spell it out, then. The mine Ricardo Cuervo stole from my grandfather is here. So, by the way, is Cuervo himself—though I'm sure you know that already. I have a plan for dealing with the man, but it's one Carlos and I can't pull off alone. We need someone to help us."

"But . . ." Kristyn hesitated, puzzled by the unexpected turn the conversation was taking. "What does that have to do with me? How could I help you?"

"The details aren't important now. Suffice it to say you *can* help—and by God, you're going to! Now I suggest you adjust your clothes. We're going to ride through town, and I don't think you want to go looking like that. I'll wait for you in the alley."

He started to leave, then paused just inside the entrance.

"Oh, and my dear, if you have any ideas about double-crossing me—don't. Because if you do, I really will put my fingers around that pretty neck and strangle the life out of you."

Thirty-Eight

Rafe was uncommunicative on the long ride from town, and Kristyn, afraid of arousing his anger again, did not press him. Only when they reached the place where he had set up camp, a secluded aspen grove a mile or two from the ravine where she had spent the previous night, did he finally speak, and then only to give her the sketchiest explanation of what was going on.

"I moved my things out here yesterday," he told her tersely. "Carlos took my place at the hotel in town. If Cuervo asks around, all he'll get is a vague description of some dark, Spanish-looking man who registered two days ago. That fits my brother as well as me. With a little luck, maybe he'll assume I haven't arrived and Carlos is waiting for me."

He did not volunteer anything further, and Kristyn did not try to question him. She waited a few minutes, half expecting him to order her to make the fire or help with preparations for supper. When he did not, she decided to take advantage of the daylight that remained, and finding a mountain creek a short distance away, she stripped to the skin, cleansing first her dust-smeared body, then the filthy pants and buckskin tunic that had already smelled foul enough when she put them on the day before.

She was feeling almost human again by the time she made her way back to camp. She had not dared to ask Rafe for the loan of a shirt and trousers to wear while her own things were drying, but she had taken a thin blanket from one of the saddle rolls and draped it around her like a makeshift robe. When she arrived, a tempting aroma of stew and fresh-baked biscuits greeted her, reminding her that she had not eaten for twenty-four hours.

She began to relax a little as she squatted beside Rafe, sharing a plate of meat and vegetables, competently seasoned with wild herbs. She could not help remembering how self-conscious she had been that first night by the banks of the stream, not at all sure how white people were expected to eat, or whether he was going to laugh if she made a mistake. Now, she was perfectly comfortable breaking the biscuits into little pieces dipping them into the stew.

It was not until they had sopped up the last of the gravy and Rafe had poured coffee into a tin mug, again to be shared between them, that he began at last to elaborate on his plans, spelling everything out in matter-of-fact tones that belied the tension between them.

"The whole thing is really quite simple," he told her. "The letters Cuervo is using to blackmail the government official are in Silver City, at least they were yesterday morning. I'm gambling they still are since Cuervo hasn't gone anyplace, and I don't think he'd trust someone else with them. You can see his dilemma. He can't destroy the documents, and he can't slip away with them, not while I'm around. Like it or not, he has to leave them where they are."

"That sounds reasonable," Kristyn agreed, intrigued enough to forget everything else for the moment. "But I don't see what good that's going to do you. You still don't know where the letters are, and Cuervo's not likely to tell you."

"Ah, but he *is*. Not directly, of course—but the way I have it worked out, he won't be able to help himself. I'm sure they're somewhere at the mine, though not in that ostentatious safe he has set up in the office. I intend to arrange a series of small explosions. Nothing dangerous, mind you— nothing that could cause any serious damage—just enough to scare the hell out of Señor Ricardo Cuervo. If he thinks the place is tumbling down around his cars, he's going to save the two things he holds most dear, his skin—and those goddamn letters!"

"Yes, it just might work," Kristyn replied, completely caught up now in what he was saying. The plan *was* simple, but its simplicity was its strength. Still, even in that quick telling, she had picked up the one glaring flaw that stood out from everything else. "I can see how you might sneak into the mine to set the explosives, especially if you do it at night when Cuervo isn't there. But how are you going to manage

when the time comes for the blast? If you're going to get
close enough to see what he is doing, what's to keep him
from spotting you at the same time?''

Rafe leaned back, smiling faintly as he stared into the fire.
She had a way of getting under his skin, the little bitch. She
was the most devious female he had ever run across, but she
had a quick mind, and when they weren't quarreling, it was a
pleasure to talk to her.

"Precisely, my dear. I *can't* get close to him. And neither
can Carlos. Even dressed in miner's garb with a few days'
growth of beard, too many things could give us away. Our
build maybe, our mannerisms. But you . . .''

He turned toward her, a darkly amused look on his features.

"I suppose I should be grateful to you for leaving in a
manner that caused such scandal. Cuervo is certain to think
there's ill will between us, and he wouldn't be far from
wrong, would he? It will never occur to him that you are
working with me. Perhaps—no, almost certainly, considering
his ego—he'll assume you came to Silver City because you
found him irresistible and couldn't stay away. Especially if
you offer him a—uh, token of your affection.''

"A . . . *token*?'' Kristyn saw the sudden hardness in his
eyes, like black mirrors reflecting the flames. "You expect
me to . . . *sleep* with him?''

"Well, why not, if you want to?'' His voice sounded a
little too sharp, even to his own ears, but she did not seem to
catch it. "Flirt with him or sleep with him, put him off or
give in—do whatever you would have if I hadn't come along.
It doesn't make any difference to me. What the hell do I
care? All I ask is that you stick close to the man when the
time comes. Don't let him out of your sight.''

He *does* want me to sleep with him, Kristyn thought, so
sickened suddenly she could hardly think straight. He had not
come right out and said it, but that's what he'd implied. His
pride was hurt when he thought she might go with a man of
her own free will, but if there was something in it for him, if
it suited his own vile purposes, that was a different story
altogether!

"All right,'' she said dully. "I'll help you find the
letters—but only because your grandfather was kind to me.
I'd do anything to help him. But if you think I can . . .'' She
caught herself just in time. *If you think I can sleep with a man*

I don't love, she had started to say—only she had just told him she slept with men she didn't love all the time, and that was exactly what she wanted him to believe! "If you think I'm going to sleep with a man I don't want, just to suit you, you are mistaken. I'll chose my own lovers, thank you very much, without any interference from you."

Rafe stood up, turning his back angrily as he picked up a long willow stick and poked at the fire. Damn the hussy, was she right? *Should* a choice of lovers be hers? He had never let any woman put shackles on *him*, never wanted one to . . .

But if he felt like that, why the devil had he married her? If she weren't his wife now, would he have minded so much?

Rafe scowled unconsciously as he caught sight of the faded denim pants where Kristyn had hung them on the low-hanging branches of a tree. They looked absurd, almost grotesque, flapping in the rising winds. The tunic she was wearing had fallen to the ground, an ugly, ill-made garment, buckskin patterned with Indian beads . . .

Indian beads?

He glanced back at it, the willow stick forgotten in his hand. Could she have found out that her Indian husband was alive? Did she know he had lied to her?

But that was absurd! Rafe heard something snap and, looking down, he saw that he had bent the branch so tightly, it had broken in two. Annoyed, he tossed it to the side. Of course it was absurd. If she knew what he had done, she would have confronted him with it, blurting it out, the way he blurted out his own angry suspicions when she hurt him.

He turned back, surprised to see that her eyes had softened. They were misty now, shimmering with traces of quicksilver in the reflection of the fire. Tears—or only the effects of the smoke? The former, no doubt, he thought wryly. Women had a way of doing that, crying, calling up all those protective instincts just when a man was sure he had his feelings under wraps.

He had told her before that he didn't care if she slept with Cuervo, and dammit, he had meant it at the time! At least, he had tried to mean it. But now, seeing her in the firelight with tears in her eyes, he knew he was playing games with himself. She was his woman, his wife, whether he willed it or not, and he had the insane feeling he would put her in a cage and hang it from the treetops if only that would guarantee his

exclusive rights to her. He would let her flirt with Cucrvo—he
had to—but by God, if the bastard tried to touch her, if he so
much as laid a hand on her, he would kill him!

"I see you've taken to Indian fashions again," he remarked dryly. "Did you pick that up at the trading post, or
have you been consorting with braves in the tepee again?"

His sarcasm cut through Kristyn like a knife, reminding her
suddenly, sharply, of the pain she had suffered that day. The
tears spilled from her eyes, and because she did not want him
to see them, she lashed out.

"I told you already, I will lie with any man I choose—and
any place I choose! Indian men are bigger than whites—did
you know that?—and they last longer. Yes, and they feel
harder inside me, too!"

Her crudeness shocked him, but it was not a sensation that
was altogether unpleasant, for Rafe had always found boldness exciting in a woman, always enjoyed it when a woman
dared to talk as freely, as vulgarly, as a man. He could
almost see her in the tepee, naked, groveling in the dirt like
an animal, and while the image disgusted him, it aroused
him, too, making him long to throw her on the ground,
proving with his own virility that all those angry barbs were
not true.

He had not wanted to desire her again. He had not thought
it was going to happen, but somehow, unaccountably, it had,
and he realized that nothing on earth could stop him from
going to her.

Kristyn, watching in silence, saw the change that came into
his face and, sick with shame, she understood what he was
telling her with that mute, moody gaze. He wanted her,
wanted her with all the hunger of their previous couplings,
and the first stirrings in her own body warned her that she
could not hold him back.

"Take that goddamn blanket off," he told her, his voice
deep and husky. When she did not respond, he repeated, a
little more harshly, "I said, take it off! I want to see what
there is about you that tempts me to lose command even of
my own soul."

Kristyn longed to fight back, but sensing his power over
her, she surrendered to the inevitable, raising her hands and
letting the blanket slip from her shoulders. What good was it,
resisting, when he would not only have his way with her in

the end, but have it with her full and shameless cooperation? He did not even have to kiss her, caress her, tease her with soft words of love. He had only to come to her, and her wanton body, against every instinct of her will, made ready to receive him.

Her breath caught in her throat as she watched him peel off his clothes, strewing them out behind him. Then slowly, he began to move toward her, and she felt herself sinking back onto the blanket, felt her legs ease apart, mindlessly opening to accommodate his passion.

Rafe did not miss the movement.

"I see you've learned to spread your legs without being told," he said hoarsely, despising himself for the throbbing pain that surged through his loins. Dammit, why was it that this woman, even at her most perverse, excited him so much? "You are becoming quite an accomplished harlot—or is that an unfortunate choice of words? A harlot, after all, has learned to please a man. You exist solely for your own pleasure."

"My . . . *pleasure*?" Kristyn felt a sharp burst of anger, and she tried desperately to hold on to it. "You think it *pleases* a woman to be used like this? Without even a pretense of tenderness? Or love?"

"Oh . . . ? This doesn't *please* you? You don't like to be treated this way? You don't crave it?"

"No, of course not. I——"

"Then why do your legs open whenever I come near you? Don't play coy, my dear. You know damn well you are anticipating the feel of a man inside your body. Or do you perhaps think I am going to lavish on you that purest, most selfless proof of my devotion?"

He paused, his mouth parted, the tip of his tongue running pointedly over his lips as he stared down at her, *there*, where those same lips, that same tongue, had toyed with her so devastatingly before.

"Well . . . why not? It drives you to a frenzy, doesn't it? And only when you are in a frenzy, *querida*—only when you are completely outside of yourself—can any man ever truly possess you."

She felt him kneel down in front of her, felt him lean forward until his face was buried in the soft, moist hair between her thighs. There was in him now none of the tenderness which had accompanied the act before, none of the sweet generosity, but in their place came a raw excitement, compelling in its own way, irresistible.

His tongue was rough as he assaulted her, but it was a roughness she could welcome. His lips were hard, almost crude, not coaxing but devouring. All the wildness of his lovemaking, the anger, even the pain, suddenly seemed a part of her, at one with the tameless, ravening passions that flooded through her body.

He was playing with her. No, not playing *with* her, playing *on* her, as if she were an instrument and he a skilled musician.

And, oh—he *was* skilled. Kristyn lay back, feeling his hands on her breasts, sliding down to her belly, and she wondered how he could know her so well, this man who had been with her only a few times. How could he use those groping fingers so unerringly to excite her? That hard, teasing tongue to drive her to such peaks of desire?

Perhaps he had been right about her after all. Perhaps she *was* only interested in her own pleasure. Perhaps she had not truly learned to satisfy a man. But she could not think about that now, she could not care. Tonight, this moment, this sweet pulsating passion, was hers. He might use her, manipulate her, do with her as he would—but he was exciting her, too, fulfilling her as never before.

Then, suddenly, just when sweet perfection seemed within her grasp, she felt him pull away, leaving her alone on the blanket, dazed and bewildered. One minute she was riding on waves of passion, surging inevitably toward that crest for which she hungered, the next she was looking up to see him standing over her, his features drowned in shadow.

"No—don't stop. Oh, Rafe, please . . . What . . . ?"

The words died on her lips as she caught a glimpse of his face in the firelight. Not brooding at all, as she had imagined, but angry, his jaw set in a taut line.

Almost instantly, she realized what had happened. He had intended only to manipulate her body, proving once and for all his mastery over her. But somehow, in the process, he had aroused his own male hunger as well, and now he longed for nothing so much as to bury himself deeply, urgently, inside her.

He had meant to make of her his slave. Instead he had enslaved himself—and that he could never endure.

Tears shimmered in Kristyn's eyes as she saw him withdraw slowly into himself, pulling away, and she realized bitterly she had lost him.

"I think, my dear," he said, his lips twisting slightly at the corners, "that you overestimate the power of a woman over a man. You need someone like me to bring out the quivering excitement in that sensual body of yours, but I don't need you. And I never will."

Kristyn could only lie on the ground, staring helplessly after him as he strode into the darkness. How could he do this to her? Use her this way? Play with her so cruelly?

Yet, even as she thought it, she sensed somewhat guiltily that she had asked for what she got. She had known all along how jealous Rafe was, but she had taunted him anyway with "other men." A part of her, that perverse part she could not control, longed to run after him, begging him to listen to her, to try to understand what she had done.

Pulling herself up, she drew the blanket around her shoulders, shivering in the chill night air. No, she thought bitterly, I can't go after him. I can't let myself do that! And I can't stay here either—not after the way he treated me!

Her pants were still hanging on the branch where she had left them, and she tugged them up over her legs, barely noticing that they were still damp and cold. Fastening them hurriedly, she put on the tunic, ignoring the smell of wet rawhide, the clammy feel of it against her skin.

The silent hills seemed to close in around her, so illusively near she almost had the feeling she could reach out and touch them. Billy Collins is up there, she thought suddenly, startled, though she knew she should not be. After all, she had known for two days he was there.

For the first time, it occurred to her that she still had at least one option left. Billy might be a desperado, but he had been her friend, too, and a friend was what she needed now. Even if he was furious when they met again—not unjustifiably, after the way she had run out on him—surely she could tease him out of it. She had always managed Billy before. She could do it again if she had to.

She turned around slowly, wondering where Rafe was at that moment and how hard it was going to be to get away. She would have to move stealthily, of course. She would have to lead her horse at least a mile or two on foot to be sure he didn't hear the hoofbeats, but once away, she ought to be able to locate Billy without any trouble. There might not be much left in her that was truly Cheyenne, but she could still track like an Indian. She would find him, and when she did . . .

She tossed her head, letting the night wind whip through her hair. When she did, she knew only too well what the cost of Billy's continued friendship was going to be. But that was something she would deal with when it happened. She could not let herself think about it now.

And anyway, what choice did she have? She could hardly stay where she was. Rafe had been right about one thing. She did need him to quench the sweet, yearning sensations that flowed through her flesh. If she stayed, sometime during the night, the hungers he had already stirred within her would swell again, too aching to ignore. Then, under cover of darkness, when her blushes could not be seen, she would swallow her pride and go to him.

And he . . . ? Lulled by sleep, coaxed by renewed longings, would he turn away from her again? He had been angry tonight, but he could not stay angry forever. There was something between them, a strong, undeniable bond, and no matter how they hated it, no matter how they fought against it, they would succumb in the end. They would humiliate and use each other again and again—unless she found the courage to leave.

Thirty-Nine

"Well, well . . . well!" Billy Collins gave an appreciative whistle as a slender figure glided down the steps of the small log shanty. "Now that's what I call a change."

Kristyn spun around animatedly, feeling better than she had for days. She had been amazed that morning when she stumbled across the outlaw camp at the good-natured ease with which Billy had accepted her back into his life—and absolutely delighted when he offered her a choice of anything in his wardrobe "if only you'll get out of those disgusting rags, for Christ's sake!"

"Do you really like it?" she teased, knowing there was only one answer he could give. She had picked a pair of black pants that fit perfectly, lying low on her hips, and a gracefully flowing crimson silk shirt. Her hair, loose and freshly washed, was tied back with a red bandanna. "You don't think I look like a cowboy?"

"Honey, if you look like a cowboy, I look like Jenny Lind." Billy grinned. "And, yes—sure I like it. It's a hell of a lot better than that outfit you were wearing this morning." He ran a practiced eye up and down her figure, enjoying what he saw. There was something about a woman in man's clothes that had always appealed to him. Especially when the woman was built like this one and the pants seemed to have been molded onto her body.

"Isn't it lucky," Kristyn asked, looking up impishly through lowered lashes, "that your things fit me so well?"

Billy obliged with a ready laugh.

"You do have a way of making free with my clothes. I didn't mind so much that you ran off with not a word that time in Kansas, but you took half my wardrobe with you. The pants didn't matter so much—they weren't anything special. But hell, honey, did you have to take my favorite shirt, too?"

"Come on, Billy, no exaggerating. That was a very ordinary shirt. And what do you mean, half your wardrobe? One pair of pants and one shirt is hardly half. Even on the run, you have more clothes than any man I've ever seen!"

Linking her arm through his, she began to stroll down the narrow path that led through the camp, delighted at the easy camaraderie they had picked up again after weeks of separation. She had not had a chance before to see much of the hideout he and his men had built in the woods, and now, glancing around, she was impressed with the clever way in which everything had been camouflaged. An old miner's shack had been reinforced on the inside to provide a small house for Billy, but the exterior was so rough and tumbledown, it looked as if it hadn't been occupied for years. The other buildings, the cookhouse and bunks, were nestled under extending ledges of rock, with loose, leafy branches covering the siding and making them almost undetectable.

Billy did not miss the direction of her gaze.

"I thought we had this place pretty well disguised," he said, shaking his head wryly. "From a distance you can't even see it. At least *I* can't—and I know it's here. But you shot that theory all to hell. How did you find us, anyway?"

"Oh, that was easy." Kristyn flashed him a quick smile. "You think I was just wearing an Indian shirt when I showed up this morning, but in reality I was stalking you like an Indian—with Indian cunning and know-how. Of course, it didn't hurt that I had noticed thick black smoke coming from your fire a couple of days ago."

"It's that visible?" Billy frowned. "I try to watch it when I'm here, but sometimes I forget. I'll tell the men to be more careful."

"Well, then, tell them to burn more aspen and oak—and less pine and other resinous woods. They don't smoke as much." She caught herself abruptly, grinning at the quizzical look Billy sent her way. "I did tell you I wasn't raised in the city, you know. Outlaws aren't the only ones who have to lay a decent fire."

They had stopped beside a makeshift corral, constructed of split rails, and now, seeing the spirited collection of horses the gang had accumulated, Kristyn forgot everything else.

Leaning over the fence, she stretched out her hand and gave a tempting little whistle. Billy, pausing a few paces behind, smiled as he watched.

She looked like a little girl, so excited at the prospect of viewing the horses she could barely contain all that lively energy. What a change from the tired-looking waif who rode into camp shortly after dawn.

But even then, she had been feisty! he thought with a grin. Even then, so bone-weary she could hardly hold up her head, she had been too proud to tolerate a pitying glance from him.

He had known, right from the beginning, that there was an unspoken contract between them. Kris was a smart one—she had a good head on her shoulders, and she wasn't afraid to use it. She knew what kind of man he was, what he would expect of a woman, and she would not have come if she hadn't been ready to accept his terms.

But acceptance would come at her pace, not at his. He had sensed that when he saw her, sensed it in the way, even in surrender, she had held something of herself back from him. Subtly, without words, she had been telling him, Don't push me. And by his taciturnity, he had replied, I won't.

And he wouldn't, either. Billy watched as she leaned farther over the fence, those absurdly tight pants stretching over her derriere, and he felt a responsive tightening in his groin, reminding him how long it had been since he had had a woman. If it were anyone else . . .

But dammit, this wasn't a woman he wanted to feel lying stiffly beneath him, submitting because she had no choice. He wanted her eyes to turn dewy, her lips to part, her breath to come hot against his cheek as she whispered, I want you.

"Tell me, pretty lady, what is a man supposed to do to win you?" Billy leaned against the fence, propping one boot casually on the lower rail. "I could tempt you with furs and diamonds, and with any other woman that would work. But you . . . ? Well, you'd do them justice all right, but I have a feeling you'd prefer one of those horses you're looking at with such sparkle in your eyes. Maybe the little roan?"

"The roan?" Kristyn looked over to see if he was serious. She had already picked out the sprightly filly as the best-looking horse in the corral. "Do you really mean that? You're not just teasing me?"

"Of course I mean it. That horse is as pretty as you

arc—well, almost as pretty—and almost as spirited, too. If you want her, she's yours. Dan!'' Raising his voice, he turned back toward the main part of the camp. "Dan McCafferty!''

A boy appeared suddenly, loping toward them with an awkward gait. His hair was even redder than Kristyn's, and his face had more freckles than she had ever seen on one human being in her life.

"Sure, Billy, what do you want?''

"Cut the roan out of the herd and put a saddle on her. That leather-tooled one Harris' brother brought up from Mexico. It's nice and light, just right for a woman.''

The boy, Dan, gave Kristyn a curious, sidelong look, but Billy did not volunteer any information, and he decided prudently to hold his tongue. Not bothering to go around by the gate, he braced one hand on the fence post and swung himself over the rail. The filly tossed her head at his approach, but she did not shy away, and he had no trouble coaxing her out of the ring.

"Oh, Billy, I think she's going to like me!'' Kristyn cried out. "Really I do! Did you see the way she was with the boy? She's eager to go for a run. And, oh, I am eager to ride her!''

"I can see that!'' Billy laughed. "You're so excited your cheeks are the color of roses. And all for a horse, you vixen! When are you going to flush like that for me?''

Kristyn caught the underlying note of desire, even in those teasing tones, and she turned toward him, unexpectedly confused. Billy had been remarkably gentle with her, remarkably understanding, but she knew that could not last forever.

"There *will* be roses in my cheeks for you,'' she murmured hoarsely. "You know there will. I would not have come to you for help if I didn't think I could give something in return. Only right now, I need—well, I just need more time.''

It was the closest they had come to speaking of the thing that had been on both their minds since she arrived, and to his surprise, Billy found he was content with that. A woman like Kris was worth waiting for. Not for long, maybe—patience was in short supply in his emotional makeup—but for as long as it was likely to take.

"Here comes Dan with your horse, and by God, you were

right. She *is* as feisty as you, and as eager to get going! Well, then, have a good ride, but don't go too far. Oh, and Kris . . .''

He hesitated for an instant. Then, snapping his fingers at the boy, he gestured for him to unbuckle his gunbelt and hand it up to Kristyn, who was already mounted on the roan.

''Never go out of camp without a gun—or anywhere in camp for that matter unless I'm with you. These are rough men I have gathered around me. Some of them may not look it, like young Dan here, but take my word for it, they are. No matter what they seem like, or how politely they treat you, don't ever forget what they are.''

Kristyn strapped on the gunbelt, feeling a little strange with the weight of it on her hip as she rode out of camp. But for all the ominous warning she had sensed in Billy's tone, the day was much too pretty, the horse too spirited and lively, to dwell on it for long.

She steered the roan up a steep mountain path, laughing at the impatience that made those prancing hooves clatter against the rocky earth, then guided her out into an open meadow and gave her her head. The wind was a biting challenge, touched with hints of autumn, and she turned into it, loving the sting of it against her cheeks, the way it tore her hair free and sent it streaming out behind her.

It was almost as if she were a young girl again, with not a care in the world. Almost as if she did not have to worry about what was going to happen when she rode back into camp and faced Billy again. As if she had never laid eyes on Rafe Valero in her life.

Oh . . . Rafe!

Even then, even in the midst of that natural loveliness, the thought of him was like a physical pain stabbing into her heart.

I can't think about him, she reminded herself miserably. I don't *dare* think about him! He's still too close. There are too few miles between us. If I think about him now, I'll be tempted to go back.

Billy was waiting for her when she returned to the hideout, standing beside the corral as he chatted with one of the men. Kristyn surprised him by running over impulsively, catching hold of his hands, and squeezing them with a warmth she had not expected.

He would have been considerably less touched had he

realized that her thoughts were not on him at that moment, but somewhere else, somewhere dark and frightening, and she was using him as a buffer to protect herself from feelings she could not face.

The men began to drift over, a little shyly, as if they were not used to being around a woman. As they were introduced, one after the other, Kristyn could not help remembering Billy's words. *No matter what they seem like or how politely they treat you . . . don't ever forget what they are.* It was easy to see now why the warning was necessary.

If there had ever been a more ordinary, innocuous-looking group of men, Kristyn had not seen them. Some were downright plodding, as plain-looking as simple farmers, others had something of the gambler's swagger in their steps, but every last one of them seemed surprisingly carefree, not dangerous or grim in any way. It was hard to believe they had anything like killing or horse-thieving on their minds.

Horse-thieving?

Kristyn glanced a little guiltily toward the place where Dan was leading the high-stepping roan into the corral after having curried her down. All the time she had been riding, it had never occurred to her to wonder where the horse had come from.

"Billy . . . ?"

He followed her eyes with a laugh.

"No—that's the only horse I ever acquired honestly in my life. I won it playing poker in Denver, and I didn't even have an ace up my sleeve at the time. Maybe that's why I saved her for you."

"Oh, Billy, that's ridiculous. You couldn't possibly have been saving her for me. You didn't even know I was coming."

"Maybe not." He laid a hand on her waist and led her toward a smallish building with a lean-to attached to the side. "And then again, maybe I did. Or maybe I was just hoping you'd come because I wanted you to."

In spite of herself, Kristyn could not help thrilling to the touch of his hand, the easy warmth in his tone. It was so good to be with a man who was not afraid to tell a woman he liked her, even if he *was* doing it mostly for effect. She had come to him out of despair, thinking she had no place else to go; now she was beginning to realize she had not made such a bad bargain after all. If she had to have a man to protect her, she could do worse than Billy Collins.

The rest of the afternoon passed quickly, for Kristyn, eager to show Billy that she was ready to do her share, took over the lean-to kitchen and began to prepare their evening meal. Wild game, mostly rabbit, seemed to be a mainstay of their diet, as it had been for Little Bear and his band, but to her surprise, she found that at least one of them knew how to prepare it, for half a dozen carcasses were hanging outside where the flies could blow them until they were tender enough for the cooking pot.

Conscious of the strong odor, Kristyn cleaned the rabbits outside, then put them in a heavy iron kettle and hung it over an open firepit at the end of the shed. Filling it halfway with water, she added a little of whatever she could find: wild onions from a nearby slope, herbs from the garden someone had started outside the door, potatoes that were ready to go bad in a sack in the corner.

By the time the men arrived, a succulent aroma filled the air and the stew was ready to be ladled into large earthenware bowls, already set on the table. With it, Kristyn served biscuits, the kind Rafe had prepared on the road, made with powder instead of soda to get them to rise, and freshly churned butter, kept sweet in the icy waters of the stream. She had even managed to improvise a salad of sorts, wild prairie turnips cut up and marinated in some wine that had gone sour, spiced and colored with cuttings of green herbs.

"Why, ma'am, I don't know when I've sat down to a meal like this," one of the men said, gulping the words between mouthfuls of stew. "Ain't et like this since my ma fed me, and that's the truth."

The speaker was a big man with the unlikely name of Red Greeley. Kristyn could not for the life of her imagine why they called him that, for his hair was as black as pitch and his skin had a sallow cast, with not a trace of ruddiness in his cheeks.

"I'm glad you like it," she said, pleased at the compliment. "I wanted to make some special flat bread for you, the way I learned down south. There's plenty of dried corn in the shed. But I'm afraid it takes too long to prepare."

"You mean *tortillas*?" one of the other men broke in. "We used to have 'em all the time, back in New Mexico."

"In Santa Fe?" Kristyn's voice was a little too sharp. The man glanced up, but if he noticed anything in her expression, he did not call her on it.

"No, ma'am. Not Santa Fe. South o' there a piece. More toward Lincoln—but the cookin's the same."

"I've heard of *tortillas*," young Dan put in. "They sound real good. I always wanted to try 'em. Maybe you could make 'em for us some other time, for a special supper. Maybe the night we come back from . . ."

He broke off, his face flushing beet red as he turned uncomfortably toward the end of the table where Billy was seated. Following his gaze, Kristyn was just in time to see the outlaw chief throw him a warning look.

Back from where? she wanted to ask, but something in the atmosphere had changed, and she sensed that questions would not be welcome. Back from someplace they did not want to discuss in front of her, that was for sure. And that could only be a job they had planned.

When the meal was over, Kristyn cleared away the dishes and stacked them on a rough wooden table beside the large washtub young Dan had filled with hot water in the lean-to. To her surprise, the boy lingered behind, offering almost eagerly to help with the dishes.

"We usually take turns cleanin' up, except Billy and Red and a couple o' the older guys. But when there's a woman around, everyone's afraid to help out. They think the others'll call 'em sissies."

"And you aren't afraid of that?" Kristyn could not help being amused by the earnest look on the boy's face. "Being called a sissy by your buddies?"

"Nah," he replied with a sheepish grin. "They call me what they want anyway. I'm the youngest, an' they're always funnin' with me. Anyway, my ma used to make me help at home. It's kind o' like bein' back with her again. Oh, not that my ma was p-pretty like you, ma'am."

He had begun to stammer, just slightly, and Kristyn, turning back to the dishes, tried not to smile at the sudden blush that spread all the way down to his neck. The boy shook out a piece of flour sacking that had been rumpled up on one of the shelves, and with the same solemn expression, took each bowl and cup as she handed it to him.

"You must miss your mother very much, Dan. Is she worried about you? Being away from home and all that?"

"Nah. My ma died four years ago. Pa just went to hell after that. He wasn't so bad before, but when Ma died, he took to drinkin' every night, and then he'd beat the shit out o' me—beggin' your pardon, ma'am. I stood it as long as I could, then I cleared out."

"So that's why you joined Billy and the others," Kristyn said. "This kind of life must have sounded very glamorous to you."

"Glamorous? No, ma'am. I wasn't lookin' for glamour, or excitement neither. It just seemed like this was the place to go."

He had stopped wiping the dishes for a moment and was staring fixedly at the rag in his hand.

"You see, the last time Pa beat me, I took the whip and beat him back. I beat him till he was dead. There ain't no place a man can go when he's killed but somewhere like this." He tilted his head up, meeting her eyes with a look much older than his years. "I ain't ashamed of anythin' I've done. I ain't never killed a man since then, and I ain't going to, not without cause. You won't never hear tell of Dan McCafferty shootin' a man unless there wasn't any other way."

Unless there wasn't any other way.

Kristyn shivered a little, though she could not help being sympathetic. And yet, in the end, did it really make any difference? *I ain't never killed a man . . . without cause.* Which of them would not make that claim? Only their causes were their own, and she'd be willing to bet they grew vaguer and vaguer every day.

"What is this job you're planning, Dan?" she asked impulsively. "The one you started to talk about before, when Billy gave you that funny look?"

Dan jumped nervously, his hand shaking so badly he almost dropped the dish he was holding.

"I can't tell you about that. Please don't ask. Billy'd whip me near as bad as Pa if he even caught me talking—"

"That's ridiculous, Dan. And anyhow, you haven't told me anything. Surely Billy wouldn't——"

"Surely Billy would!" a voice interrupted from the doorway. Turning, Kristyn saw that Billy had slipped into the lean-to.

She was surprised to realize that the sound of male voices was no longer audible and the room with the large table where they had just had dinner was now empty.

"Don't pump the boy, Kris," Billy said sharply. "That's not fair. He's scared to death to tell you—he knows what will happen if he does—and he can't stand not to! Never underestimate the impact of a pretty face on men who have been cooped up for weeks with no one but other men to keep them company."

"Well, maybe it wasn't fair," Kristyn conceded, rather guiltily. "But you're not being fair either, Billy. After all, I am curious. That's not unreasonable. Women are supposed to be, you know."

Billy lightened almost instantly, responding to her sally with a good-natured laugh.

"Actually there's no reason why you shouldn't know what we have in mind. You'd find out soon enough anyhow. We're planning to hit the mine in town."

"The mine? Not the one that belongs to . . ." Kristyn faltered, realizing that Billy would not recognize the name Don Diego El Valeroso. "The one that's owned now by Ricardo Cuervo?"

Billy gave her a sharp look. "You know Cuervo?"

"I've met the man. I can't say I really know him, and I wouldn't call him my favorite person in the world. Still, I do have a grudging respect for his power—and his ruthlessness. For heaven's sake, Billy! Tangling with a man like that could be dangerous."

"Dangerous . . . ?" He broke off, tossing a glance at Dan who was staring at both of them with frank curiosity. "You finish cleaning up in here, Dan. Then you go back and bunk down with the others."

The boy looked so disappointed, Kristyn thought for a minute he was going to protest, but Billy cut him off before he had a chance.

"Now, Dan, you wouldn't want the lady's hands to get all rough and red soaking in the dishwater, would you?"

The boy broke into a grin, probably sheer relief at being let off so lightly.

"Sure, Billy, anything you say."

He turned back to the dishes, and Billy put his hand on Kristyn's waist, steering her into the other room. Someone had turned up the kerosene lanterns, making the area brighter than before, and the table was cluttered with large sheets of paper on which pencil sketches had been scrawled.

"Billy . . . ?" Kristyn looked around, surprised. "What on earth is all this?"

"This," he said, laughing as he shook his head, "is our pitiful attempt to come up with a map of the Folly. I've managed to get one of my men inside as a miner, but he has to go in with the others and come out with the others, and he sees only what they want him to. I know there has to be a hell of a lot of cash around someplace. Cuervo has taken more out of the mine than he's accounted for to his backers, but I'll be damned if I can get a handle on where he's stashing his profits. There's an old safe in the office, but it's just there for show. A baby could crack that one."

He turned to her with a twisted half-grin.

"You say you know this man, Cuervo. Any idea how I can get into that mine to have a look at it?"

"As a matter of fact, I do." She paused, enjoying his reaction. "At least I know how *I* can get in."

"You?" Billy squinted at her dubiously. "Come on, Kris, you don't expect me to believe you're going to draw me a map of your pal Cuervo's mine?"

"He's not my pal," she reminded him sharply. "And why not? I'm very good at sketching."

"I've no doubt of that." Billy threw a wry glance at the table. "You couldn't do worse than these guys, that's for sure. But how are you going to feel when we start to use that map? You've got an honest streak in you about as contrary as the mean streak in me. Do you really think you'd be able to go through with it? Hand me a map of a man's mine when you know I'm going to rob him blind?"

Kristyn hesitated, a little surprised that the thought had not occurred to her. Somehow, with a man like Cuervo, it didn't seem like stealing. Besides, if she figured out where he was hiding the cash, she might locate those letters for Rafe, too. Not that she cared about him, of course! She wouldn't walk across the street to save his life after the way he had treated her! But she did want to see Don Diego get his property back.

"I'll not only give you that map," she said, meeting Billy's eyes, "I'll wish you well when I do it."

He still looked skeptical, and she had the feeling he was about to laugh again.

"Come on, Billy. You can't afford to turn me down. Not only can I get into the mine, I'll wheedle a guided tour of every corner of the place. Besides, men get careless around women. They think we don't have the wits to realize what they're saying or doing. Cuervo might let something slip in front of me that he'd guard with his life if a man were there."

Her logic was irrefutable, but Billy hesitated, not liking the thought that kept nagging at the back of his mind.

"Just how well do you know this man, Kris?"

Kristyn flushed. "Not as well as you seem to think. I told you before, I don't like Ricardo Cuervo. As a matter of fact, I dislike him intensely."

"I know what you told me. But that's the kind of thing women sometimes say about a man when they mean just the opposite."

"Why Billy . . ." Kristyn stared across the table, hardly able to believe that scowl on his face. "Don't tell me you're jealous?"

She had expected him to deny it indignantly, but to her amazement, he did nothing of the kind.

"You're damned right I am!" He moved around the table until he was close enough to take hold of her hand. "I haven't even had you for myself. Do you think I'm going to turn you over to another man without a fight? I'll always be jealous over you, Kris. You'll just have to get used to it. I want you enough—I care about you enough—to hate it every time you even look at someone else."

Kristyn turned her head to the side, confused and a little embarrassed by the openness of his feelings. If only Rafe had been able to say those things to her.

But Rafe hadn't said them! Catching her breath, Kristyn forced herself to look back at Billy. Rafe was not a part of her life anymore. She would be a fool if she kept on clinging to him.

"You have nothing to be jealous of, Billy," she said quietly. "I *do* despise Ricardo Cuervo, and not, I assure you, because I am harboring any deep, buried attraction for him."

"And what about Cuervo? Does he share this antipathy of yours?"

"Oh, I don't think so." Kristyn smiled as she withdrew

her hand and moved over to the hearth where a fire was still flickering faintly. "I rather suspect Senor Cuervo is not immune to my feminine charms. At least I hope not. That will make things easier when I go there."

"*No!*" Kristyn was startled by the force in his tone. "Dammit, Kris—the man is dangerous! You said so yourself. There's no telling what he'll do if he finds out what you're up to. And even if he doesn't, he's renowned for his lack of scruples when it comes to women. That might make it easier for you to get into the Folly, but it sure as hell isn't going to make it easy to get out again."

"And you think I can't handle him?" Kristyn was a little surprised to find that she was actually beginning to enjoy the idea. The plan *was* dangerous, but it was exciting, too, in a way that piqued her sense of adventure. "I have always been very good at dealing with men. You, of all people, ought to know that."

"Maybe, but . . ." Billy turned away, staring into the lean-to, dark now, empty. "Cuervo isn't exactly me, my sweet little innocent. I can be a bastard about many things, including women—but not when it comes to you, though God knows why. You twist me around your fingers, minx, and for some reason I enjoy it. I rather doubt that Cuervo is going to respond in quite that way."

Kristyn sat down on the hearth, staring at her hands, folded quietly in her lap. Billy was so different from Rafe. If *he* had only once worried about her going to the mine alone, if he had *once* told her it was too dangerous, she would have moved heaven and earth to do anything he wanted.

When she looked up again, she saw that Billy was watching her with a strange, faraway look on his face.

"My wife had red hair, too," he said softly. "Did I ever tell you that? Not auburn like yours, but a paler color. Strawberry blond."

"Your . . . wife?" Kristyn was surprised at the funny little catch in her voice. It had never occurred to her that Billy might be married. "No, you never told me that. You never even told me you had a wife."

"It was a long time ago. When I was Dan's age, maybe a year or so older. I had already joined a gang like this one, but I was naive enough to think I was going to get out of it. I thought I was just going to get myself a stake and then I'd make a go of farming. It was a damn fool idea, but she wanted it and I wanted her, so I gave it a try.''

"And it didn't work?"

"Oh, it worked for about a year and a half, after a fashion. When the crops started to fail, it seemed like we never had enough to eat, but I still had hope, and her, so I kept on going. Then the child came, and I didn't have enough money for a doctor. Do you know what a man feels like, watching his wife bleed her life away while his son is already in a box outside, and he can't do a thing about it? Not a damn thing! I swore that day I would never be poor again, and I never have.''

"Oh, Billy . . ." Kristyn stretched out her hands.

He caught hold of them, hanging on as if he were drowning. "I've already lost one woman I cared about. Dammit, I'm not going to lose another. That's why I can't allow you to go to that mine.''

"Shhhhh!" Kristyn drew his hands up, cradling them against her cheek. "Nothing is going to happen to me, Billy. I'll be very careful—I promise you that. But I have to go. The plan will never work without me.''

Something seemed to release inside him, a deep sigh she could neither see nor hear. He pulled her closer, holding her for a second against his chest, but there was nothing frantic in his manner now, nothing desperate.

As he drew back, his eyes almost seemed to be laughing.

"If I agree to this—and I'm not saying I do, mind you—*if* I agree, what will you promise when you come back? Will you stop all this foolishness and be mine at last?"

Kristyn hesitated. It was hard, even now, giving up her dreams of Rafe, but she knew she had to. It was not a secure life Billy was offering her. It might not last for long. But at least, while it did, he would be good to her.

"Yes," she said softly, "I will be yours."

Forty

Kristyn was even more aware of that same keen sense of adventure the next morning as she paused in the doorway of the mining office and peered into the room. She was still wearing the same black pants and loosely flowing red shirt, but her hair had been pulled back into a soft coil at the nape of her neck, and wispy auburn curls nestled on her cheeks and forehead. A black hat, man-style, with a jaunty curve to the brim, set off that carefully arranged coiffure, and a black silk scarf was knotted loosely at her throat.

The only man inside the office was a young clerk, who blinked up at her from thick, wire-rimmed spectacles.

"Can I help you, ma'am? If you're looking for Gamper, he's not in."

"Actually, I'm not," Kristyn replied, not having the vaguest notion who Gamper was. "At least not today. I'm looking for Ricardo Cuervo. I was told I could find him here."

"Mr. Cuervo? Well, yes, ma'am, but . . ." The boy hesitated, studying Kristyn with open curiosity. They didn't see many women in the mining office, especially ones that looked like this.

"But what, young man?" Kristyn pressed when he did not continue. "Either he is here or he isn't—and if he is, I want to see him. Señor Cuervo and I are very good friends. I'm sure he would not be pleased to hear that I have been kept waiting."

There was enough authority in her voice to prompt the clerk out of his chair and onto his feet. Cuervo had told him that he did not want to be disturbed, but if this woman really was his friend, perhaps his current mistress, it would make him more furious to have his orders obeyed than ignored.

"I'll just be a second, ma'am," he said, making up his mind. "You wait here. I don't know if Mr. Cuervo can see you or not, but I'll find out."

Left alone, Kristyn strolled idly around the room, taking in the layout and the furnishings with a mildly curious eye. Everything was much as she had expected, with nothing to catch her interest, except perhaps the old safe standing on the wall beside the window. Rafe had been right about that, she thought, amused. And Billy, too. It was obviously there for show.

Still, it was a good show. Cuervo had chosen it carefully, picking an old-fashioned, heavy-looking piece of equipment that fit in with the vaguely ramshackle air of the rest of the room. To the casual eye it might well look as if it held all the important records, perhaps even the payroll on Fridays.

"*Señorita . . .*"

A voice broke into her thoughts. Turning, Kristyn saw Cuervo framed in the doorway behind her. He was dressed in workman's denims, dark pants and a paler blue shirt that fit his lean body as if they had been tailor-made. Almost against her will, Kristyn felt her eyes being drawn toward the man. He seemed arrogantly aware of his own striking good looks as he paused in the doorway; aware, too, of the primitive, feral energy he exuded, like an animal poised to strike.

More than ever, Kristyn was aware of the heightened sense of excitement that had caught her up before. This was going to be a duel between them, a deadly duel—and she was determined to win!

Extending her hands, she took a step toward him, then hesitated.

"Dare I hope you remember me, Señor Cuervo?"

"Remember you?" Cuervo's black eyes snapped with amusement. "My dear lady!" Taking both her hands, he bent over them, pressing them lightly against his lips. "I am not likely to forget. How could I? It cannot be more than a week since I danced at your wedding *fiesta*—and what an enchanting bride you made! I remember saying to myself, He is a lucky devil, that young Valeroso."

"Valero," Kristyn corrected, tilting her head a little to the side as she looked up. "Rafe shortened his name some years ago. I suppose that is my name, now, too—legally at least. But come, *señor*. Do we need this exaggerated politeness between us? This foolish pretense? All of Santa Fe must know by now that I have left my husband. I daresay everyone is enjoying the gossip enormously. And perhaps speculating just a little?''

She raised her voice slightly, turning the words into a question. As she had hoped, Cuervo seemed to fall for it.

"Speculating? But, my dear girl, of course we speculated. We would not be human if we had not. I myself spent a great deal of time wondering about your rather bizarre behavior. You might be curious to know what conclusions I came to.''

"Yes, of course I am—*very* curious."

"Well, then, let me tell you. At first I wondered, quite naturally, if you and the young man had had a quarrel. Rafael, after all, is not known for his placid nature, and red-headed ladies are supposed to have fiery tempers to match their flaming hair. But then I said to myself, No, Ricardo, it is too soon for the young lovers to have quarreled. There must be something else.''

He paused, looking pointedly into Kristyn's eyes.

"It occurs to me now that perhaps it was a prearranged plan. Not a rift between the two of you, but something intended to look like a rift. Then, if your husband sneaked off to join you, it wouldn't occur to anyone that you were together.''

Kristyn felt her blood run cold as she realized suddenly how clever the man was. It had been a mistake, after underestimating him before, to think she could set little verbal traps and he would walk into them.

"But . . . señor . . . !'' She shook her head a little, trying to look as if she could not figure out what he was talking about. "That doesn't make sense. Why would Rafe and I sneak off when we could be together in Santa Fe? Still . . .'' She lowered her voice, conscious that she was going to have to come up with a good story, and come up with it quickly. "You *were* right about one thing. It was not a sudden quarrel that caused us to part.''

"Ah . . . ?'' Cuervo let her know with one artfully arranged eyebrow that he was skeptical but open to persuasion. "I must admit I am intrigued.''

Kristyn turned away, managing to look faintly confused.

"You say you remember dancing at my wedding, *señor*,'' she murmured. "Then you must remember another *fiesta*, too, when you stole a kiss from me in the garden. Do you think I would have responded with such helpless abandon if I had been ready to surrender my heart to another? No, I married Rafe Valero for one reason, and one only!'' She whirled suddenly to face him, eyes flashing with unexpected fire. ''Because I planned to leave him that very night!''

''You—*planned*—to leave him?'' Cuervo was so startled he lost his composure for a moment. ''But what in God's name would prompt you to do a thing like that?''

''I did it because—because I hate him! Oh, *señor*, you have no idea what it was like, how terrible it was. The pain. The humiliation! I thought then I would die. I have planned for weeks, for *months*, to get my revenge on him. At last I have it!''

''But good Lord! To go so far as all that! You *must* have hated the man. What could he have done to turn you so violently against him?''

Everything! Kristyn longed to cry out, forgetting she was playacting. Rafe had done everything to her, taken everything from her—and given nothing in return! It was he who came into the Indian camp and tore her from her family, he who caused the rift between her and her young husband. He had lied to her, deceived her, shamed her! It would be no wonder if she really had planned vengeance!

''I—I cannot talk of such things,'' she said, her voice quivering with emotion. ''Not now. The pain is too fresh. All I can do is throw myself on your mercy and beg you to trust me when I tell you I do have my reasons.''

The tears in her eyes were genuine, the tremor on that soft upper lip just subtle enough to pique Cuervo's interest. A sexual indiscretion? He could believe it of Valero. And after all, the girl must have been innocent once, with that smoldering child-woman sensuality of adolescence.

Still, he thought, eyeing her warily, something about her story didn't quite ring true.

''I have my share of male vanity, my dear, but even I find it hard to believe that one kiss could have affected you so strongly. Are you really telling me that, after leaving your husband, you journeyed all the way to Colorado just to find me?''

''Oh . . . no!'' Kristyn widened her eyes, looking shocked for a moment, then started to giggle. ''Of course not! That was the purest coincidence. I just happened to be passing through when I overheard someone mention your name. I must confess, however, that the mere thought of your being here—of your being so close—well . . . You may scoff all you like, but that one kiss has had me in a turmoil ever since. Oh, I know it meant nothing to you—you have kissed so many beautiful women—but it had a profound effect on me."

"Really?"

His voice was cool, almost mocking, but there was a new light in his eyes, a kind of greedy glow, and Kristyn realized to her surprise that he actually believed her.

Rafe had been right—his vanity *did* blind him to reason. She had been afraid she might go too far, flatter him too outrageously, but obviously where this man's self-image was concerned, nothing was too much.

"Oh, yes," she murmured breathily, "it did."

"So when you heard my name, you came running right away?"

"No!" Kristyn flashed him a hotly indignant look. "I most certainly did not! Quite the contrary, I tried to stay away from you. I tried very hard. Only I . . ." She lowered her eyes, letting her lashes tremble against her cheeks. ". . . I just couldn't seem to stay away."

She looked up, her eyes troubled. Then, she forced a little laugh into her voice.

"Besides, I've never seen a mine before. I might have been able to resist you, *señor*, especially since I did not know how you would receive me. But the lure of a mine? Now that is too fascinating."

Cuervo laughed, amused at her sudden change in mood. What a delicious little creature she was, charmingly transparent. If she had tried to persuade him that she had eyes for no one but him, he would have been inclined to disbelieve her. But that sweet confusion, those silly, muddled protests—what man would not be moved by that?

"So you are interested in the mine, eh?" he said, chuckling indulgently. "Well, well, that is different. Of course, you had to come. Tell me, what is it you want to know?"

"Oh . . . everything!" Kristyn could hardly believe how easy it was to manipulate him once she had figured out the key. "Absolutely everything. I'm dying to know all about it.

Everyone in town says it's a very successful operation, though
I suppose silver is nowhere near as valuable as gold.''

"Gold? Oh, my dear child!" He almost choked, she was
so delightfully funny. "What a singularly feminine mind you
have. Diamonds, furs, gold—sometimes I think those are the
only three words a pretty woman knows. Silver may not be as
romantic as gold, but it's every bit as profitable, I assure you.
I take out quite enough to make me a very rich man.''

"Really?" Kristyn stared at him, obviously enthralled by
those two magic words, *very* and *rich*. "Do you suppose—
well, I know it's asking a lot, but—could you show me
around the mine? Personally? I'd love to see where all that
silver comes from.''

"Well, I don't know . . ." Cuervo hesitated. Ordinarily,
he avoided going into the pits. The place was too dark for his
taste, too slimy. But those soft blue eyes were hard to resist.
And there was something about the intimacy of narrow,
unlighted tunnels. That was one of the things he loathed with
the miners, the smell of them, the coarseness when they
accidentally touched him. But with a woman like Kristyn . . .
Yes, with Kristyn it was a temptation.

There would not, of course, be any overt sexual contact
between them in the mine. But the feel of her body against
his, her hips, her thighs, perhaps even those truly magnificent
breasts in the darkness . . . ah, that would be like a fine
aperitif, whetting a man's appetite for the banquet to follow.

"Very well, if you wish. Why not? I was in the middle of
a meeting, but that can wait. It would be my pleasure to show
you around.''

Taking her arm, he led her down the long, dimly lighted
hallway and out through a door at the rear of the building.
The terrain in back was markedly different from that in front,
flatter, cluttered with rusty mining tools and other odds and
ends. A gray plank fence ran along one side, but the other
was open, leading around the building and back to the main
road. At the far end, a sheer rock wall rose almost perpend-
icularly, broken only by a gaping black hole in the center.

As they approached a sturdy-looking shed, Kristyn saw
through the open double doorway that the shelves and tables
inside had been littered with miner's gear. Cuervo picked
through a pile of helmets, choosing one and handing it to
Kristyn before selecting another for himself.

"Some of the men don't like to wear helmets," he told her. "Especially in the entry shaft or the sturdier tunnels. But I never go in without one, and I don't want you to either. It's a safety precaution, and it makes sense. Oh, and you'd better have one of these, too." He took a rough woolen jacket down from a peg on the wall. "You'd be surprised how cold it can get down there."

Kristyn put on the jacket as they headed back into the yard, trying not to notice how foul it smelled. Her own hat, at Cuervo's suggestion, had been left in the shed, and the helmet felt strangely heavy on her head.

When they were halfway across the yard, Cuervo stopped, startling Kristyn by striking a sulphur match and lifting it to her face.

"The candle," he explained, grinning at her reaction. "Every miner's helmet has one. In some places, it's the only illumination. There are lanterns in the working areas, but for the most part, the tunnels are dark. I know them pretty well by now, at least in the areas we'll be in, so we shouldn't have any trouble. But see that you stick close and don't lag behind."

"Don't worry." Kristyn eyed the entry cavern ahead with something less than wholehearted enthusiasm. The sense of adventure she had enjoyed before was dulling considerably with this talk of helmets worn for safety and the possibility of total darkness in the pits. "I have no desire to go off exploring on my own."

"Good." Cuervo lit the candle in his own helmet and, setting it on his head, led the way into the mouth of the cavern. "This is the entry shaft we're heading for now," he called out over his shoulder. "The miners use another entrance on the far side—there's a cage there to raise and lower them—but I avoid it like the plague, especially when the shifts are changing and it's crowded. Come on, now . . . watch your head."

Kristyn obeyed, ducking instinctively as she followed him through the opening. Squared-off timbers had been set against the stone, completely framing the entrance, and inside, she was aware of other braces, vaguely illuminated in the flickering light.

Curious, she turned toward them, letting the beam from her helmet play on darkened wood, so aged in places it looked as if it had begun to rot away.

"Are you sure these timbers are safe?" she asked, eyeing them dubiously. "They don't look very sturdy to me."

"Reasonably sure." Cuervo grinned again as he turned to wait for her. His features loomed out of the shadows, sharp and angular in the candlelight. "The braces *are* in bad shape in some of the other sections, and we've had a number of accidents lately. But the timbers around here are in good condition. Any area I go into, I want to make damned sure I can get out again."

"Well, if you say so . . ." Kristyn cast a skeptical glance at the beams, still not liking what she saw. And he said the timbers in other places were even worse! She shivered a little as she recalled the charges of dynamite Rafe was planning to set. He had said everything would be safe, but she couldn't help wondering if he realized how badly conditions had deteriorated.

"Actually," Cuervo told her, heading back into the cavern, "there's very little danger in any of the areas we'll be going into. As long as you keep your head and do what you're told, you won't get into trouble." He stepped over to a shadowy spot that seemed to indicate a hole or pit of some sort. Jutting out of it, Kristyn saw a smooth cedar pole, onto which short wooden slats had been nailed at uneven intervals to form a makeshift ladder. "This is the roughest part coming up right now, at least that's what most newcomers think. Once you get through here, the rest will seem easy."

He tilted his head down, directing the light of his candle into the shadows, and Kristyn was horrified to see it play faintly on sheer rock walls, then disappear into nothingness.

"We're going—*there*? But that's—why it's straight down!"

"Fifty feet down," Cuervo agreed with an unpleasant laugh. "An amusing little exercise, don't you think? Of course, there's still time to change your mind if you don't have a head for heights."

Kristyn was conscious of the warmth of candlelight on her cheeks and she knew he was shining his beam deliberately into her face.

"No . . . no, I'll be all right. It just . . . well, it surprised me, that's all."

"Okay, if you're sure." Cuervo moved over to the ladder, gripping it firmly as he searched for a foothold. Only when he had found it did he swing off the ground and begin his descent. "It looks clumsy, but actually it's quite easy. The only trick is to make sure each rung is steady before you put your weight on it. The mine is moist and the wood rots away almost as quickly as we can replace it. Just give it a test with your foot. If it doesn't hold, use the next rung down. And hang on tight."

Kristyn watched, her breath catching tensely as he climbed down the ladder and vanished from sight. Stepping gingerly to the edge, she forced her eyes downward, following that flickering light as it bobbed deeper and deeper into the abyss. When at last it was gone, she realized with a rush of panic that her turn had come.

Her hands had turned so cold they were almost numb, and she was aware once again of the temptation to turn back, so intense she was afraid she would not be able to resist. But she had promised Billy, she reminded herself sharply. And promises were made to be kept! Besides, she was determined to find those letters for Don Diego.

Leaning forward, she clutched at the pole with both hands, then began to grope for a toehold, the way she had seen Cuervo do. The cedar was slippery, moist with the cold sweat of her palms, and she tried desperately not to think what would happen if she could not hold on.

The first two or three steps were the hardest, and Kristyn, giddy with the danger of what she was doing, was terrified that she would faint and crash to her death on the rocks below. But once she had tested several rungs and found them sturdy, she felt her confidence begin to return, and rather to her surprise, she managed to move quite spryly the rest of the way.

A wave of exhilaration flooded through her as she reached for that last rung and felt not wood but solid stone beneath her foot. She had been afraid, but she had conquered her fear and done what she had to. Cuervo was right. From now on, everything *was* going to seem easy.

She felt almost lightheaded as she joined him on the sloping path that led away from that perpendicular shaft.

"Where are we now?" she asked, peering curiously into the darkness. "What do you call this part of the mine?"

"We're still in the entry shaft. The first fifty feet are straight down. The next fifty follow an inclined gallery, a slightly longer trek but less precarious for the faint at heart.

Fortunately, there's no blasting today—otherwise we wouldn't be able to come this way. The tunnel would be so full of dust and smoke, we couldn't see where we were going, much less breathe. The miners manage it because they're used to it, but I wouldn't want to try it myself.''

"We'd have to go in by the cage then?" Kristyn turned her head from side to side as they walked, focusing her beam on the walls of the narrow tunnel. "With the workmen? Or is there another entrance?"

"No, just these two. There used to be several others, but they've fallen into disuse, and I see no reason to repair them. Here now, watch your step. The ground is slippery, and loose stones sometimes fall from the roof, particularly when the men are blasting, though it can happen any time.''

"Do you blast often?" Kristyn could not help remembering again what Rafe intended to do. What if, by coincidence, his blasts came at the same time as the others?

"Sometimes several times a day, sometimes not at all. It depends on what kind of vein we've hit and how difficult it is to get at the ore.''

"But isn't that dangerous? Using dynamite in a place like this? I would think the tunnels would come crashing down around you.''

Cuervo seemed amused. "We do have cave-ins sometimes, of course. That's one of the perils of mining. But give us credit for a little sense, my dear—and a little skill. We know how much to set and where to place it. Besides, all this takes place below ground. The earth is very solid here. It absorbs much of the force.''

The walls *did* seem solid, Kristyn admitted as she let her light play on them. Yet, there was something distinctly eerie about them, too. The temperature had dropped dramatically, and they almost looked like sheets of ice, translucent, glowing from somewhere deep within.

Reaching out, she ran her fingers along the stone.

"Why, it's wet.''

"I told you.'' Cuervo laughed. "The mine is moist. Groundwater seeps in almost constantly, sometimes flooding a shaft or tunnel so badly we can't use it for months. In fact, whole mines have been known to shut down for that reason.''

"Of course! That's why the walls are so shiny.''

"Partly. But there's a particularly rich vein in this section.

We're going to begin working it actively soon. It's the silver that gives the stone its uniquely crystalline appearance.''

"Oh . . . I see." Kristyn shivered a little as she pulled the coarse wool coat tighter around her. Now that Cuervo had pointed it out, she could almost see the ore permeating the rock. "You said that silver is as profitable as gold. Is that really true?''

"Ah, profits again." Cuervo smiled faintly to himself. He had wondered when she was going to get back to that. How very like a woman. "An average yield might bring in perhaps a thousand ounces of silver per ton—a good one like this as much as eight thousand. And that, my curious little girl, can amount to two thousand dollars a day, three thousand, even more if we work around the clock.''

Kristyn turned wide eyes on his face. "And of course you do.''

"Of course." He was delighted with the way her mind worked. Transparently greedy—and intensely practical. "When you get to know me better, you'll learn that I am not a man to be satisfied with two thousand dollars a day if I can have three, or three if I can have five.''

The complex labyrinth of tunnels and vast chambers that had been gouged out of the earth was so extensive, and so intriguing, Kristyn found herself following Cuervo's every word with genuine interest. Indeed, there were times she was so caught up in everything she was seeing and learning, she almost forgot why she was there.

And just as well, she thought, grinning wryly to herself. Those contorted passageways seemed to twist and turn at random, throwing her so off balance she could not have drawn a map of the place had she tried. And really, there seemed little point to it. Coming down into the mines, seeing the size of that underground network, made her realize how futile the idea had been in the first place. If Cuervo wanted to hide something, there were hundreds, *thousands*, of places he could do it. She would not even begin to know where to look.

Everywhere Cuervo took her, Kristyn saw reminders that the mine was a working area, with activities scheduled twenty-four hours of the day. The tunnels were extremely narrow and so low in places she had to stoop to get through, but no matter how cramped, they all had metal tracks along the ground to accommodate mining cars filled with ore. A small

recess in one of the walls, opening onto another tunnel at the
far side, seemed to be a foreman's office, for it held a
battered wooden desk, littered with papers, and an old cabinet
that had been jammed to capacity with rocks and various
pieces of equipment. No one was there at the moment, but a
rusty lantern dangled from a beam overhead, casting starkly
unnatural rays over the setting.

They paused at the edge of one of the busier pits, a
surprisingly large cavern that had been gouged by repeated
blasting out of the earth. To Kristyn, the area seemed bitingly
cold, but most of the men had removed their shirts, and their
bare chests glistened black with dust and sweat. The sound of
their picks rang against the rock as they worked out chunk
after chunk of ore, heaping them onto carts that would be
hauled away by a seemingly endless procession of mules.

Kristyn's stomach turned faintly queasy at the sight of the
animals, stolid and motionless as they waited to be forced
into labor.

"That does seem cruel. The men are here by choice.
Whatever their reasons, they at least want the job. But those
poor animals never asked for anything like this."

"Hardly cruel," Cuervo snapped, impatient with the femininity that had charmed him before. "Quite the contrary, the
mules actually like it here. My—uh, predecessor got the idea
he wanted to bring them up to the surface, but they hated it.
Animals get used to what they have, just like people. Most of
these miners couldn't live any other way now even if they
wanted to."

So callous, Kristyn thought, shuddering. So utterly uncaring.
It suddenly occurred to her that the true evil of this man was
not his calculating greed, but his total inability even to recognize the needs and feelings of others.

"Well, be that as it may," she said, a little more sharply
than she had intended, "it seems a dismal way to live—for
either man or beast."

Cuervo was standing close enough to feel the tremor that
ran through her body, and misreading it, he put his arm
around her shoulders.

"I did warn you it was cold down here. Shall we go back
to the surface? I think perhaps you've had enough for one
day."

"Yes," Kristyn agreed, trying not to recoil noticeably

from that unwelcome touch. "I daresay you're right. It does get oppressive after a while."

Cuervo did not release his hold as they made their way back down the tunnel, but moved deliberately closer. Even through the thick jacket he had lent her, he could feel the tantalizing ripeness of her body. He could not help remembering how provocative she had looked before in that man-tailored shirt, too big across the shoulders but clinging so tightly to her breasts it left nothing to the imagination. Lowering his hand, he let it brush as if by accident against her bosom, testing to see if she would pull away. When she did not, he knew she was his for the asking.

The journey back to the entry shaft took no more than twenty or thirty minutes, but to Kristyn, aware constantly of Cuervo's body next to hers, the time seemed to drag interminably. It was all she could do to choke back her distaste, knowing that even now, even though she no longer needed him, she dared not let him suspect her true motives.

The sky was overcast when they reached the surface, but the gray seemed almost blinding after the total darkness of the mine. Kristyn tilted her face upward, and drew in deep gulps of cool, clean air. How good it felt to be outside again—and how easy it was to take even the simplest gifts of nature for granted!

As she returned the coarse woolen coat and hat to the open shed, a faint shiver ran down her spine, recalling the way she had felt in that last pit, watching those poor plodding mules trapped in the darkness.

Like a premonition, she thought—a warning of things yet to come.

But that, of course, was absurd. It was only the dark, the cold, the claustrophobic closeness of the tunnels that had made her imagination run away like that.

"Well, thank you for showing me the mine, Señor Cuervo," she said, forcing a laugh into her tone. "But I hope you will understand if I don't ask you to take me there again."

"As a matter of fact, I would be very much surprised if you did. I hope you will allow me to offer you a pleasanter diversion in the form of dinner tonight. And don't you think you could call me . . ."

He broke off suddenly, his eyes focusing on something in the yard behind her. Curious, Kristyn turned, but all she could see was a young man in a brown shirt, his hands jammed into his pockets as he peered through the window of an old shed, then sauntered on again.

An old shed? Kristyn's heart jumped. Glancing back at Cuervo, she was just in time to catch a look of suspicion on his features. Of course! That had to be it! What an idiot she had been to think he would hide anything he valued underground. One poorly placed explosion, one cave-in, and he could be cut off from it for years, if not forever. But an old shed on the surface, slightly dilapidated, filled with junk and discarded tools . . . ?

She was aware that Cuervo had begun to look at her again, and she twisted her features into a mask of bewilderment.

"Call you what, *señor*," she prompted slyly. "You started to say something before, but then you broke off. I had thought you were going to ask me to call you Ricardo. Did you change your mind?"

"Change my mind?" He gave her his complete attention again, grateful that she seemed too scatterbrained to notice his distraction. "I never change my mind about beautiful women. Yes, of course I want you to call me Ricardo—and anything else you might choose."

His lids drooped halfway over his eyes, accenting the suggestiveness of his tone. She had not shied away from him in the mine, not once, although she must have been as aware of his body as he was of hers. Now she was telling him with the overtness of her behavior that the idea of tonight was as exciting to her as it was to him. Soon, very soon, she would be his. But for now . . .

For now, he reminded himself reluctantly, he would have to let her go. Leaning over her hand, he touched her fingers with the barest brush of his lips as he apologized profusely for not being able to accompany her back to town. Yes, he thought, enjoying the way her hips swayed just slightly as she began to walk away from him, he had to let her go now. But tonight . . . ah, tonight, she would not get away.

Kristyn, hurrying down the hill, was unpleasantly conscious of dark eyes following greedily from above. Really, the man was an animal! She turned once, halfway down the path, only to see that he was still looking after her. Forcing an artificially bright smile to her lips, she raised her hand and threw him what she hoped was a gay little wave. When she turned again, he was gone.

As she headed toward the place where she had tied her horse, anxious to be out of there once and for all, she was surprised to catch a hint of movement out of the corner of her eye. Looking around, she saw a young man working his way stealthily through the underbrush, half crawling in an attempt to keep from being seen. It was the same youth she had seen a few minutes before, ambling with careless abandon past that old storage shed in the yard.

She took a step forward, curious to see what he was doing. Just then, he turned slightly, giving her a glimpse of his face, only partially shaded by a floppy old hat.

"Dan?" She was so startled she almost shouted out his name. "Dan McCafferty, is that you?"

"Shhh! Not so loud." The boy's voice came back in a hoarse whisper. "Billy wouldn't like it if I let anyone see me talkin' to you. Especially not that Cuervo fellow."

"No, I suppose he wouldn't," Kristyn conceded, backing off a little. "I noticed you by that shed, and so did Cuervo. He'd be suspicious if he saw us together."

Moving over to the roan, she unhitched the reins and brought the horse closer, stooping as if to adjust the stirrup.

"There," she called out, in a low undertone. "If Cuervo happens to look down, everything will seem perfectly normal. But for heaven's sake, Dan, tell me—what are you doing here?"

"There are three of us around," Dan hissed back. "Me and Red and one of the other guys. Billy sent us to keep an eye on you. I was just about to leave when I saw that shed, and it looked funny to me."

"I think you're right. Cuervo reacted strangely when he saw you there. But what on earth called your attention to it? I walked past it at least twice and I never even noticed it."

"I dunno. It just didn't look right, I guess. I could see through the window, and it was filled up with old stuff, but most of it looked pretty good. What I've heard of this Cuervo, he doesn't let nothin' go to waste. He uses it till it falls apart and then some. Why would he stash perfectly good tools away like that?"

"He wouldn't," Kristyn agreed. "You have sharp eyes, Dan. Billy's going to be very pleased with you."

"Yeah, I reckon." A slow grin began to spread across the boy's features. "I guess knowin' this will come in real handy tomorrow when it's time to set the charges and——"

"The charges!" Kristyn whirled around, completely forgetting that she was supposed to be absorbed with the stirrup. "You mean dynamite?"

"Well, sure. Billy said we were gonna hit the place tomorrow no matter what you found out. We can't hide out in the hills forever. We've already been there longer'n we should. He said we'd just grab what we could and get out while the gettin' was good."

"But dynamite, Dan," Kristyn pressed urgently. "You said—*dynamite*?"

"Billy wants to hit the safe in the office. There's bound to be a little cash in it, he says, for show. And there's one or two other spots he wants to try. Now we've got the shed, too. Heck, Kris, you know Billy! He'll make a reg'lar Fourth of July out of it. Billy'd never just go for the safe when he can take the whole building!"

Kristyn stared at the boy, so stunned for a moment she could not speak. Billy was going to dynamite the Folly tomorrow. And so, if her fears were right, was Rafe!

Only those timbers were weak enough as it was! They'd already had more than one accident—Cuervo admitted that himself. And this wasn't going to be an explosion deep in the bowels of the earth with solid rock to contain its violence. One charge on the surface might well be devastating. Two were unthinkable!

Swaying weakly, Kristyn caught at the saddle to steady herself. All those men down there, those men and those poor dumb mules, caught in pits and passages that would become deathtraps. She could not let that happen! At all costs, she had to prevent it! She could not stop Billy—trying to stop Billy would be like keeping a boulder from crashing down the mountain with her bare hands—but she might talk some sense into Rafe!

Swiftly, without giving herself time to consider, she tossed the reins over the horse's head and swung into the saddle. She had not wanted to see Rafe again, God knew—she cringed to think of the mockery in his eyes when he saw her and assumed she had come crawling back—but she could not indulge her selfish qualms now. Not when the lives of so many men depended on her.

"You go back to Billy, Dan," she called out over her shoulder as she spurred the horse into a brisk trot. "Tell him what you've seen. Right now, I've got something else I have to do."

Forty-One

Kristyn found Rafe's camp just where she remembered it, half hidden in a grove of aspens, their foliage already yellowing from early autumn frosts.

As she approached, slowing her spirited roan to a walk, she detected the faint outline of a horse through the thinning leaves and she dared to hope he was there. But when she pushed her way through the undergrowth, she was surprised to find not Rafe's powerful black stallion but a smaller animal, a dappled gray, barely bigger than a pony.

Carlos? she wondered, then brushed the thought aside. She had never seen Rafe's younger brother ride anything but his own strongly built gelding. Besides, the dainty gray hardly seemed the sort of mount a man like Carlos would choose.

She was aware of a vague feeling of apprehension as she tethered the roan and headed cautiously toward camp. If someone else was there, someone other than Carlos she might have trouble talking to Rafe alone. Yet talk they must, coolly and calmly. She could not afford even the possibility that he might be too angry to listen.

Circling around the camp as quietly as she could, she slipped up from the other side. Whoever was there—whoever she had to deal with—she wanted at least a glimpse of him before she decided what to do.

Scattered clumps of shrubbery provided a meager screen as she closed in, peering out from behind the branches. At first, the area seemed deserted. Rafe had camouflaged all traces of his presence almost as carefully as an Indian, covering last night's fire with sand and scuffing it over with his boots.

Kristyn was about to give up and head for higher ground when her ear picked up a faint sound somewhere behind her.

Whirling swiftly, she was just in time to see a solitary figure emerge on the pathway that led to the stream.

Billows of white swirled up to show glimpses of plump ankles and dainty feet clad in satin slippers. Jet-black tresses, caught on a rising wind, veiled anonymous features even as they heightened that aura of blatant sensuality.

A woman.

The realization landed with a dull thud in Kristyn's stomach. She should have known the minute she saw that frivolous little horse that it belonged to a woman! No, she should have known even before she rode into Rafe's camp that someone like this would be here! For all his bravado about not needing a woman, he must have been every bit as frustrated as she by their mutually unsatisfying encounter two nights before.

Only he, unlike she, had no qualms about finding someone else to assuage his physical needs!

Anger alternated with a totally illogical sense of betrayal as Kristyn watched the woman work her way slowly up the path. She knew she should have been glad to see her here! Relieved! If Rafe had another woman, he would not be tempted to come to her. And she would not be tempted to let him! But perversely, stubbornly, all her heart could feel was wild, unreasoning jealousy.

The woman paused briefly. Reaching up with pale, jeweled fingers, she caught at the long wisps of hair that blew across her face, brushing them back from sultry Spanish features.

Ysabel! Kristyn felt sick inside as she realized what had happened. It was not just any woman Rafe had turned to last night. It was Ysabel! She had followed him from Santa Fe, that shameless hussy—this time she had gotten what she wanted.

Thrusting out her hand, Kristyn braced it against the ground. If Ysabel hadn't been with Rafe last night, she would hardly be making herself comfortable in his camp now. She'd be back at the hotel with Carlos. And she wouldn't have that look on her face, the expression of a woman who had just been totally, thoroughly satisfied.

Damn her!

Torrents of rage seared through Kristyn's body. If it had been anyone else, anyone at all, she could have dealt with it. But this was too much!

"Ysabel!"

Leaping out from behind the shrubbery, she threw herself into the girl's path. From the day she first laid eyes on that simpering brat, she had done nothing but put up with scheming and tantrums. She was not going to put up with this as well!

Ysabel halted abruptly, her eyes widening.

"You! What—what are you doing here?"

Kristyn took a step back, eyeing her with a certain satisfaction. She could not recall having seen Ysabel at a loss for words before.

"What does it look like I'm doing?" Ysabel might think she had Rafe, but it was time she learned a few of the facts of life. "Did you enjoy yourself last night, *puta*, lying in the arms of a man who will never be yours? Or did it make you feel like the alleycat that you are?"

"Alleycat?" Ysabel's voice squeaked with shock and indignation. "You dare to call *me* an alleycat? And—*puta*? I am not——"

"Of course you are. A *puta* and an alleycat both. What do you think? That he belongs to you now? Because you spent one night with him? But he was with *me* the night before!" Her eyes narrowed as she gauged the other girl's reaction. "Or didn't you know that, Ysabel? Does it come as a surprise to you?"

"You were here? With *him*?"

"Of course I was here, you silly slut!" All the anger seemed to burst inside Kristyn until she no longer knew what she was saying. "And yes, I *was* with him!" Oh, it was almost worth the pain just to see that expression on Ysabel's face! "You don't think he really cares about you? Foolish child, he doesn't give a damn! He was only using you—because I walked out and he couldn't have me."

"That's a lie! He does care about me! He loves me. He told me so last night! And how dare you call me a slut? *You* are the slut. You slept with Rafael before you married him. Everyone knows you did. That's why El Valeroso forced him to take you to the altar. And I suppose you slept with Carlos then, too. And, of course, there was that savage——"

"Stop it! Damn you, just—just close your filthy mouth!"

Kristyn's hand lashed out, searching for the side of the other girl's face. Rafe couldn't have said he loved that lying little cat! He couldn't! Not when he had never spoken those words to her!

The sound of that slap echoed sharply through the grove, stunning them both. Slowly, an angry red mark began to appear on Ysabel's cheek, bloodlike against the whiteness of her skin, and dark flames smoldered in her eyes.

Come on, hit me back! Kristyn thought, hungry for an excuse to strike out again. It would be stupid, getting in a fight with Ysabel. It would not settle anything, but at least it would release some of the anger and hurt inside her.

Ysabel seemed only too ready to oblige when the sound of approaching hoofbeats held her back. Startled, Kristyn tilted her head to the side, gauging the speed and direction with a practiced ear.

Two horses. Coming from the vicinity of town. The sound stopped briefly, as if the riders had reined in at the edge of the grove. Then they started forward again, pushing through the tangled undergrowth to the clearing.

Rafe was in the lead, hatless, his long, wind-tousled hair spilling onto his brow. Behind him came Carlos, mounted on the gelding he had ridden from Santa Fe.

As they drew to a stop, Kristyn was aware suddenly of what she must look like, her feet spread apart, her face glowering with fury. That alone would have been enough to tell the two men what had happened, even without the telltale mark on Ysabel's cheek! Bitterly, she realized that this time when Rafe laughed at her, she would have no right to complain.

But as he dismounted, leaving his horse to walk slowly toward her, she saw in his expression none of the sardonic amusement she had expected. Instead, his jaw was set in a grim line, and his eyes seemed to bore through her.

She felt her mouth go dry as he stopped a few feet away, and she realized, idiotically, that her heart was beating much too fast. Only a second ago, she had dreaded nothing so much as his laughter. Now even that would have been a relief from the seething anger she sensed just beneath the surface.

He stood where he was a moment longer. Then, slowly, one corner of his mouth twitched upward.

"I see you've managed to find more suitable garb since the last time I saw you. Did you locate your friends in the hills? Rumor has it that Billy Collins and his gang are holing up up there."

Billy Collins? Kristyn stared at him in dismay. Surely he wasn't going to harp on *that* again?

"I didn't come here to quarrel. I came because I had to talk to you. It's desperately important. You must listen!"

"Talk? Ah . . . and here I thought you were drawn back because of my irresistible appeal." The rage was gone from his eyes, but it had been replaced by a coldness that was even more unsettling. "What a disappointment to find you interested only in conversation. Don't you think, my dear, we are a bit beyond all that?"

"Oh, Rafe . . ." Even now it hurt, that sarcastic edge to his voice! "Can't you ever be serious? Do you have to turn everything into a cruel joke? I really *do* have to talk to you. Alone."

She glanced pointedly toward the place where Carlos was seated on his horse. Ysabel, rather to her surprise, had drifted over to stand beside him.

Rafe followed her gaze, giving his brother a curt nod.

"Might as well get back to town, Carlos. There's no point hanging around here. And take that pretty little minx with you. A rough camp like this is no place for a lady."

No place for a lady? Kristyn simmered at his words. A lady, indeed! The camp had been all right for *her* that night he dragged her here, but it would not do for sweet little white-clad Ysabelita.

Only Ysabel was no more a lady than she! And Rafe knew it!

She was tempted to say something, but one glance at his face warned her she would only anger him more. Biting her tongue, she watched in silence as Ysabel scampered away, looking almost as glad to leave as Kristyn was to see her go.

Carlos waited until she had disappeared into the grove where the horses were tethered, then he turned back to his brother.

"I don't think this is the time for me to go to town. Ysabel can find her own way. She's done it often enough these past months, has she not? I don't want to leave you alone."

"You wouldn't be leaving me alone," Rafe reminded him dryly. "You would be leaving me with my wife."

"That is what I mean, *amigo*—and I think you know it. I do not want to leave you alone . . . with her."

He let his voice trail off as he faced his brother with a cool, steady gaze. For the first time since Kristyn had known him, he showed no signs of yielding.

When at last the impasse was broken, it was Rafe who spoke.

"Are you afraid for me, Carlitos? Or for her?" There was humor in his voice, but it was dark and biting, and Carlos did not laugh.

"I am afraid for both of you."

Rafe reached up, brushing the hair back from his brow.

"I recall thinking more than once recently that I would like nothing better than to put my fingers around that tempting white throat. Do you perhaps fear that that is what's running through my mind right now?"

"I do not know, *hermano*. I think you don't even know yourself. There is much anger in you tonight. So much I can't understand you anymore. Let's not put it to the test. Let me stay here."

"No. You are not going to stay." The words were quiet, but telling. "I will deal with this in my own way, Carlos. It is no concern of yours. The woman is my wife."

"And you are my brother. I cannot let you even think of this thing. I will go if that's what you want. But I will go only when you give me your word no harm will come to her."

Rafe raised a faintly mocking brow. "You would trust my word if I gave it?"

"I have always trusted your word, Rafael. You know that. I always will."

"Well, then . . ." Rafe threw up his hands in a gesture of resignation. "So be it. I promise you this much, *hermanito*— and only this. My wife will come to no harm at my hands today. For tomorrow, I cannot speak. But for today, she will be safe if you leave her with me."

Carlos nodded, his lips turning up just slightly. Then, touching his fingers to the brim of his hat, he reined his horse around and rode out of the clearing.

Rafe waited until the sound of hoofbeats faded into the distance before turning back. When he did, Kristyn was surprised to see that his eyes had mellowed, taking on Carlos' gentler humor.

This time when his lips twisted crookedly at one corner, she sensed no bitterness in the gesture.

"That shirt becomes you, my dear. Your outlaw friend has good taste."

The sudden change in moods confused Kristyn, as she sensed he had intended. Was he trying to make fun of her? Or did he just enjoy playing with her emotions, pulling her back and forth until she didn't know where she was anymore.

"Excellent taste in what?" she responded tartly. "Shirts—or women?"

The words were no sooner out of her mouth than she regretted them. But far from being angry, Rafe only laughed, seeming, quite unpredictably, to enjoy her show of spirit.

"In both, I suspect. Although I had intended to say—in *clothes*." Sitting down on a jutting rock, he stretched out his hand, then dropped it a second later to his knee. "Ah, Cristina, Cristina, what am I to do with you? I keep driving you away, yet here you are back again—and my willpower is shot to hell. Tell me, *querida*, if I locked you up in a room, with bars on the windows and bolts at the door, could I have you to myself? Or would you pine away and die, like a wild creature shut in a cage?"

Kristyn eyed him warily, not sure what he was up to, but knowing it had to be something. Rafe was capable of wooing her with tender words when he wanted, then turning around and doing something cruel!

"I would be like the wild creature!" she burst out defiantly. "Like a poor little fox caught in the traps you white men set. I would gnaw off my foot if I had to to get free!"

"And, damn you, you would, too!" He reached out, grabbing her by the arm and pulling her toward him. "What if I made you a promise, Cristina? What if I guaranteed that I would never try to put you in a trap? Or hold you against your will? What would you say to that?"

"I'd say you were lying!" Kristyn tried to squirm out of his grasp, but he was too strong and she could not get away. "You say you don't want to put me in a trap, but your idea of a trap and mine are two different things. And everything has to be by your definition!" Freedom was a tantalizing concept to him all right, as long as it was freedom for the man and not the woman. He could do anything he wanted—and he probably would!—but let her come home with one silk shirt and he thought she had slept with some man to get it. "You can make me all the promises you want, but the first time you get angry, you'll call me a tramp again. And you'll treat me like one, too! You don't——"

"Enough, woman!" Rafe tightened his hold, making her arm ache. "Confound it, you do have a way of bringing out the worst in me, even when I'm trying to be reasonable. I *do* have a hot temper, but if you had one ounce of patience in that fiery heart, you'd wait five minutes until I'd cooled down instead of setting me off again!"

He drew her closer, his fingers bruising her flesh. But his eyes were surprisingly gentle as they touched hers.

"Don't set so much store by what I say when I'm angry, *querida*. I'm not angry with you. I'm angry with myself. When I first saw you, I thought you were wild, sensual, exciting beyond belief—and that's exactly how I wanted you! But God help me, I wanted you in a cage, too, and if that's a contradiction, I'm not sure I can do a blasted thing about it. Hate me for it if you want, despise me, but don't push me away."

"I—I don't know what to say when you talk to me like that." Kristyn lowered her gaze, confused. "I only know I'd be a fool to trust you again. You've hurt me too many times. Oh, Rafe, I don't want to be hurt again. I can't bear it anymore."

"Shhh . . . shhh!" His breath was hot on her forehead, his lips achingly gentle as they played with her hair. "Why are you fighting me when we could be in each other's arms right now? You are the most contrary woman I have ever met. When I tell you I don't want you, you demand that I make love to you. And when I tell you I do, you fight me like a she-bear! Couldn't we try desiring each other at the same time for a change? Couldn't you come to me, just——"

"Come to you?" Tears flooded Kristyn's eyes. "For what? So you can treat me the way you did last time? So you can tease me, caress me, make me want you until I can't stand it any longer, and then—then . . ."

Rafe laughed sharply. "No, goddammit! I didn't enjoy that any more than you did. It was stupid, it was spiteful, it was immature. I admit it freely. Now, are you going to keep throwing it in my face, or are you going to come here and give me a chance to make it up to you?"

Something in his voice, a deep undercurrent of sensuality, vibrated through Kristyn's body, evoking a familiar warmth that spread slowly outward until even her toes were tingling. Helplessly, she realized that, no matter how brutal he might sometimes be, a part of her was always going to respond to Rafe. It was up to her mind, her reason, to resist.

Summoning all her strength, she wrenched her arm free.

"*No!* I don't want that anymore! I know you don't believe me, but this time you're wrong! You have plenty of other women, we both know that. Go and *use* one of them! Besides, I told you—" she backed away, afraid to be too close— "I didn't come for this. I came because I discovered something today. Something you have to know!"

"Discovered? From whom? Those outlaw friends of yours?"

His voice took on a certain sharpness, but Kristyn forced herself to ignore it.

"Yes! From my outlaw friends! Only—oh, Rafe, this is important. You have to listen! They're going to set charges of dynamite at the mine tomorrow. I've been terrified ever since I heard about it for fear you would set off your own blasts at the same time. I know you haven't been in the mine lately, but I have. The timbers are so rotten in places it's a wonder they don't cave in by themselves. I don't think they'd hold up if all those charges went off."

"You could be right about that." Rafe leaned back against the rock, looking thoughtful. "Well, you needn't have worried. I'm impatient, but I don't work quite that fast! And it looks like I won't have to now. Your friend Collins seems to be doing the job for me."

"Billy?" Kristyn shook her head. "But that doesn't make sense. Billy's looking for cash, not letters. Even if he finds them——"

"I don't expect him to *find* the letters, just set the trap for me. Think about it, my dear. One blast sounds very much like another, regardless of who sets it. Of course having a passel of outlaws running around might complicate things, but then again, it might make them easier. While Cuervo's guards have their hands full with Collins and his men, I'll have a clear coast to keep an eye on their boss. And don't worry . . ." He shot her a wry look. "I'm not going to ask you to do my dirty work for me. I thought better of that idea five minutes after I came up with it. I don't want you anywhere near the son-of-a-bitch. Or near the mine either, with that blasting going on. Now if I can just come up with a disguise . . ."

"Rafe, what are you talking about?" Kristyn stared at him, puzzled. Then suddenly it occurred to her that she had not told him where the letters were! "You don't have to go through all that. Believe me, you don't. You don't even have to——"

"I have to do what I think is right," Rafe cut in, suddenly impatient with the conversation. Striding over, he caught hold of her again, sliding his hands down her back until her body was wedged against his. The warmth of her, the softness, was a spur to his senses, reminding him how much he wanted her. "But that's tomorrow—I can think of better things to occupy us tonight."

"Oh, no . . ."

Kristyn could feel the pressure of his chest, taut against her bosom, and she realized, frightened, that he was not going to woo her with words anymore. He was perfectly capable of taking her by force if he had to.

And God help her, if he did, her own body, even against her will, was going to respond.

"Why are you doing this? Please—*please* . . . I didn't come for this!"

"Liar!" His arms were hard around her, his lips so close they were a distraction. She could hear the laughter in his voice, that teasing tone she both hated and loved. "I can kiss you now, just one kiss, and you won't remember what it is you claim to have come for."

"No—oh, no! That—that's not true!"

"Isn't it?" He had begun to tease her with his lips, barely touching the corners of her mouth, kissing her again and again so tenderly it took her breath away. "Prove it, then. Open your mouth to me, Cristina. Let me come to you just once, and then if you can still pull away, I won't try to stop you."

It was not a challenge, it was a demand. Kristyn felt him close in with his mouth, felt the remembered sweetness of his lips, strong, warm . . . so passionate it was hard to believe there was no love in them. Every part of her body, every nerve, every throbbing muscle, longed to surrender.

Traitor! she cried inwardly as she felt her body sway toward his. And, oh, what traitorous wretches those arms that coiled around him, clinging even as her lips parted hungrily to receive the savage invasion of his tongue. Shame. That was all he offered her. Shame—and yet, oh God, she could not keep from wanting him.

And it *would* be shame . . . when it was over. When she lay alone on the ground, weeping bitterly at the thought of what she had done. She could not forget the way he had treated her last time, the way he had touched and teased and then drawn back again.

Oh, it was wrong! Wrong that a man should use a woman like that and not pay for what he had done. For herself—for every woman who had been so brutally mistreated—she had to fight back!

Anger surged through her veins, and she clung to it, focusing on it, shutting out everything else. Someone should use this man the way he used women. Hurt him the way he had hurt her.

Her lips were quivering as she drew back, just slightly. Her body trembled, almost uncontrollably, but somehow she managed to hold on to her sanity.

"You are right," she murmured breathily. "I can't just kiss you . . . and walk away."

Her hands were coy yet bold as she ran them lightly across his chest, her fingers playing with the buttons of his shirt, slipping inside the fabric for an instant to tangle in the matted hair beneath. She felt him urge her strongly, forcefully to the ground, the sound of laughter deep in his throat telling her he was confident now, sure of himself and his hold over her. She waited until his body strained against hers, waited until she knew he could almost feel his victory. Then, with one swift, fluid movement, she pulled away and drew herself to her feet.

For a minute, he could only lie there, dazed, looking much as she must have looked that night he did the same thing to her. Then, slowly, his eyes darkened, simmering with an anger that was not truly anger at all but a complex of emotions burning in his gut.

"It seems that it is not only women like me who need a man," she said. "Apparently men, too, occasionally feel the need of a woman . . . or are you perhaps an exception?"

He glowered at her for a moment, sensing his defeat, hating it all the more because he had earned it.

"All right, dammit, you win. You are a devious, conniving, infuriating bitch—but yes, by God, I need you! Now for Christ's sake, come here and stop playing my own stupid games on me."

For a single, insane instant, Kristyn was tempted to give in. She had won, he said—and in a way she had. But the final, ultimate victory would never be hers if she showed her weakness now. If she went to him, if she let him see that she wanted him still, she would never, *never* be free.

Taking a step backward, she looked down at him.

"You made the rules, Rafe. You live by them."

Without another word, she turned and walked away, leaving him as he had once left her, alone and cold on the ground. Never again would he use her the way he had. Never would he beckon her at his whim, play with her only when he chose, discard her when he was through. She would love him all her life—she would never truly be free of him in her heart—but from that day forward her body would be her own, never again given in bondage, to him or any man.

Forty-Two

Kristyn could not have said herself what she was doing shortly before dawn the next day, standing on a hillside near the mine in the first frosty chill of morning. Common sense warned her that the Folly was the last place she wanted to be, yet some deeper, basic instinct drew her toward it and she could not force herself to leave.

She had half expected the area to be deserted, but quite the contrary, it was bustling with activity. The shifts seemed to be changing, for long lines of silent, grim-faced men were moving slowly up the hill. As the first of them reached the top, night workers began to pour out of the mine, and Kristyn watched from her vantage point as the two groups worked their way past each other on the crowded path.

She had been there perhaps a quarter of an hour when her eye was caught by a man who stood out dramatically from the others. He had come up the hill with the arriving miners, but he did not move like someone about to go into the pits, and she found herself staring at him, intrigued by something familiar in his bearing. Broad shoulders stretched the fabric of a lightweight cotton shirt, and his body was powerful but not husky. His motions, as he pulled on the bulky coat he had been carrying, were unexpectedly fluid and graceful. Surely there could not be two men in Silver City who looked and moved like that.

"Rafe?"

She was so startled, she uttered the word aloud. Rafe was here! She had known he would be, of course, but she had not expected him so early. And she hadn't expected him to come in with the miners.

Yet she should have! Bitterly, she berated herself for her

lack of foresight. What better time for Rafe to arrive than
with the rest of the men when he would be less likely to be
noticed? And if he had decided to go into the mine . . .

Well, hadn't she herself believed that that was where the
letters were? And oh, she hadn't had time to tell Rafe the
truth! She had been so angry yesterday, so hurt, she hadn't
been able to blurt out the words. He still thought they were in
the mine. That was where he could be waiting for Cuervo
when the blasts came.

And the mine was the most dangerous place he could be!

Kristyn felt her heart thump wildly against her chest. Rafe
thought the mine was safe because he assumed Billy's charges
would be no more hazardous than his own. Only he didn't
know Billy the way she did.

Young Dan had not been wrong yesterday. Billy wouldn't
blow up the safe if he could take the whole building—and he
wouldn't take the building if there was an entire hillside
waiting to be demolished!

Forgetting everything else, Kristyn began to run toward the
entrance where the miners were beginning to gather. She had
to find Rafe somehow in that milling crowd. She had to warn
him before it was too late. Yes, and she had to get the other
men out, too!

Snatches of half-formed plans tumbled over each other in
her brain as she hurried forward, stumbling in her haste. She
could hardly rush into that crowded entry area and shriek out
wild premonitions of disaster. Even if she were a man, the
others would find it hard to believe her farfetched tale. But a
woman? They would only laugh and push her aside as they
went on to their work, unwilling to lose a day's pay on such
flimsy provocation.

No, she could not do that. Somehow she was going to have
to find a man she could take aside and talk to, quietly,
urgently. A foreman, perhaps. One of the older men. Someone the others would trust.

Oh, if only she could catch up with Rafe! If only she could
make him believe her! The men would listen to Rafe. He had
an air of authority about him, a kind of commanding sureness
that prompted others to obey without question.

Only to do that—to catch up with him—she was going to
have to get into the mine!

She paused at the edge of the path, cursing herself for not

having gotten rid of the flashy red shirt and black pants she had been wearing for the past two days. The outfit was soiled now and badly wrinkled, but it was still bright enough to stand out. And her long hair, coiled at the nape of her neck, marked her all too clearly as a woman.

Well, there was no time to worry about that, she reminded herself grimly as she started forward again. Perhaps she would find a storage shed near the entrance where she could help herself to a jacket and a helmet to cover her hair. If not, she was going to have to take her chances and pray that everyone was too busy with their own concerns to notice her.

As she neared the entrance, she saw that it was considerably larger than the one Cuervo had taken her into the day before. Only one side of the long, open shed was walled in, but the entire area had been roofed over with sheets of rusty metal. A counter at the far end was strewn with old woolen coats and shiny rubber slickers, but a number of men were lounging nearby, and Kristyn dared not risk going over.

Most of the miners had congregated at one end of the shed, and Kristyn drifted closer to see what they were doing. As she approached, she caught sight of a crude openwork structure that had been erected over a deep shaft in the ground. It was empty at first, but as she watched, an odd-looking contrivance rose out of the earth and filled it up.

The cage Cuervo had mentioned yesterday. Kristyn felt the men brush against her as they headed toward it, and she moved a short distance away, pausing where she could still see it but would be less likely to be noticed herself. It was constructed of metal, with a solid floor and barred sides, rather like the cages in which Santa Fe *señoritas* kept their brightly colored birds. Only there was nothing ornamental about this device, nothing decorative in its squared-off, utilitarian lines. The gate in front opened noisily and a dozen or so men crowded in before it clattered shut again.

Wasn't that just like Cuervo? she thought, recalling the deep entry shaft at the far end of the mine. A bell clanged somewhere below, and the cage of men descended slowly into the earth. He must have known she would prefer coming in this way, but he had taken her down that rickety ladder all the same. He probably thought she was going to be so frightened she'd throw herself into his arms for comfort!

Kristyn had been so absorbed in watching the cage, she did

not notice that a man had detached himself from the others and come over to stand beside her. Now, feeling a hand on her arm, she looked up with a start.

"Carlos?" She didn't know why it surprised her to find Rafe's brother there, yet somehow it did. "Where—where did you come from? I didn't see you."

"You were so deep in thought, I doubt you could see anyone. But what are you doing here? Don't you know how dangerous it is?"

Kristyn nodded solemnly. Like Rafe, Carlos had garbed himself as a miner, only on him the outfit was more effective. A touch of white powder dulled his hair, and he had smeared dust on his face, hinting at the unnatural pallor of men who spent their lives underground. Plainly, of the two brothers, this was the better actor. Rafe was too strong-willed, too fiercely independent to submerge his own personality, even if his life depended on it.

"Oh, Carlos," she blurted out impetuously. "I'm so frightened. Rafe thinks that Billy Collins is going to set the same kind of blasts he would have. But he's wrong! Billy's going to place enough dynamite to cave the whole hillside in."

"Are you sure?" Carlos's voice was sharp, tense.

"Of course I'm sure! Billy doesn't care about human life. It's cheap to him. He's killed so many men, he doesn't think about it anymore." She faltered, sensing the skepticism on his face. Somehow she had to make him understand. "Don't you see, Carlos? They can't hang Billy more than once. And they can only hang him if they catch him. With all the chaos, with every able-bodied man desperate to dig out survivors, who's going to form a posse to go after him?"

Carlos looked worried.

"There may still be time to evacuate the men. *Por Dios*, I hope so. At least I can try." He started to turn, then caught himself. "I want you to get away from here, Cristina. As fast as you can. The last thing I need now——"

"I can't, Carlos! Don't you understand? Rafe is in there with the others! I saw him come this way. He could be killed."

"And you think that staying here is going to help him? You have already told me what's going to happen. I'll do everything I can to prevent this tragedy, but I'm going to need my wits about me—and so will Rafael! How can he concentrate on what he's doing if he has to worry about you?"

"Worry? About me?" Kristyn was startled by the brittle edge in her voice. It seemed petty, thinking of herself at a time like this, but she couldn't help it. "Oh, Carlos, I wish he *did* worry about me. But he doesn't. The only time he even thinks about me is when his precious ego has been wounded."

"His ego?" Carlos looked at her, surprised. "Sometimes, *amorcita*, I think you are as stubborn and proud as that brother of mine. You think that is all he is feeling? Wounded ego? Don't you realize Rafael is hopelessly in love with you?"

"How easily you say that," she replied softly. "As if you knew what you were talking about. But Rafe *doesn't* love me. He's never even pretended to. Not once, when we have been together, has the word *love* crossed his lips."

Carlos took hold of her shoulders, drawing her close as he looked intently into her eyes.

"Rafael does love you, Cristina, even if you don't believe it. I told you that before. Don't you remember? If I were not sure he loved you, do you think I would have given up my own hopes so easily?"

There was a ring of quiet conviction beneath the teasing in his tone, and Kristyn sensed he was telling the truth, at least as he saw it.

"But if he does love me, if he *really* loves me, why couldn't he say so . . . just once?"

"Words like that have never come easily to Rafael. Don't forget, he was raised by our grandfather, and El Valeroso, too, is very close-mouthed about his feelings. Oh, my poor Cristina . . . if your husband is stubborn and proud, and you are stubborn and proud, how are you going to make peace with each other? One of you has to give in first. One of you has to say, My dear, can we not sit down and talk this out with each other? Could that one not be you?"

He released his hold, dropping his hands with an apologetic smile.

"But this is not the time to talk of such things. Be a good girl, Cristina, and run down the hill so we will know you are safe. There will be time to make things right with Rafael tomorrow, I promise you. Don't be so afraid.''

He turned away, leaving Kristyn to watch helplessly as he pushed through the crowd, heading toward a passageway that seemed to lead to one of the other buildings. Was that where Rafe went, too? she thought, feeling a sudden lump in her throat. Was he just out of the range of her vision? Or was he already deep in the mine?

Don't be afraid, Carlos had said. Only how could she not be? Any minute now, any second, the whole place might collapse in a series of violent explosions, and then how was she supposed to "make things right" with him?

Oh, Rafe . . . *Rafe*. How it hurt to think of him, down there with the others. Even if Carlos managed to find him, what good was that going to do? Rafe would get the miners out all right—he had too much respect for life not to move heaven and earth to do that—but would he come himself? Or would he stay in the mine, facing death in one last brave, stubborn attempt to find the letters?

The letters that weren't even there!

Terrified, Kristyn realized she had to do something. Somehow, she had to get to Rafe and tell him that it was pointless going down into the tunnels, that he would be risking his life for nothing.

But Carlos had told her to stay out of the way.

Kristyn hesitated. If Carlos caught her, he would insist on taking her out of there himself, and that would cost precious time he needed to evacuate the miners.

Still, Carlos didn't need to know what she was doing. Backing out of the shed, she darted across the yard toward the central building. She dared not risk waiting with the men in front of the cage. Carlos might come back and see her. But she could go in that other entrance, picking her way through the labyrinth of tunnels and open, gaping pits Cuervo had shown her yesterday. If she was fast enough, if she managed to remember the way, there might still be time. If not . . .

Shuddering, she forced the thought out of her mind. She could not let herself dwell on the consequences of her failure. If she thought about it now, she would never find the courage to go on.

The hallway that ran through the main building was empty, as was the yard in back. After a quick glance around to make

sure no one was lurking in a shadowy corner, Kristyn hurried
over to the shed where she had gotten her jacket and helmet
the day before.

Once there, she wasted no time. Spying a bulky lantern on
one table, a box of matches on another, she struck a light and
touched it to the wick. She could not risk carrying the lantern
down that awkward ladder, but she could rest it on the ground
in the entry chamber, making the first hazardous part of her
descent a little easier. In the tunnels themselves, she would
rely on the beam from her helmet.

She had no sooner started to search through the jumble of
headgear on the nearest table when her ear picked up a sound
in the yard outside. Gripping the lantern tensely in one hand,
she eased over to the door and peered out. As she did, a man
rounded the corner. Gusts of wind blew thatches of yellow
hair back from his face.

"Billy!"

Kristyn stepped out boldly, knowing she could not sneak
past him across the yard. Her only chance was to try to outwit
him.

"For God's sake—Kris!" Billy's eyes narrowed as he
caught sight of her. "What do you think you're doing?" He
took a step forward, but Kristyn backed off.

"You stay where you are, Billy Collins! If you come
anywhere near me, I—I'll throw this lantern in your face!"

"What the hell?" Billy stopped abruptly. "Dan told me
he'd seen you come in here, but I didn't believe him. What's
going on? Those charges are set to go off any minute now."

"I know that—and there are a lot of men in the mine who
are going to be trapped when they do." Kristyn met his eyes
evenly. "I can't let this happen, Billy. I can't let you do this
terrible thing. I'm going down there."

"You're going—*down there*?"

"I've got to stop this somehow. I can't let you kill . . ."
She hesitated, realizing any mention of the man she loved
would only make things worse. "I can't let you kill innocent
people. I have to do something to stop you!"

"Stop me? Dammit, Kris—no one can stop me! Putting
yourself in danger isn't going to save those miners."

"Maybe not, but at least I can warn them. Maybe there's
enough time to . . ."

"There's no time for anything! It's already too late! Don't

you realize that, you stupid little fool? What do you think? That I'm going to back down when I see you in danger? The charges are already set. I couldn't stop them if I wanted to."

Couldn't? Kristyn wondered sharply. Or wouldn't? She doubted if Billy even knew himself.

"Aren't you tired of all this killing?" she burst out bitterly. "When are you going to weary of taking out your rage, your pain, on decent people who had no share in your hurts? It tore you apart when your sister was killed by your father's cruelty. I know it did. Hasn't it occurred to you that it's someone's brother you'll be killing today? Or husband, or father? I can't let you do it!"

She spun around swiftly, praying that the abruptness of the gesture would take him by surprise. As she scurried across the yard, she could hear his voice calling after her, begging her to come back, but she did not let herself listen. She needed all her concentration now, all her strength for the task that lay ahead.

She hesitated only a fraction of a second at the edge of the pit, letting her light shine into inky blackness that seemed to have no end. Then, clutching the lantern in one hand, she forced herself to reach out with the other, catching hold of the pole as she balanced her feet on shaky rungs.

It was dangerous, she knew, trying to go down that make-shift ladder one-handed, but she dared not leave the lantern behind. Nor could she pause to contemplate what she was doing. It would take Billy a minute to find a helmet or lantern for himself in the shed, a minute more, if she was lucky, to discover the matches where she had left them. Two minutes at most—and in those two minutes she had to be down the pole and well along the sloping gallery that led into the mine!

The wood felt slick beneath her grasp, and she cursed the awkwardness of the lantern, but she could not let it go. Without light down there, without even the few visual clues she might pick up in the gray sameness of the rocks around her, she could never find her way.

Besides, there were too many pits, too many yawning holes that seemed to spring up from nowhere. She had to be able to see where she was going.

She had no time to try each foothold, no time to do anything but step down and pray the wood was sound. If only it hasn't rotted since yesterday! she thought desperately. If only those flimsy slats will hold just long enough to see me to the bottom!

It seemed an eternity, but at last she felt her foot land on something hard, and she realized she had reached solid ground. She paused for a second, listening tensely, not expecting to hear anything but testing the darkness anyway. To her surprise, she detected a faint scuffling somewhere above. A slow, steady sound told her that someone was moving down the ladder.

Billy!

Terrified, she realized that once again her outlaw friend had done the unexpected! He had not gone back for a helmet at all. Boldly, recklessly, he was plunging after her in the darkness.

A slow shiver ran through her body as she realized he was only seconds behind her now. And as long as she had that lantern in her hand, he would be able to see exactly where she was—while she could only guess at his position.

Trying desperately not to think, not to concentrate on anything except the need to get ahead, she forced herself down that shadowy tunnel.

The long, sloping gallery seemed even colder than it had been the day before, and the ground was slippery beneath the leather soles of her boots. Be careful! she warned herself tensely. One misstep, one stumble, and it would all be over. Billy might not be able to force her back to the surface, but he could keep her from going on. He could keep her from getting to Rafe!

The first ominous rumblings reached her ears while she was still in the sloping passage. Horrified, she stopped where she was, too stunned for a moment to move.

The sound seemed to intensify for one heartwrenching second, then broke suddenly, fading into an eerie echo of itself. Kristyn stood still, gauging the direction of it not so much by the noise as by the heavy tremors that vibrated through the earth. Not from above, she thought, faintly puzzled, but from somewhere deep in the mine. Then those weren't Billy's charges at all! They were routine blasts!

The surge of relief that accompanied the thought was short-lived, giving way to a cold sense of dread. What if the miners happened to blast at the same time Billy's charges went off? With powerful explosions coming from all directions, every part of the mine would be affected. Every pit and shaft and tunnel would be struck simultaneously by blasts so potent, she could not even imagine their force.

More frightened than ever, Kristyn pushed herself forward again, redoubling her pace. Somewhere behind her—how close? she wondered—Billy was closing the gap between them.

Within seconds, the tunnel had filled with dust, its eerie, grayish glow obscuring even the outline of rock walls inches away. Kristyn could feel it stinging her eyes, choking her lungs with every breath she took.

We couldn't come this way if they were blasting, Cuervo had told her the day before. *We wouldn't be able to breathe.*

Oh, God, was he right? *Was* she going to die in here?

The thought was fleeting, but utterly terrifying, and it was all Kristyn could do to fight her rising panic. Tugging the silk neckerchief from her throat, she wadded it into a ball and forced it over her mouth. The miners managed the dust all right, Cuervo had said. They were used to it. But there must have been a first time for them, too, and they had survived. If they could do it, so could she!

The thin fabric eased her breathing somewhat, and Kristyn found that she could take in cautious gulps of air without pain. She had begun to feel lightheaded from the lack of oxygen, and the insides of her mouth and nostrils were raw.

Glancing over her shoulder, she tried to catch some hint of Billy, but she could see nothing in that pervasive gloom. Had he been discouraged by the blast, or was he somewhere just behind, ready to reach out and grab her when she least expected it?

Don't think about it, she warned herself tensely. Don't think about anything—just keep on going! If you let yourself think, you'll go crazy with fear.

The dust had begun to settle, so slowly it was barely perceptible at first. Raising her lantern, Kristyn found that she could distinguish vague outlines in the haze ahead of her.

The path had been sloping downward at a steep angle. Now she realized, faintly alarmed, that it had tapered off and she had been walking for some distance on a level stretch. Surely she should have turned by now. Hadn't Cuervo led her to the left almost immediately after the sloping ended? But things seemed so different in the dark. Time and distance had lost all meaning.

She sensed rather than saw the gaping blackness that suddenly loomed up ahead of her. The air had grown colder, taking on a strangely menacing feel. Stopping cautiously, Kristyn picked up a kind of brooding shadow on the ground ahead of her. Reaching out with her toe, she was stunned to feel a sharp edge of rock descending abruptly into nothingness.

A pit! Tears burned her eyes, and she knew they were not caused by the dust. Off to one side, a path twisted away from her, veering not to the left, but sharply right.

She was lost.

Somewhere behind her, somewhere in those blinding clouds of dust, a fork had branched off to the left and she had missed it. Now there were no options open to her, no options at all. She could not go straight ahead, nor could she follow that path to the right, for that would take her farther and farther from the place she wanted to be. And she couldn't go back, because back was where Billy Collins was waiting.

She was not going to make it. The awareness of that bitter reality came, ironically, in the last split second before the explosions began. She had lost, and the taste of defeat was like gall in her mouth. She had wanted so desperately to find Rafe. There were so many things she longed to say to him, so much that was wrong and needed to be set right. Now it was too late, too late for him . . . too late for her. They were both going to die in that terrible dusty darkness, alone and apart from each other, and there was nothing they could do about it.

The explosion came suddenly, reverberating with the force of thunder, making the earth shudder from somewhere deep within. The first blast was followed almost instantly by another, and then another, until even the rocks seemed alive with sound and motion. Fascinated by the sheer power, too horrified to move, Kristyn stood there, watching as stones worked themselves loose from the ceiling and toppled around her. She could feel the thrust of them crashing at her feet, hear the strange hollow echo they made as they rolled into the abyss.

She knew she had to do something—she had to move, to run, to try somehow to save herself—but in that first moment of fear, her mind was numb, her body paralyzed with shock.

Then, suddenly, she was aware of a blur of motion, and a

figure burst with explosive force out of the chaos of dust and falling rocks. It was Billy. She knew it had to be Billy, but he was so gray with dust he looked like a ghost of himself.

"Kris—look out!"

The urgency in his voice drew her eyes upward. Horrified, she saw a deep crack opening in the roof above her head!

Billy did not wait for her to react. Leaping forward, he took hold of her arm, whirling her around, thrusting her with wrenching force against the far wall. The breath was knocked out of her as she struck that hard, unyielding stone, and her hands flailed wildly upward, letting the lantern fly from her grasp.

That last brief moment would be forever a series of impressions in her mind. Billy's face, tense yet vitally alive in the hazy lantern glow. The toe of his boot, defying that unutterably deep abyss, holding for a second at the edge. The sharp grunt of pain that escaped his lips as stones came tumbling down, smashing against his head. And, oh—that terrible, excruciating feeling of falling helplessly through space, as if it were she and not Billy who was hurtling to her death on the jagged rocks below.

Then the lantern crashed against the floor, and everything was black.

Forty-Three

Kristyn stood alone in the darkness, listening as the last faint echoes of the explosion died away. The silence that followed was broken only by an occasional eerie clatter as stones continued to break loose from unstable walls. The stillness was so heavy, so unnatural, she almost imagined she could hear particles of dust drifting to the ground.

"Billy?"

She called his name aloud, but she called it softly, knowing she would receive no reply. In that last second before the lantern shattered she had seen everything all too clearly. No miracle was going to restore her friend to her. No laughing voice would call out from someplace in the darkness, "Oh, come on, Kris, you didn't think you could get rid of me as easily as that, did you?"

She was aware suddenly of something in her hand, and tightening her fingers, she was surprised to find she was still clinging to the neckerchief. Wadding it up again, she pressed it against her mouth to block out the choking dust. Billy had always been so sure of himself, so ready to gamble even when the odds were against him. Had it ever occurred to him, she wondered, that sooner or later he was bound to lose?

Why had he done it? The dust seemed to knot up in her lungs, and she coughed painfully into the scarf. He would have been safe if he had stayed where he was. Why had he risked his life for her?

There had been so much in Billy that was evil and warped, yet there had been much that was good, too. In death as in life he was a contradiction. A man whose existence was based on stealing, a man who could kill without thinking twice—that was the man who had given his life to save her.

The dust had begun to settle again, or so it seemed, although without sight to aid her, Kristyn could not be sure. At least the earth was steady now, with no hint of the rumblings that had rocked it before, and she found she could breathe quite easily when she pulled the scarf from her mouth. She knew it was time to assess her situation, time to try to do something, but it was hard to make herself move, and she realized she was afraid.

It took all her willpower to force herself down on her hands and knees, groping through the heaps of dirt and broken rocks that littered the ground. If only she could get a feel for what had happened, if she could visualize the area the way it was now, perhaps she could figure out what to do.

After a few seconds, her hands found the edge of the pit and, shuddering back her revulsion, she used it to get her bearings.

The pit had been straight ahead when she came upon it. That meant that the tunnel to the entry shaft was behind her now. Turning, she crawled painfully toward it, sweeping the ground with her hands as she advanced, trying desperately to find the opening where she knew it had to be. But every time she reached out, she encountered only more rocks, more rubble, blocking her in every direction.

It was several minutes before she admitted the truth. She was not going to find the tunnel because the tunnel no longer existed. The explosion had loosened the support beams, collapsing them until nothing remained of the narrow passage but stone and shattered veins of ore.

And the other tunnel?

The thought clutched like icy fingers at Kristyn's heart. What if the other tunnel, too, the one veering off to the right, was blocked? There would be no way out then. No way she could even call for help through that massive stone barrier. She would die here. She would sit down and wait for suffocation or starvation to overtake her, and no one would ever know what had happened.

Fear rose in her throat and, desperately, she choked it back. The other tunnel would not be blocked! They couldn't both be blocked!

But the surge of relief that flooded through her as she crawled forward and found the tunnel open was replaced abruptly, irrationally, by a moment of blind panic. The tunnel had been her only hope, her only chance for survival, yet the thought of forcing herself into it was suddenly more terrifying than everything that had gone before.

If it had been the other passage, the one that was blocked, she would not have minded so much. She had seen that passage with her eyes. She knew what to expect. But this one? What if it led to another wall of rock? Another deep, impassable abyss?

Well, wherever it goes, she reminded herself grimly, I have to follow it! And I had better do it now.

She had not realized until she stood erect and forced herself into the mouth of the tunnel, groping for a foothold with every step, how hard it was going to be to leave Billy behind in the darkness. The reaction was not at all logical, she knew, but still it was hard to turn and walk away.

She recalled suddenly a windy afternoon on a craggy tor rising above the streets of Dodge. Boot Hill. How she had hated the place, but Billy seemed to thrive on those bleak, weathered rocks. These are my kind of people, he liked to say. Someday I am going to lie among them.

Only now, for Billy, that someday would never come. There would be no open hillside for him, no dubious friends to keep him company. Only a deep, lonely pit, never warmed by shafts of sunlight, never parched by the dry winds that swept across the plains.

Blinking back her tears, Kristyn forced herself to focus on the tunnel as she started forward again. She would mourn her friend later—right now she had to concentrate on the task at hand. Billy had given his life for her. The least she could do was see that his sacrifice had not been in vain.

The tunnel continued on a fairly level plane, easing sometimes to the right, sometimes to the left, until Kristyn no longer had any idea where she was or what direction she was moving. The walls closed in at times, brushing her shoulders, and she had the terrifying feeling it was all going to come to an end. But somehow it never did and she managed to go on.

The cold stone seemed to grow damper and damper with each passing minute, and she could almost feel water trickling down the walls. A soft splashing sound marked every step she took, and her feet were numb with the moisture that seeped into her boots.

"Oh, *please*—don't get any deeper!"

She whispered the words aloud, not because she expected anyone to hear, but simply because the sound of a voice, any voice, was a comfort in that terrible darkness. What was it Cuervo had told her? The tunnels sometimes flood so badly they have to be shut down? What was she going to do if she rounded the next corner and found the passage so deep in water she had to turn back?

Oh, if only Rafe were there with her! If only she could feel his arms around her, hear his voice one more time in her ear. If only she could know he was safe!

It tore her heart apart to think he might be dead or dying in some far corner of the mine at that very moment. She had made such dreadful mistakes in her relationship with him. She had run away from problems when she should have stayed and faced them. She had to have a chance to work things out with him!

The path had begun to tilt upward, so subtly at first Kristyn did not recognize it. When at last she realized what was happening, she stopped abruptly, gaping into the darkness in amazement.

Up! The path was going up. And *up* led to the surface!

She began to move more rapidly, her step quick and eager for the first time. Surely if the path was going up, it must connect with an entry shaft on the far side of the mine. And she might reach it at any moment!

She was half running now, stumbling in her haste to get ahead, not even caring what was underneath her feet. Only when she felt her toe jam against a large boulder did she force herself to slow down.

Next time it might not be a rock, she reminded herself grimly. Next time it might be a gaping hole deep in the earth!

She did not know how long she followed that gently sloping path. It could have been an hour or two, it could have been half the day—she had no way to tell. She only knew that time, which seemed to fly before, was now beginning to drag again, each new second bringing new fears that her optimism was ill-founded. What if the tunnel did not lead to an entry shaft at all? Or even worse, what if it was not really going up? What if it was only an illusion, reinforced by her need to believe?

Even her eyes had begun to play tricks on her. Up ahead,

she could have sworn, just for an instant, that she caught a brief flicker of light, glinting off the stone path.

Too many hours in the darkness, she thought helplessly. Too much straining into inky blackness. Now she was beginning to see things that weren't there. But, oh, God, it *had* been tantalizing. Soft whispers of gold, seeming to glow in the shadows, like a ray of sunlight shimmering on moist gray stones.

A ray of sunlight?

Kristyn felt her body tremble as she realized suddenly that the image was not an illusion, not a mirage at all, but a real beam of light. Natural, beautiful sunlight filtering down from above.

Her heart began to flutter wildly as she raced forward, barely able to believe her good fortune. After all those hours of imprisonment, those grim hours of fear, she was safe at last!

But the cry of triumph died on her lips the instant she entered that narrow shaft and looked up. The light was there all right, and it *was* sunlight—but it was hopelessly out of reach.

She could have wept with weariness and frustration. It was so close—the end of her agonizing ordeal was so achingly close—yet it might as well have been a thousand miles away. The shaft was barely twenty feet deep, but twenty was no different than a hundred when there was no ladder in sight and the walls were made of hard, slick stone. The opening at the top was partially sealed with decaying boards and covered with a thick layer of weeds, mute evidence that no one had come that way in months.

Tears shimmered in Kristyn's eyes, but she forced herself to blink them back. She had come too far to give up! She might not be able to climb those sheer walls, but she could scream her lungs out and pray that someone would come. The main entrance to the mine must be at least a mile away, and in all the chaos, she could not imagine that anyone would hear, but she had to try!

Her shouts echoed shrilly off the walls, sounding eerie and unreal, more like an animal in pain than the cries of a woman needing help. Common sense warned her that no one was there, but the will to live prompted her to call out again and again, even when her voice was raw and she knew it would soon give out.

She was nearly ready to dissolve at last in a fit of helpless tears when she became aware of sounds coming from somewhere outside. Shouting? she wondered. Hoarse shouting, as if someone had heard and was calling back. Catching her breath, she fell silent, straining her ears into the deepening shadows.

At first she could hear nothing, and she was afraid she had imagined it. Then it came again, louder this time, clearer, the same strong, masculine tones she had heard before. Only this time she was sure they were calling—Cristina.

"Oh, Rafe! Rafe, is that you? I'm here—in an old abandoned mine shaft!"

He was alive! The tears came spilling out of her eyes, running openly down her cheeks. Rafe was alive, and he had come to find her! She was sure of his voice now. He was so close there was no mistaking it. And he *was* calling her name.

She could see hands clutching at the crude wooden grating, ripping it away, and a sudden stream of sunlight flooded into the shaft. The brightness blinded her for an instant and she could barely make out the faces that peered over the edge, but she knew one was Rafe, the other Carlos. Two voices called out in unison.

"Cristina? Are you down there? Are you all right? What's happened? Have you been hurt?"

"No, no—I'm fine," she shouted back. Now that she could see him clearly, she wanted to laugh through her tears. His face was so smudged with dirt she barely recognized him. "But, oh, Rafe—I was so afraid. It was dark down there and the lantern went out and I—I thought I was never going to get out."

"Hush, darling, hush! Don't be afraid. We're here now. We'll take care of you. We're going to have you out in no time, I promise."

He was as good as his word. Kristyn could hear sounds coming from above, then a rope dangled over the edge and Rafe was swinging down it, one-handed, letting that rough cord burn through his fingers. She would never be sure in all that confusion just how it happened, but suddenly she was in his arms and he was holding her tightly, protectively against his body.

"Oh, Cristina, Cristina—I thought I had lost you." He

buried his head in her hair, the aching in his voice muffled by thick, dusty tresses. "I've been such a fool, my darling. Such a damn, stubborn fool. Can you ever forgive me?"

Could she forgive him? Kristyn laid one hand on each side of his face, tilting his head back so she could look at him. Were those tears she saw in his eyes?

"You *are* a fool, Rafe Valero," she murmured huskily, "if you need to ask that."

"Oh, my darling, I love you. God help me, you'll probably twist my heart in your fingers, but there it is—I love you."

Whatever he said next, whatever questions he asked, Kristyn barely heard him, and while she answered automatically, telling him what had happened, she was not even aware that she was speaking. All she could focus on, all she could think of, were the words he had said before. He loved her! Rafe loved her, and he was not afraid to tell her so!

Rafe turned out to be surprisingly solicitous, refusing to let her climb up the rope even though she assured him she was as nimble as a monkey and could manage quite easily. Instead, he insisted on knotting it securely around her waist so Carlos could hoist her out of the pit. Any other time, Kristyn might have protested, but today she was so happy to be with him, she could not bring herself to quarrel about anything.

He finished tying the knot and gave it a sharp tug to make sure it would hold, wincing slightly as he did. Startled, Kristyn recalled the way he had swung one-handed into the pit.

"Oh, Rafe—your arm! You're hurt!"

"It's nothing. I wrenched it trying to get some of the men out of the shaft. It'll heal by itself. Come on, now—up with you."

Rafe boosted her up, and Carlos hauled her the rest of the way in a matter of seconds, tossing the rope back for his brother. Kristyn could not resist a little smile as she saw Rafe loop it around his wrist, disdaining to secure it at his own waist. Holding on with his good arm, he braced his feet against the wall and walked up it with a show of athletic grace. He might have yielded enough to tell her he loved her, but that stubborn male pride was still intact!

The next few minutes seemed like a dream, and Kristyn almost felt as if she were sleepwalking. Rafe's arm was around her and he was guiding her away from the shaft, urging her down on the earth beside him, not letting go of her for an instant. Everything that had happened, all the fear, all the pain, flooded away, and she was conscious only of the comforting strength of his body next to hers.

"Oh, my darling," she whispered. "I was so afraid for you."

"*You* were afraid?" Streaks of dirt and sweat gave his face a wry look. "I had forgotten how perversely feminine that mind of yours is. *You* were worried about *me*? Did it ever occur to you, my sweet, that I might have been practically out of my mind with fear for you when I learned you had gone down into the mine?"

"You knew I was there?"

"Of course I knew. What do you think I was doing over here? When we couldn't get through the other way, I remembered this tunnel and hoped it wouldn't be blocked. But, for God's sake, whatever possessed you to do such an insane thing? You knew it was dangerous. You had just told Carlos as much."

"Yes, I knew—but I was worried about you! I hadn't told you about that shack, or Carlos either when I saw him, and I was afraid you'd be looking for the letters below . . ."

She broke off, realizing suddenly that she wasn't making sense. Forcing herself to speak slowly, she told him everything that had happened from the time she first discovered the shed to the flood of fear that raced through her heart when she came to the Folly at dawn and saw him in miner's garb.

Rafe's features clouded over as she finished.

"You mean you went down there for me? Because you thought you could help me?"

"It was my fault you were there in the first place. I should have told you about that shed yesterday, only we—well, I was just so mad I couldn't think straight! And then I saw you this morning, and I knew I had to get you out of the mine somehow before——"

"But I wasn't *in* the mine." He gave her a funny, teasing look. "You persist in thinking of me as a fool, though God knows why. Could it be the way I have occasionally behaved with you? I would never have gone into those shafts with half the hillside about to be blown away, even if I did think the letters were there—which, incidentally, I didn't. They were much too valuable for Cuervo to stash them someplace where they could be buried under tons of rock.''

"Then you knew they were aboveground all along? Did you know about the shack, too?''

"I suspected it, yes, though it was only a guess. The place looked exactly as it had years ago—even the things inside were the same—but there was a brand-new lock on the door. Still, I couldn't be sure enough to risk breaking in, not until this morning. Cuervo was just arriving when the explosions started, and the minute he realized what was happening, he took off like a bat out of hell. I didn't have time to follow him, but I saw where he was going.''

"And you couldn't stop him? Oh, Rafe . . .'' Kristyn felt suddenly very tired. "Then he got the letters after all—and he got away with them. I know how much the Folly means to you. You were willing to risk your life to get it back. Now he's going to hide them someplace else, and you'll never be able to find them.''

"Not exactly.'' Rafe drew back, studying her intently for a minute. Then he rose and held out his hand to pull her up. "You're going to have to see this sooner or later. Might as well get it over with now.''

Kristyn followed him mutely to a spot a few yards away where a slightly elevated clearing offered an unrestricted view of the terrain below. At first she had the odd feeling that he had taken her to the wrong place, for the area she was looking at did not seem even vaguely familiar. Then, slowly, she realized what had happened.

Rafe had not been exaggerating when he said that half the hillside was blown away. Below her, the land was marked with open, ugly scars where rocks had been wrenched out of the earth. Isolated areas, surprisingly, remained intact, and the long entry shed with its elevator cage, was virtually untouched. But the central building where the offices were located had been demolished by a massive avalanche. And the place where the shack once stood was nothing but a heap of dirt and stone.

"Cuervo was—*inside* when it happened?''

"Yes.''

"Then he is dead?''

Rafe nodded grimly. "He had just gone in with one of his men when the whole thing came crashing down on top of them. I doubt if he even had time to get at the letters. They were probably buried somewhere under the floorboards. We won't know for sure until we get into the place and dig it out. Maybe not even then.''

"What happens if you don't find them?"

"I don't suppose it will make much difference. The official who falsified the records is basically an honest man. Now that Cuervo is dead, I daresay he can be persuaded to do the right thing. Not,'' he added, glancing wryly down the hill, "that I expect anyone to dispute my ownership. There isn't a hell of a lot left to fight over.''

Kristyn could hardly disagree. Looking down at that mutilated hillside, she thought sadly that she had never seen anything so appalling in her life. Perhaps, in the end, something might be salvaged. Cuervo *had* hinted at rich veins that had not yet been tapped. But for now the destruction was awesome and complete, and she sensed that the Folly would never be the same again.

And what good had it done? Billy didn't have the riches he had sought, and Rafe had lost his mine. All that earth torn up—those men buried in the tunnels for nothing.

"The poor men,'' she said softly. "I wonder how many were as lucky as I.''

"We did what we could, Cristina.'' Rafe took her by the shoulders and turned her around. "Fortunately, the working areas weren't badly hit, just some of the tunnels. The night shift was already out, thank God, and we managed to keep most of the new men from going in. There will be loss of life, of course, but it would have been far worse if you hadn't found Carlos when you did and alerted him. You can at least take comfort in that.''

"Comfort? Well, maybe . . .''

It was hard to find comfort in the midst of such sickening devastation, hard to think only of the men who had been saved when even now she could see long lines of people working their way up the hill from town. She could not make out their faces from that distance, but she knew they were gaunt and harrowed with fear. How many of them would recognize the features they searched for in that dusty throng of miners? And how many would go home again weeping and alone?

This was Billy Collins' legacy. The thought saddened her,

even more than his death. When people talked of him in days
to come, they would not remember his laughter, as she did,
his boyish recklessness, those sudden, unexpected fits of
generosity. They would remember only the evil about him.
The man he had shot one bullet at a time, inching closer and
closer to his heart. The mine he had blown out of the side of
a hill.

"Well . . . at least he paid for this."

"He?" Rafe threw her a quizzical look.

"Billy. He died down there."

The instant the words were out of her mouth, she felt him
pull away, and she regretted having spoken. They had been
so close these last few minutes, she forgot how jealous he
could be.

"Oh, yes—your friend Collins. You say he died in the
mine? Do you by any chance expect me to grieve for him?"

"No, of course not, but . . ." Kristyn faltered, suddenly
ashamed of the way she had reacted. "But *I* do! I'm sorry,
Rafe—I know how you feel, but I can't deny Billy just
because you want me to! He *died* for me down there. He gave
his own life to save mine. I'm not going to ignore him, as if
he never existed. No, and I'm not going to pretend I didn't
care about him either!"

She turned away, a little confused by her own outburst.
Why did they have to quarrel like this? Why did they keep on
jabbing at each other even after they admitted their love?

He moved up behind her, laying his hands lightly on her
shoulders.

"Peace, Cristina—I have no desire to stir up all the bitterness again."

"Nor I, love." She turned back, smiling a little as she
caught sight of his face in the fading afternoon light. How
funny he looked, with smudges all over his cheeks and nose.
"But I think it might be wiser to talk of other things. Anyway,
I really am curious about something. How did you know I
was in the mine?"

"One of Collins' gang told us. A young boy. A redhead.
He seemed to have a fit of conscience at the last minute—or
maybe he was worried about you, my sweet. He's just the
right age for developing a crush on an older woman."

An older woman, indeed! Kristyn tried to scowl, but succeeded only in giggling.

"That would have been Dan. Dan McCafferty. He's a good boy at heart. I hate to think what's going to happen to him."

"Oh, I imagine they'll go easy on him. He did come to us before the blasting started and turned himself in voluntarily. As a matter of fact, he helped us locate one of the charges and defuse it. I don't suppose he can look forward to a hero's reception, but he ought to get off all right."

"If it were just this one thing, maybe. But there is something else, too. Something in his past."

"This is the West, Cristina," Rafe reminded her gently. "Many men here have pasts, and they've learned to live with them. The boy couldn't go through with this violence today. That shows good faith on his part. I rather doubt, in light of that, that anyone is going to delve into his past. I think he's going to be fine."

"Oh, I hope so. It would be so much easier if I could only believe that something good was going to come out of all this."

"Something good has already come out of it."

Rafe smiled as he caught the puzzled look on her face.

"We have come close to each other again, and what could be better than that? I know there are still things to be settled between us, but we have time, darling. All the time in the world."

He took her in his arms then, tenderly, reassuringly, telling her once again, without words, that he loved her and everything was going to be all right. Only when he felt the last tremors ease out of her body did he look up to acknowledge his brother, waiting patiently a short distance away. Even then, he seemed reluctant to leave.

"I'll rejoin you later," he promised. "When things have settled down at the mine and Carlos and I have done everything we can for the men who are trapped inside."

He had taken only a few steps when he turned back, a lopsided grin spreading across his face.

"See that you wait for me at the hotel. I want you there when I get back! Don't run away from me again!"

Kristyn laughed softly as she stood alone on the hillside, watching him disappear into the shadows. As if she would ever be tempted to run, now that he was hers at last! She could not believe how tall he looked, so strong and straight-

backed, even though he must be as exhausted as she. Only
when he was finally gone and she could no longer see him
did she turn and begin to make her way into town.

He was right, she thought as she cut through the undergrowth toward the road. There *were* things that had to be
settled between them, hurts to be assuaged, but she was not
afraid of them now. Rafe loved her—he had told her so at
last!—and she had always loved him. Nothing could come
between them again.

Dusk had already begun to gather by the time Kristyn
reached the outskirts of town, and the natural darkness was
intensified by black clouds massing on the horizon. A scatter-
ing of people was still on the road, hurrying in the direction
of the mine, women for the most part, in calicos and faded
gingham skirts.

She was half a block from the hotel when the wide double
doors swung open and a slender figure darted out. Ysabel was
dressed in the same white gown she had worn the day before,
but somehow on the dusty main street of a Colorado mining
town it looked almost grotesquely out of place.

Kristyn hesitated, half tempted to step into a convenient
doorway until the girl had passed. But one look at the stricken
expression on those usually sullen features was enough to
make her ashamed of the impulse.

Why, she's scared to death, she thought, surprised. She
loves Rafe, too—and she's terrified that something happened
to him in the explosion!

And after all, Ysabel was no threat to her. Rafe had just
told her he loved her! Surely she could be generous with a
vanquished rival.

"They're all right, Ysabel," she called out. "Rafe is
fine—and Carlos, too. I just left them a little while ago."

"You were with them?" Ysabel stopped a few feet away,
tossing her head with a strangely defiant look. "*Both* of
them?"

"Of course, both of them," Kristyn replied, puzzled by
the emphasis in the girl's tone. "They just rescued me from
one of the mine shafts. Now they've gone off to see about the
others."

The color left Ysabel's face, returning slowly in the form
of two red splotches, one on each cheek.

"You enjoy that, don't you? Having two men to come to

your rescue, not just one. Doesn't it bother you at all, sleeping with two brothers? Playing them off against each other even though you know you'll poison their relationship?"

"Oh, for heaven's sake, Ysabel." Kristyn was so tired, she could only manage to be mildly annoyed. "I'm not playing them off against each other. I thought you knew that. I only want one of them, and you're upset because he's the one you want, too. Well, I'm afraid you can't have him. He's mine—and I'm very sure of him now."

"You're sure of every man you sleep with, aren't you? Rafael, Carlos—even that outlaw who's responsible for all this! Well, you'll have one less lover in your corral after tomorrow when they hang that Indian you call your husband."

"When they—what?" Now it was Kristyn who turned suddenly pale as she tried numbly to grasp what the other girl was saying. "They're going to *hang* Little Bear? But how can you . . . Are you sure? Where did you hear that?"

Ysabel glowered angrily. "I don't know anything about this Little Bear. But the one you called your husband—the one with the funny name, Man-with-the-Wolves or something like that—was caught yesterday near Fort Avery. They say he's going to hang in the morning, but I don't suppose that matters to you. You'll just find yourself another admirer to take his place. How about Ricardo Cuervo? He was sweet on you. Or maybe he'll be too busy now with everything that's happened at the mine!"

Without waiting for a reply she began to stomp childishly down the street, heading back the way she had come. Dazed, Kristyn stared after her, watching as she disappeared into the hotel.

Little Bear? . . . Captured?

She had always known that one day she would hear those words, but that did not make them any easier to accept. Little Bear to hang in the morning? Wearily, she wondered if it was ever possible to prepare oneself to hear something like that.

She could not condone the acts her young husband had committed, any more than she could find excuses for Billy Collins, but she could understand the pain that had driven him to them. She had loved him deeply once. In a way she loved him still, loved him with the part of her that was yet a little girl and remembered everything they had shared together. She could not bear to think of him locked up in a cage like an animal, waiting to die among strangers.

Impulsively, she spun around, scanning the deserted street
with her eyes. She would never be able to make her way
through the crowds toward that place on the hillside where
she had tied her horse, but there was a sturdy, long-legged
bay tethered to a hitching post in front of the county jail. If
she leaped on his back now, not stopping to think of the
consequences—if she rode all night without resting—could
she reach Fort Avery by dawn?

She hesitated only briefly as she untied the horse, standing
for a moment with the reins in her hands.

See that you wait for me at the hotel, Rafe had told her.
Don't run away from me again.

She had already run away from him twice, once on their
wedding night, again on the night they had quarreled so
bitterly. He had managed to forgive her for that. Could he
forgive so easily again?

Oh, Rafe, Rafe, she thought miserably—oh, my darling.
He had swallowed his pride once to admit he loved her. Once
was enough for a man like that. She cast a last, hasty glance
down the street, but as before, no one was there, and she
realized helplessly that she would never be able to find
anyone in that empty town to take a message to him. Any
explanations would have to come when she returned—if he
was willing to listen.

It was a terrible chance she was about to take, but she
knew she had to do it. Little Bear was her husband. Rafe had
known that when he took her to the white man's altar, even if
he hadn't seen fit to mention the fact to her. He might be
ready to overlook her obligations to another man, but she was
not. She had to go to him now.

It was ironic, she thought as she flicked the reins over the
horse's head and swung into the saddle. Rafe would have
been the first to tell her there were things a man had to do if
he was going to live with himself. Why was it so hard for
him to understand that a woman had to be true to her honor,
too?

She had done little enough for her husband while he lived.
The least she could do was stand by him at the moment of his
death.

Forty-Four

Fort Avery was a sturdy rectangular enclosure, composed primarily of barracks and military offices arranged around a large, unpaved court. As Kristyn paused briefly just inside the gate, she saw that the central yard was almost eerily empty. Only a single officer cut across it, kicking up a trail of dust behind the heels of his smartly polished boots. Along the periphery, crude boardwalks groaned under the weight of too many people as frontiersmen in rough buckskin crowded in beside black-clad shopkeepers and farmers' wives with broad-brimmed sunbonnets.

She was too late!

Kristyn's heart sank as she saw the size of the crowd. It was barely past dawn and the newly erected gallows at the end of the yard was empty, but people had already begun to cast impatient glances in that direction, as if they expected the show to begin at any minute. She had counted on having time with Little Bear, an hour at least, two or three. Time to talk of memories and feelings, time to reestablish a sense of the past and find an acceptance of the present—time to say all those things she had rehearsed so carefully on the long ride from Silver City. Now it was too late.

The feeling of futility was reinforced a few minutes later when she located the commandant of the fort and told him in a few terse sentences what she wanted. Even had there been a full day before the hanging, she doubted that he would have considered her request. He was a man of average height and rigid military bearing, with scant traces of gray in close-cropped hair and not a hint of compassion in his eyes.

"You want to see the prisoner, madam?" His voice was as

599

clipped as his manner. "Privately? I'm afraid that is totally out of the question."

"But, captain, I *must* see him." Kristyn was embarrassed to feel tears well up in her eyes. "*Please*—you must help me!"

The captain remained unmoved. He had less than his share of patience with overindulged females, and his profession had made him well-acquainted with the type of woman who was unnaturally attracted to savages and criminals.

Still, he had to admit, running a practiced eye up and down her figure, this woman hardly seemed the type. She was roughly dressed, and as dusty as if she had been on the road for a week, but there was a kind of dignity about her, a quiet self-possession that in his experience usually indicated good breeding.

"I am afraid I cannot allow that, madam," he said, softening his voice a little. "I have strict orders not to allow anyone to see the prisoner. Publicly or privately."

"But couldn't you make an exception in this case? You see, this man, Little Bear—the one you call Man-Who-Lives-with-the-Wolves—is my husband."

"I beg your pardon?" The captain was shocked enough to drop his military stiffness. He had a sister who looked a little like this woman. A much younger sister, maddeningly annoying at times, but quite fetching, too, when she wanted to be. If any man ever suggested that she had been touched—much less *bedded*—by an Indian, he would have killed him. "Surely you don't mean that this—this savage is your husband?"

Kristyn tilted her chin up as she met his eyes. They were all alike, these Blue Coats! So intent on killing Indians, they didn't even look at them as human beings.

"I was stolen by the Cheyennes when I was a little girl," she retorted sharply. "I don't expect you to understand how I feel, but I lived among those people most of my life. I grew up with the man you are going to hang today. We were children together, we came to adulthood together—and we fell in love. I have returned to my own people now, but I cannot forget him or turn my back on him in his moment of need. Tell me, captain, would you have more respect for me now if I were less loyal to my husband?"

The captain shuffled his feet uncomfortably. This woman

was looking more like his sister every minute, a hot-tempered vixen, but unaccountably winsome for all that.

"I'm sorry," he murmured awkwardly. "Really I am. But there is—well, there's nothing I can do."

Kristyn heard the reluctant finality in his tone, and she knew she ought to give up. But somehow she could not bring herself to leave, not without trying to make him understand.

"My husband was educated by the whites, captain. His people sent him to the mission school when he was very young so he could learn the ways of the conquerors and fit into their world. But the only thing he learned there was that he would never be accepted, no matter how properly he dressed or how well he spelled his words or said his prayers. He did not belong. His manners were perfect, his speech flawless—but the color of his skin would always be different."

She paused, not certain whether his silence meant she had touched him or only that he was embarrassed by her unexpected frankness.

"But you see, captain, when he came home, he found that he did not belong there either. He was tainted in the Cheyenne world, as he had once been tainted in the world of the whites. Tainted by his contact with a culture the others could not understand. I know what it feels like to be an outsider among your own people, and I assure you it is a painful position. That's why he did what he did. To carve a place for himself with his people."

"By killing others?" The man's eyes widened. "By slaughtering innocent women and children?"

"By living as an Indian, captain. And dying as one."

She was vaguely aware as she turned away that he had not heard a word of what she was saying, but it no longer mattered. Plainly he had never understood the Indians, and he was never going to. Would she be like that one day, too? she wondered sadly. So wrapped up in her own concerns she forgot what the rage was all about? The pain?

To die like an Indian. Perhaps that was a concept no white man could ever understand. To couple your own death with the death of your people. To stand up and meet your fate, strong and free to the last. She had begun to understand dimly that that was the only path Little Bear could ever have taken, perhaps the one she would have chosen herself if she had stayed with the Cheyennes. The end result was the same.

Death was death, no matter what. But his would be a death of
fire and fury, not the slow spiritual strangulation of the
reservation.

She found a relatively uncrowded spot on the boardwalk
not far from the main gate and took her place there to wait
quietly for what she now accepted as inevitable. She had not
detected bars on any of the windows opening onto the
courtyard, and she dared to hope they would be bringing her
husband in from outside the compound. If they did, if they
came by the place where she was standing, perhaps after all
she would be able to speak to him. Perhaps he would pause
for a minute—a second—just time enough to say a word or
two.

It was not much, a brief word in passing, but it was all she
could hope for.

She felt her eyes being drawn with a kind of morbid
fascination toward the scaffolding at the far end of the yard.
It was a simple structure, no more than a crude platform five
or six feet off the ground with a flight of steps leading up to
it. She sensed it had been hastily erected, perhaps the night
before, for it still had the naked look of new lumber about it.
A sturdy beam ran across the top, and from this a rope now
dangled, the noose at its end silhouetted against the streaked
gray backdrop of a cloudy sky.

The clearing, which had been so empty only a minute
before, now began to fill with soldiers as men in blue uni-
forms took up their positions every few feet along the
boardwalks. Their presence seemed to have an effect on the
crowd for the level of conversation fell, and in that subtle,
unexpected stillness, Kristyn's ear picked up the rhythmic
cadence of marching boots outside the enclosure. Turning
toward the gate, she was just in time to see two columns of
soldiers move with military precision into the yard. They
formed themselves smartly into a long double line, then
halted, marking off the edges of a narrow walkway leading to
the gallows.

Kristyn's heart stopped beating, then started again with a
wildly thumping sound. It's beginning, she thought. It's
beginning—and I can't do anything to stop it!

A child darted suddenly out of the crowd, dodging between
a pair of soldiers and plopping himself down on the dirt.
Almost immediately, a distraught mother started after him,

but one of the Blue Coats waved her back and strode forward himself. Picking up the tot by the back of his shirt, he carried him, flailing and bellowing, back to where the woman was standing.

"But I can't *see*!" the boy screamed as the soldier thrust him back in his mother's arms. "I can't see *anything* from here!"

Ghoul! Kristyn thought. Monster! She hated the child at that moment, hated the mother who had brought him there, hated the soldier who hoisted him good-naturedly onto his shoulders. They were all ghouls, these people who came to wallow in the macabre spectacle of a man kicking his life away at the end of a rope!

Yet even as she cursed them, Kristyn knew she was not being fair. Some of these people were farmers. They lived in isolated houses scattered throughout the countryside, much like the farmhouse she herself had seen only a few days before. Every morning of their lives they got up knowing that a war party of Indians might be somewhere just outside. Was it any wonder they had come to cheer the death of this man who brought such terror into their everyday existence?

A silence fell suddenly over the crowd, a kind of expectant hush, followed within seconds by a ripple of sound as people began to nudge their neighbors, turning with excited whispers toward the gate. Kristyn turned with them, knowing even before she did what she was going to see.

Little Bear was standing almost exactly in the center of that wide entrance. Blue-coated soldiers were stationed on either side, but they stood a little apart, almost giving the illusion that he was alone. His hands had been tied behind him, but his back was proud and straight, his shoulders set in a defiant line. His eyes were turned toward the gallows, but it seemed to Kristyn they did not focus on it, almost as if he were staring through that crude structure, beyond it, at things that no one else could see.

They had taken the eagle feather from him, but his hair was tied back with the same red bandanna, and a faint breeze blew it lightly away from his face. Like the day he rode home from mission school, Kristyn thought, her heart catching in her throat. Like the day she had run down that hillside, eager to welcome him back. Only then, when he had leaned down to look into her face, she had seen laughter in his eyes.

He paused briefly in the gateway, then began to move slowly forward. There was a quiet sureness in his step, a kind of composure that neither Kristyn nor the watching crowd had expected, and she could feel them shrinking back, frightened by something they could not understand in their midst.

She waited quietly, just at the edge of the boardwalk, until he was halfway between the gate and that double line of soldiers. Then, pushing past the startled guards, she ran boldly into the center of the clearing, stopping a few feet away.

She could not have said herself what she expected at that moment, but whatever it was, it did not happen. Little Bear broke pace for an instant, but if he felt any emotion on seeing her, if he was surprised, glad, angry, it did not show. There was no more expression in his eyes now than she had sensed before when he stood at the gate and trained them blankly on the gallows.

On, please, say something! she thought. Say I should not have come, say you are angry with me—say you hate me if you want—but don't leave me with this terrible, empty silence!

He seemed to stiffen just slightly, but his lips did not move: his eyes were still unblinking as he started forward again, with only that one faltering step to acknowledge her presence. Sick with shame and despair, Kristyn stood alone for a moment, staring after him with eyes so dimmed by tears she could barely make out his retreating form.

She should not have come! The realization was like a dull pain cutting through her. She had given up so much, *risked* so much, to offer him this last proof of her loyalty, and he didn't even want it. It made no difference one way or the other whether she was there!

Perhaps, she thought bitterly, he had not even seen her. Not really. Perhaps he was so wrapped up in his own thoughts, his own feelings, she no longer existed for him.

She was only vaguely aware of curious eyes watching as she pushed her way back through the crowd to the rear of the boardwalk. She could not bring herself to leave, even now, but sensing that her presence would be an intrusion on his privacy, she slipped behind a nearby post. That way, if he looked up to scan the anonymous crowd of faces, he would not see her.

The gesture was lost on Little Bear, for as he continued

with measured paces toward the gallows, he did not allow his gaze to deviate right or left. He had begun, almost mechanically, to gauge the distance between himself and the base of that short stairway, and he let his mind focus on it now, marking it out in intervals. Forty yards . . . thirty . . . twenty-five.

The coolness that had impressed the watchers before was not altogether a facade, for that calm resignation extended inward as well. He had anticipated this day for a long time. He was ready for it. He even welcomed it in a way as the natural end of the life he had chosen for himself. His mind was not afraid, his heart was quiet, and yet—something in his muscles tightened as he looked up and saw the gallows, now twenty yards ahead.

They had killed a badger the night before they set out on that fateful raid. It was an ancient superstition, one he had never believed in, but for some reason the old customs had drawn him of late, and this time he had officiated over the preparations himself. Taking a clean, sharp knife, he had slit the animal's belly, spilling out the entrails and laying the carcass upside down on a bed of wild sage so the blood would gather and congeal in the cavity. The next morning they had filed past it, each man naked, his hair hanging loose and unbraided to his shoulders. The warrior who looked into that dark red mirror and saw himself as an old man with white hair and wrinkled skin would be assured that he was going to survive the day's violence and live to a ripe old age. If he visualized himself scalped and bleeding on the ground, it was an ill omen and he remained behind.

Little Bear had seen neither image. He had leaned over the badger and all his eyes had picked out was the same youthful face he saw so often in rippling forest streams. Oddly enough, the vision had been a comforting one. He was not going to be killed on the raid, he had told himself. He might not live to earn a single wrinkle on his brow, but he would not die that day.

And he *hadn't* died. He had been captured!

His lips contorted into a faint grimace, the only expression that had touched his features since he entered the yard. He should have recognized the warning. He should have known in advance what was going to happen and been wary enough, sly enough, to stave off his fate one more day.

Twenty yards. The gallows had been twenty yards away before. Now it was barely ten. Little Bear was surprised at the twists his mind was taking in these, its last moments of existence. He had expected a hundred images to flash through his brain, a thousand memories to tantalize him with their sweetness. Instead, he had only one thought now, one conscious regret—one thing yet to do before he left the earth forever.

Glancing ahead, he picked out one of the soldiers, a young corporal with a faint line of blond fuzz on his upper lip. He waited until he was abreast of him, then startled the boy by pausing to speak a few curt words. He was a little surprised himself, for they were not the words he had expected, but he did not try to question them, knowing that whatever slipped out of his mouth now came from somewhere in his heart.

It took him only a second or two longer to reach the foot of the scaffolding. There he paused one last time, sensing a kind of numbness that seemed to spread through his limbs as he looked up and saw the rope waiting for him. He tried to keep his mind a blank, tried not to count the steps as he mounted them, tried not to see anything but those faintly grayish clouds in the sky above. His body was going to betray him. He knew that now, and he hated it. He was going to feel a basic, primal fear at the moment of his death. But he was not going to let himself show it—not in front of the crowd that had gathered to exult in his weakness. They had come to see an Indian die. They would see him die with dignity and courage.

He refused the blindfold they offered him, standing quietly, facing the courtyard, his head held high as they slipped the noose over his neck and tightened it. The scent of new rope was sharp in his nostrils, faintly resinous, and the roughness of it scratched his throat. He was aware, fleetingly, of the irony of knowing that his last sensory impression on earth was to be the feel and smell of the white man's rope.

But there were other impressions, too, subtler instincts that had nothing to do with the senses of the moment. They seemed to come back all at once, those feelings he had half expected before, as sweet and yearning—and comforting—as he had dared to hope. The smell of the pine forest after a soft spring rain; the feel of the bowstring, taut against his fingers; laughter at the fireside, just after dusk had fallen; the cries of children as they raced into the fields to play their endless games; wind catching at a shimmering red mane, blowing it back against the hands that held the reins . . . the first morning light on blue eyes wet with tears.

He had been wrong. His body was *not* going to betray him. He was not going to be afraid in this, his final moment. He was going to die as he had wanted, with a quiet inner dignity that no man could take from him.

He opened his lips one last time, singing the words Cheyennes had sung for generations and would continue to sing as long as one of their race was left on earth, celebrating not his death but the continuity of life that went on forever.

> "It is a good day to die!
> All the things of our life are here,
> All that is left of our people are here.
> Cheyennes, it is a good day to die."

Kristyn kept her head buried in her hands long after the raucous sounds of the crowd had faded and she knew it was safe to look up again. She had turned coward at the last moment, unable to share, as she had intended, that final agony of her husband's death. The body of a hanged man, they said, writhed and kicked at the end of the rope, his muscles continuing to react even after his brain had ceased to send out signals. Grace and quiet pride had always been a part of Little Bear's existence. She could not bear to see him subjected to that gross indignity.

She was glad he had not accepted the terrible black hood they wanted to place over his face; glad, too, that somehow they had found enough humanity at the end not to force it on him. It was enough that he had to go to his death with his hands tied behind his back, as if half a hundred rifles against the shoulders of as many soldiers had not been sufficient protection against that awesome public menace. An Indian should die free and unfettered, with the wind in his face and his eyes open to the sky.

By the time Kristyn finally looked up, the crowd was dispersing, and soldiers had begun to cut across the courtyard, going about their everyday business. Little Bear's body was dangling motionless on the gallows where it would remain for the next several days, a symbol of the white man's triumph over his enemies—and an object lesson for any Indian or half-breed who came to the post to trade.

It was intended as the final insult, but it was, ironically, the final solace as well. Had they cut him down quickly, hastening him off to an unmarked grave, his soul would have been trapped forever in the darkness of the earth. Now, when night fell and the first stars came out, Kristyn would at least have the comfort of knowing he had begun his long journey toward a land where forests were still thick with trees and the white man and his gallows did not exist.

She paused one last time at the gate to look back. But in that inert, lifeless form hanging from the scaffolding, she could detect no traces of the man she had once loved.

Where had he gone? The little boy who had crawled under the tepee liner to peer at her with curious eyes that first morning in the Indian village? The playmate who had scowled so fiercely at letters in the sand, determined to figure out what they meant and how to put them together? The youth who had sat cross-legged on the ground in his new tunic and blue denim pants, and laughed when he could not remember how to whittle an Indian arrow? The gentle suitor-turned-husband who had had so short a time to initiate her into the secrets of love?

When had she lost him? Not today, surely, for today there had been nothing left of the Little Bear she remembered. How could the boy have died so completely within the man? The youth with all his dreams? The tender, considerate lover? How could time have taken him away, moment by precious moment, and left only this shell of a stranger whose life she could not share—and whose death touched her only in a terrible abstract way?

She was aware of a heavy feeling of sadness as she turned back toward the gate, sensing in that final gesture not so much a parting from the man himself as from a way of life that had once held her heart. She had been, for a little while, like the others, a Cheyenne. But her identity had been too entwined with theirs, her sense of self tied to a sense of them, and with their passing, with the loss of Brave Eagle and Buffalo Calf Woman, and now at last of Little Bear, she had lost the Indian in herself as well.

"Ma'am?"

The voice startled her. Looking up, Kristyn saw a young

corporal hovering a few feet away. He was leading a horse on a rawhide thong behind him. A powerful red sorrel with long, perfectly shaped legs and a spirited look to his eyes.

Fire-Wind. Kristyn did not know whether she wanted to laugh or cry. In all her anxiety these last hours, she had not even had time to wonder if he was safe. Now here he was, standing docilely—well, as docilely as Fire-Wind ever stood! —behind the young officer.

"Yes, corporal? You wanted to speak to me?"

"Well, yes, ma'am. It's about the horse, ma'am. You see, it belonged to the Injun. The one we just hung."

"I know," Kristyn replied, conscious suddenly of a faint chill in the air. She could not forget the look on Little Bear's face when he told her he would shoot Fire-Wind himself before he would let a white man have him. How bitter it must have been, going to his death with that vow unfulfilled.

"Well, you see, ma'am, he said it was really yours. I reckon he must have meant he stole it from you. Something like that. Anyhow, he said you ought to have it back. I asked the captain about it, and he allowed as how it was probably true and I ought to see to it."

Kristyn stared at him for a moment, feeling the cold even more as it seeped into her veins. She recognized the officer now—the young man Little Bear had stopped to speak to before he mounted the gallows.

So he had not gone to his death with the vow unrealized after all. He had turned Fire-Wind over to her, knowing she already had his last instructions!

"He didn't steal the horse, corporal," she said dully. "I gave it to him. But yes, now that he is dead, I suppose the animal is mine."

Numbly, only half aware of what she was doing, she took the reins and began to lead Fire-Wind through the gate. What a grim last jest her husband had played. And what a bitter choice he left her! Destroy a fine, spirited horse she loved with all her heart—or spend the rest of her life knowing she had betrayed him one more time.

"Oh, ma'am . . ."

The corporal's voice stopped her again. Kristyn turned back, waiting for him to speak.

"He did say one more thing, ma'am, though it doesn't make any sense." He had begun to stammer a little, embarrassed to go on. "He said to tell you not to take the horse out and shoot it. Said there wasn't any point in that now. Well, I ask you—who would shoot an animal like that anyway? That's the plumb craziest thing I've ever heard! Does it make any sense at all to you, ma'am?"

Kristyn stood absolutely still, resisting the temptation to look back at the gallows, knowing Little Bear would not have wanted her to. So he *had* seen her in that split second their eyes met. He had seen and spoken, if only her heart had been able to hear.

Perhaps, after all, there had been something in him of the little boy who once thrust a puppy into her arms. The youth who looked at her with such glowing pride the day she won the horse for both of them.

"Yes, corporal," she said softly. "Oh, yes—it makes a great deal of sense."

She laid her hand on the sorrel's neck and led him out through the open gate, reveling in the gusts of wind that had seemed so cold before. At least now there was something left. Some small, tangible part of a life that had been achingly beautiful and would never be hers again.

Traffic on the road outside had thinned considerably, and as Kristyn led Fire-Wind over to the place where she had tethered the bay, she became aware of a solitary figure standing a short distance away. He was dressed all in black, a black gunbelt over tightly fitting black pants, a flaring black shirt open at the neck. His left arm was bandaged loosely in a sling.

Kristyn's heart gave a little leap as she caught sight of him. She had not hoped—she had not *dared* to hope—yet there he was, obviously waiting for her. With a soft cry, she started toward him, then caught herself, sensing intuitively that it would be better to let him come to her.

He paused a few steps away, his hat clutched awkwardly in one hand, his bearing strangely subdued, almost humble, for the first time in his life.

"I think it's time we had a talk, Cristina. Can we do that—at last?"

Forty-Five

Rafe kicked at the fire, stirring the coals into leaping yellow flames before he tossed another log on them. The late afternoon shadows had begun to lengthen beneath tall pine trees, and the glowing warmth felt good in the autumn chill.

He was smiling as he turned back to Kristyn. No, not smiling, she thought—grinning was more the word. Whatever humility he had shown for one minute outside the fort was gone now, and he was his old self again.

"You look like a poor little chimney sweep," he said, shaking his head. "I don't believe I've seen so much dust and grime on any one person in my life."

"A chimney sweep, indeed!" Kristyn laughed softly as she nestled deeper in a thick bed of pine needles, covered with the old trail blanket Rafe had spread out for her. "You're a fine one to talk, Rafe Valero. You were twenty times as dirty yesterday when you pulled me out of that shaft. Only you've had a chance to clean up since then and I haven't! Tell me, husband, shall we delay our little talk until I've had time to take a bath in the stream and wash the mine dust out of my hair?"

"No, we shall not!" Rafe crouched down beside her, reaching out to take hold of her hand. "I rather like you as a chimney sweep—you have a certain winsome appeal. Besides, we've put this talk off long enough. I have the feeling if we don't settle things between us now, I could go off to gather firewood and come back and find you gone again."

Kristyn smiled as she raised his hand and laid it on her cheek, but she did not try to argue. They were so close now it was hard to believe anything could ever come between them. But then, they had felt close before—and the illusion had all too quickly shattered. Rafe was right. It *was* time to put their relationship on a solid footing.

"But you have to satisfy my curiosity first. You haven't told me how you managed to find me. What made you think I'd be in Fort Avery?"

"Ysabel."

"*Ysabel*?" Kristyn felt her eyes grow round with astonishment. Of everyone who might have helped reunite her with Rafe, Ysabel was the last one she would have suspected. "But Ysabel hates me, Rafe. Why would she tell you where I was? Or did she do it inadvertently?"

"No, just the opposite. She came to me deliberately—and of her own accord. It looks like the little minx is developing a conscience, or perhaps she's finally beginning to mature. That's what Carlos thinks, and for his sake, I hope he's right. At any rate, she came to me in tears and told me everything she had done, right from the night of our wedding when she found that newspaper and showed it to you. She seemed genuinely sorry, and I think, to give her credit, she was honestly trying to set things right."

"Well, perhaps . . ." Kristyn replied dubiously. "People can change, I suppose, and Ysabel and I do have a way of bringing out the worst in each other. But even if she's sorry, that doesn't make up for what she did."

"No, of course not—but dammit, Cristina, this wasn't all Ysabel's fault. Why didn't you come to me right away? Why didn't you cry or curse me out—or something! If we'd talked it over then, we might have been able to work things out without going through this hell."

"I—I suppose I should have, but I couldn't, Rafe! I was too—it *hurt* too much!" Even now, the memory was raw enough to bring tears to her lashes, and she turned her head aside, embarrassed to let him see. "I thought you didn't love me. You never said the words. Not once! I thought you'd only married me because your grandfather bullied you into it."

"Because Grandfather *bullied* me?" Rafe tucked a finger under her chin, tilting her face back to him. "You've said that before, but I'm afraid I didn't take you seriously. Be honest, love—in all the times you've seen me with my grandfather, have you ever known me to do anything simply because he told me to? By God, I'm stubborn enough to do the opposite just to prove my independence! No, sweet little skeptic, I married you for one reason, and one only. Because I loved you to distraction, and I couldn't bear the thought of letting you go.''

"But I couldn't know that, Rafe. Not if you didn't tell me. And that night your grandfather told you to marry me—well, you just stood there and stared at him with the strangest look on your face. Then you stomped out of the room without a word, and oh, you were gone such a long time.''

"I had a lot of thinking to do,'' he reminded her. "Don't forget, I knew I was keeping a secret from you. A secret that had the power to destroy our lives.''

"Secrets have a way of doing that, I think,'' Kristyn replied softly. "You said before that *I* made things worse by not coming to you. But isn't that what you did, too? Why couldn't you just tell me the truth? Right from the beginning?''

"Why?'' He threw her a darkly amused look. "Ask me a difficult one, why don't you? You make things so easy!''

He rose and moved a few steps away, staring out at the twilit horizon. Kristyn, sensing his need to withdraw into himself, sat quietly on the blanket and waited until he was ready to turn and speak again.

"I never meant to lie to you, darling—at least I don't think I did. I just started reading that blasted newspaper article and my eye skipped ahead, and—well, I couldn't bring myself to spit out the words. I tried to believe I was doing it for your own good. You *would* have insisted on going back to your husband, you know, even though he had turned into a renegade. I was only trying to protect you—or that's what I told myself. But . . . oh, hell!''

He came back, squatting down on the blanket beside her.

"I didn't know then, and I don't know now, if that was the truth. Maybe it was, in part. Or maybe I just couldn't stand the idea of sending you off to someone else.''

"So you told that first lie . . .''

He laughed harshly. "You're beginning to get the picture. Yes, I told one lie—and it kept on growing until I couldn't control it anymore. When I was tempted to ask you to come back with me to Santa Fe, I didn't dare for fear you'd find out what I had done and never be able to forgive me. That's the same fear I was feeling the night I paced back and forth in the garden outside your room, trying to decide what to do. Be honest and risk losing you, or lie and bluff it out.''

"And you decided . . .''

"Shhh!" He laid a light finger on her lips. "Don't berate me, even if I deserve it. I know now that I was wrong. I should have told you the truth. But God help me, if I had it to do all over again, I'm not sure I wouldn't make the same mistake.''

"Yes, you were wrong." Kristyn looked away, surprised to see that it was almost dark now and the distant hills had half disappeared. "You were wrong . . . in a way.''

But in a way he had been right, too. Brave Eagle and Buffalo Calf Woman had told the same lie because they understood that it was time for her to go back to her people. If Rafe had been honest with her—if he had blurted out the truth that day at the hotel—she would indeed have returned to Little Bear, and the sacrifice of her Indian parents would have been in vain.

She was a little surprised, as she turned back, to see that the seriousness on his face had been replaced with hints of gentle laughter.

"Do you know when I first fell in love with you, *querida*?''

"No, when?" Kristyn leaned back against the blanket again, loving the way his eyes had begun to play with her, only half teasing. "When you first saw me?''

"No, you vain little creature. I was fascinated, I admit—I don't think I'd ever seen such smoldering sensuality in my life—but I'd hardly classify that as love. Desire? God, yes! I wanted you desperately that night by the stream, and I'd have had you, too, if you hadn't fought me like a wildcat! But love? No, my darling, I fell in love later, not by firelight but by candlelight, as I stood at the bottom of the staircase and watched you float down in a sinfully seductive red gown. I thought then, and I still do, witch, that there was something basic and primitive about you—and I am a very basic man.''

"So it was the color of my gown that captured you." Kristyn glanced down at her hands, wondering why the words made her feel so strange. "Or perhaps it was the cut of it. You never really accepted me, did you? Not until you saw me dressed up like one of the proper, well-bred white women you were used to.''

"Ah . . . is that what you think?" Rafe's lips twisted into

an amused expression. "Did I give the impression just now that when you came down those stairs you looked like a young lady of fashion? Hardly—and if you had, I wouldn't have looked at you twice. 'Ladies,' I assure you, hold no particular appeal for me. Oh, you wore your finery with a certain defiant flair. I won't take that from you. But I was aware every second of the half-tamed savage just beneath that beautifully manicured surface."

"Savage?" Kristyn smiled faintly as she looked up. "You've called me that before, and I never quite know how to take it. Though I must admit, on your lips, the words come out less an insult than *lady*."

Rafe started to laugh, then turned solemn again.

"I'm not being fair, am I? I love you for the savage that you are, and yet I persist in trying to turn you into a lady—which, by the way, would bore me to tears. I revel in that unquenchable passion of yours, I thrill to it—I wouldn't want you to control it any more than I want to rein in my own desires—but the mere thought of you in someone else's arms, sharing that same urgency, that same——"

"Oh—oh, Rafe . . . !" Kristyn put her hand over his mouth, laughing a little as she realized suddenly where the conversation was going. That silly jealousy of his. And it was partly her fault for being so spiteful that day he made her angry! "Haven't you figured out yet that there isn't anyone else? There never has been. Not since the night I first saw you."

"No—don't do this!" She was surprised by the hardness in his tone. "Don't lie to me. I can handle everything else. I don't know how, but I'll work it out. But I can't handle it if you lie."

"But I'm not lying, darling. It *is* the truth. You really are the only man in my life. I was completely innocent that one night I went to my young husband—and I was almost as innocent when I came to you. There hasn't been anyone since."

"But what about Collins . . . ?"

"Oh, Billy wanted me, I won't try to deny that. He was quite emphatic about it the first time, as a matter of fact. But once we got beyond all that, he treated me with respect. I think he was looking for something—*someone*—to believe in.

At any rate, I was never with him, not the way you fear. I never even kissed him . . .''

She broke off, blushing a little as she recalled the one kiss she had been guilty of.

"And I never intended to let Cuervo touch me, either. That just happened before I could stop it. I only went walking with him in the first place because I wanted to make you jealous!"

"Well, you succeeded," he remarked dryly. "But dammit, Cristina . . ." He hesitated, fumbling uncharacteristically for words. "You told me yourself you'd been with other men. You were very specific about it."

"Well, that will teach you," she replied, "not to believe every word a woman tells you. Especially if she's a savage—and no lady at all!"

"But for God's sake! Why would you lie about something like that? I'd understand if you said you hadn't been with other men when you had. Women do that all the time. But why lie and say——"

"Why?" The word burst out of her lips. "*Why*, you ask me? How many times have I told you I cared? How many times have I said you were the only man for me? Did you ever believe me? No! But I lied once and told you I'd slept with dozens of men—and you believed me *just like that*! Why should I tell the truth when it's so much easier to lie?"

Rafe looked dumbfounded for a moment, then burst out laughing.

"Touché, wife. You seem to understand me all too well. And I'm afraid you've learned to deal with me too, minx! You couldn't have devised a more perfect punishment if you'd sat up all night dreaming of ways to torture me. By God, all that time, imagining you writhing in some other man's embrace—and you were saving yourself chastely for me!"

"Which is more than I can say for you," Kristyn retorted, recalling suddenly that he had things to explain, too. "You've hardly been sitting around all these months just dreaming dreams of me!"

"I've never pretended to be less that a man," he countered, somewhat stiffly. "I was raised as a man in a man's world, and taught to take my pleasures where men find them—as long as I didn't dally with a social equal, or the daughters of my grandfather's friends. I'm not going to apologize for what

I am. But I will say this—and it's a confession, my sweet, coming from a man like me. There has been no excitement for me in any other woman since I first laid eyes on you. You have spoiled me for everyone else."

"Well . . . that may be," Kristyn replied, eyeing him dubiously. "But you certainly didn't turn that little cat away when she came to you. And you can't tell me Ysabel isn't your social equal!"

"Ysabel?" Rafe looked surprised. "I've been with many women, my love—I just admitted as much. But never with that *diabla*."

"Oh, Rafe . . ." Kristyn felt the sting of tears in her eyes. "You asked me not to lie to you before. Please, don't lie to me. I know Ysabel was with you in camp. I knew right away when I saw her! She was so smug, so self-satisfied. A woman like Ysabel would never look like that if she hadn't just been with a man!"

"Oh . . . and you thought that man was me?" Rafe had begun, very softly, to laugh. "Well, then, it seems I had my revenge, too, that is if jealousy tears you apart the way it does me. Ysabel didn't come to camp that night to seek me out. She came because she finally realized, as I have suspected for months, that it's Carlos she loves, not me. It was he she spent the night with—and a damned uncomfortable night it was, too! I was forced to take my blanket higher in the hills to give them some privacy. I didn't get a wink of sleep."

"But—but, Rafe . . ." Kristyn knew he was trying to make her laugh, but she couldn't quite manage. "I—I can't believe that. Why, she said herself . . ."

Or had she? Kristyn broke off, trying to remember what Ysabel's exact words had been. Had she said *Rafe*—or had she simply said *him*?

"Oh—oh, my goodness . . . !" Ysabel had said *him* and so had she—only they were talking about two different people! "Oh, no wonder we hated each other so much!"

They were both laughing then, Kristyn because she finally felt free of the doubts that had tormented her, Rafe simply because he sensed her change in mood and knew instinctively that everything was all right. When they fell quiet again, they found suddenly, though neither of them quite knew how, that they were holding hands and looking into each other's eyes.

"Is it all over then?" Kristyn asked softly. "Have we laid our ghosts to rest at last?"

"The ghosts we share—yes, I daresay we have. At least, I hope so. But I think you still have ghosts of your own yet to exorcise."

Kristyn smiled as she shook her head.

"No, I've come to terms with my own ghosts. They're still painful, of course. But I can live with them."

"With the memory of your husband, perhaps. And the years you spent with the Indians. But what about your parents? Have you thought about them?"

"My parents?" Kristyn pinched her brows together in a frown. "Oh . . . you mean my *white* parents."

"They must have been frantic with worry when you left without a word. I know you don't feel close to them—and perhaps that's their fault—but they wouldn't have tried to find you in the first place if they didn't care. Don't you think you could at least get in touch with them and let them know you're all right?"

"Yes, of course." Kristyn agreed without hesitation. "I think I'm beginning to understand them a little better now." If even Rafe had looked on her as a savage, how must her parents have felt when they stood on the doorstep and watched her get out of that wagon? "I did write once from Kansas, but I'd like to try again if you'll help me. Only what do you mean, *I* have ghosts to exorcise? Don't you think you have at least one of your own?"

"Me?" He looked surprised.

"I was thinking of your grandfather. He really does love you very much, you know. Are you going back to Santa Fe to be with him?"

Rafe shook his head. "Don Diego is much too feisty to be a ghost, darling. And, no, of course I'm not going to Santa Fe. I only considered it for a few mad days because I thought I could keep the truth from you there. But my destiny is here. In Colorado."

"Even with the Folly gone?"

"The Folly was never as important to me as you seemed to think. I intend to start it up again—the town can't survive without it, and those people have suffered enough as it is— but it'll be years before it shows a profit again. I have a few things to keep me occupied in the meantime."

"And you don't feel guilty? Abandoning your grandfather?"

"I'm not abandoning him, my love. I don't think even he looks on it that way. Carlos is perfectly capable of handling things in Santa Fe, and he's earned the right to try. I rather doubt El Valeroso ever thought I'd stay there. Why do you think he sent me to Colorado in the first place? It was his way of helping me get a start in life, though of course he'd have died before he'd admit it."

"Rafe, what about Carlos?" Kristyn had never been able to respond to that young man's gentle flirtation, but she liked him and she couldn't bear to think of the position he might be placing himself in. "Do you think Don Diego will ever be able to accept him?"

"Oh, I think in his own way he always has, though he wouldn't admit that either. Still, he's more open now, more honest about his feelings. And that, my sweet, is your doing."

"Mine?" Kristyn stared at him, astonished. "But I haven't done anything, Rafe. Why, I never even tried to discuss Carlos with him."

"Perhaps not, but you did bring things out in the open. You're the one who coaxed him to talk about the past. Neither Carlos nor I had ever heard the name Luisa before." He raised her hands to his lips, kissing them gently, then letting go again. "Besides, you brought a touch of spring into his life. You made him feel, for a moment or two, as if he were a young man again—and the young have a capacity for seeing things from a new perspective. I don't suppose he'll ever be able to forgive my father for what he did, nor will he forgive the woman who took my mother's place while she was ending her life in a lonely convent. But I do think, for the first time, he's able to see Carlos as his own man, not an extension of his parents and their failings. I think his relationship with his younger grandson will be a good one from now on."

In the silence that followed, Kristyn was keenly aware of the closeness of him on the blanket, the tempting warmth of his body next to hers. She longed to go to him, longed to throw herself into his arms, but suddenly, somehow, she felt shy . . . a little awkward.

"Will you go back there sometimes?" she asked softly. "Just to visit?"

"To visit, yes, and often. But my life is here now. This is my home—if you will share it with me."

He held out his arms then, the invitation she had needed, and she was only too ready to accept. Everything else was forgotten, the pain of the past, the heartaches, the doubts, as she went to him at last.

"I will share anything with you, husband. Any place. As long as you want me by your side."

Forty-Six

Their lovemaking was gently sweet, as it had never been before, unhurried now that they were sure of each other and knew they had a lifetime to express their different moods and feelings. Afterward, languid and satisfied, Kristyn sat in the darkness, her knees tucked up to her chin as she looked down at Rafe, stretched out on the blanket beside her.

She could not believe how much she loved this man. Loved everything about him: the stubborn way his jaw insisted on clamping together, even in half sleep; that deceptively boyish look to long, dark lashes, curling against his cheeks. Life would not always be easy. Two such strong-willed people could never hope to exist without clashes. But it would be good, and she would be happy.

The night sky had turned almost breathtakingly clear, velvety black studded with the diamond-bright shafts of a thousand stars. Raising her head just slightly, Kristyn looked up, losing herself for a moment in the sweet perfection of a world made for love.

Beside her, Rafe stirred on the blanket, opening his eyes to gaze up at her. Her profile was somehow touching in the moonlight, her lips slightly parted, like a little girl about to make a wish on the first evening star. It seemed to him her eyes were misty. With love? he wondered. Or tears?

He reached out to lay a hand on her arm, gently, so he wouldn't startle her.

"What are you thinking?"

She smiled, but she did not look down.

"I was thinking of that first night by the stream, when I told you about the Hanging Road and how it led, star by star, up into the heavens. It saddened me then, thinking of my young husband making that long journey alone. But tonight I am at peace. Tonight I know that he is safe—and on his way home."

The softness in her voice stirred something deep inside Rafe, a nameless fear he had not recognized until that moment.

"Do you mind so much?" he asked hoarsely. "All the things you had to give up to come to me?"

She looked down at him then, her eyes gentle, luminous.

"What things, my love?"

"I don't know. Living in tepees, maybe. Hunting buffalo—gathering water every night from a different stream. Whatever it was you loved about that life. Whatever it was that made you run from me when I came to take you away."

"Not living in tepees, surely." Kristyn laughed. "Houses are much more comfortable. And women don't hunt buffalo. Only men do that. But I know what you're trying to ask. There is something about that life I will always miss. Not the tangible things so much, but the intangible ones, the ones I can't quite define. A certain smell in the air sometimes, the way the wind feels when it touches my cheek, memories of the senses that remain even after the mind has forgotten."

She paused, her eyes turning dreamlike for a moment, then smiled again.

"Only I am not giving those things up for you, Rafe. Nor am I giving them up now. They died in little pieces in my heart with the people that I loved. With my father on a battlefield on the plains . . . my mother on a lonely hilltop . . . Little Bear today on the gallows. I am not a Cheyenne anymore, except possibly in my deepest dreams, and even those one day will fade. I am a white woman now—and I belong completely to you."

"Completely?" He caught her wrists, one in each hand, gently but firmly, and pulled her down beside him. "I wonder."

"Oh, I think I can prove it." She let her lips play with his, lightly, teasingly, knowing he was hers at that moment and reveling in the thought. "But I have to warn you, my love—I can be quite a savage at times. My own husband once told me that. And . . ."

She drew back just an instant, her eyes touched with lights of laughter.

". . . I think he might be right."